"Military SF is growing increasingly popular, and there are enough battles in this to please most readers, helped along by Ingrid's fine storytelling ability and crisp prose. . . . Rousing action in the grand tradition."   —*Science Fiction Chronicle*

"Highly recommended, outstanding selection . . . showed wit, skill, innovation . . . thoroughly satisfying entertainment for SF fans."
—*The Midwest Book Review*

"Ingrid has a knack for striking nightmare imagery."   —*Publishers Weekly*

THE SAND WARS

VOLUME ONE

SOLAR KILL
LASERTOWN BLUES
CELESTIAL HIT LIST

VOLUME TWO

ALIEN SALUTE
RETURN FIRE
CHALLENGE MET

THE SAND WARS
VOLUME II

ALIEN SALUTE
RETURN FIRE
CHALLENGE MET

CHARLES INGRID

DAW BOOKS, INC.
DONALD A. WOLLHEIM, FOUNDER
375 Hudson Street, New York, NY 10014

ELIZABETH R. WOLLHEIM
SHEILA E. GILBERT
PUBLISHERS
www.dawbooks.com

First Paperback Printing, February 2001
2   3   4   5   6   7   8   9

DAW TRADEMARK REGISTERED
U.S. PAT. OFF. AND FOREIGN COUNTRIES
—MARCA REGISTRADA
HECHO EN U.S.A.

PRINTED IN THE U.S.A.

ALIEN SALUTE

PROLOGUE

Where in the hell was their transport? What had happened to recall? Jack fought the maddening impulse to scratch inside his armor, as sweat dripped down, and the contacts attached to his bare torso itched impossibly. To scratch now, the way he was hooked up, he'd blow himself away.

Damn. Where was that signal? They couldn't have been forgotten, could they? If the pullout had happened, they would have been picked up . . . wouldn't they?

As sweat trickled down his forehead, he looked around.

Sand. They had been dropped in a vast sea-gulf of sand. Everywhere beige and brown and pink dunes rose and fell with a life of their own. This was what the Thraks did to a living world. And the Knights, in their suits of battle armor, trained and honed to fight a "Pure" war destroying only the enemy, not the environment, were all that stood between Milos and his own home world lined up next in a crescent of destruction that led all the way back to the heart of the Thrakian League.

So far, they'd been lucky here on Milos. Only one of the continents had gone under . . . still, it was one too many as far as the lieutenant was concerned. The Dominion Forces were losing the Sand Wars. And he was losing his own private struggle with his faith in his superior officers. They'd been dropped into nowhere five days ago and had been given the most succinct of orders, gotten a pithy confirmation that morning and nothing since. Routine, he'd been told. Strictly a routine mop-up. You don't treat Knights that way—not the elite of the infantrymen, the fastest, smartest and most honorable fighters ever trained to wage war.

Jack moved inside the battle suit. The Flexalinks meshed imperceptibly and the holograph that played over him sent

the message to the suit and, in turn, the right arm flexed. Only that flex, transmitted and stepped up, could have turned over an armored car. He sucked a dry lip in dismay over the reflex, then turned his face inside the helmet to read the display.

The display bathed his face plate in a rosy color and his eyesight flickered briefly to the rearview camera display, just to see which of the troops were ranged at his back. The compass wasn't lying to him. "Five clicks. Sarge, have they got us walking in circles?" His suit crest winked in the sun as he looked to his next in command.

"No, sir." Sarge made a husky noise at the back of his throat. Sarge wore the Ivanhoe crest—a noncommittal comment on what he thought of his lineage and his home world, but it made no difference to Storm. The men who joined the Knights came from every walk of life and the only criterion was whether a soldier was good enough to use a suit. If he was, and if he survived basic training, his past became a sealed record, if that was the way the man wanted it.

The sand made Jack thirsty. He waved his arm. "All right, everybody spread out. Advance in a line. If the Thraks are here, that'll flush 'em. Keep alert. Watch your rear displays and your flanks."

The com line crackled as Bilosky's voice came over in sheer panic. "Red field! Lieutenant, I'm showing a fracking red field!"

Storm swiveled his head toward the sound, cursed at the obstruction of the face plate, and re-turned a fraction more slowly so that his cameras could follow the motion. "Check your gauges again, Bilosky. It's a malfunction. And calm down." The last in a deadly quiet.

Bilosky's panic stammered to a halt. "Yes, sir." Then, "Goddammit, Storm—those Milots have pilfered my suit! Every one of my gauges is screwed. I'm showing a red field because I'm running on empty!"

Storm bit his tongue. He chinned the emergency lever at the bottom of the face plate, shutting down the holograph field. Then he pulled his arm out of the sleeve quickly and thumbed the com line switches on his chest patch so that he could talk to Bilosky privately. Without power or any

action to translate, his suit stumbled to a halt. The Flexa-links shone opalescent in the sun.

"How far can you get?"

Not listening, Bilosky swore again. "Goddamn Milots. Here I am fighting their fracking war for them, and they're pirating my supplies—I ought to—"

"Bilosky!"

"Yes, sir. I've got . . . oh, three clicks to go, maybe. Then I'm just another pile of junk standing on the sand." He turned to look at his superior officer, the black hawk crest rampant.

Storm considered the dilemma. He had his orders, and knew what his orders told him. Clean out Sector Five, and then stand by to get picked up. The last of Sector Five ranged in front of him. They could ration out the most important refills for Bilosky once they got where they were going. "We'll be picked up by then."

"Or the Thraks will have us picked out."

Storm didn't answer for a moment. He was asking a man with little or no power reserves showing on his gauges to go on into battle, in a suit, in full battle mode. Red didn't come up on the gauges until the suit was down to the last ten percent of its resources. That ten percent would carry him less than an hour in full attack mode. Not that it made any difference to a Knight. Jack sighed. "We're on a wild goose chase, Bilosky. You'll make it."

"Right, sir." A grim noise. "Better than having my suit crack open like an egg and havin' a berserker pop out. Right, Lieutenant?"

That sent a cold chill down Storm's back. He didn't like his troopers repeating ghoulish rumors. "Bilosky, I don't want rumors like that bandied around. You hear?"

"Yes, sir." Then, reluctantly, "It ain't no rumor, lieutenant. I saw it happen once."

"Forget it!"

"Yes, sir."

"Going back on open air. And watch your mouth." He watched as the other lumbered back into position. Then, abruptly, Jack dialed in his command line and watched as the miniscule screen lit up, his only link with the warship orbiting far overhead. The watch at the console, alerted by the static of their long-range comm lines, swung around.

The navy blue uniform strained over his bullish, compact figure. He looked into the lens, his nostrils flaring. The squared chin was cleft and its line deepened in anger. A laser burn along one side of his hairline gave him a lopsided widow's peak.

"Commander Winton here. You're violating radio silence, soldier. What's the meaning of this? Identify yourself."

"I'm Battalion First Lieutenant," he said. "Where's our pullout? We were dropped in here five days ago."

"You're under orders, lieutenant. Get in there and fight. Any further communication and I'll have you up for court martial."

"Court martial? Is that the best you can do? We're dying down here, commander. And we're dying all alone."

The line and screen went dead with a hiss. Suddenly aware of his own vulnerability, Storm pushed his right arm back into his sleeve and chinned the field switch back on. His suit made an awkward swagger, then settled into a distance eating stride. Fighting wars would be a hell of a lot easier if you could be sure who the enemy was.

Bilosky and Sarge and who knows who else were talking about berserkers now. The unease it filled him with he could do without. He squinted through the tinted face plate at the alien sun. Strange worlds, strange people, and even stranger enemies. Right now he'd rather wade through a nest of Thraks than try to find his way through the rumors surrounding the Milots and their berserkers.

There was no denying the rumors though. The Milots, who had summoned Dominion forces to fight for them against the Thraks—those same low-tech Milots who ran the repair centers and provided the war backup—were as despicable and treacherous as the Thraks whom Storm had enlisted to wipe out. And there were too many stories about altered suits . . . suits that swallowed a man up and spawned instead some kind of lizard-beastman who was a fighting automaton, a berserker. Rumor had it the Milots were putting eggs into the suits, and the heat and sweat of the suit wearer hatched those eggs and then the parasitic creature devoured its host and burst *forth*—

He told himself that the Milots had a strange sense of

humor. What Bilosky thought he'd seen, whatever every trooper who repeated the gossip thought they were talking about, was probably a prank played at a local tavern. Knights always took a certain amount of ribbing from the locals, until they were seen in action, waging the "Pure" war.

Ahead of him, the dunes wavered, sending up a spray of sand. His intercom burst into sound.

"Thraks at two o'clock, lieutenant!"

Storm set his mouth in a grim smile. Now here was an enemy he could deal with. He eyed his gauges to make sure all his systems were ready, and swung about.

Thraks were insects, in the same way jackals were primates or ordinary sow bugs were crustaceans. They were equally at home upright or on all fours, due to the sloping of their backs. Jack took his stand and watched them boil up out of the sand from underground nests and launch themselves in a four-footed wave until they got close enough to stand up and take fire. Thraks were vicious and dedicated to a single purpose . . . at least, fighting Thraks were. Diplomatic Thraks, so he had heard, were as vicious in a far more insidious way.

He cocked his finger, setting off a burst of fire from his glove weapons that slowed the wave. The line of Thraks wavered and swung away, even as they stood up and slung their rifles around from their backs.

On Milot, they had the slight advantage, having gotten there first and having begun their despicable planet transforming. Even a slight advantage to the Thraks was disastrous to the Dominion. Milot was already as good as lost. Battalions had been wiped out, forced into the deserts, to make as graceful a retreat as possible. Inflict as many casualties as they could, then pull out. Jack's job, as he understood it, was to make the toll of taking Milos so heavy, so dear, that the Thraks would stop here.

Storm's grim smile never wavered, even as he strode forward, spewing death as he went, watching the gauge detailing how much power he had left. Bodies crunched under his armored boots.

They were mopping up. They were to distract the Thraks and the enemy cannon long enough to let most of the troop ships—almost all of them coldships—pull out, and then they would be picked up. That was the promise. . . .

He strides through the line, knowing the wings of his men will follow, and seeing that the front is not a front, but an unending wave of Thraks. What was reported as a minor outpost is a major staging area, and he's trapped in it, wading through broken bodies and seared flesh. He sweeps both gloves into action, firing as he walks, using the power boost to vault walls of fallen bodies and equipment.

Somewhere along the way, Bilosky lets out a cry and grinds to a halt, out of power. He screams as his suit is slit open with a diamond cutter and the Thraks pull him out. Jack ignores the screams and plows onward. He has no choice now. The pullout site is ahead of him. He has to go through the Thraks if he wants to be rescued. Ahead of him is the dream of cold sleep and the journey home. The dream. . . .

He lives long enough to fall into a pit, a pit ringed by Thraks, surrounded by what is left of his troop, and by stragglers from other battalions. They stand back to back for days, firing only when absolutely necessary, watching the unending waves of Thraks above them. And he sees a suit burst open, days after its wearer expired with a horrendous scream and the armor halted like a useless statue in the pit. He sees the seams pop and an incredible beast plow out, and charge the rim of the pit, taking fully a hundred armed Thraks with it, even as it bellows, striking fear in those beyond its reach. He knows he is dreaming that he has seen a berserker, and tries to ignore the empty shell-like suit with the crest of Ivanhoe left behind in shards and settling into the sand.

Even as he stands and fires, he thinks of what it is he wants to dream. He wants to dream getting out of there alive, with his men. That is what he wants most. Then he wants to be able to scratch. And he thinks he hears something inside the suit with him, something whispering at his shoulder, and he knows he's losing it. Aunt Min back home always said that when the Devil wanted you, he began by whispering to you over your shoulder. Storm is scared to turn around. All he wants to do is find his dream of going home. And when the recall comes, he doesn't know if he's hearing what he's hearing or not . . . or if he can even be found behind the wall of Thraks.

And then he realizes he is cold sleep dreaming, on an endless loop, dreaming without beginning or end until someone finds and awakens him.

But that was then. This is now. . . .

CHAPTER 1

The aged freighter hardly qualified as a transport ship, let alone a cold ship, but none of the nearly five hundred people crowded into it complained. They stood and shivered and talked quietly to each other in knotted groups, looking pale and shaken as they waited for processing.

Only one man had an expression of triumph seized out of the jaws of the defeat that had forced them into exodus. Tall, made massive by his opalescent battle armor, he looked the crowd over now, and his eyes flashed with eagerness even as he assessed the results of the evacuation.

"What if the emperor offers you the command?"

He made a noise of anger. "Kavin's hardly cold in the ground."

The woman with the questioning, gentle brown eyes remained composed under the wash of his anger, tilting her head slightly to one side as though to veer away from it. "But we have to consider it, don't we?" She kept her hand on the Flexalink sleeve he supported her with. Beneath her fingers, she felt the smoke and grime of battle, and her delicate nose still scented blood faintly though most of it had been washed away. They'd both witnessed the violent death of his commanding officer and friend. They stood intimately close in the immense hold of the transport ship that vibrated loudly under their feet. "And I need to talk to you . . . I need time to tell you what happened."

The man's helmet was off, hanging from an equipment hook at his waist. Sweat darkened his sandy blond hair and fatigue washed out his blue eyes. Even with his strong cheekbones, he was plain-faced, ordinary, but there was something commanding in his features. Tiny lines were etched at the corners of his eyes and into his forehead, for all he appeared at the prime of his twenties. His avid gaze deflected from his field command to her, and softened as he took her in. The reflection of her image in his eyes was as intimate as an embrace. "You don't owe me an explanation. I just thank god you came back."

A shiver swept over her, setting off the intricate blue patterning of the tattoos that covered her—that made her alien from her lover. These tattoos were only a small portion of what she had suffered when the religious wars had swept across Bythia and forced the Dominion settlers to flee. But she knew Jack was most concerned about facing Emperor Pepys. "You've got two months of chill time to think about it," Amber returned. "You'd better have an answer for the emperor by the time we get home."

"If he offers it to me, I'll think about it."

"Not good enough," she said, and streetwise savvy edged her tones. They were among the last of the evacuees to be processed. "You have to accept, if Pepys asks you. You're the only one left who knows how to fight a 'Pure' war. Anyone can wear a suit—"

He looked down at her and his mouth twitched.

"—well, not anyone, but no one understands the warfare the way you do."

"I know," he said then, heavily.

The freighter seemed to groan around them as it picked up acceleration speed. It would take days to hit warp speed, weeks in transit, and then days of deceleration. Those days would pass as if in a dream to the vast bulk of its passengers.

Amber pressed her fingers into his armor. "And then we can talk."

Storm shifted his weight uneasily. He did not like the prospect of cold sleep, never had, never would. A nurse came by, still in sterile greens, and Jack stepped out to block his passage.

"I don't want any of these people on a debriefing loop."

The nurse came to a startled halt. His face was narrow and his chin pointed, giving him a feral look. "We take our orders from Emperor Pepys—"

"Not now you don't. I don't want any of those evacuees stressed out. They won't forget what happened." He felt Amber shudder at his side. As if any of them could forget the bloody civil uprising out of which they were being emergency lifted, compounded by the ever-present, ever-dangerous Thraks and the rumors of war.

The nurse sniffed. "Of course, commander." He hurried past then, skirting around the battle-armored man with caution.

Jack smiled. Too tired to do so, he couldn't hold it, and the expression faded rapidly from his face.

Amber relaxed a little. "Thanks, Jack," she said softly.

"Not just for you. I don't trust the debriefing loops." He looked out over the hold as another small group of evacuees pressed forward into the medical bay. Far ahead of them stood St. Colin of the Blue Wheel, watched over by his lumbering bodyguard and aide, Jonathan. The Walker prelate leaned on a cane, injured but hearty nonetheless. Fine gray and chestnut hairs strayed across a balding head, but his chin was square and his massive hands gestured as he talked to the group surrounding him. His preaching voice reached Jack. The man in battle armor shifted his weight, temporarily warmed by what Colin was saying. Nearby stood young Denaro, also a Walker, but looking sullen in his uniform, weapon belts crisscrossed over his chest, his militancy a kind of insult to his affiliation. Storm frowned as he watched Denaro a second longer. The Walker ministry had suffered a profound loss on Bythia. Denaro did not look as if he would tolerate it for long.

Amber must have sensed his thoughts. Her chin pointed in the militant's direction. "I hope Colin keeps an eye on that one."

"He'll have to," Jack answered. "I've done all I can. I've got the Thraks to worry about now." He'd escorted a wave of humanity aboard the shuttles to the transport. The Thrakian warship orbiting Bythian space was momentarily distracted by the necessity of getting its own personnel off-planet. He had time, but only a little, and he didn't like seeing it wasted. The column shuffled forward. He and Amber were at the rear and would be last. "Amber . . ." and he hesitated, because what he said next the young woman would not want to hear, and he knew it. "I don't intend to be chilled down."

She pulled back. "I have to go alone?"

"Yes."

"I don't—"

"You have to. Just as I have to stay up and alert."

Amber looked up at him. Her chin jutted defiantly, and then her jawline softened. "You don't think the Thraks will let us go?"

"Not if they don't have to. This transport is a load of potential hostages. Colin, my command, almost everyone on here is of value to the League."

"It would be worth even more if you could have gotten that bushskimmer out alive."

Jack had no answer for that. He'd lost a valuable witness in the Sassinal riots, a man who could testify to the fire-storming of Claron. But that was over now. At least he'd heard the testimony . . . words he'd never forget. He looked down at Amber. "It's over," he said.

She nodded. She grabbed up his gauntleted hand and held it tightly and even though he wore battle armor, he could almost feel the chill of her grasp through it. "What if they insist on cold sleep?"

Her question suggested that she knew instinctively what also worried him: the transport pilot was in command here now and not Jack. He shrugged. "It'll take a lot more men than Harkness has got to hold me down."

Now she knew why he hadn't removed his armor once they'd boarded.

Amber laughed briefly. "I hope I'm awake when they try."

"You run a sloppy ship."

The pilot twisted his head to peer at the tall man . . . seeming even taller now that he stood in the bulkhead framing. Sandy blond hair swept back from his brow and his faded eyes reflected disapproval. The ship shuddered with the vibration of engines thrusting the vehicle nearer and nearer warp velocity. Harkness grumped and slumped lower in his chair. "And if I do, it's my business," he said.

Around the chipped and battered plastic table, the navigator and engineer got up quickly and left. They did not look the intruder in the face as he moved to let them shrug past the bulkhead.

Harkness' voice sounded thick and lumpy as if it needed to be strained through a filter before issuing out of his mouth. He pointed at the interloper. "I'll chart no interference from you," he said. "Or you'll be chilled down yet and shipped like the rest of the stiffs. This is a cold ship transport and don't you forget it."

The intruder had eased a wide shoulder against the bulkhead. He smiled pleasantly. "You've already tried it once," he said. "You have other worries. We slipped out of Bythian space easily enough, but you're a sitting target coming out of decel, and there's a good chance the Thraks will be waiting for us. There's a war on now."

Harkness' eyes narrowed. He reached for his bag of whiskey and poured a level glassful. "I took out a contract to lift a shipload of evacuees and return 'em to Malthen. I did not take out a contract to listen to your mouth."

The man's smile did not vanish, but neither did it warm his clear blue eyes. "Not yet," he said. "But you will." The man lifted his shoulder, shifted his weight, and removed himself gracefully from Harkness' vision.

The pilot scowled before lifting his drink. Too full, it washed over his fingers before he got it to his mouth. With a curse at his shaking hand, he slogged the whiskey down.

Jack walked the cryogenic bays where his friends and fellow soldiers lay asleep yet not asleep, their pale bodies seemingly devoid of life under sterile white sheets. He stopped at the plastic shield of a privacy crèche and paused to look inside at Amber, lying there, her dark honey colored hair a-tumble about her face. The sheet covered her from ankle to neck, but it could not hide her beauty which was all the more exotic for the bizarre tattooing. She'd said she wanted it removed the minute she got to Malthen, if it could be done. Jack looked at the dialysis shunt in her ankle, preparatory to the stage when she would one day be awakened and, unable to help himself, he shuddered before looking away.

Only Amber knew if he was a really a hero or a coward for refusing to be chilled down with the rest of them.

He paused now and spread his hand out over the plastic shield as though he could touch her face and share her dreams with her. It had been another battle to keep psychological debriefing loops from being hooked up to her cold sleep dreams, but he'd won that one, too. The human mind should have some dignity in cold sleep, even if the body did not. He looked at his four-fingered hand, at the scar where the little finger had been sheared off. It had been amputated, a victim of frostbite from a cold sleep occupied too long. Seventeen years too long.

Two months of real time was not too much to be added to his years, Jack thought. He'd endure it, waiting for the end of the voyage and the beginning of the war, his war, with the Thrakian League. Endure it, hell, he'd welcome it.

His emperor, the traitor, was another matter.

Jack dropped his hand from the shielding, took a deep breath, and continued his journey through the frigid hold, not pausing to look at his men who lay like fallen soldiers. He did not stop until he reached the gym where he stripped off his shirt and began to exercise, chasing his thoughts like demons from his mind.

The gym was ill-used, but that hadn't surprised Jack after a look at Harkness' crew. The surprise was that the transport even carried a gym. He winced a little as he flexed. Deep, purpling bruises still covered his torso. He'd be healed by the time they pulled out of hyperdrive and began to decel though . . . one valid reason for not being chilled down. His peculiar susceptibility to cold sleep fever was another.

The action on Bythia had not injured him badly, but it had cost him the life of his commander and friend. Jack would be long in forgetting Kavin. Besides their friendship, the two had shared the common background of being battle armor Knights, infantry soldiers who were mobile tanks, fighting ground warfare designed to annihilate the enemy and not the planet they fought upon. Virtually no one beyond the two of them was now trained in "Pure" warfare, although the art of wearing battle armor had recently been recommissioned by Emperor Pepys. Now Jack stood alone.

He would have to find a way to carry on.

Sweat tickled its way down his skin. He counted off his sets mercilessly, whipping his body back into shape, until he was too exhausted to move.

Jack woke, groggily, on his back on one of the exercise mats, his face still clammy with sweat. Jack looked up, his neck stiff and cramped, and stretched. Over him stood a

white suit of battle armor, opalescent Flexalinks muted by
the dimmed lights of a ship in downtime. The deadly gauntlet, powerful enough to crush his skull, each finger the firing
barrel of a destructive weapon, was poised, curving over
him as though in benediction.

Jack smiled, grasped the gauntlet and got to his feet.

Hi, boss.

"Hello, Bogie. Feeling better?"

The regenerating being that now occupied his battle
armor paused. *I'm cold.*

Jack bent over to loosen the muscles in his legs preparatory to finding the refresher and cleaning up. He craned
his neck to look back. "It's standard temp in here, buddy."

He returned to his standing position and frowned. He
knew little about the creature in his armor except that it
was as fierce in fighting nature as a Milot berserker, but
hadn't, thank god, the cannibalistic, parasitic tendencies of
the giant saurians. Jack had not been sure about that at
first, and had been haunted by the growing sentience of his
battle armor.

More than microscopic, regenerating out of a square of
leather that ought to have been dead tissue, Bogie had
been implanted in his suit on Milos during the Sand Wars,
twenty-five years ago. It was hot in a suit. Jack had welcomed the adaptation by his Milot repair technician. The
circuitry and gear inside occasionally poked and prodded
at his back, and the weight of a field pack with a small-
muzzle laser cannon could dig holes in his flesh. Many of
the Knights hung a leather chamois. It had been the death
of a lot of them. Their body heat and sweat could nurture
a berserker into parasitic life. By the time a Knight knew
what was happening, he was a consumed man, trapped inside his suit of armor like it was a meat locker.

Jack looked at his own suit of battle armor.

Bogie had a small towel draped across his left wrist. Jack
took it and mopped his face, wondering briefly where the
Milots had gotten the leather chamois they used for his
infestation, thinking that they were implanting a berserker
and giving him Bogie instead. He tossed the towel in the
corner.

Unlike a Milot berserker, Bogie had soul. In fact, his
mind and soul were forming far more quickly than his phys-

ical being. The chamois hanging inside the armor showed little change from when it had originally been placed there. It was a little thicker. If Jack held it between his fingers, he could sense a pulsing life. Bogie was like an embryo and neither he nor the sentience knew what it was he had to have to finish regeneration. Berserkers ate their way through blood and flesh. Though there was no denying that Jack's presence in the suit vitalized Bogie, neither knew how. Because of that, and Bogie's hardwired-like psychic hookup with the suit circuitry itself, he had not removed and incubated the chamois. He feared killing the creature that way.

From a liability, Bogie had become an asset. From a parasite, he had evolved into a companion. Jack didn't like the armor's coldness and considered the fragility of life that was Bogie's present state. The only way he knew to warm the suit was to wear it. He looked about the massive ceiling of the gym. It had once been part of the freight hold, he decided. He had room.

"How about we suit up and go through some basic exercises?"

I would like that.

Jack unsealed the seams and got in. He spent some time clipping leads to his bare torso before settling in and then sealing himself up.

The holo came up, a soft-tinted rosy glow that read his muscular movement and relayed it to the suit, through a step-up transformer. A blow meant to swat a butterfly could conceivably crush a small mammal. Such was the power of a man once inside a suit.

There was more now. Jack felt the immediate enveloping embrace of Bogie, close and intimate, like a lover.

Only this being was born to fight, Jack knew. Just as he had been sworn to.

Jack smiled tightly to himself as he finished suiting up. "Okay, Bogie. Let's pretend we're killing Thraks."

Kick ass, boss, the armor responded.

He began to drill.

Neither man nor machine saw the twilight wrapped shadow that watched from the far recesses of the hold as, with a muffled burp, Harkness reeled out of sight and lumbered back down the corridors of his command.

*　　*　　*

The navigator frowned at his blipping screen. "I don't like it," he complained to his employer.

Harkness hawked and swallowed it down. "Quit whining," he said. "What do you want me to do, pull out of hyperspace and make a fracking coordinate change? We might end up inside solid rock."

Alij stabbed a pointed nail at his screen. "Sir, we might anyway. Something's happening out there, and I don't like it."

The pilot straightened. He scrubbed a hand over his patchy head of grizzled hair. The slim brown navigator glared at him. That arrogant Dominion Knight son of a bitch had warned him it would come to this. The pilot shrugged. He reached for the com system and thumbed it onto page. "Captain Storm, your presence is requested on the bridge."

Alij sat back in his chair and hid his startled expression in the glow of his screen, but he was the first to jump in eagerness when the bridge doors *schussed* open minutes later to admit the soldier.

There was not a man in Harkness' crew who hadn't at one time or another spied on the Dominion Knight, particularly if he could be found drilling in the gym. Most of the Knights aboard had had their equipment destroyed before retreating. The crewmen had a morbid fascination in watching the battle armor at work after having faced it themselves when they'd tried to subdue Storm. It was a killing machine, no doubt about it. Now, Alij watched warily as the man entered the bridge.

"Problem, pilot?"

Harkness growled in his throat again, then said, "My navigator says he's getting feedback through his hyperspace readings. Any idea what could be going on?"

Jack looked at the pilot. He knew the grudging expression for what it was. Capitulation, fueled by worry. He looked to the navigator. "When are we due to pull out and decel?"

"Beginning of next watch. Say, twelve hours. We're two weeks out of Malthen, putting on the brakes all the way."

"Close." Without edging the pilot out of the way, Jack squeezed in as close as he could to the instrumentation board. He was no pilot. His skill was warfare, specifically, the infantry. But Harkness was a transport pilot, a man used to handling freight and the occasional cold ship. Jack could not read what he saw on the screen either, but he didn't like it.

He wondered if the Thraks could be waiting for them at the edge, having calculated their most likely reentry point from hyperspace. The Thraks knew they'd been at Bythia— hell, that was the incident that had started the war six weeks ago. It would take about that long to begin mustering forces.

Harkness' cold ship would be priceless to them because of its cargo locked in cold sleep. Jack frowned. He looked at Harkness and the copilot swiveled in his chair. To the copilot he said, "Bring up the subspace bulletin board."

"Sir, we haven't got time to put out a call and receive an answer—"

"I know, officer. I'm looking for bulletins, not placing a call."

"What?" Harkness practically gargled in his sputtering rage.

Jack ignored him until the monitor scrolled up the info he wanted. "There!"

The copilot froze the screen.

Some subspace ham had spread the word the best way he knew how, and Jack's face tightened in appreciation. He had no way of knowing yet if Thraks had attacked anywhere, but here at least were corridor coordinates of the latest warship placements. "Navigator—"

"Alij, sir."

"Order up a graphics overlay. I'll bet my armor you've got Thraks sitting there, waiting for us."

Alij moved to the computer and made his verbal requests.

"Damn." Harkness smacked a beefy fist on the back of his chair. The bridge quivered in response. "Any chance of collision?"

Jack said, "I doubt it, but they'll be firing as soon as they can track us."

"They'll never catch up with us."

"They won't need to. They'll catch you turning the corner for braking, and trap us on the right angle, during the vector changeover."

Harkness' expression flickered. Grudgingly, he said, "Thought you weren't a pilot."

"I'm not. But I've fought Thraks before and I know how they can attack vessels."

The pilot said nothing. He looked to Alij as the computer began to show graphic overlays of corridors and windows. Alij, without knowing what he was doing, began to nod vigorously as Jack's suspicions were confirmed. "Yes . . . yes . . . here they are . . . yes . . ."

The pilot squeezed his bulky body upward into a firm stance. He nodded at Jack. "Thank you, captain."

"You're welcome, Harkness. We're not out of this yet. A transport vehicle like this is most vulnerable when it pulls out of hyperspace and turns that corner to begin braking . . . and it's my bet the Thraks aren't going to blow us out of the sky."

"No?" A bushy eyebrow went up.

"No. I'm afraid what they'll have in mind this time is taking prisoners."

The copilot broke the silence with a hoarse whisper. "We'd be better off dead."

CHAPTER 2

"Giving up already, Leoni?" Harkness growled.

"No, sir." The sallow-faced man straightened hunched shoulders. "Have you ever seen a sand planet, sir? After the Thraks have come in and taken over?"

Jack stood quietly, listening to the exchange. He was very careful not to let emotion flicker across his face.

Harkness shook his head.

"Well, I have. About ten years ago. The crew I was on had to bring in a load of supplies under treaty. Not that the bugs need much on a sand planet, but trade is trade, right?" His brown eyes blinked guiltily. His employer did not respond. Leoni plunged ahead. "It's eerie. My guess is the planets don't survive long, with the whole ecosystem shot like that . . . the oceans are there, but most of the vegetation is gone. It's been eaten down into these coarse granules, beige and rust colored. I held some in my bare hand. It felt like bugs were in it, squirming around. My skin stung for weeks. The Thraks lay their eggs in the stuff, and the larvae eat the sand, sort of. I remember looking at it and thinking, this used to be grassland, once. Or maybe a forest or someone's farm. No more."

Leoni looked around the control room. "I could stand there. I could still breathe the air even though it had thinned out some. But I wouldn't want to live there. It's my idea of hell."

"You were lucky," Alij said. "I heard about a trader run that stayed—the bodies of its crew added to the supply list."

"That's an old story," Harkness countered. "I've never heard proof of it."

"What proof would there be? We know from the Sand

Wars that the Thraks have little use for prisoners. Even if they wanted us, we wouldn't be kept in very good shape."

"Then we need to make sure it won't go that far."

Jack let his breath out slowly. He felt their gazes upon him. He looked about the control room. Harkness cleared his throat.

"What are you going to do?"

He took it in before responding, "What kind of weaponry do you have?"

"Four guns, two mounted on each fin aft. Not much."

"Is the firing circuitry mounted on a single board, or do you have to have a man at each gun?"

"They're tied in."

"That helps. Anything else? Mines?"

"No. My reputation is my best defense. Everybody knows I don't carry much of any worth," Harkness said.

"And this ship maneuvers like a garbage scow." Jack saw the pilot wince, but did not apologize. He looked over Alij's shoulder to the computer screen where the graphics overlay brilliantly detailed the window of their exit and the likely placement of the Thrakian warship waiting for them. "We have some time," he said. "I need to think." With that, he left a stunned silence behind him on the bridge.

He sought the gym and Bogie. The battle armor hung on its rack, quiet and yet deadly. Jack approached it and sat down cross-legged in front of it.

The battle which the transport crew and the Thraks were about to engage in was not in his line of expertise. He knew that and surely Harkness' crew comprehended it—but perhaps not. He fought on the surface, a man-shaped mobilized tank, a machine meant to slog through the lines of the enemy. He was, in so many words, a weeder.

The thought creased into a smile. Some weeds were tougher than others to pull.

He stood up and went to the suit. He needed to think and there was only one way he could do it without interruption. Bogie blossomed open to him and, after kicking off his boots and stripping off his jacket, he stepped in. Inside, he kept himself occupied clipping leads to his torso and taking care of the other details of suiting up. He tried to ignore the chamois at his back as it settled about his shoulders like some bat-winged creature. He closed the seams and snugged the helmet on with a half-twist to seal it. The world immediately became muffled. Isolated. Refined to the visor and the target grid.

"Bogie," Jack said. "I need to remember."

The sense of welcoming surrounding him pulled back in surprise. Then, *Jack, do you not remember on your own?*

How could he explain what had been done to him in the name of the Dominion? The seventeen years he'd lain in cryogenic sleep, adrift on a lost transport, his mind locked into a military debriefing loop. Those years had stripped away most of his memory of his youth and his beginnings, just as the Thraks had physically stripped away his family when they'd attacked Dorman's Stand and reduced it to a sand planet. The corner of Jack's mouth twisted bitterly. Nor had he been well-treated when found. There had been ugly hints that perhaps his mind had undergone indoctrination when being brought out of cold sleep and treated for the side effects those seventeen years had wrought.

Jack had one recourse left to capture those years—Bogie. He had no way of knowing for sure if the creature had been alive enough while first incubated on Milos to absorb any of Jack's conscious or subconscious memories, but while on Bythia, there had been some indications of Bogie's ability to do so. It was Jack's only way to regain what being a soldier for the Dominion had stolen away from him.

He could feel the warm and comforting presence of the chamois across his shoulders and back, almost as though a fatherly figure had put an arm around him.

"Bogie," Jack said quietly. "Your memory is all I have left of Milos and before. If you can remember, if you can give it to me so that I can remember, then. . . ."

Then what?

"I'm not sure. Then I'll know why I fight. Why I hate. Why Amber is in danger just being a part of me. But today I have to remember all of what I know about how Thraks fight. I remember most of it . . . but it's overshadowed by the Milots and their damn berserkers." Jack plunged to a halt. "Dammit, I'm not a computer. I don't have access to old files."

Neither am I. I . . . cannot do what you wish of me.

"Bogie, you remember, I know you do—you kept me

going on Bythia, and what you remember may be piece-meal but it's better than nothing! It's mine. *Give it back to me!*"

I have no control. I don't understand things well enough yet. I'm still new, Jack.

Jack stood inside his armor and suddenly felt alien to this piece of equipment that had been his second skin for as long as he could remember. *Could remember*, dammit, that was the problem. He stretched and felt the Flexalinks move with him. Because he had no solace other than in movement, he fell into a drill routine.

The armor moved with him supplely, far more gracefully than most would suspect looking at its rigid links, but that was part of its effectiveness. The rest depended a great deal on the man wearing it, for the structure took care and maintenance and a man was only as good as his mechanical ability in the field.

Bogie said suddenly, in his undervoice which sounded like rocks tumbling over one another in a deep-running stream, *I can give you this.*

Jack had hit the power vault before hearing Bogie, and as the memory hit him, he doubled over and the suit slammed into the hold flooring, but Jack barely felt it, for he was burning inside his mind.

Fire swept across a verdant world. Peace and healing disrupted in the middle of the night. The skies vibrated as warships came down, and their weapons struck. A firestorm sweeping across Claron, charring all in its path—his breath caught in his throat. Fear again. The suit, his escape, his tumbling in freefall in deep space without hope of ever being caught . . . the horror of knowing this memory came courtesy of, not the Thraks, but warring factions within the Dominion itself where he should have had no enemy.

"Bogie!"
Jack.
"Stop it," Jack ground out, his body curled tightly in pain, his temples throbbing, his gut sucked to his backbone in the nauseating panic of endless freefall.

As abruptly, the memory left.

Jack caught his breath first. Sweat dripped off his fore-head. He had no idea the memories he'd asked for would be vivid recreations of what he had gone through. Before he could say anything else, Bogie said, *Perhaps this will be better.*

He was swept away again. . . .

Dust motes swirled in the air, and he sneezed as he leaned over a row of greens, the sound of the automatic harvester droning in the background. The sky was the color of his mother's eyes, brilliant yet everchanging blue, even to the clouds which wisped across. The dirt gave up the smell of growing things, leafy greens hybridized from what had been collard greens on old Earth, Home World, but which Jack was just used to seeing heaped up in his mother's crockery, steaming under butter as greens. He liked them well enough. They were a staple product of his parents' farm. Jack preferred the orchard though he could not climb in any of the trees except for the windbreaks.

He pinched at a leaf now, examining the underside critically for sign of mites or fungus, frowning in an expression which he knew imitated that of his father. His father stood far away at the fields' end, carrying his keypad in the crook of his arm, varying the harvesting pattern of his machinery as he worked.

Jack stood up. He looked down the row of growth and saw, almost beyond his eyeshot, a nest resting under wavering, wilting leaves. The harvester loomed beyond, darkening the horizon with its presence.

He moved so quickly he almost lost his cap. His brother's cap, too, and not only would he catch hell for wearing it, he'd catch double hell for losing it, he thought as he bolted forward. He pitched forward, scampering down the irrigation trough, even as the nesting bird dove past his face, wings fluttering and beating at his eyes. Jack ducked away and tugged his hat on tighter.

He stopped a few meters from the nest and stood, his chest heaving from the run. His shirt clung wetly to his back. Dust swirled around him and then settled. The noise of the harvester battered against his ears and he looked up, watching it head straight at him.

His dad was beyond sight and hearing. Jack would have to save the nest on his own. He eyed the creamy black and white swirled shells. The mother would come back—she'd just been nipping at his ear—and if she perceived him as a real threat, she'd cover the nest, feign a broken wing, then try to lead him away.

It was the nest covering movement he waited for even as the harvester bore down on them, blocking out the sun's rays as it came.

Jack stopped squinting as the shadow fell across them. He reached up and took his brother's cap off as he waited.

The bird wheeled about him once, her gray and speckled body arrowing across the field. He caught a glimpse of white-ringed amber eyes, piercing and alarmed.

If only Dad hadn't taken the safety off the harvester, it would have perceived him and halted. It was a drain on the batteries, Dad said, and so he'd removed it. Who would be stupid enough to stand in front of the machine, anyway?

Salty sweat dripped into his eyes and he brushed the sting away with the back of his hand, wincing as his vision blurred. From the corner of his eye, he saw the mother bird drop frantically to earth and attempt to cover her nest with both her body and any stray twigs she could scratch up.

Jack pounced, cap in hand.

He could feel the heat reflecting off the harvester's grill, waffling off his face. He'd have freckles for sure after this!

The cap swooped down, locking over fowl and nest. Jack shoveled in his other hand underneath and plucked the nest from the ground, a mere meter from the harvester's whirling blade. He turned and ran.

He didn't stop running until he reached the windbreak. There, he found a tree with a comfortable fork that he could reach if he shinnied up high enough. It was tough going with the nest in hand, but he made it, locked his legs around the trunk and deposited the nest. He left the cap on it and fell back to earth.

The grass here was lean and stringy, half-browned by the sun, and it did little to cushion his fall. Jack leaned back on his spare hips and bruised elbows—always bruised, he remembered—and watched the nest. The cap joggled and dimpled as something under it moved.

He had to leave it alone now, leave it alone or risk chasing off the mother bird for good. He knew that. He knew almost as much about the local creatures as he did about

his father's farm. So he watched as the mother bird
emerged, fluffing her wings out indignantly, and knocking
the cap off herself. It fell to one side and hung on a slender
twig. He thought of what he'd tell his brother to get him
to come out of the house and see what had happened to
his cap.

The mother bird looked over her nest and appeared to
be satisfied with conditions. Jack caught his breath. He, too,
was satisfied. As he got ready to get to his feet and dust
himself off, the twig broke and the cap slid down to land
at his feet. Jack grinned and picked it up. All in all, a
good day.

Jack sat up. The suit moved with him. Bogie said, *I
cannot control it.*

"I understand," Jack answered. He drew in his breath.
His brother. The farm. His father. He'd forgotten most of
that. He leaned his head forward, touching the cool shield
of the visor to his forehead. He had his nightmares of the
Thraks. He'd encountered one or two as a free mercenary.
He knew what he had to know to face them.

He got to his feet. The gauntlets flexed as he balled his
hands. Nine fingers clenched. Ten in his memory of a boy
scooping a nest out of the path of destruction. How close
had that blade been? Perhaps it would have been only a
matter of time until he'd had that finger sheared off, for
he'd cheated the blades that day. The scar ached in
response.

Again, Bogie said.

He wanted to tell her she was free, but he was afraid
she'd smell the murders of two men on his hands, and so he
decided to wait until morning to gift her with their deaths.

"Amber," he said, to capture her attention. "Look at
me."

Her face turned. She used her hair to veil her thoughts
from him, its strands sweeping down and covering half her
face. One soft brown eye watched him warily.

He could think of nothing else to do and nothing that
he wanted to do more. He crossed the room and knelt
beside her on the pillows, and took her in his arms. Gently
he swept back her hair.

The expression in her eyes shocked him. "You love me," he said quietly, and was surprised to hear his voice waver.

Amber shook her head. "Dammit, Jack. It took you long enough to see it."

"I haven't been looking."

"No." She reached up and traced the side of his face where a very faint scar swept into his dark blond hair, all that was left of a laser burn she'd doctored for him long ago. "And if I were looking, what would I see?"

A heat rose in him and he found it difficult to answer, "The same, I hope."

She hugged him tightly again, burying her face in the curve of his neck where it met his shoulders. That was all the answer he needed.

The pile of pillows shifted, covering the floor near the Bythian courtyard window as they lay back. Jack fought for control, trying to move slowly, his hands seeking out, then holding the curves of her body. She answered, biting his lower lip gently, then moving away so that she could open his shirt. She uncurled the hairs on his chest as though they were buds and found his own nipples, and caressed, then kissed them.

She took her robe off. Bare skin touched bare skin. The port wine dark sky without sheltered them in privacy. A house lizard skimmed the curtains as Jack moved over her. She tangled her fingers in his hair, drawing his face close to hers, gentle brown eyes widening in the mystery of their first lovemaking.

Even as he moved to open her, lightning struck his mind. Its blue fire silvered through and he stiffened, unable to move without pain. All desire was seared from his flesh even as Amber moved to draw him closer. Paralyzed, his senses darkening, he could say nothing as he slipped from consciousness, knowing Amber's mind had struck to kill him.

He came to, sweat cascading down his torso, and Bogie said, *I am sorry.*

Jack's throat had constricted and he could not respond for a moment.

I don't understand these memories, Bogie added. Then, *Again.*

"No!" Jack cried, as a crimson wash flooded his eyesight, and his body froze in catatonic reaction as Bogie fed him one last memory. Thrakian forms rose before him.

Harkness leaned over Alij's shoulder. He straightened and looked out over the bridge. "Where the hell is he? Is he going to do something or not? We're out of frigging time."

Leoni said tersely, "He's still suited up in the gym. He's been motionless like that for hours."

"Maybe he's meditating or something before battle. I heard about those Knights," Alij added.

"Meditating." Harkness made a sound deep in his phlegmy throat. His response was cut short by the opening of the bridge portal, and then the opalescent glare of the whitish battle armor filled the bulkhead. The man could not move all the way inside; he was too large for the compartment.

Jack took his helmet off. Fresh air tickled across his face. Sweat plastered his hair to his head as he cautiously ran gauntleted fingers through it. He smiled briefly in memory of a bald sergeant who swore he'd lost his hair that way, lasering himself with his own gauntlet.

The three officers looked at him.

"Well," Harkness rumbled. "What are we going to do?" He stabbed a finger at the screen where the edge of sub-space now defined the clear presence of a Thrakian warship waiting for them.

Jack said, "I suggest we surrender."

CHAPTER 3

"Surrender?" Harkness straightened his bulk, a half-growl smothering in his throat. "I knew it the minute you wouldn't go into cold sleep. I should have known it the minute I saw the lot of you straggling in, your butts whipped. You're a goddamn coward."

Alij had gotten to his feet, resting a slim but trembling brown hand on the back of his chair. "Pilot," he said to his employer, but Harkness was advancing on Jack, battle armor or not.

"You're afraid of the deep sleep and you're afraid of them, out there!" Harkness jerked his head. Spittle hung from the corner of his mouth that he did not bother to wipe away.

"You're a damn fool if you're not afraid of the Thraks," Jack said evenly. He carried his helmet under his left arm like a second head. Removed, but not inactivated, faint noises came from the gear.

"I won't lose my ship to Thraks!"

Jack arched an eyebrow. "I don't think you have much choice, pilot. This . . . ship . . . is not equipped to fight. Leoni, am I correct in my assessment of the cryo bay as a lifeboat unit that can be detached?"

"Yes, sir."

"How long is it equipped to maintain life support?"

"Four weeks."

"With its cargo awake?"

"No, sir," Leoni said, ignoring Harkness' look of spite and hatred at him. "Awake, a little less than ten days."

Jack looked back to Harkness who stood, his beefy frame shaking with ineffectual rage. "Ever docked with the lifeboat before?"

"What has this to do with anything, you ball-less wonder?"

"Everything." Jack pressed against the bulkhead, leaning in as far as he could, until his broad-shouldered armor stopped him. "You do have a pilot's license, do you not?"

"Yes. Yes, goddammit, I've got a license."

"Then, sometime in your career, you must have passed the exams to do so. Could you do it again?"

Harkness' face worked even as the veins went from red to purplish, mottling his expression. "I could," he said, finally, defeated by his inability to vent his anger adequately. "You damn son of a bitch."

Jack ignored him. "Alij, I need you to set up coords for some alternate windows."

Cat-quick, the navigator sat back down. Harkness spat and then said, "Belay that order."

"Do it, Alij."

The navigator looked from Jack's quiet insistence to his pilot. He stopped, unsure of what to do next.

"I need those coords now."

"No, goddammit! This is still my ship!"

"No," Jack said. "Not now it isn't. Now it is damn near the Thraks' ship and the longer we argue, the closer we are."

The pilot's ham hands folded into fists. "I won't let you do it!"

"Sir?" Alij looked from face to face.

"You stupid son of a bitch," Harkness threw at him. "He means to jettison the cold bay and let the Thraks scuttle after it."

The two subordinate officers stopped in their movements and looked to Jack, shock livid on their faces.

Jack shook his head. "No," he said. "I mean to set them free in subspace, before the Thraks know we've done it. It's their only chance. We'll still be the main target." He waved a gauntlet about the cabin. "The main lifeboat gone, we'll still have considerable left of this hulk. Most of it empty, isn't it, Harkness?"

"You're my only contract this run," the pilot grumbled reluctantly. His mottling began to fade and his small eyes showed a flicker of interest instead of rage. "I still think you're a son of a bitch, but I'm beginning to think you're up to something."

"Good," Jack answered. "I am. Set the crew to readying the lifeboat for detachment. As soon as Alij has coords to show me, I'll be picking out the release point."

"Where do you want them to be?" Alij asked as he swung around in his chair and prepared to manipulate the computer.

"Away from us and the Thraks. Preferably behind them, if they'll have the trajectory. Pilot, come with me."

Harkness' rage was gone now, replaced by wariness. "Why?"

"I need you to give some orders, and a tour." Jack smiled, but it was not an altogether pleasant expression. "I want to see what's left of this shell with the main lifeboat gone."

Jack doubted if Harkness had ever heard of a Trojan Horse or would appreciate the strategy if told of it. The pilot gave orders to cast off the lifeboat without further question, but was uncharacteristically silent as he waddled along beside Jack's armor. Most of the transport was dimly lit, if at all. Jack paused a moment and waited for their footsteps to stop echoing inside a corridor.

He looked down at the pilot. "No wonder you're a poor man, Harkness . . . all this space and only one contract for the run."

The man flushed again, red bursting all the way into the wattle of his neckline. He spat to one side. "What do you want from me?"

"I want to know where you keep the contraband. The corridors and holds." Jack rapped sharply on a metal plate. "Like behind here."

With a noise that was more growl than hawk, Harkness reached for a bolt and twisted it. The panel slid open. Jack aimed the sensor-tripped lightbeam from his helmet into the area. It was empty. He looked at the pilot.

Harkness shrugged. "Figure it out," he said. "I had to make the run empty this time. Pepys didn't give me a chance to pick up any other cargo."

Jack pursed his lips in thought a moment as he examined the interior of the hidden hold. He stopped his inspection long enough to reply, "And that just might save your life, Harkness. Now show me the rest of the tunnels."

The pilot shook his head, not in denial but in puzzlement. He looked up at Jack, one eye narrowed as if trying to focus on him better. The pilot's intense gaze swept across Jack's face. "Where the hell does Pepys get his Knights from?"

Jack smiled tightly. "You'd be surprised, pilot. You'd be surprised."

"I already am. Follow me," Harkness returned and then continued waddling down the corridor. He did not seem to notice that his gripper boots made far more noise than those of Jack's heavy armor. "It occurs to me that I might owe you an apology."

"For thinking I'm afraid of Thraks? I have a healthy respect for them, and the damage they can do. If I didn't, I wouldn't even consider casting the cryo bay off."

"Then what do you have in mind?" Harkness stumbled to a halt, and his eyes narrowed. "You're going to let them board us."

"Yes."

"And we'll hide like smugglers."

"No," Jack corrected. "You'll hide like smugglers. I'll be hunting."

"Jay-sus," Harkness blurted. He rubbed his hand over his face.

"Now," Jack finished. "Show me the whereabouts of the backup lifeboat."

This request the pilot didn't even try to figure out. He just turned and led Jack to it without another word.

Jack sat in the gym, the only place really large enough to accommodate him when he was equipped, and he studied the information Alij and Leoni had brought him. The copy lay across his lap. The shortness of time niggled at him when a buzz of static came across the intercom and Leoni intoned, "The cryo bay's ready for cast off."

Jack stood. The copy sloughed off his lap and drifted to the floor, but Jack did not pick it up. The information was branded in his mind and it was not likely that he could close his eyes for the next few weeks and not see it emblazoned across his vision. He traversed the corridors to the

bridge where Harkness and the other two awaited him.
They were standing double-watch, and the stress of the
command showed in their bloodshot eyes as they watched
him fill the doorway.

He told Alij which coords he wanted used, and the navigator repeated them to the computer.

Harkness had his head tilted, listening. "That doesn't
give us much time," the pilot remarked.

"No. Nor them." Jack cleared his throat. "Before it goes,
I want you to tell the nursing staff to start waking the
sleepers."

"What? What in the hell are you thinking of? They've
got four weeks' supply with sleepers. Less than ten days
awake, or maybe you didn't hear Leoni earlier. And that's
just an estimate. If any of those Knights are as big as you
are, the demand's stronger."

"I heard," Jack said. He felt the pain etching itself into
furrows across his forehead. "But I won't condemn anyone
to drift into death asleep."

"If the Thraks take us," Harkness persisted, "it'll take
two weeks to get Dominion needlers out here to pick them
up. They can't make it awake, you've got to leave them
chilled down."

"Then," Jack said, "I'll just have to make sure the
Thraks don't take us." He turned and left the bridge, but
he could feel the fear and hatred in their eyes washing
after him.

Jack felt the lurch and plunge of the transport as the
cryo bay left it. He moved to the portal screen and watched
it drop away suddenly, its inertia carrying it on a different
voyage from that of the mother ship as Harkness fired ret-
ros to change the course of the transport. He felt Amber's
and Colin's nearness torn away from him as if, even in
sleep, they had been close in their dreams and thoughts.
Don't let this be a mistake, he thought. Then he straightened. Ten days and counting. Amber had ten days of life
left for him to defeat the Thraks and relocate the cryo bay.

As painful as it was, he did not stop watching the
tracking blip until the screen lost it. Instead of ordering it
to fine tune on the blip and follow it, Jack let it go.

*   *   *

He hooked up the suit in a way it hadn't been since the Sand Wars. He paused as he reached the dead man circuit. That little device was to prevent the armor being taken from him by enemies on the battlefield. Remove a dead or wounded Knight from his armor without knowing how to disarm the circuit, and the suit self-destructed. He would be facing the enemy now. He looped the circuit in. He was nine days and counting when the freighter erupted out of subspace and began braking for Malthen, and the Thrakian warship flared into being beside them, tractor beams on full, and the two ships shuddered as they made contact.

Then he smiled.

CHAPTER 4

Amber wore her thermal sheet about her like a cape. It kept her warm. Her clothes weren't enough; cold sleep permeated the entire atmosphere of the bay, and her skin was peaked with goosebumps that refused to go away, even when Colin dropped his arm about her shoulders. His presence was enough to light a fire normally and she gratefully shrugged into the added heat although nothing would help the emptiness of waking up and finding Jack gone.

"Your hands are ice cold, child," the older man scolded after reaching for and cupping one. "You came off dialysis too quickly!" His handsomeness had softened into aged good looks, but his square chin jutted in concern.

"No! No, it's not that." Amber cut him off from summoning the nurse. She darted out from under his embrace with a quickness born of the streets. Colin watched her impassively as, now facing him, she remembered their shared past together, how the two of them had met, and knew he also remembered. She had the grace to flush. She'd been stranded on a very wintery and inhospitable frontier post and she'd tried to roll the Walker prelate. His aide had caught her—her punishment had been that Colin took her in and helped her in her quest. That time, after basic survival, it had been to find Jack.

A cold tremor swept through her. Colin put his hand out to her again. "Come on," he said. "You'll feel better when we find Jack. We'll both feel better."

Amber shook her head even as they moved off together. "Jack's not here," she said.

"Nonsense. Maybe he's not up yet, but we'll find him."

Amber stopped in her tracks, forcing Colin to a halt also. "Colin, Jack didn't go into cold sleep. *He's not here*." She added softly, "I think we're detached. That's why the nursing staff isn't letting us disperse to transport quarters. This bay and the three rooms—that's all there is."

"Detached? You mean we're floating free?"

"I think so. Jack thought this whole bay looked like a lifeboat. Something's gone wrong and they won't tell us until everyone is awake." Suddenly, the thermal sheeting had done its work. She felt warm, burning, and she let the sheet fall to the deck. The shame of being left behind by Jack flushed through her being. He didn't trust her—how could he? Somehow he must have learned that her mission on Bythia had been to kill him. And although the snakeskin Hussiah had taught her well, had peeled away her subliminal training to kill, he had also brought her psychic assassination abilities to the surface. Her rescue by Jack had saved his life as well as her own. But . . . had he known? Did he doubt her still? She rubbed at her blue-dyed arms as if she could chafe away her past and her fears.

Before she could say more, a young man detached himself from the group forming at the interior bay doors and strode their way. He wore the rich dark blue uniform of a Dominion Knight. Its color set off the white-blondness of his looks, silken hair in a defiant brush, eyes that were blue without compromise of gray or green, fair skin that had acquired a sprinkling of freckles from exposure to the Bythian sun. He drew near them, a wrinkle across his young forehead from his earnest expression. A look passed between the Walker saint and this young soldier. He paused as if he'd intended to speak to Colin first, then turned and looked at her.

"Are you all right?"

Amber looked at him. She tried to quell her rapidly growing anger, but Rawlins evidently felt it. His blue eyes showed his pain. She shook her head. "I'm sorry, Rawlins. Jack isn't here."

"I know that, ma'am. The commander told me he was staying awake."

"He *told* you?" Amber thought he'd told no one but her.

"Yes, ma'am. He's been anticipating action from the Thrakian League. I'd say from our present situation that we've been cut loose from transport and as we lose momentum, we'll be coming out of subspace shortly. I'd also say he's had some of the trouble he's been looking for." Rawlins flushed across the cheekbones as though he'd relish sharing that trouble.

Colin frowned. His wrinkles, unlike Rawlins', were permanent. "What's our situation here?"

"Air and rations for about ten days. Maybe more if we stay relatively dormant. We're on a kind of autopilot but without the navigational equipment we need to redirect our course." Rawlins' gaze flickered and he looked toward Amber. "I came by to ask if I can help. I'd like to . . . look out for you."

Amber was hugging herself and staring off at a plated wall of the bay as though her gaze could burn a porthole through it. She brought herself back long enough to meet Rawlins' gaze. "I'm all right."

"Are you sure?" He bent quickly and picked up the thermal sheeting. "Cold sleep fever can be awfully hard on some people."

"I don't get it," Amber said tightly, as though her throat had closed up.

Rawlins looked back to the older man. "St. Colin?"

"I'm fine, thank you, lieutenant."

"I never had a chance to thank you, sir, but I'm told you saved my life."

There was a strange faraway look on the older man's face, but he gave only a short nod and said, "I was pleased to do it. You came to my aid in a difficult situation."

"Yes, sir. I don't remember much. I guess I just acted in a rush . . . but I'm glad I could be of help." Rawlins straightened but stopped short of snapping off a salute. "I'll be back if you need me."

Colin waited until Rawlins was out of earshot, then chuckled. Amber broke away from her inner thoughts long enough to glare at the Walker saint. "What's so funny?"

"Ah, my dear. It's you. You're breaking hearts again."

"I am? Oh." She stared off after Rawlins who'd disappeared into the ranks of now awakened Knights. She said nothing further, but folded herself up and sat down cross-legged on the cold floor. Jonathan detached himself from the medical quarters and, lumbering bearlike through the crowd, came in search of his minister. Colin sighed as he saw his bodyguard approach and looked down at her. "What are you going to do?"

"Meditate," Amber said.

"That sounds like an excellent idea. I could do with a bit of prayer myself." Unceremoniously, Colin joined her on the floor.

The old ship creaked and groaned as it was invaded. Jack leaned back inside his suit and listened through his mikes, picking up movement despite infamous Thrakian stealth. The short hairs along the back of his neck prickled. A rivulet of sweat started down his bare back between his shoulder blades, but the chamois that was Bogie's regenerated life soaked it up greedily.

The waiting would be the hardest. He had no qualms about that. Killing them would be difficult, but waiting for them to penetrate the various traps and deceptions he'd planted throughout the ship's hulk would be the hardest. That, and wondering if the Thraks would simply kill off Harkness and the crew once Jack's work began.

It was the little glitch in Jack's Trojan Horse plan which he'd forgotten to mention to the pilot. The Thraks might forget they were looking for Dominion Knights and simply take out their anger on the nearest human captives. Harkness and the crew would be easy for the Thraks to pick up, if they hadn't already. In a ship riddled with hideyholes, Jack had left them no place to hide. Jack had had to categorize the ship's crew as expendable. He'd had no choice. But that didn't mean he liked having done it. He wanted surety he'd be able to retrieve the cryogenic bay and Amber safely.

A hair thin thread of noise reached him. Jack's palms began to sweat. The gauntlets tingled at his wrists, indicating power up. He set his teeth.

He could hear them now. Their measured tread along the corridor flooring. The occasional metal clank as they probed the plates. Soon. Very soon now the two of them exploring this corridor would discover a hollowness where there should be none. They would, of course, investigate. Thraks might be alien, but they were not lacking in curiosity.

Metal and plastic sounded as the plating was drawn back. Jack braced himself as his target grids suddenly registered two blips. He was hidden. He wanted the Thraks within this hold before he killed them.

And he wanted to kill them as quietly as he could.

A blinding white beam Jack's visor could not screen out quickly enough swept his face plate. Vision seared, Jack swore and fired automatically, trusting his targeting grid. With a high keen, two forms thumped to the decking. He could hear their muffled death throes.

Blinking until he could see through his watering eyes, Jack stumbled out of the back of the hold. Both Thraks lay still, their chest plates punctured by his glove lasers. Lucky shots.

No. Not lucky. Instinctual.

He stared down at their huge bodies. Not quite insects. Supple, within their own dark brown and sable body plates. In death, their face plates had gone slack, exposing leathery skin and gaping mandibles. He supposed that would count for an expression of surprise. He'd never seen a Thrakian face without its face plates carefully held in a masklike position. Each mask indicated an emotional nuance, very formalized in its positioning. Diplomatic Thraks were more theatrical than the warriors, but even warriors used their masks as if they were shields.

Jack kicked the forms aside and left the contraband hold, making his way to the next trap.

He encountered his next victim in the corridor. As the creature seemed to sense him and turned, Jack hit the power vault and kicked. His foot connected with a sickening crunch. The armored boot knocked its head bouncing down the dim aisleway where it rolled into a crevice. Jack caught up the spasming body and carried it with him to the next hold where he threw it as far as he could into an empty corner. Ichor splashed as he did. Jack stepped into a shadowed far corner.

They sent another trio after him six hours later. Jack jerked awake from his doze as Bogie said, *They're here, boss.*

"Where?"

Three meters down the corridor, according to the sound grid.

Jack blinked hard. He had grit in the corners of his eyes.

Carefully, he rolled his shoulders to ease the tension in his back. "Thanks, Bogie."

Don't mention it. The warrior spirit's voice carried an edge of irony. *If you'd done it my way, we'd have been out of here a long time ago.*

"If I'd done it your way," Jack retorted, looking over his screens, "we'd have the whole Thrakian League on our necks, you bloodthirsty old pirate." He had time enough to wonder how many more his booby traps had picked off before the cubbyhole's plate was wedged aside.

No lights this time. The corner of Jack's mouth twitched. They knew he was stalking them now. The Thraks were aware enough of human composition to know that lighting might give Jack something of an advantage. What they were unaware of was that the power of their beams could blind him.

He could hear their clicking and chuckling beyond the opening. They seemed to be discussing who would penetrate the hold first. His twitch stretched into a half smile.

He watched as the first Thraks eased into the hold, slope-backed, on all fours, supple and quick, as cautious as a canine with its back up. It could not see him, Jack realized, and watched as its deathmask gaze swept his shadowy corner several times. Feathery antennae erected at cheekbone height from behind the mask.

Jack had never seen antennae on Thraks before. Adjunct sensory equipment? He watched the creature as it reared up into a fighting stance.

A second Thraks moved in, clacking angrily. It shadowed the first. Jack looked over their shoulders to the third, hovering in the background. He'd bring that one down first—its body would block the exit. As soon as it leaned in closer to its fellows. . . .

There was an immediate reaction when the first Thraks discovered the shell of a companion in the corner. Jack had a split second as the third Thraks reared in the doorway.

He shot, rolled, and stood up, fingers pointed, and blasted the other two even as they pulled their weapons into position.

A fiery beam glanced off the side of the helmet as the last Thraks went down, its mandibles white with froth.

From fear or anger?

Jack stepped over the bodies as he left the hold and shut it behind him. He could have walked through them to relish the crackle and crunch, but he had no way to clean the stain off his armor just yet.

He made his way deeper into the bowels of the freighter to yet another contraband hold, and closer to his ultimate objective, and waited for the next to the last time.

If his plan held.

The wait gave him time to think, and remember, and compare. He could not ever remember having seen antennae before, but then, he'd never stalked Thraks before. And he'd never before had the sensation he hadn't even been *seen*.

What was different this time?

Nothing. Not a damn thing that he could think of.

Perspiration beaded his upper lip. Bogie had flooded his mind with memories of the Sand Wars. If he had enough time to sort them out, perhaps. . . .

But his time was not his own. There was Amber to think of, and Colin, and his command of Knights, and his obligation to the evacuees.

They sent a whole damn company after him this time.

Bogie spoke just as the target and sound screens lit up.

"I see it," Jack told him.

You'd better be quick.

"Or I'll be dead. I know."

He had only a split second in which to notice that the antennae had gone out again, quivering after him as eagerly as dogs sniffing after a scent. Were they sniffing him out?

He did not have time to know if they'd succeeded, for his plan called for him to make himself a living target.

"Here I am," Jack called, and stepped out into the open.

Now you've done it.

Jack was too busy to retort.

He hit the power vault, spraying fire down below as he soared toward the cavernous roof of the cargo hold. He caught the hatch doorway above, and was through, in a wash of laser fire that turned the suit red-hot. He broke out in a sweat as he slammed the hatch lid down and secured the bulkhead, sealing the bay. The outer door below closed automatically as he set off the sensors, sending the last remaining lifeboat into launch sequence. The armor cooled as he waited for the inevitable.

The stripped down shell of what remained of the transport shuddered as the lifeboat powered off. Jack waited until the shuddering quit, then began to make his systematic way to the bridge.

He stopped a last time as the freighter quivered again, and he heard the sound of the Thrakian warship blasting off in pursuit of the lifeboat and its lost company of men.

A miserable, grubby lot of men awaited him on the bridge. They turned pale and battered faces toward him as he filled the bulkhead opening.

Harkness spat.

"It worked," he said. There was blood in his phlegm. "And at least we're alive."

"Now," Jack said, "Let's find our cryo bay while they can still say the same."

CHAPTER 5

Rawlins tapped Amber gently on the shoulder. She felt his touch as though she had been asleep underwater and even though she opened her eyes, she viewed him through a murky veil. It had been days since she'd first awakened to find the lieutenant following her like a white shadow. She brought a smile to her face and let it shine for Rawlins, though underneath, her emotions knotted. Amber found him smiling back as she came fully out of her meditations.

The air stank now. It spoke of bodies too close together, and water too scarce for bathing, and the air itself, too used up to be recycled well. It spoke, too, of time running out.

Her stomach echoed the speech.

Rawlins grinned as he lowered himself cross-legged onto the decking beside Amber. He held out a savory smelling bundle, wrapped about by a disposable cloth. "Last of the hot food," he said.

"Thank you." She did not have to fake warmth in her voice as she reached out and took her rations. "Did you eat?"

"Yes," he answered, his gaze flickering off toward the quiet people surrounding them.

She thought, in that second, that Rawlins was a great deal like Jack, able to be alone and private even in a crowd where privacy was nearly impossible. She also thought that Rawlins, like Jack, had probably given her a portion of his dinner. She would not insult him by asking further, and she ate her gift with swift, clean bites.

Rawlins flexed his back as though tense. Amber swallowed the last of the meat pie, then said, "What's wrong?"

His shockingly blue eyes flickered back to her, then he frowned. His brows were almost as milk-blond as his hair, but he'd darkened them with a liner. She could see the dye across the fine hairs. Then she realized part of what was so startling about his eyes: the lashes were nearly transparent, giving him a wide-open look.

Rawlins cleared his throat. "We've had no word from the freighter."

"Have they picked up our homing signal?"

"Not that we can tell."

"What do you think it means?"

"It means that, if Thraks did attack, the freighter may not have survived. Or that they can't get within range to find us. Or . . . we're on our own while they decoy the Thraks away."

"Or," Amber teased, "the world ended yesterday and we just don't know it yet."

He flushed. "And you're not worried?"

"Yes. But Jack has a way of surviving, even when he shouldn't. And we're alive today. So that counts for something. And I've just had dinner. That counts for a lot." Amber grinned.

"Is it true what the guys talk about?"

"That depends." Her grin faded. "What do they say?"

"That you're a street brat. That you grew up in under-Malthen."

"That I did. So my philosophy is easily explained. Live for today. Tomorrow, take care of tomorrow. Or something like that."

Rawlins shook his head. "It must have been tough."

She paused, squinting her eyes in recall. Rolf, the man who'd kept her and trained her, had not been a good person. But she'd had her freedom most of the time . . . a wild, flighty creature who would be recalled to her accounting only at sunset. A fey thing, with flashes of intuition that kept her alive, and successful, and protected her from Rolf. Her mind could, and would, kill. She'd almost killed Jack the night he had reached for her in love. The fear that she had, had driven her away in Bythia, straight into the arms of the holy madman Hussiah. The guilt burned her still. How could she face that happening again? There was no way of knowing if she had purged herself of the instinct to kill without intention . . . until the moment came again. Amber brushed her hand across her face as if looking for a stray bit of hair that tickled. The movement brushed away her thoughts. "It was . . . different," she answered. "How about you?"

"I'm a timber man. Or was, until I decided to become an officer. Then when the Knights expanded, I applied to join them."

"That's rare. Pepys doesn't like to recruit out of Dominion ranks."

"I know. But I'm good in armor."

She appraised him. Jack had mentioned Rawlins' ability many times. But the young man's soft declaration now was not boastful, merely confident. "So I've been told."

He colored then, and ducking his chin down, turned his face away.

Amber laughed, and put her hand on his arm. "I'm sorry, Rawlins! Really."

"Don't worry about it. Here I am with orders to be a tower of strength for you, and you're the one comforting me."

"Orders?"

He looked at her. "You know."

Indeed, she did. Jack thought of everything . . . but had he thought of the fact that she would find Rawlins strangely appealing? That he awoke in her an echo of what her feelings for Jack awoke? This was dangerous, Amber thought, and did not continue to meet his gaze. "Tomorrow," she said, "you can be a tower of strength for me." With a deep breath, she dropped back into her meditations, not only to control her usage of air, but also to calm the turmoil of emotions rising within her.

Rawlins watched her consciousness recede until he could no longer reach her. Around them sat or lay dozens of people in similar conditions, though Amber was a master of the deep trance. St. Colin had instructed them all on meditation in an effort to conserve air and keep stress under control.

He had no place else to go, and he wanted very much to be where he was, so he made himself comfortable and tried to drift away.

"There she is," Harkness said grimly. "We'll be in docking position in about six hours. It's going to be tight, commander."

Jack stood behind him, looking over the pilot's shoulder, at the com screens. "Better late than never," he said.

"Maybe. Maybe not. Depends on how levelheaded our lot has been. Pinned up in those three labs . . . we're going to have a squirrelly bunch."

"A good number of the evacuees are soldiers," Jack told him. "I think I can vouch for their actions. And St. Colin is quite a man. If you haven't seen him in action yet, I recommend you do so. He'll have been talking with them."

"I've seen you in action," Harkness growled. The purpled mottling of his face had deepened, but the swelling had gone down. "That's enough for me. Shall we mark the homing signal and let them know we're coming?"

Jack's gut tightened reflexively. He would like Amber to know he was close to her, but he did not want to give the Thraks any more information than he had to. "No," he said.

Harkness' head swiveled about to look at him, one frizzled eyebrow raised.

"No," Jack repeated levelly, meeting the pilot's gaze.

"Right," Harkness said, and looked back to his command. "Right." He cleared his throat. "We're close to a sand planet."

Jack had been on his way out. He stopped in his tracks as though he had been shot. "Which one? How close?"

"Opus. One of the last the Thraks took. I understand the nest ain't been too successful. It's damn near abandoned. We might be able to find some supplies if we go in."

"No. No, dammit, that's probably where that warship's from. Let's scoop up the lifeboat and get the hell out of here before they track us. Our call for Needler coverage has been out long enough. They should be close now."

"It's a gamble."

"One I'm willing to take."

The pilot chewed on the inside of his cheek before answering slowly, "Then it's one I'll take as well."

Jack looked at Harkness. Animosity was banked inside the bulky body as though it were some kind of slow-burning fire. "I'll see," he said, "that your freighter is re-outfitted."

Harkness took the information with a nod. He was the first to turn away. Jack waited another moment to see if the pilot had yet another bomb he wished to drop in Jack's lap, but the pilot said nothing more. Jack ducked back through the doorway and left the bridge.

What was left of the transport had been thoroughly cleaned down, but the stench of Thrakian dead seemed to have permeated everywhere. Jack found himself snarling as he walked back through the hulk to the vast gym.

If she had been here, Amber would wonder with Harkness why Jack hadn't destroyed every Thraks he could get his gauntlets on. He didn't know if he could explain to her that he did not want to send other Thraks into a frenzy of vengeance, that his only goal had been to make occupation of the freighter too expensive. Setting loose the second lifeboat had ensured that the Thraks would cut their losses and go after their remaining search party while they could. The Thraks were not berserker fighters. They had a calculated strategy behind much of what they did, even if it was incomprehensible to their enemies.

They were, after all, Jack mused, alien.

It was more surprising to him that there had been a sand planet one could classify as a "failure." Had it been too close to the Dominion territories? Had the Thraks been unable to complete terraforming? If so, why? A defeat to the Thraks was a victory for the Dominion and the Triad Throne, even if accidental. The trick was to find out what had happened so that it could be duplicated. Was what had happened the reason the Thraks stopped expanding so suddenly and sued for peace?

He stopped before his armor and eyed it critically. He'd been unable to strip and service it properly since leaving Bythia. Traces of warfare from two engagements stained it where he'd been unable to cleanse it better. Jack reached out and traced over the crudely painted over insignia on the suit's chest plate. There would be a day, soon, he promised himself, when he'd show that insignia again. When he returned to Malthen this time, he did so with full knowledge of who had been responsible for ordering Dominion troops abandoned on Milos.

Pepys, emperor of the Triad Throne. He hadn't been emperor then, of course, but the savage losses of the Sand Wars had been one of the major factors propelling Pepys into power.

And when Jack faced Pepys again, it would not be as a loyal Knight reporting to his monarch.

And Jack knew that Pepys knew it.

Bogie awoke under Jack's feather-light touch as he brushed the insignia. *Jack.*

He did not respond to his alter ego. Bogie's mental strength washed over him like an inexorable tide, probing, and then ebbing away into silence as the being sensed that he did not wish to converse.

The quiet left in Bogie's wake was shattered by a tone from the intercom monitor.

"Commander, it's not necessary to come up, but I'll feed this to you. We've never seen anything like it."

Again, Jack thought, as he went to the monitor and watched it flicker into life with the computer's projection. And this time, as last, the vision chilled his blood.

His silence was his answer and after a brief moment, Harkness said, "You don't recognize it, either."

"No."

Alij put in, "That sucker's big enough to inhale us and never notice it."

"Moving how fast?"

"It'll overtake us before we dock."

Jack looked at the screen. The Thraks had nothing in space like that as far as he knew, and neither had the Dominion. But the Thraks hadn't been to war openly in twenty years. Who knew what they could have been developing? He wet his lips. "What's their course?"

"I don't think they plan an intercept." The intercom was silent a moment before Alij added, "They don't need to to blow us out of the water."

"I know." Jack stood a moment, hating the feeling of being totally helpless. "Leave the intercom open. I want to see the computer simulation of that the second it becomes more than a blip."

"Will do."

Jack sat down and waited.

He waited until the hour when the computer simulation came on and showed him outlines of firing turrets. Then he went over and suited up, unsure of what else he could do. Then he went to the bridge.

Harkness noted his looming presence at the bulkhead, and gave a nod. He said to Alij, "How close?"

"Mark, one half hour."

"How close are we to rendezvous?"

The brown-skinned navigator gave Jack a nervous look. "Do you want me to split hairs?"

"If necessary."

"It should be simultaneous. But . . ."

"Yes?"

"But I don't think they intend to ram either us or the lifeboat." Alij laughed a little too sharply. 'That's just a theory."

Harkness gutturalized deep in his throat and spit into a cup at the side of the control board. The pilot said nothing, deeply intent on the computer simulation of a docking process happening at his control screen.

"Why do you say that?"

"Because, well, because we'll be making some minor adjustments in speed and trajectory to match those of the lifeboat. And I don't see the unknown making adjustments. If they continue on their course, and we continue on the course Harkness has set, they'll just brush over the top of us. We'll miss by maybe two hundred feet."

The hairs prickled at the back of Jack's neck. He watched Harkness simulate a docking.

"Then we'll just have to wait and see."

Harkness' lip curled then. The computer showed a successful interlock, its picture flashing in triumph. He looked over his shoulder at Jack.

Jack nodded. "Nice job, pilot. When it comes time for the real thing, don't forget to account for the wash of the unknown's drive . . . if they miss us."

Harkness blinked. Then he nodded in return. "Will do, commander." He turned back to the screen. "Alij, you'd better be tracking very closely."

Amber awoke to a prickling of every sense in her body, all over, like a heat rash. No veil clouded her eyes as she looked up and then stood. Every hair on her bare arms stood out and she rubbed her forearms gently for warmth. Across from her, Colin awoke as well. He got to his feet agilely for an older man who'd spent much of the last twenty-four hours cross-legged in meditation. He patted down his blue overtunic and searched in a leg pocket of his miners' jumpsuit for a candy. He broke it in two and gave half to her.

"What is it?"

"I don't know," she answered. Around them, less sensitive people began to come awake, still groggy in the bad air. The candy brought moistness back to her dry mouth. Information had been scanty, and she knew it wasn't entirely the fault of those who had taken over the running of the lifeboat. Some of the equipment had apparently been in disrepair. They were running blind and would stay that way until rejoined with the freighter or . . . or until they ran out of supplies.

The decking underneath her feet reverberated as though they'd hit a bumpy road.

Colin put his hand out and they steadied each other. Rawlins broke through a mass of sleepers and waved at her from the other side of the bay. He trotted over to join them.

"Sergeant Lassaday says it could be a tractor beam or a docking maneuver."

Amber smiled at the word sent by Jack's bullet-headed sergeant. Colin's hand on her shoulder flexed.

"Can he tell for sure?"

"No. The screens are out. But he'll swear by it."

Lassaday swore by his nuts, Amber thought. She smiled widely at the memory. A giddiness swept her. Then she thought, *It's nothing but bad air. Euphoria. I should know better.* Aloud, she said, "Do you think it's Jack?"

"I pray it is," Colin answered. He let go of her as suddenly the vehicle shuddered under heavy and clumsy contact. Metal sounded.

And when it should have been quiet, the bay continued to shudder and echo violently. Denaro, the militant Walker, came to his feet. He'd been shorn of his weapons belts for cold sleep, but his posture now told that he could use hands and feet if nothing else. He was prepared to fight. Colin snapped his fingers and Jonathan left his side with a quickness belying his massive build. When he came to a halt, it was to overshadow the young and rebellious Denaro.

Like an earthquake with no end, the decking rippled

under her feet. It brought her to her knees, Colin tumbling down with her, and those still standing screamed and lay down in fear. The bay was filled with cries of panic which tailed off to a sullen, sobbing quiet.

The side of the bay gave out a ring as though it were an instrument that had been struck.

Then silence.

Amber knew the bulkhead was opening. She could almost hear it. Sensed it with other than the five senses DNA had given her. She stood up, alone, and headed to the bulkhead.

If it was Jack, she wanted to be the first there.

She prepared her mind.

If it was not, she wanted to strike with the only weapon she had.

CHAPTER 6

Guthul was still cursing the cleverness of his enemy when his adjunct entered his quarters. The adjunct's quivering face plates signaled his excitement.

"What is it?"

"We have a sighting, general. I've been requested to bring you to the bridge."

The general stood. Even for a Thrakian warrior, he was impressive. He arranged his mask into one of dominance and victory, no little feat considering his defeat at the hands of the Dominion Knight. The adjunct quailed as the general passed him, headed for the bridge nest.

Guthul was aware of the attention directed on him as he loped into the bridge and stood erect once more. He eyed the sensor screens. No one had to point out the object of concern. It ruled their sector of space as he did the control nest. His face plates shifted as he put on a subtly inquiring mask.

"What is it?"

"Our grids have been unable to identify. It is a dreadnaught of unknown origin."

Guthul homed in on the sighting as he came closer. His chitin rustled. "Between us and the Dominion freighter."

"Yes, general."

"And between us and the Opus crèchelands."

An audible gasp hissed through the control compartment. Guthul looked about him in anger and surprise. "Had you forgotten? I have not. A sign of leadership is to remember our defeats as well as our victories. We conquered Opus . . . but our nests have failed. Still, the crèchelands deserve our vigilant protection. Queen Tricatada expects nothing less from us. Adjunct."

"Yes, sir."

"Continue pursuit." Then, as Guthul swept around and prepared to leave the bridge nest, he added briskly, "And be equally prepared to break off pursuit if necessary. I'll not risk another defeat this trip."

The adjunct brightened. "Yes, sir!"

So much sweat pooled on Harkness' brow that Jack wondered how the pilot could see. Leoni bent over and mopped his employer's brow, but a new puddle beaded up as fast as he wiped the last one away.

Alij looked to Jack. "They're almost on top of us."

"Any sign that the turrets are moving into firing position?"

"None, but . . . smaller weaponry is activated easier and faster. We may not get that notice."

"I know." *Goddamnit*, he knew. Knew better than the navigator. This close the alien ship didn't need its big guns to blow them apart. And this close to the lifeboat, Jack didn't want to engage in protective fire without clear sign of hostile activity from the unknown.

Alij had returned his attention to the screen and said, "Uh-oh."

"What?"

"I'm getting an echo from behind the unknown . . . that or—"

"Or what?" Jack leaned into the bridge, shoulder armor scraping the bulkhead. Bogie protested. *Watch it, boss. I don't like crimps.*

"Or the unknown's so big it's been eclipsing another ship." Alij gave the computer another set of coords, and the viewscreen shifted slightly. "Damn. There it is."

And this one the two of them recognized. The Thraks were right on their heels.

Harkness interrupted, "I've got it."

Alij called out, "They're close enough to spit on us," but Jack barely heard him, already on a run to the interconnective bulkhead as the transport clamped its lifeboat back into position.

The docking crew worked in deepsuits, and motioned him forward as the bulkhead began to open.

*   *   *

Rawlins reached Amber's elbow, but she shook him off as the bulkhead creaked ominously with pressurization from the other side.

"We don't know who's boarding. Get back," he urged in her ear.

Amber swung on him. She didn't know what he saw in her eyes, but it was enough to make him draw back slightly. "Get the others back," she said. "I'm staying here."

Lassaday was propelling the evacuees gently into the crowded bays behind them. Rawlins hesitated, then went to join his sergeant. Amber pivoted back around and waited. A trickle of sweat made its way behind her ear and down her neck.

The bulkhead eased open, revealing a flash of white, and it took no more than that for Amber to be certain. "Jack!" she cried and threw herself forward.

The massive battle armor suit gathered her in as though she were a fragile doll. Even as Jack caught her up, a rumbling and trembling began and the lifeboat shifted suddenly as though not secure in its newly reestablished berth. The bay filled with screams.

"What is it?"

Jack smiled grimly. "We're being buzzed," he said.

"The Thraks?"

"We don't know who," Jack answered. "And they're in no mood to be asked. Let's hope this junker holds together."

Amber held on tight, her hands clasped at the back of Jack's neck, so glad to see him she forgot to be angry, and when she remembered, too frightened to keep it up. Pressure plates groaned and creaked until it seemed the freighter would split apart. Then, she realized, it had peaked and was beginning to ebb.

Gradually the rumbling and shaking quieted, and then all was silent. Through the open bulkhead, voices called, and the din began again as the evacuees realized they had been rescued a second time.

Jack carried Amber through the doorway and into the main body of the freighter. She thought she could hear his heart pounding in his chest, but knew that was impossible. Flexalink armor and equipment was between them. The odor of blood and sweat and ash seemed to be embedded in the suit. She wrinkled her nose.

"You've been fighting."

"The Thraks boarded us shortly after we jettisoned the cryo bay."

Amber looked at the tense line of his jaw, saw the pulse jumping, and knew he did not want to answer the questions she needed to ask. But she did anyway. "Why did you have us brought out of cold sleep? You knew we'd expend supplies."

"If we couldn't get back to hook up, I couldn't just leave you adrift. Awake, you had a chance. Asleep . . ." his voice faded.

Asleep, she'd have been locked into the nightmare Jack himself had lived. No. He wouldn't have condemned her to that. She pinched the back of his neck. "Well, next time you think of heroics, don't think of doing them without me."

"Unless you're thinking of enlisting, there won't be any way you can join. There's a war on."

"Mmmm." Amber caught herself as he swung her down outside the bridge entry. She could hear Harkness' thickened voice giving orders.

The massive pilot turned and motioned to Jack. "Commander, you'll need to see this."

Amber helped Jack shuck the armor and they left Bogie lying in the corridor, seams open, as the control com screen filled with an incredible sight.

"What the hell is that?"

"The unknown. It's just irradiated Opus."

Amber caught her breath as she watched the corona flare out around a planet, dominating the screen. She did not register its name, only its demise.

"Who did it?"

"We're pretty sure the unknown vessel, but not positive. The Thraks are still in range, but we can't view them now, they're on the far side of the planet."

Jack wiped his hand over his face. There were reddened crimp marks over his bare, sweaty torso where leads had been clipped on. His tanned skin was streaked with dirt and ash, his sandy blond hair darkened to brunette by hours of perspiration within his helmet. Amber was caught by the way his presence dominated everyone on the bridge without effort and without intention, and she caught herself thinking, *He's twice the man anyone here is,* even as he said, "How bad is it?"

"We don't know. We'll keep the readings, but we'll have to find an expert dockside to examine the readings. One thing for sure . . . there's no Thraks alive down there now."

Jack watched the corona flare into a subtle aura. This was different from watching a planet burn—he'd seen that, too. He did not know if he was watching homicide—or suicide.

He could think of only one thing to do. He tapped Harkness' shoulder. "Let's go home."

CHAPTER 7

Interlude

He came to her when the ship had quieted, to the tiny cubbyhole given to her as private quarters. She had her caftan slipped down off one shoulder, her bare arm out, as she applied a balm the nursing staff had given her. The brilliant blue tattoos remained unaffected, but their heat diminished and Amber was basking in the calm, when she suddenly caught her breath.

She sensed him beyond the metal portal. His warmth washed through, touching her, sending her thoughts into turmoil even as the bulkhead opened and he stepped through, massive in the battle armor, smelling of sweat and war . . . and something more, a musky undertone.

He stopped, wearily, and looked down at her as she caught up the fold of her robe and brought it back up over her shoulder. His tiredness showed in the depths of his rain blue eyes, shadowed by the dimmed lights of downtime. But her senses, heightened by her ordeal on Bythia, caught much more and she came to her feet involuntarily, her hand out to him, even as he said, "I'll leave if you want me to."

"No." Her fingertips brushed his gauntlet. Bogie's senses as well as Jack's flooded her. She shrank back at that— Bogie had changed so much she scarcely recognized the sentience. Wisdom encompassed his ferocity and though she knew he overrode Jack's emotions now, it was with Jack's permission, for they were no longer parasite and host, but companions. So much had happened to Jack on Bythia that she felt that she rather than the alien Bogie was the stranger, the outsider.

Jack pulled back, as if perceiving her hesitation, and Amber stammered, "Don't go."

He dropped his gauntlet back to his side, brushed the

glove over his helmet, and then stood there ill at ease. Amber closed her eyes briefly as she felt what he did.

He found the sight of her suddenly hitting him like a swift blow to the stomach, stirring feelings he almost did not recognize. Her tawny hair was disheveled and tumbled about her shoulders along the silken caftan and the glimpse he'd had of her made him tense his jaw for a moment.

She opened her eyes to see the tiny tic along his cheek.

Jack cleared his throat. "I wanted . . . I wanted you to know why I did what I did."

She stood in front of him, glad the caftan concealed the trembling that had begun in the hollow of her stomach. "I know why," she answered softly. "Didn't you know that I would?"

"Let me talk."

"If you'll let me talk about what happened between us." Without trying, she caught his thoughts again, musky flashes of emotion that seared her as, suddenly, he wondered what the tattoos looked like under her robes. He had an intense desire to trace the designs with his fingers, wherever they might go. The wonderment surged through him and Amber's head jerked up, and her eyes met his quickly, widening in amazement.

She took a step back. "No. Please. Last time. . . ."

The sweetness of the last time surged through him, melding time and place until he no longer knew if he was in memory or in reality. He shook his head to clear his thoughts and got out, "That wasn't your fault."

"It never is! But that doesn't mean that I can . . . that you and I. . . ."

"It doesn't mean we can't." He found himself moving forward. Amber put her hand out to stop him.

For an electrifying second, the three of them were one. One pulse raced in desire. One heat rising to the inevitable as they moved into each other's arms.

Amber drew back slightly. "I refuse to make love to more than one man at a time."

Jack stopped, his mouth agape. She tapped his armored chest. "I think this is one experience Bogie doesn't have to share with you." Deftly, she began to strip him of the armor until he stood alone. Jack kicked his gear to one side and reached for Amber.

He held her so close to him now that he could feel her heart pounding wildly in her chest, her nipples quickening through the fabric of her caftan. "I'll have to leave you behind again, I won't have any choice. And I can't promise you I'll come back to you."

Her breath grazed his chin as she answered, "I know."

"I think we've waited long enough."

"God," she whispered and looked up at him, her neck arching gracefully and a pulse beating in the curve of her throat. "What if I—"

He did not let her finish her protest. His mouth covered her last words, and she met his embrace with one of her own, and his body felt the sense of her from her long legs to the fragrant strands of her hair. When she moved back, it was to let her caftan drop to the deck. She stepped out of it, bared to his touch.

He hesitated a moment, drinking in the beauty of her young body, breasts high and round, her thighs smooth beneath the blue patterns of the alien artist, the hair of her pubes just as golden and fragrant as that about her face. Wordlessly, she reached for the fastenings on his pants and he let her undress him, feeling his hardness surge forward as she stripped his breeches away.

Then they moved close together, he tracing the feathery, erotic designs upon her skin, and she following the bunching of muscles and tracks of scars from other wars and other times until she gathered in his maleness and he bent to trace his lips rather than his hands about her breasts . . . and from there, he could remember little thought as their heat swept them away.

He awoke, her silken body curled next to him. The room was still darkened and her soft breathing soothed him. He could not sleep without fitful awakening, haunted still by the nightmare of being trapped in dreams without end. As great as his need for Amber was, having her did not cure him. He lifted his head slightly to look at her sleeping next to him and knew that even her love could not sate his need for vengeance.

There wasn't a part of each other they had not caressed or claimed, and he lay with his eyes half-open, consummated, yet somehow still lacking and wondering why.

Amber moved her head along his bicep, her cheek brushing his arm, then turned and curved in another direction. Gently, he eased his arm from under her.

Amber had given him new life. Always, from the moment he had met her. He was reluctant to leave her now, but, compelled, he continued to ease his body away from her until he could stand.

As he stood, enveloped by the musky smell of her balm and their lovemaking, he realized what it was that drove him away. Amber had made love to a man with only half a past, and not much of a future. Bogie had the key to the other half, and Jack could not rest until it was restored to him. With that past in his grasp, he could offer Amber a future of her own.

And find a way to extract his revenge upon Pepys and the Thrakian League.

With the stealth Amber herself had taught him, he dressed and left her alone.

CHAPTER 8

It was an ill-kempt, sour-looking group that was cut away from the evacuees upon docking on Malthen. Pepys watched his security force neatly separate the ones he'd called for from the rest of the group after the old transport landed and then cracked open like an old, rotten eggshell.

As motley as they looked, unbathed, tired, the man he sought stood head and shoulders above the crowd. Even without his armor.

Pepys made a noise in his throat. He was unaware it had been heard until a hand fell on his shoulder.

"That is him?"

"Yes."

The captain was in dress blues, his own perhaps or someone else's, poorly fitting, his muscles pulling against the seams. He'd put on bulk since leaving for Bythia. *Just a boy, still growing,* Pepys thought. *What would it be like to be growing into your prime once more?* As the World Police troops quickly rounded up the man and the lithe girl by his side, and the group of Walkers led by Colin into a second car, he saw Storm pause and look over the docks.

It was as though he were a hunter or a hound and he'd winded something. "Look at that," Pepys cried fiercely. "He sees the staging. He knows."

"Knows what?"

"Knows we're readying for war."

The man behind him said blandly, "A soldier's soldier."

The camera work faded out as the vehicles pulled away toward the palace.

Pepys paced his inner rooms. He wore a shirt of flowing sleeves to hide his spindly, birdlike arms, but his hands hung out like those of a gangly adolescent boy, and he flopped them unconsciously when he walked. His trousers and boots were plain, but of the finest material. Wealth gleamed deep within their manufacture. He pulled up short to stare at his new minister. Baadluster did not return the piercing look, he was in a world of his own. The minister was homely, tall and pasty pale, with lips too thick and ears too large, poking out from limp brown hair, but the man had eyes of coal black that, once focused, could burn you to the core.

Pepys erupted back into motion before Baadluster could focus on him. He had needed a new minister, now that the Thrakian League had declared war. Baadluster assumed those new duties overtly, and, covertly, those of Winton, Pepys' head of the secret service, who had died on Bythia in Jack Storm's hands.

Literally, if the reports he had gotten were true. Jack had taken Winton's head in his gauntlets and squeezed until it had exploded like a ripe melon.

Pepys was unsure how to credit those reports. The Knight was an enigma to him, to be sure, but he had never sensed a violent or brutal streak in the man. Still, Winton, being Winton, had perhaps elicited that response. Winton would have made a saint come undone.

The Emperor of the Triad Throne stopped at that thought, and ran his liver-spotted hand through his hair. The frizzy red strands rose with a static electricity all their own as he did so. Pepys reminded himself of a legendary Medusa, every hair on his head determined to snake about as though alive. He kept his own hair because it pleased him to do so . . . gave him a disarming and boyish look . . . kept his foes from staring him in his cat green eyes and realizing the schemes that lived deep within them.

He worried for a moment about what Winton might have told either Jack Storm or Colin of the Blue Wheel before he had died. He had not sent Winton off to Bythia to attend to either the Knight or the saint; the man had been about his own machinations, but that did not make him less knowledgeable about Pepys' intentions. And, then, of course, there was always the question of how much Jack already knew before Winton exposed himself and suffered the consequences.

He told himself this was no time to worry about losing power.

Pepys impatiently looked over the local bank of scanner monitors. The emperor took a deep breath that spasmed somewhere inside.

"I've cleared my agenda for him. I don't have time to waste."

Baadluster appeared to wake, though his eyes had always been open. "Perhaps traffic. . . ."

"Traffic!"

"The man has returned from a planet caught up in civil war and out of the hands of the Thraks to report to you. He *will* be here."

Pepys looked up, into Baadluster's eyes. The minister met his gaze levelly for a moment before looking away. Because he looked away, Pepys did not have to hide his smile of triumph. But he said, "Of course, you're right, Baadluster." He lowered himself to a chair built to suit his wiry, slight frame. "We're agreed on this course of action."

"Yes, emperor."

"Do you think it wisest?"

Baadluster considered him. The coal dark eyes stayed flat. Cool. "Not wisest, perhaps," he said, "but best. And that's all we can do, is it not? Make the best choice available at the time."

Pepys' attention was riveted on the minister. "And what, do you think, is the wisest?"

"Kill them both. Though, in retrospect, that might make a martyr out of Colin, which you would want to avoid at all costs, even if the evidence pointed toward the Thrakian League as the murderers. A spiritual network such as the Walkers have can endanger your own."

Pepys said nothing aloud but his eyes reflected his thoughts. *Yes, it would. And I don't want that.* He had never wanted that. Damn the Walkers. They'd seemed harmless, but during the decades of Pepys' reign, they'd been everywhere, looking for archaeological proof that Jesus Christ had gone on to walk other worlds. The religious affirmation had yet to come, but the sites being investigated had other, more tangible importance. The digs had established outposts which had gone on to establish frontiers, all steeped in Walker philosophy. Pepys could point at a half dozen major treaty infractions with the Thrakian League over the last decade that involved Walker sites. And when you had a saint who could actually work miracles, as Colin had. . . .

"There'll be hell to pay, Baadluster, if we're wrong."

Baadluster did not answer, but his black eyes fired up even as security rang through to tell Pepys that Captain Storm had arrived.

The Knight arrived alone, as requested, separated in the outer halls from his companion. Colin would also arrive separately, later. The vibrancy of the uniform faded his eyes to an honest blue. His sandy blond hair was beginning to recede slightly above his brow. He was young, half the age of the man he was destined to replace, but Commander Kavin had had implicit trust in Storm's abilities.

Pepys cleared a drying throat at Storm's appearance. Winton had had no such trust. *The man is one of our lost Knights,* he'd told Pepys. *I'm sure of it! He knows what we did in the Sand Wars.*

Then where had he been for the last twenty-five years, showing no sign of the passage of time?

Where?

In the hands of the Thraks, perhaps?

Or one of the several factions working very hard to put Pepys and the Triad Throne out of business permanently? Sweat broke out in the emperor's armpits as he thought of the Green Shirts.

He had not bothered to tell Baadluster that he and Winton had already tried to have this man killed several times. Storm was too damn lucky to die.

Pepys got smoothly to his feet. Jack still wore his insignia of captain, his promotion to commander not official yet.

"Emperor!"

As Jack saluted, Pepys leaned forward and snapped off the insignia and held the gold-threaded decorations in the palm of his hand. He felt gratified at the mild surprise awakened in the Knight's eyes.

"Commander," Pepys answered. "You'll have your new rank emblems before the day is out. Bureaucracy is always slow to keep up with field promotions."

"Thank you, sire." Storm inclined his head.

As he looked up, Pepys indicated Baadluster. "Commander Storm, I'd like you to meet my new War Minister, Vandover Baadluster." He guided the soldier to a pair of waiting chairs.

The two men sized each other up. Pepys admired Baadluster for the noncommittal expression retained by the minister. He might know nothing of the soldier beyond the ordinary barrack gossip. Storm showed only a mild curiosity.

Jack turned back to his emperor. "How ready are we?"

"Congress drags its heels, but we'll be ready. The Thraks have not yet officially declared war, but they've been busy dismantling their diplomatic posts. We'll hear soon. Or perhaps just slightly after." Pepys smiled maliciously. With the Thraks, one could not depend on being told until after the first strike. "We, of course, are doing the same."

"In the meantime, Thrakian cruisers are still in the trade lanes, where the Treaty allows them to remain." There was disdain in the new commander's voice.

Pepys looked at him with a long measuring glance, then said deliberately, "I made that Treaty. I'll see it enforced as long as it still has life. If there is a way to turn back after all this . . . if it can be done, I will see it done."

A normal man would have flinched. Storm returned the Emperor's look levelly and answered, "The Thraks have no such compunctions. Never have had, never will."

"Nor, sir, had you. Without your actions, we might not be in the position we're in now!"

Baadluster stepped between them with a movement so smooth it seemed almost accidental. The minister forced Pepys to sit back in his chair.

"My actions," Jack said, "have always been with the Triad Throne and the Dominion in mind."

"I know that," Pepys answered impatiently. "Else I would not give you the Dominion Knights."

Storm stopped in his tracks as though momentarily taken aback. Pepys' gaze met Baadluster's with a gleam of triumph. The emperor knew the soldier now knew he was going to be offered the command of the Dominion Knights, and that he had not expected it originally. Pepys had him where he wanted him.

The soldier shifted his tall muscular form in a chair built for Pepys' comfort. Jack placed his hands on his thighs and leaned slightly forward. "And what do you want me to do with them?"

"The Dominion Knights will be fully reinstated. We've stepped up recruitment and training. I don't anticipate any problems from the Dominion Congress accepting either our troops or my leadership of them." Pepys gave a tight-lipped smile. "They may call us mercenary, but the Congress knows what we can do. We both know this war won't be fought in the sectors of space. We can try to put weapons' platforms into orbit outside each and every target we wish to attack or defend, but that is a logistical impossibility. No. Like the Sand Wars, this will be fought planet to planet, without destroying the land we both covet, and we'll have no choice but to follow the Thraks' lead. We need the infantry to fight this war, commander, and the Knights are the best we have to offer."

Jack watched Pepys, realizing the electricity with which the fine red hair rose and fell as though on a tide, was a signal of the man's level of intensity. He was intense now. Very intense. But not over Jack and Jack was grateful for that, aware he tended to give himself away too easily even with Amber's street savvy training. Jack inclined his head in slight affirmation of his emperor's statement. "I accept."

Pepys sat back in his chair. "You understand, of course, that your command of the Knights will be secondary to my and Baadluster's orders, and also probationary until you give me proof of your ability to win in the field. I don't, however, anticipate problems in that area."

"The Thraks were all but unstoppable before, sire," Jack answered levelly. "They may prove so again, but I can guarantee our best effort."

"Good! All I can ask. Our relationship with the Dominion is an odd one, but we are all human, and that binds us together. We are woven like a net, a fishing seine, and the Triad worlds are the floats that keep the net buoyant . . . but the Dominion is the strand that makes the weaving. If the strand comes undone, eventually we, too, will be left adrift." Pepys blinked furiously and Jack was astonished to see dampness well in his emerald eyes.

The emperor shook off his mood as Baadluster cleared his throat. Jack looked to the tall, pasty-complected man who towered over them and who had no chair to sit in. The new Minister of War returned Jack's gaze, and Jack saw the heat smoldering in the depths of flat black eyes.

He knew then that Vandover Baadluster could be as terrible as Winton had been.

"Commander," Baadluster said. "Please tell me, in your own words, what happened after Bythia."

For a moment, Jack felt a stab of panic, razor sharp. Technically, he was now an officer stripped of rank. Pepys could do that to him, if he wished. Jack had no illusions as to the strategies the emperor might employ, but he let his breath out slowly, giving way to the rationale that this was no: one of them. Just the same, Baadluster noticed the flicker of his gaze toward Pepys. And misinterpreted it.

"Come, come! Don't look to him for permission to answer. I'm your commanding officer now."

Pepys, however, wore a pleased expression. "Don't badger him, Van. He's my man, as he should be. That's what it means to be a Knight."

Jack felt bile at the back of his throat. Pepys had no idea of what it meant to be a Knight. The amputation scar of his little finger went livid as his fingers pinioned his right thigh. If he had been able to bring alive out of the Bythian disaster the man who'd told him that it had been the Triad Throne itself which had ordered the fireburning attack on Claron, Pepys would not be sitting across from him. No, Pepys had no idea of what it meant to be a Knight. Jack hesitated too long in answering and an unfathomable expression flickered across the emperor's face.

Pepys lifted his chin slightly as Baadluster intoned, "He says it without words, but he says it none the less. He wonders if you know what it means to be an emperor."

The faint sheen of sweat on Jack's brow turned icy.

A silence fell on the room.

Pepys smiled tightly. "And now, Minister Baadluster, you may leave us."

The limp-haired man had been hovering over Jack. He straightened and looked at his emperor. For a moment, Jack thought he was going to argue. Then the thick lips thinned, and Baadluster turned and left the private hall.

Pepys keyed his remote and the taping banks shut down one by one. Jack watched the displays go dark, knowing the gesture was being made to impress him, and knowing that nothing kept Pepys from recording secretly. But he was supposed to think that Pepys would not stoop to that, although Jack knew he would.

The emperor waited for several long minutes, bright green eyes peering at Jack over the steeple of Pepys' hands. Jack forced himself to wait coolly.

"Why did you murder Winton?"

Jack looked into Pepys' shaded eyes. "I did not murder him. I killed him in self-defense."

"A man in battle armor against a man without?"

"Winton was not helpless."

The emperor dropped his hands into his lap. "No, I suppose he was not. He was not the sort of man who would ever be. He did not trust you, Winton didn't."

They stared into one another's faces. Jack thought of Amber and how much she would relish this game of words and facades. He did not. He shifted his weight in the chair from one lean hip to the other. "Why?"

Pepys' hair crackled upward. "I'm sure I haven't an idea. He was in charge of the World Police. It is possible he thought you were a security threat."

"I haven't been on Malthen long, your highness—but I've never heard that the WP was shy when it came to arrests or trials."

"No." Pepys gave a twitch of his lips and looked away briefly. "Your interest in the firestorming of Claron always bothered him. You championed it when you first came to me. The . . . incident of Claron was a regrettable one. For reasons of security, what happened there can never be revealed, and yet you don't strike me as one who would accept that as an answer. Give me reason to believe that Winton was wrong about you."

Although Jack's face did not twitch, his gut screwed tight. Damn Pepys for making him trade off Claron's lease for new life against the greater good. Damn him. It was the Thraks or Pepys, and Pepys could thank god that he was the lesser of two evils at this point. He made a choice. "No."

Pepys' face went whiter still, verging on gray, but his eyes lit up and he leaned forward in the chair. "What do you mean?"

"I mean, your highness, if my service as a Knight is not evidence enough for you, I can't please you."

"Can't or won't?"

"My point is made."

"But not mine. Do you like your commission?" the emperor asked abruptly.

"I appreciate it," Jack answered.

The emperor thrust himself out of his chair and began pacing. "What am I to do with you, Jack Storm?"

"Send me wherever you want the Dominion Knights to be stationed. Then let me do my job."

Pepys turned at the edge in Jack's voice. "You imply, without interference."

"If necessary. You tried to keep Kavin on a short leash. To paraphrase, he hung himself on it. He died fighting, not the enemy, but Winton."

"I know that."

"Then you should not have allowed it to happen."

Pepys brought himself up. His pointed chin trembled for a second, then dimpled as he fought to calm himself. "As if anyone could control Winton. He plotted against everyone. Even me."

"A dangerous man."

"Less dangerous to have under one's nose than a galaxy away." Pepys cut the air with the side of his hand. "I won't be judged by you."

Jack did not respond.

Finally, Pepys dropped back into his chair. "What happened after Bythia? What do you know about the Opus incident?"

"Only that the monitoring equipment aboard the freight transport was primitive, at best. The Thraks had done their best to board us. I couldn't allow that to happen. I think they intended on taking hostages. When they attempted to overtake us, an unknown interceded and shortly after, our readings indicate that the planet was irradiated."

"The Thrakian League claims it was done by you."

Jack could not keep the surprise from surfacing. "What?"

"They've filed an official protest."

"We've never operated like that. And Harkness' scow is incapable of such an action. Did they mention the unknown?"

"No. I have only your report that such a vehicle existed

and, under the circumstances, it sounds as though you are trying to smokescreen the situation. General Guthul claims that the transport had jettisoned a lifeboat and appeared to be on an erratic course, out of control, coming out of hyperdrive. When he attempted to come to your aid, he was fired upon, missed—and the weaponry used annihilated Opus." Pepys drummed his wiry fingers on the chair arm. "He has support in the Dominion Congress. He has just enough of the truth to give credence to his claims."

"A Knight would never jeopardize planetary environment to win a battle."

"Yes." Pepys gave him a long, slow look. "Yes, there is that. And, small though it was, you seized a victory for us. I won't forget that and I won't let the Congress forget it either."

"There may be other advantages to the encounter."

"Such as?"

Jack barely hesitated, then continued. "The Thraks stalking me seemed to have difficulty sensing my armor. If there is an advantage to be had from the encounter, other than beating them at their game, I believe it is the discovery that there is a property peculiar to norcite which baffles their sight."

"Really?" Pepys' impatience faded abruptly into curiosity. "Are you asking for permission to research and test this further?"

"I think the project has merits."

"All right then. Proceed. But obtaining Thrakian subjects for field tests are your responsibility. Brace yourself for a long week. Baadluster has arranged for a visiting senator to oversee the drills."

"From Congress?"

"Yes." Pepys looked perversely pleased. "May I remind you that politics has been the death of more good soldiers than war?"

"I'll try to be discreet, sir."

"I'm counting on it." The emperor turned his back on him, and Jack knew he had been dismissed.

Jack left. He knew for certain they had been recorded, for Pepys had feared to ask him the obvious questions. Who was he? Where had he come from? And was he going to try to topple Pepys from his ill-gotten throne?

CHAPTER 9

Over the years, Emperor Pepys had received St. Colin of the Blue Wheel in many different ways. He'd been hustled in the moment he'd asked for audience, and he'd been ignored for months. He'd been both paraded in and hidden under cover. He'd been received with respect and scorn and, once or twice, desperation.

He'd even been met once by the secret police, their shackles ready.

So he was prepared for almost anything when Pepys summoned him the third day after his return from Bythia.

Raised to conspicuousness from humble beginnings, Colin wore miners' jumpsuits under his brilliant blue overrobes. He kept the jumpsuit pockets filled with many things: credit disks to satisfy filching hands on the street, religious tracts, a hand beam and even a handgun. Today the palace gate screening discovered the gun, a WP man removed it, examined it critically and gave it back.

"What if I shoot him?" Colin asked mildly.

"Then we'll know you did it," the guard answered sourly. "He's waiting for you in the private audience room."

As Colin threaded his way through the magnificent, if cold, rose obsidite corridors, he reflected that he knew the private audience room well. The location of their meeting gave him not a clue as to Pepys' frame of mind. It could not, however, have been good. Colin had been the Ambassador Pro-tem on Bythia. He should have been summoned the first day back, regardless of his age and need to rest.

At that thought, Colin pounded to a stop and harrumphed at himself. Age, indeed. Just a step past middle-aged.

Of course, death throws a long shadow and he'd nearly met it months ago.

As he rounded the bend, he could see that the door to the audience room was thrown open, and golden daylight from outside windows cast a gleam across the flooring, making it the color of a glorious sunrise. He gathered his thoughts and his life in his hands, and entered.

The twilight of the catacombs embraced him as General Guthul listened to the buzz of protest left behind at the end of his address before the councils. They sounded as though they had just left the nest, he thought to himself, even as he arranged his mask into one of triumph and confidence. And they might well be outraged. He had just laid before the League a plan of such outrageous action that they might as easily behead him for treason as rustle their chitin in amusement.

And, if he were very, very fortunate, one or two of them might have the military background to call him genius. It was those one or two upon whom he now staked his whole career.

They clicked him back into the assembly much sooner than he expected, shaking him out of his hum of meditation upon the whole, and he hastily checked to make sure his facial planes were arranged properly before returning.

One or two nearest him took offense at his mask and rattled their bodies angrily, antennae up and trembling. He took no note. They were conservatives, always the first to rattle and the last to take action. They seemed to consider taking alarm part of their contribution to the council. The rest of his peers he found alert and resting on their forearms across their slanted benches, awaiting his next words.

"Continue, general. We have considered your speech and decided that it is not the prattling of a deranged being. We have weighed it and found it worthy, if unorthodox."

Guthul pulled himself up, aware that he was a fine specimen of military breeding, and he looked about the semicircle of the assemblage. "There is no more to say," he husked. "I am done. Either back me or court martial me. I demand my due and I demand it now. The time for hesitation is past."

Another trilling ran through the council. "You suggest putting us well within reach of the enemy if we strike as you demand."

"Yes. It is the only way to draw out Commander Storm. The risk is great, the advantage considerable if we can put the commander down now. I must remind you, however, that if we attack on the Dominion fringes, where we are safe to hit and run, we also put ourselves within reach of the Ash-Farel. That the great and ancient enemy is upon us once more."

Parthos, the newly recalled ambassador to the Triad, opened his face mask and then closed it tightly, a shocking display of emotion and anger. It generated the effect he intended as attention immediately swung from General Guthul to the diplomat. As Guthul was a fine specimen of warrior breeding, Parthos was an equally fine one of diplomatic genetic structure. He snapped his lower mandible into place and the strength of its clack echoed throughout the chambers. "I suggest we vote for Guthul's plan. I stand in favor of it, knowing that if Guthul is to fail, he will pay the price, and applauding that he is Thrakian enough to risk all."

As Guthul heard the speech, he was very careful not to let the joy and personal triumph he felt move his mask of leadership. But it was difficult. Very, very difficult.

Now he could contemplate squashing the Dominion Knight like the plasmic worm he was.

The samovar of tea had cooled, cookie crumbs had been swept away, and Pepys' fine hair had crackled down to a moderate aura before the emperor's emerald eyes fastened on him with their usual predatory stare. Colin put his cup down.

"Animal, vegetable, mineral, or friend or foe?"

The emperor rocked back, visibly startled. "What?"

"The game we're playing today, my friend."

Pepys caught the joke and laughed before putting aside his cup. "Neither," he said. "You're here because it was necessary to talk to you before removing you as ambassador."

"I removed myself, already."

"So you did. But as my subject, it's necessary for me to formalize it." Pepys stayed lolled back in his chair, watching as Colin rose and strode to the window. The window held a rare view of a singular aspect of Malthen . . . untamed land ranging over a sere group of foothills. Colin thought of Bythia.

He turned round.

"You did me a great disservice, Pepys."

The emperor nodded. "And myself as well."

"You urged me there, with several hundred of my most militant followers to protect our findings. That gave you leave to send a like number of your Knights, to keep an eye on me. But did you anticipate that my men would be slaughtered and your numbers halved before we got out?"

Pepys put out a freckled hand and played with the gold rim of his teacup. "No," he said shortly. "Your men, yes; mine, no. I knew the Thraks were playing a deadly game there. I did not know the Bythians were on the brink of holy war."

"On the brink no more. They blazed through my ranks like wildfire." Colin sighed. He shoved his hands into his thigh pockets as he leaned against the windowsill. "I know you. I should have seen it coming."

"The militants were doing you no good, Colin. We weeded them out before. I merely saved you the job of doing it again."

"Militant or not, they were men with souls! Sometimes I think you think very little of that."

Pepys did not answer, through the movement of his finger upon the cup's rim sent out a tiny belling. Finally the emperor looked up and he smiled, a gesture that did not warm his eyes. "Very few men would talk to me as you do."

Colin ignored the warning. "Very few men have the resources to frighten you," he responded. He stood up, removing his hands from his pockets, and in one change of posture went from a benevolent, fraternal man to a man of dignity and fathomless potential.

The pupils of Pepys' eyes widened at the change. The emperor straightened in his chair. He lifted his hand from the teacup. "I want Denaro."

"What is he to you? He's only one of a handful you failed to have wiped out."

"Give him to me," said Pepys.

"No."

"Then I'll take him for treason."

"You couldn't prove the charge."

"No, but I could tie up your time and attention doing so, and have him anyway."

Colin felt the lines at the corners of his eyes deepen. "What game is this you're playing?"

"The game of empire. Denaro's as dangerous to you as he is to me. Give him over and we'll both have done with him."

Colin thought deeply. The sunlight at the window had shifted a fraction before he finally answered, "I'll let you know." He headed for the audience room door even though Pepys had not dismissed him. He heard Pepys' voice, at his heels, as the door closed.

"Do that."

Denaro stood at attention before Colin, his muscular body bulging the seams of his jumpsuit, belying all attempt of the humble cloth to make him seem a simple Walker disciple.

Colin sighed and looked down at the hardcopy Denaro had brought him. The implications were obvious and the man's request not unreasonable.

Not unless the prelate were to consider Denaro's militaristic tendencies and the splinter factions threatening to tear the Walker religion apart. Perhaps Pepys had been right in trying to arrange for the collapse of the Walkers. God knew that Colin feared a holy war among the Dominion worlds and other outposts of mankind far more than he feared anything else in his lifetime. If he sent Denaro on his way to set up a dig, the hotblood would be free to build his army as well as set up a frontier outpost to support the Walker investigations. And then, there was Pepys' request.

The emperor and the reverend had been friends once. Colin had seen his friend grow apart and disappear into a mesh of alliances and entanglements, a web where every word and action tied into another, pulling here and there until he had become an emperor.

And what had Colin stayed behind to become? A minister, thrust into sainthood by a miraculous action he could not explain and had, only once since then, been able to duplicate. If he had not become a saint, would the Walkers have held together? A question he could not answer and yet asked himself time and again. Should he, as Denaro and others insisted, pull together the strands of their influence and make a genuine empire of their doctrines or should he continue to hold those strands loosely and let fate bear them where it would? He knew Pepys spied upon him as a rival.

However, it was Denaro's chafing that occupied him at the moment.

Colin rubbed at his weary eyes. He did not have the energy of his youth, and the incident at Bythia had drained him far beyond expectations. It was worth it to have healed the heroic Rawlins, but Colin wondered if he would ever regain his own vigor. Perhaps it was not meant to be. Perhaps this was the price God extracted from him for resurrection. If so, then the next would be his last . . . if ever there was a next.

The hardcopy report fell into his lap. Colin shook his head. "No, Denaro, I do not think this outpost a fit assignment."

The youth said nothing at first, but a nerve jumped along the thick sinews of his neck. As the silence drew out, Denaro broke it. "Doubtless," he said, "your eminence has some other position in mind for me." He showed his surprise as Colin smiled kindly at his words.

"As a matter of record, I do," the older man said. Lines of character deepened in his cheeks and about his eyes. "Come with me."

CHAPTER 10

Communion. Storm watched the troops moving below and moved as one with them, and Bogie overrode his thoughts until the blending edge between his personality and the alien's disappeared for a moment. He brought himself back with difficulty.

We're ready, Boss.

"To fight? Nearly."

The being responded with surprise. Jack shifted inside the Flexalinks, saying, "First we must have an enemy."

Thraks!

"Maybe."

Another thrill of surprise from the deep warrior voice echoing inside his mind. Jack smiled widely in spite of himself, a grim smile. "We're waiting for them to declare themselves."

There was a split second of humbled silence, then Bogie rumbled, *Thraks declare themselves the moment they crawl out of their crèche.*

"Yes."

You fence with words.

"Sometimes it's all that keeps us from being as savage as the enemy."

Sometimes being as savage as the enemy is all that will allow you to defeat them.

Jack made no answer to that, and Bogie's mind-speech lapsed as if the being knew he wished to be alone with his thoughts.

He'd had precious little time to be alone with himself the past few days. Around them, the equipment shops and immense hangars being erected for staging filled the training grounds with such a din of noise it was only possible to find quiet with a helmet on and the mikes off.

There was a muffled vibration behind him. He turned and saw Colin entering the bridge, his grayed and balding head bowed against a wind only the Walker prelate seemed to feel. Jack took off his helmet and closed the observation booth windshield, baffling the sounds so they could talk. The reverend carried a report under his arm, plastic edges ruffling as he walked. He straightened, saw Jack watching him, and came to a halt, wearing a calm if worried expression.

"What brings you here," Jack said, "past security points that ought to have stopped you."

"I have friends in many places," Colin chided him. He looked down off the bridge. Jack, following his gaze, saw Rawlins at the gates looking up to make sure that Colin had reached his goal before re-securing the grounds.

The two men looked at one another. "There's a story between you and Rawlins," Jack said.

"Perhaps. He saved my life. That sort of action often forms a bond." Colin set his lips together and made it apparent he was not going to say anything further.

Jack looked back to the grounds. Below, armor flashed, glinting in the Malthen sunlight. Colin seemed content to let him watch the drilling for a few minutes, then there was a rattle of papers. Jack turned back.

"What can I do for you, Colin? I've got an appointment in a few minutes."

"Then I'll get to the point, Jack. Take Denaro in as a Knight."

His newly fashioned composure as a commander broke. "You want me to what?"

"Accept Denaro into training."

"As a Knight? Or as a Walker?"

"Both. Denaro is willing to swear allegiance to Pepys. But I feel that . . . that in the undertakings ahead of us, we are wise to have formally trained personnel. Bythia would not have been the disaster it was if the men we'd had posted there had been trained militarily as well as spiritually."

"Pepys would never allow it."

Colin looked past Storm's broad shoulders to the training grounds. "He has already given me permission."

Jack thought he knew a lie when he heard one, but he had never heard Colin lie before. "Impossible."

"No. Not really." Colin smiled. "I quote, 'It's better to have your enemy under your nose than a galaxy away.' He said you would find the quotation familiar."

Jack made a noise at the back of his throat. His armored presence dominated the control booth, but Colin did not seem intimidated. Jack had a sour taste burning in his throat. "If the emperor has given his permission, then you don't need to talk to me."

"No need perhaps, but I wanted to."

"To explain why you're handing me a live wire?"

"That. And," Colin handed him a copy of the printout he held, "this."

Jack took it in his gauntlets, handling the plastic copies as deftly as with his bare hands. He skimmed it. "Looks like a survey report."

"It is."

"Anyone else seen this yet?"

"No. Walker surveys are quite confidential."

Jack tapped a wavy line. "You're going to establish another dig site."

"If finances and personnel allow." The Walker prelate paused a moment. "And if I have the coverage I need."

"You're expecting trouble again?"

"You showed me the signs yourself. Look here, at this spectrograph. These hills here . . ."

"Rich in norcite."

Colin nodded. "Probably. And that means. . . ."

"For whatever reasons, Thraks will probably be as interested in the site as you are. At least they were on Lasertown and Bythia."

"And it also means I'm not likely to find the archaeological evidence I'm looking for. We may find . . . once again . . . something else."

Jack looked at Colin. "But you're willing to take the risks."

"I must. Those other sites may not be what we're looking for, but I can no longer blindly ignore the evidence. There is a pattern here, there must be. And if there is another sentient, space-faring race, I can't turn blind eyes to it. Can you?"

"No," Jack said. "Nor can I give you Dominion protection."

"Not overtly. But I think I can guarantee you that Denaro will go AWOL as soon as he feels he is proficient in a suit."

Jack scrubbed his armor gloved hands through his dark blond hair. "I don't need that," he said.

Colin sighed and answered, "Neither of us do. But I can't think of another way. With the Thraks about to declare war, we may be way out there all by ourselves."

Jack shook his head. "I won't let you go all by yourself. All right. Denaro is in. Lassaday's in charge of Unit 3, it's just begun training. We'll install him in there. But if he turns up missing, I don't want to remember we had this conversation."

"Nor I," returned the saint, with an unheavenly glint in his mild brown eyes. He left when Lassaday climbed to the bridge.

The sergeant looked after the reverend as he left. "And wha' did he want?"

"He blessed the recruits."

"A practical man, that Walker." Lassaday rubbed his callused palm over his tan, bald, and profusely sweating head. "I'd give my left nut to have a thousand more like them."

Jack did not let humor twitch the corner of his mouth as he looked at the training grounds. The sergeant was too right. They needed a thousand more like this. "Don't let the senator hear you say that."

"A senator?" Lassaday's lip curled. "Jesus, commander, that's all you need. If I were you, I'd weld him to Baadluster and let the Minister of War take the heat."

"I would, but it seems Baadluster's done just that to me. They're getting restless down there. Better get back."

"In a minute. I heard some scuttle."

Jack took a moment to look closely at the veteran. He'd been through Lassaday's none too gentle but capable hands for Basic. On the grounds, Lassaday wore a silver mylar jumpsuit to catch the eye, but his sun-darkened face wore a no nonsense look now. "What is it, sarge?"

"I got the word there's a lot of subspace chatter going on. My son is into it, posts to th' bulletin board all the time. It looks like the Thraks are massing."

"Really?" Jack smiled tightly at that. Would fortune smile on him twice by tipping the Thraks' hand? "It would be nice to anticipate an attack before they break out."

Lassaday beamed. "Thought you'd like that, commander. Be there waitin' for 'em, a little reception committee, like."

Jack nodded, and Lassaday left the podium, passing by a brilliantly coated gentleman who was approaching the bridge. The man could be none other than the senator, short and compact, with arms and shoulders that looked as powerful as a bulldozer, fair-haired and with the florid complexion of a short-tempered man. Well-muscled thighs drove the man across the bridge to Jack's side where, though much shorter than a man in armor, he was not out-massed.

"Commander Storm."

Jack offered a gauntlet. "Senator Washburn. Your aides?" He looked around, anticipating a brace of aides/bodyguards.

"Sent them away. Told them you'd either be responsible for me or you weren't worth the price of scrap for your armor."

Jack found himself with a genuine smile for the short, feisty gentleman. "So that's the way of it," he said. "Good. I have no more time for you than you have for me."

Washburn's thick blond eyebrows wagged up and down. "Commander, I have all the time in the world for you, but I appreciate the frankness. What have you got for me?"

"Team drills. This is Unit 1, the team I went through training with, and we're all fairly seasoned now, but most of us had to be reequipped coming out of Bythia, and new suits take time to get used to."

"Any trouble getting the optimum out of your gear?"

"No, sir. I think you'll be pleased." Jack waved his left gauntlet and the troops waiting below went into motion.

At the end of an hour's time, Senator Washburn turned to Jack. "I'm impressed. But what makes you think this type of land war is what we need?"

"Senator, we all know maneuverability in space is greatly hampered. Basically, we have one pass and that's it. We'll be slugging it out on land because that's what matters to both us and the Thraks. We don't breed in vacuum. On the whole, we don't nurture our young out there, nor grow our crops or mine for manufacturing. We're still land-based and that's where we'll be fighting because it's our land they covet. If we fight them from space, we'll be polluting the very terrain we're trying to save."

Washburn's right eyebrow bristled up. "It's the old Sand Wars mentality."

"Perhaps. Who says it was wrong?"

He grumbled deep in his throat, and said, "My colleagues won't be easy to convince. We were soundly beaten in the Sand Wars."

Jack could say nothing back to that. A familiar ache of having been betrayed and left without hope arced through him, but he did not let it show in his expression. He remembered Lassaday's information.

"Perhaps," he said, "I can arrange a demonstration."

"That would be greatly appreciated, commander. And don't be shy with the budget. Get yourself some new armor—that set looks a little worn to me."

Jack's lips twitched a little. "It has its purposes."

"Don't stint yourself, commander." The senator gripped the railing, leaning forward until his nose pressed against the windshield. He took a deep breath. "God, I love a wartime economy."

Baadluster's pasty complexion pinked. "You want to what?"

"Follow the lead that the subspace call-board is giving us. I want to be entrenched on that planet when the Thraks hit. I want to be waiting for them."

"We've got no confirmation that Stralia is targeted. We're still waiting for an official declaration."

"And that attitude gives them first strike capabilities."

"Perhaps." Baadluster's teeth nipped at his too thick lips. "Stralia is under our noses. Surely the Thraks would have better sense than to attack us there, scouting activity notwithstanding."

"I have a hunch otherwise."

The minister stood there, his slender hands twitching at his sides for a moment, before he pivoted to look at Pepys. He did not fling his hands into the air, but he might as well have.

Pepys put a hand up to his chin, somewhat disguising the

amused set to his expression. "Just what," he mumbled out of his half-hidden mouth, "do you propose to do?"

"If we go, we go now. Even though we're closer, we'll have no way to beat them out of subspace if we don't. I'll take Rawlins as my second and leave Lassaday here to keep taking the edges off Units 2 and 3. I'll leave Travellini as my back-up officer."

"The Knights could be ruined almost before they've been reinstated."

"Never. And Washburn intimated that the Dominion Congress doesn't want to hire ineffectual, outdated troops. He all but told me they wanted to see us in action."

Baadluster hissed in disgust. Pepys waved him quiet. "How soon can you be ready?"

"By the time you have a transport ready for launch. The suits are already in the shop being stripped down and re-powered—that's customary after any training exercise. We can be on a shuttle before nightfall."

"Then," and Pepys' red hair crackled with the force of his words, "You had better say your goodbyes. You just be sure to give me Stralia and give them their victory."

Jack saluted. "I'll do my best, your highness." He turned to go, remembered something and turned back. "I swore in a new recruit this afternoon. He'll stay behind with Lassaday."

"A single recruit?" Pepys' eyebrow went up like a fuzzy red caterpillar. "Who is it?"

"A former Walker by the name of Denaro, your highness. Colin brought him to me. Said you knew all about it. He shows a lot of potential."

Baadluster's frustration seemed to boil over about then and Jack thought it wise to retreat.

Jonathan lumbered into the middle of Colin's afternoon meditations, a harbinger of reality. Colin looked up at him, saw the knifelike frown creasing his aide's ursine face, and dispensed with scolding him for interrupting.

"What is it, Jonathan?"

"Commander Storm is here. He demands to see you."

"Ah." Colin nodded. "Give me a few minutes, then send him in." He stood up and stretched, then reseated himself. He had thought to himself more than once that the commander's name was not so much a name as a prophecy and he thought it again now, knowing that Jack would be bristling with indignation—and rightly so.

The room shuddered slightly when Jack entered, though he was dressed as a mere soldier and not in battle armor. Colin set his teeth. The resonance of the meditation room would bear the shock waves of the commander's obvious anger for days.

"Jack. I've been expecting you."

"You're damn right you have. How long did you think you had before I found out about Denaro?"

"Not much longer than this. All I needed, actually, was long enough to get him sworn in," Colin said mildly.

Jack halted in the middle of the room, in front of the burled wood table and the chair where Colin sat. His light blue eyes had darkened and the wind had torn through his straight hair, tumbling it about. The man had few lines on his face . . . his shoulders broad, his frame erect, but Colin could never shake his feeling about Jack—the eyes were older than his mid-twenties body. He had a maturity about him that belied his youth. There was a mystery buried somewhere in that man that Colin was not privy to, and Colin wondered if he would live long enough to see it unfold.

"I don't like being used, especially by someone I consider a friend."

"And if I had told you, would you have accepted Denaro?"

The commander hesitated. He frowned, the expression pressing lines into a face that did not yet have them permanently etched in. "I don't know. But you didn't give me a chance to make that decision, did you?"

Colin stood up. "No," he said, regretfully. "I'm afraid I didn't. And you're right, Jack. I should have. I should have known you well enough."

"What happened?"

"Pepys wanted Denaro."

"Why?"

The Walker prelate strode a few steps away, to look at a mood painting on the wall. Its swirl of blue colors formed and dissolved in a constant, if gradual, shifting. "I'm not sure why except that Denaro is a militant, and Pepys is afraid. He wanted him where he didn't have to worry about him anymore."

"Maybe Pepys is right." Jack's voice was calm now. "Denaro has and could cause the two of you a lot of trouble."

"Could. Just as you could cause him a lot of trouble. I'm sorry, but it's not in me to condemn anyone for what they could do. But I couldn't disobey, either. After all, Pepys is my emperor. So I gave him Denaro in the best way I could." Colin tired of the blue painting and turned. His blue robes fluttered, giving Jack an eerie sensation that the older man was just an extension of the painting's possibilities.

"Denaro is safe from persecution as long as he's a member of the Knights."

"Yes. I think so."

"What about when he leaves us?"

"We'll have to face that when it happens. In the meantime, Pepys has a war to run. He should be sufficiently—distracted—I hope, to forget about Denaro."

"Never," Jack told him. "The man never forgets an enemy."

Colin paused, then said, "I'm sorry, Jack. I did not mean to add this to your burdens. You're right. If you wish, I'll recall Denaro. We'll let Pepys take whatever course he intends."

"No." Jack made his way to the room's entrance. He stopped at the door. "He's one of mine now, and he's going to be good. But next time, saint," and Jack smiled crookedly. "Talk to me first. We might both be on the same side"

Colin returned the smile warmly as Jack gave a half-salute and left. The older man's smile faded. Unlike Jack, Pepys did not know a good man when he had one. It might be the death of his friend.

CHAPTER 11

Amber stared around the immense compound, an uneasy feeling at the nape of her neck, which she couldn't dispel. Since returning, the pace of their lives had been frantic. The entire barracks was on alert, packing for shipping out even as they trained. She chafed her bare arms as she waited, tracing the feathery blue patterns drawn there. As long as the alien dye permeated her skin, alien senses invaded her soul.

She sensed the visitor before he reached the front portal, had it open, and was waiting as the street savvy urchin darted out of the courtyard shadows, beyond the view screens of the panning security cameras and within arm's length of her.

He skidded to a halt and tossed a palm-sized package at her. "Here's your jammers," he said. His upper lip curled in a sneer.

Amber suppressed her smile, knowing that she'd surprised him, but he wasn't about to reflect it. She flipped him a three credit disk. "Thank Smithers for me," she said.

"Don't bother with it, lady. He's sending you the bill."

"I'm sure he is," she returned, but the boy had pivoted and dived back into the shadows, his grubby hand closed tightly about the money.

She'd embarrassed him because he thought she'd seen him coming. What would he say if he'd known he'd set off every sense she owned: smell, touch, hearing and thought, as well as sight? Amber palmed the door shut and stood a moment, her eyes half-closed. These were extensions of the sensory perceptions Hussiah had given her. Would they wear off with the tattooing? Or would she be driven insane first?

Amber forced her eyelids up and ripped open the package the street brat had delivered. Two jammers blinked in her palm. One discreetly placed to the fore of the suite and one to the rear . . . even though the apartment had been swept, she knew that the jammers would keep long-distance ears from hearing them. With a wry smile, she paced the double suite and installed the chips, knowing that Jack would never have thought of it.

Paranoia can be good, she told herself, and returned to the front door, her silken caftan flowing about her as she paced tensely back and forth until she again sensed a visitor.

His heat flowed out ahead of him like a swiftly moving fire. Amber hesitated as she went to the door, knowing it wasn't Jack unless he was furious—and Jack did not have that temperament unless he was in armor and linked with Bogie. Then who—? She keyed on the viewscreen.

A rawboned man halted in front of the door, brushing his limp brown hair to one side with an impatient hand. His thick lips pursed as he reached out. Amber instinctively disliked the look of the man, but she recognized the cut of his clothing. One of Pepys' courtiers, probably. What would such a bureaucrat want here?

She opened the door cautiously. The caftan sleeve slid along her slim arm as she did so, revealing the blue tattooing. His black eyes drifted toward the sight, took in the phenomenon with a ferocity of interest that almost seared her as he looked back.

"I'm looking for the young lady who accompanies Commander Storm."

"That would be me." She blocked the door with her form even though the man hardly looked as though he would force his way past. Looked, but not sensed. No. She felt his heat wash over her. Heard the race of his pulse. Could pick out a stray thought even though he kept his mind locked down well. He would do whatever he had to to get what he wanted. She braced herself. "Jack is not here at the moment. He's working with the troops."

"I know. If you would allow me . . . I'm Vandover Baadluster, the new minister." She said nothing, but the man's dark eyes glittered as though he knew what she'd been thinking.

He waved a long-fingered hand. "May I come in?"

He set her teeth on edge, but Amber inclined her head. "It's your street," she said, her words an echo from her past.

"Street? Ah. Yes." Baadluster eased himself in. "From that standpoint, I suppose it is, but the emperor would never want you to feel as though these apartments were other than yours."

Amber said nothing. Whoever he was, this man had not come here to make her feel at ease on the palatial grounds. Nor had he come to be silent.

Baadluster rocked back on his heels. "Have you settled in?"

"As well as can be expected." She moved back uneasily, knowing that the man had not come to her to exchange pleasantries. "I . . . am busy, Minister Baadluster. If I can help you?"

"Perhaps. I have been investigating the records of my predecessor, Commander Winton. I was distressed to see that you were implicated in several assassinations."

Amber felt her skin grow cold and pale. "I was not found guilty. Evidence suggests that the assassin who died on Bythia when he murdered the Ambassador was the same man who struck here."

"Unfortunately for you that evidence is never to be available to us again."

"I can't be tried!"

"No. And there is probably no chance you ever will be. But," and Baadluster held the word in his teeth a moment. "But future transgressions will not be so easily dismissed."

"I'm not an assassin."

He looked around the apartment for a moment. "Winton suggested otherwise."

"Winton was crazy."

"Perhaps. It would have been easier to tell if Storm had brought him back alive, wouldn't it?" He looked back to her. Then, so quickly she couldn't evade him, he grabbed her wrist. His fingers felt like live coals on her skin.

"You come from under-Malthen," he said. "You've no implanted ID. You come and go past the security systems as if they don't exist."

She wrenched her arm away. "Old habits die hard."

"Indeed. Are you and Storm a team, or are you using him?"

Amber palmed the door open. "Get out."

"I've not finished our talk."

"I have."

Baadluster flushed, a purple mottling of his pasty flesh tones. "You play, but I do not."

She straightened and threw her head back, feeling her chin settle into pointed stubbornness as she did so. "It would really be naive of me to think that we're on the same side, wouldn't it?"

"Yes," the Minister of War answered. "It would. And it would be even more naive to think that Jack Storm will not suffer for his association with you. Or you from his."

"What do you want?"

Baadluster curved his plumpish lips into a semblance of a smile. Amber concealed a shudder as the nape of her neck tingled. "A word now and then," he said, "might convince me of your loyalties."

She stood for a long moment, running through the possibilities of what Baadluster wanted, then fixing on it in shock. "Why?"

Vandover smiled. "Because you will want to."

Amber gathered her thoughts. Jack would not be surprised that they were suspicious of him—they had to be, after these last few years. But without proof, and with Jack in the position he was in, with war looming on the horizon . . . he'd probably never been safer. She cleared her throat. "I won't do it."

"Of course not, my dear. I didn't think you would."

Her stubborn chin dropped slightly.

Vandover Baadluster smiled widely. "But it was worth a try, and neither will you tell him I contacted you. Pepys is a liberal emperor, but nothing in regulations says that a soldier's whore has to be allowed to stay with him."

"I'm not his whore!"

"No?" His brow arched. "Perhaps they have another word for it in under-Malthen."

Amber moved away from the portal as Baadluster neared it. "And I'll give you this, for free." Her angry gaze met his amused one. "Just like me, you aren't safe anywhere, either."

For the briefest of moments, she thought he was going to hit her, and fought every muscle in her body not to pull back until she sensed the muscular heat of his arm bunching. But Baadluster did not move. The darkness of his eyes seemed to flare but whatever it was he might have done, Rawlins interrupted.

So filled had her senses been with the man before her, she'd never heard his approach, but the young Knight filled the doorway suddenly, his milk blond hair tousled from the wind, and his fathomless blue eyes drinking her in.

"Amber. The commander has word for you." Rawlins blinked slowly as he looked from her to the minister. "I'm sorry," he said, "if I interrupted you."

"No matter, lieutenant."

Amber cleared her throat to say, "Rawlins, this is Minister Vandover Baadluster, the emperor's newest adviser."

Rawlins saluted.

"Lieutenant. I'm finished here. For now."

She held her ragged breath as the man inclined his head slightly and left Jack's apartments. Even with the portal closed and locked behind him, she could still feel the feral heat of his body and his thoughts.

If she could have, she would have disinfected the room.

Amber pressed her hands to her lips for a moment and found herself trembling. Angrily she dropped her hands to her sides and clenched her fists. They would never have dared approach Jack like this. Never.

And because he wears armor, Amber thought. *You won't jerk him around because he wears the armor!*

Rawlins looked thoughtfully out the portal as he opened it to leave himself. "Trouble?"

"No."

"You're sure?"

"Yes. What does Jack want?"

"He'd like you to come out to the training grounds."

She frowned. "Why?"

"He wants to talk with you."

A chill ridged up her spine. "Why didn't he use the com?"

Rawlins would not meet her eyes as he said, "Some things are better said face to face."

Amber shivered as the coldness from the room seemed

to gather inside her. Rawlins sensed her withdrawal and moved back from the door. He made as if to touch her comfortingly on the arm, but did not complete the gesture.

"It's our job," he said.

"No" She returned his gaze, thinking of Jack and how far they'd come to reach this point. "No, I think it's his destiny."

CHAPTER 12

Intercepted

Baadluster shadowed the emperor as Pepys looked over the subspace call report.

"Have you made a record of this?" he asked of the minister.

"Nothing official. You won't be able to keep it down long. There's bound to have been other messages that were gotten out."

Pepys sighed. As he looked up, he rubbed his fatigued eyes. "It will be blamed on the Thraks."

"I think so. But there's no doubt in my mind from the description given here that it's someone else. Perhaps even a twin ship of the unknown Storm encountered."

Pepys blinked his eyes back into focus. "Another planet gone. Hundreds, no, thousands of colonists . . . so far out on the rim that we barely had contact. Why?"

"Shall I inform your officers?"

The emperor sat there, caught by the stark realization that there might be somebody out there bigger and badder than the Thraks. Were they waiting around to pick up the pieces? Or did they even care if there were any pieces left?

"Your highness."

"What? No. I don't want anything official said about this. Let's wait and see if any other messages got out. Perhaps not. This . . . massacre . . . seems to have been pretty efficient."

"Your highness, I'd suggest the star fleets be notified, if not the Knights."

"No."

Baadluster drew himself up. "Very well. Good night." He withdrew, his gangly shadow mingling with, then dissolving among the other long shadows in the emperor's private chambers. Pepys scarcely noticed his leaving.

CHAPTER 13

Jack looked up from his reports as a flicker of movement outside his private berth caught his eye. He keyed the tapes to pause and a faint hum of static filled his ears as the audio dimmed as well. The shadow of movement coalesced into Rawlins, waiting nervously beyond the privacy panel, and Jack made a movement to let him in.

"What is it, lieutenant?" Disapproval faintly edged his words. With the ship nearing their destination, they had barely enough time to prepare themselves for the coming drop. Rawlins should not be wandering around.

The young man came to a stop. His milky white hair spiked back from his high forehead, and his blue eyes seemed to beg Jack for reassurance. Jack did not need to hear any words to read the unease in Rawlins' eyes. Forty-eight hours would not be enough to prepare this man for war. Maybe a lifetime wouldn't.

Jack hated to go into battle with hesitation like that riding his men. But he knew Rawlins wasn't a coward—he had never seen that in him before. So it was something else that gave the young man doubts. Evidently Rawlins thought Jack had an answer, or he wouldn't be here.

But Rawlins stood poised, his fear unvoiced, as though speaking of it would give it shape.

"Come in, lieutenant. There just might be enough space for you to sit down if you do."

That thawed his second's vocal cords. "Yes, sir." Rawlins stepped in past the privacy panel's track and squeezed his lean hip onto a chair flap. "Did I disturb you?"

"Just going over the terrain. We'll stay in orbit on the far side, keeping the planet between us until the Thraks commit to a landing pattern. Then we'll position the drop. I don't know where it'll be, but I have a good guess based on past performance." He had a damned good guess and he didn't need the tapes to inform him. His communion with Bogie was feeding him a storehouse of information. Now he had more than his instinctual gut level hatred of the Thraks to fight them with. More than his nightmares of locked-in cold sleep. More than Baadluster's vague stratagems. And he could only pray it would be enough.

Rawlins stretched his legs out restlessly. He looked up at Jack from under dark brows. "It all depends on us, doesn't it?"

"No."

The brows went up in surprise. "But I thought—"

"You thought we had something to do with gravity and magnetic attraction, with rain and wind and fire and DNA? Come on, lieutenant. The only thing depending on us is whatever sector of land I give you to hold onto. That's it."

"I've never seen a sand planet, sir, and I don't want to. Claron was bad enough for me. But I thought that the Dominion . . . that Congress' support of the war . . . the whole circuit . . . was in our hands."

Jack took his tapes off pause and shut the whole system down. He took his headset off. "I don't think any Knight alive is armored well enough to carry that kind of load, do you?"

"Well, no, sir. Not really."

"Then you can relax, soldier, because you're not being expected to." Jack leaned forward slightly. "What you are being expected to do is study your briefs so that when I give you your assignment, you can carry it out."

Rawlins' color came back, and so did the glint in his eyes. He nodded. "Yes, sir. I can handle that."

"Good. Now get out of here or you'll wish Lassaday had come along instead."

Rawlins grinned in tribute to their tough and feisty NCO. "Yessir!"

Jack watched him go and sat for a long moment as the privacy panel closed after him, leaving the berth in silence. As he finally moved to replace his headset, he thought of what rested on his shoulders, and what didn't.

Amber had had little for him in the way of goodbyes other than the immense sadness welling in brown eyes flecked with gold. She had stood in the curve of his arm for a long time after his words had died away, and they watched the training grounds empty of troops eager for combat, until there was nothing left but dust whirls and the spartan barricades. Because of Bogie, he felt her presence through his second skin, every nuance of movement and heat.

He felt the sighing moving through her just before she said, "I don't mind you going so much . . . it's just that I always get left behind. And I never thought I'd be jealous of a pile of scrap . . . but Bogie's the lucky one. I may share your bed, but he shares your soul."

And with a faint whisper of a kiss, she'd left him on the command bridge to make ready to go to war.

She'd been right, of course. And that was one more wrong he carried with him until he found the Thraks who could purge him.

CHAPTER 14

"No, no, you stupid son of a bitch," Lassaday bellowed, his voice breaking into static over the com. "Keep that up and you're going to blow your ass off! Now step in line and remember, the suit's carrying you, you're not carrying the suit. Quit flexin' your muscles like some overgrown ape."

Denaro fought the wild gyrations of his armor to a standstill as the sergeant's rough voice washed over him. Beneath it, he imagined he could hear the jeers of the other recruits. His heart thumped loudly with anger and he took a deep breath, retreating into the meditations of the Blue Wheel to compose himself.

St. Colin had promised him a hard but rewarding road to travel. How hard, the old man could scarcely have guessed. But, and Denaro steeled his jaw, the empire would not get the best of him. He had been given his mission and he could not fail in it. He was in exile until he mastered the armor or it mastered him. Sweat dripped off his brow and down his bare torso, where leads pinched uncomfortably to his skin. He took a deep breath and, almost as if Lassaday sensed he had composed himself and was ready to try again, the sergeant rasped, "Get the lead out, boy."

The session over at last, Denaro stumbled into the tunnel corridors leading to the locker rooms and the shop. Jostled and bumped around by recruits more in tune with their equipment, he sagged against a wall and let them run by him. He ached in more muscles than he thought God had ever created as he reached up and unscrewed his helmet.

Malthen air poured in, tinged with a smell of hot concrete and dirt, but it was sweet compared to the sour aroma of his own body.

"Rough day?"

Denaro was startled, in spite of himself, and smothered a groan as a calf muscle threatened to cramp. He half crouched down to rub it, realized he couldn't get to it through his armor and settled for stomping his foot on the ground several times until the muscle unknotted. He glared at the woman who shared the corridor shadows with him, until he recognized the commander's woman.

His mother had taught him that the ungodly feared a fight and to "stare the de'il in the eyes until He backs down." The commander's whore was no exception and so he stared at her until she came out of the shadows and he could see her better.

He had stayed away from her on the evacuation transport. There, Jonathan had been by St. Colin's side and it had been Denaro's job, in the background, to keep the evacuees away from the prelate. He had been in disgrace, the majority of his company overrun by Bythian snakeskins until less than one man in twenty had survived. It was none of his business that the reverend seemed to enjoy the woman's company. It was, perhaps, a minor reflection of his humanity and flesh that he did. But Denaro did not like to profess such a weakness himself and though he stayed rocksteady as she glided within arm's reach of him, he could feel his nostrils flare.

The thundering passage of the other recruits faded away and the two were left alone in the corridor without even an echo to disturb them.

The woman jerked her head slightly, indicating over her shoulder. "They have an advantage over you."

"Three weeks of training," he said warily. He knew the Devil was going to offer him something and he wondered what it might be.

Amber smiled. He saw then she was no older than himself. "Jack said you had potential."

The Devil himself! But Denaro felt a tinge of pleasure at the praise, nonetheless. "Did he?"

The girl-woman said nothing further, but began to circle him slightly until Denaro had to crane his neck a little to keep her in view. She unnerved him.

"I've been with Jack a couple of years," she said. "You

might say I've got the theory while you're getting the practice."

"Theory?"

"On how the suit works. How it should work, how to mesh its power with your ability."

Denaro froze as she went behind him and then returned. The dim light of the tunnel caught the feathery tattooing on her bare arms ... she wore her jumpsuit with the sleeves cut off as though daring people to look upon her disfigurement. He shivered even as he made his mind up that he'd let the imp tantalize him enough. He straightened and tightened his grip on his helmet.

She laughed, a breathy, mocking sound. "Denaro! I think you're afraid of me."

He shot her a look that lesser disciples of the Blue Wheel would have quailed at, and she laughed at him a second time. Then, astonishingly, she stretched out her hand, palm up as if offering peace.

"I could help you through the rough spots of the next few weeks," she said.

"You? Why?"

"Colin has been very good to me. Let's say I owe him."

Denaro relaxed slightly. "St. Colin is a man of many virtues."

"You can say that again."

He scarcely noticed as she entwined her arm about his Flexalink sleeve and began drawing him down the corridor with her. As the perfume of her tawny hair dazzled his senses and blurred his vision slightly, he was deaf to her last words:

"And I've always wondered what it would be like to wear armor myself."

The staging hold vibrated as the ship began to descend into an orbit. Around the shop, soldiers in various stages of hook-up looked up briefly. Their glances flickered toward their commander. Jack was aware of it and ignored it as he continued donning his armor. Steadied by his presence, the men went back to their tasks. Most of them had never made a wartime drop before and it did not help that the few who had were keyed up. Jack tried to ignore the shaking of his own hands as he wired himself to stay in the suit, plumbing and all, for the next few days.

The surging through his nerves was not fear though, it was adrenaline. Pure, unadulterated. His pulse sang throughout his body as he outfitted for battle. His ears rang with the buzz of his readiness, and with Bogie's tide of ferocity which grew by the second.

"Commander Storm."

"Yes, Whitehead." Jack looked up. The fleet pilot's face filled the screen, his helmet masking all but his wide nose and dark eyes. The pilot looked unhappy.

"We're approaching the far side as requested, commander, but we've picked up a blip."

Jack's skin tingled. "What is it?"

"I'm not sure, sir."

"Give me your best guess or relay the picture."

Whitehead gave him a measuring stare over the com. "I'd say there's somebody waiting for us."

In a corner, one of Jack's men muttered, *"Shit."*

Jack stood up and finished shrugging into the suit. "Give me the overview."

The pilot fed it in.

The shadowy blip grew in size until there was little doubt.

"It's a trap," Rawlins said.

Jack felt himself growing cold. The Thraks were waiting for them. But he smiled. "Good."

CHAPTER 15

"Good?" echoed Rawlins.

Jack ignored him. "Whitehead, are they in orbit or maintaining a fixed position?"

"Doesn't look like they've got much drift."

"Okay, then pull a right angle turn here. Put us in orbit, but keep them on the edge of vision. I want to know the second they move."

Rawlins was still in shock, his half open suit making him look like some kind of exotic flower. His piercing blue eyes were fixed on Jack. "Sir."

Jack said to Whitehead, "Give me a picture of those sectors we were looking at earlier." With a brief glance over his shoulder, he said, "Thraks dug in are a lot easier to find than Thraks being dropped in. We may not catch them coming out of hyperdrive, but this'll do just as well."

He scanned the data coming in over the screen. "Freeze it there." The computer obeyed. "There's sand. Not much. But a Thraks never digs in for a fight without some sand. They store their food in it, like a larder. This is where they're dug in tightest."

Rawlins thawed out, shrugged into his sleeves, and sealed his armor to the neck. "Then that's where we hit."

Jack shook his head. "No. That's suicide to hit 'em there. We'll land here and here," he windowed the screen. "And spiral inward. It won't be easy. That's rough terrain and they'll hit us with everything they've got once they see we've pinpointed them."

"How do you know that's them? Maybe that's a desert or something." Garner, dark bushy hair in disarray and with disbelief on his feral face, moved across the bay. He and Jack had been at odds during Basic, but Jack had won his loyalty once before, and Jack did not fear having the soldier at his side now. Garner's face showed no malice, but he looked to Jack for an answer.

"It shows on the spectroscope. Believe me, it's Thrakian sand. *I know*." And he did.

"Yes, sir," Garner acknowledged. "Then what's below it?"

"Depending on how long they've been here . . . nests, an armory, and possibly even catacombs. It doesn't take them long to dig in." Jack picked up his helmet. He looked around the ship's hold. Fifty-nine men paused to meet his eyes. "Whitehead, put me on broadcast."

"Yes, commander. Tied in."

He was now being watched on the two other ships by another 120 men. Jack said, "We're ready for drop. The Thraks are here, waiting for us. But they don't know that we don't care. We're ready for them. And we're going to take them out. This is how we're going to do it. Listen carefully. Drop time in twelve minutes." And he began to detail the drop zones, sector assignments and ever-tightening spiral they were going to throw around the heart of the Thrakian infestation.

When he was finished, there wasn't a man who doubted they could do it.

He smiled tightly, a grim smile for which he had, unknowingly, begun to grow famous. "All right now. First team drop units, Red Wing, Blue Wing, Green Wing, let's go."

He made a motion and Whitehead cut the com screen transmission. The pilot's face filled the screen once more.

"Break a leg, commander."

"Don't worry," Jack said "I want you to watch that mother ship. Turret movement or orbit change. If it flinches. . . ."

"I'll go in and burn its tail feathers for you." Whitehead bared his teeth in anticipation.

"Do that," Jack said. "But don't forget you've got to haul our asses out of here when we're done."

"Commander." Whitehead sounded mildly aggrieved. "That junk is no match for a needler."

"The general of that junk may surprise you." Jack said nothing else as he locked his helmet on. The ship shuddered as Whitehead took it down to where Jack wanted it.

Team One went into the drop tubes. It would take six passes for Whitehead to get them all down. Jack wanted to be on the first one, but he was scheduled for the last, just in case the Thraks had changed techniques.

The Thraks hit them as soon as they chuted in. Jack was pleased. It gave him a chance to blood his men right away, rather than have them walking about the landscape all spooked until they met action. Wondering about the enemy was more dangerous than facing them. His com was crackling with messages as he plummeted in, cut the chute and let his power vault absorb the shook of hitting.

"Quiet down out there and get to work," he ordered, cutting across the chatter. The com lines went quiet. Then Rawlins, with Unit 3, called out, "Oh my god! Here they come!"

And it was busy after that.

He doubted if any of his men had really seen a warrior Thraks. The Thraks that came in on the trading ships were really drones, mottled gray or sable, impressive enough until compared to their bigger brothers. But a warrior Thraks was bigger, more massive, his natural body armor far denser, his ability to run slope-backed on all fours making him much more agile than the drones. They were most insectlike when still. In movement, they became vicious carnivores and Jack didn't want his men underestimating them.

"Red Wing. We're being flanked."

"Then turn. Keep your grids on, and put your locators on memory. We'll fall back into pattern later," Jack said.

"Man down! Man down!" a voice shrilled, and cut off abruptly.

Jack waited. "Rawlins, Garner, Peres. Anybody know who that was?"

A young voice quavered back, "This is Simons, Commander. That was Joe Henkley. He had trouble after the drop . . . something inside the armor broke loose . . . he'd been trying to get it hooked back up."

"All right, Simons. Thanks for the data. Keep your chin up and your eyes peeled." Jack let the rosy glow of the holo bathe him as he searched for movement. He wasn't disappointed. In two seconds, he was very busy, as the choppy, green-brown terrain of grass, brush, and hillocks, suddenly exploded with Thraks.

They didn't go down the way they used to. Bogie sang in his blood as Jack fired and ran, fired and vaulted, return fire ricocheting off the armor. He saw one stumble down in the wave of chitin rearing up against him, even as he turned and ran, drawing them after him into the arms of his soldiers holding the sector behind him. Bogie roared his disapproval of the maneuver until Jack turned and stood, flanked by Rawlins to his left and another Knight to the right.

He pointed his gauntlets and laid down a spray of fire. Another Thraks tumbled, but a dozen more jumped it, throwing themselves over and coming up mean.

"Holy shit," Rawlins muttered. "What stops 'em?"

"This does," said Jack, and blew the leader's head off. It took a precise throat-shot just below the mask to do it. But it could be done. He took the legs off three more and said, "Let's go."

Bogie roared his approval as Jack ran toward the Thraks, vaulted their line and came down behind them, sending havoc into their ranks.

From the chatter on the com, he could tell that his men were settling down from their first startled reactions. He cut into the transmission, saying, "Don't waste your fire. Now that you know what they're like, make every shot count."

Garner huffed back, "Jesus, commander, these bugs are *tough*."

"Yes," Jack returned. "But you're tougher. Remember, Garner. We're here to kick ass. We want 'em to think twice about going to war with us."

He began firing single shots until the Thrakian line either went down or fled.

Then, still smiling his grim smile, he set his locator to find his original destination and resumed course. Ahead and behind him, flanking him, just within hailing distance, his men did likewise.

Third day. His mouth felt dry and the sweat trickled persistently, maddeningly, through his chest hairs and down to his sweatsoaked trousers. At his back, the chamois that was Bogie's regenerative form lay coolly against his shoulders, absorbing heat and moisture there, and protecting him from the chafing the field pack always created on an armored back.

He almost hadn't ordered field packs. He was glad he had. Thraks had been bred tougher. They fought better than they had in the first Sand Wars. They'd taken their beatings and learned their lessons.

But then, so had Jack.

Twelve percent casualties weren't bad. And they were now targeted toward the interior of their spiral pattern. From the attacks in response to their raid, he knew he was right about the location of the nests and main armory. Wipe that out, and the mother ship just over the horizon would pull out in a hurry. Whitehead and the two other needlers and been doing a little dance with the Thrakian behemoth, nothing serious, but most of the bombing to soften up the Knights had been kept to a minimum. So far, so good.

Although, if he had it to do over, he'd have Lassaday here as well. And Travellini. Holding 180 hands to get his troops through this was tougher than he'd thought. His throat had gone dry and raspy sometime last night and Bogie had mournfully informed him that morning that their water supply was depleted. It seemed the old suit had developed a minor leak. The recycler was keying in on the leak as humidity and drying it out almost faster than it leaked, leaving Jack without water and with a paper dry throat.

It made it difficult to give orders. He'd spread himself too thin, knowing himself to be the only true veteran among the suits. There were mercenaries, of course, who'd been through a variety of actions, but nothing in a sustained, contained situation like they faced now.

All in all, they'd done well. He was proud of them. Any minute now, the Red Wing should hit the leading edge of the sand as the spiral tightened. When they did, with Peres leading them, Green Wing and Blue Wing would have to get their asses in gear for Thraks would literally erupt out of the ground, determined to protect their headquarters. Not too long now.

Jack licked his lips and wished he could mop the sweat off his forehead.

Almost as if reading his thoughts, Peres said, "What's it going to be like, again?"

Jack checked his tracking grid. Peres should be southwest of him. That put him facing into the wind. "Grit," Jack answered. "In the wind first, like dust. Then you'll get close enough to see patches of it on the ground. Eventually, you'll hit the dunes and from there, Robbie, you're going to be too busy to be a tourist."

A short laugh. Jack added, "And I don't want anybody slowing down for souvenirs. I only need one body and I'll handle picking that up. Everybody else concentrate on clearing the field. We blow the armory and get out."

"Yessir." He heard a wave of echoes.

"Anybody showing a red field?"

"No, sir."

"Good." Inwardly, he was greatly pleased that no one had exhausted their power supplies though he had suspected there would be dead suits. Although technically they could stay in the field much longer, in reality it depended on how much firepower they'd expended. And how much firepower they'd expended depended largely on how inexperienced and scared they'd been. They'd done very well to get this far.

Peres said, "There's grit on the wind, sir."

"Good." Jack checked his gauges over. "Give a yell when you hit the first patches. All Wings, all sectors. Listen up. When Peres signals us, tighten the ranks. We're going in. Any of you with expended field packs, *drop 'em*. I want you lean and mean. Got that?"

An echoing wave of assent.

Ten minutes later, Peres' hoarse voice came over the com. Jack never heard what he said, but he launched forward into a run, closing up the ranks and bringing his spiral pattern into a stranglehold.

He heard the whoops and cries as Thraks exploded out of the scrub brush and dunes of sand, intent on protecting their last holding grounds.

The Knights crossed the leading edge of sand that encroached on the Stralian soil. The line of Thraks wavered for a moment and gave way. Jack could not see far enough over the dunes, but in a few hours, he should be able to meet with Peres as their deadly circle closed.

He kept firing and striding, breaking the ranks of the Thraks before him, his boots doing almost as much damage as his gauntlet fire. His left gauntlet muzzle jammed, leaving Jack with scorched fingertips inside the glove as it overheated. With a mild curse, Jack pulled out his laser rifle from his field pack and cradled it, the first time he'd had to use the pack. He'd been saving it for the coup de grace, but no matter. Nothing was going to stop him today. He saw Rawlins following him in, and then picked up ground sight of the rest of Blue Wing. Laser fire dazzled his sight as another wave of Thraks reared from the ground and charged.

Their bodies crunched when he strode over them. Flecks of green and yellow ichor flew up to splatter the white armor. White. A deadly shade of armor unless one were buried to the hips in white and beige and pink sand.

Then, he became part of the landscape, unlike the sable and more somber colors of armor the others wore. Jack's armor had always been designed for war with the Thraks. He was going to win this one. He had no doubts.

Not even when the ground opened up right under him and he plunged into darkness.

CHAPTER 16

"Shee-it, commander!"

Jack's ears echoed even as he dropped and hit the power vault to land. He landed, and went to his knees, Flexalinks complaining. It had been like falling off a cliff. Even worse had been the plunge into Bogie's thoughts—the berserker clawed at him from the inside. He swam in raw panic. His breath rasped through his clenched throat as he fought to take possession of his mind, of rational thought. Bogie weakened and Jack immediately squelched the light sensors, not wanting to advertise his position, and came to rights.

I'm blind, boss.

"Loosen up, Bogie. I'm not."

Then he broadcast, "I'm okay. Nobody panic. I'm in an underground cavern or catacomb. Maybe Thrakian, maybe natural, hooking into their network. I'll take one or two volunteers with me, the rest of Blue Wing go on to their rendezvous." His voice sounded normal, even cheery to himself, no thanks to Bogie's fear that still attempted to claw its way out of him—and take over everything he knew.

"Ah . . . commander?"

"Yes, Rawlins."

"What are you likely to run into down there?"

Jack smiled tensely. "I'd say, lieutenant, I'm likely to run into a lot of Thraks. On the other hand, if they're coming out after you, I may just run into a lot of luck." Bogie's panic bled away as Jack began to examine his surroundings. He stood cautiously, thinking to himself that the new suits had automatic sounding equipment, with periodic readouts. His armor had it, too, but he had to instigate the function. He'd been just too damn busy to bother.

Getting old, boss.

"Not me," Jack answered him. "Just you."

Maybe. The sentience's inner voice was weak. The suit's gauges were swinging into low. Was Bogie feeding off the suit's power and causing both of them to run short? *It's cold.*

"And dark." Bogie would no more admit his emotional lapse than apologize for stepping on a Thraks. Jack cut the conversation short, as he relocated his original path and saw the cavern widen out in front of him accommodatingly. All right then. He'd take the low road as long as it led where he wanted to go. The berserker's mental shiver acknowledged his decision.

At his back, two heavy thuds announced recent arrivals. Jack panned the rear view—one was Rawlins. The other a new recruit by the name of Aaron. Aaron was a curly headed, snub-nosed kid with innocent blue eyes that shaded the devilment hiding just under the surface. But Jack hadn't seen anybody technically better with a suit, even if he wasn't as athletic as some. Aaron made a lazy salute before casting about the cavern. He then dimmed his lights to follow Jack's lead.

Rawlins was an ebony shadow among the darkness. His visor glinted briefly, then a low beam issued out.

Knowing he couldn't ask for better men at his back, Jack went into the unknown.

It was like being swallowed whole, Amber thought, as she stepped into the fawn-colored armor. It smelled, too, and she wrinkled her nose slightly, thinking of sweat factories and other memories from her not too distant past as a street hustler.

Denaro's face had pinked. "There's no plumbing for—ah—someone like you."

Amber peered out at him over the neck rim as she finished sealing the seams. She had to crane her neck to do so. She was tall, but Denaro was vastly taller even for a soldier and the suit was greatly oversized for her. She thought that, suited, Denaro would be bigger than Jack. "That's okay, Den. I'm not going to be in here all day . . . right?"

"Ahh. Right." The Walker shifted his weight from side to side.

Amber waved a slim hand at him. "Don't worry, Lassaday won't catch us. Besides, you've been authorized to log extra practice time."

He cleared his throat. "Just don't . . . ah . . . dent it or anything."

"You'll have it back in no time. Come on, walk through the tunnel with me." Frowning slightly, Amber concentrated on slipping her feet into the boots and her hands into the sleeves and gauntlets, where a mesh of circuitry immediately gripped her fingers and, for the first time, she understood a little about the gauntlet weaponry. *Just like pointing a finger*, she thought. Strange that her first time using a suit would be in ordinary armor, not Jack's where both Jack's presence and Bogie's could embrace her. She'd been in armor before—under extremely cramped and difficult circumstances. This was entirely different. A feeling of power swept her.

"Are we powered up?" she said, aiming her right index finger at the locker room wall. Before Denaro could answer, the laser rayed and a pan-sized area blackened.

Amber jerked her hand out of her sleeve in reaction and stood, wide-eyed, looking at the sooty wall.

"Yes," Denaro said, his voice anticlimatic. "On low power, but be careful." He held out the helmet. "You'd better put this on. If you're spotted like that, they'll know it's not me in the armor . . . but they won't be able to tell through the visor screening who it is."

"Don't worry," Amber said grimly. "We won't be spotted." She reached for the helmet.

Jack had never known Bogie to feel cowardice, but as he strode through the earthen caverns, he could feel the presence quaking about him. The chamois along his shoulders and the back of his neck fairly shivered, sending harmonic feelings along the tiny hairs back there. "What is it?"

Cold, boss. Cold and dark.

Jack looked over his power gauges. There was a nearly imperceptible drain. He wasn't expending that much energy in the suit. "Bogie, what are you doing?"

I . . . don't know.

"Watch my power outage, okay?"

There was no answer, but another tremor upon his shoulders.

Behind him, Aaron and Rawlins matched his steady walk. Jack surveyed the cavern as well as he could with the amount of illumination he wanted to use. Dirt wall, unshored . . . as if a gigantic mole had dug it. Under their feet was a layer of clay sediment, broken by small rocks and pebbles, all dry. Perhaps an underground flood wash, of some sort. No rocks or minerals to speak of. He could feel a deep-rooted vibration overhead.

"What is it?" Rawlins broadcast.

"I know what it is," Aaron's still high, very young voice answered.

"Aaron?"

"Yessir. That's the rest of Blue Wing. There's a rhythm, like someone jogging."

Dust and pebbles shivered down from the roof. "If you're right," Jack murmured, "watch your heads. We're liable to have visitors."

The cavern narrowed to two abreast width, then made a Y. Jack paused at the fork, checking his map. The screen flashed him a direction, and he went to his right, slightly off course by a degree, but then again—no one had promised him a direct road.

The vibration overhead paused. All three of them came to a stop.

Jack tilted his head even though it did no good . . . the mikes were directional . . . his stance was unconscious. "Fighting," he told the two. "Come on, we're missing all the fun." Bogie's chill had transmitted to him and as he surged forward, his teeth began to chatter. His sweat covered torso had gone icy. He charged into the tunnel, certain that they were almost within striking distance of the Thrakian nest.

Amber skidded to a stop at the tunnel mouth. Her heart pounded and her pulse sang. The Bythian tattooing—which had faded to a tenth of its original intensity so it looked like a network of fine veins marbling her fair skin—burned with her delirium as power of one kind spoke to power of another. "Oh, my god," she murmured to herself, for she'd left Denaro in the dust. "Jack must feel like a god." She leaned against the left seam of the suit, heedless of the circuitry and wiring poking into her.

Denaro came panting up. His dark hair stood all on end. "Milady!" he cried, as if she were deaf inside the armor. "Are you all right?"

"I'm fine. Don't get your bowels in an uproar."

His ashen face now grimaced at her retort. He wiped his forehead with the back of his hand. "I've seen a recruit blow himself away in a suit. Perhaps you could use a little more theory, too."

She ignored his sarcasm. "Don't forget, Denny, my boy— I'm the brains and you're the brawn. Now what direction do I head this scrap heap in?"

"The obstacle course is that way."

Feeling invincible, she surged out of the tunnels and on to the fields.

Feeling invincible, Jack spotted the light curving from the end of the tunnel, alien though its illumination was, and knew he'd been right. "Use everything you've got, boys," he said to Rawlins and Aaron. "Including your boots. Stomp what you can't laser. Don't let 'em tear your field packs off, you'll need your rifle." He took his out of the cradle of his right arm and lifted it. "Let's stir up a hornet's nest."

He broke into a run for the fifty yards remaining, his momentum and the power of the suit carrying him at an incredible rate. Thus it was that the three of them broke into the underbelly of the Thrakian occupation force, kicking through wafer thin cellular walls, ignoring the cocooned nets hanging from the ceiling as they fired. Aaron let out a squawk of indignation as one bundle swung into his helmet and Jack heard an "Oh, shit! That was part of Fielding!"

Rawlins ducked as a Thraks picked up what was left of a fellow warrior and threw the blasted torso at him, ichor spraying wildly. "How the hell can you tell?"

"I'd know that hairy, tattooed arm anywhere! What is this?"

Storm waded through bodies, kicking and shattering anything that twitched as a chittering wave of Thraks backed away from him. "Let me give you a hint, Aaron," he got out as he laid down a spray of fire that seared chitin and left a smell like burning hair on the air. "They don't take souvenirs, either! This is their pantry."

He thought he could hear Aaron gagging and added, "Keep going, boy! Watch 'em. Here they come at two o'clock!"

The Thraks boiling away from them were unarmed and frightened. The Thraks flooding downward from the other end of the tunnel were armed to the masks and madder than hornets. They did almost as much damage to the unarmed Thraks as the three Knights did.

Jack swung his field pack around, grabbed two grenades, tore the pins and chucked them as far ahead as he could. The concussion battered the suit and the mikes, leaving his ears ringing. Two blurs to one side of his helmet told him either Aaron or Rawlins was following his lead.

He got his heading. Bits of chitin filled the air even as the first of the line to get through reached him. He set his rifle in his armpit and laid down an even spray of fire. "Rawlins, Aaron. I want you to kick your way out and get up there!"

"What?"

"Use your power vault and grenades, dammit! Get dirtside and do it *now*."

"Yessir!" they chorused as Jack set his teeth and boots. Provided there was nothing alive at his back, he ought to be able to hold this tunnel mouth indefinitely.

Or at least as long as he still had firepower.

The ceiling came down behind him and for just a moment he was cloaked in a fine cloud of smoke and dust. The Thraks piling into the tunnel drew back in wonderment.

For just a second.

Then, with a terrible clacking of mandibles and spurting of their rifle muzzles, they plowed forward again.

Jack smiled. It had obviously been a long, long time since any of them had faced a Dominion Knight.

CHAPTER 17

"You ought to be proud of our boy," Pepys said, swinging about in his chair. "He's handed us a decisive victory."

Baadluster's upper lip tightened as though his teeth gave him some deep and stabbing pain. He paced away for a second or two, then turned and faced his emperor. "That he has," he said grudgingly. "And now Stralia's fate will be decided quickly in the Appellate Courts. The sooner it is freed to be colonized, the better it will be able to defend itself. Or had you overlooked that piece of property?"

Pepys shrugged indolently as he threw the report over one shoulder where it slumped to the ground and lay, plastic sheets akimbo. "I gain more in the long run for the Dominion to have confidence in me as a war leader and provider of troops. My claim to Stralia was poor at best and fourth or fifth in consideration. A wise man, my dear Vandover, knows when to cut his losses and take what he can get. And look what our commander's given us! Just look! Damn near one-handedly."

"Then," and Baadluster drew near. An unhealthy pallor cloaked his skin. "Perhaps you'll consider what I have to suggest. You face a full Congressional hearing with regard to the budget and appropriations."

"I do," Pepys agreed. "All it takes is enough of them to decide I have them by the monetary shorthairs and we'll be providing no troops."

"Send in your hero. If we work with him, we should be able to overwhelm the Congress with emotion, sway the dissenters, and get the budget through before anyone notices that we're going to own them completely."

Pepys' indolence faded rapidly as he straightened in the chair. He looked keenly at Baadluster. "You're talking about giving him a public forum."

"He's a soldier, not a politician. Feed him what you want him to say."

Pepys tickled the corner of one eyebrow with a fingertip. "Storm," he replied slowly, "is his own man. But it could work."

"Surely he's not naive enough to believe all we require of him is to fight Thraks."

"I think perhaps he is."

Baadluster smiled. "Then we can't allow him to stay that way. There are concerns he must deal with . . . building the troops and generating the propaganda necessary to authorize their use. I have leverage I can use if your highness finds it difficult to persuade him."

"Leverage, Vandover?"

The Minister of War towered over the emperor. Pepys waited for enlightenment, but none came. He smiled tightly. "I see you've been busy filling Winton's shoes."

Baadluster gave a slight nod.

Pepys sighed. "Well, then. I suggest you get hold of our hero. We have only a few weeks to make preparations." He waved his hand, dismissing Baadluster. The minister lingered a few seconds longer than was in good form, as if to show Pepys that he did not have the control he wanted. Pepys watched the lanky man's disappearing form until the closing portal hid it from sight. Then he took a deep breath. He had stayed true to his adage that it was better to have an enemy under your nose than out of sight, but he wondered if he had done a wise thing. Rumors reached him now and then. Rumors that Baadluster had belonged to a splinter faction of the Green Shirts though Pepys had not been able to unearth recent activity. Had the Green Shirts been too radical for Baadluster . . . or not radical enough? Pepys closed his eyes, thinking that when he had been younger, he could not rest until he had the throne. Now that he had the throne, he could not rest keeping it.

Lassaday stalked about the locker room. "Dammit, Trav," he muttered to Captain Travellini. "Do we tell 'em or not?"

"We have no proof that anyone's been breaking in. The security systems show nothing."

"I know that! I'd give my left nut to know who—" he

broke off as a buzzer rang in, overriding his words. "What is it?"

"Moussared here, sir. The racks check out."

"Right." He looked to Travellini. The captain stood at attention, slender, darkly handsome, a single wing of premature silver along one temple. "Nothing there. But I know what I know, even if I can't prove it."

"Then you'll have to tell the commander and let him take over, sarge."

Lassaday's thick chest rose and fell in frustration. "Th' freebooters'll wait for no one! By the time I get enough proof, they'll be gone, and our suits with 'em!"

Travellini spread his hands out. "Our only other choice is to shut down training altogether until we find out where the missing suit is, and who's been breaking in. I don't think we can afford to do that."

"Damn right. Well, th' commander's back tomorrow. I hear the emperor's got a call in for him. I guess we'll be next in line, eh, Trav?"

As the good-looking captain nodded assent, Lassaday slammed a locker door in frustration and left, eyeing the security camera with an evil glare for its failure.

Jack hardly had two words for Amber when he returned. He went to see Pepys first and then Lassaday cornered him, and when he came back to Amber, telling her that he would have to leave with Pepys in a few weeks, all she had with him was the night . . . and the night she shared with Jack's nightmares.

He rarely slept through. She knew that from years of association with him and the one or two times she'd nursed him through injury and illness. But she thought perhaps it had lessened, or even faded altogether, that night-startling bolt from sleep into wakefulness, his eyes wide and his breath shuddering in his chest. He did not fear death, she knew that. He feared the inability to be allowed to live . . . his dreams deep scars from the seventeen years he'd been locked helplessly in cold sleep. She tried to soothe him back to rest, but their lovemaking had already spent his energy and though he lay down beside her, she wasn't asleep when he got up and left.

She knew where he'd gone. Her slender fingers kneaded

at the blankets as his warmth faded from beside her. He'd gone to the suit, to Bogie, to commune in a way he'd never reached out to her.

Amber threw herself out of bed as if to follow, then stopped herself at the bedroom door. She couldn't follow. She knew that. She turned her restlessness into pacing, then stopped. Bitterly, she repeated what her hated Rolf had often told her: "You can't lose what you never had."

She returned to the now cold bed. She might not have him now . . . she might never have him . . . but she would not let him face his destiny alone much longer. At the back of her closet, behind a false door, hung a suit of armor that she was very close to mastering.

Lassaday grimaced. It sent rivulets of sweat running down his bald pate. "I don't like yer leaving so soon, sir. Not with the trouble and all."

"It can't be helped. I don't like it either." Jack looked out over the parade grounds. The troops looked good, but he knew after Stralia that they had a hundredth of the manpower they needed, and with the attrition rate of training . . . he might never have the Knights at full muster. He disliked the duty he'd agreed to perform for Pepys, but it had one advantage. The Knights would gain the publicity they needed to gather new recruits. And the Stralia incident bothered him more than he wished. He could not shake the idea that the Thrakian League had been waiting expressly for him. Did they think that the Knights were nothing more than an extension of himself, now that Kavin was gone? If so, he must do everything in his power to make sure they were not right. Lassaday, Garner, Travellini, Rawlins and the others must be able to step in. He was the last true Dominion Knight . . . and it was in his power to correct that, to make certain that it did not remain true.

But it would take time, time he found hard to gather. The upcoming trip would delay him even more.

Yet he had also found evidence on Stralia that he could not ignore. The Thraks had not just been waiting there for him . . . from the depth and size of the catacombs, he was certain the Thraks had been based, on and off, on Stralia for some years while the Dominion Congress argued the colonization and ownership rights. He did not like the implication of the infiltration which had taken place right under the noses of the Triad Throne and the Congress.

A buzzer sounded and Lassaday grimaced again. "Th' bugs are ready, sir."

Jack looked down at the portion of the parade grounds that had been sectioned into a blind maze. Shields thinly glazed with norcite were set in place among the other walls.

Lassaday sighed. "We've got a bloody fortune down there, sir."

"I know." But it would be worth it if he could prove what he hoped to prove about the Thraks. If they had a blind spot he could capitalize on, the war would come to a quick and speedy halt.

They'd brought three Thraks back and, so far, kept them alive. Now he heard the portal doors opening, loosing the warriors onto the parade grounds. Lassaday leaned over the bridge railing with him, knuckle-scarred hands tightly gripping the bar.

"What if this doesn't work, sir?"

"Then we try again," Jack said. He watched as the Thraks stumbled out into the white-hot light of Malthen's ever-burning sun. For a moment, he thought he saw confusion on the masked faces. Then the Thraks fell on each other with a fury that saw two tear each other apart. The third turned and made a gesture to Jack and that was indisputable, despite the language difference, and tore its own throat out and toppled, splattering ichor onto the parade ground sands before anyone could stop the suicides.

Lassaday growled deep in his throat. "Nasty beasties," he said. "Well, that's the last of 'em."

Jack stepped back, gorge rising in his throat in spite of himself. He wondered if he would have exhibited similar courage under Thrakian captivity. He swallowed hard. "There'll be another time, sarge. Store those norcite shields where they can't be vandalized. We'll find a way to use them."

As he stepped down from the bridge, he tried not to let the failure bother him. He could not be wrong about what he'd observed aboard Harkness' freighter. He could not!

CHAPTER 18

"We're on final approach now, your highness."

Pepys wiped off the fine sheen of nervous perspiration from his forehead. He looked askance at his cabinmates, Storm and Baadluster. Storm looked calm and composed, almost meditative. Baadluster's attention was fixed on the viewscreen showing the descent.

Pepys wrenched his thoughts from his nervousness and focused on the screen. The cloudy luster about the planet faded for a moment, as if a wedge had been cut into it.

"The shields are down," Jack said.

Pepys looked to the windowscreen. His air sickness fled in the moment he realized that the center of the Dominion was wide open, vulnerable to their descent. He smiled wryly then, thinking of all the times in his dreams when he'd willed such a thing to happen for his attacking troops, and had never been able to force it. The shields could be brought down, that was true, but at great risk and expenditure.

It was not surprising the Thraks struck only at outlying, ill-defended planets.

The shimmer returned. They were through. Pepys cleared his throat, rapidly picking up composure as they returned to his element. His battlefield, by necessity, was the Congressional hall awaiting them.

Dreams of conquest here were disguised behind his politics. He took one last look at his Dominion Knight and hoped to god he and Baadluster had not underestimated the man.

Baadluster seemed to sense Pepys' thoughts. He turned from the viewscreen as the capital came into sight, its visibility partially veiled by scattered clouds and a light drizzling of rain over portions of the immense city. "Rest today, Storm," the minister said. "Tomorrow we go back to work."

Jack looked at the city, thinking that the Dominion capital was everything Malthen was not. Clean. Beautiful. Unfettered. Green streaked the walkways and park areas as if the forest had returned, unconquerable, to the pavements. The domed rooftops of the many buildings glittered in cobalt blue or in the green patina of weathered bronze. Pink and white tile. And windows, everywhere windows, as if the restriction of mere walls were too much to bear. He liked what he saw. He looked forward to the following day.

Pepys said, "Good timing. The Thraks have formally declared war. Now let's see if we can get the Dominion to join with us in answering them."

A shiver of anticipation ran down the back of Jack's neck.

The chamber was huge. In hushed tones, Baadluster said, "It's said to have been patterned after the old Terran Congress."

Home World. A beginning so far away that, in the end, only it might be safe from the Thraks. Jack felt himself squaring his shoulders back as he stepped into the wing, awaiting his introduction.

The senators and representatives were anything but quiet. Many sat, listening to the speech being presented to them, but equally as many conferred in groups, sitting or standing. There were young men and women at com lines, taking notes or transmitting messages, calm islands in the benevolent chaos. Overhead were the trade logos and city state banners as well as world flags of the Dominion, the Outward Bounds, and the Triad Throne.

Jack sucked in his breath, calming himself, and rethought his decision not to wear his armor. He missed the edge of Bogie's righteous anger but not the subtle power struggle that underlay their communication. Diplomacy was going to be difficult enough. He caught sight of Senator Washburn, a prism of activity, settling a wing of senators in their seats, hovering over each one and speaking confidentially before moving on to the next.

He also saw Pepys, sitting in the visitors' gallery. The red-haired emperor had worn his regal robes, and was outfitted as Jack rarely saw him, in red stones and gold threads that made him look like a barbarian throwback. In the midst of all his splendor, he looked a bigger man than he was. Five WP men rayed around him in formation. Jack recognized three he'd had dealings with under Winton's regime; he felt his lip curl in instinctive dislike.

At Jack's side, Baadluster intoned, "I'll be leaving you now. I must join Pepys. You're sure you're set? Have the speech with you?"

Jack nodded. He palmed the disk lightly, thinking that he still did not feel comfortable with the contents hammered out by Pepys and Baadluster. Senator Washburn stood up straight and looked at them. Their time must be close. Baadluster hissed something under his breath and faded away from Jack's side.

Jack's tension left with the minister. He looked across the hall, wishing that he could somehow find and isolate Amber's face in the ocean of faces, but knowing he could not because she had been left behind. As he saw the security and broadcast cameras panning the hall, he knew she'd not have felt at ease here. Anyone appearing here would be forever stored in too many master systems. As he looked up into the domed roof and eyed those cameras, a thought occurred to him and began to slowly expand.

One of Washburn's aides came up behind him. "Almost ready?"

He looked at her. Expectancy shone from dark eyes set off by warm brown skin. He nodded.

She took his hand. "Just feed the disk into the podium as you step up. The speech comes up on that transparent screen down there . . . the words are color-coded to be invisible on the broadcast. Looks spontaneous, but isn't. You can move your eyes slightly, the screen moves with you to a certain degree. Unless, of course, you have your speech memorized."

He nodded again.

She smiled widely. "Say something," she said., "The senator will have my head if you've lost your voice from stage fright. Destinies are decided in here."

"Damn all Thraks," Jack rumbled in amusement.

The aide laughed. "Good enough for me."

The audience hall began to applaud and the noise moved

in waves, baffling off the acoustics of the chambers. At first, Jack thought they might have been heard, then he saw that Senator Washburn had gained the podium and was preparing to introduce him.

The thought that had begun grew until it seized him, and he scarcely heard Washburn's speech leading up to his introduction.

The aide pushed at his right elbow lightly. "That's it, you're on."

Jack stepped out of the wings and moved toward the podium. A hush rippled across the floor following applause for Washburn's words. *What has Washburn promised them in me?* he thought briefly, as he stepped onto the dais. He felt a catch deep in his throat, a momentary flutter of nervousness that he shrugged off. The AV equipment responded to his weight in front of the podium and flashed READY, awaiting his disk to be fed in.

The audience had quieted, awaiting him, and as he hesitated, they began to clap again, as if urging him to relax and deliver his words. He looked across the floor, where Pepys' planned splendor caught his eye once more, and then a grim determination settled over him along with a deadly calm.

He held up his right hand, four-fingered like a badge of courage, and knew the cameras were broadcasting close-ups of him, and the speech disk winking in his palm. To hushed murmurs, Jack flexed his hand and the disk folded into an unusable mass. He tossed it to the foot of the dais.

Instantly, the air became electric. The audience knew whatever they were about to hear was not a prepared speech. Uncontrolled. Alive. Anticipation snapped toward him, and he knew he had better not disappoint them. Baadluster half rose to his feet in the visitors' gallery. Pepys dragged at his sleeve and brought him back to his seat.

"Congressmen and representatives, ladies and gentlemen, and honored guests."

His voice brought quiet to the chambers. Even without the sound system, he would be heard clearly. No one, short of an assassin with Amber's powers, could stop him now.

Joy filled his voice as he began to speak.

"I have been introduced to you as a commander in the Dominion Knights, the battalion newly reformed by Emperor Pepys. I'm his sworn man, a soldier who wears battle armor. Many of you will listen to my testimony with bias, believing what you have already been told is the truth.

"You've been lied to."

Voices raised in pandemonium. To one side, Jack could see Washburn pounding a gavel for silence. Pepys sat up straighter in his booth, his auburn hair a crackling halo about his grim face.

"I swore to Pepys, but before him, I was sworn to another. A man whose name since his death has come to mean defeat and shame. I'm an honorable man, but I can hear you asking how can a man be loyal to two masters? If you're not, you're all damn fools."

"But I know where I stand because I never swore to the man, but to what he offered."

"First let me tell you who I really am."

"I was born on Dorman's Stand."

Another burst of noise and disbelief. The senators still standing about in the back galleries began to move closer, finding seats. He could see an aide racing across the upper balcony, in pursuit of what, he wondered briefly, as the audience calmed yet again to hear him.

"You heard me right. There's been no human born on Dorman's Stand in the last twenty-five years. It fell during the Sand Wars. It's a sand planet, lifeless for our people. But I was born there, and I remember the way it used to be, and I grew up there following in my father's footsteps until it came time for me to believe in another man." A fleeting, wry smile, passed over his lips. "I was a raw recruit then."

"I enlisted as a Knight under Emperor Regis."

This time, there was no wave of noise. Instead a deadly silence fell over the people before him. He caught sight of their faces and knew he had them.

"I'm probably the last living true Knight still in commission."

Baadluster and one of the WP men abruptly left the visitors' gallery, but Jack felt a keen edge of joy, for it was too late now.

"I enlisted to fight the Thraks, thinking we could stop them. I was sixteen and you must understand what it was like to be me then."

He took them back, among the finely threaded memories Bogie had given him, because he had no choice. Otherwise they would never believe him. He was unsure if they believed him now. He only knew that no one stood any longer, and that even the aides at the com lines had turned to him, listening, their lips and fingers stilled.

"And so, I swore to Emperor Regis.

"And so it is that I'm here today. For if we had not been betrayed on Milos, if the Knights had not been left without backup, we could have held Milos. We could have stopped the Thraks then and there.

"But Regis wasn't secure in his power, evidently, and there were factions working to unseat the old warrior. We Knights became the pawns in a petty struggle and Milos was the mortal blow."

An incoherent shout interrupted Jack. He paused and looked toward the wing from which the sound had issued, but no one followed it up. He took the opportunity to press his fingertips along his brow, mopping up a few drops of sweat he hadn't known had rested there. He took up the unseen challenge.

"How do I know? *Because I was there.* I was one of the thousands scheduled to be left behind. The fleet was ordered out and the Thraks swept in. I was one of only a few hundred to make it to the three transports that somehow managed to come in. All three of them were hit heavily by Thrakian fire while trying to lift off."

His gaze swept them now. He challenged them. "I can see you remembering. Facts, you might tell me, easily scanned on any library computer. Perhaps. But I lived them.

"Two cold ships never made it past the League offenses. A third did . . . so heavily crippled it went adrift, its cargo locked in cold sleep. Eventually, its damaged systems could no longer function. Backup systems faltered. Those asleep died.

"Seventeen years later, the ship was found and one man remained alive—alive, but not untouched."

Jack held up his scarred hand. "I suffered frostbite. Cold sleep fever. And they tell me I could have been saner. I lost an entire lifetime while the Thraks took the planets they wanted, and, Emperor Regis became a defeated old man who fell prey to an assassin.

"I spent four years in the Knights. Seventeen asleep. And the last five years learning the truth.

"The truth, ladies and gentlemen, is that the Thraks have no regard for your right to life. The truth is that we once had the means with which to stop them. To teach them respect for dealing with us. And we have those means again. I swore, not to Regis and not to Pepys, not to an emperor.

"I swore for peace through war.

"I stand by my oath.

"And I ask you to give me back the means with which to achieve it."

With those words, Jack stepped back.

There was an absolutely stunned silence. He dared to look at Pepys, knowing that both the expressions on his face and the emperor's would be covered by close-ups. The emperor sat motionless in his booth.

Haltingly, the applause began. It grew in spurts, hampered by the sound of the audience getting to their feet. They stood in waves until not a man was left sitting.

Not even Pepys.

CHAPTER 19

"A goddamn pacifist."

Jack sat down wearily, throat dry after hours of interviews following the Congressional speech. "Why else would you make war?" he said quietly and tried to ignore his emperor pacing before him.

Pepys came to a stop. His face went through several expressions before settling on a frown. His mouth likewise opened for retort, then closed. He looked to Baadluster.

"All is not lost," the minister said. "They're still debating out there."

Pepys shook his head, his frown obscured by a cloud of fine red hair, and stalked away again, his ceremonial robes practically afloat. He cast a look of loathing at Baadluster as he passed him.

He stopped at the far end of the room as though he had needed to put a distance between himself and Storm.

"I am your emperor," he said, his voice modulated with effort. "Why did you not tell me?"

Jack looked up. His eyes of rainwater blue met Pepys' cat green ones. "I thought you already knew."

Pepys made a gesture with his hand, the side of it cutting air as though it were a sword. "How can I trust you?"

"Or I you."

"Don't fence words with me! You weren't found by one of my ships or I would have been told."

"I'm a Dominion Knight," Jack said. "That should be enough. I am what I am, and I do what I've been trained to do. No more. *And no less.*"

"That's all I get? That's all? I could have you removed as commander."

Jack inclined his head. "If that's what you want. But I don't recommend it." He stood up. Under the lines of his dress blues, his frame carried the powerful muscles it took to wear and use a suit of battle armor. "Now you know me for what I am. Remember that I have always known you for what you are."

Pepys' body had been seething with indignation under his ceremonial robes, but the tone of Jack's voice froze him in his place. Baadluster cleared his throat as inconspicuously as he could, yet the emperor shot him a hard look and the minister shifted away from him slightly.

"Are you threatening me?"

"No," Jack said, as he moved closer. "But I think it's time we understand one another. Winton feared me, but for the wrong reasons. The Thraks didn't have me. If I was in the hands of the Green Shirts, then they couldn't accomplish what they wanted to. It had already been done, my emperor, by seventeen years of cold sleep, locked into a debriefing loop. I have lived and relived an eternity of betrayal. I know who I hate." Jack paused. His hands flexed. "Give me the freedom to go after the Thrakian League."

Pepys had been holding his breath. He relaxed now, nearly imperceptibly. "And then?"

"Reclaim Claron. Winton had it firestormed to rout me out. He duped you into okaying his actions because of the survey showing Thrakian infestation."

Baadluster said, "What kind of accusation is this—" but Jack gestured, cutting him off.

"Winton used freebooters. They can't be controlled."

Pepys sighed. He pulled out a chair and sat down, suddenly. "I bear the onus," he said. "All right. Terraforming for Claron. However long it takes, whatever the expense."

"In exchange for what?"

"Your silence? No." Pepys took a deep breath. "I am, in spite of all you might suspect of me, still the emperor of the Triad Throne. You can't prove what Winton ordered, I know that, but that does not mean I condoned it. Then or now. Let's just say I'm doing what I am doing to gain your loyalty."

A tiny muscle ticked along the line of Jack's jaw. He straightened. "I am a Knight. You either already have my loyalty or not. I can't be bought."

"No," Pepys answered him, smiling tightly. "Perhaps

not." Anything further he might have said was interrupted by Senator Washburn bursting into the room. He was followed by a slender young man in the uniform of an aide.

"This is my son, Brant," Washburn blurted. He inserted his square, massive frame between Pepys and Baadluster. "Jack! Jack, my boy, I couldn't have done better myself!" He turned to Pepys. "Brilliant! Absolutely brilliant! His tongue would snap if he tried to lie! And a pacifist at that."

Pepys said irritably, "What is the news, Washburn?"

"What else could it be? Pepys, you astound me. No wonder you sit on the Triad Throne. If you'd given us a warmonger, we'd be out there arguing still . . . probably until the end of the session. But when you gave us a peaceful man who knew the time had come to fight—well, you lasered the opposition in their tracks."

Baadluster interrupted. "We have the appropriations?"

"Yes! Yes! We have a probationary war, gentlemen."

Jack watched them from across the room. He had won the battle for Claron, but he felt curiously hollow inside. It was not victory enough. Amber would probably have agreed with Washburn's assessment of his tongue and lying. He had learned long ago not to lie if he could help it.

So he simply had not told all of the truth. Pepys seemed reassured, but he would not be if he knew Jack's thoughts. First the Thraks. Then the emperor.

CHAPTER 20

"Drop in twenty minutes."

Jack rubbed the back of his neck and tried to ignore the computer voice. He keyed back, "Just get us in there."

The fleet pilot came on with arrogance in his voice. "You think this is easy?"

"I think," Jack formed his words deliberately, "that the bulk of the enemy is dirtside and if you want to fight a war, you've got to get us where the action is."

The warship waggled, and every man in staging found it hard to keep his footing. A buffeting followed and Jack knew that last burst had been close.

The pilot made a noise of contempt and closed off the com line.

The man suiting up nearest Jack paused. He frowned. "They never give us any respect."

Jack shot back, "Just do your job. We get in there, clear the sector so the shield crews can be dropped and get pylons built and the shields back in place. That's what we're here for. Do your job and the respect will follow."

The soldier's face paled a little under Jack's harsh tones, but he nodded. "Yes, sir."

Jack lapsed into uneasy silence. He looked across staging and realized he knew very little of the men fighting with him this run. Who would watch his back? Garner, across the bay, his spike of blue-black hair standing up defiantly, had his back to his commander and was instructing a green recruit on the niceties of a first drop. Jack could not hear what was said. He touched the cherry picker that held his own suit.

Boss. Are we ready?

"Nearly."

It's been a rough campaign.

"I know." This was Jack's third drop in five days, but they were going to regain Oceana and get the shields back up, dealing the Thrakian League another severe loss.

They can be beaten. A step at a time, but they can be beaten!

Jack opened up the seams, picked up a probe and began to test circuitry, automatically, out of habit, even though Bogie had been fully powered and tested twenty-four hours ago. He frowned. There were minute power shortages. Bogie had been pirating again. Jack rubbed his temples. The finding strengthened his resolve to get new armor fitted when they returned to Malthen. His old suit was no longer reliable . . . and there was another being fighting him for control of it. He couldn't tell Bogie yet nor could he predict what the sentience would do if he found out Jack would no longer share the suit or companionship with him.

Would it be the death of Bogie? Jack knew that the possibility existed, for the sentience was struggling now to regenerate as he had never had to struggle before. Perhaps the being was more closely related to a parasitic Milot berserker than he realized. Perhaps it needed more than Jack's warmth and sweat.

Perhaps it needed to begin feeding.

Jack jerked the probe out of his suit irritably. Across the way, Fostermeir, his NCO for this drop, began the countdown. "Gentlemen, suit up! And let's not forget the dead man circuit, boys. We don't want any Thraks pulling armor off the casualties to take home and have fun with."

Premonition prickled at Storm. *Well*, Jack thought. . . .

". . . there's no time like the present." Denaro straightened, his helmet under his arm.

Amber shook her head. "I can't go with you."

"You damned well can't stay here. We may have five thousand recruits roaming around now, but I can tell you that they *know* there's been rogue activity. It's just a matter of time until you're caught."

Amber's mouth curved just a little. Denaro glared at her. He threw his shoulders back.

"All right, all right," he said. "I've been a pain in the ass. I have my duty to St. Colin and the Blue Wheel. And I'll admit I thought you were a she-devil at first, come to tempt me with all your wiles. But I'm a soldier and you're a soldier, and the emperor's army is no place to be caught. If you're going to fight, fight a war that counts. With someone honorable."

"Jack's honorable."

His jaw moved, then the man said, "From what I've seen of him. But Pepys is not, and a Knight has to be the emperor's man. Come with me."

Amber hesitated. Then she said softly, "No. I won't leave him. But you needn't worry . . . no one will find out from me where you've gone."

Denaro stood poised one second longer as if arguing with himself, but his lips clamped tightly on the words he might have said, and he ducked out of the locker room, leaving Amber alone with the words she might have said.

She stood alone with the echo of receding footsteps and wondered if, when Jack came home, he would come home to her.

Or would he really be coming home to his obsession with the armor and his fight against the Thraks?

Since the day of his speech to the Dominion Congress, her loneliness had been incalculable. It was as though a ten-meter metal plate had dropped between them. She had finally moved out of his bed, into the second bedroom in the apartment, and he had not even noticed.

Or worse, if he had, he had not objected.

"Ah, damn," she whispered, and the strangled sound of her own voice startled her. What was she lacking? What was it that she couldn't give Jack? If she could only find out.

She hung her helmet on its hook; thinking that it looked more than ever like a disembodied head, and began to strip her armor from her body.

"Red Wing down! My god, they're all gone."

"Pull yourself together, Garner."

"Jack! They're gone!"

"I've registered the hit, mister. Now pull your team together and get out of there." Jack moved his chin and took a sip of water that did little to ease the ache of loss he felt. The Thraks were getting used to fighting them again. They were taking a terrible toll.

He moved forward, tall buildings blocking his soundings and his readings on the target grids. Broken concrete and twisted beams prevented him from getting a fix on either his men or his enemy. Tile and fallen brick obscured doorways. Window shards lay scattered on the ground, sliver sharp and jewel bright.

This had been a city once, before Thrakian bombardment reduced it to rubble. Jack moved through it and tried to keep the devastation from moving him to despair.

Bone shards were almost as prevalent as glass shards. Evacuation had come too late for some. Ruins of transports and hovercars lay on their sides, gutted with fire, lanced with skeletal remains. He was all right as long as he did not remember they had been human. The countryside was scarred even worse: the Thraks had spent days knocking out the power systems and the shields. Days before the Knights could get here. Days and nights of aggression against a planet unprepared for the act of war. He did not look down as he strode through an alleyway, his mikes echoing the sound of his own steps back at him.

His gauntlets tingled at his wrists, reminding him they were powered up. Jack halted just before the intersection with the main tube. He had a hunch the Thraks that had taken out Red Wing were now realigned out there, waiting to ambush Blue Wing.

He looked at his mapping grid. "Fostermeier, Blue Wing, count off, with street positions."

"Yes, sir, approaching corner of Tenth and Galway."

"Garner, angling up eighth toward Galway."

"Peaches here, in the alleyway intersecting Mendoza."

"It's Aaron, sir, and I'm scaling a foundation . . . I think I'm near First Street."

And on down the line, as they all approached Galway.

He called it a hunch. Amber would call it intuition and curse him if he paid no attention to it.

"Don't enter the tube. I think we'll run a little interference first. Back off."

"What is it, commander?"

"I think they're in the subway junction under the Galway Main tube. Thraks like to go underground." Jack felt the rightness of it the moment he said it. Yes, of course, the subway system! Like home to the Thraks. The moment Blue Wing entered the main street, they would boil up out of the subway entrances just like they boiled up out of sand.

The question was, what was he going to do about it?

Static buzzed in his ear. A faint transmission fed in. "Commander Storm, this is Gold Wing."

"Who's that? Where's Captain Bosk?"

"He's down, sir."

"Dead?"

"Well . . . he wasn't, sir, but the dead man circuit got him when they pulled him out of his armor."

They wanted armor. And they wanted it badly. That confirmed Jack's fears. No longer would the Thrakian attitude of natural superiority be on Jack's side. The Thraks were going to find out all they could about the enemy they were facing.

"Commander?"

The young voice pulled his attention back. "Who is this, mister?"

"Lieutenant Vega, sir. We're on the outside of the city, near the open country. I remembered the lectures you gave, sir. There's sand around here somewhere, there's grit in the wind."

Already. Jack made up his mind. "Hold on, Vega. We'll be backing you up just as soon as we can pull out of here." He toggled onto his main frequency. "Fostermeier, I want a river of flame down there."

"What?"

"Fossil fuel, whatever you can find. Or, a volunteer with all the grenades he can handle."

"That's a death sentence, commander."

Jack felt the sweat trickling down his back. "Not necessarily, sergeant. I'll do it myself, if I have to."

Aaron came in over the corn. "Ah . . . commander? I'm presently standing on the first floor of what appears to be a brewery. The storage tanks are still intact."

Alcohol? Not a very hot burn, and difficult to start, but their lasers ought to be up to it and it was better than nothing. "Garner, get over there and help him. Peaches, you, too. I want to funnel it down in flames. The rest of you men, home in on me. We're going to be decoys. And Fostermeier, if anything happens, I. want you to take the rest of Blue Wing out to Vega's position. Where there's sand, there's the main infestation. It'll have to be taken out. All right, let's go. We're on a timetable for the construction crew drop. I want those shields back up before they can bring their mother ships down!"

They formed a wedge. They marched, the shocks from their armored boots vibrating through the asphalt and pavement. Jack smiled grimly. He knew that the Thraks knew they were on their way.

He only hoped they couldn't count that well.

Garner came on. "We're set here. Shit, Jack. This stuff is 120 proof . . . but we can pour it right on top of 'em. We've stopped the storm drains, the street will be full in a second."

"Then it'll burn well. We're almost in position. On my mark . . . now." Jack right-angled, making his way toward the brewery.

A fighter streaked overhead, leaving a sonic boom in its wake. Jack craned his neck back, helmet cameras catching its blurry image. At the edge of the city, explosions erupted, and he could see a dark cloud of smoke and glowing ash rise crimson against the destruction.

"We've got no time left, they're bringing in the big guns."

"It's on the way," Fostermeir said.

Jack strode out onto Galway. Two degrees to his left, he could see the cavernous mouth of the subway stairs. He was in a concrete canyon, with nowhere to run if his tactic failed.

Amber liquid washed past him, curling about his boots, and swirling on down the street, blue alcohol flames nearly invisible. It spilled down into the subway, where it burned hotter and he could see the gout of flames turn orange and roar back up from the mouth of the underworld. Thraks filled the stairway. Jack braced himself and began to shoot, cutting them down as they attempted to hurdle the wall of blue and orange flame.

Something slapped at the armor. He staggered back.

Boss, they're using projectiles. I suggest we not make a target of ourselves!

Beside Jack, Fostermeier blossomed. He dropped, visor down, into the dwindling river of fire.

With an angry whine, something slapped at Jack's armor again. He felt the pinch of crimped Flexalinks along his upper arm. "Sergeant!"

He's gone, Boss.

Jack hit the power vault, clearing the NCO's still form easily. The alcohol flames, quickly spent, guttered out. He scanned his screen, saw another two of his men down in the street. A field pack lay burst open between them.

With two strides, he reached them. Jack plucked out three grenades. He turned and headed for the subway entrance.

I don't think I'm going to like this said Bogie.

"I think you're right," Jack answered. "Garner! Head for the outskirts, now, and that's an order! Home in on Vega and go for the nest." He keyed the start sequence on the grenade and, even as he walked into the field of fire, he wondered when Bogie had gotten a sense of self-preservation.

Something slapped him high in the left shoulder, hard enough to pivot him around on his boot heel and leave him staggered. He righted himself and keyed the second grenade, then lobbed them both.

Smells flooded the suit as if he'd cracked his helmet, yet he hadn't. Sounds followed—an earfilling chittering of Thrakian alarm. A wall of Thraks reared in front of him as Jack punched in the last code. He rolled the grenade across their front, hit the power vault, and was in the air and behind them when the shock wave hit.

He could smell the explosion. The scorched chitin. The hot ash. As he hit and landed, a racking pain skewered his left shoulder.

"Damn," he said. "I'm hit."

No kidding, boss. You're leaking.

Projectiles. The norcite coating on his armor had taken him farther than Fostermeier and his other two men, but he wasn't completely invincible. Jack got to his knees and then stood up. The constrictions of the armor prevented him from surveying the exterior damage.

From the inside, it felt gooey. He started to look down and thought better of it.

"Get a patch on it, Bogie, and let's get out of here."

The chamois which always lay along his back and neck, edged over to his shoulder. Jack felt a gentle warmth begin to drive away the icy pain. He turned and panned the street. It was empty.

He broke into a jog, the battle suit eating up the distance. The throb in his shoulder kept time with the jolt of his boots.

He wasn't going to go unless he could take the nest with him.

Bogie settled gingerly over the torn flesh. He was cold, always cold now, and the power reserves of Jack's armor no longer fed him the energy he needed to maintain a status quo, let alone to regenerate. Blood welled up around him, soaking naturally into the porous nature of the chamois. Bogie refocused from the battle they fought to his own inward nature.

He tasted life. He knew the flavor. It sang in him, gave him heart.

He knew that Jack was dying, even as he sensed that he had begun to live again, for the first time in long, cold months.

It was the blood. The crimson fountaining up from the damaged flesh. It had to be.

He stemmed the life flow. He dared not taste it again.

He dared not.

Jack's pulse thundered in his senses. He could heal Jack somewhat, set the edge of puckered flesh next to the edge of puckered flesh and begin the healing. Clot the bleeding, scab the wound.

And he could carry Jack to safety within the shell of the battle armor, if there was safety to be found anywhere on this planet.

Or he could touch life himself and grow again.

His soul trembled.

The chamois quivered. Tiny cilia erupted. Hairlike. Feather light. Questing for the life font it desired. No, craving was not strong enough! In every particle of his newly reforming body, Bogie had to have what he had tasted.

Bogie pulled back from the wound, not trusting himself. Jack neither knew nor cared as he cried out hoarsely, "I have the sand targeted. All Teams, all Wings, home in on me, we're going in!" even as he staggered forward.

Jack's destiny was moot, Bogie decided. He let the cilia creep forward in quest of whatever life might be left.

CHAPTER 21

Amber woke screaming, her voice clawing its way out of her throat, her bed covers thrashed and wet with sweat—or was it tears?—about her. She shivered into silence, her throat as lacerated with her terror as if she'd tried to swallow a power blade. Her chest heaved for air, and then she *knew*.

"Oh, god. It's Jack!"

She threw aside the covers and, in pitch darkness, stumbled out of the bed. There was no time, no time to waste at all. She opened the com lines to Colin and prayed for a speedy answer.

It was the middle of the night, but the Walker prelate answered on the second ring. She recognized his meditation chamber surrounding him. His eyes were tired, he was still fully dressed, and she realized he'd been working late.

"Amber. What is it?"

"It's Jack. I know it is. Oh, god," she got out, before a paroxysm of fear stilled her.

"Where is he?"

"I don't know! Fighting somewhere. But I think he's dying . . . or dead."

St. Colin closed his eyes briefly, as if in remorse, then looked back at her through the screen. "He's a soldier, dear heart. He knew the risks."

"He can't! It's not his time yet. Not without me. He can't!"

"What do you expect me to do?"

And in that moment, hope seized her nearly as keenly as the fear had. He had not said, *there's nothing I can do.* He'd asked, *what do you expect me to do,* as if he could do something. With one hand, she swept her disheveled hair back from her face.

"What can you do?"

He winced. "A prayer, perhaps?"

"I'm not religious."

For a long moment, he closed his eyes again, before looking deeply into hers. His deep sable eyes were pensive. "I'm helpless, Amber. If I were with him, perhaps . . . but he's far beyond my limited capabilities."

"I can help."

"You'd have to be with me. Do we have much time?"

She snatched at the remnants of her dream. "I don't know—but it's better than nothing. You stay—I'll get there."

Colin keyed off as she broke the connection and his screen went dark. He sat back in his chair. He'd been up most of the night in his meditation chamber, not worrying, barely thinking, merely attuned to the elements of the room. Renewing himself. Perhaps even readying himself. When the natural time for sleep came, he had used a light trance instead, waking when Amber called. *Did I know?* he asked himself. There were those Walkers who would insist he had . . . the ones who called him saint. But there were others who would disagree, the same Walkers who would have felt that Denaro had defected. He knew there might be trouble at any moment, precipitated by the militant's actions. It was only logical to stay alert.

And there were a precious few who would say, what happened, happened. Why question it? Simply accept it as you find it.

Colin rubbed his temples, thinking that he preferred to side with the last group. He knew he had erred in speaking with Amber. A deliberate or an unconscious error? Was it recognition of some unvoiced feeling that if he could save any friend he had, he would save Jack? Perhaps. What was done, was done. He slipped back into his trance and it seemed like a matter of moments before a sleepy, rumpled Jonathan was escorting Amber into the chamber.

Her very presence resonated in the chamber. She wore her Bythian caftan and had tied her tawny hair back in a knot, but tendrils of it had escaped to frame the tense lines of her face. She barely waited until Jonathan left, then she crossed the room and grabbed his hands. Her fingers were chill.

"He's still there," she said, and her voice was husky. "But I'm losing him."

He made her sit beside him, and then he said, "You think I've promised more than I have."

Amber looked closely at him. "I think you have promised all that you can do."

He knew she had caught him. He was silent for a long moment. "Very well," he said. "Do you know why I am called a saint?"

"I looked you up once," she answered, with a mischievous grin that was far more like the old Amber he knew than this worried young woman who sat next to him. "You were rumored to have raised the dead."

"No rumor," he said, feeling uncomfortable. "But he'd just died in my arms. Doctors do it all the time."

"But you were at a Walker outpost."

"Yes. Relatively primitive conditions, and don't ask me how I did it because I don't know. I just know that, suddenly, I was filled with this outrage that he should have died, and I was determined that he shouldn't suffer the indignity of his broken body . . . he'd been in a cave-in, trying to reach a group of school children who'd gone in to see some artifacts just as a minor quake hit. They were frightened but safe, the area they were in had been shored up well. He was killed in an after-shock. I was very young then. I was angry that someone so good should have died so horribly." Colin looked away from her then, filled with the memory. "I remember holding him very tightly as I prepared the body for his widow to see. The esophagus had been packed with dirt. I cleaned him out, straightened broken limbs, and washed him. Then the outrage hit and I held him tightly one last time, thinking—and I've never told anyone this—thinking how pissed off I was at God that it had happened."

"And then he began to breathe in my embrace."

Colin took a deep breath himself and turned back to Amber. He had not quite told her all of it, but some things were between himself and his God.

"And so that's why they call you a saint."

"I presume so. It cannot be for holding my temper in

check. Amber, I cannot guarantee it would ever happen again. It would be a mockery to do so. God heals, not I. I can't guarantee God's manifestations."

She pushed the silken sleeves of her caftan up in determination. The light blue tracing of her tattoos seemed alight. "Maybe not. Now tell me what happened to Rawlins."

His jaw fell. "What do you mean?"

"What do I mean? What do you think I mean? The two of you walk into an ambush at the Thrakian embassy and the two of you walk out alive? The only thing wrong with you was broken ribs. I knew something had to have happened to Rawlins. He was in a daze for a month, and now he follows you around as though you had a psychic leash on him. We all have our histories on Bythia. I simply couldn't figure out what yours was."

Colin shook his head. "He took a chest shot meant for me. I healed him. He . . . was not dead."

"But dying."

"Perhaps." He felt very old, suddenly. "Amber, I'm not the man you took adventuring to Lasertown. I'm not even the man who went to Bythia. It . . . it takes a toll, perhaps one I can't begin to pay any more."

"That's why I'm here. Please. You've got to help me try. Together."

Colin looked at her. Night pressed in about the room, even though there were no windows. He could feel its presence, very close. Her heat warmed his right side, but nothing could keep the iciness of a soul at ebb tide from his left. "All right," he said quietly. "Take my hands and see if you can find your way to him."

Amber took the older man's hands in hers. She could feel the age in his skin. Wrinkled. Not elastic like hers, springing back after each touch. And the pads of his hands were callused and broad, like a man who had worked with them each and every day of his life. She wondered at that even as she felt the tiny drum of his pulse under her fingers. Anchored by his steadiness, his age, and his wisdom, she flung herself into the void in search of Jack.

She expected cold. She received nothingness, a stretching of herself until she felt vast and incredibly transparent, a sprinkling of mortal dust that the first solar wind could scatter irretrievably. She had to make the effort to pull herself together before she mingled forever with the infinite possibilities of the universes she encountered. She was a kite, soaring, and Colin was the flier, far behind her, yet connected by a tenuous string of simply *being*.

Her perception of herself and Colin was so altered from what she'd expected, that she had no idea of how to look for Jack. Would he be dust also? Or a rock, like Colin?

No, she thought. She remembered him from her first impressions, locked in his white armor, hot with vengeance. *He was a sun*. She knew that and went in search of a planetary flame that burned as brightly as any solar disk.

Condensing herself, she trailed across worlds in a track that had no signposts, no maps, no indication of where she had been or where she was going. She found a flame or two, tasted them—not Jack . . . not even human. She flew onward.

There was a tug at her string. She looked back and saw Colin's anchoring of her self grow a little weaker. Time had no meaning. *How long?* she thought. And then, *how far?* He reeled her in until she hovered, not in her body but close enough to see out her eyes and once more feel the touch of flesh upon flesh. Her ears were filled with song, a thousand notes and vibrations, some discordant, most melodious.

"Here," Colin was saying, and his voice was so thin, so far away, she could barely catch the sense of it. "Amber, can you hear me?"

Her lips opened. "Yeeesss," she whispered.

"Jonathan's located the current campaign. Star maps will do you no good, but I have something. This was made for me by a Walker congregation from Oceana. Use it to home in on."

He pressed something into the palm of her hand. Her impression of touching it was double-layered: the faint, gritty impression of rock and cloth upon her palm, and a closer, much more intent impression upon her ethereal body. She grasped it and flung herself away again, this time with a lodestone for her direction.

To that, she added pain, for, previously, she had forgotten to look for war, and although every planet she touched echoed with strife, she looked for immolation.

She reached a world and slowed, uncertain, felt a gigantic brush of another body past hers, and saw, was seared by, the impression of an immense warship coming to, turrets swinging around, and the planet below, trembling under the blast it received.

She quailed from the uprush of death and pain and fear, alien though it was, for the planet being destroyed was not inhabited by humans. She heard their cries in her mind and tumbled away, letting the backlash of the weaponry sweep her away.

Quiet hovered behind her. The warship thundered out of orbit and left, the planet wrapped in an aura of radiation. Amber held her lower lip between her teeth as she took one last look back, over her shoulder.

Sand, she thought. A sand planet but sand no more. Its atmosphere rippled in a prism of color.

She had no time to wonder. The lodestone in her hand jerked to the right, and she soared, and found another solar system.

The white flame she sought guttered low. Fear coalesced in Amber's ethereal body as she drew near, and found a physical world, torn by battery placements and shelling and laser fire—all scars that would heal quickly, unlike the world she'd seen irradiated. Below her stretched a cityscape, half in ruins, flames licking at it, gray pavement streaked with crimson. Beyond it, she saw countryside, its green trampled, ground broken, trees snapped and flung aside. Men in armor ranged it, moving quickly. She saw the sand waiting on the horizon, sand and the abhorrent touch of Thraks. Drawing in upon herself, she swooped down, no longer having to search for Jack. She was air and he was fire, and he sucked her in as though she existed only to fuel him.

Her last gasp was to reach for Colin.

Colin felt the sharp jerk on his soul. It nauseated and frightened him because it felt as if something was trying to suck him out like a raw egg from its shell. Amber's chill hands convulsed within his, and then he was gone; his mind ripped out of his body, and he found himself confronting . . .

It was not death. He knew death. It was Jack and something different, something primitive and feral, something desperate to do anything to maintain its life . . . yet something with an ultimate form that shimmered on the edge of Colin's senses like a golden curtain of intelligence and benevolence. He was reminded of an embryo's selfishness in its mother's womb, launched toward a life it could not possibly comprehend yet.

Amber enveloped him. *Can you help? Dear god, hurry, I'm losing it . . .*

Colin sensed Jack's wound, but the second presence fended him off, would not let him near, and, worse, this thing knew and understood the plane they inhabited, the spiritual self. It could and would destroy Colin on this plane. He approached again, and was rebuffed so solidly it made him gasp and pant in his physical form and his senses whirled, torn between what he experienced in his two selves. He was fading from Amber's grasp. All he could do was offer the second presence a glimpse of the life awaiting it, before their contact exploded and he and Amber were flung across the galaxies.

CHAPTER 22

Jack staggered and went to one knee, jarring himself inside the armor. A lead broke loose from where it was clipped to his torso, and he swore. But the sharp pain did some good. It broke the lethargy riding him. His shoulder sent a jag of agony throughout his body, broke sweat out on his forehead, and raised bile to the back of his throat. He righted himself. He listened for Bogie to goad him onward, but the sentience was uncharacteristically silent.

Around him, return fire kept him pinned down. He checked his target grids, uneasily aware that he'd been about to walk right into a crossfire and wondering what his mind could have been on. That's when he knew just how badly he'd been tagged. He was losing it. . . .

"Jay-sus, commander, you've been hit!" Garner hit the dirt field next to him, ducking his helmet behind a barrier of mud and rock thrown up by the earlier pounding the installation had taken.

"How close are we to getting in?"

Garner's helmet swung to face him. Through the sun-screened visor, Jack had difficulty seeing if there was humanity within. But Garner's voice held a trace of his fierce, biting humor.

"You and me and Aaron, and three or four well-placed grenades should do it. They'll be facing a fatal distraction . . . if you can do it."

"Don't worry about me." Carefully, Jack reached around to unsling his field pack. He left it and the laser rifle within it lying at his feet as he stood, keeping the outcropping between him and the main nest.

"Commander—"

"No more weight than necessary," Jack said. "Take what you need and leave the rest. If this works, there won't be enough left of the Thraks to matter. If it doesn't . . . the team coming up behind us can use it. Where's Aaron?"

"He hit the dust over there." Garner pointed. Armor could be seen lying amongst charred and broken ground, grass clumps still attempting to wave feebly despite damage and trampling, like a forlorn banner.

Aaron's young voice came in faintly over the com. "—Com trouble, but I'm ready when you are—"

"Ready." Jack keyed his grenades. "On your feet. I want to see if you guys are good enough in armor to keep up with me." He surged out of hiding and charged the Thrakian battlement.

Bogie felt the renewed heat of Jack's blood. He lay against Jack's skin, listening to the thunder of his pulse as the man launched himself against the enemy.

And within the armor, Bogie fought another war. He felt the touch of something he could not identify, something . . . celestial. It offered him so much more than mere life. It gave him a view of the being he might grow to be out of the baseness he was now.

But not a being sprung out of blood.

No.

And as Jack threw himself at the nest, laser fire rippling off his armor, Bogie drew back his cilia, denying himself. He did not have the strength to heal Jack the way he once could have. Instead, he worked at stemming the flow by blocking here and here . . . doing what he could to make sure the man who nurtured him might live.

But there was no way either of them could block the barrage from the remaining Thraks.

Jack flung his grenades, hit the power vault and somersaulted in midair, away from the resulting explosions. The burst flung him, as he'd intended, out of the line of return fire. He heard Garner yell and Aaron bite off a curse that sounded much too vehement for his youth. Then the mikes went dead, overloaded by the following blasts. He landed, and a shock wave tumbled him over. Garner landed well. A laser blast blossomed in the middle of his chest plate. Crimson and ebony blocked out his rank insignia and Garner crumpled slowly.

Sound bled back in. Jack stood. He heard the ricochet

whine even as the projectile slapped him again and he felt
the pain tear through his right thigh. *Damn*, he thought, as
he went to one knee, and twisted around. *I'm never going
to get out of here in one piece!*

Then, all was silent . . . except for a piercing screech that
became louder and louder. He looked up and panned the
darkening sky. A Needler whipped in overhead, lower and
lower. He saw the canopies hitting the air below it.

The shield crew.

Jack withdrew his right hand very slowly from his gauntlet and sleeve and wiped his face. His skin was clammy.

Static crackled. "Thank you, Commander Storm. All
clear now, shield crews dropping. Stand by for pickup.
Acknowledge."

Jack cleared his throat, his thoughts still fuzzy. "This is
Commander Storm. Please repeat."

A laugh. "What's the matter, Jack? That last salvo
scramble your brains? There's nothing moving down there
but Dominion armor. Get your shit together and make the
rendezvous point. I understand there's a few of you guys
need the doctor."

Jack blinked. He realized then that the dancing lightning
of laser fire had ceased around him. He pulled Garner to
his feet. The man came up, air burbling in his chest. Jack
assessed the damage. He reached into the armor and made
Garner place his own hand over the wound to staunch it.
It wasn't sucking air, so the man just might make it. Jack
felt a surge of fierce joy as Aaron helped him brace Garner
from the other side. Once more they'd beaten the Thraks
at their game. He heard the Needlers screaming overhead.
"Let's go home."

CHAPTER 23

Interloper

The warship swept in before the tertiary alarms even had a chance to go off and the factories had no time to download for red alert. Young Brant stood at the con tower, unable to believe his comp readouts.

"It can't be in under the shields."

"Affirmative. Unidentified aggressor, bearing six-zero-niner—"

"Shit," he muttered and hit the manual alarms.

Later, the records would show he was a full thirteen minutes ahead of the tertiary system.

Brant then opened the general com lines. The armory factories could blow half the planet up if they went, and there was no doubt in his mind that the incoming wasn't friendly. As he opened the lines, he said to the computer, "I want a Thrakian ID."

"Negative," the comp replied smoothly. "The unknown is not Thrakian according to data bank."

"It has to be!" Brant stood on one leg and then the other. "Answer the com, dammit! Answer me!"

A low thunder began to rumble. His fair blond hair stood on end. The tower vibrated.

"ETA fourteen minutes," the comp said. "Air to land missile approach."

"What?" Brant's voice went up half an octave. "Oh, shit, oh, shit! *Answer the com!"*

A light came on, but the screen stayed dark. "Good afternoon, this is Washburn Industries. If you wish to talk to personnel, key 1. If you wish payables, key 2. If you wish—"

Brant screamed into the receiver, "We're under fire! Emergency!"

Then he ran for the underground silos. Behind him in the tower, the comp said smoothly, "ETA seven minutes."

And another comp replied, "If you wish to talk to customer service, key 5. Thank you for calling Washburn Industries."

Brant erred. The unidentified assailant did not take out half the planet. But the predominant continent in the northern hemisphere suffered severe casualties. Washburn Industries, along with two grenade factories and Beretta Laser Rifles, were pulverized.

Even the underground silos.

Only the "black box" remained intact to tell the story after the first impact.

CHAPTER 24

"You can let me walk across the quad. I'm not going to break in two, goddammit."

Amber said scornfully, "An overnight at the hospital and you think you're healed. If you don't behave yourself, you'll be *sleeping* in the quad. Colin, talk some sense into him!"

The Walker stood, Jack's arm draped about his shoulder, looking as though he was bolstering the man's weight while Amber wrestled to set up a four-wheeled cart. The early morning breeze ruffled Colin's light fringe of hair and he took a deep breath. Malthen might actually have rain today, he thought as he inhaled. He no more supported Jack than Amber did at the moment and the two men exchanged a glance.

Face pink, Amber straightened. "There. You sit. Or you go the hard way, facedown on a gurney."

Jack made as if to shrug, then winced and thought better of it. He sat down in the small cart and adjusted the handlebars to a comfortable reach. He started the cart. Colin and Amber did not find it difficult to match its pace as he drove across the palace grounds.

"You know," Jack said, "the medics didn't say this was necessary."

"The medics," Amber retorted. "The same medics who also released Garner this morning? Just before he collapsed?"

"That's different. Garner spent the trip back in a cryo tank. They thought he'd healed more."

Amber stretched her long legs and strode out in front of the cart, bringing Jack to an abrupt halt. She looked down at him. "I hear one more complaint out of you, and I'm

going to tell Pepys and Baadluster you're out early, and
you can spend the day with *them*."

"Now that," Colin observed, "is a potent threat."

Jack smiled wryly. He held his hand up. "I surrender."

"Good. Now point that thing in the right direction and
get going."

Colin caught up with Amber. In a voice pitched so that
Jack could not hear it over the hum of the cart's motor, he
offered, "You shouldn't be so hard on him."

Her nose was pinched white, belying her attempt to
smile. "I know," she answered. "But when a miracle can't
even save him . . . when you know there's nothing you can
do, that you're absolutely helpless . . ." She stopped at the
edge of grass that was brown and brittle, as desperate in
its need as she was in hers. "I've just got to knock some
sense in that thick farmer's skull of his. I know what it's
like inside that suit . . . you think you're unstoppable. Well,
he's not. And the sooner he realizes it, the more chance
I've got that he's going to keep coming back to me."

Colin took her words in with a deep sigh. He reached
out and took her hand, pulling her along with him as he
hurried to catch up. "That's why, my dear, so many of
us believe in God." At the outside walk to the officers'
apartments, he took his hand from hers and gave her a
chaste kiss on her cheek. "I'm going no farther. This is a
sensitive area at best, and I want no more friction with
Pepys than necessary."

Amber threw a look over her shoulder to make sure Jack
was waiting for her before he stood up. She looked back.
"Have you heard from Denaro?"

The old man smiled. "Now that would be telling,
wouldn't it? I'll talk to you two in a day or so." He gave
a graceful half-bow, then turned and left them.

Amber helped Jack stand. If he noticed her new strength
and firmness of muscle, he said nothing. What he did say
was, "Where's Bogie?"

"In the shop. There was a lot of damage, Jack. I went
in yesterday after I left you. But he's okay. Just, I don't
know. Different."

Jack paused, leaning his weight on her shoulder, his
warm breath grazing her face as he talked. "I think he's
dying. I can't give him what he needs to grow anymore."

"Jack!"

"I don't know what to do. We could turn him over to one of the university labs, I guess."

"We couldn't! He'd die anyway without us. And what lab could you trust?"

Jack's silence confirmed her fears. She shouldered his weight a little better. "Come on. Let's not stand out here and talk about it." With her free hand, she checked the security seals. All were intact.

He made himself smile. "You just want to get me in bed."

"Keep thinking positively," she shot back, and palmed the door open. He found it necessary to lean on her more than he'd thought as his newly healed thigh and shoulder weakened on him. Inside the apartment, he took a few short breaths to quell the pain and dizziness as Amber left him long enough to lock the door. She left all the shades down and the lights off and he blinked, waiting for his eyes to adjust to the dark.

"Can you make it to a chair?" She thumbed at an unresponsive light switch. "Damn light sensor's broken."

A third voice caught them in the dimness. "Don't bother, Amber. I can see just fine."

When Amber had pulled the shades, Jack could see the golden mesh ocular piece glinting at them. The rest of the face had changed . . . harsh angular lines biting into heavy jowls. The tousled black curls were going a dirty gray. The intruder rested a handgun on his thigh lightly, its red charge button shining at them. But Jack knew the man well. Long ago deserter and underworld scoundrel, Ballard.

He clenched his fist even as he fought to stay upright, solid, menacing. "How did you get in here?"

Ballard glanced at Amber. "She knows we have our ways. She bought jammers a few months ago. Simple enough for me to slip in a microchip that made your home easy for me to unlock. Thought I might need it." He held up a thick hand. "Before you tear me apart, Storm, let me say that I had nothing to do with what happened last year."

Jack had little reason to believe him. "The terrorists carried an unusual calling card. Your prosthetic eye." Sour memories of threats and beatings filled his throat.

Ballard made a noise, half scorn and half as if painful remembrance. "That bastard Winton set them up. Me, too. He tore my eye out, then sent me on my way." He smiled without any warmth. "I didn't think I'd be able to get another one put in. But Winton also paid me well. I found a good surgeon this time. I hid out until I heard you'd killed him on Bythia." Ballard shifted in the chair.

"What made you crawl out from under the rocks this time?"

"The war." Ballard waggled the gun. "I was taking libation in a bar, looked up, and there you were in Congress. You did us proud, Jack. I was the first to call you what you are, the last remaining true Knight. I want you to remember that. I want you to know that I knew who you were, and even with my eye gone, I didn't tell Winton. He had his suspicions, but he never had the truth from *me*."

Jack shook his head. "You deserted and took your armor with you. Don't be proud of yourself now."

Ballard hawked deep in his throat, turned his head slightly and spat on the rug to his right. "Listen, hero. If it weren't for scum like me and Amber, you wouldn't have survived two weeks in Malthen."

Jack moved then. He launched himself across the room so quickly that Ballard could not react, wrapped his fist in the front of the intruder's short jacket and shook him as if he were not even human. The gun fell to the floor and Amber snatched it up.

Ballard's teeth rattled. He blurted out, before Jack could say a word, "I'm wrong there. Amber's not scum, never has been. Dammit, man, let me go. I came here to help you."

Jack staggered back on his heels as he gave Ballard one last shake and dropped him.

The chair cracked as it took the man's weight and Ballard sat, panting. He brushed a limp curl off his gold screen eye.

"Say what it is and get out."

"All right. Amber—" the man's good eye flickered visibly toward her.

"She can take care of herself."

Ballard shrugged. "It's not good, Jack, getting her involved. All right." Gingerly, he reached inside his short jacket. "I brought you something." He flipped the recording disk in the air and Jack caught it.

"What's this?"

"*This*, my Knight, is something you should know about. Rumor has it that the new Minister of War makes Winton look like a saint. There are more things in heaven than you or I can dream about," and Ballard smiled crookedly. "Thank me for it later. If you need a witness, let me know." Ignoring Amber, he got to his feet and lumbered toward the door.

Amber trained the gun muzzle on him. Her finger began to tighten on the trigger sensor. But Jack waved. "Let him go."

She gave Ballard a poisonous look as he reached the portal. "Don't ever confuse me with yourself again."

Ballard paused, a massive wreck of a man. He reached out and chucked her under the chin. "No. I won't make that mistake again. I owe you a sincere apology, little one." His gaze flicked over Jack once, quickly, then back to her. "Let's just say that a small and jealous man can make bitter remarks." Amber wavered uncertainly and he took the opportunity to leave.

Jack held the recording in his palm. "Let's see what the hell this is."

The recording faded into silence. Amber looked up from her kneeling position on the floor. "What's going on?"

Jack stayed in the broken armchair. It had gone lopsided after he'd dropped Ballard's mass into it. He drummed the padded arm beneath his hand. Three fingers and a thumb, drumming, a discordant noise. "It means that whoever it was got in under the primary and secondary alarm systems and past the shields. The computer had to have been right: they couldn't have been Thrakian. It took a week's worth of pounding to break the shields on Oceana before they got to go dirtside. No one I know has the technology to circumvent shielding as if it wasn't there." The face of the war was changing before his very eyes.

"Then why weren't you told?" Amber countered.

"I don't know. It could be they don't trust me since Denaro defected: I could kill Colin for getting me involved in that." He stopped drumming his fingers and, instead, rubbed his thigh as if the deep gnawing pain he still felt from the wound could be eased that way. "It sounds to me like the same outfit that got Opus."

Her golden-brown eyes widened. "Them?"

"I think so. Don't get me wrong—it could be freebooters, there's none of them above a little looting during wartime, when the majority of the fleet is distracted elsewhere—but there's no one, no one, with that kind of technology yet." He stood, still a little wobbly, and made an effort to hold himself tall. "I think that we're facing brand new players, and we can't begin to know the rules or stakes until we know who or what they are. Ballard says he can get me witnesses. Contact him. I want to meet with them. I don't think there's a way in hell we can trust Pepys or Baadluster to tell us the truth if they even know it."

CHAPTER 25

Pepys looked at the report. "Another one," he said, wearily, and rubbed his eyes. They had lost their emerald brilliance from fatigue. His freckled face was puffy.

Baadluster stood at the window, looking out to where a light rain attempted to clean Malthen's air, water its greenery, and purge its technology. He held his hands clasped loosely behind his back and, perhaps intentionally, perhaps not, his voice sounded a little smug as he answered the emperor. "No one else has seen this yet, not even the Dominion Security Council. If you wish me to arrange it so . . . no one will."

Pepys looked over a copy of the transmission one more time. Then he said, "What about Washburn?"

"We may have to take him out to keep him quiet. That was his son making the recording." Reluctantly, Baadluster turned away from the sight of the rain.

One carrot-colored eyebrow arched. "Surely someone would notice the absence of four major defense industries."

"Accidents happen. We could release news of a Thrakian strafing."

"On a shielded world?"

"A traitor let down the forcefields," Baadluster said blandly. "Washburn or his son. It would not matter, to the dead." He turned back and missed Pepys' shudder.

The emperor took a deep breath. Then he said, "Whatever is quickest and easiest to arrange. Do it neatly. I want no connections to be made."

"Don't worry," said Baadluster smoothly. "If anything comes back, it will lead to the Green Shirts. Now, as to the other matter we spoke of, I believe it's time to come off the defensive. I think we should look to beating the Thraks on their own territory."

"When?"

"I think we can have the new recruits up to it in two weeks."

Pepys stood up and stretched his wiry body. "What about the new recruiting centers?"

"Up and operational. Commander Storm appears to have a certain amount of charisma. They're still lining up for enlistment. We'll have all three centers fully equipped for basic training by the end of the week. Five thousand more graduates in six months."

That brought a smile to the emperor's face. He stepped to the window, deliberately blocking Baadluster's line of sight. It was, after all, his view. "I never thought I'd see the day the Dominion willingly donated ground to me, to my troops. I wonder if they'll like the flower that grows from that seeding!" He laughed. "All right then. We can afford to take the offensive. What about our new commander? Will he be well enough?"

Baadluster stood behind the emperor. The man was small enough that the minister could easily see over his head. He had, in fact, a better panorama than Pepys did, and he knew it. His too thick lips thinned cruelly. "If not, he would never admit the weakness. One way or another, he'll accomplish what we want him to. And if we're lucky, the Thraks will rid us of him."

CHAPTER 26

Jack fingered the Flexalinks. He curled a fist and pounded the shoulder plate, unhappy with the feel of it. It might have just been his imagination, but he felt the give in it. The weakness. The edges of certain links here and there retained their crimping in spite of having been pounded out.

Good as new, boss.

He did not answer Bogie. The armor was not as good as new. Could no longer be repaired as good as new. And, he knew from previous outings, its obsolescence impaired his leadership. Leadership, hell, it impaired his very *survival*.

"Ever think of moving, Bogie?"

Huh?

"Never mind." He dropped his hand. What could he do? "Still cold?"

The sentience was slow in answering, then, *Yes.*

He slapped the armor sleeve. "We'll think of something." He turned to leave. The shop was quiet. It was midshift, in the middle of the night, and he'd left Amber alone in the bed once again to come here. Soon, even in midshift, the shop would be filled as staging began for the operation to invade the Thrakian League. He approved of Baadluster's decision and that filled Jack with the faintest of misgivings, but he could not deny himself the sweetness of a strike at the Thraks. He turned away, and was caught by the edge of Bogie's thought.

What is life?

Jack said ironically, "You ask me? Maybe I should haul St. Colin in here and let you grill him."

I am serious, Jack. When you were injured, I . . . tasted you. I tasted your life, and it was warm.

The sentience had to mean blood, not life. Jack thought

of the Milot berserkers and how they were born into existence. He shuddered. Was Bogie then, if not an actual berserker, a parasite as he had once feared? Did he fight the possibility of being first possessed, then consumed, every time he wore the armor? He fought the revulsion the idea brought to him. "You're alive, Bogie. You're thinking and aware."

Only through you. Take you away from me, and I am nothing.

That was what Jack feared most. Did the alien sense the inevitable choice Jack was being forced to make?

Jack took up some tools and sat down, helmet in hand, while he worked. The feeling of having something to do while he talked settled him. Finally, he said, "That will change when you've grown."

I can't grow any more. What will feed me? Blood feeds you. What will feed me?

"Blood isn't the only thing that feeds me. I breathe air. I like the feeling of sun on my skin. A bottle of good beer and a medium-rare steak now and then. I need to feel good."

You need Amber's love.

"That's one of the things."

Bogie was silent for a long time. Jack finished checking the circuitry he was working on. He did a minute bit of soldering and cursed when he burned his fingertip. He ought to let the technicians handle this, he thought to himself. It's too bad Bogie wasn't a seed. He could just transplant him. Or a seedling that could be grafted somewhere. He looked up. "Other things grow differently. A seed takes sunlight and water. Photosynthesis. It grows that way."

Explain.

Jack tiredly brushed his hair from his forehead. "I can't explain. Listen. Feel." He reached out and held the armor's gauntlet and remembered his family's agra station on Dorman's Stand. The rows of growing things. The ATH moving down, harvesting, its bulk and its roar. Roots being pulled from the soil. The smell of dirt and heat.

There was a lingering moment when Bogie tried to hold onto him even though Jack was finished and was attempting to pull away.

With a shuddering sigh, he broke contact, and saw the

white-hot rays of first sun under the shop door. Half the night had gone in what had seemed a few moments. He stood. His injuries had stiffened and he moved to stretch them, carefully, mindful of the weeks of healing still to come. The gauntlet moved after him, curving for a grasp on his arm. Jack paused and let Bogie touch him, aware of the effort it took the sentience to animate the battle suit.

Let me feel the sun again.

Jack felt the wash of heat against the shop's garage door. "Feel it yourself." He braced his good shoulder against the equipment rack and shoved it across the begrimed concrete flooring, until they were up against the door. He palmed it open and heard the servos begin to whine.

As the door rolled up, Jack blinked. The sun, almost too harsh for human eyes, flooded his senses. He tugged the rack after him and wheeled it outside.

I never realized, Bogie said. Wonderment tinged his rough tones.

Jack felt the new day wash over him. Recent rains had cleansed the air somewhat. No brown tinge hung over the cityscape, cloying the horizon, and the pink tinge of sunrise had already burned away. It was not as beautiful as Dorman's Stand, or even as beautiful as Oceana had been, destroyed though it was.

But it was, indisputably, alive.

What a fool I was, breathed the alien sentience.

Beside him, Jack felt the sleeves move as, haltingly, Bogie held his hands up to the sunlight.

This is life.

It was not the celestial brilliance that had brushed him when he thought of bleeding Jack. But it was of the same stuff, and it flooded him, fed him, warmed him.

"Sunlight?" Jack said. "But you've been out in the sun—" he stopped short. What was different? Why did Bogie feel energized now?

They stood in the wash of the sun's rays. Jack still held the helmet in his hands. He reached over and screwed it down.

Almost immediately, Bogie gave a muted cry of frustration. The rending sound echoed in Jack's mind.

Gone!

Jack reached over quickly and took the helmet off. He

grinned. "Not gone, Bogie. There's solars in the helmet . . . their job is to absorb the energy and channel it into the suit batteries. All you've got to do is learn how to tap into the circuitry. You've been doing it—I've got power drainage every time we go out, but what you're getting isn't solar energy. If that's what you need, there's no reason why you can't bypass the solars. We only need that if we're on extended field maneuvers. I'11 work with you on the rewiring."

I can have the light.

"All you need. It'll just take a few days. Can you wait that long?"

His answer was a shout of fierce joy.

Amber waited until the sound of Jack's leaving had faded from the apartment and his warmth from the blankets before she got up. She would not sleep much more this night and there was no profit in tossing and turning. She dressed quickly, pulling on a dark blue jumpsuit and glove-soft leather boots. She had dreams of her own to pursue in the middle of the night. Raking a brush through her hair, she tied it back in a love knot and made a face at herself in the mirror. Soon, very soon, she'd show Jack what she could do. Then he would sooner leave his right arm behind than leave her.

Outside, the courtyards were half-illuminated by the security lights and she stayed in the shadows, working her way toward the training grounds. The closer she got, the harder her task got. New recruits swelled the facilities. Temporary dorms and lockers were being installed and Pepys had had a hundred acres of abandoned housing razed for a new obstacle course, just outside the wall of the old grounds.

Amber paused to catch her breath. The excitement of the deception set her pulse racing. It was a flaw in her, a fatal flaw, that she would always have to walk a tightrope, live on the edge, to have this feeling. Even loving Jack did not give it to her.

Excitement gave way to poignancy and she was standing there, hesitating, when a hand gripped her arm.

"Milady Amber. Out late, are you not?"

She looked up into the pasty white face of Vandover Baadluster. Her heart took a fluttering beat, then steadied.

"When I can't sleep, I walk."

"Understandable, but not wise," the Minister of War said as he steered her away from the shadowed outside walls. "The new recruits are many, and a rowdy bunch. I've been told rape is just as distasteful to a one-man whore as it is to a virtuous woman. I suggest you not make yourself a target."

His words took her breath away. She stood, momentarily speechless, feeling her nostrils flare in sudden hatred for the man. He sketched a bow. "Besides," he said, "we suspect sabotage. We've been monitoring activity and tonight have set a trap for the unwary Knight."

She kept her expression steady. "Sabotage?"

"There's been an intruder. He's been discreet and he knows the security systems well enough to bypass them, but there's no denying there's been unauthorized activity among the ranks. If we're very lucky, he's just an industrial spy gathering information on the armor for another manufacturer."

"And if you're not lucky?"

Baadluster pursed his thick lips. "Then we have a traitor on our hands. Commander Storm's latest reports show the Thraks have regressed to projectile weapons, a strategy unwarranted unless the enemy has made an extensive study of the armor."

A trap set for a traitor. Amber shivered as she realized she might have walked into it.

Vandover made a consoling noise at the back of his throat. "You have nothing to worry about, milady. But one would suggest a return to your apartment which is, undoubtedly, more secure."

She tilted her face slightly as she looked up at him. He knew that she knew that he meant he could not make any recordings off the security monitors. "Thank you, Minister Baadluster, for your concern."

"Not at all." He touched her again, a fleeting gesture that stopped her in her tracks. The harsh dome of light accentuated his homely features even more, and his dark eyes were like burning embers. "You might reconsider the offer I made to you earlier. Commander Storm is in an awkward position, whether he acknowledges it or not. His friendship with St. Colin borders on treason itself and though we cannot associate him with the defection of Cadet Denaro, he does himself harm by thinking himself free of blame."

"Jack was not even on Malthen when Denaro went AWOL."

"No. But his induction of Denaro into the Knights borders on collusion. You are aware, are you not, that St. Colin had been ordered to turn the man over to Pepys for investigation of suspected treason? That the two of them instead buried the man as a recruit, knowing the emperor could not at the time afford the scandal such an investigation would cause. So that now, months later, Denaro has taken irreplaceable equipment and vanished. No, my soiled beauty. Your commander has not made wise choices in his career."

"Jack doesn't play your kind of politics!"

"No? Then what kind of politics does he play at? A Green Shirt perhaps? How do we know where he spent those seventeen years of his life?"

Anger made it difficult for her to breathe. She felt her eyes narrow. "Pepys has a fool for a Minister of War."

He stepped close to her. She could feel his heat as if it were an open flame. Her Bythian tattoos telegraphed danger to her, but she stood her ground.

"You have one chance," he told her, quietly but firmly. "And one chance only. And that chance is that Jack is as naive as he is brave. Tell me. Tell me of who he sees and what he does so that I may guide him in the months ahead, because, webbed lady—" His stare pierced her as if he could see the faint markings on her skin beneath her clothing. "—I am no fool and neither is Pepys, and you know that. Confide in me or Jack will be so tangled in the schemes of others that there will be no possibility either of you can survive."

She wished then, with all of her heart, that Hussiah had not taken from her the art of killing. If she had any way of shaping her thoughts into an arrow and aiming them into the core of Baadluster's being, she would do it. Him she would kill with even less conscience than Jack killed Thraks.

Baadluster read her expression and took a step back. "One day, milady, we'll meet again, and you will remember that I offered this opportunity to you, *and that you refused it*."

"You give me nothing! I can't spy on Jack."

He bowed his head. "It is late. The grounds are secured. I suggest you return to your apartment. We have work to do here, and you are detaining us."

Amber turned on her heel and left as swiftly as she could without making it apparent she was fleeing him. She only had the satisfaction of knowing that Baadluster's trap would be empty tonight for it had been meant for her, and he himself had told her of it.

Later, in the cold bed, she curled up in the silken caftan she'd brought out of Bythia, and, feeling her skin crawl with mystic patterns, she cursed herself for having lost the ability to kill. Not only that, but as the patterns continued to fade, they took the last of her psychic talents with them. Soon she would have nothing left . . . nothing to bind her to Jack and Bogie. No weapon of her own to help them fight in their struggles to live. She had only her wiles left. And the clandestine training as a Dominion Knight.

Pepys was awake when Baadluster returned empty-handed. The emperor sat in his easy chair, sipping tea from a fine bone cup that was reputed to be over one thousand years old, and he did not refrain from a mocking smile even though Baadluster gave him a look indicating he wished, among other things, to smash that ancient cup.

"No quarry?"

"No. But we know there is trouble. Even Lassaday admits it, and Lassaday is Storm's man, as loyal a soldier as the commander has."

"There's no indication that the commander is involved."

"No."

"Good. Then let it be."

Baadluster glared at him. "Let it be? I have been reduced to catching spies and then you say, let it be?"

"The strike at Klaktut is far more important." Pepys put the teacup down and mopped his upper lip.

This brought a halt to Baadluster's ill-tempered pacing.

The minister locked gazes with the emperor. "Then I can return to strategic planning."

"Of a certainty. After you place a call to Queen Tricatada."

Baadluster protested angrily, "We are winning, Pepys. You cannot throw it all away by telling the Queen we plan to hit one of her major nests!"

"No. No, I don't plan to tell her what we're doing." Pepys stood and smoothed down his clothes, preparing for a morning of judgment hearings. "With her embassies and consulates shut down, our network of information is greatly hampered. It appears that we both are under attack from a third party, and I'd like to know what she knows of that."

"A Thraks would never tell you."

"No." Pepys smiled. "Like anything else, Baadluster—it's what they don't say and how they don't say it that's really important. Go put in the call. When it's completed, come and get me from the chambers."

Vandover made a sardonic bow as Pepys left the room.

CHAPTER 27

The Rusty Bolt had changed little through the years of Jack's acquaintance with under-Malthen, except perhaps to get mangier. A sallow faced lump of a man smelling of *ratt* sidled through the privacy curtain and looked at Jack, the whites of his eyes gone yellow like a hard user with his liver about to give out.

Showing rotting teeth, the man said, "I'm supposed to say 'Ballard sent me.'" He put his hand palm up on the table and Jack pressed a hundred credit disk into it. The man looked at it, then pushed a small circuit card across the table. "That's for Amber. Ballard said she ordered it."

"Talk. I haven't a lot of time."

The man shrugged and his rotting teeth showed wider. "Neither have I, man. Ballard says you're supposed to hear about what happened to Washburn Industries."

"So tell me."

"Gone. Pulverized. Enemy incoming hit it, and internal explosives did the rest. I was supposed to be on shift, but I took a long lunch break . . . about two days earlier." The man shrugged.

"So if you weren't there, how do you know?"

"I wasn't there when it happened, man, but that doesn't mean I wasn't there. I got my scooter back in commission and reported back to work. Like, I was the first one to find the ashes. I got there even before the firemen. They had to come from half a continent away. Too hot otherwise."

Jack stared. The man had to be dead in his boots . . . and he knew it.

Another shrug. "Either this way or th' *ratt*. I prefer th' *ratt*."

"So would I."

The informant nodded.

"How did you get out? They must have cordoned off the area pretty damn quick."

"So fast I blinked and missed it. And then Washburn came in. Never saw him leave though. Heard he killed himself when they found his son's body in th' lower silos. His son's supposed to have been th' one let the shields down for the Thraks."

"Is that what you think?"

"No way. That kid was so straight, he was a real pain in the ass. Besides, I know better. I saw it."

"Saw?"

"That's right. It evidently hung around, scouted us before it left. I saw it planing over the Wide Windy . . . that's a desert area outside the defense state."

This was what had been hinted to Jack. He pushed a drawing over the table. "Like this?"

The sallow-faced man looked at it for a split second and shook his head.

Jack pulled another sheet from his short-jacket pocket. "Or this?"

Blackened nails tapped the second picture. "That's her." The man sniffled and rubbed at his nose. "Gotta go, all right?"

Jack nodded. The man stood. Jack hesitated and then pressed a second credit disk into his palm.

He looked at it. "Five hundred credits?"

"You earned it." That was enough money to buy enough *ratt* to O.D. The two men looked at each other levelly.

The second broke contact first, unable to meet the rainwater blue gaze holding him. "Thanks, man," he mumbled. "I mean it." He wove his way out of the Rusty Bolt and Jack watched him go.

The Thrakian ship he'd put aside immediately. The second drawing was a fairly accurate computer rendition of the unknown that had gotten Opus. So whatever had happened at Washburn Industries was known, only Jack hadn't been told about it. He was staging Operation Nest short of rifles and grenades, plagued with inexplicable back orders, and he wasn't going to be told the truth. Storm didn't have to worry about Baadluster or anyone else getting his hooks on the informer—he wasn't going to last any longer than it took him to get another load of *ratt*.

On the other hand, it was better than the lingering death that had been facing him.

Jack pushed his dirty glass aside, got up, and left the bar.

He traced the last of the tattooing over Amber's soft skin. She lay quietly under his touch, her eyes closed, not immediately responding to the news that he was leaving in the morning, news that no one had known for sure until an hour ago. Her pupils moved slightly beneath the transparent blue veining as she responded to his caress. *Even there*, he thought. *That snakeskin bastard had touched her even there.*

"How can you go, knowing that?" she asked, finally.

"I have to go. With Washburn dead, our backing in the Congress is very tentative. We have a 'probationary' war. It's the one thing I agree on with Baadluster and Pepys. I have to show how effective we can be against the Thraks."

She arched her back as he drew his fingers down across her stomach, her loins and then her thighs. "You're being *very* effective right here and now," she murmured.

He slapped the flat of her stomach lightly. "You're upset."

"Of course, I am! Every time I take a deep breath, you're being taken away from me. And, dammit, Jack, you're making it harder to follow."

He smiled at her as he lowered his body over hers, pinning her to the bed, and she gasped a moment in pleasure, then thrashed her head to one side. "Don't you change the subject."

He began to move, very slowly, inside her. "I'm not," he said softly. "You are. I was talking sex."

He watched her bite her lip as he prolonged his movement.

"How can you go to war if you're not even sure who the real enemy *is?*"

He entered her again, deeply, and she took an intense breath. He kissed her. "I think," he said into her ear, biting her earlobe gently, "that this is a poor time to be discussing it. At the moment, I only care about who my *lover* is."

Amber sighed. He could feel the anger dissipate from the silken body cradling him. She wrapped her arms about his shoulders. "Who am I," she answered, "to disrupt peace negotiations?" And she pulled him closer.

Two weeks in hypnosleep with subliminal isometrics. No cold sleep this trip out. The engagement was too important. Cold sleep made them sluggish. Dull. Occasionally you'd find your best man was susceptible to cold sleep fever. No. Jack was taking no chances with any of his three ships this time. He was even going to allow himself to be put under after one last computer simulation. Operation Nest was too important to allow anything to interfere.

He ran the simulation through and sat, the illumination of the screen playing upon his face as he watched. Three thousand troops, though only five hundred of them were seasoned, but it was enough, and his Wings spearheaded the drops. Hit and run. A devastating blow to a major Warrior crèche. It worked. It was perfect. Jack sat back unhappily. Nothing in life was ever perfect.

Amber was the one with the psychic ability, but he'd never been one to discount the feelings he had from time to time. He couldn't put his finger on it. Maybe it was the unidentifieds that showed up from time to time, though he saw no way the assault on Klaktut could be tipped off. They would come out of hyperdrive, so close that a hair's miscalculation would mean disaster—turn the corner and they were *there*. The Thraks wouldn't even have a chance to react.

He sat back in the chair, searching through the meager memories Bogie had been able to give back to him. He found one and held on to it for a moment: his father, looking out the screened-in porch, while a field full of crops was being destroyed by clouds of hail. "It's like this, son," he'd said, and pulled Jack close. "You do all you can. Right fertilizers. Mineral balance. Natural herbicides. And then you plant and watch it grow. But sometimes, no matter how much good you do, something bad happens."

"What is it, Dad?"

"Flood maybe. Or brush fire. Or a plague of insects you can't possibly fend off. We call it an Act of God. Watch for it, Jack. It'll happen to you someday. All you can do is withstand it and get ready to start over."

An Act of God. Jack watched the computer simulation

and wondered if it was too late to program one in and study the contingencies.

Unfortunately, there was no telling what kind of Act it would be.

CHAPTER 28

Jack stood wearily in the hallway. He'd not even been given a chance to bathe or get out of his armor. The stink of war and death hung palpably about him. Bogie throbbed against his shoulders and he thought, not for the first time, that soon there would not be room for the two of them inside the white armor. He carried his helmet in the crook of his left arm and his shoulder wound pulsed, a reminder that he had not completely healed. He looked down at the aide.

"Last time I was here, I spoke in appeal to a joint session of Congress. What's it called this time?"

The young man flicked a scornful glance at him, then looked back at the doorway for a signal. "It's called a Congressional Hearing," he said, briefly.

"Ah." Jack rocked back on his heels in fatigue. He dared not close his eyes. If he did, the nightmare might overwhelm him.

"Retreat! Retreat! Make your rendezvous point at all costs. Those Needlers are losing their asses coming in for you!" Jack cleared his throat, knowing his hoarseness made his commands bleed out over the com lines. Around him, the sky was rimmed with laser fire, an aurora borealis of war, and around him lay armor laden corpses that would never rise again.

A total rout. If he had not known better, he would think that the Thraks had known they were coming.

Three o'clock, boss.

Jack pivoted wearily and laid down a spray of fire. The tingling at his left wrist told him power was ebbing. Not expended yet, but he was at his last stand. It might not have been so disastrous with seasoned troops, he told himself. Perhaps.

A shuttle settled just out of his range, the land burned to obsidian glass, fused by previous landings.

"All right," Jack yelled. "Get on, quickly, that's it, let's *go!*" He watched the wave of soldiers making toward the shuttle, some running and others staggering, and a handful carrying comrades. He watched the horizon for a sign of incoming salvos, but the air was still and silent for now.

The shuttle filled, labored to a takeoff and was gone.

He took a deep breath. As long as he had power enough to fire and strength enough to stand, no one alive was going to be left behind. He no longer had any doubt that they had difficulty targeting him and when he returned, he would insist that norcite be glazed over every piece of armor in operation. If he returned.

Incoming, Bogie whispered in his mind.

"Hit the dirt, boys," Jack screamed.

The world splintered apart around him, but they missed the landing point, and another shuttle hesitantly hopped down.

He could hear Lassaday's guttural, "Hut, hut, let's move your asses or the Thraks will have 'em for you. Let's go!"

A glad noise shuddered through Jack. He had not known, until that moment, whether the sergeant was still alive. He got out, "You, too, sergeant, or I'll have your balls in a sling."

"Commander! That you, by god?"

"It is. And those were orders."

"Yessir!"

Jack braced himself. "How many more out there, sarge?"

"A hundred more, coming up the hillside. Let me stay out, commander . . . see if we can take some of . . . some of *them* with us. We've got room."

"No."

There was a flat silence on the com, then Lassaday said, "But, Jack . . . they're *human.*"

"No. Not as far as they're concerned, Sarge. Now move it out!"

"Yessir." And this time, the belly of the shuttle muted the transmission and Jack knew the NCO had gone aboard the next to last shuttle out from this Thrakian hell.

It was not the sergeant's fault the new recruits had gone to pieces on their first mission.

Nor even Jack's.

No amount of war intelligence had mentioned or could have prepared them for the sight of Klaktut.

Jack had expected a sand planet, totally metamorphosed for the needs of the Warrior crèche. But Klaktut was not sand, except in those isolated nests. The rest of the planet was verdant, agraformed, domesticated. And humans were among the primary domesticated stock, facing the Knights dropped in for battle, staring as dumb-faced as any animal as the battle armor strode across their fields.

But that hadn't been the worst of it. As the fighting grew desperate and the Knights inexorably spiraled in to take out the major Warrior crèches, human flesh had formed the last ditch walls between the crèche and the invaders.

Jack could not blame the boys who'd signed on for honor and glory when they broke at the sight.

It filled his gorge also. He'd always been told the Thraks took no prisoners.

It redoubled his determination to get every Knight off Klaktut alive that it was within his power to do.

And, in the long run, only the retreat was a victory.

Jack thought, swaying with exhaustion as he waited in the corridors of Congress, that he would not even be allowed to savor that. Perhaps he should have allowed Lassaday to bring back one of *them* so that the inquiry he faced would have some idea of the horror of those days.

His stomach swam. He'd never made hyperdrive so fast, barely forty-eight hours after being docked with the shuttle. He'd slept the sleep of the dead in his armor. Luckier than some on board, who'd slept and not woken up . . . dying of their wounds, but at least not left behind to be buried in some alien soil.

Or worse.

It was naive of him, he reflected, to expect to be commended for his efforts. With Washburn dead, a major source of support for the probationary war was gone. Still, he'd beaten back the Thrakian attacks. It was only their initial invasion on the League's own turf that had gone sour.

The Congressional aide touched his armored sleeve. "It's time, commander."

He moved forward.

No applause this time. He heard dimly, as he moved forward, a muttering that followed him like a hungry and discontented mongrel, nipping at his heels. He moved to where another aide, a young lady who would not meet his eyes, indicated he should sit.

No podium. No telecast audience. As he sat and looked across the chamber, he saw Pepys and Baadluster standing in the visitors' gallery, where they talked as if unaware he had entered.

A man stood. He had hair of silver and skin as dark as the void. When he stood, the room quieted.

"Tell us, commander, in your own words, what happened."

As he was still hoarse, Jack moved the mike sensors a little closer, and then he began to speak.

He told the truth. He did not play for sympathy or support. He thought, perhaps, that they ought to know that in war there would be winners and losers. But when he finished, when they had asked their myriad of questions, he realized that he was wrong.

It showed in their faces. They no more understood defeat than they had really understood his victory.

Jack swallowed painfully and hoped for an end to the questioning. He watched as Pepys took a seat on the dais.

"Thank you, Commander Storm. I yield the floor to Emperor Pepys of the Triad Throne, our noted ally and warlord."

Pepys stood. Jack was aware that there was movement to the rear of him, in the audience room doorway behind the dais, where he had originally waited months ago to make his appeal to the joint session. A cool breeze touched the back of his neck. His muscles stiffened. He winded a scent on the breeze, a smell of old enemies, and wished that he'd had time to take his armor off, or at least cleanse it of its stench.

"We can be thankful," Pepys said, "for Commander Storm's skillful handling of the retreat. We can be thankful, as well, for his quick assessment of the situation. As few lives were lost as possible. As for the invasion itself," and Pepys bowed his head, "I will bear the hubris. It is mine and mine alone. And because it is, it is fitting that I am here today."

In a fog of exhaustion, Jack wondered what it was Pepys was leading up to. Why should he apologize for an offensive maneuver that could have, if successful, put a major dent in the Thrakian war effort?

"It is well, in these days of nearly instantaneous communication, that more sensible heads than mine prevail. While Commander Storm has been in transit to Columbia, a major decision has been discussed and reached. Congressmen and representatives, ladies and gentlemen. The past few days you have all seen and discussed the evidence that there is another aggressor in our space."

Jack lifted his head. *By god, he had told them!* Jack would have liked to have heard what was said, certain that he had not had all the evidence.

"I did not, therefore, refuse to discuss alternatives when first contacted by Queen Tricatada. I brought my reservations here and tabled them in these sacred halls where not only laws are made and upheld, but differences are met and melded. Because we kept open minds, we learned of the Ash-Farel, the ancient enemy of the Thraks, and the peril that faces us all."

The hair prickled at the nape of Jack's neck. He took a deep breath, and readied to turn in his chair as he heard footsteps behind him.

"Ladies and gentlemen. It is not only my wisdom but your own which has led us to this landmark moment. May I present our new allies and their representatives—Queen Tricatada, her warlord General Guthul who will become supreme commander of our allied forces, and the new second in command to Commander Storm, Admiral K'rok!"

As Jack staggered to his feet and stood, facing the Thrakian contingent, the huge Milot soldier stepped forward slightly and gathered him, armor and all, in an immense, furry, and smelly hug.

"I be glad to see you, Knight Jack," the Milot traitor grinned. "Now you be saluting General Guthul and I be saluting you!"

CHAPTER 29

The giant Milot dropped Jack back to the dais and stepped back, saluting smartly as he did so. The scent he had winded had not been his imagination and it threatened to overwhelm him now.

At Jack's back, the Congressional session had gotten to its feet, applauding. The sound was ironic to his ears; how many months ago had it been for him?

Behind K'rok, General Guthul stood, his mask horrific and dignified, and Jack had no doubt it was stylized with all the nuances of meaning a Thrakian war commander could arrange. Behind them, a lesser Thraks stood and Jack recognized the implants in the soft wattle of throat exposed by an inferior mask. An interpreter.

He then looked to the Thrakian queen. He'd never seen one before, nor any Thraks he could identify as female, though there must be many as the Thraks were incredibly prolific.

Did they even know the natural life span of a Thraks?

She stood, a brilliant and deep cobalt blue, iridescent wings coiled at her back, her body a pearshape meant for breeding. Her mask was streaked with color, although Jack could not tell if all the streaks were natural coloration or if some were cosmetic. Her height topped that of Guthul, making her a phenomenon even among Thraks.

She carried a scent, too, a dark and musky scent that stirred Jack for a moment until he realized he was responding to it. She stared at him, her faceted eyes like sapphire jewels, distinctly feminine—and totally alien. She trilled something and the interpreter stood forward.

"My queen says you have been a worthy adversary and now she hopes you will be an equally brilliant ally."

Jack inclined his head. He had been so worthy an adver-

sary, he had scared the Thraks into suggesting alliance—
and Pepys had been backhanded enough to accept! He
closed his lips on any reply he might have made. He—all
of them—had been betrayed. There was no answer he
could think of to make to that. K'rok put an arm about him
and drew him around to face the Congressional audience.

Quietly, in his ear, K'rok said, "My sorrows, Jack. This
be a bad way to conquer an enemy."

Jack straightened in his armor. He put on a smile and
answered back, out of the corner of his mouth, "I'm not
done fighting yet."

Lassaday rubbed the dome of his bald head in frustration. "A week of alliance, ser, and them bugs have done
everything but move into my bed! They've got more out
of Pepys and the DC than if they'd beat the pants off us!"

Jack overlooked the parade grounds from the bridge, listening to his chief NCO vent his frustration. Lassaday was
right. Not only were the Thraks back in the chief star lanes,
and the inner planet trade lanes, but they were in the fleet
and now Jack was expecting his first Thraks battalion to
join the Knights. They were infiltrating with greater success
than if they had conquered.

He didn't like it any better than Lassaday. Worse, it had
been kept from public knowledge. Amber knew something
troubled him, but had been unable to nag, wheedle, or even
seduce it out of him. Pepys and the Dominion Congress
planned to make a public announcement in another week,
when all facets of the alliance had been sealed.

But Jack worried at it as if trying to get at the marrow.
He knew of no fleet officers invited aboard the Thrakian
vessels—the atmosphere and dietary demands "too complex" to allow that interchange. Thraks were more adapt-
able, they'd been told.

Nor had Jack had any of his officers assigned to League
Warrior crèches. Again, humans were not compatible with
Thrakian conditions. But he was expecting two dozen
Thraks, hand-picked by Guthul himself, to arrive in less
than forty-eight hours. Modified suits were to be molded
to them and they were to be trained, if possible. When Jack
thought of all the raw recruits and wounded Knights killed

by dead man circuits to avoid just such an eventuality, his gut clenched.

Lassaday said, "Sir? Sir?"

"I'm sorry, Sarge, what was that?"

"I said, ser, that we've isolated that wing of the barracks like you told us."

Jack smiled at that. Amber had provided him with jammers, but she had nearly burst from the effort of trying to find out why. The Thraks would be unable to broadcast information unless they used official channels. He had no control over that, but he knew Pepys. The emperor might have sold out, but he had no intention of going around bare-ass naked in front of the Thraks. Pepys would be manipulating the official channels. Jack nodded. "We may have to have guests, but nothing says we have to make them welcome."

Lassaday saluted smartly and said, "I didn't hear that, ser!"

"On your way, sergeant."

Lassaday brushed past Amber and Colin on the way down. Sensing trouble from the purpose in the Walker's stride, Jack left the observation railing and went into the privacy booth.

Colin followed him in, Amber on his heels. She gave Jack a worried look and sat down in the corner to watch for intruders.

"To what do I owe this visit? Rawlins let you in again?" There was no point in telling Colin he'd breached some heavy security. The man had eyes and he'd probably seen for himself. If he hadn't, there was little doubt in Jack's mind that Amber had pointed it out to him. She sat now, with a faintly guilty look on her face, and he wondered if she'd disliked compromising him. He hoped so.

Colin sat down, folding his brilliant blue robes about him. Today, his miners' jumpsuit was a faded charcoal. To Jack it brought the grayness of Lasertown to mind. He had not thought of Lasertown much—it was as if the months of shanghai and enforced servitude had been pushed out of memory—but K'rok had brought it all back as if it had been yesterday. The Thraks had invaded the dead moon mining colony to take over the norcite mining operation as well as a Walker dig site. What he, Colin, and K'rok had seen embedded in the dead moon's surface before its destruction by Thrakian agents defied description to this day. Colin stayed silent, watching Jack's eyes, as though sharing in the same memories. He waited respectfully for another moment before speaking.

"We have a history together, you and I."

Jack smiled. "You must have some problem to start dredging all that up."

Colin smiled too, a crooked expression that belied the age of a man edging past his prime. "It was a place to start."

"Why don't you start with what's bothering you?" Jack gazed out over the parade grounds. "My time here is short."

"What's going on? The base is locked down, and so is the city. I've been told by a few of my aides that the spaceport is all but impossible to get in or out of. Have we been beaten and nobody told us yet?"

Amber stirred. She put her chin up and pushed a wave of tawny blonde hair back off her shoulders. "He won't tell you. If he won't tell me, he won't tell you."

Jack wondered briefly why she hadn't used her psychic sensitivity to ferret out his secrets, but said to Colin, "No, but we might as well have been."

"I know some of it. I've been saying eulogies all week. The Knights took a beating. Almost half of them didn't come back."

Amber gasped. Jack looked at her. She hadn't known. He made a diffident gesture, not denying what Colin had said.

"What can you tell me?"

"You should be asking your old friend Pepys."

Colin snorted. "Pepys is as much an enemy as a friend. I had hoped never to say the same of you!"

"I can't tell you," Jack said, "officially." He made a movement that Amber understood. She got up and quickly checked the room's security screening. He waited until she was satisfied and sat back down.

"We didn't get beat in the war. We lost a battle, yes, badly, yes. But we didn't get beaten. We were sold out."

"What?"

Jack said bitterly, "It appears to be a trademark of

Pepys. At any rate, we'd hurt the Thraks badly enough that they came to him with a suggestion of an alliance."

"An alliance?"

"Against the unknown aggressor."

As Amber made a noise of triumph, Colin appeared to deflate and sagged back in his seat. He put both hands to his face briefly, an eternal gesture of grief. It was touchingly effective.

Then he lowered his hands. "I should have known." He got to his feet and began to pace about the privacy booth. "I should have known."

"How could you? I didn't begin piecing bits together until after it had been done." And Jack told them about the disastrous drop on Klaktuk, and ended with the Thrakian League triumvirate's appearance before the Dominion Congress.

Amber had gone ashen. Colin stopped pacing, his tired face alert, as if he dared the years to slow him now.

"I never thought Pepys had that kind of nerve."

"He may not have any choice. You said we had history together. Well, so do K'rok and I, at Lasertown."

"He took over the mines. He used the Milot berserker to keep you laborers in line." That was Amber, her voice high and unsteady.

"More than that. He was as intensely interested in the Walker dig site as the Thraks were. He told me that, in his years as an officer after Milos had been conquered, he'd come to the notion that the Sand Wars began because a bigger, nastier enemy than the Thraks was pushing them out of their traditional breeding grounds. That they swept through our worlds because they were running from an enemy they couldn't beat. He was convinced an artifact from that enemy might be found on the moon."

"We found nothing," Colin said, "but the body of a beast."

"Maybe. Maybe not. K'rok disappeared while the site was being destroyed. I don't know what else he might have found or where he might have gone. I thought he might have been destroyed, too. But the Thraks gave their enemy a name: the Ash-Farel."

"So K'rok was right."

"I think so. He's been made my subordinate officer. He'll be my second in charge of the Dominion Knights."

Colin scratched his chin reflectively. "Do you trust this Milot?"

"Not as far as I can throw him which, even wearing a suit, won't be far. Since the Thraks have allied with us, they expect us to operate on the basis of 'an enemy of my friend is my enemy also.' "

"Convenient," Amber muttered.

"More than convenient. The attitude is the whole purpose of the alliance, I think. That, and the deep infiltration of the Triad and Dominion systems which they could never achieve before. When the wraps come off this alliance in a week, Colin—you'll think we've been invaded successfully."

"That bad?"

"Worse."

"Then I've come to the right man." Colin straightened. "You remember the report I showed you."

"Vaguely."

"I've got Denaro there starting the basics of a dig. We discussed it, and we discussed my fears regarding the operation. If we've allied with the Thraks, Jack, they've given no indication of it on the outer rim. We've been harassed to the point of open strafing. I came to ask you to send an independent detachment to cover my people before I have a slaughter on my hands."

Jack felt pain in his expression. "If you'd asked me two weeks ago, I'd have had the authority. Now General Guthul is over me. I'd never get orders past him and Baadluster. How recent are your transmissions? Hostilities should have ceased."

"Oh, Jack." Amber sank down.

Colin shook his head. "I talked to Denaro last night. The Thraks are bold and nasty, according to him."

Jack spread his hands. "There's nothing I can do."

Amber got to her feet and went to the door. She paused at the portal and looked back over her shoulder. "The Jack Storm I knew wouldn't have let that stop him."

He looked at her. The scorn on her beautiful face pierced him. He felt it wrenching his gut somewhere just behind his navel. Hadn't he told himself a variation of that ever since he'd left the dais on Columbia, without even an attempt to kill either Tricatada or Guthul? He felt a spasm in his left eyelid.

"There's more to it than you know, Amber."

"I know *you*," she bit off. "And I know that if you have doubts over the Ash-Farel and the Thraks, that they're well-founded. I have never seen you hesitate to do the right thing, no matter how hard or difficult it was. *Until now*."

Colin put his hand on her elbow. "Amber, dear heart—"

She shook him off. "Don't dear heart me! I'm not your little street girl anymore! I'm a woman. I sleep with him and I love him and goddamn it, I can't even look him straight in the eye any more! So don't tell me what to do. *Tell him*." With a strangled sob, she bolted out the door of the privacy booth.

Colin looked at Jack with a stricken expression. "She didn't mean it."

Jack swallowed. It was difficult. He returned, "I think she did. And she's right. I don't have much time this afternoon because I'm waiting for a contingent of Thrakian warriors to come in. They'll be blended in with my Knights. I'm supposed to give them *armor*, for Chrissakes."

"I didn't know."

"No one does. I haven't even had the heart to tell the rest of my men yet. They died in droves on Klaktut. They saw things no one should ever have to see. And now I have to go and tell them that the enemy is now our ally." Jack broke off. His chest felt tight. He hadn't even worn his armor since they'd come back, unable to take the mental punishment Bogie had given him. Bogie felt that he'd surrendered on Columbia without even a fight.

But he'd told K'rok he wasn't finished. He just wasn't sure of the right time or place.

He looked at Colin and saw the Walker watching him. Watching him with a speechless pity etched on his handsome yet aged face. "Dammit, Colin, don't look at me like that!"

Colin shook his head. "Amber's right," he said, wonderingly, and made a move toward the door.

Jack said, "I could only send ten. And they'd have to leave tonight. No word, no warning."

Colin smiled. "I can pilot a corsair."

"What?"

He shrugged. "I'm a man of hidden talents."

Jack thought rapidly. A corsair was much faster than a needler—in and out of hyperspace—quicker because of its smallness. A thirty-man crew was its capacity. Ten or eleven of them, with armor and field packs, would equal that mass.

"And," Colin added smoothly, "I don't know about the alliance yet."

"No." Jack felt himself smiling in return. "You don't. It would be difficult for me to withhold troop protection from you without telling you my reasoning."

"And," the Walker added, "you could go along to make sure diplomacy doesn't get out of hand."

Jack nodded. "Find a corsair and it's a deal."

"Good." Colin opened the portal. Amber stood beyond. She grinned. "When are we leaving?"

CHAPTER 30

To give her credit, she didn't look surprised when Jack answered, "There's no 'we' about it. You're staying here. We're taking a corsair. There's room enough for me and Colin and seven Knights."

She brushed her hair back from her face and said nothing as Jack pressed a button, then bellowed, "Lassaday! Get up here!" and turned back to her. "No arguments?"

She looked to Colin. "Even a saint needs a bodyguard."

The older man smiled wearily. "Ah, my dear. You've done a better job protecting this old husk in the past than I have—but I bow to Jack's decision. This is one trip it won't be easy getting back from."

"Since when has that ever stopped me?"

"Since now." Jack's eyes darkened and she stilled her tongue, knowing when she'd gone far enough with him.

Lassaday came panting onto the bridge. "Yes, sir?"

"What's the last word on our new recruits?"

"Th' bugs, ser, are in quarantine now. They'll be waitin' for pickup just after darkfall."

Colin said, "I'll go get ready."

Lassaday let him pass and looked at his commander with a quizzical expression.

"Can you get along without me for a few weeks?"

"With that stinking bear of a humanoid and those bugs?" Lassaday made a face as Jack looked at him, then said, "If I have to."

"Good. I need seven volunteers, a suicide mission, seasoned only—and men who can keep their mouths shut. And no one, such as yourself, vital to keeping a chain of command here at the center." Which, Jack reflected sadly, left out Lassaday, Travellini, and Rawlins.

"I'd give my right nut to go with you," Lassaday returned. He sighed. "When d'you want them?"

"We leave at dusk."

The sergeant crossed his bulky arms over his chest. "What's up, commander?"

"Our renegade Walker saint is about to embark on a mission which will seriously jeopardize our new alliance with the Thrakian League. Since I cannot reveal the treaty to him at this time, I have no choice but to accompany him in hopes of settling whatever grievances may occur without serious diplomatic breaches."

"Ah." Lassaday smiled widely. "I sincerely hope you get a chance to kick ass, ser."

"Me, too, Lassaday, me, too."

Jack looked the ground shuttle over. Colin sat next to him, muffled in a work jumper that neatly hid his Walker robes, which he had politely declined to remove in favor of being inconspicuous. Now, dressed as a port traffic director, he was in danger of being drafted to dock vehicles, but at least he was somewhat disguised.

The ground shuttle vibrated as seven Knights in full armor got aboard. Jack checked them out.

"Aaron."

"Sir!" His voice betrayed the tension his young face hid.

"Garner." No surprise there, the grizzled streetwise veteran hardly missed a chance to follow Jack into the tough spots. "Feeling fit?"

"Guaranteed, sir."

"Tinsdale."

"Sir."

"I asked for experienced men."

"I was a mercenary, sir. One of the few you missed when you took out General Gilgenbush's fortress satellite a few years back."

Surprise flooded Jack. Those were survival days when it was just him and Amber against the system. "Is this a grudge, cadet?"

"No, sir. I hate Thraks damn near as much as you do."

Jack had to live with his qualms. If Lassaday had singled out the man, Jack had to trust the sergeant.

"Maussaud."

"Sir."

No problem there. He'd gone to Bythia and back with Jack.

A lean Knight in deep blue armor sat. Jack didn't recognize the battle suit. He pointed. "Sound off, cadet."

"Skyler, sir." The voice was a trifle hollow.

"Experienced?"

"Lassaday sent me, sir."

Jack fought a smile. "All right then." He saw two gray suits move into the other bank of seats on the shuttle.

"Rodriguez, sir."

"And Patma."

Jack nodded to Colin. "There's our lucky seven."

The prelate returned a shaky smile. "Let's hope so."

And me you get as a bonus, Bogie remarked.

Jack looked down the back of the ground shuttle. "We're stealing a corsair. We're going in under the pretense of taking out the twenty-four Thrakian recruits who've been sent to us under the new alliance exchange program. That will get us in past security. What will get us out is keeping your cool and following my lead. Colin is unarmored. Protect him at all costs if any trouble breaks out. But I don't want any heroes. Understood?"

The affirmatives echoed. Jack put his helmet on. He sat down to drive.

WP security took a long look at Jack. Finally, he removed his helmet to look the man in the eye. The sentry was framed by needlers and corsairs at his back. Jack sorely wanted to walk over him and be on his way. "I was told quarantine was lifted."

The man shifted unhappily. "Yes, sir. You understand, commander, I have to be careful."

"I understand that you're holding us up. You've got the port screwed down and locked tight, but the longer you hold those Thraks bottled up here, the more risk you run that someone's going to see them. I got the impression we've been trying to avoid that." Jack leaned on what he knew of World Police procedure.

Unhappiness etched deep into the WP man's face. "You got that right, Commander Storm. And that one ton Milot is eating us out of the cafeteria. All right. Berth 41."

Jack eased back into the driver's seat and pulled the shuttle around the security post.

He waited until he was out of earshot before muttering, "Good. Berth 41 is out in no man's land."

Colin was scanning the printout Jonathan had given to him before leaving.

Jack looked over at it. "Where in the hell did he get that?"

The reverend looked up. "I don't think hell had a thing to do with it. I don't know where Jonathan gets things like this. I just know he does." Colin tapped a plastisheet. "There's a corsair being reoutfitted in Berth 17. It's the best bet of five listed here. It's supposed to lift midday tomorrow."

"That means the crew is still out enjoying the sins and virtues of Malthen tonight. Sounds good." Jack checked the overhead map and steered toward Berth 17.

As he pulled toward the cradle where the slim silver form rested, a hairy black object lumbered in front of the shuttle. Jack hit the brakes, throwing Colin forward against the dash. His helmet went rolling on to the asphalt, and the form bent to retrieve it.

"Jack, my commander. I be thinking you'd never get here in time for dinner." K'rok grinned at them over the dash. Behind him, in the distance, a contingent of WP trotted, weapons up.

"Shit." Jack helped Colin up. "Make a run for it. They're after K'rok, but they'll stop anyone who looks suspicious. Garner, the rest of you, let's go!"

The Milot paused. The whites of his eyes showed. "What be this?"

Jack took his helmet. He looked at his old foe and friend. "I don't think it would help you to know. We talked once, on Lasertown. I have the same doubts you do."

But K'rok nodded. "You are leaving?"

"I'm on escort duty, but I didn't have time to ask Guthul's permission."

"Nor did you intend to." The ursine form sighed heavily. "We have secrets, you and I. I have lived long under the Thraks. I have never been liking it."

Jack slapped K'rok's shoulder. "You run the Knights for me until I get back."

"I will. I be running a little interference for the Thraks, too." K'rok stepped back. He saluted.

But Jack was looking over the Milot's shoulder at the wing of WP guards which was now on the run. He slammed the Milot over even as laser fire pinged the ground shuttle's hood. K'rok hit the ground with a heavy thud and had the sense to lie still.

Jack put his helmet on as he ran.

Patma went down just outside the main lock. Jack vaulted his still form. He could see from the damage that he'd lost a man already. Even as he dove through the main lock, the corsair shuddered.

Colin was powering up for launch. The lock closed on his heels as two of his men grabbed him and pulled him into the main corridor.

The irrevocable had begun. Ten days in hypnosleep, and then they would see what Colin's new world had to offer them.

The corsair slipped out of hyperspace and Colin sat back with a heavy sigh. "So far, so good."

"What are we looking for?"

"Denaro's got coords pretty well set up. The norcite deposits are in the mountainous area I indicated to you earlier. And locals had superstitions about the regions."

"Locals?"

"Yes. None left. Colinada is a plague planet."

Jack sat down, feeling none too sharp after days of hypnosleep. "Colinada?"

"Denaro wanted to name it for me. I insisted it be feminine. A planet is a lot like a woman, I think. They all have hidden beauty and dangerous wiles."

There was a sharp movement in the cabin behind them where three of the Knights were up and about.

"What's this about a plague?"

"The locals were wiped out about forty years ago. The Dominion sent in their best anthropologists and xenobiologists, but the predominant mammals couldn't be saved. It's been quarantined ever since."

"And it was your bright idea to break the quarantine."

Colin rubbed the back of his neck before answering, "Actually, no. We became interested in it after the Thraks did. A few years after their survey, we made one of our own. Plague or not, after Lasertown and Bythia, I could hardly ignore it."

"Right." Jack slumped lower in the copilot's seat. A red panel went on. "Looks like I'd better get back in armor. And I want you in a deepsuit."

"When the time comes, I'll be ready."

Jack felt Colin's gaze as he left the control cabin. He barely had the suit sealed when he felt the first blow. The corsair rocked. Jack screwed his helmet on and ran forward.

Colin was getting hastily into a deepsuit. The instrument panel blinked, and Jack could see blips coming across a target grid.

"Shit."

"Amen," said Colin. "We're going to have trouble getting in."

Jack looked over the screens. "Not if you're any good at sewing."

"What?" The Walker stared at him in astonishment.

Jack tapped the target grid. "It's called 'Threading the Needle.' If you can do it, you'll get us past the Thraks."

Colin did a double take, then sat down. His hands shook slightly as he reached out for the controls, taking the corsair off automatic pilot. "This is a young man's game," he muttered. Jack stood behind him and finished sealing up the vacuum suit.

"You asked to be a player."

"So I did, heaven help me. Buckle down back there. This is going to be a little rough."

Colin was not normally given to understatement, but the corsair bucked and twisted. Jack swore and reached out to steady himself as the slender vehicle attempted to outrun and outmaneuver the immense Thrakian mother ships riding herd over Colinada's orbital approaches. He was uncertain whether the old mercenary offensive pattern would work . . . but it was better than no chance at all.

There was a high-pitched scream of metal and the ship shuddered violently. Colin thrust out, "Sweet Jesus, we've punched through!"

Jack twisted around.

"Damage?"

"In the tail section."

"Anybody back there?"

It was Garner's shaken voice that answered, "Not now. And the bulkhead's sealed off."

The five remaining Knights fell silent.

"Who'd we lose?"

"Tinsdale, sir."

Jack took a deep breath. An uneasiness lifted from his shoulders. He never wanted to lose a man, but he had not wanted to trust the ex-mercenary. "All right," he said.

The blue Knight got unsteadily to his feet, made his way across the corridor, and disappeared inside the toilet. A sound of retching followed his retreat.

The flight of the corsair smoothed considerably. Colin inhaled deeply. "I'm picking up Denaro's homing signal."

"Good. They're on our tail, reverend."

"What?"

Jack shook his head. "You didn't think it would be that easy, did you? And these are Talons. Keep it on manual and you can outrun them."

Colin mopped his forehead with the back of one hand, muttering, "And I thought I had faith."

Jack laughed. It was punctuated by an explosion and he had just enough time to grab his helmet.

CHAPTER 31

"All right, get your chutes on. We're going to take this just like a drop." Jack braced himself in the cockpit hatchway as the corsair shivered again.

Garner and Aaron had hold of Skyler's limp form between them as they dragged him into the corridor. Jack sized up the situation and decided they had it well in hand. Skyler's blue gauntlets twitched as he became semiconscious. "But, commander, this is—"

"No time to argue. We're breaking up. Get going!" Jack grabbed the two of them and steered them toward the belly of the hold.

Maussaud and Rodriguez needed no urging and fled past him. He reached out and stopped Colin in the passageway. "Where the hell do you think you're going? Get a chute on, you're dropping with us."

Colin smiled secretively. "We have some baggage on board we might want to take with us." He turned and trotted toward the forward hold.

This was no time to be touring the corsair, but Jack followed him. He stopped in the portal as a familiar sight met his eyes. "Holy shit. These fellas were gunrunners."

The Walker patted the casing of a mobile laser cannon. "Do you think you could hold onto one of these?"

Jack threw a chute at him. "You go first. I'll follow." He bent and hefted the equipment. When the Talons came at them, he would have something slightly more effective than stones to throw at them. He caught up with the prelate. "Do you think Jonathan knew about this?"

Colin's voice was muffled as he stepped into the cargo hold, where Garner had opened up the bay doors. They were already so deep into the stratosphere that the ground below could be seen breaking through the cloud cover. "I wouldn't be surprised," he replied.

Garner and Aaron still held the unconscious blue Knight between them. "Commander, I think you should know—"

"Can you manage his chute between you?"

The two veterans nodded. Distracted, Garner looked up and sputtered, "What th' hell have you got there?"

Jack grinned. "Firepower. Altitude?"

Rodriguez was nearest the gauge. "Twenty thousand and dropping."

"How close?"

"Ten thousand should bring us closest to our original target area."

Aaron made a funny sound. Then he said, "How are we going to get off dirtside?"

"The Walkers have facilities here. They're just having a little trouble with the Thraks."

"Eighteen thousand."

The wind whistled into the open bay as the corsair plunged downward. Jack's armor grew cold. Bogie complained.

"There!" Colin pointed. An orange flare pierced the horizon. "Denaro's responding to my transmission."

"Fifteen thousand."

"Shit!" Garner broke in. His gauntlet pointed. Jack could see a brace of Talons outpacing them on each flank. Any man chuting down would be an easy target.

Jack put the laser cannon down. He reached into his equipment belt and pulled out a grenade. He keyed the firing sequence.

"Ten thousand."

"Go, go, go! I'll keep them busy."

Colin shuddered as Rodriguez and Maussaud pulled him out of the bay, their armor and his deepsuit arrowing into the high winds. Then Garner and Aaron went, dragging Skyler between them, who showed groggy signs of coming around.

Jack felt the chill inside the armor bite into his grin.

He tossed the grenade into the back of the hold, picked up the cannon, and jumped.

The corsair exploded into a fiery ball behind him, taking one Talon with it and sending the other into an out of control plunge. Jack wasted precious seconds freefalling to watch it go. Then, one-handed, he was very busy popping his chute and guiding it after the others. Much heavier than the others, he dropped like a rock. He was the first to see the third Talon sweeping in after them even as they approached the dissipating orange smoke of the flares. The Talon curled around them, and he could see the shots that took out Aaron and made Garner dance in the air like a broken puppet.

The warplane rolled in midair and swept around for a second run.

The ground came up fast. Jack braced himself and hit it running. He ripped off his chute so the ground winds couldn't carry him over. The rest of the chutes came tumbling down.

Rodriguez hit a cliff.

Then there was only Maussaud and Skyler ripping off their chutes and helping St. Colin to his feet. Jack felt his throat squeeze shut for a split second. Then he hefted the cannon and broke into a run to meet them.

Skyler's helmet had popped off and lay on the ground. The Knight hadn't bothered to replace it yet, too busy untangling Colin from his chute. The Walker's complexion had grayed, but he kept insisting, "I'm all right. I'm all right."

Amber didn't stop fussing over him until she had the chute off and could pat down the deepsuit for herself. The fierce ground wind of Colinada ripped at her long tawny hair, so Jack could not see the expression on her face as she turned when he joined them. The whine of the approaching ATV overrode his first words.

He didn't repeat them, but, instead, reached out and grabbed her in a fierce hug. She mumbled, "Garner and Aaron tried to tell you. I knocked myself out in the john. They must've put my helmet back on and dragged me to the bay. Shit, Jack. They didn't have a chance."

He curled his gauntlet and traced a gouge along her blue Flexalinked shoulder. "You didn't have much more of one." He swung on Colin. "Did you know about this?"

The prelate was hanging his helmet on his equipment belt. He looked up. "Cross my heart, I didn't," he said. With a devilish grin, he added, "I wouldn't be surprised if Jonathan did, though."

The ATV braked to a screeching halt in a hail of dust

and gravel. Denaro stood up in full armor, broadcasting, "Here they come again!"

Jack panned the sky. He could hear the high-pitched whine of a Talon descending rapidly.

"Let's go!"

They hung onto the ATV wherever they could fit as Denaro ground the gears and put it back into motion. Colin said mildly, as they bucked across the wilderness, "How do you keep going?"

"We've gone underground. They strafe us daily, but we've got a fix on the site, your eminence. We may never get out of here, but we're going to see what it is they don't want us to."

"What about your ship?"

"Intact. But with them guarding the windows, it would be a suicide run to try to leave, sir."

Jack ground his teeth against a hard jolt, then said, "We'll have to see what we can do about that."

"What?"

He looked at Amber. "Lure the Talons in, damage them, then the mother ship will get mad enough to come close. I ought to be able to singe her a little with our contraband friend here."

Denaro looked back to see the cannon, then wrenched the wheel, narrowly avoiding a rather solid looking tree. Its lower branches whipped about the battle suits. Sparse forest gave way to outcropping, and Jack could see the sod-roofed underground installation. The ATV skidded to a halt.

Denaro reached for the cannon. "I'll take that."

In the flush of sunlight, Jack reached for the cannon, and Bogie stopped him.

Let him have it. The sentience wrapped around him, quelling the movements of his gauntlets.

Denaro looked at him, then took the cannon gently. "I'll get you the homing beacon."

Tell him it won't be necessary.

Jack could feel Bogie swelling along his shoulders. "What is it?"

It calls to me, boss. This is one of the memories I've been dreaming of. I know where it is.

The site on Lasertown had had its siren song, too, pulling unwary miners to their death trying to answer it. Jack hesitated.

Amber looked at them. "What is it?"

"Mutiny, I think." Jack swallowed. "Denaro, give me your armor."

"You can't ask him to make a stand without a suit!"

But the Walker militant was already stripping. He stepped out of the dark armor proudly, clad only in his trousers, and Jack was reminded of those moments on Harkness' freighter and of the young man who'd been undefeated even in that time of retreat.

Jack climbed out of his white armor. He sealed it back up and screwed the helmet on. "It's all yours, Bogie."

Maussaud scrambled back in shocked silence as the battle armor animated. Colin watched, his expression masked by the deepsuit helmet, as Jack's armor began to move. Its contortions were herky-jerky for a moment, then the suit walked off ten paces. It beckoned.

"God's balls," Denaro said, then flushed. "What have you got there?"

His elder pointedly ignored him. His helmet swung toward Jack. "Sentient computer run?"

"Not exactly. If we get through this, I'll try to explain it to you. Just take it that we need all the firepower we can get, and he's a big boy now." Jack stepped into Denaro's suit, the only armor big enough to accommodate him.

Amber unscrewed her helmet and popped out a small circuit board. "Synthesizer," she said as she palmed it. "So you wouldn't recognize my voice." She went to the opalescent battle suit, took off the helmet and installed the card. She talked for a few minutes and Jack wondered if she was explaining to Bogie how to utilize the circuitry. She screwed the helmet back and stepped away.

"Follow me," said Bogie within the armor. His voice was not the deep, grating voice Jack knew, but basso profundo, melodious—and joyful.

The Talon swooped over them.

"Get out of here," Denaro yelled, and dragged the cannon into position by the outcropping that hid the Walker installation. Maussaud hesitated, then said, "I'm staying here, commander."

Jack nodded. "All right."

They ran after Bogie.

* * *

It was like running after a child who'd just begun to walk. As they approached the hills, Bogie gained ability. He stopped only once, to spread his gauntlets as if drawing down the sun's rays to him.

"What's he doing?" Amber asked, her voice breathy as she tried to catch her breath.

"Refueling, I think."

Colin said nothing, but went to one knee, with his head bowed. Jack could hear him gasping over the com lines.

"This is no time to pray," Amber said, and tried to help him up.

The older man shook his head. "You've got power suits. I've got nothing. Forgive me, Amber, but I'm still an old man."

She looked at him in shock, then began to strip the vacuum suit off.

"What're you doing?"

She met Jack's stare. "It's no protection to him now! It's just weighing him down. And this way, we won't have to carry him as soon."

There were dull explosions in the background. As Jack pivoted, he saw the golden lance of the laser cannon's reply. The Talon veered off sharply.

Colin coughed. "It had better be worth it."

They looked over the horizon. They'd come up a steep incline of shale, and now looked out over a meadow lush with spring grasses and tiny yellow flowers. Bogie began to stagger down the slope, heading toward the mountain facing on the valley's far side.

"I'm here!" he cried out.

Jack reached for Colin's elbow and Amber took the other side as the air thundered over them. The three of them looked up. The Thraks were determined that this discovery not be made. If Denaro failed to hold the enemy, all of them would die here in this valley. They ran as the white armor ahead of them fetched up against a wind and rain exposed cliff, with eons of time written in its stratas.

Bogie scrabbled away at the sod and rock until he found a fissure, then tore at it with his gauntlets. The cliff face peeled away as though it had been chiseled to do so, in one slab which went to dust and pebbles at the battle armor's feet.

Amber caught her breath, but it was Colin who murmured, "Good God Almighty."

The white armor froze for a moment, its glove curved over the monstrosity exposed by the soft ground.

"What is it?"

"It's what we saw on Lasertown," Jack told Amber. "At the digging site, before it was destroyed."

Bogie's curved gauntlet fell downward in a gentle caress over the mummified being. A sound came over the suit mikes, a sound Jack had no other word for but *wail*, yet it was short and smothered.

"It called to him," Colin said. "Just like the dig site at Lasertown called to so many unfortunates. Even after death. Even these hundreds, maybe thousands of years later." He turned to look at Jack. "What is that inside your armor?"

"A gift from Milos."

A hissing intake of breath. "Berserker?"

"No . . . I don't know. I don't think so, but whatever it is, it's regenerating itself from a square of hide, a chamois, inside my armor. It's a small bit of flesh, but it thinks—and cares."

"And interacts with your circuitry."

"That, too."

"Alive," Colin murmured. "And aware, and called." After a slight hesitation, he moved forward to touch the mummified creature himself. Bogie's gauntlet went out as though to stop him, and then fell back.

It was saurian. No doubt of that . . . the skin retained its scaly pattern even through its crust of age and dirt. It looked upward, as though destruction had rained from the sky, catching it unawares. The head was broad, the eyes like a horse's . . . no sight directly to the front or rear, but well-set for vision otherwise. The teeth, bared in a death grimace, were sharp at the corners but well rounded otherwise. Colin touched them.

"Not carnivorous, at least, not strictly. These are for grinding, not tearing. Look at the hands."

For hands they were, not paws or toes, fully exposed as the find reared up.

"Bipedal?" Jack said and moved forward, as drawn by

the beast as Bogie and Colin were. Amber stayed on point, watching the scene over one shoulder.

"It looks as if he was. And look at this." Colin reached for something wedged in the dirt, something held in the hand on the far side. It came loose easily from the beast's fingers.

"It's a nonbiodegradable polymer satchel."

Amber made a faint noise. Jack grinned. "It's a plastic bag," he told her.

She mouthed an indistinguishable curse.

Colin held it in his hands for a moment. Jack saw that they trembled. He looked up at Jack.

"Should I open it?"

"And have what's inside disintegrate when the air hits it?"

"Maybe. Maybe not." The Walker looked out over the hills, toward the reddening sky. "We may never get away from here to open it under better conditions."

Amber muttered, "Just seeing it may have to be good enough for you. Jack, I'm picking up blips on the long-range target."

"ID?"

"Not yet. We're out here in the open."

Bogie mobilized then. With movements almost too swift to follow, gauntlet fingers chiseled out the body and he lifted the fragile remains in his arms. "Boss, let's get out of here."

"You can't take that with you!"

"I feel him in my mindsong. I was meant to come here, to find him, to bring him . . . home. Jack—" and Bogie held out his arms, pleading.

The mummified form seemed to shift in the cradle of Flexalink sleeves. Jack sensed it and lunged forward too late. The mummy began to cave in upon itself, dust unto dust, ashes unto ashes, and rained through Bogie's helpless fingers as the sentience cried.

He did not stop until the mummy had finished disintegrating and was nothing more than particles upon the ground. Bogie stood still, his arms outstretched toward Jack.

"I'm sorry, Bogie. The exposure . . . it wasn't meant to be."

Amber said, *"Jack."*

Bogie turned his gauntlets over, emptying dust from his palms.

Then Jack added, "Your helmet cameras recorded the find. We'll have pictures, at least."

Then Bogie spoke, from the hollowness of the armor he inhabited. "At least," he echoed. He looked up. "Amber is right. We've been targeted."

Jack felt the rumbling then, a deep subsound that prickled the hairs on the back of his neck. A rumbling like the one that had awakened him in the middle of the night when warships firestormed Claron. Or the rumbling a soldier hears just before a drop of enemy troops. By the time the sound became fully audible, it would be too late.

"Shit."

He grabbed Colin by the elbow. "It's time to think about getting out of here."

Amber loped by them, her armor glinting in the first blue rays of sunset. "Past time," she muttered.

Bogie shadowed Jack. "Boss, I'm getting three blips. Two gunboats and a third, much larger ship."

The broken terrain made any speed difficult. He kept a hand out to Colin's elbow as the older man stumbled now and then, and a too bright flush pinked the prelate's face. His thin fringe of chestnut and gray hair ruffled in the wind, and he puffed a little as he endeavored to keep up with Jack. But the Walker kept a death grip on his plastic bag.

He could hear the sky's envelope giving way to the gunships that were streaking in. Colin staggered to a slow jog.

"Don't stop now."

"How far?"

"Far enough." Jack looked over the hillocks. He said to Bogie, "Which ones are going to reach us first?"

"The third ship, at this rate."

He stooped and looked up. "Then I think we're going to be okay." He pointed as the Ash-Farel swept over and the Talons disintegrated in its wake. His shout of welcome was swallowed by the thunder of its passage. He frowned then.

"How did you know?" Amber breathed

"I didn't," Jack answered her. "And I've changed my mind. We may not live to tell the tale."

CHAPTER 32

He thumped Colin on the shoulder and grabbed Amber by the elbow. "Run for it. We need to get as far underground as possible."

"What is it?"

He took off his helmet and hung it from his equipment belt. Denaro's armor fit him well, but he didn't wish to meet Colin's gaze through the sunscreen darkened visor. "Curse me for a farming boy—Amber's right. I'm too thickheaded to play these games. We're just part of the bait in a trap."

Overhead, thunder rumbled, but the sky did not smell of rain. Soon, it would stink of battle. The three of them, tailed by a shambling Bogie, began to walk out of the valley.

"I don't understand," Colin said, between gulps of air.

Jack shook his head. Sweat had been trickling down his brow and now drops flew into the air. "I wondered why the Thraks kept you pinned down here instead of just blasting you off dirtside. This is a plague planet, after all—not too many people would even know you'd been here." He took Colin's elbow to ease the older man's efforts. "They were waiting to see who would show up."

"They wanted you."

Jack smiled wryly at Amber. "No . . . in fact, they're probably disappointed I came in so quietly. I'm willing to bet they figured I'd come in force, warmonger that I am."

They paused on the crest boundary to the valley.

"What they wanted was a tremendous battle—what they wanted was to attract someone's notice."

"Whose?"

Jack pointed overhead as thunder drummed. "The Ash-Farel." A lightning strike obscured his next sentence, but it was not a natural phenomenon. With a curse, Jack grabbed both Colin and Amber and threw them down, protecting them with his body. He was aware of Bogie joining him, and then the heavens split open.

Afterward, he would curse himself for not leaving his helmet on—but his deafness was matched by Colin's as they shouted back and forth and tried to explain. Then, all he knew was that the sky went white-hot, and the air burst as the ships came streaking in over them.

It had been a trap, and a well-laid one. The golden ship of the Ash-Farel had little chance as the Thraks streaked in and crippled it. They harried it across the horizon and Jack watched sadly as the ships disappeared. The Thraks would not even give the Ash-Farel a mercy stroke.

Tears from the brilliance of the fight streaked Colin's dirty face as he lifted his chin to peer after them.

"Why," he said. "Why don't they finish them off?"

"They want it down," Jack said. "They want it down and cracked open like an egg."

"Why?"

Jack looked toward Amber. "The Thraks want to know what it is they're fighting. They're taking prisoners and gutting that ship for all the technology they can get their claws on."

"But—" her tawny hair swung about as she looked back in puzzlement. Bogie crawled back and lifted her to her feet.

"I think we'd better hurry," Jack said, his voice gone hoarse. "They bought us a little time. Let's hope it's enough." He sacrificed further explanations for speed as he called ahead. And when they got there Denaro had the dig corsair waiting in a launch silo.

The Walker holding of Farseeing was comfortable and homespun. They were welcomed as honored guests and soon forgotten in the fervor that surrounded Colin's presence. Amber found Jack quartered in the men's wing, packing to leave on the second day after their arrival.

"Rumor has it the Thraks have extended an apology to St. Colin for their grievous actions." She dropped down on his cot. "I still don't understand. The Thraks are our allies now, but you acted as if you thought the Ash-Farel were there to help us."

"Perhaps they were."

"But they've attacked Dominion colonies, too."

"I think they're attacking war efforts, whosoever they belong to."

She tilted her head. "Maybe. And so the Thraks found the norcite dig—"

"A site which has been known to attract Ash-Farel attention before—"

"And created a disturbance big enough to bring a warship in—"

"And sprang their trap. We, of course, got an apology. The Thraks are our allies, after all, and had no intention of harming us. We merely . . . got in the way while they were repulsing the enemy."

"They must have had this planned even before the treaty."

Jack nodded. "Having an alliance just made them do an extra little dance to explain themselves."

She shrugged. "And speaking of explanations, how do you plan to explain that?" Amber said, nodding her chin toward the fully animated Bogie.

"I don't."

She tossed her head, sending her tawny hair in ripples over her shoulders and down her back. She was dressed in borrowed clothing, the modest blouse and long, full skirt of the Walker women. The colors of the Blue Wheel sect suited her. "Come on, Jack. You can't just explain away fully automated, fully powered battle armor. Robots we've got, but sentient computer-grounded war machines, no. They've been banned. And you can't tell anyone the armor's inhabited. The xenobiologists will go crazy trying to dig him out, like he's some kind of oyster."

Jack raised an eyebrow and her torrent of words came to an abrupt halt as she realized why she had caught him packing. "Oh, no," she said. "Oh, no—not without me this time. You're not leaving me again!"

He grabbed her shoulders. "I have to, Amber. Where I'm going, you won't be able to follow. I can't take you and I don't want to have to worry about you."

Fear muddied her golden-brown eyes. "What are you going to do?"

"I'm going to desert. I'll be taking my suit and Bogie with me."

She went limp between his hands and only his strength kept her upright. He held her as though his very life depended on it. "You have to go back. You have to watch Pepys and Baadluster for me. And I have to go."

Baadluster scared her. "But why?"

"I think we're fighting the wrong enemy. And I have to know if I'm right, and if I am, I have to be able to bring back proof."

Bogie added, "And I must follow my mindsong." The synthesizer gave depth and sorrow to his basso voice.

Amber straightened. "What about Colin? He's never been more at risk."

"I know. And that's another reason I'm leaving you behind." He loosened his grip on her and ran the knuckle of his index finger along her jaw. "You'll have to fight the part of the war I can't."

She tilted her chin up as though it would stop the flow of tears brimming in her eyes. Baadluster would hound her, perhaps even imprison her, but she couldn't let Jack know. She would not be responsible for stopping him.

"I'll try," she answered, her voice barely above a whisper. "Where are you going?"

"That I don't know yet. It's better if you don't know, anyway."

She nodded. The tears splashed down in spite of her efforts. She raised a hand to dash them away. "Dammit. I've become a regular shower since I met you!"

He lifted her chin back to its customary insolent tilt. "No," he said softly. "You've become a beautiful woman."

A shiver ran through her, but she lifted her face away from his touch and glared at the white suit behind him. "You!" she called. "If you let anything happen to him, I'll rip you out of there and throw you in the deep freeze!"

Bogie just laughed, a deep rumbling sound. "Yes, ma'am," he said and saluted.

"How will I know how you are? How will you contact me?"

Jack looked at her. "That's up to you. You've kept your

power shuttered ever since Bythia . . . but it's the only way we'll be able to keep in touch. You're going to have to reach out for me and hope you find me."

"Telepathically? Not over those distances." Her tremors reached her throat and spasmed her muscles, threatening to shut away all sound. Hussiah had not only taken away her ability to kill, he'd taken away her ability to reach out to Jack. "I can't—" Her voice failed her, as she'd feared.

He saw the doubt in her eyes. "Then you'll have to trust me, Amber. You'll have to trust me that no matter where I am or what happens to me, I'll come back to you."

She denied him, shaking her head.

He nodded then, and reached out, pulling her roughly to his chest where she could hear the thumping of his heart. "We have to believe it," he promised. "I'm going to fight this war and I'm going to win, and then I'm going to come back to you for good. Nothing is going to stop me. Nothing."

RETURN FIRE

To Donald A. Wollheim,
the man who made science fiction possible. . . .

PROLOGUE

Pepys, emperor of solar systems, sat in his communications web like a bloat-bellied spider, his frizzy red hair alive about a face furrowed in concentration and worry. His fingers twitched as his mind communed, but he found nothing he wanted in the data he combed.

He broke silence with a furious yell that echoed throughout the obsidite rose-pink hallways until his minister heard him and came running, security cameras panning every flap of his somber black robes as he answered the call.

Pepys was unplugging from his computer network when Baadluster gained the chamber. The emperor looked up, his pale, freckled complexion drawn in anger over the skeletal bones of his face. Vandover paused, thinking to himself that, underneath the anger, Pepys did not look well. An unwell emperor boded ill for the Triad Throne as well as for the Dominion, for Pepys was the war leader and main creditor of the armed forces. He was a brilliant man, but he had always reminded Baadluster of a small star shining brightly just before it went nova. The ambitious side of Baadluster found the realization enlightening. He produced a smile.

"Can I help you, your majesty?"

Pepys pushed himself out of the chair holding his frail looking body. "Find him."

Baadluster lost his smile. Pepys' battle with the commander of the Dominion Knights was a war that had already drawn in and destroyed one ambitious successor to the throne. Baadluster might be found out and defeated, but he had no intention of fighting a losing battle not his own. He said cautiously, "Commander Storm was reported lost in the skirmish on Colinada. Although I give the

Thrakian report as little credence as you do, your majesty, it appears the information is correct."

"And Saint Colin walked out of there unscathed while the best soldier in battle armor was blasted into ashes?" Pepys gave a snort of disgust.

"Then ask the Walker what happened. As a religious man, he should be predisposed toward lying."

"I have. He confirms the Thrakian story." Pepys shrugged into an over robe, its threads woven into a nearly impervious fabric. Its weight did not seem to tax the emperor's slight shoulders. The red-haired emperor had a wiry strength often overlooked. Pepys looked up, cat-green eyes glittering. "Jack is an idealist. I lost his trust when I made an alliance with the Thrakian League. In his eyes, we've sold out to our worst enemy. He understands diplomacy about as well as you understand the emotion of love. If you can't find him, find the girl. She'll find him."

"I know the whore has returned to Malthen. More than that—she doesn't carry an ID chip. She can go anywhere without being recorded." Baadluster shrugged. "He'll know she's being sought. He'll find another whore."

Pepys paused in the doorway of the chamber. He looked back, lips thinning. "Your assessment of Amber's relationship with Storm proves me out. The lady may be many things, but not a whore. I want Jack Storm found."

"Then just what do you suggest I do? I'm a Minister of War, not head of the World Police." The ambitious man who had lost his life trying to nail Commander Storm had been head of the security network. Baadluster had wasted no time in tapping into Winton's position, but it had all been unofficial. He spread his hands, large, flat appendages, in the air. "The Ash-farel keep me busy."

Scorn smoldered color back into the emperor's pale face. "Try the Green Shirts. He may have gone looking for the underground." Pepys drew up a corner of his robe, wrapped it nervously about one freckled hand, and smoothed it there. "He says he has full knowledge of who and what he was twenty-five years ago, but I doubt him. He's exhausted his options here—he'll have to go to them for answers."

Baadluster inclined his head, thick lips pursed in a noncommittal expression.

"And Vandover."

The minister looked up from the delicate, threadlike cable he had begun to roll up and put away. "Your majesty?"

"Spread the word that Storm is on an infiltration mission. If he reaches the Green Shirts, they won't trust him either."

"Yes, your majesty."

"I want him dead. If we can't find him and do it, perhaps they will."

Baadluster straightened. "Pepys—there appear to be two invincible forces operating in our space. The first is the Ash-farel, who are dangerous enough that they drove us to ally with the Thraks, and the second is Jack Storm. I respectfully remind you that opposing Commander Storm may not be wise. You've tried to take him out before. This time, he may feel free to return fire."

Fury filled the emperor to the point where he seemed to gain height. But he said nothing, turned heel, and left.

Baadluster found he'd been holding his breath. He looked at the fine cables draped over his fingers and dropped them on the communication chamber floor. Let the janitors clean up Pepys' messes. He followed after his emperor.

CHAPTER 1

Colin bowed his head and bent his shoulders. A dank wind blew thinning strands of hair across his brow, but it was not the element he cut his way against as he crossed the parking grounds toward home. Before he lifted his eyes to meet theirs, he could hear the clack of chiton and carapaces as Thraks shifted into a guard position, meeting him at his own door as though he were the enemy and not they. He met them squarely, the trio who had replaced his own long time bodyguard at the gated entrance to Walker headquarters, his rugged cross thumping upon his chest at his abrupt halt. He smoothed it down, aware the faceted eyes of the aliens accosting him watched every movement keenly, their expressions hidden behind kabuki masks of beetle armor.

The self-made minister to thousands swallowed a bitter taste in his mouth, reminding himself that they were no longer enemies, but allies. He no more believed it than he believed the lies of his long time friend Emperor Pepys, author of this misalliance.

"Identify yourself," said the Thraks to the fore. Dark sable throat leather bulged with his implant.

Colin sighed. "Colin of the Blue Wheel," he said, disliking the way his voice sounded the moment the words were out. Old. Weak. Dispirited. He clenched his hand deep in the vest pocket of his overrobe. Had he traded all he'd once valued just to coexist?

The Thraks reached forward spindly fingers, crab claws with agility, bowing over him from its superior height. "Pass," it said.

The Walker saint thrust his jaw forward and moved between them forcibly though they had stepped aside to let him around them. With the clicking sounds of their alien flesh, they jostled each other to let him through, as averse to touching him as he was to touching them. Once inside his gates, burly Jonathan met him with warm hands, steadying him.

The ursinelike aide also topped him, but Jonathan exuded the milk of human kindness and, perversely, Colin felt smothered. He almost preferred the Thraks to this attention.

He snapped, "Leave me be."

"Your holiness . . ."

Colin came to a halt inside the foyer. He waited until the security doors slid shut and then said, "I'm sorry, Jonathan. You didn't deserve that."

The massive man's face closed in an expression that agreed with him. He moved to take Colin's outer vest, but the older man hugged it about himself, saying, "It's a little chilly. You can taste winter's edge out there—it may even rain later. I think I'll keep this on a while."

"I've got your apartment warming up. Shall I send up tea?"

Tea sounded good. "I'll take it up with me," he said. "I've the eulogy to work on. Tell Margaret to hold all my calls this evening." His aide nodded briskly and turned away to the kitchen

Alone at last, tea tray balanced in his hands, Colin mounted the steps to his private apartment. Audiences with Pepys were beginning to sap him, as though the emperor were a parasite of some sort, a devious being Colin must constantly spar with. Nor was Colin happy about being pressured into doing the eulogy for Commander Jack Storm, late of the Dominion Knights. There would be the inevitable military rites, all the more poignant because Jack was missing in action—his body had never been found. And, God willing, it never would be.

Taking the staircase an incline at a time, feeling his knees creak and watching the chinaware jiggle on the tray, steam puffing from under the teapot lid with each sway, Colin approached the only sanctuary he had left, a small but comfortable apartment hidden deep within Walker headquarters.

He set the tray down on the burled wood table from old home, long ago Terra, his knuckles brushing the polished surface. There was life in that touch, the life of wood still vibrant. With a sound half-sigh and half-groan, Colin lowered himself onto the comfort of his settee.

The room was deeply shadowed in late afternoon, but he did not call up his lights, preferring the comfort of dimness as he poured a cup and sat back, sipping the heated contents gingerly. The settee cushions embraced him.

"You're getting old," he muttered to himself. "Tolerating the enemy at your doorstep."

"I've never known you to tolerate anything," a shadow spoke back to him, and a man separated himself from the darkness of a corner.

Colin juggled his teacup, cursing as the hot liquid splashed on him. With a laugh, the tall man joined him and helped to blot up the disaster.

The minister sat back in exasperation. "Good God! What are you doing here—you're dead."

A sandy-colored eyebrow arched. "Rumors greatly exaggerated?"

"No, by God! I perjured myself, Storm, to give you a second chance. What are you doing here?"

Jack lowered himself into an expansive chair across from the couch. "I'm grateful for everything you've done."

"And we're both ruined if anyone saw you come in."

"I'd not be much of a Knight if I couldn't get past a few Thraks."

Colin's mouth twisted as he steadied his hands and reached for his teacup again. Pointedly, he did not offer his guest any. Storm did not need an invitation. He scooped up a cup with movement suggesting his long-fingered hands, one of them oddly missing the smallest finger, had handled much more delicate instruments. Colin had wondered for years how his friend had injured himself, but there were some questions one did not ask a free mercenary. And now, of course, Storm was no longer a mercenary, but a sworn Knight, a fighting man mated to the technology of battle armor. But now Colin also knew, had learned, what had caused that injury, and others, which haunted the man. Being confined in cold sleep for seventeen years had taken its toll. Frostbite here, and other, more subtle and devastating changes elsewhere.

Jack waited for Colin to down half a cup. "What makes you so melancholy and testy this late in the day?"

St. Colin made a most unsaintly face. "I find myself faced with composing a eulogy."

"Ah." Storm added compassionately. "It happens to all of us, sooner or later."

"You should know," the man said dryly. "It's your funeral."

"What!"

"Don't tell me you didn't know. And here you are, making a liar out of me."

Storm put his teacup down, stood, and paced, the wood table an uncertain barrier between them. "It's only been a few months."

"The Thrakian ambassador has been pressing to take you off the MI list and have you officially laid to rest. Then he can press to have K'rok instated as permanent commander in your absence." Colin watched as Storm halted and several expressions flitted across the Knight's face.

"K'rok?"

"Who else?"

"I thought perhaps one of the Thraks—" he paused. "No. Milot or not, K'rok is probably the cagiest being for the job they want done, although I don't know if the Thraks know what they've got a hold of—"

"They certainly didn't know with you," Colin interrupted. "But Milos has been under their claws for twenty-five years—"

Humor reflected in Storm's rainwater blue eyes. "Not long enough. K'rok was born free, and he grew up fighting Thraks. He only stopped to avoid extinction, and as soon as he finds a way to throw off their yoke, he'll do it. No, K'rok is as good a choice as any to head up the Knights. I think I'll stay dead."

Stress lines in Colin's face visibly relaxed as the prelate sank back among the cushions, teacup balanced on his knee. "I'm glad I was able to persuade you."

Storm paused in mid-stride, the irony not lost on him. He looked down. "I wouldn't have exposed you unnecessarily," he said.

"Thank you. *I* wouldn't have lied about you unnecessarily, but I seem to remember us coming to an agreement on that strategy. And, since we did, what the hell are you doing back on Malthen?"

"I think I've gotten you in enough trouble already." With a flexing of a young body still well in its prime, Jack sat. He did not reach for his teacup. "But I think I see an easier way of accomplishing what I need to. When's the funeral?"

"The day after tomorrow."

"You'll need a retinue?"

"Of course, I—" Colin plowed to a stop. He shook his head. "Oh, no. You're not sneaking in behind my robes."

"It's not for vanity. I need to get in. And I don't want to jeopardize Amber by contacting her."

"And do you honestly think, if I did bring you inside the palace grounds with me, that you'd escape *her* detection?"

Jack grinned. "I should hope not. But if she finds out, she'll play her part anyway. You know that."

"This . . . opportunity . . . you're looking for. It must be awfully important to risk coming back here."

Jack smiled thinly. "It is," he said. "It's my initiation into the Green Shirts."

The teacup bounced off the redwood table and shattered at Colin's feet. He did not seem to have noticed, all warmth fled from his face. "That's unconscionable. They're murdering scum, Jack—you're better off dealing with Pepys directly. He has to put on a public facade and that at least makes him maintain a veneer of civilization."

"They may be terrorists—but I haven't forgotten that they were the ones who found my cold ship and thawed me out."

"To make a pawn out of you," Colin pointed out.

"But they didn't succeed."

"Not yet anyway. It depends on what you've agreed to do for them. Destroy the Knights?"

Now Storm's weathered face paled slightly. "Never," he said, his answer clipped. "And you should know better than to ask."

"I do what I feel I must. I thought Pepys was your target . . . bringing down a corrupt administration is one thing, but replacing it with a terrorist organization is another. Every man has his price. I wonder what yours might be."

"They're giving me the name and location of the doctor who found me."

The two men looked sharply at one another. Then, softly,

Colin asked, "Why? Why do you want to know after what they attempted to do to you?"

"Because he had to have kept records. The cold ship carried my looping—and I want that back. I want my goddamn memory back, intact, whole. I want my past. I want myself."

"That's a lot to ask," Colin murmured. "Are you sure it's what you truly want to face? There's a lot of us who would give anything to forget what happened yesterday and beyond." He cleared his throat. "And I hate that you must deal with scum."

Jack interrupted. "Odd. They speak very highly of you. I was given your name here on Malthen."

Colin surged to his feet with a strangled, "What?"

Before either man could say another word, the apartment com line signaled. Colin visibly gathered his wits, then answered, "What is it?"

The screen brought Jonathan into focus, but not before Storm deftly stepped out of viewing range. "I'm sorry to disturb you, but Denaro is here—"

Colin grabbed up his remote and thumbed on the mute. He looked at Storm. "He must know you're here."

Jack shook his head. Colin looked back to the monitor. "What seems to be the problem?"

Jonathan shrugged. He said confidentially, "He's armed to the teeth, your holiness. He seems to feel you might be at risk." He moved aside and the monitor camera panned a massive young man, dressed in trooper fatigues. Jack noted three weapons on his upper torso alone, not counting the cross hanging upon his chest which could be used in ways holy men had never intended.

"Tell him I'm in meditation and not to be disturbed."

Storm made a hand signal and Colin paused.

"He might be of use," Jack said.

"Not if he finds out you're in league with the Green Shirts."

The two men faced each other. Jack had trained Denaro to wear battle armor even though the militant Walker had ideas of his own about duty and honor and obedience.

"If you add me to your retinue, he'll have to know sooner or later."

Colin hesitated a moment longer but knew that if he had

an honor guard escort of Walker priests, he'd also have a flanking pair of bodyguards assigned by Denaro and one of them would probably be the aggressive young man himself. "He won't be much use to you, Jack. Pepys has had him watched ever since he cashiered Denaro from the Knights."

"Then have him come back later. He won't be at ease until he sees you're all right."

That seemed appropriate. Colin nodded. He took the com off mute and said to Jonathan, "I've had a rough day. Give me an hour, and then I'll talk to Denaro, if he'll wait."

No answer was needed as the young man took up a chair in the corner of the lobby, staring intently through the monitor as if he could see into Colin's apartment. The com line hung up.

Jack said, "Denaro helped you cover for me."

"No question about that. He won't mind finding you here—but if he ever finds out you're associated in any way with the Green Shirts, your life is forfeit."

The sandy-haired man grimaced. "He'll have to stand in line behind Pepys and Baadluster and half a dozen others."

Colin took a step, heard the grinding of shards underfoot and looked down. He seemed to realize for the first time that he'd dropped his cup. With a dismayed cluck, he bent over and began to pick up the pieces, muttering, "Genuine porcelain."

"Does Denaro still have his armor?"

"No. Baadluster keeps an iron grip on the equipment. If there's any black market to be had, he probably runs it." Colin straightened, his attention still on the fragments in the palm of his hand. He stirred them. He looked up suddenly, with renewed fire in his brown eyes. "What do the Green Shirts say about me?"

"I was told to tell you I deal in artifacts, and that you might know a broker."

The fire quieted. "Ah. I do know a thief or two in that area. Did they intimate I was a Shirt?"

"No. And that I was to use discretion in inquiring." Jack tilted his head to one side, eyeing the Walker saint.

"And well you might, this or any other time." Colin cleared his throat in satisfaction. "I do not collude with the enemy!"

"You don't have to tell me that. But as to brokers. . . ."

Colin closed his fist over the shards of porcelain he held. "Unfortunately, religious artifacts are bought and sold like any other commodity. Well, the best man I know is a real scoundrel in under-Malthen, a man named Gibbon."

Jack nodded in satisfaction, saying, "Then that's probably the man I need." He began to fade back into the long shadows from which he'd emerged.

Colin looked up abruptly. "Will you be buying or selling?"

"Selling," the man answered. "As soon as I steal two suits of armor."

"Your price of initiation. You know what the Shirts can do with weaponry like that."

"All I need to do is get in, make the contacts I need, and get out. I won't leave functional armor behind. You won't believe how difficult it is to man a suit unless you've been well-trained."

"I see."

"I hope you do. Talk to Denaro about me. I'll be back later. In the meantime, I'd like you to watch something for me." Jack had been blocking Colin's view of the shadowed far corner of the living room. Now something loomed beyond . . . battle armor, in all its rugged and massive glory, its white Flexalink scales shining like nacre.

"In the name of God, man, you can't leave that here!" Colin fairly shook with agitation.

"I can't leave him anywhere else." Even as Storm spoke mildly, calmingly, the armor raised a gauntlet hand high as if in salute.

"Jack—God alone knows what kind of alien flesh is regenerating inside there, hooked up to your circuitry and power systems. Bogie's an embryo, a child, with the ability to destroy anyone and anything it doesn't comprehend—and not truly alive yet, how can it comprehend life?"

Jack let his right hand fall upon the Walker's shoulder. "I can't leave him alone. And because you know what he is—as much as anyone does—you know there's a soul there, as well as flesh. If anything happens to me, I'd like to know he's in good hands."

"Godfather to an abomination." Colin sucked in his breath. "Someday he could destroy you, Jack."

"Eat me up and spit the gristle out, like a Milot berserker? Maybe. But in the meantime, we have an understanding."

"You still wear your armor?"

Jack nodded. "He's all I've got. The little memory I have is from shared consciousness. And . . . we need each other. He's a warrior spirit, Colin, whatever else he is—and if that means that someday he has to turn on me in order to finish his regeneration, that's a chance I take. I think he'll give me warning."

"And then what . . . what will you do when he needs to feed?"

Jack gave a sinister smile. "Feed him Thraks."

Colin seemed to deflate under his hand. "All right," he said, "but only because he's too dangerous to leave untended."

"Thanks. I've some arrangements to make. But I'll be back later, and I'd like to know if I'm going as bodyguard or priest."

"All right," Colin agreed. Before his eyes, Jack seemed to fade from sight. The prelate listened, but could not really discern the Knight's manner of exit from his apartments, though the older man knew he should have been alert, for if Jack could get in or out, sooner or later someone else could. He looked down at his hand, and saw the shattered remains of his teacup still clenched within it.

He cupped both hands together and shook them lightly, the shards of his cup rattling about for a few seconds. When all was silent, he opened his hands, and smiled at the whole teacup resting within. Then a thought shadowed his pleasure, and his face. If only healing Storm could be that easy.

CHAPTER 2

"You'll go as a priest," Colin said. "Make that a reverend. Certain of the Walker sects are of monkish persuasion—you'll be in a hood and cowl. There's nothing very humble about your size—" the older man eyed Storm. "We'll put you next to Jonathan to shrink you somewhat. Denaro agrees with me, though. It's sheer folly to let you go and suicide to aid and abet."

"But you'll do it."

"Of course I will. What do you think I've been talking about?" Colin's speech lapsed as he lowered himself into his chair. For a moment, Jack perceived a flash of what the future would bring: the man grown older and feeble as the chair appeared to swallow him up, body hunched in weary surrender. But then Colin squared his shoulders and the future disappeared, his age apparent but not victorious as yet. He rubbed one hand across the knobby knuckles of the other in thought, then added, "We've only Amber to worry about."

"She knows I'm here."

"You told her?"

"Not directly—we both know that doesn't mean she doesn't know. And why would you not want her to know?"

Colin opened his mouth as if to say something, thought better, and shut it. But the hesitation did not go past Jack. He stood over Colin. "Is there a problem?"

The prelate did not look up. He said quietly, "There's always a problem somewhere, if one looks hard enough. Pepys and Vandover deserve more consideration than you've given them."

Jack dropped into the chair opposite Colin. For a moment, it looked as if he would lean back and put his heels up on the priceless burled table, but instead, he leaned forward intently, upper body resting on his forearms braced by his knees. "Don't kid yourself. I've given the emperor *every* consideration. I haven't come this far to walk into his hands now. Or ever."

"I didn't mean—"

Storm waved his four-fingered hand. "I know, I know. But consider this . . . with the Thraks infiltrating everything they can, at the behest of the alliance, Pepys is a dead man. Dead if the Thraks turn against him, dead if the Green Shirts can get their hands on him—dead if I expose him for the ambitious traitor he is."

Colin had not meant to flinch, meant even less that Storm should see it, but the clear blue gaze didn't miss much. He stopped, "I'm sorry, Colin."

"You've nothing to apologize for."

"I'd forgotten you and Pepys were close, once."

The older man scratched the corner of his temple, where his graying eyebrow had recently begun to sprout. The irony of it—fewer hairs on his head, more on his chest and in his brows—reminded him constantly of the contradictions of aging. He dropped his hand. "That was a long time ago," he said.

"And yet you're not surprised at what Pepys has done."

"Of course not. He's the emperor, isn't he? I've seen few emperors, or presidents, or even rebels for that matter, get where they are without walking over a lot of bodies. And you are very naive if you think otherwise."

"What about you?"

They considered each other, then Colin smiled gently. "Unfortunately," he murmured, "you'd find a sacrifice or two under my feet as well. But as few as I could possibly get away with—and no one who didn't know what they were doing."

Jack inclined his head. "Fair enough." He took a deep breath. "When do I get these reverend's robes?"

"Jonathan will bring them up. We've a few hours yet. Denaro will be in full equipment, in the honor guard. He says to tell you that he won't be using the dead man switch, whatever he means by that."

Jack considered the information with surprise that he quickly muffled. In answer to Colin's raised eyebrow, he said, "If there's trouble, and a man goes down, the armor is equipped to destruct if the man is pulled out before disarming the suit."

"What's he telling you, then? That he's not using the switch."

Jack nodded, saying, "In case of trouble. If he goes down, if I can get to him, I can use the armor without worrying about disarmament."

They sat in easy silence for a moment, as if aware of the commitment made to each other, then Colin reached over the burled table, which felt to him like another living thing, and took Jack's hand. "I'll tell you now," he said, "for I may not have the time later. Once we leave these apartments, I'll not look at or talk to you. May God go with you."

Jack gave a sudden, lopsided and boyish grin, quite unlike the even baring of teeth in a battle smile which Colin had seen so many times. Colin had the eerie sense of seeing into Jack's very soul in that expression. "I hope he's quick—because once I get my hands on the armor I need, I'll be running like the very devil's on my heels."

Colin let out a short burst of laughter, then caught himself and quieted. "Denaro left this for you." He fished into a deep thigh pocket of his miner's pants and pulled out an address disk. "It's encoded with the current whereabouts of the fence you mentioned. He suggests that you visit him as soon as possible—the man's not going to be in business very long." He sighed. "I'm as naive as I've accused you of being. Pepys has to know of Gibbon's background—and I nearly hanged myself by associating with him. They found my weakness—both sides—and used it neatly."

"It's not your fault. That's what a Walker does . . . search for religious evidence."

Colin frowned. "We're more than that, much more. But you're right. It won't stop my looking. I shall simply be more circumspect about my contacts in the future. Be careful with Gibbon, Jack. You know the faction Denaro works with—fanatics are difficult to control. Denaro has left orders that will give the man time to deal with you and pass you on to the contacts within the Green Shirts—but whether he can exercise those orders or not. . . . Find Gibbon and make your contact. And hurry."

"I will." Jack's hand closed neatly about the address disk.

Jonathan's heavy footsteps and large presence could be felt outside the apartment door. Storm smiled briefly. "Thank you. For everything."

Colin got up even as Jonathan rang for admittance. "Just," the older man warned, "don't criticize the eulogy."

Jonathan entered to laughter, and the great, burly man hesitated a moment, his gentle face frowning slightly as if he wondered if the laughter was directed at him.

A gray curtain of rain slanted across the parade grounds. It fell in spurts, wind-driven, a chill rain soaking the funeral procession. Far lightning struck. It illuminated the figures standing in the rain, and one of them lifted her head, turning slightly toward the electric glow.

She stood to the side, flanked protectively by taller figures, her face veiled from the cameras and audience, her thoughts her own. Thunder rumbled outside the city.

"It's almost over," the man at her elbow murmured. He was bareheaded, protected by the canopy overhead, a few wispy hairs of dark chestnut and gray ruffling across the top of his head, his strong jaw sagging a bit, but his eyes dark and full of challenge. He wore a dark blue overvest covering his plain miner's jumpsuit, various pockets flat and smooth for once. A simple cross hung against his chest and, unaware, he stroked it once before reaching for the slender young woman's hand. "It's almost over," he repeated.

She nodded. The veil shuddered with her movement. Then she said, "He would have liked the storm. Jack liked rain."

St. Colin did not respond except to tighten his fingers about her chill ones. Anything he might have said would have been drowned out by the military display coming to attention before them.

"Right, HARCH! Company, present!"

The ground trembled under the weight of battle armor. Faces obscured by their visors, the Dominion Knights filed past, their movements slow and somber, Flexalink shining dully in the overcast light. In a ripple, they began a salute to the woman in black and held it for their red and gold clad emperor as they passed the dais.

She did not turn toward Pepys as the armor passed, but he watched her. She knew it. She could feel the intenseness of his cat-green gaze upon the back of her neck and the slimy feel of that other's gaze—Baadluster. She leaned slightly toward Colin as if gaining strength from the man and repelled by the emperor and minister.

"Company, HALT! About face!"

The ground trembled one last time as the unit came about and stamped to a halt. Raindrops danced and glistened off the multicolored armor, massive and crude embodiments of the manpower it encased. Nowhere was there white armor—only one man she'd ever known had worn white. The veil across her face trembled. She could spot the few and scattered alien presences within the armor as well as those posted within the gates. Thraks, even here, even now. The corner of her mouth curled bitterly and she licked lips gone suddenly dry.

Colin loosened his hand from hers and stepped forward. The funeral began.

Vandover Baadluster stirred at his emperor's side. "She gives a very real performance," he commented, low-voiced.

Pepys sat up straighter within his voluminous red and gold imperial robes. The rain had taken the ever-present static from his red hair and it lay about him, restless, hovering, about to burst into its aureal state, but for the moment quelled. Not so the electricity of his cat-green eyes, and his stare flicked briefly from the presentation to his Minister of War's face then back again. "Do I detect sympathy?"

"No"

"What then?"

Baadluster stood, his gaze fixed upon the military rite before them. His thick lips molded into a noncommittal expression as he ignored his emperor's jibe. "I am not sure," he answered finally, reluctantly.

"Good. You give her the flag. I have business elsewhere." Pepys gave a diffident wave of one hand. If he noticed the sudden tensing of the minister's body, or the clenching of his hands, he gave no indication, instead smothering a yawn as St. Colin of the Blue Wheel began a eulogy. True to his word, as the funeral ended, he left his throne quickly, ostensibly to avoid a new curtain of rainfall slanting across the skies toward them, and Vandover found himself with the triangular folded company flag across his hands. He glanced at Amber.

She stood taller than he remembered, a distinctly regal aura about her slender figure, her face obscured by the dark veil. The fall of her tawny hair had escaped the veil and hung about her shoulders. She turned toward him expectantly.

He felt a jolt when their fingers touched as he transferred the flag to her palms. His chin jerked up, his gaze meeting the opaque veil searchingly—hadn't she felt it?

She closed graceful hands about the flag and said, "There are Thraks present, minister. They disgrace the armor. May I remind you it was the Thraks which killed Commander Storm?"

His nostrils flared. "This is not the time or place. . . ."

"No. Of course not. I forget that it was you who welcomed our enemies into our ranks." With a convulsive movement, the young woman hugged the flag to her chest. "He died so that we would all remember who our enemies are."

He leaned close. So close that he imagined he could clearly see her wide-set, expressive eyes—mellow brown heavily flecked with gold, amber, like her naming. "You mock the emperor, and you mock me. Storm is not dead. And I intend to find him."

Her words taunted him. "I hope you do, Baadluster. Hell isn't big enough for both of you. Perhaps Jack'll get sent home." She whirled on her heels and left him at the dais edge. The entourage of St. Colin's ministers closed ranks about her and followed.

Keenly aware that he was being watched by the troop and cameras, Baadluster drew himself up. He received the dismissing salute with dignity as well as hatred.

The sky rumbled, and rain began to fall in earnest. The video crew began to strike their equipment hastily, and, falling out, the troop broke into a jog leaving the parade grounds, their suits churning the area into waves of mud. Baadluster bowed himself against the elements and left swiftly. He did not notice that one of St. Colin's retinue splintered off.

Jack broke the lock code to the shops and stepped in quietly, looking around. No one from the dress troop would be in here yet, nor any of the support techs, for that matter. The locker rooms would be filled to the brim as they stripped the muddy suits and sluiced them down before loading the equipment racks. He had time to do what he'd come for.

The sight and smell of the shop rooms gave him pause. Memories flooded him of all the time he'd spent in shops like this, stripping down, cleaning, and repairing his armor. In makeshift tents on frontier Milos, in the mercenary shops side by side with his friend Kavin, now dead. Even here on Malthen where he'd sworn false allegiance to a false emperor. He felt no guilt for what he did now because the loyalty he'd sworn was only valid if the ruler also upheld his oath.

Jack stirred. The security systems would be picking him up soon, whether he wore the white light shield clipped to his belt or not. Besides, he did not have the faith in electronic gadgetry that Amber had. He swiftly located the inspection and racking area and found what he needed.

New suits, never worn, one still lying in its packing crate. Jack deftly resealed it and found a crate for the second, then loaded them on the power sled for transportation. He coded them for delivery to a blind address, where help he'd hired would redirect them, making tracing difficult if not virtually impossible. He jimmied open the dock doors and watched the power sled disappear into the darkening afternoon. He should follow them out, but the loading docks were strictly automated and his body heat would set off alarms and consequences he'd be better off avoiding. He sealed the double doors shut again and, passing through one of the diagnostic rooms, paused, then pocketed one of the new probes racked there, thinking Bogie could use some fine tuning.

He had almost made it back to the entry when a voice stopped him in his tracks.

"I just headed up a memorial service for you, commander. I didn't believe the rumors."

Hair prickled on the back of Jack's neck. He'd half-expected to meet someone in the shops—he'd hoped they'd be Thraks or Sergeant Lassaday. Thraks he'd kill cheerfully and Lassaday, with a bit of explanation and persuasion, could be expected to let his commander pass.

But the voice was young, strong, and clear—and he turned to face a man who was everything Jack might have been, had he not been betrayed. Rawlins stood in a corridor entrance, the dim light shining off hair that was silver-blond, eyes the intense blue of bottomless pools watching him in accusation, whole and unscarred of limb and soul. Jack was a soiled mirror-image of the young man, his own hair muddied, his blue eyes lightened, grayed by truth rather than innocence, he liked to think. He'd always found it difficult to face Rawlins, and this meeting was no less painful.

"Rawlins. Seeing ghosts?"

"Sir." The officer shifted weight easily, then said, "It is you. I thought so, but I hoped—from the back—I could have been mistaken."

Jack studied the distance between them, gauging not only how quickly he could get to Rawlins, but to see if the blanking shield would cover them both. His calculation was uncertain. In any case, he could not afford to stand here and attempt to repair the damage done to Rawlins' idealism. "I'm going out the door, Rawlins, and you will not have seen or talked to me."

"Is that an order, sir?"

Jack shook his head. "No. A request, one that will benefit you perhaps even more than it will me.

The jawline tightened. Rawlins looked pale in the twilight illumination. His eyes glittered. "Then it's true. You've gone AWOL."

"Nothing is ever exactly as it seems." He took a half-step back, toward the door.

Reflexively, Rawlins' hand went toward the weapon he carried. Jack stopped.

"Tell me what is true, then."

Jack shook his head even before the other's words finished ringing in the corridor. He half-raised his open, weaponless right hand, the four-fingered hand scarred by cold sleep. "There isn't time, and it's better you don't know."

"Is it the Thraks?"

Jack didn't answer, unwilling to lie, even partially. His defection was in part due to the Thrakian alliance, but there was so much more.

"Nothing is that uncomplicated," he told the former aide.

He searched his memory of Rawlins and found a way out. "One of these days, when you have time, and you think you can handle the consequences of knowing the truth . . . you might discuss it with St. Colin."

Rawlins' face blanched. Jack was unsure of what he'd touched off there, knowing only that his aide had had ties with the Walker reverend during their campaign on Bythia. Rawlins would believe what Saint Colin deigned to reveal, and Jack knew he could trust Colin to be discreet. Jack took another stride backward, hand still upheld.

"There isn't time," he said, "to tell you more."

Abruptly, Rawlins nodded. His posture changed to one of defeat, his chin dropped. Then he looked up.

"Take me with you."

"You can't go where I'm going. You're still a Knight." Jack's voice sharpened, a whip crack across the space between them. "Sometimes the hardest enemy to fight is the one that walks shoulder to shoulder with you. We all do what we have to do, lieutenant."

"Captain," corrected Rawlins softly, but he gathered himself. "Yes, sir. Thank you, sir." He turned heel and left.

"No," Jack added softly to the emptiness. "Thank you." He found the door and escaped.

CHAPTER 3

"He got in all right?" Colin paced before Denaro, not looking at the captain of his private army, but well aware of the heavily armed and armored man taking up the majority of room in his apartment.

"No one followed him, your holiness," Denaro said. "I could not observe without attracting attention."

The Walker prelate ignored the disapproval flavoring Denaro's words. He had already been through this argument with the young warrior, and he'd already made his position clear. Storm was to be given whatever aid he needed. Discreetly if possible, openly if necessary. "Good. Then he'll be making contact with Gibbon this evening. Pass the word. Gibbon's offices are to be kept clear until Storm's done his business. Then, and not before, you can shut him down."

There was a slight hesitation before Denaro answered in the affirmative. Colin met his gaze. He said nothing, but he knew that he was faced with a man who might have plans of his own in the working. If so, there was nothing he could do about it now. To vent his suspicions now might be extremely foolhardy—and destroy what confidence Denaro had in his leadership. To wait might lead Jack into a trap—but Colin could not avoid that, no matter how he wished. Trust was all. He looked into Denaro's deep black gaze.

"Good. Then all we have to do is wait. If all goes well, Jack will be back before he goes off planet."

Denaro burst out, "That's stupidity. He'll risk incriminating you."

Colin scratched a bushy eyebrow. "Maybe," he answered slowly. "But I have something he wants and needs very badly." He looked over Denaro's shoulders to the hulk of white armor waiting silently and sullenly in a corner as if it were a living, thinking thing.

Which, in many respects, it was.

Colin sat down, crossed his legs, and picked up his meditation studies. He looked up briefly at Denaro. "Relax," he advised. "It's going to be a long night."

Jack took almost as many blind routes as the suits did before he gathered up the power sled, transferred the two large crates to yet another power sled, and keyed in the address to Gibbon's disreputable offices. Nightfall had curtained even this section of under-Malthen which was now garish with neons and a never ending stream of humanity looking for and fulfilling vices in a variety of ways.

Gibbon was a quiet, hardworking businessman. The neighborhood he'd chosen to do business in was the same. Jack approached the loading dock in the rear cautiously, scanning the building's eaves for security systems panning the vista.

He saw none, but that didn't mean he wasn't being observed. He put the power sled on idle and knocked on the door.

A synthetic voice droned out of the speaker. "We're closed."

Jack was in no mood for argument. He looked at the silver mesh which hid the source of the voice. "Green Shirt" was all he answered.

The door snapped open immediately, and then the loading dock slide as well. Jack put the sled on auto and stepped through the doorway.

Gibbon was a massive slab of a man, head sunk into a pair of shoulders that seemed as wide as the loading dock doors. His eyes glittered as he looked Jack over. Jack caught the bloodshot glow of greed in them.

His right ear was a rack of jewelry that chimed softly as he looked toward the crates being delivered into his storeroom, and then back toward Jack.

"I may or may not have been expecting you," the man said. "But some things are damned stupid talking about on the street." He opened a beefy hand and waved Jack into the depths of the store.

Jack looked about the scatter of crates and shipping cartons, dim corners and far recesses. Under his heel, he heard the echo of a false floor, and smiled thinly. "Some things are damned stupid doing," and he shook off his host's invitation.

Gibbon's thick hand clenched. The jewelry quivered noisily, and his eyes boiled with anger. "Are you here to do business with me or not?"

"I thought you were closed."

"I thought you were someone else." Gibbon swallowed convulsively.

"I might be yet," Jack said. "Or you might be."

"Ah! Is that the reason for your shyness? Well." The shopkeeper's closed expression opened up, and he gave a sardonic laugh. "Good enough. What shall I do to identify myself, for it's obvious you don't know anyone who knows me. I'm not the sort of man easily forgotten or duplicated." He threw his arms out and did a pirouette, in the graceful way the very large sometimes have, as though it were the sun and moon that orbited around them instead of the other way.

Jack felt a moment of guilt that this man would cease to exist shortly after doing business with him. He offered his hand. "Call me Jack," he said.

"I will. And you may call me Gibbon. And who sent you to me?"

"Saint Colin of the Blue Wheel."

"Ah! Aha! That confirms it. And these two lovely cartons contain my shipment."

"No."

Gibbon had turned and was making his way to the office portion of his warehouse, a room Jack could barely glimpse through a privacy curtain, a room no less cluttered than the docks. He came to an abrupt stop.

Jack gave an apologetic shrug. "There is a matter of payment. . . ."

"Ah." Gibbon nodded heavily. "Of course. *Then* it becomes my shipment."

Jack smiled.

From inside the cuff of his sleeve, Gibbon produced several short plastisheets. Jack caught the flash of a surgery scar, across the wrist flesh where ID chips were usually implanted, and was in the process of reaching for the plastisheets when they, and Gibbon's hand, disappeared in a laser flash.

Jack cried out and hit the floor, and began to crawl backward toward the dock gridway. Gibbon grabbed his stump of a hand with a bloodcurdling scream and did a dance upon his false-bottomed floor. It rolled under his bulk with the sound of thunder.

The lights went off, replaced by an orange gleam. He could still see Gibbon's vast body in a black silhouette ballet as a second bolt caught the man in the chest, yellow-white, lighting up the storeroom for a moment. Then the false flooring gave way under Gibbon's weight, and the man disappeared from view with a crash.

Jack heard the shouts and cries of disappointment as men filled the storeroom.

A half-melted, charred piece of plastisheet kited across the floor and under Jack's hand as he backed farther into the loading dock. Convulsively, he picked it up and shoved it inside his jacket. The Green Shirts had promised him considerable payment for delivery of the suits: credit, IDs, maps leading him to further contact. He had no time to see what minor scrap of the payment had survived.

A hand reached out and prevented him from moving.

"Give it a minute," the soft voice whispered in his ear. "I can guarantee Gibbon will come up firing. When he does—we're out of here."

The voice he would know anywhere, the owner he would trust with his life. Jack felt his face crease as he gave a genuine smile into the twilight.

"I told Colin you'd know I was back."

"Damn right," Amber said. "And you're in trouble as usual." But she didn't sound angry with him.

Amber graced the sofa of the saint of the Blue Wheel, her slim form reclining across the furniture as though she didn't have a bone in her body. The pose was a sham and both Colin and Jack knew it. She radiated nervous energy the way the Malthen sun radiated heat, and she watched both men as they talked quietly.

Colin ran his hands through his thinning hair one more time. "I feared Denaro might pull something like that. It was unforgivable of me to send Amber after you . . . and to think he could be trusted."

"Don't apologize for him. I'm out of it. They left the shop burning, and for all he knows, I burned with it."

"Which you would have," Amber pointed out, "except Colin's tongue would snap off before he could tell a lie. I know that section of town. You had no business going in there without me."

The two looked at one another across the room, various passions revealing themselves on Amber's expressive face.

"I know," Jack answered softly. "But I also know the emperor's probably watching you. I didn't want to make things more difficult."

"Difficult was leaving you six months ago so you could play dead. Hell is living as though you are dead." Amber looked away suddenly, as if she'd said too much.

The Walker cleared his throat and muttered, "Damn the boy, anyway."

Jack's clear blue eyes pinned Colin momentarily. "He could have been protecting you."

Colin blinked. "Or had motives of his own. I'm not forgetting the militarist faction among my followers. You've got to get off Malthen as soon as you can. I can't shield you any longer. He'll know once he sees the armor missing anyway. He'll know you survived and took it with you."

At the mention of armor, Jack's gaze veered off to where it stood. He said, "I can't leave Bogie behind."

"Then I'll have to learn how to control Denaro." Colin paused, and examined the plastisheet Jack had given him. "And to answer your second question, yes, I have the resources to reconstruct this, but you don't have the time. What is this, anyway?"

"It's my payment for turning the battle armor over. I requested some information and was also promised a lead to joining with the Green Shirts officially."

Colin frowned. "You know my feelings on that."

"And mine as well. But I can't bring Pepys down without them, and we need to know as much about the organization as we can . . . or we'll just have replaced one evil with another."

"Then you'll have to act on what can be read. Do you know who you're looking for?"

Jack gave a bittersweet smile. "Oh, yes. This is the man who brought me out of seventeen years of cold sleep."

Amber sucked in her breath. "He won't want to see you coming."

"I know. That's one reason we're taking Bogie with us."

CHAPTER 4

A dirty night rain had pelted the streets and concrete lots of under-Malthen, washing away a thin veneer of misery. It left behind a sheen of grit and oil that muffled sight as well as sound, embracing stealth which was well for the denizens of under-Malthen, to whom crime was like air.

The three unlikely figures hid in the shadows outside Mentech's security doors. Slim and lithe, the first, in dark colors and hooded, worked intently at the computer alarm system. She had breached the conventional security system and seemed unaware of the camera she had not detected, or the vision it relayed. The second, a tall, big-shouldered man who took no pains to conceal either his plain, strong-featured face or sandy hair, bent over the figure clothed in black. The last, shadowing the pair, was a massive thing, white armored, opalescent in the thinning light of the moon. A robot, perhaps, or a cyborg, though from its size and armory, it was not a civilian machine. That thing had been built to win wars.

All three made an impact on the two men watching them through the monitor's hidden screen.

The tall man made an impatient gesture. "Why can't we hear them?" The sleeve of his plastic lab jacket flopped extravagantly about his thin, bony wrist.

"They've got a white sound barrier up."

"How did they get so close before the monitors picked them up?"

The gray-haired little man in a uniform of gray as dull as his hair color hunched into himself. "I don't know, doctor. Professionals. I would suggest the one in the fore is a thief. . . ."

"We have nothing worth stealing here!" The doctor held his arms folded defensively across his chest, one hand free to rub the side of his large, thin nose. That was not strictly true but he had no intention of letting his security personnel know of the wealth as well as the experiments protected inside the lab buildings. He sucked in his breath. There was no time to waste: his operation had been made and whether the trespassers were illegal or enforcers made little difference. He had no idea who they were or what they wanted—but they triggered his decision. He decided to cut his losses. It had had to happen one day. Today was as good as any.

"Hold the door," the doctor said. "As long as you can." He walked away, leaving his employee nervously watching the one monitor the thief had not decommissioned. His voice drifted down the hallway. "There'll be a bonus in it for you."

The doctor's mistake. At that promise, the gray-suited man told himself he would not lay down his life for his employer—otherwise, how could he collect a bonus? But he would do everything else in his power. He keyed open the storage yards for the android intruder force.

Five doors slid open. Five pewter colored machines glided out. Servos whined smoothly, joints flexed, weapons charged. The security patrolman fed in the images of their targets, his fingers flying over the keyboard. Then he sat back to watch his job being done.

The doctor took the first corridor hover he could find. He keyed on his belt com. After a slight crackle, a hoarsely feminine voice said, "What?"

"We've been made. Shut the labs down and burn them. Start with 1, 3, and 4. I'll be taking care of 2 personally."

"What?" Her amazement crackled over the line.

"There's no time, dammit! Do what I said. All that matters is that the two of us and our records get clear."

"Right. Labs 1, 3, and 4. I'll meet you in 2—"

"No. Outside the buildings, in the back lot."

The voice quavered a bit, then said, "It's that bad?"

"Yes."

"We can't fight for it?"

"No! Stop arguing."

Her voice, tinged with loathing, protested, "Jeez, I hate that tunnel. All right. Be careful."

The doctor paused a moment before squeezing off the

com button. "You, too," he said faintly, his voice off the air. He leaned with the hover as it turned a sharp corner.

Amber said irritably as the massive piece of battle gear shuffled his boots impatiently for about the twentieth time, "Three more connections and we're in. Just hold on."

"Onto what?" the armored structure said, his voice deep and resonant, a being of operatic tones inside a personified tank.

"It's a figure of speech." Jack spoke as if instructing a young child. "Be quiet so Amber can concentrate." He stood closest to the woman and could feel the tension generating in every fiber of her being as she cupped the alarm system. It did not help that she knew he would be leaving as soon as he got what he wanted, that he would not allow her to continue on with them. She had argued long and loud her value to him, and her presence here and now confirmed the fact that he needed her skills.

She had her mane of dark honey-colored hair tucked away inside that skintight hood, but he could still smell the fragrance she used as he leaned close. It made his thoughts wander. . . .

"Give me room," she whispered. "One wrong connection and we'll have sweepers all over us. I don't need the police—and you're supposed to be dead."

He stood back slightly.

"Not," she added out of the side of her mouth, "to mention that a lot of people have gone to a lot of trouble—"

"I know" he interrupted her mildly.

As if she read his thoughts, as indeed she might have, Amber said, "It's worth it, if we can break the Thrakian alliance and Pepys."

"It's a web," he answered. "The way they've tangled themselves up in everything, it'll take a lot of unweaving. A lot of strand-breaking."

She repeated. "Worth it." She hunched over a moment and made a slight noise in her concentration. The sound deflector on her belt continued its pulsation.

The armor at his back brushed his shoulder with a gauntlet and left it resting there. He patted the gauntlet. "Soon, Bogie." The alien used the battle gear casually as an eggshell. Jack both befriended and feared that entity, a situation as close to fatherhood as he'd ever gotten.

"Got it." She straightened up and saw him watching her. "Ready?"

"As we'll ever be. Now remember, the grounds are massive. I want Dr. Duryea, no one else."

Bogie rumbled. "Use stun?"

"Yes."

There was an echo of disappointment from the armor. Childlike though he was, Bogie had the blood lust of a Milot sand berserker. Amber smiled faintly, the lines of tension erased from about her gold-flecked brown eyes. Jack passed her the palm laser he'd been holding. He had his own weapons, gauntlets to the wrist not unlike Bogie's firing power, gauntlets scavenged from another suit of armor, and stripped down. His pants hid the power lines running to his Enduro bracer armored calves and boots, power supplies jury-rigged there. Amber's slight frown returned as she looked down.

"One misstep and you'll blow your own foot off."

"Never. I know what I'm doing." Actually, she was quite possibly right. He had done his own jury-rigging. Although a soldier knew his armor intimately—it was, after all, his life—a soldier didn't have to be an engineer to wear one.

"Open sesame," Amber said mockingly, reaching around and slapping her hand on the lock. "What are you going to say to the good doctor when he finds out we've broken in."

Jack grinned fiercely. "Thank you."

There are times when every soldier expects to see his life pass before his eyes. Transport ships from military zones and engagements routinely use a debriefing loop to extract information and destress troopers during cold sleep. It was routine—nothing should have gone wrong. But it had.

It had started with the Thrakian invasion of Milos, an invasion which the Dominion forces could have turned aside. Would have turned aside if they had not been betrayed and cut off. Storm had been one of the few men left alive to make it to a transport. And then, that ship had been damaged during lift-off and gone adrift, lost.

Lost for seventeen years. Faced with his memories of a disastrous military engagement for seventeen years. Memories that burned out the deeper recall of his youth and his family, now dead by Thrakian hands.

Now he was about to face the man reported to have found him, sole survivor on a burned out hulk of a transport ship, and thawed him out.

"Thank you" was only one of the things he meant to say.

Mentech's access door snailed ajar, releasing a draft into the night air that smelled of disinfectant and other, more foreign, less identifiable scents. Bogie lumbered forward with an impatient growl and ripped the door off its track. His gauntlets crumpled the plating as if they were plastisheets.

Dismayed, Jack caught a glimpse from the corner of his eye down the right corridor, reached out and slapped Amber down even as he yelled, "Take it off stun, Bogie! Take it off stun!"

All hell broke loose as the intruder force opened fire. Jack felt Amber under his shoulder as he elbowed himself up. Laser spray passed over him, a hot curtain, sparks floating down from the metal and plastic framework it seared. He cocked his gauntlet. Power tingled along his bare wrists inside the armament. Without coming up off the floor, he fired back.

Bogie had caught one of the robot force dead center. Its smoking ruins had come to a halt in the corridor lobby, half-melted, its pincer arms at spindly half-mast. Even destroyed, it looked deadly.

The other four moved so fast Jack couldn't track a target. Under his shoulder, Amber made a muffled noise.

"When I roll," Jack told her, "run for it."

She made a noise like a spitting cat. "Damned cheap contraband," she added. "My gun shattered when we hit the floor."

He couldn't let her go unarmed. If even one of the sentries got past Bogie and him, it would track her down through the streets. "I'm going to the right," he said then.

"I'll shadow you."

A silver spider whirled past him. Jack kicked out in reflex, knocking its weapon out of alignment and the plasma blast intended to dispose of them instead ripped what was left of the door out of the framing. He got to his knees and felt Amber skittering past behind him. He fired once, aimlessly, to cover her.

Mentech's lobby was all business; ten paces across he spied double doors with palm locks and a face plate that probably read retinal patterns. Bogie's handiwork left an unusual sculpture in the center of the room. To the right was the wall, and to the left a corridor that disappeared around the corner—a corridor that undoubtedly led to a storage room where the intruder force had been stored. Jack now had his back protected by a corner.

Bogie knew where they were, had tracked them the moment they moved, and did not fire in their direction. He pivoted to his left and his gauntlets burst in rapid fire. A second robot exploded in sparks and smoke. Jack flinched away from the eye-burning sight even as Amber grabbed his shoulder and screamed.

His hand came up in reflex, pointed, and squeezed. They were showered by metal and smoldering plastic fragments and he realized the thing must have been overhead.

Through the smoke, he could see two more pewter objects bent toward them, skirting Bogie. Why didn't the armor draw them?

He must have muttered aloud, because Amber's voice hoarsely answered, "Heat! They have to be heat sensored."

And Bogie was cold. The only heat he possessed was his weapon fire.

Jack sighted and fired at a five-armed beauty only a mechanic could love. It staggered, rocked back on its tread, then came on again.

Bogie snagged the last machine and, awash in its laser fire and impervious to the weaponry, began to take it apart.

Jack and Amber bolted to their left. He went down on one knee, skidding, felt his jury-rigged wiring pop—he hoped it was his wiring—and fired a second shot even as the wall opened up in flame where they'd just been. His left gauntlet went dead, his wrist ice-cold.

A tensor arm shattered. The robot skewed around, bringing its undamaged arms and turrets into play.

"Shit," Amber said, and he heard a noise at his heels that sounded like she'd flattened full out on the floor.

Bogie literally had his hands full. Jack eyed the machinery coming at them, well-oiled, smooth, deadly, and targeting them.

He picked its locomotion out and fired. The robot ground to a halt, its base shattered. But from the turrets and muzzles facing them, Jack had no doubt he was well within range.

"Run!"

"No," said Amber, muffled. "Just quit playing around and frag that son of a bitch!"

He laid down a spray across its chest, even as he dodged to his left, his knee giving out completely. A muzzle melted. Laser fire limned the wall where his chin had been. He felt it like a close shave and fired back.

He missed, but it drew Bogie's attention. The white armored being paused, hands in the air, the netlike remnants of a robot hung between his fingers.

Amber reached up, grabbed Jack by the throat, and jerked him down even as their sentry fired. He felt the heat sear across the back of his head.

"Close," the girl muttered, "but you're not bald yet."

They lay in an entangled embrace. Jack hugged her close as servos whined and they were targeted once again.

Bogie fired. The robot paused, as though absorbing the energy. Then, abruptly, it shattered.

In his arms, Amber let out a ragged breath. Her warm, dry lips brushed his cheekbone before she said, "I think they know we're here."

Jack got to his feet and pulled her up. He bent over to examine his left bracer. The wires had been severed—his left hand firepower was out for the night. He'd have to make do with the dwindling charge in his right glove.

"What are the odds they have more of those babies around the corner?"

Amber shook her head, and trembled within his loose embrace. Bogie kicked over a tarnished hulk and crunched his way toward them. "Which way, Boss?"

Jack looked over Amber's shoulder toward the double doors.

Amber leaned against the computer clipboard in the wall next to the hand lock and examined it critically. Her nose wrinkled slightly across its bridge. "Your doctor's been a bad boy," she said, as Jack looked into the small, sealed lab, the third of its type they'd come across.

"Find the access code?" he asked, without turning his attention away. The gleaming counters, the suit-waldos waiting to penetrate an entrance from the side walls, the incubators full of petri dishes . . . research interrupted. Bogie leaned a shoulder against the sealed door. Jack felt his ears pop as the suit interfered with the pressurization. He touched the Flexalinked elbow. "Leave it," he said, and turned his attention to Amber. "Are you in?"

"I'm in, and the news isn't good. You don't want in there—or anywhere. Dr. Duryea is a genetic engineer, and an illegal one, if these notes are right." She shuddered. "We're going to end up with something real nasty if we break those seals."

"No kidding." Jack took up a stance behind her, reading the computer clipboard.

"Uh-oh." There was a line break across the flow of information. Amber dropped a hand to his wrist. "These labs are rigged to blow."

"What?"

"Somebody's set them in destruction sequence." She turned off the computer. "At least these babies aren't getting out of here alive."

"How long have we got?"

"Seven minutes."

Jack stepped back into the corridor. He made a sweep. "Bogie, take that T-intersection. Stun for the doctor, full power for anything else."

The opalescent armor turned and went the way he'd indicated. Amber watched critically. "Sure that was a wise thing to do? His judgment is a long way from being developed."

"No worse than yours, guttersnipe," Jack returned.

She made a face at him, an expression that belied the handsome young woman she'd grown into and reminded him of the panhandling youngster he'd first met years ago. "Then I'm going with you. If this is an indication of what Mentech is up to, we're likely to meet something nasty and full-grown just around the corridor."

As they jogged, his gauntlet up and ready for anything that might cross their path, he said, "What was the firing sequence?"

"This wing from front to back lot, and the wing Bogie took."

"That's it?"

"There's another wing, an L section." Amber considered and jabbed a thumb in the approximate direction. "According to the schematic, that's not been given the sequence yet."

Jack smiled. "Then that's the way we go."

She gave him a chill look. "Maybe," she said, "fire won't kill what's in those labs."

He pretended he hadn't heard her.

Duryea paused at the hydra's tank. He ran a gloved hand fondly over the molded lip of the container. There was a stirring within. "Sorry," he whispered. "Another job incomplete. But your owner will be just as delighted with my research report. Cheaper, but still conclusive." He reached up and turned off the respirator pump guarding the inflow to the covered tank. There was nothing for a moment, then the liquid within began to froth furiously. Eventually, lavender blood tinged the foam. Duryea watched as the roiling liquid slowly calmed. He heard a muffled explosion and knew the destruction sequence had begun in Wing 1. He popped a chip out of the wall clipboard and slipped it in his pocket.

The sealed doors behind him opened and he said, without turning around, "I thought I told you to wait beyond the tunnel—"

"Sorry, doctor. You didn't leave instructions at the door."

Duryea whirled and saw the tall man and the thief blocking the doorway. In the muted laboratory light, he identified the thief now as a woman—and a nicely curved one, beneath the black cloaking. "Everything's destroyed," he said. "There'll be no evidence."

"We hardly look like sweepers," the young woman answered, her voice heavy with irony. "Now, do we?"

"It matters little." The palm laser hanging in the depths of his right lab pocket seemed to shift of its own accord. Duryea casually began moving his hand downward. "You've seen what I do here. I scarcely want police attention any more than you do. Who are you?"

The tall man shifted. He tilted his head back slightly, and the doctor got the full impact of his clear blue gaze, eyes the color of lake water on a good day. He knew those eyes. . . .

The flicker of recognition had been seen by the other. He smiled ever so slightly. "You do know me, doctor."

"What are you doing breaking into my labs?"

The man took a step closer. He wore massive, armored boots and gauntlets, and there was the stink of laser fire about them. The doctor shrank back instinctively against the hydra's tank, knowing them for weapons. "I just came to say thank you, but you're a suspicious man. All this research, up in smoke."

"Thank you?" Duryea kept sliding his hand lower, dipping it closer to his pocket. The man was his target, the young woman appeared unarmed. A clean shot to the throat, and he was out of there, before his lab joined the destruct sequence.

"Yes. You found a transport drifting out of range." That rainwater gaze looked about briefly, appraising the lab. "I suppose I should be grateful all you did was revive me. I could have been spliced into something more . . . unusual."

Duryea felt his heart convulse in his chest. He grabbed for his laser, but the other outdrew him, and he found himself on the floor, in a puddle of hot, wet substance. It was difficult to breathe.

"Storm. . . ." the doctor got out.

The named man went down on one knee beside him. "What the hell did you do that for," he said angrily. "I didn't come here to kill you!" He frowned as he searched Duryea for other weapons, and his palm skidded on fabric growing steadily bloodier. "You haven't got long. Who pulled me out and why? Why wasn't I reported to the Dominion as a troop survivor?"

Duryea felt his throat fill with fluid. He gargled and spat, so that he could speak. "We're all weapons in the war—" he said.

"Green Shirt?"

Words failed. The doctor found the strength to nod. Yes! For all his sins, he'd done something right. He'd been a member of the revolutionary Green Shirts.

"And you hid me."

The doctor nodded again.

"I was a Dominion Knight!"

Duryea's right hand began to quiver convulsively. It danced among the blood and gore upon the flooring. "Pepys . . . had the Knights destroyed. You, too, if. . . ."

"What about my *mind*? Where's the tape of my debriefing loop? Was it taken off the transport? Who's got my artifacts?"

Duryea's chin met his chest. It was sticky and smelled like burning meat. The doctor felt his thoughts become dizzy and spin off, one by one. He got out, "The Countess has it . . ."

"Who?"

"The Countess," the doctor repeated. "Find her, find yourself." He coughed, and there was no breathing through that gargle. He followed his last thought into darkness.

"Jack," Amber said tightly. "We've got about ninety seconds to get out of here." The display light from the lab's wall clipboard illuminated her face with a ghastly glow.

He stood. His boots glistened with the doctor's blood. He keyed on his belt com. "Bogie—get out of here *now!*"

He took Amber's hand.

"Be careful what you ask for," she said faintly. She put a boot toe in the doctor's rib cage and nudged gently. "You just may get it. Has it occurred to you that if he couldn't alter you directly, he may have edited the looping tape?"

Jack took her by the elbow and led her outside. He left the door open.

"That's a chance I'll have to take, isn't it?" Jack listened to the explosions, growing louder, more destructive.

"Suppose you remember a long lost lover?"

He looked down then, and met her gold-flecked eyes. "Then I guess she'll just have to stay lost," he said softly. "For the night, anyway."

Amber smiled and slipped her hood back, loosening her hair. The hall drummed with the sound of battle armor running toward them. She sighed. "I don't suppose there's a way to turn him off for the evening?"

"He'll never notice," Jack answered. "He's more interested in the vidscreen anyway."

"Good. I have in mind a rather long farewell."

"You could wake a dead man," Jack told her, as he gathered her in, war and Bogie and the past unimportant for the moment.

CHAPTER 5

An immense cavern. A world of mist and rain without, a clean rain, sprouts shooting upward at its touch, a pioneer world barely touched by civilization and unaware of the dangers of Thrakian sand. Yet, on the far side, a canker growing, an ever exacerbating sore, was the cause that drew this council in the cavern. A sleek, sable-coated humanoid paused before the cavern's maw, wiped his whiskered face neatly with supple hands and looked about. His only concession to clothing was a pair of slicker yellow shorts, bulging with various full pockets, and a tail slit for his sable appendage. He was one of the otter-folk, calling themselves Fishers, and this, their world, was meant to be one of mist and rain.

But it was the canker that drew them together. Skal was the last of the arrivees and, though he could hear the chatter of the bickering Elders within, he had little desire to join them. He looked out across the high plateau, across the mud flats and pastures blowing in the wind like seas of grass, and gave a sigh.

"Deep thoughts," said a husky Fisher voice at his back, and Skal swung about, his body a sinuous ribbon of movement, to face the female, her own sleek coat a rich and rare cream color, like the mystic fogs of their waterways.

"Yes, they are, Mist-off-the-waters," Skal answered. He patted her arm.

"They're waiting for you."

The younger, in his Fisher prime, gave a bob of his head. He knew well that he was the guest of honor. "Let's go in then. I'm as braced as I will ever be." He took a last deep breath of water-laced air, and headed into the cavern, his tail stiff and resolute behind him.

They did not chant or pass the pipe for him, and Skal

was just as glad. He sat, nose down, unable to look in the eyes of his Elders, though every Fisher orb was luminescent as the moon, bright with anticipation. He gathered what it was he had to say, having come straight from the trading post with its subspace vid-screen, one of the planet's only links with civilizations far more advanced than theirs. He knew what it was the Elders were going to ask of him and, worse, he knew what answer it was he was going to make.

A one-armed Fisher, silver at his muzzle and ear tips the only blemish in his raven black pelt, broke off niceties with a grunt. "Let's quit farting around," he said in his deep-throated rasp. "We've a problem. Let's solve it."

Around the circle, russet, sable, and gray muzzles turned to him. Mist twitched a little and blinked, her blue-black eyes showing little white and a grave expression. "Trust One-arm to get to it quickly," she said, and gave a humorous Fisher shrug.

The youngest Fisher there, one who had earned the title Elder by virtue of her experience rather than her age, bore a remarkable scar. It was a laser burn, across her brow, pink tissue furrowing to ear tip, an alien scar from times they remembered but seldom spoke of. Her name was Little Fish and she gave a light, polite cough, before interrupting. "Someone had better speak," she said. "The wound at Three Falls widens daily. Men fester it like swamp bugs. Their poison grows to threaten us all. And, I'm told, twenty leagues south at Deep Hole, a cubling with two heads was born."

A hiss rumbled about the circle, tumbling the woodsmoke from the fire in its lazy curl to the ceiling.

"This cannot be true!"

"It is, I swear to you. I have seen it in the smoke myself. Poisons washed away from the wound fill the earth . . . soon the world."

"Off-worlder poison. . . ."

"Aiiii." One of the Elders rocked on her haunches, her arms over her head.

A black and russet muzzle hissed, "We must rid ourselves of them!"

One-arm growled. "I am right!"

Mist laughed softly, and the other Fishers turned to look at her in amazement, shock over the two-headed cub still in their eyes. She shook her head, curbing her feelings. "At last," she said. "We are all agreed on something!"

A thickly russet-coated male who had not spoken yet, leaned to his right, lifted a hind-leg and passed wind, before saying with a grunt, "Give Skal his assignment."

Mist nodded.

This was what Skal had feared, and he would not look up as the ivory female spoke to him.

"Bring back the Sun. Find the Warrior and bring him back to Mistwald. He showed us his might, and spared us from it. Now he must fight for us again."

The Fisher would not meet Mist's eyes as he said, "We cannot start a war with the offworlders. We already know the price it would mean paying."

"Would you die from woundfester?"

Skal leaped to his feet. The pelt at the back of his neck bristled. That which had wounded him as though it were a hook or talon in his chest pricked at him now: the death of his once-foe, once-comrade. Hero to them, friend to him. He did not wish to speak of Storm's death, for it would crush the hopes of the Fisher-folk, but now he could not avoid it. "It cannot be done. He is dead! I myself saw the ceremonies across the stars when he was laid to rest."

Mist said softly, "Not so."

He met her gaze then, his own fierce brown eyes practically ablaze. "Ask any at the trading post. We watched it through the smoke screen from sub-space." He stammered to a halt then, his own emotions choking in his throat. "I brought him to you once, *but I cannot bring him to you again.*"

One-arm muttered, "We are lost. The poisons will spread. Can nothing be done?"

Mist got to her feet also, her tail lashing angrily from side to side instead of balancing her weight. She showed neat Fisher teeth as she barked out, "Will you give up, then? Never!"

Before the entire circle of Elders, she thrust her hand into the fire, deep into its red and orange flames, without a cry as the blaze angrily licked at her pelt.

When she drew her hand out, a small, carved knife lay in her palm, and she was untouched by the burning. "You gave the twin of this knife to Little Sun. If he were dead on Mistwald, what would happen to that knife?"

"It . . . would no longer exist."

"And this is the knife's soul. Does it exist?"

He stared at the object in her hand. "Yes, but—"

"Do not contradict me! You see the knife's soul!—it exists. Therefore, the knife exists, therefore Little Sun still lives! Find him, Skal."

A spear of hope lanced through him. "He's not on Mistwald."

Fat, burly Croaker laughed. "If he were, we would not have our deathwound opening up. You must go where the knife's soul takes you."

Skal looked about the cavern. Tallow candle stubs guttered low. Late afternoon had fled to deepest night outside, he could see the bowl of the sky, deepest velvet, star littered. "Even if it means off-world," he said, acquiescing to the council.

"Wherever it leads you," Mist answered, though he had not questioned. "Wherever."

CHAPTER 6

"No," Amber repeated softly. "I won't go with you." She tucked her chin in, and her hair fell about her face, shielding her expression. Silently, Colin watched both her and Jack, reserving his opinion for the moment.

"No? You're one of the main reasons I came back."

"Me . . . and the Green Shirts. I'm not fool enough to think you can find them and protect me at the same time."

Jack stopped and rocked back on his boot heels, grinding down on the edge of the Walker reverend's priceless carpet. "You don't need protection."

"Damn right, but you'd try to give it to me anyway." The young woman added gently, "I would have given everything to go with you, but there's work to be done here. Duryea gave you a lead, one that you can't follow if you're going after the Green Shirts. If there is a countess, she won't be easy to tie in, and that means she won't be anywhere near where you're going to have to go."

"And where am I going?"

Amber looked from Jack to Colin and back again. "Are you serious? You have to head for the Outward Bounds— the frontier is full of young rebels. One or two are bound to be the serious type."

Jack looked at Colin. "Did you tell her?"

The saint shrugged. "Did I have to? She just told you. The only thing she didn't tell you is that you're going to be using Bogie for the bait."

Amber shrank back in the chair, tucking her long legs under her. "Use Bogie? Oh, Jack."

"I haven't any choice. The wreckage at Gibbon's had been combed through—there's no sign of the two suits I had shipped there. Bogie's all I've got."

"What if they slit your throat and take him? He's just a baby."

"That baby is as bloodthirsty as most Thraks—and you know it." Jack scrubbed his hand through his sandy-colored hair. "I'll leave him half-powered and disconnect the deadman switch. That's about all I can do. And what about me, lying there with a slit throat?"

She wrinkled her nose. "I thought I taught you better. If not—" she broke off and gave an eloquent shrug.

"You can take the girl out of the street, but not the street out of the girl," Jack said to Colin.

The older man said nothing, but the fierce wrinkles at the corners of his mouth were testimony to the effort it took to restrain himself. Jack finished pacing, stopping at the far corner of the room.

"So once I'm at the Outward Bounds, where do I go?"

"The junkyard," Amber answered promptly. "The strip shops, the retreads. One flash of Bogie and you'll attract all the attention you want. From there . . ." She spread her hands.

"And as for you—"

"I'll keep an eye on her," Colin said abruptly.

She gave him a wise look. "You won't have to. Vandover will be watching out for me."

"Trouble?" Jack asked.

"Nothing I can't handle." She hid her fear with a toss of her head.

He knew better than to press her. If he had to leave her behind, he had to trust that both of them could handle it. He knew Colin well, and the older man would never knowingly let Amber come to harm. The Walker structure had a range almost as far-reaching as both the Dominion and Pepys' Triad Throne combined—and an admirable spy organization within it. If and when Vandover Baadluster came to conclusions about Amber, Colin would know about it almost as quickly as the Minister of War concluded it.

"How are you working your way toward the Outward?" Colin asked smoothly.

"The same way I got here. Odd jobs, hitchhiking. To do it any differently is asking for trouble once I've contacted the Shirts. They'll be able to monitor me since I 'died' on Colinada."

"Time's against you."

"I know. It might be quicker to go in as contract labor, but I'd have no control over where they'd send me and," here Jack smiled grimly, "I've an aversion to chilling down."

"Why not ship out on one of the Walker supply barges?"

That offer took Jack a moment to consider, then he shook his head. "Denaro's likely to have tapped into your freight lines—and since we're unsure at the moment where his loyalties lie, it wouldn't be safe for either of us."

"We haven't established that Denaro is working at cross-purposes."

"No," Jack said smoothly. "And I don't have time to wait while you do. It's not fair to him or your organization to start an inquiry now, anyway. You might create what you've been trying to avoid."

Quietly Amber said, "You could go freelance mercenary again."

Again, Jack shook his head. "Bogie's too conspicuous. If I go as a mechanic, he's just another trunk of tools. But I'd have to use him if I freelanced. Pepys would have me collared as soon as I applied for work. No. I think I know what I have to do."

Amber pushed herself out of the chair. The dark blue jumpsuit she wore tailored to her curves echoed the suppleness of her movement. "You know I don't like long good-byes, so I'll say them here and now." She looked intently at Jack. "You never promised me it would be easy, and I won't have you making stupid promises now. So I won't make you any either. Just do your best."

"You know I will—"

She turned away abruptly, bolting to the door. In the moment she waited for it to slide open, she blurted, "I know that. I also know it could get you killed one of these days," and the door let her out before he could answer.

Colin stood up and put his hand on Jack's arm, restraining him lightly. As Jack turned an accusing gaze on him, the man said gently, "Let her go. It's not safe for you beyond my apartment walls anyway."

They watched the door shut out the vision of Amber fleeing.

After a long moment of silence, Jack shrugged off his friend's hand. "That's not like her."

Colin turned away, gathering up his overrobe before seating himself once more. "Of course not," he said. "Jack, you're a straightforward man, and if you have any fault at all, it's that you deal with people on the same basis."

Jack sat opposite him. He leaned forward, tracing the redwood burl table with a blunt forefinger. "I'm riddled with faults," he said. "What's that got to do with it?"

"Amber was trained to be a child of subterfuge and you tend to forget that."

"Amber," Jack answered dryly, "was trained to be an assassin."

"Be that as it may, she bolted out of here so that you would not begin to question her about what her activities would be."

He stopped tracing the rings of life grown on a faraway planet and looked up, frowning. "What do you mean? She knows her way around under-Malthen. She knows how to access the information we need without causing trouble."

"Maybe. Maybe not."

"What do you mean?"

"The biggest source of information to tap here, or just about anywhere, is the emperor."

Colin had Jack's complete attention now. "Admittedly, Pepys has a web strung just about everywhere—for that matter, so do you."

"And he watches his enemies closely. Almost as closely as he watches his friends. She may inquire in under-Malthan, but I'm willing to wager she'll end up trying to tap Pepys' files."

Jack licked dry lips. "You'll be watching out for her?"

"Indeed, I will. And actively dissuading her from trying such a course. But I think it's important for you to know that you're not the only one at risk."

"I never thought I was."

There was a pause, then Colin nodded. "I should not have thought that of you, Jack." He rubbed one hand across the back of the other, soothingly. "I only pray that you all succeed." He stood up. "Before you leave, I'd like to show you something . . . something I didn't want Amber to view." He keyed on his large wall screen.

On edge, Jack sat back, wondering what the Walker was

about to show him. The wall unit came on, and he recognized a recon satellite's view of a planet—a water planet, and he guessed he was watching one of the outer colonies.

"Thasia," Colin said. "Mainly inhabited by Walkers."

"Heard of it," Jack told him. "A dome world. Looks good, but the temperatures are a little extreme."

"That's it. It's far out. May never have been suitable for massive colonization." Colin sighed as the recon focus brought the world in closer.

"Never have been . . ." Jack repeated.

"Watch," Colin told him.

And Jack did. Watched as the recon satellite, on the edges of its broadcast image, caught the fringe of an incoming fleet. A warship like nothing he'd ever seen before, and even as he said, "Who the hell's that?" to Colin, the view screen showed domes cracking like egg shells, the precious life they protected suddenly exposed to the hostile environment.

That attack was over in minutes.

Colin watched even after the screen darkened to black. "They never," he said, with great effort, "even got out an alarm. The satellite was destroyed on their way out."

If he expected a similar reaction from Jack, he didn't get it. Storm got to his feet and moved close to the wall unit. "Run that back again."

Colin, wide-eyed, opened his mouth as if to protest. Instead, he keyed out his request, and the video ran back. "Tell me when."

"All the way to the beginning." Jack watched intently as Thasia was destroyed. "Freeze it there."

Colin did so. Jack tapped the back of his hand on the screen. "No defense? Any word from Baadluster or Pepys?"

"No. But it's early yet. I should hear from Pepys tomorrow morning."

Jack looked back to the freeze-frame. "This was done by the Ash-farel."

"That was what we concluded."

"A Thrakian League wing was in that quadrant. They should have been in there, on defense."

Colin cleared his throat. "Unless the Ash-farel came through them first."

"Doubtful." Jack paced back and forth, his shadow momentarily interrupting the projection. He halted again. His forefinger stabbed the close-up of destruction. "I don't know who the hell they are, but we've been told a lot of lies about them."

"Lies? Lies?" Colin's voice went up a notch. "They've wiped out thousands of innocent people."

"And left the planet virtually untouched. They're fighting a 'Pure' war, Colin. That planet, in a year or three, will be perfectly habitable again. The Thraks have been lying to us about the kind of destruction and fighting the Ash-farel are doing."

"Lives, human lives—"

"Damnit, I know that! But we're not talking about total destruction. We're not talking about firestorming, like what happened to Claron. I'm a Knight, and we were trained to kill humans, flesh, war machines, whatever it took, like killing vermin—but always to leave the planet clean. Habitable."

Colin snapped the projection off, and the wall went dark. Jack stared at it for a moment longer, as if he could still see the image.

" 'Pure' war or not," his friend said, "they're killing us off. They can get through our defenses and the Thrakian defenses—and they won't be stopped."

Jack smiled then, a short, grim smile that made Colin shiver. "But that's the key to them. They're not destroying the planets. They've a moral or ethical standard that we might even begin to understand, if we could contact them. And, whatever the Ash-farel are, the Thraks are afraid of them. Very, very afraid of them."

"And they fight a 'Pure' war."

"Exactly. It confirms my gut feelings—the reason I deserted my command. We may be allied with the Thraks in order to face the Ash-farel, but I think we're fighting the wrong enemy."

Colin's lips tightened. "That may be—but human lives, souls, are not vermin to be cleansed off a planet's surface."

"That all depends on your point of view," Jack answered.

CHAPTER 7

"Duryea's been reported dead, and his labs destroyed." Baadluster's tone of voice implied that he was not unhappy to be rid of the man.

Pepys did not stir in his communications web. He did roll an eye toward his somber Minister of War. "I know," he said shortly, as though part of him were listening to another voice—which it was.

"There was no record of the experiments he was conducting for you. You'll have to begin all over again."

"I know," the emperor repeated patiently. "What I don't know is who attacked him."

Baadluster gave a slight bow of acknowledgment, saying, "I've men working on it. If we can discover how the labs were blown—"

Pepys waved a negligent hand. "Forget it. Duryea destroyed them himself. I know his handiwork, seen it before. He doesn't like to leave evidence behind when he's forced to move. Particularly evidence that he might not get paid for."

"I see."

Pepys did stir then, rising from his chair and removing his crown of probes. "As well you might." Released from its imprisonment, his red hair began to waver in the slight air currents caressing the room. "Tell me what you find out as soon as you can. The Green Shirts usually protect their own. This time they didn't. I want to know why."

Baadluster made a full bow this time, and turned to leave. His departure was interrupted by Pepys who made a loud noise, flung his arm out, and snapped his fingers for Vandover's attention. His cat-green eyes were fixed on the bank of monitors. He pointed a shaking finger at one.

"There! Just coming in, subspace relay. The Ash-farel are attacking." He pulled his crown of input leads and probes firmly onto his brow and, white-faced, sat down to watch. Vandover hovered at his side, knowing that he should be in the domain of his own board room to see this, but he stayed, also knowing his aides would be recording the broadcast.

Pepys sat transfixed for the brief duration of the action. Suddenly the satellite went out of commission, and the screen went to test pattern at the abrupt cessation of the signal. Pepys' hands whitened as he grasped the arms of his chair.

"What happened? Who's on the defense line there? Why were there no shields up?"

Vandover scanned the coord information on the bandline still riding the top of the monitor's screen. He said flatly, "That's a Walker colony, your highness. I would assume shielding was too expensive for such a modest population. The domes would have been enough   ordinarily."

"Damn." Skin over the whitened hands pulled taut until knuckles showed through, each an individual death's head. "How long can we keep this from Colin and his damned council?"

Vandover stretched his neck and scratched a tiny mole upon it reflectively. "In all likelihood, he already knows. His spies are at least as good as yours."

Pepys turned in his chair and eyed his minister with a baleful green stare. Vandover shrugged. He had told the truth. If the emperor started taking offense at the truth, there was little he could do. The emperor licked paper thin lips. "I want to know whose quadrant that was and how the Ash-farel got by—and if they survived, why."

"Your wish is my command," Vandover said ironically. He bowed deeply in his black robes, the better not to see Pepys' mouth flex bitterly at his words. He turned and was halfway out of the portal before he straightened, the better to hide his own elation.

Pepys slammed the portal shut fast, but Vandover had already eased through it. He caught not even a scrap of the man's elusive black robes.

The emperor sat back in his chair. The bank of screens before him showed a myriad of activity worlds over. Nothing interested him. None of them would show him what he really wanted to know. None of them could broadcast the future.

CHAPTER 8

Skal huddled against the counter as his prospective employer frowned and took the Traveler's disk Skal had paid much for—almost as much as if it had been a genuine passport instead of counterfeit. The human Skal faced dropped the disk into a reader and studied what his monitor displayed for him.

The pitted hull of an off-world ship in its cradle loomed behind them. All about them was the bustle of the port, barely dimmed by the wall of plastishield between it and them. The Fisher felt almost as though he was right in the midst of the cradles and ships, dodging hand trucks and cargo walks in order to be interviewed. But all that bustle was actually beyond the shield. In here, inside the monstrous domed hall, were cubicles of business. Skal's whiskers twitched. He could not have guessed at the liveliness of the trade here, inside a dome where Fishers were not allowed, even on this their own world.

A computer/printer rattled frantically to his right, on the other side of a wall which he could see over if he stepped up to it and pushed his muzzle atop. Although curiosity tickled his insides as though he'd swallowed a live fingerling, he dared not look. The cubicle next door housed a lawyer and his computer was researching/creating a contract before the very eyes of his client. The machinery was similar but different from the computer at the trading post which not only sold goods but inventoried them. Still, Skal was pleased he had recognized the technology for what it was: he would hate to have sat waiting like a half-tailed cubling, muzzle twitching with never-to-be-sated inquisitiveness.

None of the cubicles had a ceiling; partial walls separated them but did not offer real privacy. Higher up the dome were the blister window office cubicles for true privacy. Up there was where Skal would rather be, but he would not spend all the funds he had for the price of his ticket at one time. He had no idea how far he might have to go to find Jack Storm. The yellow flake from his rivers was worth a certain amount. Just how much, he was not sure, but all metal, no matter how base, had a bargaining worth.

His prospective employer gargled in his throat. "According to this, I'm all but ordered to take you off-world, if you want to go. You've been appointed Ambassador-At-Large."

The very tip end of his proud tail moved slightly, but Skal did not worry that he had been unmasked as the deceiver he was. His brief association with humans had shown him that they were not adept at reading Fisher body language. Instead, he gave a half-bow. "True, but would you rather not get value for your passage? I'm prepared to work for the journey."

The human on the other side of the counter had a massively round face, like that of the full moon, and little hair to decorate it with except for bushy eyebrows that moved fluidly up and down as though they were hairy-bodied caterpillars. "You're in a hurry."

Skal smoothed down his whiskers with a right palm. "Of a certainty. I cannot wait for a liner. Besides, your vessel has an itinerary appealing to me."

The captain laughed. It was much the same as his gargle, but louder. "I run a garbage scow!"

"You, sir, haul a scrap barge. You go where technology lives off its own carrion. You may not have noticed, but—" and here Skal leaned forward confidentially, "Mistwald is a low-technology world." A shiver of apprehension ran its way through his deep sable coat, mottled with amber dapples. If he was not taken on now, he would have to wait until after the barge cleared port before he dared show his disk around again. It would be a terrible delay if that came to pass.

An eyebrow arched, fatly and proudly. "I thought you Fishers liked it that way."

"I might remind you that the Dominion rejected us, not vice versa."

Captain Obe sat back in his chair. He had been leaning

on his plump elbows on the counter. He smiled. "Now I understand. You not only want a trip, you want an education. Well. Scrap boy doesn't pay much—"

Skal shrugged, an eloquent Fisher shrug which rippled his supple body all the way to the tip of his foot claws. "I don't ask much," he said, and opened his muzzle in a wide grin.

Rain left under-Malthen stinking instead of cleansed, damp and mildewed. Piles of garbage that occasionally mummified and disintegrated into dust to blow away were now rotten and putrefied. Welcome, Amber thought, to the rainy season. Jack's funeral and brief visit seemed a lifetime ago, in the few days of storm that preceded the actual rain by several weeks. She slogged through the gutter, clutching a light plastic wrap about her body, her hair tucked in under its hood. Without seeming to, her body wove a pattern along the sidewalk, eluding most of the views of the security cameras. Old habits died hard.

A light hand skittered over her buttock. Amber whirled, spotted the wide-eyed child, and snarled, "Beat it, Skag!" and pivoted again so quickly that she caught the real perp by his wrist, trying to pick her waist belt. The boy's lip curled in a grimace.

"Amateur night," Amber told him, and thrust his arm away from her, freeing him. "Wait for the streets to fill up."

The teen spat out, "Nobody's out today."

"They'll be out. You've just got to know when the traffic flows. Learn what you're doing." Amber moved swiftly again and caught the first child, a girl, probably his sister, in the midst of trying to pick her boot shank. "You two just don't give up, do you?" she asked, her fingers entwined in the child's greasy hair.

The girl gave a yelp, but her partner merely shrugged. "Times is rough," he said.

Amber nodded. "Times *are* rough." She dropped a five credit bit in his hand. "Get some hot food."

They bolted so fast that the girl left hair wrapped in Amber's fingers. She stood pensively on the sidewalk, in the darkening light, and shook the strands free on the wind. Times were rough. She'd made Jack promise her years ago that he'd never bring her back to under-Malthen, but here she was, of her own volition, living in hell.

With a shudder, she began to walk again, seeking the neighborhood of her old apartment. Better here than in the barracks, where Vandover Baadluster made no apology for the shameless recording of everything she did and everything she said. And there was a bank of charlatan psychics working in the palace for Pepys who would have liked to have reported on everything she thought as well. When she'd lived with Jack, she'd gotten away with jamming the cameras and mikes, but now she knew she walked a thin line between what Pepys would allow and what he wouldn't.

As for the psychics, so few had any real talent at all that she'd never had to shield her powers. As for now . . . with the power burned out of her, she no longer had to worry. Not that Baadluster had given up hunting her. No, even though the war effort diverted his attention, he would be locating her soon enough. Amber made a mental note to move again this weekend. She'd keep Baadluster guessing as long as she could. That was not psychic intuition—it was common sense.

Her wrap tangled about her knees as she turned the corner to catch the back lift to her rooms. She stumbled and caught herself against the rough siding of the building. Her breath stuttered in her chest. She pulled back into the shadows, lower lip caught in her teeth as she stifled her surprise.

Like a bitter wind piercing her, she had caught a flicker of presence in her rooms. A rank, low, and muttering presence. Baadluster.

He had already caught up with her.

Amber hugged herself as she went cold in that bitter wind. He would be at the window, watching for her. It had been pure luck that she'd caught scent of him first. No, not luck . . . the last, burning flicker of her psychic abilities. She eased past the edge of the building and looked up. A shadow briefly interrupted the golden glow of the interior lights. She'd left them on, knowing it would be dark when she returned. Left them on as proof against just such an intrusion as she now faced. The shadow moved. Vandover, pacing in his impatience. One of the few traits he shared with Jack.

She hesitated only a second longer, as she decided where she would go now. Yes—the labor district, on the edge of the border between Malthen proper and its shadier environs. A favorite housing for the high-priced technicians, particularly hospital techs, who could not quite afford the best. Pepys would not look for her to move closer. Besides, she had exhausted her connections in this part of the city. It might be more convenient to be closer. She might find herself with her own hands in the emperor's pockets, so to speak.

The sky grew completely dark, and a shower began pelting out of the oppressive cloud cover. She left in its protection.

CHAPTER 9

Jack woke for a second time that night, the stale taste of failed *mordil* rank in his mouth. He reached out instinctively, but the anti-grav hammock had him securely and he wasn't going anywhere accidentally. Someone made a noise in his sleep, and Jack stilled, aware that they were packed in close quarters and his restlessness would easily be transmitted.

He laid his head back, pillowed it on his left hand. The small vial of *mordil* could be felt in one of his left leg pockets, like a thorn pressing in. He wouldn't take any more tonight. Sleep would come or it wouldn't. Either way, he was accustomed to it now. After seventeen years of involuntary cold sleep, his body refused to let normal sleep come quietly. He was used to the phenomenon by now and getting addicted to *mordil* wasn't any more attractive than being awake.

He'd been dreaming of Claron—wild and unsettled, new frontier, as he'd enjoyed it before the firestorming. He'd dreamed of the damned rascally boomrats and their persistent raids on the brewery malt fields. Somewhere in his gear lay a shiny green stone, a pebble really, left in barter by one of the wily boomrat gang leaders. Had any of the creatures managed to survive the firestorming? By any stretch of the imagination, could he picture their warrens deep enough underground to resist the heat and flame? That they would have been the type of animal to lay aside stores of grain and nuts against future shortages of food? Could there be life stealing back into Claron even though he had failed to persuade Pepys to terraform what was left? If so, it would mitigate a few of his nightmares.

Lying there, he became aware of the stench of the barracks—of rancid sweat and unwashed bodies. He caught a whiff of *ratt*. Now there was a drug he stayed as far away from as he could. So did anyone with half a brain. He thought he could pinpoint who was using it and made a note to stay away from the man on work details. He would be violent and paranoid and erratic any one of which could get a man killed on a staggering old vessel like the one they rode.

The *New Virginia* had, at one time, been a proud warship, but now was a gutted hull outfitted to run the most cargo—be it agra, flesh, or scrap—it could hold. Amenities were a luxury on any warship, and light-years away from this one. She creaked when she made FTL, shuddered when she turned the corner coming out of FTL. Pipes throbbed whenever anyone turned on the water and the heads damn near flushed directly into deep space. Her pitted outer skin shed heat tiles like dandruff every time they spun into a landing orbit. And Jack wouldn't have been on her if he'd had any place better to go.

The *New Virginia* was only slightly better than shipping out chilled down as contract labor. Besides his aversion to cold sleep and cold sleep fever, there was the added disadvantage of being unable to control his downtime. He might be shipped out and awakened in three months—or three years. Assuming, of course, that the Thraks and Ash-farel had left anything behind of the human-held worlds in three years.

A spindly hand grabbed through the hammock netting and caught his ankle. It jolted him out of his thoughts. "Asleep, m'boy?"

Jack fought the recoil reflex. "No," he said softly.

"Didn't think so. Out of there, m'boy, and come sit my hand for me." The viselike grip loosened and Jack peeled out of his hammock netting to swing down to the deck.

He landed cat-light, leaving other sleepers in their dreams as he joined Heck by the bulkhead. In the twilight illumination of the corridor beyond, the elder man looked more skeletal than ever. His twisted height barely reached that of Jack's shoulder yet the impact of his personality was such that few disobeyed Heck's oblique requests. Storm was used to commanding presences from his time in the military. He obeyed Heck when he felt like it. Tonight was such a night. A game of cards would be a pleasant diversion when stacked against nightmares.

Heck peered up at him, dim light reflecting in the yellow-white of his eyes.

"Good game?" Jack asked, stepping past him into the corridor.

"Fair enough," Heck answered. He scratched a rooster-comb thatch of gray hair. "Bet what you like—but if you've made a dent of more than fifty credits in my winnin's, I want it repaid."

Jack nodded his understanding as Heck led him along the cluttered walkway to the galley, the only place with enough room for recreation. Heck was Shop boss. He still wore his greasy coveralls from the day shift and the suit hung from his bone-thin frame.

"Taking a break?"

Heck nodded as they approached the galley. "Stamina ain't what it used to be, but I won't let *them* know it."

Jack felt a grin tug at the corner of his mouth. Heck must be playing with the flight officers again, hence the automatic siding of "us against them." As one of the mechanic crew members, Jack found himself in a decidedly under strata layer of respect on the *New Virginia*. It was about the only circumstance that could make allies of Jack and Heck.

Heck threw back scrawny shoulders and sauntered into the galley, calling out, "This here's Jack. He'll be sittin' in for me while I make my constitutional."

MacGrew, Jack recognized him as one of the navigating staff, threw back his head and snorted a laugh. "Constitutional, hell. Old man, you're going to take a nap."

"Maybe I am and maybe I'm not." Heck pulled out a rickety chair for Jack to sit in. "But this boy's going to hold my place. Any objections?"

MacGrew pointed a blunt finger saying, "You just heard one—" but his voice was overrun by the other three at the table muttering their approval. MacGrew sat back, his heavy face flushing. Jack straddled the chair and their eyes met, and then MacGrew grinned.

He shrugged as if in apology for his temperament. As the deal went round, Jack caught up a handful of cards, their plastic edges frayed and brittle. Heck stayed a moment, pacing back and forth behind him.

MacGrew looked up, but it was the young, pale-haired, dark-eyed officer next to him who said, "Go ahead, Heck, beat it. And get something to eat while you're at it. I can't stand looking at those bones of yours."

Heck cackled obscenely, then added, "Fun me all you want, boys—but when the Thraks come get us, they won't be eatin' *me*!" He left to further hoots of derision, knobby back stiff.

Only Jack was silent, staring after him. Only Jack and the men who'd been with him on a disastrous run at a Thrakian sand crèche knew that the Legion kept humans as fodder for their larvae. Where in the hell had Heck been, and how much did he know?

The pale-headed officer tapped his shoulder. "Let's go, Jack. I haven't got all night to get my money back. Ante up."

With difficulty, he wrenched his thoughts back to the cards.

Even with FTL, it would be a few weeks before they landed dirtside at the most likely of the Outward Bounds' retread shops. Jack knew he would have to take his time and stalk Heck patiently, or the canny old man would avoid him entirely, Shop boss or not. His suspicions were validated the next shift when he found his stint traded arbitrarily for another shift. Starting a game wouldn't get him closer to Heck, so Jack spent most of his work period shifting through ideas on how to isolate him effectively without scaring him off.

A tone sounded and the lights flashed. Jack looked up, then massaged the back of his neck. He was on free time now. He cleaned up his workbench, keyed in the equipment he'd left soaking in a mild acid bath for the next shift, and looked around to find himself alone. The swing shift was a fairly solitary work period. Squaring his shoulders, Jack slapped his palm against the portal lockplate and waited to be let out as the lights dimmed down.

A jackhammer slammed against his collarbone, and he was lifted off his feet, then dragged sideways. Jack went limp as the fabric about his neck drew taut. He recognized

the half-wheeze of the man who had him even as he coiled
for a strike. Surprise kept him still as the old man dragged
him into a side bulkhead with amazing strength.

As the fabric went slack and the grip loosened, Jack
pulled himself to his feet. He towered over Heck, who
seemed suddenly reduced.

Heck stuffed a handful of credit disks into Jack's hand.
"Your share of th' winnings, m'boy." He wheezed three
quick breaths, then gulped hard, as if trying to steady his
breathing. He looked up, and there was a feral glint in his
yellowing eyes. "They all laugh at me, allus have. But you
didn't. You hide it real well, boy, but I *saw*. It was in your
eyes. You knew what I meant, didn't you? Who the hell
are you?"

Jack looked down at the old man. Probable answers ran
through his mind, and he discarded most of them. He said,
"What does it matter who I am?"

Heck fairly shook with agitation. "They laugh at me.
They know nothin' about the Thraks. You do. How? Have
you seen what I've seen?" He pointed at his bleary eyes,
hand cocked as if he held a palm laser.

"Let them laugh," Jack told him. "They don't know."

"But you do."

Jack looked down at the bony man. Just how old was
he, under that skin like leather? "Maybe."

"Don't jack me around, boy!" Heck seemed to shoot
upward in height, as he straightened and threw his jaw forward. "You might be found floatin' in one of them acid
baths come morning shift."

Jack stepped out of the bulkhead frame. He drew himself
up, taking the same stance he would if he were wearing
armor, a presence he had not allowed himself to exhibit
for weeks. Fear was suddenly mirrored on Heck's face. He
stepped back involuntarily as Jack said softly, "Is that a
threat?"

"Now, now. Don't be hasty. We're all of us salvage on
this heap o' scrap. No last names, no questions. There's
metal in you I didn't see before, that's for sure. I spoke
out of turn."

"Now that you see it, listen. I've fought Thraks. When
and where is unimportant. What's important is that we both
know part of the secret lying behind those beetle-masks. I

intend to find out the rest—you can tell me, or not. I'll find out one way or another."

The will that puffed Heck up evaporated. The old man sank into himself, seeming even smaller than usual. He sagged against the bulkhead for support, hooking an elbow over a massive bolt to keep himself upright. "It's a long story," the Shop boss capitulated.

"I don't sleep much on my rest shift anyway."

"And it's not a pretty story," Heck continued as though not hearing Jack. "M'boys—if they'd lived, would be about forty now. We were Treaty breakers, an' with the Alliance now, what's left of my life is forfeit if anyone ever finds out."

The corridor lights dimmed and stayed low as Heck told his story. He and his three sons were scavengers . . . salvagers with little sense of duty or obligation. They made their living taking the pickings from the planets the Thraks had conquered . . . combing the sands to salvage the installations left behind by the original colonies and the military. They had outfitted a light corsair to stay one step ahead of the Thraks, and under cover of the newly negotiated treaty between the Thrakian League and the Dominion and the Triad Throne, which once again gave the Thraks access to the major trade lanes, the sand planets were not closely monitored. Humans shunned them. They were wide open for the kind of hit and run salvage techniques Heck and his three sons practiced.

Jack felt the hair crawl on the back of his neck as the Shop boss described their various deeds. A planet conquered and disintegrating into Thrakian sand was not a pretty sight—but he'd had no idea of the parasites like Heck who crawled over it, picking and plucking at the carcass with its precious bits of life left. He felt no sympathy for the man who now described the growing and inevitable Thrakian awareness of what they were doing.

It was greed that led to their downfall. Stupidity, too, Jack told himself and tried not to reflect that in his expression. But Heck wouldn't haven't noticed. He was too wrapped up in his tale of woe, and in the loss of three proud sons.

Though they hadn't been proud when they were captured by the Thraks. No. They had offered the worth of their cargo and corsair for their freedom. But since the Thraks had already taken that, they had nothing with which to bargain. The Thraks were interested in something else.

Heck sighed. "That something we didn't know until we were taken to th' larder camp, near the Windshears."

The sentence lanced through Jack, as though he'd been half asleep and was now chillingly awake. "Where?"

Heck smirked. "You wouldn't a-heard of it, m'boy. It's on Milos, and nary a man's come back alive since we lost it to the Thraks."

"What is it? An installation?"

"Naw. A mountain range, so sharp-edged to a hellacious wind that it damn near slices it—and aircraft comin' in there—in half." Heck rubbed his eyes wearily as if the talk was slowly draining him of what life he had left.

Jack hoped the movement would hide the tumble of emotions racing through him. He and K'rok had survived Milos . . . separately, although the Milots had called in the Dominion Knights to ally with them in the ground war. Jack was one of the few who had made it to transport. The ground sweep had been a rout. He was not sure if he wanted to hear the fate of even a few of the forces stranded by orders given by a young Pepys, even then in search of emperorhood.

"Not that that bothered the Thraks. They snugged right up against th' foot of the Windshears and started making sand. M'boys and I were marched in to join the rest of the food supplies. We had hopes of getting out, though. Thraks like their meat as fresh as they can get it. My sons were all big, brawny bucks, but the Thraks thought they could fatten up my bones a little, too. There was two cold sleep transports just outside th' base, buried up to their launch cradles in sand, but we thought—we planned—to get inside and see if we could take them up."

"Transports?"

"That's what I said. Grounded as plain as anything, for all the sand drifted over their hulls."

The implications of what the old man told him washed over Jack. Cold ship transports had been grounded instead of lifting troops off Milos—leaving thousands of men and hundreds of Knights to the enemy. Grounded at Pepys' command, given through the now-dead officer Winton. But any ship kept an automatic computer log, a bank, of its instructions, the infamous black box, the origins of which were now lost in legend. If Jack could get to such a ship, and if it had not been stripped by the Thraks, he would have in his hands proof of the betrayal perpetrated by Winton and Pepys in order to gain an emperor's throne. It would mean going back to Milos—back to where his nightmares had begun. "But you didn't make it," he said, and got a grip on his thoughts.

"No. They picked us off one by one. I got out because I was the only one left—I was always the wiry sort. I stole a hover and got picked up by another scrapper. Had to leave my last boy behind, meat for the grubs like the rest."

Heck took a wavery breath. "What's the matter, boy? You look a little peaked. Did you think that Milos would die a cleaner death than th' rest?" Heck gave a harsh bark of a laugh. "Nothin' those bugs do is clean. No. We found our boys hanging from meathooks in ice caves underground, just waiting for the nest to warm up enough for—"

"I know," Jack said flatly, cutting him off. The tone of his voice made Heck pause and clear his throat as though thinking whether to venture further and not.

Finally, with an unsteady hand completely leeched of the strength it had earlier, Heck touched his arm. "You've seen it, too."

"I have." Jack took a cleansing breath, then added, "You'd be wise to forget it."

"How can I?" Heck asked in a piercing whisper. "*How can I?* There's no one about with the balls to tell the truth anymore. Pepys all but sleeps with the Thraks, and the Dominion trots behind on his leash. Even th' Green Shirts lay down and died, ever since the Liberator disappeared . . . now all they do is take piss-ant bites out of Pepys whenever they can."

"Liberator?" repeated Jack.

"Oh, don't raise your eyebrows at me, pup. There was a day, about th' time you were born, when the Green Shirts were a glorious group. I hung on their jet stream for a while, but I wasn't good enough for them. I don't know who the man was who headed them, but his tag was Liberator, and he had balls enough for the whole lot of 'em. He's been gone twenty years or so now . . . and so has the heart of the movement. There was a day, boy, when scum like me wasn't good enough for them, and that's the way it shoulda stayed." Heck turned and began to shuffle away. "That should give you something to think about."

Jack watched him leave, fading into the grayed shadows of the old ship. Something to think about. Indeed. None of it pleasant.

CHAPTER 10

Vermin was too good a word to describe the inhabitants of Victor Three. They lived off a boiled scab of a world that even the shipbound crew didn't care to visit. Heck was the only one who cared enough to walk Jack off the *New Virginia*. They both took a look around the port—it had the look of having been strafed or firebombed and Jack wondered if they'd had a berthing accident or crash. Haphazard reconstruction was going on, while the existing concrete walls were black shadowed from the heat that had seared them.

Heck stopped, sucking at a tooth. "Strafed," he said, as if that explained it all.

"Who by?"

"Pepys, probably. No reason not to. Victor's a freebooters' planet. Doesn't hurt to remind 'em now and then who's the real boss." The Shop boss seemed even more shriveled than usual, as if his talk with Jack had bled him of whatever will to live he possessed, and he wheezed with every breath. At the berth's edge, he paused while Jack fetched a hand truck and loaded Bogie's trunk onto it.

He eyed the container. "Must be quite a collection of tools."

"It is." Jack dropped the trunk on the platform as gently as he could and programmed it to follow him at random.

"Must be a sight to see. Never seen a lock like that for tools."

"Probably not." Jack squinted, looking the port over. It was sloppy—vessels slipping in their berths, repair crews leaving equipment in aisles that ought to be kept clear, thrust pads dirty.

Heck scrubbed a callused hand over the front of his overalls. "What are you lookin' for here?"

Jack turned back to him. He let a faint smile come out. "Whatever I can find."

The old man spat to one side. It pooled in a puddle of grease. "You're no mechanic, m'boy. You're good—too good. You work on equipment as if your life depended on it, not your job."

He looked down, meeting the rheumy gaze. "You never complained before."

"It's a closed ship on board. What comes in, eventually goes out. I covered for you—but you'll never make it here. Too slow, too thorough. They'll cut you down to scrap."

"Who says I plan to stay?"

Heck hunched up a shoulder. "Well, that's it, ain't it," he responded. "You're too good for hereabouts, and they've got you spotted. Already, I'd say."

Jack watched the slidewalks as the crew pulled the joining ramps into place for loading and unloading. He felt an itch between his shoulder blades, a familiar feeling, as though the enemy already had him in their grid. He wished he was wearing his armor instead of trucking it. He looked back at Heck, who was scuffling his boots on the pad. "If I asked you for advice, would you give it.

The old man looked up greedily. "Been a lot of years since a boy asked my advice." His faded eyes brimmed. "It depends on what you're looking for."

Jack decided to go for broke. "The Green Shirts."

Heck recoiled a step. Then a crafty expression passed over his seamed face. "Show me what you've got stowed in there, and I just might be able to point you in the right direction."

Jack let himself hesitate a fraction of a second, then he went down on one knee beside the massive trunk. Heck crowded against his shoulder. Jack shielded the trunk's combination, a triple keying sequence, and opened the lid very slightly.

Bogie lay quietly in the compartment, Flexalinks glimmering in the dim light of the port. The battle armor was on its back, legs bent and knees drawn up to fit in the trunk, helmet resting on the stomach of the equipment. Jack snapped the lid shut as Heck sucked in a wavery breath.

The old man narrowed his eyes. "That's armor!" he spat out, his voice barely above a whisper.

Jack made no motion other than to straighten up. "I'm waiting," he said calmly.

Heck made a physical effort to restrain himself. Finally, in a choked voice, he said, "Skagboots'. It's the only shop I know of where you can find what you want. Not that it's the only place, mind you—but the only one I know of for sure. Mind your step, m'boy. They'll slit your throat for that." He gave a jerky nod toward the trunk.

"I know." Jack held his hand out in farewell. The Shop boss stared at it a moment, uncomprehending, then reached out and took it.

The old man's clasp was deathly cold.

The city outside the port was gray as slate, dirty and unwashed, littered with garbage too precious to recycle and too worthless to repair. Jack skirted his way through the prefab sheds, some for storage and some blinking with the strobelike flare of welding lasers, shops too small to stand up straight in. Trash ought to be as colorful as the people who discarded it, he thought, but the scrap here on Victor Three was drab and pitted. Warehouses leaned against one another, with no thought of fire walls and noise ordinances. Their ribbed bulk all but hid a light blue sky, striped with the charcoal exhaust of smokestacks.

The hand truck rattled behind him, staying where it was programmed to, in spite of all the obstacles to foot traffic. Jack tried to walk through as though he did not know he was being observed, palm resting on the butt of the hand-laser he had holstered at his right hip. The flickering weld-lights would pause a moment as his shadow darkened doorways, and then begin again.

He did not begin his search until he was through the fringe areas of the retread shops—he was not looking for penny-ante operations. When the industrial buildings grew big enough to blot out the sky, he became interested.

A live sentry leaned indolently in the frameway of the first shop he approached. It was automatic that here, among the scrapyards, human labor would be cheaper than robotic. Robotics were a byproduct of their labor—humans arrived here daily like so much flotsam from the rest of the

Outward Bounds. The man looked as if he had never seen a comb, and his application of second-rate depilatory left a permanent day-old scrub of beard that looked tough enough to use for filings. He looked up diffidently as Jack approached, but the man missed nothing, not even the complaining hovers of the hand truck as it endeavored to keep its cargo afloat. Greed surfaced in the sentry's hazel eyes.

"What can I do for you, boss?"

The hand truck stopped at Jack's heels, literally nudging the backs of his calves. "Looking for work," Storm answered.

The sentry's gaze brushed over the trunk. "Delivering or employment?"

"Employment."

Interest died down a bit. The sentry rasped a thumbnail along the underside of his jaw. "Nothing here, boss. Labor's cheap."

"I have my own tools."

The sentry raised an upper lip, showing teeth in what might have been a smile. "There won't be any work here—probably not in all of Victor Three. You're too clean—which means you're trouble. You're here because you have to be. Want some advice?"

Jack's eyebrow went up, but he stayed silent, giving assent.

"Sell your tools and catch the first shuttle out. You're going to lose 'em anyway, might as well get some money for them."

"Lose them?"

The sentry leaned back against the framework of the factory doorway. "Lose 'em—or have 'em taken from you. It's all the same."

"Not to me. I'd have to be dead first."

"Wouldn't be the first time," the sentry returned. He shrugged. "Talk is cheap."

Jack palmed a credit disk and showed it. The afternoon sun, from somewhere behind towering buildings and smokestack exhausts, struck a glint in it. "Maybe not."

They clenched hands over the disk. Jack let the other pry it from his fingers.

The sentry tucked it in a secure pocket. "Well," he said.

"I like a man who knows what a finder fee is. What are you looking for?"

"Skagboots'."

Fear abruptly washed the greed out of the other's eyes. "A couple of clics east. You can't miss it. Look for the mural on the side, called 'A Thraks Crucifixion.'"

The other's discomfort brought a tight smile to Jack's face as he said, "Sounds distinctive."

"It is." The sentry stuck a thumb in the portal lock, keying it. It slid open just wide enough to admit him, and he disappeared from Jack's sight.

As Jack turned about to sight his direction, he noticed that the sun was beginning to drop to the horizon, and that purple shadows were lengthening rapidly. He snapped his fingers to bring the hand truck about, and began walking east.

The scrap shops gave way to a junkyard, heavily fenced with sonic posts as well as wire. The yard seemed to be one continuous unit, hinting at a scrap operation far bigger than any he'd seen yet. There was heavy equipment here, tractor tows and berthing cradles, even a corsair, laser scarred and deepspace pitted, at rest among the mundane scrap of businesses and households. The size of the junkyard forced him to skirt it, unable to approach Skagboots' directly—unless this was part of Skagboots'. The thought instilled a certain amount of healthy respect in Jack.

A ragged purple shadow nearly hidden among the other shadows kept pace, and Jack finally separated the creature from its cover—a lumbering, man-sized lizard, with four hind legs to walk on and rather fearsomely clawed front legs at the ready at its chest. It raised its shovel head from time to time to look at him, and Jack knew he was looking at the equivalent of a junkyard dog. He wondered if the beast was a denizen of Victor Three or imported.

He also decided he wasn't going to get close enough to find out. The fencing and sonics were discouragement enough for him.

His stomach was grumbling by the time he reached the corner of the fencing and could see workers in the yard, scratching among the junk, selecting a bit here and there and tossing it onto slidewalks that led into a maw in the building's flank. Jack watched for a moment, thinking that he was hungry and thirsty, even as he tried to determine what motivated the selection of junk. There were no criteria that he could see. Beyond, bottom framed and fringed by towers of scrap, he could see the mural the sentry had told him of. It was not a pretty picture.

His stomach clenched fitfully. It had been a long time since he'd had a decent meal, and the *New Virginia* had not held a mess for departing employees.

The hand truck nudged at his calves again, faithful mechanical dogs, and whined under protest at the trunk's weight. Jack strode toward the front gates. They were open, the gateposts installed with monitors showing various videos about buying and selling scrap, or having repair work done, on a front monitor. Uninterested, he brushed past.

"Hey!" The Sentry camera lens snaked out, eyed him closely, and recoiled back into its station. "What are you doing?"

"I'm looking for Skagboots'."

"No Unauthorized Personnel."

Jack gave his tight smile, said, "Tell him Pepys sent me," and kept on walking.

That should bring some action at the front door.

He signaled the hand truck to flank him and keyed open Bogie's lock as he walked up the slight incline to the front shop doors. Underfoot, old plastic, brittle and broken, crunched beneath his boots. He could smell lubricant and cleansers, pungent on the air. He saw the remains of several hand trucks littering the path, and the machine flanking him made a chuffing sound as if headed toward the same fate, or in recognition of cold workmates. He stopped at the doors and saw himself reflected in the skin. Gone was the workman's demeanor adopted over the last several months, ever since he and Colin had fabricated his death. He stood tall and aggressive in front of Skagboots' monitor and dared them to come get him.

There was a flurry of sound on the other side, and when the door slid open, he looked into the muzzle of a good-sized rifle. The owner snarled, "What do you mean Pepys sent you?"

"This," and Jack kicked open the lid of his trunk.

The late afternoon sun caught the dazzle off the Flexa-links. It shone in the trunk as though made of white-fire, and the rifle holder flinched back a step, to shade his eyes. "Where in the hell did you get that?" issued from deep in the burly man's chest.

"Now that would be telling if I told you, and then we'd both know, and then you wouldn't have to talk to me to find out."

The man spat out an invective, then half-turned in the doorway. "Boots! Bootsie, c'mere!"

Bootsie was a robust woman, her chalk-fire hair pulled back in a tail, her lean hips and oversized bust filling a jumpsuit the way a sausage filled its casing—tight and appetizing. She stopped behind her guardsman, put her hands on her hips and eyed him with appraisal, aqua eyes outlined with kohl and sapphire powder. She paused when she looked into the trunk, then said, "Call in the crew and close the gates down."

"It's not dark yet."

"Do as I said." Bootsie gave Jack a dazzling smile. "I'd invite you in, honey, but we're not secure yet."

"I'll wait," he answered. She had a perfume that he could not identify. It was not overpowering, but definitely unique, underscented with pheromones because her presence was stirring his senses in a way that only Amber could. But Bootsie cheated.

Jack held onto his small smile and waited.

CHAPTER 11

He could not see all of the crew that gathered, but his neck hairs let him know he was being targeted from all directions, despite the stacks and vats and shelving that filled the warehouse vastness beyond Bootsie. Barrels of wire and tubing overflowed onto the ground as though the building were some great, disemboweled animal. Jack could hear Bogie's deep tones rumbling through his mind.

Boss, you in trouble?

"Not yet," Jack answered back, and sized up the forces, seen and unseen, answering Bootsie's summonings.

From above, high in the cubicles hung down from the rafters, a tinny voice called, "What's up, Boots?"

"Secure for strafing," she yelled back, without taking her large, emphasized eyes from Jack.

The air filled with the rumble of fire doors being closed—all but the doorway Jack stood in. He had no doubt that the gates down the lane were now shut and locked. A small wave of panic washed through him, that he had gone too far, naked as he was without his armor, but he ignored the fear as soon as he recognized it.

Yet he could not silence the echo in his mind: *Shit. We're in trouble now.*

Besides the rifleman, four sweat-streaked workers moved up to flank Bootsie. Any one of them looked pumped up enough to attempt lifting the equipment trunk and heaving it across the warehouse. They eyed him, various weaponry trained in his direction. Jack half-raised an open palm but refused to give way.

Bootsie cocked a coal-black eyebrow. "Well, you've got a foot in the door, as they say."

Her rifleman grunted, "They also say, move it or lose it."

Jack shook his head. "I'm here to do business, but if the

deal falls through, I want to know you have an open door policy. This way I'm ensuring it.''

Noises of equipment moving in the rafters drew a flicker of his attention. He could see movable cranes in motion along their tracks. One of the hooks came to a stop overhead.

Bootsie smiled. "Now we're secure, honey. Let's talk.''

Jack shrugged. "I'm not much for talking. You've seen what I've got. Either you're interested or not.''

She stretched, a languid movement that rippled muscles Jack didn't know women had. She looked overhead at the massive hook and then back. "I don't know what you've got until I see it. You could have it gutted and nothing but the shell there. Let's bring the cherry picker down and hoist it for a look-see.''

Jack kicked the lid down, saying, "Let's not.'' Mentally, he told Bogie to be prepared to be up and running if anything happened to him.

The rifleman gave a snorting laugh and added, "This guy a virgin or something?''

The shop echoed with crude humor. Jack rode it out, his gaze staying level with Bootsie's. She did not smile until the noise died down. When she did smile, it was a cold stretching of wide, sensuous lips, an expression that did not warm her eyes.

"All right,'' she said. "All right, what do you want?''

"I'm looking for the Shirts.''

The warehouse grew cavernously quiet. Jack thought he heard the woman's heart skip a beat, then quicken.

"And the suit is just a tease. Bait.'' Bootsie turned on one well-heeled boot, her hip jutting out at him.

"No tease,'' he said to her before she walked away from him. "I intend to wear it for the Shirts.''

She gave him a look over her shoulder. "And you think we know where to find them?''

"Now who's being coy?''

The woman stopped in her tracks again, and swiveled about. Her gaze fixed greedily on the hand trunk and its cargo. "Suppose we do know how to find the parties you're looking for. What's in it for us?''

He shrugged. "I'll leave the building standing.''

There was a sharp hoot from the rear. Bootsie put up a

finger, and the laughter quieted. She paced slowly about Jack and the trunk, eyeing both very carefully. He had no doubt that she was memorizing every detail she saw. She halted when she was back in front of him.

"All right," she said. "I can find the Shirts for you."

He shook his head. "Not good enough."

Her face paled almost enough to match her platinum hair. "What do you mean, not good enough?"

"Let's drop the pretenses. My contact was taken out before I could find out where to go and who to see—but I got your name instead. I'm here with a suit, a suit that can be duplicated, in time, to meet Pepys on his own ground. Or do you prefer taking daily target practice from him? Last I saw, the port had been hit and it's only four clics from here. That doesn't exactly put you out of ground zero range if Pepys decides to stop toying with you. He'll stop discouragement and go right to annihilation once he finds out Skagboots' is the place he's been looking for."

The rifleman put him in his sights. His lip lifted as he said, "You ain't gonna tell him."

"Stop it," Boots said. She looked down, staring at the ground, as though she could read an oracle scratched in the dust. Then, with a sigh, she beckoned Jack out of the doorway. "Come on in. I personally guarantee safe passage out of here. But we can't talk until the door's closed down. It's too risky."

Jack eyed her. "Suit, too."

"Suit, too. Now come on in, mister, and don't be shy. Word is, there's going to be another run late today, and we don't want our asses hanging out in the breeze, do we, honey?"

The rifleman introduced himself as Gus. As the rest of the crew faded back into the shadows, Boots called out work assignments, adding, "Keep the shop secured. It's early, but better safe than sorry." She did not look back at Jack until the sound of air drills and other shop noises began.

She looked overhead and then said, mockingly, "I don't suppose I could induce you into going into my office?"

He shook his head no. Bootsie shrugged, an erotic gesture with movement all its own, pulled up an unidentifiable piece of scrap and sat down. "Then let's talk. What do you want out of me?"

"I want to be passed along, down the chain—to a base where I can do some good."

She pulled a drugstick out of her sleeve, and lit it, inhaling deeply. Its incense fragrance drifted toward Jack. Finally, she said, "That may not be in your best interests. As far as duplicating the suit goes, I have a lot of resources right here."

"It wouldn't take much for Pepys to put you out of commission—and once the suits are made, I need to train wearers. You won't be able to keep a secret here."

Gus stood by, cradling his rifle in the crook of his arm. "He's right about that, Boots."

Without diverting her gaze from Jack, she said, "Shut up." She tapped the ash from her stick. "This isn't the only Skagboots' facility. I have one in the . . . country."

Jack answered, "Did you know lying adds years to your face?"

She frowned briefly and interrupted the expression by taking another deep draw on the drugstick. Finally, she said, "Who are you, anyway? And how did you get the armor?"

"I'm a Knight, or was, and how I got the armor follows. My name isn't important and I don't intend to give it to you any more than I intend to give you the suit. I don't wear an implanted ident chip and if you think to pull me down and take the suit anyway, be aware that it's fully powered and the deadman switch is in operation."

"You're definitely no virgin." Blue-gray smoke curled out of her pouty lips. "Damn that switch."

"It is an inconvenience." In actuality, Jack had all but permanently decommissioned the deadman circuit, knowing that Bogie could take the suit out of traitorous hands be they human or Thrakian. He didn't want to risk blowing up the armor if he could help it.

Boots crossed her legs, a stance that somehow cantilevered her breasts still further out of her jumpsuit. She gave him a measuring look before saying, "I don't know if I can pass you along the line that far. If you've been looking for us at all, you already know that we operate in three-person cells. Only one of those three knows anyone in another cell and so on down the chain."

He nodded.

She got to her feet, the swelling in her bosom fell victim to gravity, and Gus came to alert. "Show him around, Gus," she ordered, "while I put a call through." She grabbed a metal cable and ascended the line like a trapeze artist, hanging by a loop about her wrist. Jack watched her in faint admiration.

Gus poked him in the ribs. "Follow me."

"Only as far as the hand truck can make it," Jack told him. The rifleman nodded.

The shop was a compendium of any shop Jack had ever been in. Degreasing vats next to lube pits, cubicles with workbenches clear or workbenches cluttered, according to the habits of the mechanic, hoists and overhead racks as well as the massive cherry pickers hanging from the massive framework of the building, the air pungent with the smell of solder. The degaussers were vintage, but the probes on the electronics benches were the finest technology out of the market. The later, he reflected, were probably stolen. There was a network of parts running through at a slow but constant pace, baskets swinging alluringly with their contents at eye level. Jack dipped a hand into one and came up with a couple of chips the size of his fingertip. He read the parts code and an eyebrow went up.

Gus laughed. "We got everything, boss," he said. His actual voice and tone was a physical echo of Bogie's, and made Jack smile. He made as if to drop the chips back, but Gus waved. "Keep 'em. You might need 'em someday."

Jack doubted he'd ever have to repair a laser cannon, but sealed the chips in an upper pocket.

The floor space became more and more crowded until Jack became aware that the hand truck could no longer follow. He stopped and Gus turned around, puzzled. "This is as far as I go."

The rifleman gave a nod, saying, "We got a lot of equipment stacked around." They retraced their journey to where they had begun, the hand truck hovers whining as if in protest over the unnecessary trip. Jack leaned down, reset the controls and let it settle.

Bootsie came down the cable as spectacularly as she had

ascended, a slight frown marring her white-blonde beauty. "I've got my man on the line," she said. "And I'm to see the suit out of the box."

Jack had expected as much. He opened the lid as Boots summoned a portable cherry picker. He attached the hoist and let it draw Bogie to his feet. He held the helmet as the Flexalinks came to its full height. The Shop boss sucked in her breath admiringly.

She spoke to her handset. "I'd say he has the real thing." She read the reply and her glance flicked to Jack. "All right," she answered, closed the handset and clipped it on her belt.

She was in the process of saying, "You're cleared—" when all hell broke loose.

The air rumbled overhead, thunder low and mean, and Jack pulled Bogie down off the cherry picker as the building shook. Gus yelled, "Jesus, it's a strafing-run!" and took off, rifle in hand as the boom, boom, boom of the shelling rattled the shielded warehouse. It was obvious the shields wouldn't take much more of a pounding.

Bootsie disappeared down a trap door previously obliterated by dirt and scrap. If anyone noticed that Jack did not need the hoist to hold the suit up on its own, they said nothing. He peeled open the seam, cursing Pepys. If he had to shoot the damn place down himself, he wasn't going to take any more.

Bogie crouched against his shoulder blade, lift functions a nearly imperceptible purr in his ear as he settled himself in the armor. He normally did not wear boots inside the armor boots, but now he had no choice. He tore his jumpsuit open from neck to waist, baring his chest to clip the leads on. This would be a messy suit-up, but time was of the essence. He seamed up. His wrists tingled, telling him his gauntlets were powered up and ready. As he bent to reach for the helmet, there was a screaming boom above, answered by a rending of metal, and smoke and fire poured in through the torn roof. One of the massive hoists tore lose from its track and dropped ponderously to the floor where scrap and machinery collapsed under its weight.

Through the roof, sky and smoke streams showed. He jammed his helmet on and looked up, even as the Talon's shadow began to dapple the skyline, the sun behind it cast-

ing the darkness of betrayal ahead. Jack had target probability locked on before the strafing fire began again, and he
fired his own wrist rockets into the hellish miasma
whirling overhead.

The entire building creaked as the Skagboots' own crew
answered the Talon's fire as well. The shadow fled amidst
flame and laser scoring, but the helmet tracking told him
that two more attackers were approaching. He targeted the
best window for placing a hit. It was not likely his weaponry
could bring down both planes, but they were overconfident
and coming in far too low. He could do some heavy
damage.

The helmet told him his targets were locked on as he
raised his gauntlets to the correct trajectory. "Help me hold
it steady," he told Bogie, and the sentience locked his
armor into position.

Sweat began to trickle down his forehead. Then the helmet released his wrist rockets, and he was shoved back on
his boot heels by the force of the release.

Metal screeched. Air exploded. Water flamed. A cascade
of smoke and fire poured earthward. Jack had only a brief
instant to realize the overhead roof, what was left of it, was
coming down on top of him.

The suit had taken worse, but not much, and his helmet
was not screwed into place. As the machinery came down,
sweeping by, catching him in a comet tail of cable and
track, he lost his footing and his head.

CHAPTER 12

Amber hugged the shadowed ruined walls closely, her breath a whisper to her own hearing, her heart a pacemaker that the close-circuited security scanning must surely pick up. But she sensed no alarms and with a final step or two, knew she had breached the cordon about the bombed out wing. Her fingertips went to the choke collar about her slender neck and brushed the microcircuitry entwined there as if in thanks for its part in keeping her safe from detection. Pepys and his World Police were the height of security, but the black market managed to stay just one step ahead of them. And Amber never bought anything retail if she didn't have to.

Though the bombing had been blamed on the Green Shirts, she had thought for several months that the location had been more than coincidence. There had been no effort to either repair or raze the damaged section, almost as though Pepys were afraid to touch it. The Lunaii wing had housed the late Commander Winton's operation . . . some of it under the zegis of Pepys and some not, for the man who'd helped Pepys betray the Dominion Knights on Milos had had machinations of his own. Perhaps he had even aspired to replace the man he'd helped become emperor. As she eased farther into the pattern of broken shadows and shattered walls, she felt a tingle of ice down her back and halted.

With every sense she had left, she probed the area about her, and fought to stay hidden in this night that was death-dark.

Her thoughts briefly winged those of the psychics Pepys kept chained to his patronage in another wing; even they were unaware of her, and stayed so. Smiling ironically, she decided her sense of impending disaster was overdeveloped and the longer she lingered in the ruins, the more likely she was to be found.

She slipped a pair of glasses down, and the black night instantly faded to gray. Confident, she moved toward a passageway and down it as though she herself were a ghost.

The console room had been blown from within like an eggshell. She ran a hand over a jagged plastic relic, its edges as sharp as tempered metal. There was little enough left of the room to identify its purpose, but Amber saw the melted lumps where plugs and leads had been, and barely recognizable shards of electronic equipment. Her nose curled at the still-rank odor of smoke, melted plastic and metal, the fumes of electric fire, and more. Winton, if he had lived, would probably have died in this room. It gave her satisfaction to know that Jack had, at least, been able to kill the man who'd hunted him. But as they'd both come to know, as despicable as Winton had been, he was no more than a hound to the man who'd controlled him.

And that man was Pepys.

Amber left the com room. Winton had been a deeply deceptive man. Wherever he kept his access terminal to his own computer files, it would not have been in the com room.

As she made her way down the crumbling corridor, she noted that the main structure of the wing was basically intact. The third story above her was gone, devastated by the main bank of blasts, but this second story was sound and the first story virtually unharmed except for the electrical fire that had swept through, and the smoke and chemical-dampener damage.

She passed a virtually untouched portal door and paused, in spite of the insignia showing it to be a janitorial area. Amber impatiently pushed her glasses up on her forehead and ran her fingertips over the door's seal. Faint blue sparks marked her intrusion. She jerked her hand back as though shocked. Her body flinch brought the glasses back down across the bridge of her nose where they landed smartly. She blinked at the abrupt change from darkness to twilight.

She put her hand out and touched the portal seal again. The glasses showed no sparking, but she felt as though she had touched something—slimy. Amber wiped her hands on the thigh of her pitch-black pants leg. Then, gathering her wits, she bent down to see what needed to be done to unlock the door.

The lock was simple and yet complex. A sound lock, with a retinal pattern for final release. She'd anticipated that and had brought along a hologram projector with Winton's pattern on it. The sound lock though—could be anything. And yet, as she stood, she smiled.

Why would such a locking system be on a janitorial door?

She looked back down the corridor. Close enough to the com room to be convenient—anyone seeing Winton about his daily business in this area would assume he'd be en route to the corn room, especially. if they knew him well. That included Pepys' spies within the palace as well as any outside spies. Before Winton's death and the bombing, the com room had been secret, secret enough to hide the real center of Winton's power.

All she had to do was break the lock to find out if she was right.

All she had to do was stand in the corridor and make the right sound to begin the unlocking sequence. The right sound out of all the thousands upon thousands of sounds a human could make or command to be made.

She could eliminate a number of them. Whatever noise Winton would make in this passageway to gain entrance, he would want it to be swift and inconspicuous. And, it would probably not have to be in his own voice, in case a subordinate needed to get in as well. A sound or noise anyone could make.

She canted her head, smiling wryly to herself, as she narrowed the field down from thousands and thousands to merely hundreds. Just in case she could get that far, she pulled the palm-sized projector out of a side pocket and affixed it over the lens plate for the retinal identification.

The man who had hunted her and Jack for years had been an impatient, snap-judgment personality, intensely shrewd and private. Knowing all of which gave her no clue as to the sound lock.

She could try to pull the lock out, like pulling the ignition from a hovercar, but it was likely the room was booby-trapped, like a deadman switch on armor.

From another pocket, she pulled another small piece of equipment, thumbed it on, and placed it over the lock. The tiny screen flat-lined, showing her no movement within the locking mechanism.

"Not yet," she muttered, as she checked the hologram's alignment. She laid her cheek against the cool door, thinking of the sound or word that might be the key.

Then, with a smile, she straightened and said the most unlikely word she could think of that would ever be heard within these walls.

The screen began to dance with life and as the retinal plate came on, and took a reading from the hologram projector, it spiked into frantic activity.

The door slid open quietly. Amber moved within its shadow among the shadows, snapping her equipment loose from the door before its slide into the frame could dislodge some very expensive equipment. She secured it among her pockets and brought her glasses into place once again before she moved into a room that was clearly not a janitorial locker.

The terminal equipment set up was sophisticated and functional. With a smile she sat down in the com chair. Now the real work began. She leaned forward to test her ability to access Winton's most private files.

She left in failure, knowing only that someone else, from another terminal, had a program running break-in possibilities for a tie-in as well. She could only guess that someone was either Pepys or Baadluster. To lift the program might give her more access, but it would also set off an alert. She had no choice but to make some inquiries among the people she knew, and return to try again. And again, until she either had what she wanted, or she'd been caught infiltrating.

As she passed through the cordons, she caught a flickering frame of thought and looked up, freezing to immobility. She knew that smoldering touch and searched the edge of the ruins, expecting to see Vandover Baadluster waiting for her.

But the thought curled away unexpectedly and she let her breath out.

Hugging her chilled hands to her ribs, she left the

bombed out wing and made her sure way across the palace
grounds. She knew where she was now and no one was her
equal getting in and out of the grounds undetected. She
wove her way in and out of security areas, dodging that
smoldering flame of thought as much as she did camera
eyes and heat scans. There was no quick way to do it. It
was three steps here, a dart there, a painstaking pattern to
be woven.

She nearly screamed when a heavy hand dropped upon
her shoulder from behind and spun her about. She shoved
a fist in her mouth to smother her noise and looked up, up
at the burly phantom confronting her.

Before she identified him visually, her nose told her who
it was. K'rok, Milot commander of the Knights, puppet
commander of the Thrakian League. The musky scent of
the ursine beastlike being invaded her senses and she
blinked away a watering tear.

"Thought I had a thief, I did," K'rok rumbled. He
dropped his pawlike hand from her shoulder. "What be
you doing here, Lady Amber?" Faint illumination from beyond the barracks picked up a glimmer in his eyes as he
stared down at her.

Before she could find a probable answer, he took a step
closer and she felt enveloped by his presence as if he'd
embraced her.

"It is not safe, friend of Storm. They be looking for you."

"I know," she got out, her voice thin and strained.

The Milot sniffed. She knew as if it was a certainty that
he could smell the smoke and destruction on her clothing
and in her hair. He rocked back a half step. "What be you
doing in the Lunaii wing?"

"Let me go, commander." She shifted her weight imperceptibly to the balls of her feet, preparing to run.

He shook his massive head. "Not yet. I be thinking a
while." And he stood in silence, as if that was just what he
was doing.

Amber had nothing on her that would bring down a
Milot, nothing she had access to any longer, and she felt a
desperate sense of loss over the psychic powers she had
once had. Even of those powers she had once tried with
K'rok and which his alien thick-headedness had turned
away.

The Milot put his hand out suddenly, gripping her shoulder again. His voice lowered. "I feel in my heart that Jack is not dead. Knowing this, I feel also you must be doing work for him." With a sigh, the Milot lifted his head and she sensed that he looked in back of her, toward Pepys' palace. "I wish you luck," the being finished. "You must be careful. I am not trusted here by any being and cannot be helping you, except with well wishes." He turned her about, giving her an encouraging push toward the forest that edged the grounds and marked the final boundary of her freedom. "Good hunting," he said as she took to her heels, heartbeat thudding in her ears.

CHAPTER 13

The ache in his throat and lungs brought him awake. With every breath he took, it felt as though he'd been burned, the air rasping through seared tissue. He coughed, gasped with the pain, coughed again, and writhed with the effort except that he was pinned down and could do nothing more than toss his head. His eyes watered so heavily that he could not see, and he could not free his hands to wipe them.

It was somewhere in the middle of this misery that he realized he was still alive and that it was the suit which kept him so.

Jack wrinkled his brow and eyelids tightly, trying to wring his eyes dry enough to see. When he opened them finally, he got a hazy view of smoke and flame, of metal still hot enough to glow in the dark, and of a jagged portal to the evening sky. He heard low moans and cries. Plastic fumes stank on the raw air. He ducked his chin, found the drinking nipple operative and took a tiny sip of water. It stung all the way down, but the second swallow was easier.

He lay back, cradled in the armor, and concentrated on feeling his body, every contortion and ache, though in the gloaming he could see nothing below his neck. Half the building must have fallen on him. His feet felt numb until he realized it was the double booting constricting him. The realization halted the panicky drum of his pulse—he had thought he'd been crushed from the knees down.

His helmet was gone, torn away. It must lie beyond him, out of view and reach—and, he hoped, unnoticed by the scavengers which were probably already crawling all over the shop. Even as he began to assess his options, he could hear grunts and rattles, and a piece of sheet metal falling away, to crash on the flooring to his left. The noise echoed in his pounding skull. Jack closed his eyes tightly and prayed for the pain to go away so that he could think clearly.

Boss. . . . Bogie's voice, faded to a thready reflection of his normal hardy tones.

Jack realized that the comforting softness he pillowed his sore neck and head upon was Bogie. "Are you hurt?"

No. Hungry. . . .

The sentience was growing rapidly now, and his regeneration took all the sunlight he could absorb. Usually, through the suit and the built-in solars, it was no problem. But having been locked up, Bogie must be feeling drained. Though sunlight was his preferred energy source, Bogie could—and had—taken from Jack. How hungry was the alien?

Jack felt a cold sweat bead up, on his forehead. "How bad is it?"

He sensed a peevish echo as Bogie only answered, *Hungry.*

His stomach clenched at the thought. "Me, too, Boog." With the helmet gone, he could not see his readouts. "Are we powered up or do we have a red field?"

Being buried would not drain the armor, but damage and shortage might. Although he did not smell the acrid scent of burned out circuitry within the suit, the air was full of it. There was no answer. Hair tickled the back of Jack's neck—was it sweat trickling down or was Bogie moving imperceptibly there? He had a sense suddenly of just how close and how warm the pulsing of his blood through his jugular veins might be.

Time to see how much power remained in the suit. He flexed his arm, felt weight shift about him, then slide away unstably. He quieted as he heard someone scrambling through the dark. Abruptly, to the far side of the shop, an arc light came on. Its blinding white light made the shadows darker on Jack's side of the destruction. It brought out, in sharp silhouette, two men crouched about five yards away from him, and ten meters up.

"I tell you I saw him put the armor on—"

"If he's dead then, so much the better."

Warningly, "Boots will want 'em in one piece."

The pile of debris shifted with an alarming noise. Bits of

dust and particles sifted through the air, caressing Jack's face. He spat to one side and blinked painfully to keep his vision clear. His right leg cramped as he tried to flex the armor. He made a noise through gritted teeth as his calf tightened and his leg convulsed in reaction, and missed part of what the gravel-voiced man said to his partner, the one with an accent he couldn't identify. Whatever it was they said, he could tell from the tone of voice it mattered little at this point what the shop boss wanted.

". . . get a light over here."

"Shut up and keep looking. He was close to the front door." A beam cut the air, not an arm's length from Jack's nose. "That's all that's left of the fracking front door."

A splintering rip, and a yell, and the light beam disappeared with a wild thrashing. The mountain of scrap groaned and swayed and Jack could hear large pieces breaking off and crashing to the floor. A pressure lifted off Jack's legs, one he hadn't known was there, but before he could drag himself free, the load shifted and he felt it settle down once more.

"Reyes! Where are you?"

A curse, and a moan. "Lost the fracking torch! Damn near got swallowed up. Give me a hand."

From across the shop, he could hear a shout, "Get me a block and tackle over here!"

The two men, intent on their own salvation, moved together, ignoring the command from elsewhere. Jack ground his teeth and concentrated on flexing his legs, carefully, without bringing down an avalanche.

"Where's the torch?"

The accented voice: "Frack the torch. You fish for it. Some of this scrap is sharp enough to take your arm off. Let's find the suit and get out of here."

"Suppose it's buried under this crap?"

Scornfully. "Then I suggest we start digging!"

There was a sliding noise, followed by the thud of feet hitting the floor not four paces from where he lay. "Here! I'll hand you down. Damn that arc light . . . this is like working on the dark side of a moon.

The voice Jack had come to identify as Reyes said, "I think I hear Quincy moaning . . ."

"Forget that ape! You're in with me and don't forget it."

"Yeah, but—suppose he's the one they need the block and tackle for. Maybe he's under something."

There was a scuffle. Breathing heavily, the gravel-throated speaker said, "You threw in with me, and don't forget it. I want that suit!"

"But Casper—Boots is only gonna split with you."

"Forget Boots! I've got my own scrap deal working and there's more money in it than you'll ever see if you stay with Skagboots'."

A sharp intake of breath, and another slight scuffle. The lighter, younger voice of Reyes made a breathy agreement, and then Jack heard footsteps moving in his direction.

There was another sound, a light scramble toward him, from another direction. Jack turned his chin toward it, unable to distinguish whether it was the debris shifting again or if something moved with purpose. Whatever it was, it was on a collision course with him and the two salvagers.

Light filled his eyes. He jerked his head back from the palm-sized beam, a small but handy tool he'd seen Amber use before.

"Shit! He's still alive."

"Then slice his throat and pull him out of there."

"Casper, he's got a small mountain on him. We ain't getting either him or the suit out easy."

A third voice, light and easy. "Actually, you're not getting him at all."

Jack blinked, squinting, unable to see forms other than as harsh black and white silhouettes. Two of them met with a clash. He smelled the warm scent of blood as something splattered his face.

The second man, his voice fairly dancing with pain, yelled, "Shit, I'm cut, I'm cut!"

There was a hiss of breath. "Back off! We saw him first."

The light and easy voice, a cavalier tone Jack almost knew. . . . "Ah, but possession is what counts, isn't it? And I found him first. That's a nasty cut. Perhaps you should concentrate on getting that taken care of?"

The rumbling voice Jack had tagged as Casper answered, "We're going. But we'll be back."

The cavalier man answered, "I don't doubt that. Your friend looks a bit pale . . . he's lost a lot of blood. You'd better hurry."

There was a lot of shuffling as the two men helped each other out the wreckage of Skagboots' front door.

A mellowed light beam switched on, as the third man illuminated both himself and Jack and bent down.

"I think we'd better see how we can get you out of here." The face wasn't human.

CHAPTER 14

"It pleases me that the rumors of your death have been greatly exaggerated," the muzzled and sable-furred face said, with humor. "Although you seem to be in some trouble. I do, however, remember the time you dropped an entire dam upon yourself. Is this some obscure human death wish?"

The familiar tone was nearly washed out by the smell of fish. Jack recovered and said to the Fisher, "Are you going to get me out of here, or wait for someone else to come by to carve up?"

Skal's wolfish grin increased. "Perhaps that astonishing woman. There is something about her that stirs even my Fisher blood, though I doubt that sex between her and me would be possible or even desirable. No, great warrior, I am here to pull your fish out of the fire. I've been looking for you."

"How? How did you find me?"

The otter-man gave a rippling shrug. "Mist-off-the-waters sent me. She told the Elders the story of your death was untrue, and sent me . . . with this." In the moon-pool of light, the Fisher showed a bloody handknife in his palm, and Jack recognized the twin to a knife he had been given years ago.

Jack swallowed tightly. "That was a time ago," he said. Kavin, his mercenary friend and commander, had been alive then. So had the treacherous head of secret police, Winton. And Amber had been just a streetwise girl for whom his love could not be expressed.

"Water under the bridge," Skal returned and gave a barking laugh. "Now we must get you out of here!"

"I've got power enough to do it—but I was worried about getting reburied."

"I shall then mark the spot," Skal said. He stood, and the moon-pool of light moved with him. It shrank until Jack could no longer see it. Skal gave another laugh. "Jack! Your helmet!"

"Good. Secure it and stand clear."

The Fisher said wistfully, "I would be standing all the way home on Mistwald, if I could, my friend. Hurry."

Jack read the tone of his voice and knew that the Fisher mystic known as Mist-off-the-waters had not lightly sent Skal off-world into a society they scarcely knew. Skal had come to get him because they needed him.

Even as Jack tightened his muscles and prepared to use the suit to move, he knew he would have to put his own needs aside for the moment. The Flexalink answered his muscle command as it was meant to do, with the strength of hundreds, and the tons of scrap and debris shivered as the earth quaked below it.

"Money for passage is no problem," Skal told him over a mug of beer, and licked a few droplets of foam from his whiskers. "I have metal flake from our rivers that you people seem to value highly. It has its uses, I suppose, though it's too soft for metalworking other than jewelry."

Jack smiled at the Fisher's appraisal of gold. He'd seen Skal pay for the evening's round of drinks and food with a nugget. He set his mug down. "All the same, I'd keep that pouch of yours out of sight. Victor Three's a cesspool of cutthroats."

"Spoken by a man in a position to know." Skal took a deep draft of his drink, neck muscles rippling gracefully with every vigorous swallow. The otter-man seemed at home in the dingy, tacky bar.

"What sort of transportation do we want, then?" Jack hitched himself up gingerly in his chair. His stiffening muscles told him he'd be one massive bruise from head to toe come morning. A dented tool chest of considerable size rested next to his chair, and he put a boot foot upon it.

"I want the best and swiftest ship to Mistwald." Skal's laughing face sobered, merely by the lowering of his brows and flattening of his whiskers. "There's no time to waste."

"At least two weeks, with acceleration and decel—and that's if you have a Corsair or Talon. It's not likely we can

get military transportation—" not to mention, undesirable
to Jack in his present situation, but there was no need for
Skal to know that, "—so we may have some waiting
around. Who goes in and out of your sector?"

"No one but traders—and the despoilers."

"Traders take their time, it's less expensive that way,
especially if they're hauling barges. And despoilers sound
real difficult to buy passage from."

Skal blinked slowly. "You make fun of me, Jack."

"No. Not really. Who are these guys and what's the problem?" He paused to take a fresh bottle of beer from the
little servo wheeling about their table and Skal did the
same. "I know it's important or you wouldn't have come
off-world looking for me."

"If we knew who they were, we would know how to pull
their leashes—who to complain to in order to get them off,
but we do not. The few spies we've sent after them have
been sent back—dead. Very messily dead." Skal paused.
His eyes glistened. "They have burned a wound into the
land that cannot be healed. Their base is small, but growing, and we do not know if it is our world they want—if
so, how could they treat it so carelessly?—or if they are
using us as a stepping stone."

Despite the warmth of hot food and pleasant brew, Jack
felt a chill. "Not . . ." he leaned forward, "not Thraks."

"No. This much I do know—they appear to be men such
as you. Or alike to these Fisher eyes."

"Has the Council tried raining them away?" Jack remembered his days on Mistwald and the remarkable powers of
the Elders with the weather.

Skal nodded. "Useless. They simply move to higher
ground, and the stain of their existence spreads. An ulcerat-
ing sore along the riverlands. My own people can do nothing but send for you."

That must mean the Fishers were in an incredible bind.
Jack had fought alongside Skal during their civil wars. The
otter-folk had considerable ingenuity and courage. Or perhaps it meant only that anything off-world daunted them.
They'd had a look at Jack's armor and knew the destructive
power, far beyond their own, it held. They were brave,
not foolish.

"Get me there," he said, "and I'll see what I can do."

Skal looked at him over the brim of his mug. "But," he answered, "I interrupted you on a quest of your own."

"It can wait."

Eyes that were much more than animal and yet different from his own looked at him closely. Then Skal said, "I bow to your wisdom, and thank you for your decision."

Jack picked up his mug. "Drink up. Port's open in the morning and we can see what's available then. In the meantime, I want to be drunk enough to sleep well—tomorrow's going to hurt."

Skal gave that barking laugh, his whiskers flared forward, and he met Jack's mug with his. "I hear you!"

They found an ambassadorial flagship from the Dominion that was willing to take on passengers. Jack had been in Dominion territory only twice in his life—both times to appear in Congress, but he had learned from Amber that people were slow to recognize other people; they saw what they expected to see. In Skal and Jack, the ambassador's aide and pilot saw an alien with an indentured mechanic, neither of any particular interest, but with enough gold flake to pay the berthing bills.

"Thus," observed Skal, "one hand scratches the other's back."

"Something like that," Jack answered. "And neither of us have to go into cold sleep." The flagship was nearly as fast as a military vessel, and he'd been asked to do some minor shop repairs instead of chilling down to save food and energy. Because of Skal's somewhat dubious physique, cold sleep had been bypassed altogether for him. The ship was well taken care of. Neither Jack nor Skal would be worked hard. If anything, the trip promised to be boring. Skal filled in the time making maps for Jack of the terrain around "the wound" and they discussed the various methods of approaching and observing without suffering the same fate as previous spies.

Skal twitched his sleek tail. "As if," he mumbled, "they had not been men!"

"Skinned?"

"Yes," the otter-man admitted, with a note of surprise.

Jack rubbed his four fingered right hand absently. The Fishers had beautiful pelts—he would not put it past these freebooters, whoever they were, to go after those pelts. The thought made a hard, sour ball in his gut that bothered him for nights afterward.

Having his usual trouble sleeping, he finally got up one night and hauled Bogie's trunk down to the solarium. There, he shielded his eyes with a visor helmet and opened Bogie's case to all the glory of the nearest sun and let him bask in the energy. For his ears only, the alien sang a song of bloodthirsty happiness, warrior spirit that Bogie was.

Skal found him there, hand resting on the edge of the trunk much as if he had paused in rocking a cradle. He said nothing, but got a helmet to protect his own eyes from bedazzlement and sat down close to Jack. "We have been warned that we'll be entering warp speed by the beginning of next shift."

Jack nodded his understanding. The solarium would be closed down then—there being no sunlight in FTL. He sat, thinking that his journey was nearly half over, and Skal merely watched the greenness of the garden area, no doubt also thinking of home.

Then, after a long quiet, he said, "You have found that which lives in your armor."

"Yes."

"Mist told me of it, not long after you left us. She says it is a spirit being made flesh, like a cub in a womb."

"I think so." Jack took his hand from the lip of the trunk. "But what it is, I don't know."

"It's not one of you?"

Storm shook his head. "No. Nor one of anything I've ever met. It was given to me on Milos."

"I heard of that world . . . a sand planet now, is it not?"

"Yes."

Skal's tail flung angrily from side to side and he stilled it with great effort. "I did not mean to interrupt," he added.

"You didn't. I fought on Milos, a long time ago. The Milots didn't have a lot of faith we would . . . beat the Thraks. They have great saurians there, berserker lizards, big murderous beasts, and they decided that the berserkers might be able to finish the Thraks off better than the infantry. They seeded our armor with the parasites. We didn't even know they were with us until too late. First they'd infiltrate our systems and then devour us. And when grown, they burst out of our suits like they were some kind of womb or egg-sac and they were really something to see." Jack paused, his mind filled with the horror of watching a berserker burst forth from what had once been a fighting comrade. "Berserkers are mindless fighters . . . killing machines . . . but even they couldn't save Milos for the Milots."

"And you thought your spirit was one such."

"Yes. And he may be akin to them. I don't know how much longer I can wear my armor. Right now he drinks light. Later, things may be different."

Skal sat back. "And yet this relationship is not all one-sided. I sense he helps you in many ways."

"Oh, yes. He can take over some of the minor suit functions. He has a mind of his own . . . I can hear him, sometimes. He lends me his warrior spirit when I need it."

Skal pulled his muzzle apart in a smile. "One hand scratches another back. May you and I share such helpful companionship."

Jack laughed at the Fisher's favorite fractured saying, pulled out of his reverie once and for all, and did what his friend obviously desired. The otter-man sank into blissful grunts all the while directing the scratcher. "A little higher there—just under the shoulder blade. No . . . now down. Aaaah."

The flagship came screaming out of warp drive, torquing into decel in the maneuver known as "turning the corner." The gravity of the movement pinioned Jack to his cot as if he'd been nailed there, his stomach somewhere about his sternum. Missing decel was about the only advantage he could think of to cold sleep. It was not enough of an advantage to make him use it any more than absolutely necessary.

Skal gave off a groan from the far hammock.

"Hang on," Jack told him.

"I should not have had that last beer for lunch."

"This is no place to be sick. Did your mother whelp a stomachless cub?"

"Ah, Jack," the Fisher moaned. "We've been together too long. Now you talk like I do."

"I won't be worried until I *eat* like you do." Jack lay

back as the pressure moved to his forehead, to a spot between his eyebrows, and nailed him to the center of the universe. His stomach did a slow roll as it settled back where it belonged. His ears popped and he could feel the braking of the flagship.

Skal gave a noisy belch. The stench of stale beer flooded the cabin. It did not bode well for either of them.

"Hang on," Jack repeated. "Think of home."

"Yesss," said Skal. "Home . . . only days away."

Home. Skal touched Jack on the forearm, motioning him to the hover. It was not raining over this flatland of Mistwald, not far from the lands he and Amber had so lightly called Swampberg, but the air was heavily dewed. Bogie was self-motivating behind him, and the armor lumbered to a halt. They were going to Council, but Jack was armed, in Enduro bracers, his weapon rigged. Security at the port had been heavy—what Triad authorities were looking for, neither Jack nor Skal knew, but neither of them had come all this way to fail now. Skal's authority on his homeworld became obvious when neither of them had to pass customs, a quarantine, or a Triad sweeper.

"What is security for," the otter-man said philosophically, "if it works against you?" But he had taken care, nonetheless, getting Jack cross-continent and past the growing stilt-cities, including Swampberg.

The sun shimmered prismatically off the air as Skal said, "It will be raining soon."

Jack glanced across the gray clouds dappling the purpled mesas he remembered would be their destination. Though Skal had not summoned them, or told them he would be coming, they both knew the Council would be waiting for them. He was often sorry he had not brought Amber to them, for the mystic or psychic world was second nature to them, and they might have helped her with her own tortured powers if only Jack had thought of it. Instead, she had gone a more damaging way for help. He took a deep breath. The world was alive, verdantly so. It would be a damnable shame if either man or Thraks should ever ruin it.

He shook off his memories and thoughts of Amber as Skal straddled the hoverbike.

"Will that carry all three of us?"

"Maybe not," the other answered. "Would you rather walk? Or float upstream, perhaps?"

Though it was a four passenger bike, the armor's weight was more than equivalent to two. Jack motioned Bogie to mount the last seat, and he settled behind Skal. The hover whined irritatingly as the Flexalinked alien sat down, but it stayed afloat. "Not high," Skal said. "Or fast. But steady." His hand-paw squeezed the brake off and away they went.

They gained the last mountaintop with a great deal of difficulty, but Skal would not hear of putting Jack down and leaving him to follow after with the armor. His muzzle tightened and his whiskers went flat.

"They sent me after you," he said, "and I'll be fried before I'll come back empty-handed."

And so they walked in together, Jack ducking his head, their presence filling the massive cavern's entrance. Skal preceded him slightly, cupping something in his paw.

The Elders were all seated about a low-burning, sweet-smelling fire. A waft of the smoke stung Jack's eyes, but he saw Skal approach Mist-off-the-waters and drop a bloodied handknife into her palm.

It disappeared into a curl of smoke itself and she puffed it into the air.

The cream-colored otter-woman smiled, saying, "Welcome, Jack Storm. Sit and talk with us."

Jack told Bogie to stay by the cavern entrance, and then did as he had been bid.

CHAPTER 15

Minerals caught the glow of the fire and reflected it back from cavern walls, giving the impression of a thousand tiny stars caught in stone. Niches were filled with tallow candles, squat and low as he remembered them, as if they burned down but never out. Their light pearlized the armor standing on guard at the cavern's mouth. The reflection caught Jack's eye—for a moment he wondered as he knew what it felt like to see the armor for the first time. He had been mistaken for a messenger of a god before. Now he knew why.

Mist put her hand-paw on Jack's arm, drawing his attention. She said, "You know many of the Elders from before."

Jack nodded as the silver-muzzled Fisher opposite him in the circle scratched his rump with his one hand. "One-arm," Jack said. "And Little Fish who is now gracefully grown. Bald Top here has lost a little more fur, but looks well—"

The knobby russet-furred otter-man blinked large, wet eyes and looked at him without a word.

"And Mist, of course. And I remember two or three more of you, though I was never given your names beyond that of Elder."

Bald Top gave a grunt then, saying, "Well met, Little Sun."

The nickname made Jack flush. He felt his skin grow warm, and he wondered what sport the Fishers made of him this time, as well as last, for he did not understand his name. He settled for, "Well met," in answer.

Skal reported, "It took nearly all of the metal flake to bring him here."

One-arm waved his still raven-black arm. His body was

silver-tipped with age, but where his pelt stayed dark, not a single light hair marred it. "No matter, Skal. It served its purpose. You were long, but not as long as we feared. As Mist has explained off-world to us, you could have been lost forever among the stars."

"I would have come back, no matter what."

Little Fish spoke up, "We know." She brushed her whiskers back with the palm of her hand, as Skal did, and continued a bit farther along her scar tissue.

Mist had not taken her hand off Jack's wrist. Now she squeezed a little as she said, "We apologize for taking you away from your business. We understand that you are sacrificing for us."

"It's no sacrifice, Mist. I wasn't having much luck finding what I was looking for, anyway." With Skagboots' destroyed, he'd lost his trail for the moment. "Tell me what's been happening here? Have you found any patches of rusty dirt, sand that is not normal?"

The Elders looked at him without answering.

"Can you try describing the ships they're using?" Briefly, Jack sketched out what a Thrakian warship looked like.

Bald Top lifted a gum, showing teeth only slightly worn by age. "Man, we know only that they use airships—we cannot help you there."

Frustrated, Jack shook off Mist's hold. "I can't help you blindly," he said. "I can't fight an army, no matter how powerful you think that suit is."

One-arm said, mildly, "We saw you melt a mountain with it last time."

"That wasn't a mountain, it was a boulder—you all saw it—" He looked about the circle and saw sleekly furred faces devoid of any expression he knew how to read. He began again, ended up muttering, "Damnit."

Little Fish said bitterly, "Do not despair. Ours is the despair. The land, poisoned. The river, a bitter drink of death . . ."

"How? Just tell me how."

She blinked. "If we knew how, Little Sun, we would not have needed you."

He sat cross-legged. He dropped his hand under his knee and clenched it. "Tell me what is happening. Skal calls it a wound, a canker that will not heal. Don't smoke the sweet-smoke and give me your mystic farseeings. Tell me what's happening."

"Fish, dying. Cubs downriver, born with two heads."

"What?" Jack swiveled to look at the Elder otter-woman who'd finally spoken. She wore a leather apron and he recognized the avocation if not the Fisher—she was a miller. The chaff and husks of rin, a ricelike grain, dusted her apron. "Are you certain?" That sounded more like radiation leakage, but he'd never been on-planet at the start of a Thrakian invasion. Leakage from landing perhaps? Fishburg had been somewhat advanced, using breeder reactors for electrical energy. "Skal, is there a reactor in the area?"

"No . . . and our detox programs and filters are functioning well at the other operating stations. I thought of that, too, when the canker first began. But there is no doubt it came with the strangers."

"Have you tried setting up a filtration system on the river, just in case?"

"We cannot get close enough," One-arm snorted. He thumped his chest and released a belch. "They could be floating turds downstream for all we know."

Jack looked at Skal. He could find no motivation for freebooters to be doing anything the Fisher claimed was happening. "You could be wrong. They could be Thraks instead of men."

The Fisher lashed his tail. "You are worried about *sand*, then?"

He nodded.

Mist said, "These Thraks are old enemies of yours?"

"Very old. Sand—the type of sand they make for their eggs and larvae—is devastating. If it's started here, it must be stopped immediately. Or else there is no hope for Mistwald." The sandmaking microcosm, once unleashed on a widespread basis, was virtually impossible to stop. He hoped desperately that was not the case here. "Have you been to the ambassador here? Or your emperor—what's his name?"

"Shining fur-grinning tooth is in charge still, but he is embroiled in trading pacts. Up to his fat neck in 'free samples.' He has turned away from his people and you can expect no help or hindrance from him. As for others—one stranger is the same as another, eh?" And Skal shrugged. His dark fur undulated.

Jack heard the unsaid honor in Skal's voice. He alone was not "a stranger." He alone they had hoped would help them. He took a deep breath and looked across the cavern at Bogie. One man against a Thrakian base installation was a pretty tall order. He exhaled. "I think I'd better have a look at this 'wound' as soon as possible."

Mist protested, saying, "I must read the smoke for you first, Little Sun, and give blessing—"

He didn't want to know what his future was. He'd fight better without knowing. "It's better I not know," he told her.

Her eyes widened. They had appeared merely dark in the gloaming of the cavern, now he saw and remembered their midnight blue color. She sat back on her haunches at the implication of his words.

But another Elder took it as insult and jumped to his feet. He palmed the hilt of a wicked looking hunting knife sheathed at his belt. "I demand an apology," the Fisher snapped.

Skal held up his hand. "It is not necessary that Jack apologize. It is we who should apologize to him, for forcing our customs upon him."

"But he slurred Mist—"

"I'm sorry," Jack interrupted. "I did not mean to slight any of you. But there is much ahead of us, and many outcomes, and I would rather not have one vision blinding my sight."

Mist got up. "He speaks rightly. The smoke only tells what it wishes. Storm has come to help us, as we asked. I suggest we let him." Her ironic tone fell on the short, rounded ears of the folk.

The skimmer groaned as much as it had before. Skal navigated by the stars in a now clear sky, a sky that was as velvet blue as Mist-off-the-waters' eyes. "You might as well rest," he said to Jack, who pillowed the back of his head on his hands and watched overhead. "We've a night's travel."

"That far?"

"The other side of the continent."

"About as far away from the spaceport as it can get?"

Skal nodded. "If it were not for the trouble in our own remote outposts, we might never have discovered its presence until the wound was much greater.

A shudder moved through Jack. He covered it by sitting up. "I don't suppose you intend to fly in?"

The Fisher threw him a sharp-muzzled grin. "Of course not. We land downriver and circle inland."

"Across mud?"

"Not so lucky. 'We'll be in a fairly dense rain forest. You'll be able to keep your boots dry, but it might be a tight squeeze for those broad shoulders." Skal flipped a thumb back at the armor.

What a Fisher and what Jack considered dry footing were two different things. He settled down on the work skimmer seat moodily. A rain forest meant rain. Several times a day, if the season was right. And it was always rainy season on Mistwald.

He was glad Flexalink couldn't rust.

Jack and Skal finished tugging the skimmer into a branch lean-to for camouflage. Bogie provided most of the power to move the transport, but he was like an uneducated robot—he had the strength and absolutely no idea of what to do with it—completely without a clue as how to apply himself. Jack had shouted himself hoarse giving instructions until Skal looked at him and said, "Don't let him pull. Make him push." And they guided it in. The last pink-purple cloud of dawn faded before they were done.

As Jack tugged the last branch over, the Fisher looked at him, and his brows went up. "Why not wear the armor? You are a soldier and it is your equipment."

Jack pulled his pack out of the skimmer and began unpacking his Enduro bracers and weapons belts, both the waist and the shoulder belts. "Normally I would. But I'm going to be outnumbered anyway—this way there's two of me. Bogie is short on a lot of concepts, but he knows how to stand and fire."

Skal moved his gaze in Bogie's direction. "I just wondered who chose the targets. I have a gun, but I would not trust it to aim itself."

Jack read the unease in the other's voice. He straightened and clipped the last bracer onto his left arm. "I cannot explain to you the way we work. We've not done it often this way, but we have done it. My enemies are his enemies." He checked his energy clips and threw the empty pack into the skimmer.

"All the same, I would guard my back if I were you," Skal said. "Perhaps he is tired of sharing the armor with you when he must." The Fisher brushed past him, hiking up the riverbank toward a fringe of heavy, dark foliage that seemed as tall as a small mountain—the edge of the rain forest.

With a sigh, Jack called out, "Follow me, Bogie."

"Yes, boss," the armor replied in its deep and mellifluous voice, utilizing a synthesizer inside the suit. "The sun feels good."

"Enjoy it while you can." Jack hiked his shoulder belt into a more comfortable position across his chest and set off after Skal, who was moving across a grassland through stalks up to his neck.

Skal had not warned him of the clouds of insects, the winged variety, though not of the kind that enjoyed bare skin. Still, he finally fashioned a veil across his face to avoid breathing in the small, translucent green ones, with wings of such delicacy he wondered how they could survive the rain. The insects flew in layers, until the topmost skimmed the height of the rain forest, fewer, but with wingspreads that equaled the reach of his arms, and each layer occasionally dipped downward to feast on lesser flyers. He had never seen such brilliant colors.

"Bogie, make sure the suit cameras are on. I'd like to tape this for Amber."

"Recorder on." The armor lumbered after him, with a sound of grass being ripped out by the roots as it tangled about the boots and Bogie walked on, oblivious.

Skal met them at the forest's edge. He tugged playfully at the lower edge of Jack's veil. "Now you know why I have whiskers."

"Is that why? I thought it was to strain the river for fish."

Skal broke out in his laugh, until his amber eyes streamed. He mopped them with the back of his hands and reached out to slap Jack on his shoulder. In quite a different voice, he said, "Two of our scouts met their death in this forest. Good hunting to you, my esteemed friend and foe, and take care." Skal stepped away and literally melted into the forest shadows, his sable fur with caramel mottles as good a camouflage as Jack had ever seen. If it were not for the bright yellow slicker shorts and weapons belt, he would be invisible.

Sobered by what Skal had said, Jack ducked his head under a branch and entered, hoping that he had enough firepower to not need invisibility.

The sun, if there was one, Jack thought, must be overhead. He could feel a kind of smoldering green heat filtering down toward him through the layers of insects which were only slightly less dense than they had been over the grassland. Only here there were more predators . . . flutterers disappeared with regularity at the flick of a sticky tongue, but Jack had yet to see what caught them. He eyed overhanging branches frequently, but the dimness of the forest made it damn near impossible for him to get a clear look at anything. The dry footing Skal had promised was here, but he was sweating enough inside his boots to float his ankle bracers off.

Behind him, the armor moved with surprising delicacy as Bogie learned to negotiate a passage through without tearing branches off to do so. Skal's ears moved forward and back and he complained about noise, but the complaints and the noise had both trailed off.

Jack called out, "Where are we?"

"Close to the other side."

Jack had no such feeling. If anything, he thought they'd been going in circles. He said to Bogie, "Check your compass."

The alien asked, "In reference to what?"

Damn. He'd not set an initial coordinate and Bogie had nothing to draw the primary median on for reference.

Skal had come to a stop and watched Jack over the top of a bar of what looked (and smelled) like dried fishmeal. "If you have a problem," he got out, "take a sighting from above." His whiskers trembled with humor.

Jack knew a dare when he heard one. He looked up, selected a tree, and said to Bogie, "Give me a leg up."

The armor stood motionless for a moment, then stood on one boot and ponderously held the other leg in the air.

Jack shook his head. "No, no. Give me a hand up."

Bogie righted himself on his feet and spread his gauntlets.

"No," Jack said. "Listen." And he thought an image to Bogie, of being given a boost.

Obediently, the armor bent and did so. As Jack shinnied to the limb above him, Skal said. "That's the dumbest robot I've ever seen."

Before Jack could say anything, Bogie reached over to Skal, picked him up by the Fisher's weapons' belt and neatly deposited him on the bottom branch.

"I'm learning," rumbled Bogie gently.

The otter-man hooked an arm about the tree trunk and said to Jack, "I think I'll just wait here for you."

Hiding his expression, Jack kept climbing.

The tree was a slender, fragrant growth, with a light brown skin that peeled down naturally to creamy white. He had to take care it did not peel away too vigorously under him, making handholds and footholds chancy. The branches were spaced wide apart at regular intervals, making it a natural for climbing. The scent of its bark was heady and Jack thought of Amber wearing its perfume. She'd like it.

Below, Skal made a hiss between his teeth, saying, "Watch where you put your hands, Jack my friend."

Distractedly, Jack looked at his right arm, extended for a pull up and saw the brown and cream lizard not a finger's length from his hand. The reptile's tongue wagged out, and then the beast turned about on the branch. A shambling run, a leap with all legs spread, the wattle on each catching the air, and it parasailed to a nearby branch.

"That one leaves a nasty bite, but it's also timid," Skal offered to the treetops.

"I'll remember that." Jack kept climbing.

As the tree broke the forest ceiling, the wind that the forest had shunted away took hold and swayed it, and Jack could only balance on a slender branch and embrace the main trunk. He marked the direction Skal had been taking—the Fisher's sense was leading them where he said it was.

His sweat dried quickly in the stiff breeze. As Jack half-turned to head back down, he saw a good-sized clearing in the rain forest—and his heart skipped a beat.

Rust! Nothing—where there should have been trees or at least grass, there was nothing but rusty dirt.

Sand. He could not be wrong.

Jack rubbed a free hand over his face, tired from the half-day's walk. He looked back toward the destination Skal guided them to—and saw a thin curl of smoke on the horizon.

Habitation of some sort. Yet the sand was here, in the forest.

Jack got down the quickest way he knew how, which was halfway between sliding and a controlled fall. Skal saw him coming and bailed out of the tree first with a startled yelp.

"Are you bit?"

"No." He reached for Bogie and unscrewed the helmet. "Computer, mark this location as a return target." He replaced the helmet, saying to Bogie, "The in-suit circuitry will mark that. Just follow the readings on the way back."

Bogie, who could not actually see but made his way by rightness and wrongness of various suit readings, answered, "Yes, boss."

Skal's whiskers were up, like hackles. "What is it?"

"There's an installation that way, over the ridge. We'll get an overview of it when we break clear of the forest. But I don't understand why because there's sand that way—" Jack thumbed the direction. "They don't leave the sand once they plant it. Usually they'll dig a below ground nest, infiltrate there, and then start the sand."

With a worried frown, the Fisher said, "We're going to see?"

"Yes."

Skal let him take the lead.

An hour later, bare head wet with perspiration, Jack knelt by the patch of Thrakian sand. Skal also knelt, his lips wrinkled with disgust.

"This *sand*—it's not natural."

"No. It'll ruin Mistwald, the way it did Milos and my world, Dorman's Stand, and a handful of others. But it's been abandoned here." Jack stood up slowly, and surveyed the damage. The patch was large, and he could see burn marks along the leading edge. And no Thraks. But why?

"All right, Bogie. Take us back to the return target."

The armor led them back. Skal and Jack sat down and took a short break. Skal had fishbars which Jack refused, but he also had a rich fruit and grain bar, one that had Jack licking his fingers when it was gone. They shared a waterskin and got up, ready to go on.

Mistwald's sun was penetrating the rain forest at about two o'clock high when they broke cover. The forest was elevated, and the grassy plains broke out from under them, rolling down to more knolls and a set of falls, three of them, boiling water into the air. At their edge, Jack saw the installation. Jack sucked in his breath in at the size of the runway being cut into the green field even as he watched, domes going up, a crude cutaway of dirt taking a bank of fire as a squad lined up before it. The air stank with the fumes and rang with the noise. The base was going to be massive—it would have to be to hold three launching cradles as well as three runways. He saw Talons and corsairs, their shapely and deadly bodies resting to one side.

"God in heaven," Jack said. "They're getting ready to start a war."

"Who?" Skal asked, digging at his arm. "Who!"

"The only ones brave enough to defy Pepys and go after *sand* themselves. Those are Green Shirts down there. That explains why the sand in the forest is dying back. They've already dug out an infestation."

The Fisher made a growling noise deep in his throat. "What good is medication," he said, "if it kills the patient?"

Jack stayed at the forest's edge, watching the base crawl with fighters. Once he went down there, there was no going back. And yet, how could he help Skal without going in?

Bogie moved. The helmet visor went up as if he were a hound scenting the wind. "I smell death," was all he said.

CHAPTER 16

The Fisher had no mane at the back of his sleek head, but his pelt was stiffened, hackles up. "I agree," he said. "Now that we know who the enemy is, we shall know how to defeat him."

Jack shook his head. "Create a diversion. I'm going down there."

"You're *what*?"

Storm dropped to one knee. He began untangling grasses and ferns from the armor's boots, unwilling to meet Skal's too bright eyes. "You knew I was in the Outward Bounds on a mission of my own. Mist knows it, too. I was looking for Green Shirts, Skal. Looking for a way to disentangle Pepys from his web of power—and looking for myself."

"They despoil my world."

Jack stopped, his hands stained by the vegetation he held across them. "I know. They're careless—heedless—of the damage they're bringing with them."

Skal's muzzle wrinkled and he spat viciously to one side, just missing Jack. "You think I'm not aware of your worlds just because I remain earthbound to mine? I listen to the news. I have seen the damage inflicted by your 'careless' heroes. They are terrorists."

Jack looked up and met his gaze, as bright and hot as magnesium in water. "You're right," he said, and got up, dusting his hands on his pants. "They're nothing more than murderers and bombers. But they could be more. I think they meant to be, once. And they have helped me, in their own selfish way, and I don't have anywhere else to go for the help I need now. They have my mind, Skal, memories they took when I slept as a soldier. I need those memories, and I need to remind them who they were. Then we can part ways.

"And what of Mistwald? When you are done here, and leave—what of them?"

"They helped you here. They fought sand when you didn't even know it was here. They've taken out a vital first step in Thrakian infestation. They've done more than you know."

The Fisher said bitterly, "They despoil the wilderness . . . our forests and our water. They will kill us as surely as they did the Thraks—and without merciful quickness."

"Contact them. Tell them what they're doing. They may listen."

"If not?"

"It's them or the Thraks, Skal. You can put up filtration dams along the river and lakes—that'll solve a lot of the problems. Thraks . . . Thraks won't stop unless they're forced to."

Skal smoothed the side of his muzzle, laying his whiskers back. "I gave you a knife once."

There was a lump in Jack's throat and he found it difficult to swallow around it. "I know."

"You know nothing! Not then, not now!" Skal paced away, his tail rigid with his agitation. "That knife signifies an honored enemy. It signifies a mercy kill, if the battle is lost. I trusted you, we trusted you, to quicken our death if we lost the battle for Mistwald. I came to know you as friend as well. But you intend to go down there and join them, do you not?"

Jack had his hand on the suit's shoulders, preparing to open up the seams. He did indeed intend to go down and see if he could breach the camp's perimeters. But he would do it in armor. He paused, "Skal, you don't understand."

"I understand enough! You have betrayed your emperor, and now you betray us."

His throat constricted further, but he got out, "I haven't betrayed you, but I don't intend to make them leave. Give me time to do what has to be done."

"You're not going to fight them."

"No."

Skal took a deep, quivering breath. Jack watched his large amber eyes, searching for the expression that would tell him his life was in danger, but he found only sadness.

The Fisher said, "What shall I tell the Council? What of our dead?"

"Tell the Council I am meeting with the men building an unauthorized base here, and that I will ask for reparations if the Council will grant them authority to stay. As for your dead . . ." Jack paused. "It's possible the Thraks killed them. I don't know."

"It's equally as possible your Green Shirts did."

"I know. Tell the Elders I apologize for the arrogance of the human race. Tell them we don't always recognize the worth of another. Tell them I will see that the families of the dead are given prime trading rights, as well as an apology."

"Do humans know how to apologize?"

Jack found himself nodding. "Yes. Yes, we do."

The Fisher's sable tail relaxed slowly until it trailed on the ground. "Then, my friend," Skal said joylessly, "I will go back alone and tell of your betrayal with good intentions. If they attack you as they did my brothers, I don't think you'll be easy to pull down in your armor. But if they do, I will be back to avenge you." He offered his hand in farewell.

Jack took it uneasily. His hearing caught a high sound, just out of range, but near enough to be audible and to jar across his nerves. Even as he took Skal's hand, and began shaking, he lifted his head and half-turned on one heel.

He saw a glint in the sky. The whining pitch became clearer. "Damn! Skal, run for it. Bury yourself as deep in the forest as you can get." He swung about on the suit, took the helmet off, and collapsed the armor by opening up the seams.

"What is it?"

"And I was wondering about getting past security!" Jack sat down and shed his boots and legs bracers as quickly as he could. "Those are needlers—Thrakian warships. They've come after the base. This whole area will be—poisoned—with their weaponry."

As quickly as he shed the Enduros, Skal put them on.

"You can't come with me." Jack panted in his haste, shucking himself of his armor and weapons belts.

"You cannot tell me, friend, that they," and Skal jacked

a thumb skyward as the needlers came screaming closer, "will not target you once they have seen you."

No, Jack couldn't tell him that. This whole confrontation was beyond the Alliance, and the Thraks would react to his armor as if he were an ancient enemy and all that had ever gone between them was hatred and war.

The Fisher arched his brow triumphantly. "Someone must survive to take back your apology."

Jack shoved himself into the armor, hastily clipping on leads and feeds, checking the screens to make sure he was fully powered. Skal leaned in, nose first, and eyed the chamois that was Bogie's regenerating form.

"This is the other?"

"Yes."

"Interesting." Skal nearly lost a set of whiskers as Jack heaved the suit up over his shoulders and finished sealing the armor at his neckline.

"Check your weapons," Jack recommended as he flexed his gauntlets. "Bogie, take stun off, make all shots fully operational."

Yes, Boss.

The ground shook beneath them as the needlers' rumbling made the earth vibrate. As Jack screwed the helmet on, he watched the Green Shirts' base go to a scramble. Planes on the ground meant maximum vulnerability. Whatever they could get up after the pair of needlers made their first run and circled to come back could well be the firepower that saved their asses.

Jack checked his targeting grids and cameras. The Green Shirts had better thank whatever gods they acknowledged that this was first turf for the Thraks, or they'd be facing incoming missiles. The Thraks were limited to short-range and unbased weaponry until they felt they were strong enough to take the port with all its defenses and warning systems.

Thunder sounded. The needlers were coming in, and they'd be there long before he was close enough to do any damage himself. But he'd be there when they came in to finish the base off. He grabbed Skal by the back of the neck even as the Fisher was patting down his ammo clips, and broke into a run only the seven-league boots of the armor was capable of.

*   *   *

Colin moved away from the building's exterior monitors, a most uncharitable expression curdling his face. Those damn Thraks. Even the twilight could not hide their spindly presence. He was the same as imprisoned, and he knew it, and they knew he knew it and did not care. He clenched a fist. Then he caught a deep breath and opened his hand, forcing it to relax. At one time it had taken more than the sight of a few sentry Thraks ostensibly guarding the Walker headquarters to upset him. Now it was one more in a series of senseless, destructive acts.

Pepys had gone insane. Colin saw no other term for it. The emperor, in stretching out his authority to minor, fringe planets, was in relentless pursuit of power. As suspicious as the Walker prelate was of the Green Shirts, he saw more of the emperor's scheming behind the recent outbreak of petty infringements, infringements which by their nature made it necessary for the emperor and his Thrakian allies to step in and settle the problems. The Outward Bounds, while under the jurisdiction of neither the Triad Throne nor the Dominion, was in danger of being annexed. Walker information filtering in to him told him the freer spirits of the Outward Bounds would not stand still for Pepys' actions, even if it meant full-scale war—a war Pepys could no more afford with the Ash-farel threatening him and with his dubious alliance with the Thraks than he could safely behead himself and hope to live.

Colin waited now for the latest intelligence from Denaro. Pepys had infiltrated his own com lines—his most reliable information came in person, shielded by white noise screening—but now Colin wondered if Denaro were still reliable. Nothing had ever been said about the Gibbon incident— yet the young man surely knew, by Colin's subtle change in reliance upon him, that he had been suspect.

A step sounded behind Colin now and he turned. Jonathan had let Denaro in with little fanfare. The man stood, his frame braced defiantly. There was the natural arrogance of the young in the tilt of his head. "What news?"

"Farseeing is gone, your eminence, under the aegis of the emperor, reportedly to defend it from the Ash-farel."

The words struck to his very marrow. He held himself erect, knowing that he was under scrutiny from one who hoped to replace, as well as inform, him. "Gone? What do you mean—gone?"

"Annexed. I didn't mean—the Ash-farel veered in their attack, and left the colony clear. But they had forsworn themselves as Walkers by then, and begged for Pepys' protection."

"I see." Colin crossed his small private apartment, seeking the redwood table of old Earth, still finding solace in its burled rings of life and energy. "And were the Ash-farel indeed moving in for attack?"

Denaro brushed a hand through his untamable hair. "I can't find confirmation of it. It appears that agents infiltrated the ports first, sir, and after—readings can be altered, even falsified."

"Easily." Colin sat down, his palm on his table. "I cannot blame the colonists on Farseeing for being," and he gave an ironic smile, "shortsighted. Life is precious far from home. They did what they thought necessary."

"But your holiness—"

"Oh, damn me, Denaro. Stop treating me as if I were a fragile relic. I'm a flesh and blood man and no more holy than you are."

Denaro stepped back as though he'd been struck. He stammered for a reply and finally got out, "Sir."

"They had no more chance to stand against a staged attack than a real one. No, I don't blame them. Pepys orchestrated it well." Colin looked up, frowning. "You'd better instruct Jonathan and Margaret to contact the others and warn them of the tactic, though I doubt Pepys will try it twice."

"Yes, sir." Denaro's head bobbed. "But why now?"

"Now? Because now he is allied with the Thraks."

"But couldn't he have done the same when he was fighting them?"

"Maybe. But then, there was a good possibility the invasion would have been real. No. The Thraks are not holding off obtaining more crèche worlds because of the alliance. They are allied because they're less afraid of us than of the Ash-farel. They need us to buffer them. Fear is like an acid. The Thraks intend for it to eat through us first."

Denaro stood in silence while Colin thought a moment, then added, "What about the records?"

The young man's cheeks reddened in shame. "Nothing was destroyed. They thought—they thought an attack by the Ash-farel would take care of it. They never thought to destroy the . . . sensitive . . . material before Pepys took over."

The realization made Colin feel old. He took his hand from his table, the serenity he'd gathered washed away once more. The colony at Farseeing had been one of the biggest, most self-sufficient Walker outposts, and had been located at a crux between the Dominion planets and the Outward Bounds, as the warp drives were navigated, rather like Bythia on the other axis. The information which had fallen to Pepys would do no overt harm but it would fuel Pepys' own insecurity and insanity.

The only empire Pepys feared was the empire he thought Colin was building. It had done no good to tell his old friend that it was God's empire, and there were no boundary lines.

He said to Denaro, "Watch your step. Pepys will build a case for treason if he can."

"Tr-treason?"

Colin let the corner of his mouth twist in a bitter smile. Denaro was a militarist Walker—meaning that he was not waiting for the meek to inherit any of the planets they touched. But now that he faced open conflict with the emperor, he was shocked and unready. Good. Colin did not want a pitched battle between Pepys and the Walkers. "Yes. Pepys has long feared that I might make a better ruler than he. He supplanted Regis, and has waited his whole life for that to happen to him. We must see that his wait is futile."

"I . . . see."

Colin watched the young man closely. If Denaro truly intended to wrest the Walkers away from him, he'd just handed Denaro his head on a platter. He would be living on borrowed time.

Colin sighed and got back to his feet. Whatever would be, would be. Denaro turned on his heel as if to leave.

"Denaro."

"Yes, sir?"

"Any news of Amber?"

A slight flush of color across the square-jawed face. "No, sir."

Why the color? Was Denaro embarrassed because he failed to have news of her—or because of other reasons? Colin put his hands in a pair of thigh pockets in his jumpsuit. "I need to have her located."

"Because of her background, she can be very . . . elusive."

"I know. But she's under my protection, something I can't extend if I can't locate her." He was worried now, and it colored his tone.

Denaro drew himself up at the challenge. "I'll find her, sir."

"Good. Send Jonathan in as you leave, please." There was a cool draft through the apartment as Denaro left. Colin walked back to the exterior monitors and watched them—as close to an outer window as he could afford in his room. He thought of Amber and Jack and wondered where they were—and how they would all fare in the months ahead. Beside Denaro's news, he'd had word of yet another attack by the Ash-farel. They took no prisoners.

CHAPTER 17

It took Amber four weeks to break Winton's access code. She might never have thought of it, but if the name of the emperor he had helped depose opened the door lock, then the name of the man he owed most to and hated most would open his secret files: Pepys. There was a certain perverse logic to it. She knew that neither Pepys himself nor Vandover Baadluster would ever think of the code. It almost cost her her life to do it herself.

Winton's files were sketchy, almost in a shorthand, and she would have to be steeped in his mental processes to know most of what he had entered. They were not complete entries, but memory joggers. She did find a notation of Green Shirt activity and a search for a woman coded Countess. Winton's hunt had gone to ground just shortly before he'd left for Bythia, where he met his death.

She pored over the readouts, gleaning it for whatever he had recorded. His entries were short and cryptic. She came away knowing only that Countess had an aristocratic background and would be damned hard to find if she didn't want to be. The records confirmed that it was indeed the Green Shirts, with Winton as the prime manipulator, who'd shanghaied Jack as contract labor to the dead moon colony of Lasertown a few years ago. As a failed experiment, he was judged more dangerous to them alive than dead, and his shanghaiing had originally been a death sentence.

Even more rewarding was the revelation that Bythia had been intended as a death trap for Colin, either in direct conflict with Pepys over gaining access by the Walkers or by placing Colin into the role of a messianic figure in the Bythian culture. Instead, it had been Jack who'd fulfilled the prophecy and Winton who'd died.

It had not been Winton alone who'd thought of these machinations—but the partner was not identified.

She had just downed Winton's equipment when the automatic sentry came through the burned out Lunaii wing. The lights went out and she sat in the dark, pondering what she'd just read until:

"Halt! Remain in place and present your wrist ident."

Amber stifled her startled response. She wasn't going to give them a recording to make a voiceprint from. With a movement that the sentry's infrared sensors would interpret as compliance, she swept a can from her belt and released its contents.

The spray had a dual purpose: its particles obscured the sentry's sensor readings and chilled her down instantly, making body heat temporarily unreadable as well. As far as the sentry was concerned, it had been blinded. She was getting old—she didn't jump it before its interference and assistance alarm went off.

She lashed out as she passed the machine in the corridor, her nails catching and half-ripping out the control board. It dangled from the sentry's body, but it was still functional enough to whip around and fire a stunning shot her direction.

It washed off the walls, an eerie blue light in the char. Amber gathered her heels under her and kept running, her pulse pounding in her throat, adrenaline roaring through her the way it used to when she ran the streets. Another sonic beam splashed the wall next to her. She winced as the backwash caught her arm, cramped in spasmodic response, shook it off, and barreled around a ruined corner.

She heard footsteps and knew the sentry's alarm had brought the palace police—WPs, Baadluster's men. Amber sucked in her breath and made a leap from the half-wall down the stairwell. She landed with a jar that froze her knees in pain, grinding her teeth together against the sudden agony she felt clear through her skull. The impact stopped her for a moment, then she gasped and bolted downstairs, her flight anything but noiseless.

She grabbed a band from about her black-sleeved wrist as she ran. The micro-recorder caught the sound of her feet upon the metal stairs. She rewound it and dropped it in the stairwell, broadcasting the sound on an endless loop, as

she moved stealthily onto the ground floor corridor where
fire had not gutted the wing.

Night lighting made the obsidite flooring glow gently
rose. She moved through it as though she walked barefoot
over embers, eyeing doors as she passed them. She was
trapped until she reached the corridor's end, where there
would be access doors. Once there—Amber pushed dis-
couraging thoughts out of her mind. Even if she could get
through those doors, there would be no way she could keep
her passage from being recorded.

Amber flattened herself to the wall and leaned out to
eye the juncture. The door was open! It was closing slowly,
grit or other minute obstacles in its track, retarding its slide.
She threw secrecy to the wind and gained the door frame
as it shut, catching a pinch of her shoe sole as she leaned
outside.

Amber winced as she walked forward. The door had evidently caught her foot as well, it felt stone bruised at the
heel. She wondered if the security cameras had caught
enough of her to ID her. Jack would skin her alive for
taking chances like this—if Pepys didn't catch her and skin
her first. She rubbed her wrist, mourning the loss of some
expensive equipment. Untraceable, of course, but regrettable nonetheless.

She took a deep breath and left the security of the building's shadow. Even as she pushed away, the floodlights
blazed on, white-hot circles of betrayal in the night. Amber
dodged blindly.

A huge hand wrapped about her elbow, drawing her into
his umbra against the security floods.

"A second time ill-met, my lady Amber."

Her heart tumbled in her chest as K'rok drew her closer
against his form. She could feel the rumble in his hairy
chest as he said quietly, "Your kind are not seeing well in
the dark, I am thinking. Stand upon my feet and walk with
me—they are seeing only my back."

He embraced her even more closely, walking her across
the palace grounds. She heard shouts from behind, smelled
his ursine, musky, and slightly rank odor. The beat of his
heart (hearts?) sounded in her ear as he called back, "I've
seen nothing—off-duty I am, and leaving."

A voice instructed him to take prisoner any unauthorized

personnel he might encounter, adding, "If you please, Commander K'rok."

"I will!" Then, softly, "And it be pleasing me not.

"What are you doing?"

"Getting you away from here. You do not take warnings well."

"No."

K'rok made a noise that sounded like a growl. His immense, shaggy body dwarfed hers. He could snap her spine like a twig. "You should be knowing this by now. You must stay away."

"My business here is finished."

They were nearing the boundary sector, which was always well lit and patrolled. Amber faded into the overhanging branches of a tree, saying, "I'll be all right from here."

The lumbering Milot came to a halt. "I be thinking not. The Minister of War is no fool. Stay there. I will bring back a car." He loped away, shaggy head bent in determination.

Amber hugged the tree, bark scratching her chin. She found herself quaking in the aftermath of adrenal shock. She would have to trust K'rok, she had no one else to turn to within reach.

The car came to a halt. The door opened but a crack. She crawled along the ground and got in, twining her slim frame about K'rok's immense booted feet. In the shadowy interior, she was barely perceptible.

"Where to?"

"Under-Malthen. Any bar you want. I can alter the travel records." Her voice was muffled as she hid the paleness of her face in the crook of her black-sleeved arm.

K'rok grunted and jammed the car into motion. They were through the security gates and on the main thoroughfare when she heard the alarms go off, and all exits were closed.

The Milot let out an audible sigh, then rumbled down at his feet, "Are you going to stay there?"

"Yes," Amber said weakly. She doubted if she had the strength to move, just yet.

"Where will you go?"

"I don't know. Somewhere safe." She thought of Colin, and discarded it. Denaro was suspect, and Pepys knew she had sheltered with Colin before. She would not visit the emperor's scrutiny upon the Walker again, not for her sake. She lay hugging the Milot's boots and listening to the hovers whine in the floor under her ear, plotting her course. Suddenly, she knew where to have K'rok take her.

She had fallen asleep. K'rok nudged her gently a second time and Amber roused.

He growled, "After driving half the night, we appear to have arrived somewhere."

She sat up. The night was as dark as it could get, and the building before them stood immense, squat, and impregnable, white stone side catching what little glimmer was available from the moon. She saw the numerous security cameras, operating on filters, and smiled to herself. The woman she sought was still in residence here.

"What is it?" K'rok asked. "A tomb or temple?"

"No." She opened the car door. "Sadie is a pawnbroker." She pointed out the tunnel entrance. "This place is like an iceberg—four-fifths of it is underground." Amber shut the door and paused. "Thank you, commander," she said finally.

He nodded his head. "You are welcome. Tell me, if you would . . ." he stopped.

She knew what he wanted to ask. She smiled gently and said, "Last I heard he was still alive and kicking."

The Milot grinned hugely. "Thank you! And now, lady Amber, it is getting late. I must have time to get drunk enough to make my time away from the barracks to be believed.

She stepped away from the car and watched it whistle away, the immense frame of the Milot taking up the view through the back shield. Servos whined as cameras turned and stayed trained as she entered the tunnel gates.

"I have no appointment," Amber repeated for the tenth time. "I would just like to talk with Sadie and see if we can solve a problem I have." She stood wearily before the massive door, its overhead frame sculpted with the three ball symbol of the pawnbroker, and listened as the computer replied, "Madame is not to be disturbed—"

"Oh, but I am." The viewscreen filled with a massive woman, shot from the bosoms up, with dimples not only in her ample chins, but her bared shoulders as well. Sleep had tousled her dyed curls, but her eyes were far from puffy. Sadie eyed her alertly. "Who is it? Come out of the shadow there. I won't let you in if I can't identify you."

Amber put her shoulders back and stepped out, brushing her hood from her head, releasing her hair from its confinement as the woman muttered something about guests without manners and invitation disks.

Sadie stopped in mid-gesture. "Good heavens. Amber, is that you?"

"Yes, madam."

"Good heavens. The girl has become a woman. Where's Jack?"

She had already made certain plans while waiting for an audience. "Jack is dead."

"Posh. I know what the newscasts reported. Show me the body, and I'll believe Jack Storm is dead. I never saw a better survivor." The strangely alluring bulk of the woman adjusted on the couch. "What do you need, honey?"

"Sanctuary," Amber said, and fainted dead away on the doorstep.

CHAPTER 18

"I won't say your help's not appreciated," the base commander said, as they sat wearily down to eat in what was left of the mess. Soot darkened their faces. The work force hunched with bowed shoulders over cold rations, and their talk was muted with weariness. But they could afford to talk of victory, for the Thraks had been driven back, and only one Talon had been lost, along with a half-completed dome and two supply sheds. In the background, noise rumbled from bulldozers already back at work restoring the runways.

Staub added, "But you present me with a problem. Policy tells me that I cannot let you go free."

"I want to stay," Jack said. He paused with his fork in hand as Skal added, "Let me near a river and you cannot keep me." The otterlike tail twitched in emphasis.

The commander looked at Skal. "You, sir, as a representative of local government, should be treated as an ambassador. However, since we're not here in any official capacity. . . ." the auburn-haired man let his voice trail off and shrugged.

"You would have no capacity if we had not intervened," the Fisher returned. He looked down at his plate and stirred the rations into a stew, meat, fruit, and vegetable compounds unrecognizable. Then he lifted a forkful, sniffed delicately, and began to eat. "Might you have beer?"

Staub's hazel eyes looked a bit glazed but he said hastily. "Yes, of course. The refrigeration section was undamaged by the strafing." He snapped his fingers and a string bean of an adjutant took his request.

"With all due respect," Jack interrupted, drawing the commander's attention back to him, "I don't see how you can afford to refuse any help you can get. Consider my performance against the Thraks a demonstration of armor's capabilities. I know you can appreciate that."

"I can appreciate it, but I can't trust it." Staub was a man of easy authority, broad-shouldered, with a thick waist that might later tend toward roundness but now was flat. Despite the red hair, he had a complexion that tanned nicely, and the sun had etched a network of wrinkles about his gray-green eyes. He was apparently ten years Jack's senior. He had workman's hands: square, competent, solid. He drummed the tabletop for emphasis now with his left. "We've been told to look out for you, Storm. Word is you're operating as Pepys' agent."

As Skal spewed a mouthful of food back onto his plate, Jack said smoothly, "I'm dead, as far as Pepys knows."

"I remember you," the commander said. "The business at Lasertown was reported as underground. You have a reputation for doing an agent's work."

Jack smiled at the irony. Everything he'd done at Lasertown had been in his own interest. Pepys had downplayed the entire situation, neither disavowing it nor claiming it in his own interest. But telling the tale was not something he had time for. Staub was unsure, it was time to convince him before he made his mind up.

The aide returned with three cartons of beer. Skal made a great deal of noise opening his up before lifting the now foaming container to his muzzle. Jack took advantage of the break in conversation.

"I'd have come to you the conventional way, with even more suits, but I was ambushed at Gibbon's on Malthen."

There was a sparkle deep in Staub's eyes, but he, too, turned his attention to the beer, saying, "Who?"

Jack ignored him. "Then I found my way to Skagboots' Retreads on Victor Three. Bootsie was very interested in my armor, but we got interrupted by a routine freebooters' strafing run."

Staub looked amused. "It sounds hazardous to be conversing with you."

Jack looked up at the great rent overhead in the mess hall. "I think you're done for the day," he answered.

"Mm." The commander paused for a moment, took some updated damage reports from his aide, made some decisions and delegations, then turned his attention back to Jack. "It's a long way from Skagboots' to here."

Skal bared his too sharp teeth. "That was my fault, commander. I intercepted him and asked him to come with me. My world had a . . . pest problem . . . I was most anxious to solve."

"Meaning us?"

The Fisher nodded.

"I see." Staub took a deep drink of his beer. He made a face as he swallowed. "We've been dumping excess fuel and duds before coming back in to land. It's a sloppy habit. I apologize, Skal, to you and your Elders. I'll send out cleanup details, if you'll allow us to set up an official dump."

"What does he mean?"

"He means a plane can't come in safely carrying over-allowances of fuel or firepower. It's usually jettisoned over uninhabited areas . . . swamp or marshland. But," and here Jack scratched his temple where his eyebrow met it, "all of Mistwald is swamp or marshy. They're used to having filtration islands set up in those bog areas, to pick up the toxics. . . ."

"The method you talked to me about."

"Yes."

Skal laid his tail on the table, the portion that would reach. The gesture unnerved both Jack and the Green Shirt commander. The Fisher stroked his pelt, which was as sleek there as anywhere. He looked up. "The location is different and may be difficult to reach, but it is all one body," he said. "My grooming is as important here as anywhere." He curled the tip. "There *is* no backwater on Mistwald."

"I see what you mean." Staub reached for his beer quickly as Skal lashed his tail back, nearly upsetting the cartons. "Your—ah—point is well taken. Chrysler!"

The string bean of an aide leaned down.

"Get cleanup details formed as soon as possible. We've been polluting major waterways."

The aide nodded and left the mess.

Skal finished his rations and looked about appraisingly. He noticed the empty place setting at Staub's elbow and pointed his fork at it. "My condolences, commander, for the death of an honored one."

The redhead looked quickly, then shook his head. "That's not because of the raid. It's for the founders of the movement. We lost our leadership to the Sand Wars."

"Yet you carry on."

"In our way, though—" Staub halted abruptly, noticed the listening silence around the long table and smiled. "The Green Shirts do whatever they can."

"You didn't get where you are today by not taking chances. Can you afford to turn me and what I offer down?"

"If you're a beacon by which Pepys locates this base, I can't afford to keep you." The man met Jack's eyes with a level stare of his own. "What is worth the risk?"

"I can give you Pepys' head on a platter."

There was a startled silence throughout the mess, then Staub put his head back and laughed, breaking the tension, and Jack could hear the babble of excited voices start again.

When Staub quieted, he said, "Make a martyr of the emperor and we will never replace the chain of command."

"Of course not. But I can give you evidence first that will erode public confidence in him—start an outcry that will demand he be replaced."

"You're a Knight. Why would you want to do such a thing?"

"Because," Jack said, leaning forward on an elbow, "I didn't swear to Pepys. I was sworn to Regis."

Disbelief flickered across the commander's face. "Regis? Impossible. That was—what—twenty-five years ago? You're scarcely older than that. You'd have to be my age."

"How long have you been a Green Shirt?"

Skal sat back in his chair, holding his beer close to his chest, enjoying the conversation.

"Since the Sand Wars," Staub answered Jack.

"I don't know how the chain of command works here," Storm continued. "Or how long you've been underground. There was a captain of the Knights who spoke to the Dominion Congress last year, before the Alliance."

Staub's attention sharpened. "There were rumors."

"Good ones. I was that captain, soon to be a commander."

"The one found in cold sleep?"

"Yes, I was found on that transport, the only one who lived to tell the tale."

"My God." Staub pushed away from the table as if denying it and all that he had heard. "It's impossible."

"You heard the rumors." Jack wet his throat with the last of his beer, and waited.

"Then where have you been?"

"Staying alive," Jack answered. "At first, the Green Shirts who found me hid me for reasons of their own . . . and then I found it safer to hide under the hem of the emperor's own robe. Learning who betrayed us on Milos . . . who betrayed us throughout the Sand Wars. I was betrayed again when we allied with the Thraks."

"We were all betrayed," a smoke-hoarse voice threw in.

Jack nodded. "And now that I've learned what I have, it's time to take action, but I need help for that."

Staub stood up. "If you're telling the truth, you've one hell of a story."

"And if he isn't, commander, we can take care of him later." A wing captain, two seats back from Jack, spoke up. He drew his commander's attention.

"And if I am," Jack said, "I can give you what the Green Shirts desperately need: public sympathy, Dominion support."

"How?"

Jack paused. "We raid Klaktut."

The commander's laugh was short and bitter. "Now I know you *are* crazy. You Knights lost your asses in there last year. Raiding a crèche planet? You're lucky the Thraks didn't slaughter every one of you."

"What you don't know is that Pepys told them we were coming."

"What?"

Jack nodded. "They were waiting for us. We did a lot of damage anyway—gave them a show of strength that Pepys was counting on. It was that raid which made Tricatada decide to propose the Alliance. But what Pepys didn't count on was what we saw."

Staub sat down again, slowly. He wet his lips in apprehension. "What . . . did you see?"

"Farms of humans, bred for food and slaughter. People we assumed lost to the Sand Wars, still alive. Hopeless, but alive. We knew the Thraks were murderers. We didn't know they were human eaters." Jack stood up, raising his voice. "There is a story of courage and misery in every captive we bring back—a story of a life that was betrayed so that Pepys might bring down Regis and gain a throne. And even for those we can't bring back, a clean death might be a mercy."

"I can't . . . I can't authorize a deepspace action," Staub said. He scrubbed a rough hand through his auburn hair.

"But you want to."

"Yes. Yes, by damn. I'll take you to Klaktut."

"Then get authorization."

Staub looked to Skal. "That means more cradles and a larger base."

The Fisher shrugged. "If you can keep it clean, as Jack has told me you can, I see no reason why the Elders would not agree. As long as it is temporary."

Staub gave a savage grin. "Then excuse me, gentlemen. I have a call to put through."

CHAPTER 19

The pawnbroker's home was gracious inside, crowded with remnants of other days, some beautiful and some homely, all of them precious in their antiquity. Amber glided through the clutter with pantherlike grace. It was a game she had played before—how close could her cuff or sleeve come to toppling something without actually touching it? Sadie's eyes glittered as she watched her guest. Amber kept her half-smile hidden behind a curtain of tawny hair and came to a stop, kneeling at her hostess' chaise.

The woman touched her head in what might have been a caress. "Feeling better, I see?"

"Definitely."

"I'm sorry not to have had time to see you these past few days. I've been busy."

"And I'm sorry to have been an uninvited guest."

"But not unwelcome," Sadie said. Her voice was rich and full, almost fruity. "You've got trouble. Vandover Baadluster and St. Colin of the Blue Wheel are both looking for you. Baadluster worries me, but Colin does not. Which one of them are you hiding from?"

Amber rocked back from her knees and settled cross-legged on her rump, a more comfortable position. She shrugged. "Baadluster."

"Ah." Her eyes were a dark brown, almost black, and seemed to focus on some distant sight, as she sat for a time, deep in thought. Then she said slowly, "Even Pepys does not bother me unnecessarily. You'll be safe here. The question is: how long?"

"That's a good question," Amber answered. "I don't know."

"You'll be wanting to make other arrangements?"

She wondered what the other woman was thinking as

Sadie gestured with her hands, her nails done in gold and diamond overlay. Her crimson lips were permanently tinted and her eyes indelibly outlined. Her bulk reigned over the chaise with a majesty all its own. Yet this woman was, indisputably, powerful and dangerous. "I don't have any place else to go," Amber admitted in a small voice. "I've been out of under-Malthen too long. You're the only one I can trust."

"I see." Sadie gave a full and generous smile. "Everything has its price."

"I can't tap my accounts. Vandover would trace me immediately."

"Money is not an immediate problem. Jack even has a small account he's left open with me, just in case. But I have needs, too, Amber. You are a young lady of many talents.".

She sensed the change in tone. Her back straightened. "You need my help."

Sadie caressed the back of one hand with the palm of the other. "Yes. For which I would pay you, against the cost of your sanctuary."

Amber knew that Sadie knew her reputation for thievery. Once here, hidden behind (underneath) these solid walls, she didn't want to stray, but she did not dare refuse a request if Sadie made one. She inclined her head. "I'll do whatever I can. When will you have . . . arrangements . . . made?"

"Arrangements?" Sadie's eyes widened slightly. Then she laughed, a full-throated laugh of the variety men liked. "Dear, I'm not asking you to steal for me."

"You're not?"

"No! I need you to work in the morgue."

Jack lay in his hammock and listened to the barely audible hum of the cruiser. He'd been given a private cubicle, but if he wished to do anything more vigorous than sneeze, he'd have to leave the area. The overhead lights were dimmed to downtime, and he'd been asleep. But now he was awake, sweat-soaked and uneasy with his dreams of Thraks and *sand* wars and death still vivid in his mind. The cruiser held a wing of Talons in its gut. This was no heavily supported invasion. They were going in to make a quick strike—hit and run—they had almost as much video equipment as they did weapons. Commander Staub had agreed with Jack that the raid's main purpose would be to decommission one of the major nests and obtain the footage necessary to discredit Pepys.

He ought to be sleeping well, with thoughts of revenge for company. Jack absently patted his vest down, searching one of its many pockets for *mordil*. The vial was empty except for a glistening coat of liquid. He unstoppered it and tilted the last few drops onto his tongue. He closed his eyes and drifted, wondering if the drug would put him back to sleep.

In his half-awake thoughts, he sought comfort and found Bogie. The alien/suit was in equipment storage, resting comfortably. The helmet's solars had enough energy to keep him growing and Jack had ample opportunity to keep them charged.

Despite the voice synthesizer, Bogie had not become particularly articulate. But Jack found himself reaching a kindred spirit when they communed in this manner.

The sentience had also been thinking of war, though his memories were vaguer. He was eager and certain of victory and communicated that to Jack. *Come fight with me.*

"Fight who?"

Does it matter? The world is full of enemies and victory.

Jack walked the landscape of another world, the suit striding by his side, its normal opalescence replaced by a golden aura. That aura was Bogie's berserker spirit and it blazed so keenly Jack felt its warmth on his flank, as though he marched with a being made of fire.

"I don't like killing."

What about honor?

Jack halted. He looked around him. The landscape was so otherworldly, he knew that if he walked here in actuality, he would need environmental gear. "Bogie—I can't judge well enough to know who is being honorable and who isn't. We have a saying—there's two sides to every moon."

Meaning?

"The dark side of a moon is not dark because it's evil. It's dark because it faces away from the sun and we don't see it illuminated. Rotate the axis and the positions are exchanged. Is one more honorable than the other?"

The suit's aura ebbed and flared. *It is difficult to know.*

"Exactly."

Then where is the honor in war?

"I suppose it comes from fighting for something you believe in."

Bogie was silent for a while. Then he stopped and extended a glove toward Jack. *You are older.*

"I . . . think so."

You decide who to fight.

"Right now, it's Thraks."

He felt a rush of fury, and the aura extended around them both. *The enemy!*

It was that fury that made it possible for Jack to wear the armor. He embraced it, let it blaze in him as well. Before the fire died back, he was asleep in dreamless depths.

The klaxons woke him. He disentangled himself from the hammock, head throbbing from the *mordil*. Running footsteps filled the corridor. He slid his door back as he shrugged into boots. They slept clothed.

"What is it?"

"Unidentifieds closing in. We're on general quarters alert."

Jack grabbed his pack and followed. Bulkheads closed down behind him, securing the cruiser's sector they occupied. The hold was crowded with men, waiting, watching the monitor. Staub's face filled it.

"We are being pursued by a three-wing force of unidentifieds. Our speed is not yet sufficient to attain FTL, therefore, we remain on full battle alert. Expect an exchange of fire as they do not answer the hailing frequency."

Damn. Jack watched as the screen went to neutral. So much for sneaking up on the Thrakian League's backyard.

He half-turned and was surprised to find Chrysler, the adjutant, at his side. The lanky man grimaced.

"Bad luck."

"I'll say. Worse luck if the on-board computers can't make 'em."

Jack felt his eyebrows arch. "What have we got running us?"

"The best we could steal. We may not have much, but what we've got is the best." The adjutant's eyes were bloodshot from having been awakened and he blinked rapidly. "Number Two is too far away to do us any good."

There had been a second cruiser launched, but not from Mistwald. It had coordinates to meet them "turning the corner" just before they went into Klaktut. Jack had no doubt that Number Two was being told of the problem, Staub was that kind of commander.

The screen activated abruptly. Staub had deep lines about his jaw. "The unidentifieds have been made, gentlemen. We're looking at Ash-farel."

The hold became hushed.

The commander went on, "We have no information regarding in-flight attacks. We're still trying to open a com line between us."

"We'll outrun them," an unseen man at Jack's back said.

Jack knew better. As if in response, Staub continued, "They're closing fast. Rig for evasive tactics and return fire. If we can't talk to them, we're going to shoot first."

Jack began shoving his way through the press of men, to reach the two-way com on the monitor. Before he could gain it, there was a massive explosion and the hold rocked violently. Jack kept his feet. The Ash-farel could swat at them as if they were gnats. He knew. But he had never expected it to happen. He'd seen the aliens strike at Thraks, but never at anyone else.

He slapped the monitor and opened the line. "Don't fire back! It's our only hope!"

"Who is this?"

"Jack Storm."

Staub winced as the cruiser shook violently with a second blast. The klaxons began. "They didn't give us a chance, Storm," he answered. "Damage control report." Behind him, Jack could see the blurred outlines of the bridge. "Gentlemen, it appears we'll fight the Thraks some other time. Abandon ship."

Chrysler had come through the crowd at Jack's elbow. "Come on, sir, there's no time to waste. We don't know how many escape pods are operational."

Jack was at the bulkhead as it unsealed the hold. He started down the left corridor, but Chrysler caught at him. The wiry fingers were like bands of steel about his arm. "This way."

"My armor."

"We've no room for equipment!"

He shook Chrysler off. The cruiser shuddered a third time, like a dying animal, and blue-gray smoke abruptly filled the corridor. Jack would never make it to the equipment lockers in that direction.

He staggered after Chrysler, even as Bogie awoke in his thoughts.

Boss! I'm in trouble! The hold's on fire.

Jack had no time to answer him, as men pulled and tugged, jostled and carried him almost bodily down the corridor to the escape boats.

Boss . . .

Jack tried to dig in his heels. The river of men swarmed through a bulkhead, its framework jammed halfway open. He stumbled and went down. His last thought was that he was going to be trampled, but then he felt Chrysler's hard hands upon him, and he was being dragged through and thrown into a small compartment.

Jack sat up and spat out a mouthful of blood. He ground his teeth experimentally as the pod began to vibrate, preparatory to ejection. It was a two-man unit and he knew without looking that Chrysler was his companion.

Without shame, he hung his head and wept as the pod jettisoned, and the wounded cruiser fell away behind them, blazing in the velvet of deep space, Bogie trapped within its wreckage.

CHAPTER 20

The cryogenic vaults below Sadie's were not a morgue, but they felt like it. Cold, still, with bodies laid out on slabs, some with the modesty of a shroud, but many not, covered only by their lid. Amber walked among them with her keypad, noting vital statistics as their medical monitors gave continuous readouts.

Despite the warmth of her clothing and the delicate gloves pulled over her tapered fingers, she was chilled. She did not like the deathly quiet and never would. But the alternative Sadie had offered her was better than being one of the chilled down bodies lying here. She'd done it twice and hoped never to do it again, not unless it was to follow Jack across the stars.

Some of the inhabitants here were collateral, held against loans owed Sadie. She would not keep anyone in cold sleep more than two years so the loans were more often than not made in desperation, and the relative asleep was probably getting the kinder end of the bargain. Malthen was not gentle to the destitute.

There were cryo vaults in the rich end of town, where one could put down ten years or so, to keep off the wrinkles. More time was not advised—like Jack's, locked in the same mind-loop of dreams for seventeen years—the mind was affected. Amber knew of more than one high roller who'd accepted cold sleep as an alternative to bankruptcy—out of control finances careened to a halt and the interest earned over five or six years could bring a family back from debt.

And then, of course, there was always the sad tale of a sleeper who awoke to find his credit embezzled.

Amber prayed the readings stayed constant. She disliked the hard-faced nurse/tech and the woman stayed away unless the readouts became erratic. This was the last place Amber wanted to be found. Of course, the cryo machinery fed into its mainframe system, but Sadie kept her own records. Amber likened it to having a second set of books. She was fairly certain that all the information gathered and recorded would be brought to use someday. Sadie took painstaking effort to gather new data and match it to the correct sleeper. She had a fortune resting in these vaults and knew it.

It was the only set of records on Malthen that Amber hadn't tapped into yet—had not even thought of tapping into, until Sadie mentioned the morgue. Sadie was more than a money changer and less than a pawnbroker—she could occasionally act as a fence. The only Countess Amber knew lifted jewels once in a while. She was certain Sadie had to have done business with her. And, perhaps, Sadie had also crossed paths with an aristocratic woman who was a major power in the Green Shirts.

Her time was limited. Sadie would find out soon that her job was done, and the merchandise she'd been told to steal was waiting at a neutral delivery station. It was now or never if she wanted to get into Sadie's records. Amber left the lab floor and went to the computer room which was pleasingly warm. She let the keypad transcribe to the mother computer while she thawed out. As the data flow filled the system, she sat back and relaxed.

Sadie's work was routine, even boring stuff. Basically it was manually facilitated data entry. Hidden inside it was another program, much more insidious, intended to break the memory bank lockdown on files. Amber chewed on a thumbnail and watched the screen. She checked her time and kept on chewing.

The curtain brought down across Bogie's contact with Jack was black and sudden. The cruiser had ceased to convulse under enemy fire and was adrift, and the alien could sense fires raging inside its hulk. The cargo hold stayed dark and cold—the sprinkler system had damped out an earlier flare and now was all quiet.

Bogie could not remember a time when he'd been alone, severed from Jack's mind. There had been several times when the contact had been incomprehensible, but never totally unavailable. He was afraid. Could their fight be finished when it had hardly begun?

A metallic clank sounded throughout the framework of the cruiser. Bogie brought the suit to attention at the noise. It was a vibration that trilled for long moments, followed by a series of clanks. Something nudged at the cruiser. Then he heard the sound of air locks recycling and knew the vessel was being boarded.

Jack had come back. Bogie's thoughts heated with welcome, then cooled. The presence he encountered entering the cruiser had no similarity to Jack's. Bogie recoiled from the thought. Nothing found alive on the cruiser would be left that way. All equipment was to be examined and salvaged.

To the beings approaching him now, Bogie was life destined to be exterminated.

But first, they might strip from him the means of his existence before letting him die . . . Slowly, under inspection.

Bogie shuddered. To have come so far from death into life, to be reduced to . . . this. Within the shell of the armor of a Dominion Knight, the alien shrank in fear. Silently, he cried for aid and received no answer.

The screen came alive. Amber leaned forward and began to run her inquiries. She looked at the information coming up silently. She downed the file and brought up another one. This was not data the sleeper would willingly give anyone.

Amber swiveled in her chair. She looked through the office window at the sleepers in their bays. There was only one possibility that could obtain the information she was bringing up.

Sadie was running debriefing loops on the cold sleepers. Illegal as hell—and probably worth every credit of the risk. Anything the sleeper had ever done or thought up until that moment of chilldown was encoded on tape. It might be difficult to decode in its entirety, by anyone but the sleeper, but Sadie had dredged a few incidents out on the files Amber read. It was rape of the most insidious kind . . . yet. . . .

What were the odds that the Countess had ever been

here? And even as she thought that, the cold realization went through her that Sadie had tapes on her—as she was before Hussiah on Bythia had purged her of her ability to murder with her mind.

She could gain it back—all of it, all of the subliminal programming with unknowable targets for her assassin talents just by submitting herself to the tape again. The same type of information Jack was looking for on himself, held by the Green Shirts, the mind-loop to a past thought lost.

That shock held her in trance a split second too long to react to the presence in the doorway.

A rich, contralto voice said, "You do a job well and quickly, but I'm not impressed if this is how you repay me."

CHAPTER 21

Amber turned to meet the harsh and preying glare of Sadie. Amber stood up, gathering herself.

"You're a rapist," she said. "I've met street trash before, but this—"

"This is insurance," Sadie interrupted. "And I don't believe that you're in any position to judge me, my girl. Is this why you came to me? Why you pleaded for me to take you in? Or is this an afterthought?"

"This," Amber said wryly, "is why I needed to come here. Only I was tapping Pepys' files."

The woman's full mouth opened in astonishment. Then, abruptly, Sadie dimpled. "My," she said. "You're still full of surprises. Shut that down and come upstairs, then. It's too cool down here for me."

"I need to find someone."

"I have a terminal upstairs. If I feel it's justified and worth the price—and you can pay the price—we'll talk." With amazing grace for her size, Sadie turned in the doorway.

Amber felt it wise to obey her and followed.

Number Two found them after only three days adrift. By then, Jack had seen the Ash-farel bring in a tow, put tractor beams on the wreckage, and haul it away. He'd already lost Bogie when that happened, but he screened his portal dark and refused to watch as the mysterious enemy left them as quickly as they had come. The sundering he felt was as complete as death and what he felt went beyond mourning, for with the alien's passing, he lost the last link to what had been his life before his betrayal in the Sand Wars.

And a Knight never lost his armor. Never. Not unless he were dead first. He was party to one of the ultimate dis-

graces. He had lost his armor, and he had purposely dis-
armed the deadman switch, leaving the suit vulnerable to
whatever enemy wished to examine it. The Ash-farel did
not know it yet, but they had a prize beyond reckoning.
And what would they make of the tattered piece of dead
flesh within it?

The pods were not fired upon as the enemy left. Chrysler
sat hunched into the tiny bodyrest in front of the few manual controls the vessel had and watched in horrified fascination. Over and over he kept repeating: "Why don't they
come after us? We're just sitting here, going nowhere. Why
don't they come finish us off?" until Jack snapped, "Shut
up" at him. Then the aide sat in shock and did not rouse
until the tracker showed another vessel incoming.

The pods were scooped up one by one—and the three
bigger lifeboats. In all, only two men from the cruiser were
unaccounted for in addition to those dead from the direct
hit. Storm was given another cubicle, a ration for bathing,
a hot meal, and told to report to the map room.

Staub was already there, eyes sunk deep in a face bruised
with fatigue, talking to another Green Shirt with an unmis-
takably military bearing. They looked up as Jack came in.

"Jack, this is Captain Tronski. Tron, this is the man who
gave us our target."

"Wish I had known the Ash-farel were in the same quadrant," Jack said.

They gripped hands. Tron released first, with a thin-
lipped smile. He had the kind of face that ran to fat even
though the rest of his body was square and compact. He
wore khaki and his gray and beige hair was cropped short
and neat. Thick, wiry eyebrows shaded eyes of light brown.
He looked down at the star charts coming up on the
tablescreen.

He tapped a sector. "We think they came out of here,
but there's no way to be sure with FTL. We don't even
know if they knew we were here, or if they saw an opportunity and took it."

Jack looked at Staub. "Did you get a shot off?"

The commander shook his head. "Not a one. They had
the momentum—they closed with incredible speed."

"With that kind of speed, they were probably getting
ready to jump off, themselves."

Tron's eyebrows did a sort of dance. "That's what I thought."

"Where would they be going from here?"

"Outward Bounds or, to the other angle, Klaktut."

Staub licked cracked lips. "That leaves us with a problem, gentlemen. Do we want to proceed to our original destination if the Ash-farel are there as well?"

Jack added quietly, "Or do we want to proceed at all."

Staub and Tron said together, "We're going in to fight."

"But most of the video equipment is lost on Number One."

The two Green Shirts looked at him. He recognized a kind of weighing in their expressions. "I see. If we can't get evidence against Pepys, the least we can do is pose as treaty breakers. He'll still have trouble."

Staub nodded. "That's it precisely, Jack. We've got enough weaponry here to arm the men rescued from Number One as well. Our original objective is impossible, but we can still do Pepys a lot of damage."

"And get our boys out of there?" As Jack spoke, his mind raced furiously. He would be going into a Thrakian nest virtually naked without his armor. How could he even contemplate such a thing? These men had no idea what they were up against.

"I won't bandy numbers with you. We know our losses are going to be severe—but we've got enough Talons to pick up survivors."

Jack looked at Tron. "This is a suicide mission with those odds."

The two men looked at their star chart, and Staub said quietly, "It's all they've left us with. But it's better than nothing."

His pulse pounded in his ears, deafening him, and in his memory, he seemed to recalled a bullet-faced drill instructor, glaring at him and a thousand other recruits, saying, "No suit, no soldier."

Time to prove the lie.

Jack said, "I've got a water credit begging to be used. If you'll excuse me for the moment, I'll see you in staging."

Colin stood in the isolation of his Walker apartment, mentally taking leave. As he gazed at his furnishings, he realized that he only owned two things he regretted leaving behind: his porcelain tea set and his redwood table. The porcelain would never survive the subtle vibrations of space and subspace drive, the redwood table was simply too heavy to take along.

A man his age, and that was all he had accumulated. Colin smiled sadly. It was all he'd needed, really. As a man of God, the other furnishings were only temporary conveniences.

He was leaving things left undone, and he hoped Jack Storm would forgive him for that. Amber had been located hiding with money changer Sadie: there were locks on those doors even Pepys did not dare try to open. The young woman would be safe there until Sadie wearied of her presence.

"Sir?" Denaro stood in the doorway, waiting for him.

Colin sighed. "Just saying good-bye."

"You'll be back."

"Of course." But Colin had never doubted that before. He picked up his briefcase. "I take it Jonathan is downstairs leaving last minute memos for Margaret?"

Denaro nodded. He wore an expression Colin could not read, as the prelate brushed past him and into the corridor. "Have you done what I told you?"

"Yes. Amber will get word that Jack has reached a Green Shirt installation on Mistwald, and she won't be able to trace it back to us. But I don't understand how you know—"

"It's not for you to understand everything I do." He pressed the young man's hand. "I am not a Green Shirt, Denaro, but even you must know the Walker conscience is far-reaching."

Surprise washed over Denaro's handsome face as Colin reached the lift. That was as close as the saint had come to explaining himself for some time. But, Colin thought as the vehicle moved downward, not even Denaro understood why he was making the journey he was. Star maps and charts had been spread all over Colin's quarters for days, and the young militant was as mystified as ever.

So, Colin hoped, would the others be, their minds and thoughts rooted in subspace and FTL. Only he could stand earthbound and see the pattern. And see the pattern he had. And wondered momentarily if he was right in keeping it to himself, but he did not wish the pattern disrupted. He alone knew where the Ash-farel would strike next, and he intended to be there.

As he reached the lobby, Jonathan was standing, worry pressed into his face as visibly as his wrinkles, his bulky form obscuring the lobby monitoring screens.

"The emperor is on the line, your holiness. He would like an audience with you."

"Tell him my corsair is waiting. We don't want to miss departure time."

Jonathan frowned heavily. Colin noted with surprise the fringe of gray winging its way into his temples. "His majesty has already told me to tell you that he can postpone that departure—indefinitely."

So his old friend was going to be difficult. Colin looked upstairs, regretting having left the privacy of his apartment behind. But he did not want to return to it, not even for this conversation. He was afraid that, if he returned to it, he would never wish to leave it. For the sake of the Walker colonies, he must not do that.

"Very well. Set up a screen. I'd like this to be as private as possible."

Denaro said, "I'll be outside with the transport."

Colin looked at him as he passed, reminding the militant, "There's to be no trouble with the guard."

The young man looked at him. He fingered the wooden cross about his neck. "No," he said quietly. "No trouble with the Thraks. This time."

Jonathan was huffing as he ordered up a screen. He stopped long enough to look after Denaro. "He's been getting insolent."

Colin stepped through the booth's sonic walls, but not before he said to Jonathan, "It's the hot blood. He'll be all right."

His right-hand man frowned but could say nothing more, for Colin had passed the boundary of hearing. The monitor came on as soon as Colin seated himself.

"Good morning, Pepys," he said to the man who'd been caught unawares, looking away, his red hair in a frenzy of static activity. "How may I be of service to you today?"

"Cut the bullshit, Colin. What are you up to?"

"I am up to my neck in colonies threatening to sue for the protection of the Triad Throne. And you?"

Pepys, his cat-green eyes glittering, made a noncommittal noise, then added, "I'm up to my neck in Thraks."

"That appears to have been a choice you made."

"It does, doesn't it. Why are you leaving our fair Malthen?"

"I'm taking a constitutional. We still have one, haven't we?"

Pepys stared directly into Colin's eyes. The corner of his mouth twitched, but whether for a shout or a smile, Colin couldn't guess.

Then the emperor said, "I'm but a fisherman of stars. One or two are bound to escape the net."

Jonathan signaled outside the transparent barrier that the time was up. Colin looked briefly to him, then back to the emperor.

"You have no reason to hold me, Pepys."

"What about treason?"

Colin answered mildly, "If you really thought so, you wouldn't be calling me. You'd have the troops here picking me up. I don't covet your empire and you know that."

Pepys leaned back in his crimson and gold robes. He plucked idly at the hem of one cuff. "The Walkers existed before you and will exist after."

"I should hope so."

"Damn it, Colin, stop pushing me. If your colonies wish to be annexed, I don't see the harm to you. It's not as if they were recanting their faith as well."

Colin leaned forward to the screen. He wanted to be very sure Jonathan could not read his lips. "There is a kingdom beyond that of yours, Pepys, and that is the kingdom of God. A kingdom where taxes are not for warfare and ego, but for works toward the good of man. Push me further and I will go to the Dominion for aid."

"They'll never answer your call."

"Don't try to fool me into believing you underestimate me. We both know better."

Pepys fell silent. Then. "If I . . . back off, will you stay?"

"No. Not now. I can't just yet. I have some investigating to do."

The emperor sat bolt upright. "Good god, man, are you going after the Ash-farel?"

"You know the Walker tenets as well as I. If God's Son walked beyond, who knows where He stepped? Perhaps even the mysterious Ash-farel have heard of His passage."

"Colin, I—"

"We're losing our departure window," Colin said stonily. "Let me go."

"Colin—"

"Emperor!" And the religious leader of a vast estate raised his voice to a whipcrack.

Pepys slumped. He waved a hand. "Very well. This is not the time or place for us to wrestle. But one day, we will find out who wields the most power."

Colin did not answer. He bolted from the privacy booth, gathering up Jonathan, saying, "Hurry, before he changes his mind."

CHAPTER 22

The wreckage of the battle cruiser reverberated as the Ash-farel took it apart plate by plate. Bogie stayed in the equipment hold and shuddered as each metal-ringing clang brought them closer. His sensors told him of the radiation and decontaminant solution treatment each section was getting before they scrapped it. Nothing alive would remain when the aliens were done—not even him.

He kept the night screen visor down, giving his cameras some vision although the backup lights had gone long ago. He shuddered. Darkness was the same as death to him. He was hungry and alone. He thought of Amber. Would he survive to tell her of Jack's fate? There was a time when he could have reached out and brushed Amber's thoughts, but she had changed. Unless she was with him, her thoughts were not to be found. He was utterly bereft.

There was a scritch along the flooring. Bogie looked down, scanning. The viewscreens picked up a form. He searched his memory for it—a rodent, he thought. He flexed the armor and bent down to retrieve it. The creature gave a frightened screech and bolted away. It was quick, too quick for him. Jack had a blinding speed and grace in the armor that Bogie alone did not. Ruefully, he watched the creature sprint through the hold, dodging crates of equipment.

As though the sound of something alive in the hold had alerted them, the doors wrenched opened, and a blinding arc of light shone in. Bogie's sensors were dazzled. Blinded, he could not see the Ash-farel coming in. He could only hope—pray, the word came to memory that Jack used—that the armor shielded him from the aliens. He could only pray that he lived through the coming ordeal.

*   *   *

Jack remembered where the main crèche was. He'd brought them down almost on top it, and watched the Thraks swarm out of the mud-caked opening as he guided the parasail down. The sky was full of troopers. There were spits of orange as those carrying flamethrowers started them up even before they touched down. Jack knew one of the troopers. He had publicly stated his intention to glide over the nest, firing, before he hit ground.

It was a suicidal maneuver, but if it worked, it would give them all precious time.

He began to swing as the parasail settled down. He had both hands full collapsing the chute and shucking the harness, but he loaded up with grenades when he came up running. He'd told them what to expect, but they froze anyway at the sight of the fenced, green grass farms, and the mindless humans running naked alongside the rails to watch the action.

"Move it, move it, move it! Film it if you've got equipment, but move it!" The cords on his throat stood out as he shouted.

A trooper looked at him, and blinked.

It was the last move he made. A wave of Thraks topped the grassy knoll and one of the lopers to the fore took the Green Shirt's head off. Jack threw a grenade and rolled for cover. Dirt clods and grass divots and hard bits of shell rained through the air. He got up cautiously, unslung his rifle from his back, and went looking for trouble.

The mud-daub nest of the Thraks loomed aboveground, a landlocked iceberg of dried clay. Below, it might spread out concentrically for half a mile. He was probably running over tunnels now—before, with the weight and power of the armor, he'd dropped in. Now, the only way he could get in was if they dragged him in. . . .

It was a bad idea. He checked his watch. The chronos told him he had fifteen minutes left on the assault. Then the Talons were landing or hooking up everyone fit to retreat. He was either with them, or he wasn't.

A Thraks reared up in front of him, chitin and carapaces rattling with anger. The Kabuki mask of a face clacked and chattered at him, russet and brown, faceted red eyes aglow with battle lust. It was too close to fire, the backwash would clip it as well, so it lunged and caught Jack by the wrists.

Instead of resisting, Jack gave, crumpling, and the Thraks overbalanced. Jack kicked it in the stomach region and sent it the rest of the way over. It opened its mandibles in protest and Jack dropped a grenade down its thorax.

It choked on the bomb. Jack got up and ran as the beast thrashed and gagged. It was almost a mercy when the grenade went off.

He checked his crossed ammo belts. He had five grenades left. The orange wash of flamethrowers caught his gaze as he vaulted a fence. The nest was cracked open like a ripe melon. Men and Thraks were dying by the dozens.

Jack stopped and swallowed. A twig cracked near his flank, he whirled, and the dumb stare of a trio of cattle met his. He flapped his arms at them. "Get out of here! Go on!"

The woman stared a second longer after the two males bolted. Her breasts were dirty dugs that hung down to her waist, for all her youth. Up close, he could see the scars across her cranium that balded her halfway back into her scalp. She might have been beautiful once. Even intelligent.

He picked up a dirt clod and threw it. It bounced off one slack hip, leaving a pink mark that he knew stung. She tossed her head and bounded after the others, away from the line of fire.

He looked up and saw the withered remains of a fruit tree straggling over him. That was why they didn't want to leave. He must have been interrupting a favored snack. He reached up and snagged one of the few fruits left. He didn't recognize it and it left a sticky residue on his hand after he tossed the fruit away.

The object rolled along the ground and disappeared in the tall grass even as he contemplated the frontal assault and the best way to join it.

A low hiss interrupted Jack's kamikaze tactics.

"Go away. I don't feel like playing now."

A human voice, desperate. He recognized the central Dominion accent. Jack straightened. It seemed to be coming out of the ground. Cautiously he moved toward it, knowing that every good rat hole had a second entrance—and exit. Jack nudged a large grass divot in the same direction the fruit disappeared.

"Damn it, I don't want to play!" Grass and soft dirt

fountained as the man came halfway out of the ground. He stopped, white hair in disarray, and stared at Jack.

Then, great tears began to stream down the man's pale face. "Oh, God," he said. "Oh, God. You've come back."

Jack palmed a grenade.

The man clambered weakly out of the hole. He held half a human skull in his hand. "I've been digging," he said. He dropped the ivory bone. "I've been digging in secret ever since the attack last year. I hoped—I knew you'd be back. As soon as I heard the ships come in, I knew. I bolted for my secret tunnel."

The man went to his knees in front of Jack. "Whoever you are, please, dear God, take me home!"

"Who th' hell are you?"

"I'm . . ." a stricken look came over the man's face and he gulped convulsively two or three times. "No, wait! I'm Mierdan. I'm a—I was a xenobiologist. I was captured twenty-three years ago. Please, either take me with you for the love of God, or kill me here!"

"Oh, shit." Jack stared down at the frail, wispy-haired man. Now he had to get off Klaktut alive. This man probably knew more about Thraks than any human being in existence. He reached down gently and helped Mierdan to his feet.

The ground exploded behind him as the Thraks came after them. They clambered up like visitors from hell.

Jack lobbed a grenade, picked the little man up by the waist and slung him over his shoulder like a sack of grain. He ran, accustomed to the strength of the armor, and feeling its lack. They were both panting when the Thraks caught up and fired.

The laser rifle in his hand made a dull *twang* sound. His hand went numb as the rifle spun away. Mierdan slipped from his left shoulder and hit the ground. He began to wail in despair.

Jack tore his ammo belt off and threw it at the wall of Thraks. They acted in reflex as he hoped they would: one of them shot at the belt of grenades. Even as its arms and weapon went up, Jack dove for the ground, drawing fire from the others.

There was a second, frozen in his mind: his body in midair and the blast from the Thraks' hand gun sending blue-orange fire from its muzzle.

When he landed, the grenades went off and he was deaf and dumb until Mierdan began to wiggle and complain underneath him.

His back felt wet and sticky. With a groan, Jack rolled to his flank. Mierdan sat up, made a gagging sound and spewed bilious vomit over the grass. It scarcely showed among the litter of bodies.

Jack got up. He hurt. He'd been hit, but how badly he didn't know. Peppered with shard, if he were lucky. He swallowed hard. His chronos flashed an alarm at him. Thunder cut through the roar of warfare.

He had five minutes to make the transport. He took Mierdan by the arm and hauled him to his feet.

"C'mon," he husked. "It's now or never."

The little man didn't ask questions. They helped each other over the broken field and road to the flats where the Talons were waiting.

One man in ten came back.

But that one man came back triumphantly.

Jack handed Mierdan over to Staub and said, "This man has spent the last twenty years studying the Thraks."

They caught him swaying on his feet before he hit the deck.

CHAPTER 23

After the disinfecting, the blinding arc lights went away. Bogie's bedazzled sensors came back to a normal reading and he could see again. The hold stayed quiet. Across the deck, he could see a map etched on the wall. The language was symbolic and even he could understand that he could leave the ship by following the drawing. He moved away from his equipment rack and the crates marked STORM, J., and approached the schematic.

The sound of the cutting torches whined through the ship, and it shuddered. Bogie turned. His vessels and budding heart contracted and thudded wildly. He knew the sound from the shops he and Jack had visited.

When the bulkhead opened a second time, Bogie was ready. He launched upward from a crouch with a roar of synthetic noise, power-vaulted over the alien bodies, and ran to the escape hatches.

Two pods lay open, unused and functional. He dove into the nearest one, slammed the door shut and felt it begin to vibrate, made operational by the portal's closing. As it launched, he recoiled into himself in shock, for he'd seen the Ash-farel, and his soulmind could not comprehend the wrongness of the sight.

To have come so far, to no avail.

The Flexalinks could only curl so far, but the battle suit rolled as much into a ball as possible as the pod launched into hyperspace.

Left behind by the Ash-farel, losing FTL speed rapidly, the pod emerged somewhere in deep space.

"I thought," Mierdan said, chin propped on the edge of the medcrib, "that you'd lost that finger on account of me—but the doctor says that's an old injury. Anyway, the placental grafts are doing well and by the time we hit Mistwald, you'll be as good as new."

Jack rolled an eye at the scientist who'd scarcely stopped talking since Storm had awakened. He knew he was as good as new—he'd taken fire across his back, but his new skin only felt sunburned and he moved gingerly. He sat up in the crib. "What about you?"

Mierdan paused. He clamped his mouth shut. He was a spare, little man, with a sharp chin. He was working on growing a tuft of white beard at the point of it. He sighed. "I guess . . . I guess I'm going to be okay. I don't know." He wrapped his arms about his knees, hugging himself and looked across the hospital floor. "Until the truth comes out."

"The truth?"

Mierdan shook his head. "I lived when the others didn't. I—I stood by while the Thraks bred them and made . . . fodder . . . out of them."

"Did you help? Could you have stopped it?"

"No! No, and no again."

Jack put his feet to the deck. It was cold. He shivered involuntarily, and his back pained him from the movement. "Then you did nothing wrong."

"But I worked for the Thraks."

"You survived." Jack stood up, and leaned on Mierdan's shoulder. "We've all done a bit of that. Do you know where I lost this finger and three toes?"

The xenobiologist shook his head.

"Then listen while I tell you. Keep pace with me while I walk the room."

Mierdan looked as if he'd bow under Jack's weight, but he didn't, other than to protest, "You shouldn't be up."

Jack answered, "I'm not staying up. But I heal faster when I'm up." And quietly, matter-of-factly, Storm told Mierdan as much of his story as he deemed wise.

Mierdan limped him back to the medcrib. His dark eyes were brimming as he lowered Jack down.

"Then you know," he said, "what I've been through."

"Some of it. A little more than the next man."

Mierdan buried his face in his hands. There was a noisy sob, and then the scientist forcibly buried it. He looked up. "They kept me alive," he said, "only because they thought

I could help. I pretended to, and maybe I could have, but I didn't."

"Help what?"

"I know why the Thraks swarm."

Jack leaned back, pillowing his head on his good hand. The right one was still bruised from the shot that had torn the rifle away. "So do I. It's procreation, a mass hysteria procreation. And we've got some good indication that there's territorial rivalry with an ancient foe that drives them."

"There's more to it than that." Mierdan paused significantly. "Tricatada is the last, and only, fertile Thraks."

He broke the stunned silence. "Jack—are you all right? Do you have fever?"

Jack knocked the scientist's hand away as Mierdan sought to place it on Jack's forehead. "Are you telling me," he said, "that every *sand* planet has been populated by the one queen?"

"Yes. You can imagine how desperate they are. I've tried to explain to them that perhaps the overworking is contributing to the problem, but they're afraid she'll never produce a fertile egg. They swarm in hysteria, hoping above hope that one of the hatchers will be another queen, or even rarer, a king. When she goes, and she hasn't that long left to be producing, the Thraks begin to die off."

"Mierdan, are you certain?"

He shrugged and looked away again. "I've been her midwife for the last twenty years," he said.

Mierdan could have killed Tricatada and stopped the Thrakian League. Jack clamped his jaw shut tightly on what he wanted to say to that. The wiry man was not a murderer. Jack had no right to judge his actions.

But he did say, "We can stop *sand*."

"What?"

"You know what you know. We can use that knowledge to stop the Sand Wars."

Slender fingers tugged on the tuft of white hair. Mierdan shook his head. "She'll never agree. She can't. It—it's like stopping a birth in the middle of hard labor. It can't be done. The impetus demands that the birth happen. So her instincts drive her, and all the rest of the Thraks, and they cannot stop until a fertile egg is laid. Then she might be convinced to slow down a little."

"Do they have DNA?"

"No. At least, not that my crude instruments showed me."

Jack pointed a finger at him. "You'll think of something."

Mierdan's mouth dropped open. Then he shrugged. "Perhaps. Staub is pleased with me as I am. I can witness the true nature of the Thraks and the nature of the alliance Pepys has made." He stood up. "I've wearied you long enough. I'll be back later." He paused at the hospital portal. "And thank you."

Jack smiled. The little man hopped through the bulkhead and was gone. Jack lay back. The hope that Mierdan had given him made him want to reach out and grasp someone's hand tightly. It made the loneliness in him more palpable. He'd lost his armor. What was he without it? He felt more tired than he'd thought possible, turned his face toward the cool sheets and slept.

"—and don't tell St. Colin."

Colin heard the copilot's voice fade away abruptly as he approached the command post, and he came through the bulkhead with a wry smile. "Just what is it you don't want me to know?" He looked from Ivanoff the copilot to Jonathan, whose bulk nearly overwhelmed the area.

Jonathan frowned. "We've picked up a blip."

"Really? Ash-farel already?"

Jonathan paled visibly. "God in heaven. I hope not."

Colin was leaning over the instrument panels, searching the readouts eagerly. He stopped and turned back to his aide. "Good heavens, Jonathan, do stop that. That's why I've come all the way out here to this God-forsaken corner of space."

"What?" Dark-skinned Ivanoff paled as well. He rocked back in his command chair.

"I've come out to investigate what I can of them."

Jonathan sat down with a thud. "As near as I can tell, your eminence, they shoot first and communicate later."

"If that must be. It seems to have slipped everyone's mind that this is one of the first new alien races we've encountered in the last century. No one seems to want to find out what we're faced with."

Ivanoff muttered, "We're faced with coldblooded killers."

"So it seems, still—" Colin eyed the blip. Visible disappointment lowered his brows. "Whatever it is, it's too small for Ash-farel. I've heard their cruisers are immense."

Ivanoff came to attention. "That's an escape pod." He brought the image in sharper.

Colin looked at it oddly, then said, "I suppose we'd better fish it in."

They were all waiting in the docking area for the air lock to finish sealing the dock off. Jonathan put his beefy hand on Colin's shoulder.

"We don't know what's in there, your eminence. Perhaps you should retire to your cabin and I'll inform you."

Colin looked up. "Don't coddle me, Jonathan. I've seen more horrible sights than you can imagine. I don't intend to leave while they crack open that egg."

They watched together as two crewmen, dressed in environmental suits, approached the pod cautiously. It hissed as the portal door was wrenched open, and the two men just stared. One of them turned around and said, "It looks like a dead robot."

"What?" Colin came close to the window. The dock rotated so that he could get a look inside the pod. He shook off Jonathan's arm so that his aide couldn't feel him trembling. "Take it to my room," he said.

"Sir?"

"Take it to my room. And leave me alone." Colin pressed his lips together tightly and left the staging area.

It took four men to carry in the armor. Colin stood impassively, his hands tucked inside his many pocketed jumpsuit, and watched them. They were afraid to drop it, despite its weight. Jonathan hovered at the door.

"I don't want to be disturbed," Colin repeated. "See that I'm not."

His aide turned a puzzled look toward him. "I know that armor. . . ."

"Yes. I'm sure you do." Colin shut the door in his face. He walked to the Flexalink suit and bent over it for a moment. Emotion shook his hands so hard that he found it difficult to unscrew the helmet.

Escape pods were not found by accident in a quadrant of space where he expected open warfare. The deduction was obvious. Colin had been right about the area of the next attack. He'd only been wrong about when. This was Jack's armor, and it lay empty.

Empty of all but that other Jack both nurtured and feared.

Colin set the helmet aside and reached inward, touching the alien. It was both warm and featureless. It pulsated hesitantly under his hand.

"I'm a friend," the saint said, and waited.

CHAPTER 24

Amber woke in the night. She lay still for a moment, coiled in the warmth of pillow and blanket, and blinked, wondering what it was that woke her. She thought of Jack and the restlessness that plagued his nights. The thought made her smile. She was stretching out of her nest of blankets when the door opened abruptly and light stabbed her vision.

Sadie stood silhouetted in the frame. "There's been a complication," she said, "with your call to Jack."

"You've got an answer?"

"No. But there's been some unpleasantness—Green Shirts have been identified as raiders on Klaktut. Jack has been implicated as one of the ringleaders. I don't need to tell you the extent of the infiltration by the Thraks under the Alliance. We're in trouble if they decide to retaliate."

Amber got up, shivering. She pulled a blanket about her shoulders. "But the call went through?"

"Yes. Unfortunately, it attracted attention." Sadie moved aside, and another figure loomed in the doorway.

Vandover Baadluster shouldered the pawnbroker away. He smiled down at Amber. "An ancient adage," he murmured, "but true. 'You can run, but you can't hide.'" He snapped his fingers. The darkness at his back stirred, and she saw the two tall, insectoid sentries flanking him. He said, "Take her into custody. Pepys wants to talk to her."

"Sadie—"

The heavyset woman shrugged, her platinum curls mussed by the little sleep she'd had. "I can no longer help you, Amber. I'm sorry."

Vandover's smile spread. "I just love it when a plan comes together."

The Thraks moved forward, their faces in Kabuki masks of terror and intimidation. Amber stepped back, to the stand beside her bed, slender right hand going back for a weapon when the Thraks moved.

She'd heard Jack talk about fighting them, knew his hatred for them. But she'd not been prepared for their lightning, supple movements. There was no escape.

Baadluster put his hand upon her hair and caressed it as they dragged her past. The guards paused. He looked at Sadie. "A little visit to your cold lab. The emperor requests your cooperation."

If Sadie felt Amber's eyes upon her, she did not show it. The woman abandoned her bantering tone, and showed the cutting edge of her business side.

"Time is money, Vandover. If this is a social visit, I don't give tours through the cold vault."

Amber tensed, testing the hold of her captors. Did Baadluster know about the Countess and what she had stored with her?

The Minister of War dropped his hand from Amber's hair. "This is not a visit, madame. I have a customer for you, someone I wish chilled down." He smiled at Amber, "You'll be less troublesome that way."

Jack worked with the film editors as soon as they returned to Mistwald to piece together the footage they were able to salvage. He sat with Staub and watched the rough frames.

"Will it stand up?" the commander said to him.

"I don't know. They're not going to want to believe us anyway—we need more footage."

"There isn't any more. We lost most of the equipment on Number One."

"I know," Jack answered. There was a moment of emptiness for himself but he shook it off. He turned his eyes away from the projection. "The Thraks have already branded us as butchers."

"Did you expect to be a hero?"

Jack took a pull on a lukewarm beer. He rolled it around his mouth as if it held an answer and swallowed. Finally, he said, "I've been around long enough to know we rarely get what we expect."

Staub raised gray-flecked auburn brows. "A cynic?"

He shook his head. "A realist."

A door opened. A moon-faced young man, the fresh recruit replacement for Chrysler who had died on Klaktut, leaned hesitantly in. "We have a visitor," he said. "Sir."

"Who is it?"

"One of the locals, sir. I'm told she's really important."

Jack got to his feet. Any Fisher fitting that description and visiting would almost have to be Mist-off-the-waters. He said, "Can I go with you, Staub?"

The recruit flushed. "Actually, sir, she's come to see you."

Worry prickled through Jack, and his recent healings felt the reaction. Staub stood. "I think we'd better both go. Where is she?"

"She wouldn't be closed in, sir, so we cleared the mess hall. . . ."

Jack was gone before the recruit finished.

She had her back to the door when he entered, but her round ears flicked and he knew she'd heard him come in. She stood with bowed shoulders, her tail in a despondent curve.

Her first words to him were: "Help me, Little Sun. The false emperor has taken Skal hostage."

"What? How?"

"He was summoned for a subspace call at the post in Fishburg. But when he got there, he found agents waiting for him. They . . ." The Fisher paused. Her large deep blue eyes filled with unshed tears.

"Is he alive?"

She nodded. A tear hung from one whisker, a diamond in the late afternoon light.

"You don't understand," Jack said to Mist as gently as he could. "I've lost my armor. There's no way I can go in after him."

More tears brimmed in her eyes. "You will abandon him?"

"He's being held hostage, Mist. Shining fur-grinning tooth will hold him until he's lost his value. It will take time to arrange things—"

"He does not have time!" Mist's anger hissed through her sharp Fisher teeth, and her ivory tail lashed the air. "You're a fool, Little Sun."

Her emotions pierced him. He had never felt so vulnerable, not even under Klaktut's bloody sun. "As much as I value Skal's friendship and yours, this is not my world. Your politics are not mine—"

"To *sand* with politics! He's being held because he's allowed this base to stay in operation. He's being held because of you! Shining fur-grinning tooth is no fool. His spies have told him about the capabilities of the Green Shirts. Make no mistake—Skal is being held because of what you've done here, and if he's not ransomed within forty-eight hours, he will be sentenced to death without trial. We are barbarians here. If Skal dies, then Shining fur-grinning tooth will begin to round up innocents and condemn them, until we have no choice but to go to him and turn ourselves in."

Jack took a deep breath, figuring his options. With Bogie gone, he had few. "All right," he said. "I'll exchange myself for Skal."

Shock rippled across her otter face. "No!"

"A rescue will simply bring open warfare back. Do you want the fighting the way it was a few years ago? No, Shining fur-grinning tooth wants the rebel ringleaders he imagines and so we'll give him one. With luck he'll be so shocked to find it an off-worlder, he'll be unable to act. You get Skal as far away and out of sight as you can. Can it be done? I assume you have an underground?"

"Yes, there's still a Resistance."

"I see no other way."

Staub had been listening quietly but now he said, "You risk much."

Jack shrugged, saying, "What else can I do?"

Jack, who was so used to the simplicity of the Fisher life, found the imperial palace shocking. He had never been to Triata, even in the course of the civil wars he'd found himself in years ago, so he did not know what to expect. Mist piloted the skimmer over the city boundaries, and the clouds parted long enough to show him a city on stilts over a sapphire blue lake and river, Fishers going about their business by the thousands. No one looked up as the skimmer clouded their industry.

Mist showed her teeth. "How do you like our capital?"

She seemed unconcerned, unworried how Triata compared to off-world cities he had visited. She piloted them along the river, where the stilted huts clustered in abundance. She pointed her sharp muzzle at the terraced hillside rising ahead of them, at the farthest end of the lake. Beyond, sharp, new mountains rose, their peaks tipped with blue snow. The palace reigned at the top of the terrace, its green marble splendor a sight that captured all attention, its columns and roofs carved into jade brilliant leaves and vines and tree trunks supporting lofty branches. It had been built around a courtyard. As they flew toward it, Jack could see the blue eyes of pools, fountain spray distorting their edges. The Green Shirt base could easily have fit inside the palace grounds. Not even the rose obsidite splendor of the Triad Throne could compare to this gem of Mistwald.

Birds from the lake strolled along the terrace grounds. There were modest little brown birds darting in and out of the reach of strolling majestic birds with fan tails the color of the rainbow. They reacted as the skimmer shadowed them, giving out trumpets of challenge. Jack saw clouds of insects hovering in place until he realized they were in nets, buoyed by the wings of their captives. As Fisher guards guided the skimmer into a parking barn, she wrinkled her muzzle at the insect clouds.

"Lunch," she said, and Jack realized the nets would be released, so the birds could feed.

She snapped at a guard anchoring the skimmer. "Tell Shining fur-grinning tooth I'm here. He's expecting me."

The guard did not ask her name. Jack watched him lope off, weapons belt rattling about his black slicker shorts. He jumped out of the skimmer and handed Mist down. The ivory Fisher looked deeply into his eyes.

"Thank you," she said, but he had the feeling she had settled for that after rejecting other choices.

He nodded gravely. "You're welcome."

Both of them knew she didn't mean for the help in dismounting. A phalanx of guards came trotting up before they'd left the parking barn. There was menace in their attitude, but they fell in behind Jack and Mist as she led him to the palace steps.

There were sixty steps of cool, green veined marble. At

the top of them, sitting instead of standing, was a very battered Skal. He did not look pleased to see Jack.

His whiskers had been singed off one side of the muzzle. One eye was purpled and swollen. Mist sucked in her breath at his obvious mauling. He held a paw-hand close to his ribs. His breath whistled slightly.

For all that, he frowned at Jack. "So, my friend," he said, and his voice barely rose above a whisper. "You are my price."

Jack inclined his head. "The least I can do."

"Before you go in, I'll relay the message I received—it was intended for you."

"Me?"

"Yes. Amber sent to you from Malthen. She said, 'Tell Jack the mind-loop has been located and to come home.' "

Jack stood in stunned silence. His past—found. Amber had succeeded.

Skal licked split lips. "Any reply?"

"No. Not yet. Shining fur-grinning tooth can't hold me— I'll send an answer myself when you're safely out of here."

As they spoke, the phalanx of guards had spread out and now ringed all three of them. Mist bent over Skal and helped him to his feet. The two Fishers started down the stairs until they met the wall of guards. Jack held his breath until the guards let them through.

He turned to the guard nearest him. "I believe the emperor is waiting." The Fisher dipped his muzzle, about faced and led the way.

The palace interior was as cool and dim as the inside of the rain forest, and looked little different, except that its fronds and branches were worked in stone and jade. The canopy overhead was entwined with vines and feathers— bird and insect wings. The light and cloud dappled sky of Mistwald could be seen through the opaque stonework.

The pad-pad of the guards' feet upon the marble was as loud as drums. Jack's boots overshadowed them. He saw the heavily muscled otter-man seated on a throne at the far end of the room.

"Well, well," Shining fur-grinning tooth called out happily. "I hope poor Skal knows the kingly ransom you've paid for his mange-eaten hide."

"You were expecting someone else?"

"No. Not unless you're not Jack Storm. Skal didn't know of course, I think he rather suspected the Elders were willing to make a martyr out of him. I think he'd have liked that. Now he has to slink away with the Resistance and lick his wounds."

Jack was allowed within a good-sized leap of the throne. Up close, he could see that Shining fur-grinning tooth was a russet and sable powerhouse of a Fisher—but that he had a certain unwholesomeness about him. Jack felt an instant dislike for the ruler of Mistwald.

Shining fur-grinning tooth showed his canines. "You do realize the base is exposed and cannot be allowed to continue."

"We gathered that." Jack checked his chronos computer. "By now, it's probably been evacuated. Anything left behind has been demolished. You won't get anything useful."

The otter-man's tail whipped out in agitation, but the being stilled himself with great difficulty. Then he grated out, "I have no more use for you, Jack Storm." He turned his head.

"Take him."

Before the shadowed interior behind the throne could boil with movement, a clear, high voice called out, "Jack! Run!"

Amber's words froze him as neatly in his tracks as a stunner. Armor materialized and two massive guards caught him up before he could free himself. Jack struggled until their gauntleted hands tightened harshly about his arms and he had no choice.

Amber, Vandover Baadluster, and Pepys stepped from behind the curtains. Pepys had chosen to wear his imperial red and gold robes. The greenish cast of the Triata palace did not illuminate his pasty skin well. Baadluster looked as sepulchral as usual within the black robes he affected for his office.

And as for Amber, she wore the dark blue she loved, in a dress she would never have chosen for herself, too close about her hips and neckline and dipping low between her breasts. But she was beautiful even now, with her hair about her like a tawny cloud of indignation. Even as he watched, she twisted a hand free, went for a knife in her boot heel, and came up, knife cocked at Baadluster's throat while Pepys shouted, "Halt!"

Vandover backhanded her and it took both suits of armor to wrestle Jack to the ground. They knelt upon his back as he lay breathing hard and Baadluster was more gentle when he took the knife from Amber's hand. She placed the back of the other one against her face as if to cool the wound.

Pepys looked at the Fisher emperor. "Leave us," he said.

The being gave him a look of hatred, got down from his throne, signaled his guards, and left the palace hall.

Pepys gathered up his robes and sat down on the dais edge with a sigh. "You're mine," he said. "I can do anything I want to with you now."

"Then do it," Jack said. His chin ground into the marble floor and his back where the Knights rested hurt like hell, but he was done with running. "Do whatever it was you came for. But before you do, I want you to know we got what we went for on Klaktut. We have proof that you've made a treaty with monsters—not once, but twice."

Baadluster spoke, his voice a well-oiled machine. "I always said it would only take one honest man to turn the Shirts around. And you, your majesty, drove them together."

Pepys waved a weary hand. "If you promise good behavior, Storm. I'll have them let you up."

Jack twisted his neck to look at the emperor. "If I get up, you'll have to kill me here, because I'm damned if you're going to drag me anywhere to make an example out of me."

"And that's your promise?"

Jack glared.

With a sigh, Pepys signaled and added, "Just hear me out."

Amber went to Jack with a half-sob and helped him up. She smoothed his hair back from his face and touched his back gently, as if knowing the scars he bore there. Jack took her into the cradle of his arm. He looked at Pepys.

"You're a traitor, Pepys, and I now have proof—"

The emperor cut him short. "I know, Storm. I know. We're both traitors, and that is not important now." His cat-green eyes glittered at them. "You're both free to go if you will help me in one matter. Agreed?"

Amber said bitterly, "Where do we leave our souls?"

"No catch, my lady. No catch at all, because I am a desperate man. I killed and lied and cheated to get my throne, and I do it to keep it, but in between, I work very hard to keep a number of humans alive and thriving. So my petty grievances with you two must be put aside for the—" Pepys grimaced. "The so-called greater good. You have to help me, Jack. That is why I've come to Mistwald, why I've come to you instead of having you brought back to Malthen. So that you could see how desperate I am."

Amber started to say something else, but Jack stopped her. Pepys was serious. "What is it?"

"It is a matter that could set off a war that will make our grievances with the Thraks seem trivial. Even the Ash-farel pale beside it—human against human, with no respite but total annihilation of our race."

"What?" Amber asked, confused, but Jack felt a chill in his bones.

Pepys rubbed a weary hand over his face. "St. Colin has disappeared. He went out to investigate the Ash-farel. He met up with an empty suit of armor and took it. Where he went, no one knows. But the Walkers and others won't leave any stone unturned until he is found. No accusation unsaid. No kingdom unchallenged."

"Tell me about the suit of armor."

The emperor looked him in the eyes. "Jonathan was hysterical, but he said it was your armor."

Amber's hand grasped Jack's arm tightly, but she said nothing.

Jack eyed Pepys a moment longer. "I'll go," he said finally. "If you'll give me your resignation when I return."

The fine red hair of the emperor drifted about his face, but it could not obscure his expression. It was one of defeat. Pepys inclined his head. "So be it," he said. "The throne is yours, if there is one left."

Jack pulled himself up straight. He did not want or need a throne. But now, at last, what he had sworn to accomplish was within his grasp. With one last quest, he could finally see the end of the Sand Wars and avenge the betrayal of his people!

CHALLENGE MET

To Vincent DiFate
This one's for you, Vinnie,
Intrepid interpreter of word to vision.
Thanks.

PROLOGUE

The vehicle was little more than a coracle, thrown to the mercy of solar winds and planetary gravities. A man stood at the heavily shielded port watching the heavens pass. Intently, he viewed the planet the vehicle orbited. It was aswirl with clouds, but he could see the burned off continents through rifts in the cover. The blue of water and white-blue of cloud obscured most of the damage, yet he could see streaks of green and brown coming through. Initial reports from his far-flung organization told him that there were possibilities here once more. Clean water, grass, seedlings, along with the ores. The norcite would bring them back, if nothing else. *Resurrection*, he thought, and the thought tipped the corners of a weary smile. The expression smudged out the worry lines.

He was older, his shoulders bowed with fatigue. He wore the plain jumpsuit of the working class, a miner's suit, the trouser section lined with pockets both full and empty. Over its drab colors, he wore the deep blue, long vested overrobe of his office. A rough-hewn cross rested upon his chest, rising and falling with each breath. His hair, thinning brown strands across his broad skull, had been thick once and more tinted with auburn than it was now. Only his eyes remained the same: vigorous, alive, the deepest of browns, windows to a soul still fiery with conviction.

"Jack would be proud," he voiced aloud. "He's brought a planet back to life." He'd had to bring an emperor to his knees to do it, but the resurrection had begun. Colin watched the planet avidly, drinking in its phoenix rebirth out of ashes.

He was dwarfed by the massive battle armor behind him, its opalescent Flexalinks catching the light as it shifted nearer. "Should have brought Jack," said the armor, its voice sounding forth in magnificent basso profundo tones.

The man did not take his gaze from the portal. The armor was not empty, though it should have been, and the voice did not come from a human throat nor a computer sentience. There was alien flesh inside the armor, regenerating like a chick within its shell. That it missed the soldier who wore the armor, its symbiotic link, gave it more credence than Colin had at one time supposed.

The Walker saint replied, "Jack's busy. He'll come after us." The man did not elaborate. The machinations of humankind might stall any kind of rescue, but Colin had been prepared for that.

It appeared the armor was not. "You should have brought Jack," it repeated with the petulance of a small child. It shifted and brought up a gauntlet. The massive fist could easily crush Colin, but he did not flinch as it came to rest upon his shoulder. The petulant tone faded. "There," Bogie said. "Company."

The armor's sensors were far better than human eyes and so it was a while before Colin could see what the other registered. Then, when he recognized it, it was with a sucked in breath. His right hand went involuntarily to his cross and gripped it.

"By God," Colin whispered. "I was right."

The cross within his fist cut into his weathered palm. God was his business, not diplomacy. But it had seemed to him that mankind had no right to war with a creature they had not even met face-to-face, as terrible as that enemy had proven in the past. He was old enough to know destiny when it crossed his path.

The heavens seemed to tremble as the alien fleet moved into sight, warships thrumming with massive power. The tiny rescue coracle would be dwarfed by any vessel they sent out. Colin looked out over the fleet even as a lethal, viperous looking vehicle peeled away and headed in their direction. To have been spotted so quickly!

Colin dropped the cross and laid his hand over the gauntlet on his shoulder. "I can't take you with me," he said.

Armor couldn't flinch . . . could it?

"Alone again?" said the being.

"Till Jack finds you. He should. But I can't take you with

me." To meet with them, to have at last the evidence his Protestant ministry had long searched for, to prove to the worlds and mankind that Christ had indeed gone on to walk on other shores. There wasn't an archaeological site the Walkers delved where they hadn't also found signs of these others. They had become, enemy or not, someone he had to treaty with. Yet, as the fighter winged toward him, his dreams failed and his heart skipped a beat. What if he was wrong?

As if echoing his thoughts, Bogie growled. "The enemy."

"No," Colin murmured. "The unknown." He took a steadying breath. "You're my signpost, Bogie. You have to tell what I've told you, and point the way after. *If I'm very, very fortunate, I'll be there to meet you at road's end.*"

The coracle rocked as a tractor beam locked about it.

CHAPTER 1

The sound of being locked into a berth rang throughout the ship. Its clamor vibrated through the ship's skeleton as though it were a bell tolling the end of a journey, the attainment of a destination. After weeks shipbound, in vacuum and in FTL warp, the noise echoing through normal atmospheric pressure was deafening—and welcome.

The recycler began to shut down as the locks were opened to pump in fresh air. Jack's ears popped as the pressure changed and he swung about in the passenger lounge chair. He looked at his fellow traveler though her amber hair waving down across one shoulder hid the expression on her fine-boned profile.

"Now," he said. "The emperor shows his true colors."

The young woman could not hide her shudder from him. She looked about the cabin as she turned to him, her gaze surveying the lounge as if worried they might be spied upon, and she answered quietly, "I think you already have him scoped. We're still his prisoners."

"Maybe." He could not contain his growing excitement. "I beat him to a standstill as half a man. Think what I could do completed."

She turned back to the viewing screen, even though it had been shut down and the lounge portal was still locked for deep space. Jack felt her closeness as though she actually leaned against him with her head upon his shoulder, for she had not withdrawn her intimacy, and he felt himself smile.

The door to the lounge room opened with a faint hissing noise, and the emperor stepped through. The man was slight and wiry, fair-skinned and heavily freckled, his frizzled red hair alive with an electrical aura of its own, and the sharp gaze of his cat-green eyes rested upon Jack.

"Commander Storm," Emperor Pepys said, in a deep tone that belied his slight body. "Until you have been decommissioned, I suggest you rise and salute your emperor."

Jack Storm paused, and then, slowly and deliberately, he rose and saluted. He stood head and shoulders and then some over the older man, and if he'd been encased in his battle armor, he would have towered over Pepys, filling the entire room with his presence. The two men locked gazes, and Pepys turned away first, unable to stay with the clear as rainwater faded blue eyes of the other. The corner of Jack's mouth twitched. He remained standing.

"I've sent for an escort," Pepys said. He plucked an imaginary thread from the seams of his red and gold jumpsuit which was not his customary elegant wear but far more suitable for the journey they'd just made.

"Escort?" Amber echoed. "Or guard?"

Pepys' face twisted in ill-concealed anger. He shoved a fist into his right leg pocket. "Does it matter? You agreed to return with me, and this is my world."

Amber's lips curved shut and she said nothing although she might well have reminded him Malthen was her world, too. But it wasn't in the sense that she came from the underground, from the unprivileged society, and Malthen had never held anything for her, until it had brought her Jack.

"No Thraks," Jack said, and he moved to the back of her chair, his protection of her obvious for all that it was unspoken.

The emperor's anger became wry amusement. "Ah, yes," he said. "Let us not forget the phobia which drove you away from my Knights. Whatever else we may do here, I won't have you upsetting the alliance which I have taken such pains to reweave."

"Alliance. You've been infiltrated and conquered, but you're too blind to see it." Jack's hands, resting on the back of Amber's chair, touching but not hidden by the cascade of her hair, tightened. "They've sucked you in."

"There are considerations you know nothing of."

"If you'd care to elaborate, I'd like to know just what you've been planning."

Pepys made an exasperated sound, his lips pursed. He took his hand out of his pocket and slapped it on the bulkhead, then keyed open the com lines to the bridge. "Raise the shields."

"But, sire—"

"Riot watch notwithstanding—do as I say!"

The portal shield before Amber began to rise, and Malthen's white-gold sunlight flooded in, made bearable by the window filter. Pepys pointed outside, beyond the berth cradle, across the spaceport. Jack turned his head, and his eyes narrowed.

"It's the Walkers. They've heard my private ship was berthing today—they've come to see if I've brought back their saint." Pepys' voice was faint and bitter. "He brought me to this."

Jack straightened. A riot guard, faintly seen, but still visible at the perimeters of the landing field jostled against a wall of flesh. He could not hear the voices at this range, but the sight of Thraks in riot gear and battle armor controlling ordinary people made his flesh prickle. "They know St. Colin's missing?"

"Yes, damn it all. Word broke out while we were en route. I could not have kept it quiet much longer anyway, but I had hoped for better." Pepys stepped up, joining them at the window. "Old friend," he said quietly. "Is this the legacy you wanted to leave?"

Jack had often seen fiery indignation in Colin's mild brown eyes, but he knew the Walker leader would never want a religious war in his name. The Walker religion had been embraced for its benevolent tenets as well as its search for new worlds that Christ might have visited. It was as tolerant as any religion he knew, though he did not espouse it. The fervor he saw now, the wave of humanity dashing itself against the riot shields and inflexible, beetlelike carapaces of the Thraks, bore no resemblance to anything he'd ever heard Colin preach.

He started to say something as he turned to Pepys, but the emperor was still fixed on the sight before them, and interrupted Jack, saying, "So you may call my honorable Knights an escort or a guard or whatever you wish—but we're not leaving here without them. We'll never get through otherwise." Pepys backed away from the window. With a snap, he added, "You've agreed to find Colin for me. Cross me now, and you'll not only be court-martialed for the treasonous acts you've committed and been taken prisoner for—you'll be the one responsible for the slaughter that follows."

The emperor left abruptly. Amber tilted her head, waiting until the fall of his steps could no longer be heard. Then she said, "Nice man."

Jack made a noncommittal sound. He unclenched his hands from the back of her chair and moved them to the back of her neck, where he stroked soft and fragrant skin. "A fine pair we are," he told her. "A treasonous Knight and a thief."

She laughed and raised her arms so that she might grasp his hands. "A thief and an assassin," she corrected. "But you've never betrayed your Knighthood." Her voice sharpened. "Pepys corrupted it—corrupted them all." Her words were spat out, venomous and bitter.

He leaned over her. "Witch."

She tilted her head back, throat arching gracefully. "Hero."

Jack shook his head, laughing so softly that when she met his mouth with a kiss, she was surprised to feel the laughter vibrating pleasantly in his lips.

Springtime had come to Malthen and its underbelly, the slums known simply as under-Malthen. Green shoots ignored the still gray skies and slanting drizzle as the freezing rains of winter warmed. They pushed their insistent growth upward, fracturing concrete and perma-plast. Only the rose-pink obsidite walls of the emperor's residence, the palace of the Triad Throne, could deny them life. Here the grass retreated and settled to a life of surrender in the lawns and grounds, which was a far better fate than that which it faced on the Training grounds. No matter how brave the grass or weed, it was destroyed when hard-heeled boots of Flexalink ground it to dust. It grew relentlessly, only to be trampled by battle armor.

This day it had a respite, and pushed through the first wet splatters of rain, ignorant of its fate.

Lassaday, first sergeant of the Dominion Knights, first D.I. of the Malthen training station, his chunky body as hard as the Flexalinks worn by a Knight, his bald head darkened and weathered by the usual Malthen sunshine, hung his elbows over the observation railing and spat in disgust. The grounds were empty, on a day when the veterans and recruits should have been drilling, ill-weather or not. The Walker riots confined them all to base and he had little choice about his assignments. He could only thank his lucky stars that it had brought out the Thraks first, Minister Vandover taking advantage of the human fearfulness of the aliens to keep the dissenters at bay.

The sergeant looked over the pitted and battle-scarred retaining walls. His cheek bulged with the wad of stim he chewed and he spat another mudlike droplet over the railing when the alert came in over the com line. He answered it, taking his orders gruffly, and keyed off. He pulled back from the railing after a last look at the acreage before him and went downstairs.

The shop was as empty as the grounds, racks of battle armor in repair hanging silent. The locker rooms, permeated by an odor of fear as palpable as the odor of sweat, were vacant except for the robosweep, squeaking as it toured the aisles in its janitorial mode. Lassaday strode through, aware of the cameras following him as he made his own, sentry rounds. He heaved a sigh as he broke into the fresh air once again.

The barracks, however, teemed with activity as Lassaday approached them. Recruits and veterans sat in knots, polishing their minor equipment—bracers, gauntlets, small arms—or they stood around idly gossiping.

"Th' emperor's ship is ported. I want an honor guard of twelve volunteers, and I'm only takin' th' best of you." It was an assignment he had feared, but he would take it, and he wanted only the top Knights beside him when he did.

The knots broke up, mumbling, arguing, and he could hear the drift of their voices, the same words, the same arguments that had driven him to the solitude of the Training grounds in the first place.

He'd heard enough. Anger swelled his bull chest, and when he bellowed it out, he didn't care who heard or heeded.

"I've had it! You've got a problem, bring it to me! Pepys has th' right to call an escort. We'll be bringin' him and Commander Storm in, and, by God, if he's gonna be judged, I want th' commander to be judged open of mind and free of doubt—not by a bunch of ball-less wonders."

He stared around the compound which his bellow had brought to silence.

A young man, his chin clipped by a fresh laser scar, pink and lacy upon his skin, looked up from his workbench. "Sarge," he began. "We buried the man with full honors—now he's hauled back, alive and in irons."

Lassaday pointed a blunt finger. " 'Th'man,' " he repeated, "is your commander."

"Was," a voice rumbled from the shadowed interior beyond the barracks' doorway. "Now we've got a walking Milot furball for a commander."

There were shouts of protest including one young, clear voice saying, "K'rok's all right."

"He's alien!"

"You're kind of strange yourself," the recruit fired back, and the argument disintegrated into laughter.

Lassaday rubbed the ball of his thumb over his jaw. "Th' Milot's my commanding officer," he said, "and it's not fitting for me to talk ill of him, for all that he's part of the Thrakian League and we're Dominion and Triad here. But K'rok fills a commander's shoes and that's all that's required of him. You might do well to remember that when a Thraks goes to war, he takes no prisoners except for th' best—and K'rok's fought his way up through their ranks as well. And all that's required of you is a shut mouth and clear head when we meet Emperor Pepys. Jack Storm was a good man to all of us—the last true Dominion Knight, he is, and he deserves respect."

"Traitor," someone said, but Lassaday's piercing dark stare could not pick out the voice's owner.

His cheek bulged for a moment as if he chewed out his thoughts before he spoke. Then, reluctantly, "Some say so. But it's not been proved to me yet."

"Then why'd he fake his death and leave?"

Another recruit added, "And he lost his armor."

The growing clamor quieted at that. Someone said, "Is it true? Did he lose his armor?"

Lassaday spat to one side, scattering recruits. Then, "Yes. That much is true."

No suit, no soldier. They'd been drilled with that since the day they'd been accepted into Emperor Pepys' resurrected Knights. Those of them who'd made it this far into the service shivered as they thought of being without their Flexalink skins, their weapons, their second selves. *He'd lost his armor.* That alone was tantamount to treason.

"We can't judge what happened," Lassaday said, his gravelly voice low. "Not until we hear th' story."

A slender man moved into the doorway, and leaned against it, his captain's bars winking on his shoulder. Travellini met the sergeant's stare as he said, "And what if Pepys doesn't allow us to hear it?"

The NCO rocked back on his heels slightly at the unthinkable. "No," he answered. "That wouldn't be."

The captain traced a seam down the outside of his slacks and flicked off a piece of lint or dust. He looked up. "Nothing says Pepys has to give Jack a military court-martial. It wouldn't be the first time Storm has been betrayed by the system."

A freckle-faced recruit crouching over his boots, applying a patina like that of stainless steel, blurted out, "That's not fair."

The Dominion captain's mouth twisted at one corner as he answered, "None of us are likely to ever learn what drove Commander Storm away from here—and what brought him back. And we dare not judge him until, as the old troopers like to say, we've walked in his boots."

"Amen," echoed Lassaday, his anger soothed by the captain's calmness. The knots of men began to break up, voices quieted now, tones somber. Never before had one of their own been brought back in shackles, bereft of his armor, rumors of treason and cowardice hanging over his head.

But then, the aged sergeant thought, none of their own had ever dared to fight both the enemy and the emperor. He braced himself. "Now, all right, you spineless excuses for Knights. Which ones of you are goin' with me in escort?"

Rawlins stepped out of the shadows. Lassaday felt a prickle of apprehension run through him. He was a copy of Storm, but a pure copy undulled by time or cynicism, hair the color of winter wheat and blue eyes with an electric intensity in them, a copy that rang truer than its original because life had not yet defeated Rawlins. But the boy had never been the same since the military action on Bythia that had entangled his life with Storm's and with the

Walker Colin's. Rawlins had served as the commander's aide-de-camp and as for the Walker saint, it was said that Colin had blessed the boy, cursed the boy, and even raised him from the dead.

"Sergeant," Rawlins said softly. "I'd like to volunteer for detail."

Though he had misgivings, there was no way Lassaday could gainsay the lieutenant. He gave a short, abrupt nod. "That's it, then. Who is going with me and th' lieutenant?" He was not surprised to have to turn them away in droves, if only because there was a maudlin curiosity to see the legendary Jack Storm.

Amber was the first to see them crossing the riot lines, on foot, in full battle armor, Malthen sunlight glinting off the Flexalinks. They had not been able to bring the transports through the still pressing crowds of Walkers and other protesters. She stood up even as Pepys came into the lounge. "They're here," she said gently.

Jack had been sitting in repose, eyes closed, faint lines smoothed upon his brow. Years of cold sleep suspension had kept him much younger than his chronological age. His sandy hair was a little higher off his forehead than it had been, the laugh lines at the corners of his eyes a little deeper, and the grooves about his mouth sharper than she remembered, but his was a body still well in its prime. He looked up as a clink sounded from Pepys' hands, and his waking gaze fell on the shackles his emperor held.

He said nothing, but Amber's heart twisted as the lines in his face deepened as his sovereign approached.

CHAPTER 2

Amber walked the palace hallway, ignoring the gaunt shadow her body threw upon the walls. She hugged herself against a chill that was born not of temperature but of spirit, an iciness the black silks she wore could not keep out. The sight at the port had stayed with her, no matter how hard she tried to pace it off: the wall of Thraks reared in opposition to a wall of human flesh, people crushing forward inexorably, demanding that their saint be returned to them. White-tipped, Pepys had greeted Baadluster, his Minister of War, and the honor guard had surrounded them, swallowing them up—and if it had not been for those machines of war, she did not think they would have made their transports.

They had had only one incident of any measure—and her own heart had thudded as they had approached the transports, and she could see a familiar face beyond the guards.

Baadluster had made a low sound in his throat as if he also recognized Denaro, militant right hand of the Walker church. "You should have taken that one out," he muttered to his emperor, "when you could have."

Jack acted as if he had not heard them, but his chin went up, and his gaze met the flint dark one of the man standing beyond the Thraks. In a society where biological years often did not match years lived, because of cold sleep and other factors, men no longer measured actual ages. But they recognized *prime*, and each of them was in his. Jack had once taught Denaro to be a Knight, a wearer of battle armor.

In fear, Amber reached out and touched Jack's wrist, hoping to break their stares, for Denaro was heavily armed despite the large, hand-carved wooden cross hanging upon his chest. Her gesture had no effect and now Denaro was speaking, his voice cutting through the crowd noise as if it were a laser.

"You came back without him."

Jack stopped in his tracks and his escort slowed as well. A lesser man would have been dwarfed by the battle armor, but he was not. "Denaro," Jack responded. "If I had gone with him, he would have come back with me—or neither of us would have returned at all."

Denaro's eyes blinked slowly. He scorned to wear Walker overrobes, and his muscles flexed under his miners' jumpsuit.

"Jack!" Amber warned, even as Denaro's hand moved, but the crowd surged with a wild scream, as it caught her fear. The Thraks reared up, chitin and carapace pressing against the softer flesh of the rioters.

Something came hurtling through the air at them, moving so quickly that none of the guards could shift to catch it, even as Denaro shouted, "You serve a murderer!"

Jack shrugged off Amber's hand and snatched the object up, curling his fingers tightly about it.

As the tidal wave of security bore Denaro and the others away, the Walker shouted a last time. "Find him," he said. "And tell the truth. Or I'll do it for you."

Jack turned his hand over and opened his fist. A smaller, no less crude wooden cross rested in his palm. Amber sucked in her breath, recognizing it as one of St. Colin's. Jack looked out, searching for Denaro and no longer able to see him. He raised his hand in the air.

"I hear you, Denaro!"

The memory now chilled Amber. How close Denaro had come to inciting out-and-out riot. Pepys feared the Walkers. If not for their pressure, she and Jack would be dead now, but the emperor had a desperate need for them. Yet she knew the cloth Pepys and his minister had been cut from. Once Jack accomplished the impossible, if he could accomplish the impossible, the two of them would be discarded.

The hospital wing was deserted, a seldom used area of the palace, maintained only to preserve the health of the emperor. She paused at the clinic doorway, knowing she could jimmy the palm lock if she had to, but also knowing that the prisoner within was honor bound to stay imprisoned and that he had made her vow as well. That she thought him a fool made no difference in how much she loved and worried about him.

A noise in the hallway brought her up short. She thought she heard a scrabble, a clacking of carapaces against the obsidite flooring—and even as the hairs on the back of her neck prickled, the noise faded. When a man rounded the juncture and approached her, a tall, homely man with pasty skin, lank brown hair, and lips too thick to smile appealingly, she spat at him.

"No Thraks! You promised no Thraks on the guard duty."

Vandover Baadluster gave an ironic bow. "And good afternoon to you as well, Milady Amber. What need do the emperor and I have of guards with you on duty?"

She could feel the color blaze in her cheeks as she answered, "I won't have the bugs within eyeshot or earshot of me and Jack. May I congratulate you on your handling of our allies. We couldn't be more rife with them. You have rolled over, belly up, and surrendered."

"Harsh words from a beautiful whore," Vandover said mildly, but there was nothing mild about the flint dark eyes that blazed out of his pale face. "If you wish to worry about alien contact, I suggest you worry about the Ash-farel. The Thraks, at least, we have met·face-to-face and can bargain with. The Ash-farel are like a black hole, swallowing worlds and colonies never to be seen again."

She said nothing in answer to that, but turned away, her short cape billowing with the disdain she felt. She could feel her heart hammering in her chest, but the man did not bait her further.

Instead, he seemed to be examining the windowless door as if he could see through its panels. "The doctors should be done with him soon. I came down to tell you the tape has been updated successfully."

The hammering faltered badly. She swallowed to hide the flutter of pain it caused. "Then there's nothing to stop the imprinting."

"Nothing but Commander Storm himself, if the doctors

pass him." Vandover turned, aware that he'd drawn her attention back to him.

Amber met his burning stare defiantly. She said nothing.

The minister thinned his lips with a semblance of a smile. "The mind-loop of a seventeen-year-long cold sleep must be a formidable experience. I myself find it hard to believe that he volunteered for this. A most unusual reward for the task Pepys has asked of him, don't you think?"

Amber could feel her emotions seething, boiling just under her skin, but she lifted her chin and said coldly, "You might find it . . . difficult. Jack might find it gratifying."

Vandover laced his fingers together. They made a pale steeple against the unrelieved darkness of his robes. "Never doubt that Pepys wants Colin found. No one wishes the holy war of revenge that will result unless the man is brought back. Even I—" He paused a moment longer. "I came to ask you for your aid."

"Me? What could you possibly want from me?"

"Commander Storm's passion to regain his past is second only to his passion for you. I want you to sway him, milady. Convince him that he may be crippling himself by imprinting the tape before he undertakes his mission to find St. Colin. Convince him to wait . . . until later."

Or until you can destroy the tape, Amber thought, but did not say aloud. "We went through hell to find this tape."

"Indeed. Through that and Green Shirts. . . ." Vandover paused, as though naming yet another dissident faction left a bad taste in his mouth. "And it is, unless I am mistaken, a tape of a man going through yet another hell. We need Commander Storm sound in mind and body."

"St. Colin has disappeared so well that not one of the thousand underministers of his church know where he could possibly be. I don't think I can ask Jack not to have his memories restored before he goes after him. It wouldn't be fair . . . I couldn't do that to him." Amber fought a desperate battle to keep her voice cool, free of emotion. If Vandover wanted him to avoid the tape, all the more reason Jack needed it.

She would not let herself look at Baadluster, but she knew he watched her avidly. She could feel his stare burning into her.

"And what about you, milady? Is it a chance you want

him to take? Will you chance losing him? An imprint from a year or two ago is nothing—but this—his memories may not integrate. He may remember his life then, and nothing now. What of you, Amber? Are you ready and willing to be forgotten?"

She clenched her teeth. *Jack would not, could not, forget her.* But her mind trembled at the thought. Rather than give Baadluster the satisfaction of knowing he'd shaken her, she said nothing.

Baadluster waited long silent moments, then gave a bleak smile. "We are allies, Milady Amber, uneasy confederates, perhaps, but entangled nonetheless. I urge you to be selfish now, for whatever reasons you have, because we both desire the same result. Think on it." He paused another long moment, heard nothing forthcoming from Amber, turned on his heels and left with that hard smile still on his face.

She watched his back until he was no longer in view. Not until he was gone—as far from her senses as from her sight, did she let his words touch her.

Not that Jack had many choices in the future for himself or for her now. Perhaps Jack had been fighting Thraks so long that he was incapable of accepting their alliance—or perhaps he was right, and the mysterious, threatening Ashfarel was not the current enemy but a new race to be contacted and negotiated with despite their reputation as the Thraks' oldest and most deadly foe.

Amber let her thoughts sink into her despair. She was under no illusion that anything Jack did here and now was voluntary. What choice did he have? She knew the rumors permeating the ranks of his battalions. Coward. Traitor. Murderer. The emperor had brought him back in shackles.

Publicly Jack was dead. His emperor could do anything he wanted to Jack without fear of reprisal. But the man who thought that of Storm was greatly mistaken.

The panel before Amber opened suddenly, startling her and sending her thoughts scattering like dry leaves before a cold autumn wind. The emerging doctors blocked her view of Jack and they talked among themselves as they passed her, ignoring her presence.

"Remarkable condition, but I'd like to see those toe buds done before he leaves . . . the scar tissue will only continue to thicken until the point where we can't consider that option—"

"Forget the implants, he balances well enough without those digits. It's the mental profile that worries me, but for a man who was chilled down for more than half his lifetime, he spikes well enough, I guess. I wonder if Pepys knows what he's gotten into. . . ."

Their voices faded as they turned the corner and passed from view.

Amber turned her head slowly until the room opened up in front of her and she saw Jack sitting crookedly on a lab table, fastening the front of his tunic. Her senses flared with the sight of him, his plain but honest face unaware that she looked at him, his sandy hair darkened by exertion on the treadmill, his faded eyes focused on thoughts and events elsewhere, relaxed body still muscular from the demands of wearing battle armor. And although she'd grown up in the years she'd known him, he hadn't aged to speak of, his body, frozen by time, that of a man in his prime.

She spoke as she entered. "Vandover says your tape has been transcribed."

He looked up, not startled, having grown used to her catlike ways of entry and exit. He smiled, crinkling the sun wrinkles at the corners of his eyes. "It's going to work! I'm all cleared. Pepys should be down in a minute to discuss final arrangements." He reached out for her and pulled her close. She found it momentarily disconcerting—he sat on the lab table, and she looked down at him.

Biting down on her lip, she made a decision. "I saw Jonathan while you were in examination," she said.

Jonathan was Colin's right hand, a great big bear of a man—and he was the only survivor of the Walker's ill-fated expedition. Jack looked up, meeting her worried gaze. "He's comatose," she added. "He may not make it."

"What happened?"

"They don't know . . . there's not a mark on him. He's around the corner with more security than I've seen in a long time. Jack . . . it's not like Colin to take Jonathan with him and then abandon him."

"You worry too much."

"You've given me a lot to worry about."

He kissed her chin, a nibble of a kiss. In a low, intimate

voice that did not match his words, he said, "I'll want to see him before they wire me up for the cryo bay. They just told me they expect the playback imprint to run maybe four, five days."

"Pepys left word you're to be let in. I wouldn't." She swallowed. There was a heat creeping up her body, spreading from the point on her jaw where his lips rested briefly and then continued on, following the swan swoop of her neck down to the delicate bones below her throat where he paused again. She closed her eyes and, despite the attention Jack was giving her, she saw Jonathan's vast, near lifeless body, sheeted and wired, monitors projecting the reluctance of the life force it retained.

"Do you think Jonathan would mind waiting a few minutes?"

"Minutes?" she retorted. "You'd better take your time with me, soldier. And no, I don't think Jonathan would mind at all. He had a certain lust for life himself." And her eyes brimmed, in spite of herself. To combat the lump in her throat, she added, "I want you, too."

"There were times," Jack said softly, "on board ship when I thought I could hear you breathing on the other side of the cabin wall."

Amber shook her head. "If we'd been that close, they couldn't have kept me from you." She did not fight as he encircled his arms about her waist and drew her up on the exam table next to him, but she did grasp his right hand, his four-fingered hand, where the frostbite of cold sleep had taken away his little finger, and said, "Someone should do something about sealing this lab. We wouldn't want to break quarantine."

"I'll take care of that," and he voice-coded the lock with a phrase that made her laugh. And then he proceeded to do something very unorthodox to cool her fever.

For long moments, all the worlds and all the stars concentrated into the intimacy of two people entwined with one another.

CHAPTER 3

"I intercepted a message matrix from the Green Shirts," Vandover said, not bothering to conceal the pleased look which he knew contorted his fleshy lips.

Pepys, immersed in his control mesh, looked up with an irritated flash. "You know I'm busy."

"But not too busy for this, I trust." Vandover handed over the transcript which he had been tapping across the palm of one hand.

Pepys took it and scanned it. His red hair crackled with intensity as he asked, "When and where did you get this?"

"They attempted to pass it to Storm when we brought him through the port."

Pepys looked back down at the encoded and deciphered paper: *Situation with Walkers to be kept enflamed. Pepys needs to keep you alive.* He let the script slip through his fingers to the floor where it lay among a nest of cable wire. "Tell me something I don't know."

"We guessed. This confirms it."

"That the Green Shirts have a vested interest in Storm we've known for some time. Does Storm know a message failed to reach him?"

"I don't think so."

Pepys relaxed in his chair. An abstract expression passed over his freckled face as he listened to his com net, all the while talking to his Minister of War. "Send the word out through the usual informers that continued rioting will diminish Storm's use to me, not increase it. There may come a time when I choose to quash civil rebellion instead of cater to it."

"Yes, sire. About the girl?"

"She keeps him happy for the moment. We'll discuss her options later."

Vandover nodded. He backed toward the doorway.

"Vandover."

Baadluster stopped. "Yes, sire?"

"We know that Jack's mind-loop was retrieved through Madam Sadie. That means she was storing it in her private vaults, probably as collateral for one of her private loans. Any idea for whom?"

"Not yet."

"It's vital."

Vandover answered with only a terse nod. Pepys swiveled in his chair, a pendulum of nervous energy. Their eyes met briefly.

"The Dominion has contacted me. The president is seeking to renegotiate the interest on their loan. Financing a war effort has proven to be more expensive than they anticipated. But he has also asked for a starfleet increase and for two more battle armor units."

Vandover's dark eyes grew bright. "We can manage to provide both."

"Good." The emperor added, "This is a war I intend to win."

Vandover stood there until the extended silence informed him he had been dismissed. He tried to leave without undue haste, but he was a busy man and he had duties to attend.

Denaro stood in the public lobby of the Walker compound, his tall and muscled frame filling the open space until Vandover felt as slight and insubstantial as a shadow. He showed his teeth in a cold smile. "Thank you for allowing me to see you."

The young man did not return the smile. "This is sanctuary, Minister," he responded in clipped tones. "I hope you don't mind being confined to the public lobby. We have privacy screens, however. If St. Colin were here, he'd see you in his apartments, but. . . ."

"Indeed." Vandover gathered his robes and seated himself behind a screen. Denaro hesitated, then joined him. The young man did not sit in a chair, he conquered it, and Vandover watched him appraisingly. This was a man Storm had trained for battle armor at Colin's behest, temporarily shielding him from Pepys' wrath. Now Denaro was out from behind Colin's protection and, as the strongest contender to follow in the older man's footsteps, his own visibility was his protection. But it would not do to forget that Denaro wore armor . . . or that Storm had been his commander. He dampened his lips before offering, "I've come to see if there's anything I can do for you in Colin's absence."

Denaro's hand tightened on the arm of the chair, white knuckle lines stark against his tanned skin. But his face remained calm as he answered, "Removing our protective guard would be considerate. The compound stinks of Thraks."

"The Knights are here for your safety."

"Those aren't Knights."

"The emperor will be informed." Nothing would be done and the two of them knew it. Colin had had similar objections. If Pepys would not budge for Colin, he most certainly would not for Denaro.

"Thank you for your concern, Minister. Now, if you'll excuse me, there is much I need to do."

Vandover stood, relishing towering over the man still seated. "I understand, of course. Perhaps when Jonathan is more fully recovered, he can return to his duties as Colin's aide, even though Colin has not returned."

Denaro lost all color in his face. His jawline slacked. "What do you mean?"

Vandover feigned confusion. "Why . . . surely you were told . . . Jonathan was picked up several weeks ago and brought in by one of our Talons. He's comatose and Pepys has made him as comfortable as possible in the palace hospital wing. I'm sorry, Denaro. I thought you had been made aware of this."

The Walker got to his feet. The color which had drained from his face now returned in a blaze across his cheeks. Jonathan had been with Colin. They were both well aware of that and now Denaro was also aware that Pepys had been concealing vital information from him. "I'd like to request permission to see him."

Vandover shrugged. "It would do you little good. He appears to be in some sort of catatonic shock. He has the best of care, of course, and there is hope he will return to us. He is our best way of tracing Colin's whereabouts."

"Has Storm seen him yet?"

"The commander is a cautious and thorough man. Although I'm certain Jonathan will become one of his priorities, he has other concerns on his mind right now."

Denaro paused, apparently taking stock of what he knew. "There can be pressure brought to bear."

Vandover flicked dust motes off the sleeve of his robes. "Pepys is not disposed to tolerating any more civil disobedience," he answered slowly. "Storm knows that Jonathan is readily available. After all, a comatose man is not likely to be going anywhere, is he? There are advantages to be taken of the vast Walker empire while there is still confusion over Colin's disappearance." He lowered his voice. "Storm wants Pepys off the Triad Throne. That is no longer any secret. To do so, he'll need . . . backing. He has gone to the Green Shirts. Now he will come to the Walkers. It's to his advantage to let Colin remain missing while he consolidates his position with you before he plays hero."

Denaro let his breath out with a hiss. He looked past Vandover, across the Walker lobby, then his gaze flicked back. "You know this."

"I am Minister of War. What would I be without intelligence sources? But Pepys is my emperor and no matter how badly he needs Jack Storm, I would not hesitate to let him know he uses a dangerous and ambitious tool."

"Nor would I," the young man echoed. He set his jaw. "Thank you, Baadluster, for taking me into your confidence."

Vandover edged out from the screened area. "You are most welcome," he answered. He bowed and left, aware that Denaro's intense gaze burned into him like a brand. As the Thraks guard let him through, Vandover allowed himself a small smile of triumph.

Jack stood by the bedside—more of a crèche, really, to support the patient's functions—and thought that Amber had not exaggerated. The man lying before him was only a shell of the person he'd known as Jonathan. Vigorous, immense, yet gentle as if afraid of his own strength—all that had been bled away from him. The underlying hiss and suck and hum of the equipment that kept him alive permeated the room.

Amber stirred at Jack's elbow. He sensed her withdrawing to the entrance of the room. He looked back. "Was he this bad when they found him?"

Her face was pale, expression drawn, as if the time they'd shared together had never happened. She nodded in answer to his question. "Nearly this bad. They got him on life support as quickly as they could. And then, he just declined."

He swept his gaze over the monitors, reading the obscure displays. It was obvious even to him that Jonathan clung to life by the faintest of grips. He raised his voice. "Observation?"

"Yes, sir," the near wall answered him. Whether the doctors beyond were flesh or mechanical, Jack could not tell.

"What are his chances?"

"He can be sustained indefinitely, but whether it is worth it to do so. . . ." the voice trailed off and Jack knew he spoke to flesh. Only flesh worried about the quality of life. Machines worried only about function, on or off.

Jack looked back to Amber who stood braced by the door, her palms behind her slender hips and pressed to the wall. "Did he put up a fight before?"

She shook her head. "Jack, I don't know. Why?"

"I'm wondering if Colin was taken . . . or if he left voluntarily."

She straightened indignantly. "Colin wouldn't have left Jonathan like this!"

"Not wouldn't have, Amber—the proof is that he did leave him. I only wonder if he was forced to, or if he left on his own."

"How can you ask such a thing?"

Jack looked at her mildly. "I can ask because I'll need to know. Who found them? Did Colin take them to some faraway meeting place where he met more than he counted on? Or were they intercepted? Am I to start looking among friends or foes?"

She came toward him then. "I'm sorry. I thought—"

The corner of his mouth drew up. "Jonathan was my friend, too." He turned back to the crèche, sighing barely audibly. "What could you tell us, if you were able. . . ." Jack brushed his palm lightly over the man's limp arm, feeling the feverish dry texture of the other's skin.

The curls of Jonathan's thick dark hair stirred, as if attracted by some electricity between his head and Jack's hand. The Walker aide was pelted as thickly as some bear. He lay beneath the sterile sheets, his shoulders bared and the hair upon them was as thick as that upon his head. Jack dropped his hand upon the massive forearm—muscular potential, strong but not bulked. If he had been the type to wear a battle suit, he'd have been a behemoth.

At the touch of skin to skin, the near lifeless form convulsed. Amber's gasp echoed the clarion sound of alarms going off. Jack sprang back a step from the hospital bed as monitor screens danced with bright illumination.

"What's happening?" Amber called out, the edge of her voice thin and high with fear.

Jonathan's bulk jumped and thumped upon the bed. His convulsions began breaking and discharging leads and wires by the handful. Jack could hear sudden activity behind the observation wall and knew that help was on its way. Until then, to keep Jonathan's body from flopping off the bed, he reached out and held him down.

Time seemed to become thick and he stuck in it. He could hear Amber's voice, but not the words she said. They were too long and drawn out for him to make sense of them. She's panicky, he thought, and wondered at that, knowing that there were few things beyond her control and thought again that that must be the cause of her panic. He could not feel the unleashed energy of the life support crèche surging through himself as well as Jonathan's flailing body. He could not hear the crackle of the discharge nor sense his hair standing upon end as it did so. He knew only that Jonathan's hands were gripping him, dragging him down, pulling him close, and that the aide's eyes, ringed with white, were wide open. His mouth worked. "Help me," the sick man gasped, just before the hospital staff tore him from Jack's arms.

"A hypnotic induced coma," Baadluster said, his fleshy lips thinning in satisfaction. "Though a poorly constructed one. Jonathan might have died."

"Self-induced?"

The Minister of War shrugged, his storm crow robes moving sluggishly about his tall and lumpy form. "Perhaps.

He's not said, and the staff tells me he's resting now. You heard more from him than anyone."

Jack frowned, remembering the frantic burbling of words that had spilled from Jonathan before the staff had managed to separate the two of them. He shook his head. "He was incoherent."

"I see," the minister said, but there was disbelief in his voice. "And you?" He looked to Amber. "Perhaps you caught something in all the confusion."

"Me?" Her face was still wan, and purple shadows dappled the hollows beneath her golden-brown eyes. "I thought he was dying."

Vandover paused. Then, "And that upset you, milady? But surely, in your time in under-Malthen, you've seen many a death."

She shot him a glare, but Jack stepped between them. Jack was tall, even among a battalion of big men who wore the battle armor. Vandover had to look up to meet his eyes.

Very quietly, Storm said, "You are Minister of War, Baadluster, but I think I need to remind you to be very, very careful who you battle with. The emperor has need of our services and your . . . discretion."

Vandover's thick lips pursed without sound, but he withdrew to the doorway and stopped there. If he had paled, it could not be seen, for his complexion was always pasty. "The emperor sent me down with word that this latest development has pleased him, and he will see you tomorrow morning before your . . . procedure. In the meantime, both of us warn you that your freedom and safety is limited to this wing." He nodded abruptly. "Good evening, Commander Storm and Milady Amber."

Amber shuddered, as if throwing off Vandover's scent. She looked through the observation wall at Jonathan's still form, now resting quietly. "He was keyed to you," she said.

"I know. What if he hadn't been found or. . . ." Jack let his voice trail off. "I don't think Colin left him voluntarily. He wouldn't leave Jonathan to chance like that." He looked at her then, smiling. "We're going to disappoint Vandover."

"Oh?"

"I presume you can get me out of here."

She leaned into him. "Of course. Where to?"

"The only thing that Jonathan said that made any sense to me was Colin's meditation chamber. Jonathan mentioned it three times. Somewhere, in his scrambled memory, it's important." He dropped his arm about her shoulders. "Then we'll get there."

The Walker saint's apartments resonated with his personality. The rooms were both austere and rich . . . rich with the simple things of the worlds Colin had touched. Jack stepped into them and wiped his hands down, his palms damp with the effort of breaking into the Walker complex without alerting either Thrakian guards or Walker staff. As the coolness of the empty rooms swept over him and he looked around he thought that he had never, in his recollection, had a place to call his own. As long as he could think back, he'd been housed in temporary places or barracks.

Amber sat gracefully on the redwood burl coffee table that had been one of Colin's favorite possessions. The three of them had held many a conference over it. "I've never been in the meditation chamber," she said.

"Ummm." Jack walked around the main room, eyeing artwork and office work, noting the clean yet not too orderly status of both, as if the occupant had just stepped out for a moment and would be back any second. "He planned on coming back," he said.

"I can tell." She rubbed her forearms. "Or he didn't have time to prepare."

Jack paused at the archway to the meditation chamber where a small flight of stairs led up. He looked over his shoulder. "Coming?"

"N-no. I don't think so."

He gave her a quick smile. "All right." He mounted the stairs and disappeared from her sight.

Events in her life since she'd met Jack had all but purged her of her psychic abilities—either purged her or walled them away so well she need never worry about them again—save for moments now and then when they prickled at her like St. Elmo's fire, an invisible dancer upon her nerves. She chafed at her forearms now, as though trying to touch tattoos a shaman had once etched on her, gone now but not forgotten. She could feel the pull of Jack's presence on her like the tug of a golden rope.

Amber shifted her weight uneasily and looked about the room. She could sense Colin's presence as if it were a perfume lingering. Unconsciously, she took a deep breath, savoring it.

The meditation chamber stood half open, as if waiting for him. Jack hesitated before entering, taking a quick and practiced glance about, an action drilled into him by association with surveillance-shy Amber. He saw nothing overt, ducked his head and stepped over the threshold.

The chamber had been left set on display, for the moment he broached the field, gentle holo images came on, and he was surrounded by the worlds that man had touched since his intrusion into space. Jack never made it to the low, carved chaise longue of wood in the chamber's center where one might sit or lie down. Imprisoned by the orbit of worlds he had known, he stood, one hand half held upward as if to touch them . . . worlds as they'd been before sand or war or even man. Spinning almost into his grasp and then away were Dorman's Stand, Opus, Malthen and then . . . his throat constricted.

It spilled through his fingers like the illusion it was: verdant Claron, whose untouched wildernesses had once given him back his sanity. Jack curled his fingers, unable to hold the image of the planet that was now a firestormed bit of char undergoing the painstaking process of terraforming and rebirth.

He had done that much, at least. Unable to save his home world of Dorman's Stand or the others from Thrakian *sand*, at least he had been able to start the restoration of Claron. It had been flamed to scourge the first traces of *sand* away . . . and to remove him.

The display operating was a long one. He finally realized he should move and retired to the bench where Colin would have sat to watch and think. He watched until it came to him that he wasn't seeing what was in front of him, that he'd retreated into a near trance, his eyes no longer focusing. The sand planet Milos swirled past along with bitter memories. Jack blinked. He stood up in defeat.

"Jack . . . are you all right?"

Amber had been calling him. He raised his voice. "Be right down. I haven't found anything."

The display stopped the moment he stepped out of the sensor field. Jack stopped and looked back. Milos hung at the edge of his peripheral vision, fading away into nothingness. It was the site of his most bitter defeat, but he felt a catch in his throat as he lost it once again, before he went down to join Amber.

CHAPTER 4

Alarms shattered the night. Amber rolled from Jack's side to her feet, shaking her head to scatter the last of sleep, even as she cursed the interruption of their rest. Jack sat up.

"What is it?"

He listened, picking up security code signals in the alarm and gave a grunt as he bent to pull on his boots. They'd both slept clothed, uneasy under the protection of Pepys. "Not the emperor's wing. It's right here—with us."

Her brown eyes with their golden flecks widened. "Nobody's bothering us. . . ."

"Jonathan!"

Storm made the door first, but she was right on his heels.

The breach in the wing that had set off the alarm gaped before them—rank, scoured, and still smoking.

"My God," Amber said, as she slowed. "They blasted their way through."

"Stay back."

She halted behind his warning hand. "Why?"

"That was done by a suit."

Her response was drowned out by the rattle of Thrakian carapaces on the corridor floor. Instead of talking, she grabbed Jack's restraining hand but he shook her off.

"Thraks!"

"Answering the alarm. They're part of the guard now. They'll be here as soon as they seal off the wing." Even as he spoke, Jack moved forward into the blasted outer lab that had surrounded Jonathan's hospital room. Amber followed close behind.

In the shadowy interior, machinery sputtered and sparked. Plastic and metal crunched under his steps. Amber had not pulled on her boots. Biting her lip, she halted, unable to go farther, but past Jack's frame she could see a tall and darker shadow pulling at leads and machinery with quick, effective rips, freeing Jonathan's limp body.

"Drop him, Denaro," Jack said quietly.

The battle armored man turned, the massive Jonathan cradled in one plated arm as though the size of a child. The visor was down, screen darkened.

"He's mine. You bastards have had him long enough. If you want him, come take him."

Amber's breath hissed inward. By that faint sound, Jack placed her location as well behind him and out of the wreckage of the room, and the tension in his shoulders relaxed just a bit. The plastic and glass shards littering the floor kept her out of harm's way.

His answer was to move against Denaro, fast, quick, un-predictable—the only advantage flesh had against battle armor. He'd trained Denaro—the man had been one of the Knights' best before he'd gone rogue. Denaro had always been St. Colin's man, not a soldier of the Triad Throne, and Jack had known it when he took him in. And just as he knew who was in the armor, he knew how Denaro would react to a frontal attack.

Amber screamed then, as if realizing what she saw.

Gauntlet fire turned the dark air orange. Jack tumbled past it, just out of range, feeling the heat of it whistle by. At Denaro's feet, he crouched, grasped a dagger of jagged glass and stabbed upward, toward a chink in the Flexalink coverage, not where the back of the knee was, but where he knew it would be as Denaro power vaulted to avoid his attack.

The dagger skittered in his hand, made a screeing noise as it connected, then slipped inward. It was torn out of his grasp as the jump carried Denaro away. Jack immediately twisted backward, but he was too late, betrayed by his own body, as the other kicked out.

The heavy boot caught him a glancing blow to the chest—but even an angled blow from a suit was enough to drive him across the room where a wall stopped him the hard way. Jack let himself slide downward, forcing muscles that were convulsed in pain to relax.

Denaro came to ground, and set Jonathan aside. "Don't do this, Commander," he said. There was an edge of pain in his voice. He reached down and pulled the glass dagger out, its edges crimson.

Jack rolled over into a ball, legs under him, gathering himself. He looked up and met the charcoal screen of the visor, knowing a human gaze lay behind it.

"I can't let you do this."

"You can't stop me. I'm suited and you—you're not."

"That's where you're wrong. If you'd stayed in the Knights long enough, you'd have learned your weaknesses."

The gauntlet fired, but Jack had leapt already, inside and under it. Jonathan's flaccid bulk protected him from a second spray.

"I thought," Denaro said, and an aggrieved pant interrupted his words, "I thought you knew who the real enemy was."

"Never doubt it," Jack answered, just as he launched himself, and Amber screamed, "Don't shoot!"

He never knew if she'd meant it for Denaro, or for the hard-bodied aliens that suddenly filled the ruined lab and room. The reek of their excitement filled his nostrils even as the beam caught him twisting and brought him down. The warrior Thraks smelled like hot brass and he hated it worse than the smell of death which washed over him as the floor caught him up with ungentle force.

Amber shrilled, "Stop it! You'll kill them both!"

Denaro leaned over Jack. He picked him up by the nape of his neck, his gauntlet still warm and stinking. In the other arm, he carried Jonathan and the Walker aide's slack face stared unseeingly.

"Leave him," Storm got out. The side of his face was numb, and he tasted the sweet flat iron of his own blood. "Pepys brought me back to find Colin. I swear to you I'm going after him."

The visor showed him a blurred reflection of himself, but it was Denaro who answered, "Too late. We've waited too long." The armor shuddered and the room shifted. Jack realized he was being carried along, dangling by his neck as Denaro used him as a shield. "You should not have tried to stop me."

"Try, hell!" Jack twisted in the gauntlet and brought his boot heels up to the neck joint with a snap that forced the helmeted head back. Another snap and the seam began to give way.

Amber put her hands to her mouth, watching Jack retaliate. If there was a man alive who could fight a suit barehanded, he was that man. But already he'd paid a price too dear. She heard the Flexalinks sing in protest as he kicked up, not once but twice. Denaro rocked back and staggered through the massive hole in the outside wall.

The Thraks could wait no longer. Their quarry was bolting. Even as Jack found the vital weak spot in the helmet to suit seal, they swarmed.

Her throat went raw as she shouted them off. Jack slipped to the floor where he lay, crimson and blistered with laser fire, and the battle armor beat off a last attacker before turning and running, powering out of her sight with a speed she would not have believed except that she knew the suits and what they could do.

A second later, K'rok was there, the massive and furry Milot overwhelming her as he buffeted the Thraks into submission with his bellows. Sarge was there, too, calling for live medics.

Numbly, she stepped aside from the Guard. They'd never catch Denaro. She shoved aside a Thraks standing wobbling on one chinned leg, not caring that he crashed to the floor with a clacking and hissing as she went to Jack.

There was blood everywhere. The air stank of it and Jack's hand was slippery with it when she grasped it. The flesh she pressed was chill and passive and she looked quickly to see if Jack was still conscious. His eyes flickered and he moaned as the medics reached them and lifted his body off the shattered flooring onto a gurney.

His gaze met hers, but she could see he was having difficulty focusing. She leaned close as the medics locked the gurney into position and began wheeling it toward the operating lab.

His breath tickled her ear. "Get . . . the observation tape."

"I will, but why—"

"Get the tape before . . . Baadluster. It wasn't necessary . . ." Jack took a shallow, wheezing breath. "It wasn't necessary for Denaro to take Jonathan. He did . . .

to make sure I'd follow. The tape will tell me . . . where. Fair fight . . . Thraks did the worse damage." With a trembling effort, he closed his fingers over her hand. "Understand? Nothing's going to stop us now."

"Yes." Amber loped now, to keep pace with the gurney and the medics, unable to bend close enough to talk with Jack. The lab doors opened and the medics tore Jack's hand away from her. She stood for long minutes as the doors shut in front of her, cradling her right hand until long after Jack's blood dried on her skin.

Then she realized Jack had given her something to do, and she hurried to take care of it before someone else beat her to the tape. It was nothing to get the tape . . . it took a few minutes to rig the system as though it had malfunctioned or perhaps Denaro had tampered with it to explain the absence of any recording on the blank tape she substituted.

Seeing him in the healing crèche was little better than being left outside the operating bay. Sealed off, all she could see was his face. The rest of him was swaddled in medical equipment and a reconstruction matrix. A bright flush of fever mottled an otherwise too pale complexion. There was no rise and fall of his chest from breathing, under the matrix and in cold sleep, there could be none. Vandover shadowed her, but she refused to let his presence warn her off. *He could be dead*, she thought uneasily, *and the bastard's enjoying watching me wait.*

Vandover dropped a hand to her shoulder. She squelched the flinch of reaction.

"Because of his injuries," the man in black said softly, "he'll be under for two weeks instead of several days. The doctors asked me to tell you."

Baadluster was used to being the bearer of bad news. She could tell this revelation did not particularly distress him.

"Whatever it takes," Amber said tonelessly. He stood beside her a few moments longer, then withdrew and went about his imperial business. She waited until she was certain he was gone before she let the tears brimming in her eyes fall upon her face. She wished she could share Jack's triumph, but Vandover's continued presence set off the alarms of her faded intuition. The mind-loop was out of

her hands and in those of their uneasy allies. Jack had not
worried—but she did.

She worried that whatever chance Jack'd had to go
through imprint and come back the man she loved grew
slimmer by the day.

CHAPTER 5

He was whole again. Young and eager, though the core of him was ice as if he were chilled down—but he couldn't be, he had never been, and the army wouldn't risk cold sleep on a raw recruit . . . too expensive. He'd gotten here on his own hook, and now he was here, and in, with a spindly, potbellied NCO bellowing at him—

"No suit, no soldier! If you hear it once, you'll hear it a thousand times. Those of you who made it through Basic to get to us—you ain't done yet! We're going to winnow you again because only the best get to wear armor and you don't look like the best to me. Do you?"

"NO, SIR!"

"But if I make you the best, and the ones of you who make it through my camp *are* the best, and I do it not because I like you but because *it is my job to give the best to the Knights*, then you'll be good enough to wear the armor. And if you're good enough to wear the armor, then you'll know you're the best because there isn't anybody else on God's green lands good enough to tell you you're the best! Your ass is going to depend on that suit once you earn it. I'm going to teach you how to wear it, use it, eat, sleep, and shit in it, and repair it. You will treat nothing as well as you treat your armor, not even your mother! Do you understand, boys?"

"YES, SIR!"

His mother. Jack caught a glimpse of memory, of his brown-haired, freckle-dusted, sad-eyed mother, looking across a field of shadow and sun toward him, waving good-bye . . . and he remembered. He won the armor and lost Milos . . . and the Thraks devoured his own planet as they had half a dozen others, and her bones undoubtedly lay covered by Thrakian *dust*, unmourned until now.

He would have cried, but he was too cold to cry and the tears would have frozen anyway.

Pepys looked up briefly from his web of com links, his red hair drifting in its own cloud of electricity. He damped down the transmit as Vandover shifted impatiently, waiting to claim his attention. "What is it?"

"The lab says Storm will be coming out of imprint shortly."

"So soon?"

Baadluster controlled his emotions by fisting his hands, nails digging into his sweaty and itchy palms. "It's been twelve days."

The emperor leaned back in his chair. He was slight and, as he aged, was becoming wizened. The yellow-white sun of Malthen never tanned but always freckled him, in the garish way given to some redheads, and his emerald eyes contrasted sharply with his complexion as his stare pinioned Vandover. "And what will we have when he reemerges? Will we have a tool we can use?"

He inclined his head. He would have given his soul to hear the flow of communications Pepys controlled—to be able to manipulate the worlds of the Triad Throne and even the free and far-flung worlds of the Dominion simply through the networks Pepys held contracts on. No communication occurred that did not pass through the filter of the Triad Throne. Emperor Regis, who ruled before Pepys, had been good at wielding these reins, but Pepys was incredible. Vandover contained his fervor. "You will have a loyal fighting machine."

"Will I? One hopes. And what of Amber?"

"She holds vigil." Vandover's face hardened in an expression his emperor could not help but catch—and interpret. The words were forced through pasty-white lips which slowly regained a more natural color.

"There," Pepys said quietly, abandoning his mocking tone, "is a woman, despite what you think of her." But he knew well, even better than Vandover himself, what the man thought of her. He paused, listening to something coming in, his thoughts momentarily abstracted. Then he looked back at Vandover.

"If it worked," he said, "we have saved my throne."

"May I suggest that we are finished with milady's value to us?"

"We need her as long as I need Jack."

"You can tell him you have sent Amber elsewhere. Malthen is, for all purposes, in a state of siege. We have troops keeping the agra lanes open for food transport. Otherwise, the Walkers are doing a good job of pressuring us."

Pepys blinked, a predatory hooding of his brilliant eyes. "I would not believe us if I were Jack."

"You're his emperor."

"A free man has no emperor. Amber may be the only hostage wc have to keep Storm in line." Pepys stroked one of the fiber leads in his com net. "She's yours, Vandover—but only after Jack is off-planet. Whatever you do with her, *I want nothing traced back to either of us.* Understood?"

Vandover fought to contain the fierce heat lancing him. "A wise decision. She is, after all, a common criminal."

"Common is the last word I'd apply to her." The emperor shrugged. "Report to me when he's awakened." He spun back to his console, listening once again, fingers tapping out judgments, decisions, and notes on the keypad balanced across one thigh.

Vandover bowed himself out of the room. He wondered what Jack Storm was remembering now.

Sand blighted the horizon. As Jack exited staging, a rust and beige swath of hell met his eyes wherever he looked. Equipment racks swayed in the hot summer wind. He let out a pungent curse and the Milot techs working on the repair line looked up, bestial faces wrinkling and looking away. Solder popped and he could smell the flush from armor on the far racks. Only the Milot working lead stayed at attention as Jack walked over.

"I know it's hot," he said to the massive alien. "But you've got to keep dust out of the circuitry. You're supposed to be under the domes." Canopy sheeting overhead snapped in the wind. Its shade striped across the Milot's face.

"Lieutenant," the Milot said, his voice rumbling from a cavernous chest. "If you want to take a patrol out today, we must be working wherever we can. Dust is the least of your problems." And the being waved a probe at the barren horizon where transport ships were supposed to be fielded.

"My concern," snapped Jack, "is the welfare of my men. I don't want to hear that the suits aren't being repaired properly or aren't fully powered up. I don't want to hear that any of your crew is siphoning off supplies."

The Milot grunted. His piglike gaze flicked away and returned. "And I suppose you be believing we grow berserkers out of your men, too. You'll have your rack ready when you are, Lieutenant." He spat into the dust at their feet. "And all you have to worry about will be *sand*."

In his sleep, memory comes together in a violent clash with dream. He remembers why it is he hates Thraks and *sand* and doesn't trust Milots. What it is like to fight long after the suits run low on power, and some of them grind to a halt, too heavy for a man to move on his own, leaving the wearers to die a horrible death, entombed in the battle armor. He tastes the bitter seeds of defeat again, abandoned by superior officers who have decided to cut their losses on Milos. He knows that his emperor, Regis, has been manipulated into this decision by his treacherous nephew Pepys, and that Regis will lose his throne and his life. But this is a nightmare from which he cannot awake. The transport ships will never arrive, except for a few. Recall will not be sounded. The Knights are among those troops deemed to be expendable. And even as he remembers, has the sum total of his life given back to him, childhood, family, adolescence, a shadow follows him. Like a snake of darkness, it swallows up his thoughts even as he's fully regained them, and he can never go backward, only forward into his mind.

Desperately, he tries to confront the snake which is devouring all that he has been given back. It is hot inside the armor, and his grid is blurred by his own sweat, and the various leads clipped to his torso are more than irritating, they have become painful. The chamois at his back absorbs the salt and water dripping down.

Thraks are attacking, yes, but that is memory and this attack from within—it is reality. He has been betrayed again.

As he reaches out with his thoughts, a spark arcs out.

He is trapped by Thraks, his men are down, power going, abandoned to the sand and he feels the new life stirring at his back. It reaches out for him, a white blossoming fire that beats back the dark devouring snake.

Bogie. Bogie was alive with him, even then! And the realization repels Jack as he is caught within his mind, watching battle armor split like brittle eggshells, not to free his men, but to spit out immense saurian creatures, hatched from the helpless bodies of his men, frills spread in berserker frenzy, to attack both Knights and Thraks. The Milots, knowing they are losing their world, have indeed seeded the parasitic berserker lizards in whatever flesh they can. Barracks rumor has become nightmare reality.

And his own alien bonds flesh with him even as Jack fights to live.

The furious will to survive carries him through.

Gauntlet fire cuts down the Thraks, their carapaces popping and fizzing in the flame, and even his suit, too drained now to work efficiently, feels the heat. He has come full circle as the recall signal pulses across his com. He looks across a pit of Thrakian chiton and human flesh into a shadow, a blot of darkness across his visor and finally, stupidly, recognizes a transport.

They are being scraped off the surface of Milos like so many squashed bugs . . . all that is left of the Dominion's finest. He knows what battle fatigue is, and shock, and swims though it anyway, grabbing an arm strap from the transport hover, and stepping onto the running board as it lifts him from a pit of death—and he's the only one still up and moving. He waits impassively as the hover brings him cross-country to staging where, he can tell, evacuation is in an absolute rout.

A tech helps him peel off the suit, nose wrinkling at the smell and reek of his imprisonment. Sweat drips off him like a toxic wash. He kicks out of his boots and leaves the equipment, not looking back. The noise and turmoil of staging as they make ready to load three massive cold ships brings him back to reality sometime after the crew has checked his palm and retinal prints.

The cryo nurse puts a kit into his hand. "You'll need this, soldier. Showers are to the right. This is your locker number. Stow your kit in it before you report to the lab."

The man will not meet Jack's gaze. He says, although it is not necessary, and he knows the nurse has no time to listen. "We lost Milos."

"No kidding."

"I'm sorry. I tried."

The nurse pauses. Jack feels the impatience and weariness of the men lined up behind him. The nurse shrugs, answering, "You think you're responsible for the whole damn war? Now get a move on, soldier. We've got a deadline. We've got to get our asses out of here before the bugs know they've won."

Jack showers, luxuriating in the feel of real water, before the cut off leaves him half lathered and dripping. He towels off, dresses from the kit, general issue that fits much too tightly across the shoulders and thighs—general issue not being cut for a man who wears armor—and joins the masses in the hold as they stow their gear. Over the com lines, they receive a stream of instruction, the harsh voice falling, for the main part, on deaf ears. They are troops. They've been through this before. The only thing they want now is a hot meal—not possible before chill down—and some rest. The rest they'll get: months in cold sleep. The cold ship hold is immense and stacked to the ceiling with the coffinlike cryos. He works his way down the aisles to his locker and opens it.

The Flexalinks wink at him, an obscene pearl hanging from the equipment racks. The NCO loading the transport bellows once more, and this time he hears the announcement, "Your suits have been infested. They will be maintained in quarantine until we can determine their status and either flush or destroy them."

No suit, no soldier.

"Line up and file in, in an orderly fashion," the NCO bellows again, and around him, he can hear the tired shuffling of those still on their feet, the ones who are able enough to walk.

He tells himself he is lucky. He tells himself that thousands have died so a few hundred can make it to these transports. He tells himself that he will somehow bring victory out of this horrifying defeat. He is still a Knight, and he still wears battle armor.

The suit swings on its rack, splashed with soot and blood

and the ichor of Thraks. It smells of Milos and war. It looks like a denizen of Hell. It is bonded inexorably with him.

Just as he begins to integrate his past with his present, the devourer strikes without mercy.

The eyelids of the frozen man begin to flicker.

CHAPTER 6

The coracle rocked violently as it was released, ejected like
an empty shell into a decaying orbit. Bogie fine-tuned the
armor's sensors to listen after the Ash-farel vessel. He
abruptly damped them as a human scream cut like a laser
across the frequency. Fear and pain vibrated through his
system as he lay curled in the tiny rescue vehicle's equipment bay where, well-camouflaged, he had been overlooked
by the aliens.

Pain and fear were not unknown to Bogie. He had carried Jack through many such ordeals. Now it resonated inside him uneasily until he understood the edge of the
feeling: he, too, was afraid. The revelation was both heart-
ening and disheartening. It meant he had evolved enough,
was alive enough, to fear death. Now at last he understood
some of Jack's hesitation to fight. Death was the dark side
of war. And only a living being would fear death.

He had come far, but he did not cherish the feeling. He
was a warrior, he knew that, he savored battle and victory.
Now, in the echo of Colin's anguish, he knew he would
never be the same.

He made plans to emerge when the Ash-farel mother
ship pulled away. He would correct the coracle's orbit. He
would wait for Jack, who would come as Colin had promised he would, and Bogie would then point the way as it
was his duty to do. Until then, he would tap into the
armor's power circuit and take the energy he needed to
continue to live. He would try not to listen to the recording
of St. Colin's capture.

It frightened him too much.

"I want," Vandover said to the computer-screen, "someone disposed of in under-Malthen."

The image looking back at him showed no emotion, nor did he expect it to. The man's skin was sallow and his pupils too wide under the influence of *ratt*. "Who?" the man said.

"Never mind who. I'll give you a body . . . you make the arrangements."

"Ahhh." Illumination showed on the old man's face. "I'll need twenty-four hours' notice."

"Consider it given."

Wrinkles deepened momentarily in his contact's expression, then he shrugged. "I can handle it. What about the ident chip?"

Satisfaction broadened Vandover's smile. "She doesn't carry one," he said. "Do whatever you want."

"All right." The screen went dark as the com line closed.

With a little luck, Vandover reflected, Amber's body would never be identified properly—or even found. And if it was, all signs would point to another terrorist atrocity against Pepys by the Green Shirts. No, disposing of Amber was a strategy which would work well whatever its consequences.

He pushed away from the keyboard with long, tapering fingers that ached as if they could already feel the curve of her throat within their grasp.

A com light flickered, signaling another incoming call. Vandover hesitated. Pepys would be demanding his time and he still had field reports to evaluate . . . but anything coming in over this line would be from his own security units within the World Police or the local sweepers. A morsel of information from there was too sweet to ignore. He opened the line.

The screen stayed dark. The informant did not wish his face shown, then, but Vandover's grid confirmed the retinal pattern of the speaker and he knew immediately who talked to him.

"Minister?"

"I'm here," Vandover replied carefully. His screen did not relay such niceties of information to the other caller. Baadluster winced a little at hearing the harsh accent of under-Malthen mingled with a touch of the Outward Bound planets as the informant spoke again.

"Several years ago you were looking for . . . a custom weapon."

A chill thrilled its way up Vandover's spine. "A weapon?"

"Yes. Molded for a specific need. You went through Winton for its inception, but when he was killed, you lost track of that weapon."

"Ah," was all Vandover breathed in confirmation. This was unexpected serendipity, indeed. Then, "You've located it?"

"Yes and no. I have the weapon's identity. You'll have to go from there."

Vandover's knuckles whitened. Winton had died without passing on all of his information to his partner, even such vital information as this. Undoubtedly, the former security chief had been as uneasy in his alliance with Vandover as Vandover had been with Winton. A plan some fifteen years in the making had ground to a halt. He'd been unable to access Winton's secret files, but here, finally, was the data he needed. "All right," he said. "What do you want from me?"

The informant named a figure and added, "And passage off-planet."

"Done. How do I verify what you're going to tell me?"

There was a verbal shrug in the pause that followed. Then the informant said, "You know the subliminal programming. Trigger it. The assassinations should follow."

"Good enough. Who is my missing weapon?"

"A street hustler named Rolf had a stable of kids working for him. Usual scams. His contact with Winton was well-hidden. But the one you want is a girl called Amber. She's not on the street any more and she never carried a chip, but—"

"Never mind," Vandover answered coldly. "I know where to start looking. You'll find your money at the usual drop." He cut the call short and sat looking at the darkened screen.

All those years under his nose and he'd never even guessed. It made sense to him now why Winton had not had her eliminated, making Storm even more vulnerable. Winton had not known the targets or the programming, but Vandover didn't doubt he'd been trying to ferret the information out so that he could do the manipulation. Each of them had kept secret from the other a vital part of the plan, forcing them to work in tandem with one another, despite their differences.

Vandover stroked the keyboard lightly. "Winton, my boy, you were clever." The hit on Amber would have to be canceled. Or perhaps not. A postponement would suit as well. She was much more subdued since the evacuation of Bythia. He would give his right arm to know what had happened on that fringe planet, how Winton's plans had gone awry and gotten him killed instead of reaching fruition. Perhaps she was no longer the weapon she had been groomed to be. He had never sensed any psychic fires banked within her, yet Winton had assured him the assassin being groomed for them was a genuine talent, unlike those charlatans Pepys kept bottled up in the east wing. So genuine a talent that the strike could be directly to the heart or the brain . . . swift, unstoppable, and virtually undetectable.

He must investigate the information carefully before acting. A good place to start would be the powerful loan maker, Sadie, who'd given the girl safe harbor more than once. Sadie would cooperate. She was a businesswoman skilled in the art of compromise, a reed that would bend in the wind rather than be broken.

Vandover placed a call. He would stay the inevitable, but it would be only a delay. If the girl proved false or useless to him anyway, she would still have to be removed.

CHAPTER 7

Amber was dozing, forehead to her knees, folded up in the corridor like a chair someone had tossed carelessly aside. The rank scent of Thraks wafted over her and she heard their constant clicking become agitated chatter through her half-dreams. Doors opened and the sounds awakened her fully.

She had lifted her head, wincing as a neck muscle kinked. She had done vigils in worse places by far, on concrete and permaplast streets without soul or hope, in backwater holes with murderers skulking about, on faraway worlds where, even surrounded by friends, the agony of waiting for Jack to return was almost too much to bear.

But this morning's vigil had worn her out in a way no other had, and as she met the stare of the nurse standing across the corridor, she gleaned no comfort from the man's words.

"He's out of it. A couple of hours on dialysis and we'll be able to let visitors in."

Amber got to her feet, slender legs unfolding to hold her, unaware of the technician's masculine reaction to her grace. She carefully rubbed the sleep from one eye. "How is he?"

"A little disoriented. We put a piggyback on his tape to bring him up to date—it's been twenty-seven years since that imprint was made."

Weariness fled. "You did what?"

The nurse looked over his shoulder. His bulk blocked the lab door very effectively, and he listened to something happening behind him, before he looked back to her. His jaw set. "We added on a short orientation tape."

"I know what you meant. Who the hell authorized that?"

"Pepys," the nurse said. With that, he backed up and the

door slid shut. Hard glittering eyes watched her until the barrier sealed them off.

"*Shit*," Amber muttered, and clenched one fist. The Thraks in the corridor came to attention, their facial masks pulling into Kabuki contortions of expression. Jack had once taught her how to read them and she now saw aggression and command. "Don't worry, boys," she said aloud, wondering what Pepys had done. "But I suggest, for your own good, there be a changing of the guard before Jack comes out of that lab. He doesn't like Thraks." With a tight smile, she turned and left. There were things to do before she could end her vigil.

The Thraks had been replaced by an honor guard of Knights when she returned. She eyed them as she entered the medical wing corridor, her attention caught by their gleaming armor of many different colors. Jack's own white armor was so white it was iridescent even though it had been damaged over the years. A sudden sense of loss hit her, and she felt a fluttering inside her throat, a panicky, tickling surge as she wondered if it or Colin could ever be found.

The guard parted, exposing Vandover Baadluster. He had given up his somber black robes for those of charcoal . . . a slight, psychological change and one which she pondered as he inclined his head to her.

"Milady Amber."

"Minister," she answered. Triumph flooded her abruptly and, though she felt her face warm with its intensity, she savored it. She had managed to deal with him without Jack's presence, but the knowledge that Jack would soon be able to back her up made her stronger.

Vandover's flat eyes glinted slightly as if guessing her emotion and her triumph turned swiftly to anger. Anger she could deal with. She let her words stay in her throat. She would not lose her advantage by throwing it away.

"We've been waiting," Vandover said. "I was most surprised to arrive here and find you missing. But then, the nurse told me he had spoken with you. You look well."

Amber put her chin up. She was tall, but the Minister of War was taller. "Thank you. When can I see him?"

"Now . . . if you're ready."

She hesitated. Thoughts flooded her, too many to pin down. Jack had his victory, at last. What would it mean to him? To them? Where was he now? Why wasn't he striding out to meet her?

"Milady?" Vandover prompted softly.

"Of course." She stepped through the aisle formed by the honor guard, followed by Baadluster, the fabric of his long overtunic whispering with his lumbering gait. She barely heard the noise, yet it brought a sense of foreboding as though a legion whispered evil of Pepys' minister. *An omen*, she thought as they entered the interior lab, *and one which I don't need.*

He sat with his back to them, wearing a clean white jumpsuit which echoed the pallor of his convalescence. She crossed the portal and came to a hesitant stop, aware that she barred Baadluster and the others from entering the lab behind her. He heard them nevertheless. He put up his right hand, four-fingered, snapped off the console deck, and removed his ear set. She saw then that he'd been listening to something.

Before he even swiveled in the chair, she knew. There were lines of tension across that familiar back. Tension and apprehension. And when he turned to face her, there was a pleasant blankness across his plain, high cheekboned face and in his light blue eyes. For a moment, her heart stuttered in her chest—but then she saw the same keen intelligence in his eyes that he'd always had and knew he'd at least retained that much.

As he stood, his eyes spoke before the man did. *Who are you?*

Her knees turned to water. One shoulder touched the portal framing, bracing her, as she listed slightly. Her ears buzzed.

"You must be Amber," he said, reaching for her.

She slapped his hand away. "I'm fine." Shivering, she pulled herself upright again and let Baadluster brush past her.

The minister gave Jack a masculine hug. "Let me welcome you back, my boy."

Amber watched Jack's faintly puzzled expression over the top of Baadluster's shoulder. Vandover released him.

"Back after twenty some years of exile, one of the emperor's finest."

"Only to find a new emperor and the same enemy," Jack responded. There was very little warmth in his voice. "Though I understand we've become allies. I'm ready for debriefing when you are."

"Good. Emperor Pepys would like to see you as soon as possible."

"I understand." He caught Amber's gaze for a moment, then looked about him where two techs were still charting monitors. She became aware that leads still attached him to the lab console. "I'll be ready in about an hour as soon as the techs are convinced my blood sugar's stabilized and there's no hypothermia."

"Done." Baadluster signaled the guard, and they about faced and left.

Amber stayed. She ignored the observation monitors as she stepped closer and shivered at the stranger's expression in the eyes of her lover. Damn him, he made her break all her rules! "Don't do this to me," she told him. "I don't care what the advantage is. You're playing right into their hands. They added an imprint of their own onto your mind loop. God knows what they've programmed into you."

Anger flashed in his eyes. "God doesn't have to know," he said quietly. "I do. I can't tell you what you want me to say. I don't know you anymore—"

His name wrenched out of her, leaving her throat clenched in pain.

His face paled. "I'm sorry," he said. "I really am. They tell me I'm supposed to go retrieve the head of the Walker sect. I've got a lot to get ready. If you'll excuse me. . . ."

"Then you're still going after Colin?"

"I'm a soldier. This is my assignment. I don't have any choice."

"No," she said, and turned away blindly, unable to face him any longer. "And neither do I." She bolted from the lab and knew he would not call her back.

Vandover Baadluster snared her at the corridor's bend. His hand came out and caught her wrist. He blocked her instinctive kick and she stood, breathing hard. She strained at his hold, then paused, wild-eyed, at his restraint.

"Leave me," she said, voice low and deadly.

"Regardless of what you think and feel, I am not responsible for what happened to Jack Storm."

"You killed him!"

"Someone did, yes, I think we agree on that. But Pepys has other hands that do his dirty work from time to time." Baadluster's pasty face took on a glow. "It's not in my scheme of things to have Storm decommissioned just when we need his peculiar talent most."

She noticed then that there were no Thraks or other Knights about. The minister had had the wing cleared. She stilled in his grip. "What do you want from me?"

"I think it safe to say I want the same thing you want: not to send a reborn, *innocent* man out into a maelstrom of difficulties and war that he is only half aware of."

"And how do you propose to cure the situation?"

Baadluster smiled, his thick lips compressing. "I suggest we send you with him, dear Amber, to guard his back."

"I'd sooner ally with a Milot berserker than conspire with you."

His eyebrows arched and his icy fingers tightened about her wrist. She fought to keep back a cry of pain.

"Don't play with me, milady. I do not hold a high opinion of you."

"Nor I you."

"Then," and his voice lowered, "we understand each other. We each have motives of our own. I offer you this: Madam Sadie kept a mind-loop of you. My sources tell me that your traumatic stay on Bythia leached away many of your . . . shall we call them skills? You'll need them back if you want to be of any help to Jack. Your imprint can be done quickly. Do you agree?"

Amber's thoughts tumbled. Unsuccessfully, she tried to center them. To be reimprinted as an assassin—to have her psychic channels opened back up—to once again have subliminal programming within her that she could not control . . . she'd gone through hell to have that taken from her once. Why would she willingly ask that it be done to her a second time?

To help Jack, that's why.

And she also knew there was no way Vandover could know the extent of what he was offering her. He might

guess at the coldblooded skills of an adept street fighter
but there was no way he could know the rest of her secrets.
None. She could control her killer instinct this time. And
there was no one alive who could trigger her subliminal
programming, her list of targets.

She smiled hesitantly. "All right. We're agreed."

Baadluster's hard, dark eyes glittered. "Good," he said.
He released her wrist and then, astonishingly, brought his
hand up and stroked her tawny mane of hair once, caress-
ingly. "Good," he repeated.

CHAPTER 8

He watched the young woman leave, trailing perfumed anger in her wake. She stirred dreams in him, but he did not know her, not really. Jack turned back to the lab console, retrieved the disk that he'd been listening to and slipped it into a pocket. The thoughts on that disk, like the body he'd awakened to, were those of a stranger. He was older, without having remembered living it, scarred without knowing whose battles he'd fought, loved without understanding how to return it.

Not that he was an old man, not by any means—he guessed his age to be in the late twenties to early thirties range though his linear age was closer to his mid-fifties. And he had healed well, though skin stretched a little gingerly over his ribs and there was a knot or two there which ached. But he had been left with the feeling, since awakening that morning, that he was wearing someone else's skin, someone who had loyalties and loves he could not begin to comprehend.

The disk, sketchy at best, had confirmed as much. He apologized mentally to the other Jack Storm for usurping his life. There was nothing he could do about it now. The disk had not given him memories but warnings, dire warnings to help keep him alive if the worst should happen. Once again, Jack Storm was a man with but half a life—now he was missing the end instead of the beginning.

"Commander Storm?" The nurse technician leaned into the otherwise empty lab. "We're done monitoring you. I'm told the emperor wants to see you as soon as possible."

He nodded. Thanks to the disk, he had a fairly good idea who his enemies were this time around and Pepys was high on the list.

Amber shivered despite herself. She shut her jaw firmly and clenched her teeth, determined not to give Vandover the satisfaction of knowing that cold sleep daunted her. But to sleep the sleep of near-death in the arms of enemies was a far different prospect than doing it in the embrace of friends.

The Minister of War brushed shoulders with her. She recoiled from the contact, but he seemed not to notice as the taxi bumped to a halt, its hovers whining. He dropped a cassette into her hand.

She closed her hand over it without looking. "No unexpected surprises?"

"You'll find Madam Sadie's seal on it."

Amber dropped the cassette into a hip pocket. Sadie had once been an unflappable friend. Now a traitor. She did not find the information assuring.

"Do you wish me to accompany you?"

"No."

The minister did not look surprised. "Very well. I'll be back for you tomorrow." Unspoken was the warning for her to be here, awaiting him. Amber did not rise to the bait. She would be waiting. For now, she had nowhere else to go.

Pepys was waiting in the audience hall. It was empty, banners slack upon their rods in the domed ceiling, daises empty, he sitting almost forlornly in a chair to one side. Jack recognized him only because he'd been shown photos of him. Yet as he approached, a familiarity prickled him like pins and needles. Yes, he'd known the frizzy red hair would drift finely about the man's head as if filled with static electricity. And he'd expected the hard green gaze of the imperial eyes.

He approached the man in the chair, came to a halt, and saluted smartly. There was a hard knot of pain on his right rib cage, where a burl of scar tissue reminded him of a newly healed wound. *Old man*, he thought. *You didn't take very good care of our body.*

Pepys looked up at him, an appraising expression on his tilted face. "At ease, Commander," he said.

It took a moment for former Lieutenant Storm to realize he'd achieved promotion in his lost years. He relaxed. The knot of pain slowly unraveled itself and went away after one or two jolts as he breathed. He'd been told he'd tackled a man in full dress battle armor with nothing but his hands. *There are old soldiers, and bold soldiers, but no old, bold soldiers*, he thought as Pepys stood up and trailed away, evidently expecting Jack to follow.

The privacy cubicle was barely large enough to hold a table and two chairs. There were white cup circle rings on the empty top. Pepys dropped into the larger chair, curling into it with the wiry grace of a small man. Jack took a look around before taking the second chair.

The emperor gave a little smile. "Old habits die hard."

"Habits?"

He waved a hand at the room. "No security in here. White sound screens up . . . no recording but our own fallible memories."

Jack felt uncomfortable. He *had* been searching for equipment, a reflex as unthought of as a sneeze or a yawn. Who had taught him to do such a thing?

Pepys patted the tabletop. "I'm told you've absolutely no memory of the last seven or eight years."

"I'm told the same thing," Jack answered wryly.

"Too bad. In the past you've worked both for me and— perhaps saying against me is too strong—for yourself. You must have thought it was worth it if you took the risk. As for myself, I'm pleased to be able to welcome you back into a time when the Knights have been not only resurrected but redeemed. There was a twenty year period when there was shame instead of glory. . . ."

Jack said nothing though the sudden tension in Pepys' languid form told him the emperor expected a reply. He had no memory with which to judge. "I'm told I have you to thank for that."

Pepys' intense gaze flickered a little. "Told, but not necessarily accepted. What can I say to put you at ease, my boy?"

Jack's muscles bunched. He knew instinctively he was not Pepys' boy. Though, if current memory served, he had sworn allegiance to Regis and this was Regis' successor. The audience chamber they sat in suddenly felt crowded, filled with dark and fleeting shadows. Pepys did not seem to notice them and, as Jack moved involuntarily away from

them, they dissipated. *Ghosts*, he thought. *But whose?* "Tell
me why we were in disgrace." And, as he watched a range
of emotions move over the emperor's freckled visage, he
knew why the Knights believed in a "Pure" war. The environment, the planet, must never suffer for the sins of the
flesh that occupied it. Nine months and another Pepys
could spring up to take the place of this one. But there
would never be another Milos, or Dorman's Stand.

"Because you did not keep Milos," Pepys replied
smoothly. "And as for the why—we hope you can tell us.
Baadluster, in his capacity as Minister of War, will be here
shortly, and then we'll move to a room where you can be
recorded. You see, you're one of the few living survivors
of that battle. The Thraks moved in so quickly, we have
few tapes and documents of what actually happened." He
held up a thin hand. "But you need only tell it once."

Jack could feel the thin sheen of sweat that had erupted
suddenly across his forehead. They were asking for his
nightmare and they *would* have it. So be it. What would
they give him in exchange? His last few years? He doubted
that. *Trust no one*, the disk had whispered in his ear. *If you
would know the truth, find St. Colin.* "Then tell me about
the Walker you want me to find."

"Ah." Pepys shifted in his chair, moving his weight from
one hip to the other and leaning on the opposite arm. "We
knew each other well once, before he became a Walker
and went on his missionary way, and then became a saint.
He's a good man and, damn it all, that's the basis of all
this trouble. If he were not, we and the Walkers jockeying
for position to replace him could be rid of him." Pepys
grimaced at Jack's expression. "Speaking too frankly for
you?"

Jack felt at a loss. He sensed the layers in the emperor's
speech and knew that this man had reasons upon reasons
for everything he did. As for Jack, he was just a foot soldier. Nothing more, and nothing less. His gut reacted for
him. "A good man is worth the trouble."

Pepys sat upright in his chair. His hair fairly sparked as
he ran a hand through it. Then he grinned as though the
joke was upon himself. "Yes, I guess he is."

"The question would be," Jack added slowly, "why he
hasn't come back on his own."

"What are you up against? Commander Storm, I think it likely you're up against nothing less than the Ash-farel. As recent as your emotions for the Thraks are, and despite the fact we've maintained a delicate balance of truce for years, the Ash-farel are the enemy now. We know nothing of them except that they come, they destroy, and they leave. We can't communicate with them and we haven't had much success fighting them, either. Whatever they are, they're fierce enough to have driven the Thraks into a swarming frenzy right down our throats."

Jack found the Ash-farel in his memory. The update tape, he supposed, for it was accompanied by emotionless pictorial records and nothing he'd personally experienced. Those records showed him planets cleaned of all life . . . and yet, as he mulled the information over, he knew he saw a race which fought as he had been trained to fight. The planets themselves had not been damaged environmentally beyond a point where two or three years would see the worlds healed. Brutally efficient, like cleaning house without damaging the house itself. He'd seen what they'd done to shielded worlds. It was unlikely one crusader could have stood up to them, had he met them.

He crossed his legs and tapped the arch of his right shoe sole idly. "What is the likelihood," he asked, "of my finding Colin alive?"

"We both know it has to be none. Nor are you likely to even find relics enough to bring back—but Colin has never been a man to whom the expected happens. I think, I *feel*, he's still alive." Pepys leaned forward. "If you're to find him, you have to believe that, too."

"He has my armor."

"We believe so."

Jack tapped his foot harder. His armor had been contaminated, possibly still was. The berserker parasite inside was as big a menace to the holy man as the enemy he'd never met. "I'll need new armor."

"You've been fitted already. It's ready when you are."

"And volunteers." Jack gave a slight smile. "You brought me back as a traitor, a deserter. They may be a little difficult to find."

Pepys thrust himself abruptly out of his chair. "You told me you had no memory."

Jack stood, as well. Muscles, bones, and nerves newly healed cried with dull pain, and he felt their weakness holding him back, but he still towered over the red-haired emperor. "I have none. But I have ears, and the guard you had on my doors talked. I don't know how I became a commander in your Knights, Pepys, or why I then decided to desert my duty, but I'm not so fresh out of the dirt fields that I will accept gullibly everything you tell me."

Pepys' mouth twitched. Then, amusement replaced the anger in his brilliant eyes. "Good men," he repeated wryly, "are a lot of trouble."

Vandover's appearance interrupted the emperor's quiet laugh at himself. The minister stood respectfully outside the chamber, but his shadow cast itself over them. Pepys stopped smiling. He leaned close and put a hand on Jack's forearm.

"I suggest," he said quietly, "that you trust to your memory and not to gossip when you speak in front of Baadluster." Then the emperor moved past him swiftly, saying, "Vandover! You're late."

"I had business, your highness, which detained me."

Jack watched the two of them bend their heads over the leaflet of plastisheets in Baadluster's hand and realized he could not hear what they softly discussed. And neither had Baadluster heard the emperor's last words to him. But his memory was flawed.

He was not a subtle man, but he felt the emperor had just told him that such a flaw might mean his life.

CHAPTER 9

The thrumming vibration brought him back to awareness. Bogie let his damped down sensors come back to full strength and his chamois self pumped in excitement as he recognized the approach of a major vessel. The coracle shuddered as it was captured once again. Bogie triggered open the shield door to the equipment bay. He stretched out his massive armored body and stood eagerly, waiting to hear Jack's voice broadcast.

But the com lines stayed quiet, except for a static chittering that he could not comprehend. The coracle quivered as if buffeted by a wind or tide and he could hear that it had been taken in, was now docked in a hold of some kind. Outside, vacuum was being bled away and air pumped in. He could feel the difference in the soundings through the hull.

He faced the main air lock, anticipating its opening.

His mission as a signpost to Colin's whereabouts was nearly fulfilled, but even more important, the expectation of a reunion with Jack warmed him. War had torn them away from each other, but Bogie had never doubted that fate would bring them together again. Helmet visor forward, he scanned the portal eagerly.

But it was not opened, it was blown away. The armor rocked back on its heels, sensors flooded by heat and the blast—and the nightmare Kabuki-mask faces of the invaders as they climbed in, their chitin aglow in the explosion's wake.

He'd been found all right, but by Thraks.

If memory served him, Jack would have showed his teeth grimly and waded in, suit gauntlets laying down a line of fire.

Bogie brought his arms up. He'd circumvented his safety

and had been fully weaponed for some time. Now he activated the Dead Man circuit so that if they pulled him down, the suit would not last beyond the first crack in its sealing. These were the enemy.

He aimed and strode forward.

CHAPTER 10

It was like putting on a shabby, beloved old coat with pockets full of memories and past humiliations, all indivisible from one another. Or maybe it was like sitting on an alien beach, letting brilliantly colored sand run through her fingers and trying to decide if one color was good and another bad—there was no real way to separate them or make a judgment. And what if the most beautifully colored grain was perhaps the end result of the most terrible memory? Would she, now that all was said and done, throw it away?

Amber lay in quietude, her chest barely moving under its sheeted cover, feeling her life in all its layers, her mind far more active than her body yet still aware of her awakening state. Memory came back like feeling . . . prickly, painful, yet welcome pins and needles. She felt her breath bolt through her lungs and issue out in discharge, chilled by her still, cold interior. She began to shake, teeth chattering.

A nurse appeared, warmed blanket in her arms, and tucked it around Amber. She checked her ankle shunt to make sure Amber had not kicked off the dialysis shunt, murmured an encouraging sound and passed on. Amber barely noticed her. Her mind was too busy.

Like a kaleidoscope, the shards of her life fell and tumbled about her, pretty pictures with sharp edges, and yesterday was among them. She had lost nothing and gained everything. As the warmth of the blanket penetrated, she closed her eyes and slept a second time.

"He's yours," Vandover said quietly. He squeezed his hands together slightly, the only movement which betrayed his emotions. "He has no memory of your previous agreement and so, therefore—"

"Neither should I," finished Pepys. "Think you?"

"Think? He scarcely blinked in debriefing. He holds you in the proper respect and awe a recruit might be expected to . . . we should have thought of this long ago. Storm defused, but still valuable to us."

"Yes." Pepys tapped a curved fingernail against the teeth of his smile. "And now he's going after Colin because *I* command him to, and not because of their friendship. I'm in control now."

"Which is as it should be." Vandover paced beyond the seated emperor, turned and came back. "It worked as I told you it would."

"I am glad," his emperor returned. He looked up with his verdant eyes. "If not, you would have killed him, wouldn't you?"

"No. But I would have had him killed, for you." Vandover took a deep breath. "He's still dangerous. He doesn't like being manipulated."

Pepys waved a negligent hand. "An emperor commands."

Vandover nodded. He paused in the doorway as Pepys added, "What about the girl?"

"She's mine."

Pepys inclined his head, indicating his answer. "As we discussed."

"Then I will do nothing, for the moment. Although he doesn't know her, he has an almost . . . instinctual recollection of her. I've seen it in his eyes. Why create suspicion unnecessarily if she disappears too suddenly?"

"And if she corrupts him?"

Vandover's lips tightened. "She'll never get that close to him again. Now, your highness . . . I have other appointments."

"Of course. Don't let me keep you any longer."

Baadluster gave an abbreviated bow and left the chamber. Though he quickly turned down a right-angle corridor and left the chamber far behind, he could still feel the emperor's burning gaze upon his back.

* * *

His own chambers were much more somber than those of Pepys' and dominated by readouts and listings of the skirmishes between humans, Thraks, and Ash-farel. The Triad Throne took pride in its mercenary troops, but the news was not favorable. The clandestine activity between Thraks and humans was showing an ominous uptrend. Nor was he any closer to pinpointing the origins of the Ash-farel or to predicting their patterns of aggression.

Vandover frowned, looking closely at his screening of the latest graphics. Did Pepys not fully comprehend the danger? If so, why did the emperor continue his dance with the Walkers? What could a threatening civil war possibly avail him at this point?

He scanned the information he had posted, knowing that there was a pattern here, if he could but decipher it. He opened his com line to the aide-de-camp on watch.

"Sir?"

"Make an appointment with Commander K'rok for tomorrow."

"Yes, sir."

Vandover sat back in his chair. The Milot kept his thoughts close to his chest, but there was information to be had there if one was skillful enough. Bridging the gap between the emperor's mercenary troops and those of the Thraks, as K'rok was technically a Thrak himself, left the Milot in a position to discern happenings even the Minister of War was unlikely to know. Unraveling K'rok would be a challenge. He bridged his fingers over his nose and sank deeper into thought.

He swung about in his chair to find out he was not alone.

"Good evening, Baadluster."

She had dressed in black and a blue so deep in color its iridescent shimmer was almost black. He didn't see her at first, not until she moved out of the shadows of the corners. Even then he would not have seen her except that she was in motion. Her tawny mane had been tamed: combed and braided at the nape of her neck. She moved with a confidence that inflamed his blood and raised the bile in his gorge at the same time. Vandover halted, gathering his thoughts.

"I was going to send a car for you."

She perched on the corner of the desk console. "I was ready to leave tonight. I saw no reason not to." She turned the full attention of her amber gaze on him.

Vandover felt a quickening in his guts. The fire to his spark was there now, he saw it in her. How could he not have seen it before, the psychic energy that coursed through her body as hotly as her blood? Yes, she had dimmed it, banked it, possibly had even quenched it; now he had brought it back to life. It was as though he had created her anew.

Amber leaned close. She wore a subtle perfume that was perhaps no more than the shampoo scent in her hair. He responded in spite of himself. "I wanted you to know," she said softly, "that it would be dangerous for you to think we have a partnership or that I will be grateful for what you've done for me."

His ardor chilled, but not his pleasure. Vandover allowed himself to smile. "Milady," he answered, "you underestimate us both."

She stood abruptly. Tensile strength replaced slender grace. "I'm done playing games with you. You call me 'milady,' but your voice says 'whore.' I'm not yours to jack around, Vandover, and I've come to remind you of that fact. I'm going back to Jack and whether he remembers me or not is immaterial. I'll fight for what's mine."

He got to his feet. "Commendable. Commendable and predictable. But do you think this is safe, declaring yourself and drawing a battle line between the two of us? Are you really so sure that we are done with alliance?"

"I'm sure."

It was late in the palace. The nighttime lighting from the corridors glowed into the room. Vandover reached out to his console and keyed the chamber doors shut and locked. Amber took a step back, but high color outlined her cheekbones as the chamber lights came up.

"Now," he said, "we may speak privately."

"If you think those doors will hold me—"

Vandover laughed. "You'll stay, and not because of the doors or even locks."

Her gaze narrowed. "I could kill you," she told him.

He laughed again, genuine mirth filling him. "I know!" he said triumphantly. "How well I know! I'm the one who had you programmed!"

CHAPTER 11

Amber recoiled from him. The control and menace that had been hers now suddenly became Baadluster's. She took a breath. He couldn't know. She fought for composure and found it. Before, she had been close to killing the minister for Jack's sake. Now it meant her own survival. "What do you mean?"

"I mean that you should not threaten me. I know who and what you are. I know your innermost secret. I have the key." Vandover swung away from her and paced the chamber's length, checking the door seal before turning back to her. "We have things to say in private."

"I have nothing to say to you!"

"No? Then perhaps you'll listen. Even Rolf did not know which was the genuine trigger I had instilled in your neuro-lingal programming. My wishes are buried so deeply, so subliminally, you'll never know—what makes you kill. Do you want to hear it, Amber? Are you ready to fulfill your destiny?" He still smiled widely. Then, as if reading her thoughts, added, "And what do you want to bet I can trigger you before you can kill *me?*"

She unclenched her fists. With studied movements, she returned to the console where she had been perched before and resettled herself. She caught the momentary hesitation in his eyes. He couldn't be sure . . . just as she couldn't. "Why do you think I contain this . . . trigger?"

"You belonged to the pack of street kids Rolf had working for him."

"Half of under-Malthen could probably make that claim."

The light in Vandover's eyes seemed to flare. "This is no claim. Jack defended you from him on several occasions until the man was killed."

She shrugged.

"I hired Rolf to find me an assassin. Not just a street lethal child to be groomed—I wanted a special child. I wanted one with abilities difficult to measure."

Amber tilted her head, listening. She found herself unwilling to meet the blaze in his eyes any longer. She did not want him to see the despair she felt was undeniably in her own.

"Shall I describe those abilities to you?" Vandover licked his lips. "Cunning, of a surety, but then almost any feral child on Malthen's streets has cunning. Quickness and glibness, too. And a temper to match the tongue. Do you recognize yourself yet, my lovely Amber? Do you?"

She felt the hatred warm in her, running like a hot wire just under her skin. Her hair felt heavy upon the back of her neck. As she reached up and began to loosen it from its bonds, the knife in her wrist sheath flexed uncomfortably to remind her of its presence.

"Shall I continue?"

Amber paused, her hands up, fingers unknotting her hair. "No," she said softly. "I'm not the one you think I am."

"I know you are. Rolf had his tastes and desires, he did. He preferred children. He told me once just how he'd found his candidate for my assassin." Baadluster came close, closer, weight balanced on the balls of his feet. "He'd tried to rape the child, and found himself knocked on his ass for it. Psychically, not physically. The child had made himself unapproachable. That's what threw me for a number of years when I began to search for the information myself. A simple matter of gender."

Her glance flickered up in spite of herself, in spite of the man's heat which crested higher and higher. His voice pounded at her. "But I kept searching. You should thank me for my diligence, really. If it were not for your newfound usefulness to me. . . ."

Her hair freed, she dropped her hands to her lap, slender fingers close to the cuff of the sleeve which hid her knife. "You have no proof."

"Shall we see if you can be raped?"

"I'll kill you first." The calm breaths she had been forcing now grew ragged.

"Perhaps." He leaned closer. "But not before I can

speak the words you fear most. You will do that which
horrifies you most. You will murder without cause or
need."

The knife handle was so close to her fingertips she could
sense its field. "I would never kill for you."

"You'd have no choice!" Vandover spun away. "Get out
of here. Go to the man who commands your heart. I've got
the rest of you now, body and soul." He touched the console and the doors opened.

She paused at the door. "You're wrong."

"No," he said softly, menacingly. "I saw it within you.
You're mine, milady, and I will have satisfaction."

Amber fled into the abandoned corridor.

He dreamed of a dark-eyed angel. Not the softly
rounded, beneficent angel he'd seen depicted in the paint-
ings in the Walker compound. No, this one raged with righteous justice, her white robes torn and ragged as storm
winds held her aloft on spread wings which were as shot
with dark and lightning as the tempest. Her hair spread
about her angry face almost like a second pair of wings
and the glory of the anger in those dark eyes—

Jack jerked awake, thinking of Amber. In the lightless
confines of his apartment, he thought he saw her, dressed
in her favorite blue caftan of Bythian make, her fair skin
tattooed with the veinlike, intricate patterns the shaman
and prophet had drawn upon her. She drifted toward him,
arms opening for an embrace and he, desire quickening,
sat up to take her in.

As quickly as the memory touched him, it fled. He sat
on his soldier's bunk, the mattress hard under his lean but-
tocks, grasping at thin air, unaware of what he was doing.

Then, dizzily, the memories came back. He was not one
man but two, yet they were the same. His mouth cottoned.
He put one foot on the floor to steady himself. His pulse
thundered through his skull and then quieted. He *knew*,
and knowing that, understood that his life and those of the
people he loved were in even more danger.

Pepys had warned him. Had Pepys known that his memories would overlay themselves and begin to integrate again?

They had tampered with him, Pepys and Vandover. Had
one conspired to undo the machinations of the other? Rage

filled him. He tore the bedsheets aside and swung his other leg out of bed, body in motion before his mind had even decided on vengeance. The touch of his warm foot on the cold floor stilled him. The bastards couldn't leave him alone. He was not even left time to savor the long-lost memories of his home and family, now restored.

A ghost stirred in the corner of his apartment, saying gently, "You still don't sleep at night." Amber came toward him, inseparable from the shadows that hid her, except for the soft illumination that highlighted her face and golden-brown hair. There was as much hate as love in her expression

"How did you get in here?"

Sadness curtained the other's emotion. "You used to remember how I do things like this."

He wanted to tell her that he *knew*, and couldn't. It knotted in his chest. Until he understood what had happened to him during imprint, and what schemes his emperor had entangled him in, he would only endanger her as well. He made his face go blank and could only hope that his eyes did not mirror his thoughts. "Should I remember that you're a thief?"

She sat down at the foot of the bed, crossed her legs limberly, and propped her chin in the palm of one hand. "You sound like you've been talking to Vandover." She wore black with a dark blue shimmering, and he thought of ravens' wings, flashing as the birds flew over his father's fields on Dorman's Stand.

"I've been talking to a lot of people these past few days. You're the only one who seems to be an expert on my sleeping habits, however." The desire which had faded since his first awakening gave him a dull throb.

Her gaze searched his face. "You really don't know me, do you?"

"No.

For the briefest moment, it took both of her hands to hold her face. Then she seemed to gather herself and looked up again.

Suddenly, Jack knew what Colin described as hell. He could not comfort her. He could not brush away whatever demons she was struggling with, and he knew that she was fighting a mighty battle somewhere within herself. He knew it because his love for her told him and yet he dared not help her fight that battle.

The moment passed and Amber took a deep breath. "We're a fine pair," she said, with a touch of bitterness, "to think about saving worlds."

"I'm just a foot soldier," he said, to his own surprise, and knew his younger, restored self was speaking. "I do what I can."

Amber thrust herself to her feet. "I'd better go now, before I find myself suggesting that I try unorthodox methods to remind you who I am."

"I wouldn't mind," Jack said, and felt himself smiling in the darkness of the bedroom.

"I'm sure you wouldn't." Amber leaned forward and kissed him. Her lips were hard and fervent. Then she stepped back. "Somewhere inside of you, buried, it has to be buried because I can't accept the fact that it's gone, somewhere inside of you is the man I love who loves me."

Jack cleared his throat. "If he comes back, you'll be the first to know."

She eyed him fiercely a second longer. "I hope so. Because we both need him desperately." She turned, and then she was gone, almost as if she had never been there.

Jack fisted his hand. "Damn!" His voice sounded gravelly, choked by the knotted emotions he'd kept back. Amber was in trouble and he was unable to help her. He spoke to the night. "Your throne's not enough anymore, Pepys. I want your guts for this one."

CHAPTER 12

There is life in prayer, Colin thought, the hard mat of the flooring pounding new bruises upon the bruises already on his knees. He reflected also that the pain of it might add more potency though he normally found prayer very comforting. Now it was the only conversation he had, and as he levered himself off the cell floor and laborously sat down upon a crude three-legged stool he had manufactured, he wondered idly if his captors had been recording him.

He spoke aloud constantly to facilitate their knowledge of his language, but he'd never been given any sign that they were even hearing beings. He could not reach them or if he did reach them, they cared little. Why then did they keep him? What did they see when they looked at him?

Colin sat within his cell, watching his dim, obfuscated reflection stare back. The walls, ceiling, and floor were of a material he was not familiar with: light as plastic sheets, but metallic and enduringly tough. Because of the material, he thought he was in a temporary holding area that, like a tent, might be folded and taken down when not needed. He wondered how long he might be allowed to prolong that need.

He spread his hands over his aching knees and rubbed gingerly. The bones and sinews showed clearly. He was losing flesh. The Ash-farel recognized in him a need to eat and drink and flush his system accordingly, but never gave him enough. His mouth was constantly dry and his lips chapped. He felt hunger almost as intensely as the pain of his wounds.

"You are," he told himself, "a foolish old man." The warmth of his spare hands lent him some comfort, but it would not last.

It was vanity that had sent him to the Ash-farel, a sin of

the ego for which he was now being punished. He could expect no less. He had thought to communicate when no one else had, yet what conceit had told him he could? He had thought to quell a war, yet left behind him a situation poised on the precipice of civil insurrection.

"Always clean your own house first," he murmured, still watching as he kneaded the aches and pains of his joints. Jonathan would be furious with him for both the state of his health and his garments. He wore scarcely more than rags though the cell seemed to be kept at a temperature that warranted little clothing anyway.

Colin had tried every method he could conceive of to communicate with: sight, sound, color, scent, even music. The only reaction he had ever garnered was when he had been initially taken and they had begun to dispose of him as though he was a particularly squishy and pestiferous bug. He had fought back with every fiber until they had finally contained him and then jailed him. The efforts he'd gone through to get a chamber pot and then food had practically killed him.

Small triumphs, Colin thought, as he rubbed his knees a last time. It was God's will that he could be triumphant at all. Pepys was right. He had forgotten his humble beginnings, where it was a victory just to grow up fed and clothed and sheltered. It sobered him. Perhaps he had been seeking for the Kingdom of God in all the wrong places.

He smiled to himself. A lesson learned late was better than no lesson learned at all.

CHAPTER 13

"We've located Denaro," Vandover said, self-satisfaction evident in his tone.

"Where?"

The man in black bowed in deference to his emperor. "In the Outward Bounds. He's leaving a clear trail."

"As predicted. He wants to draw Storm after him." Pepys scratched the side of his head, and his aureole of red hair crackled with energy as he did so. "The only surprise here is that it's taken you so long to find him. Is it confirmed?"

"Yes."

"Then be sure Jack gets the word as well."

"He'll be even more ready to leave than he is now."

Pepys gave a brief, bittersweet smile. "Be assured, Vandover, that I intend to send him on his way as soon as I can. I want the audience hall opened up again. Let every legitimate spokesperson for the Walkers in."

Baadluster's jaw fell agape. Then, "But your highness—"

"If I don't let them in, they'll beat the doors down sooner or later. I rule here, not the mob. This is a throne room, not a boardroom. Let's see if we can't put Storm in the forefront and let him take some of the heat."

"The Walkers want your blood," Vandover responded. "I don't advise this, if for no other reason than we want to keep the commander inaccessible."

"He's my shield man, and as such, I can't afford to keep him inaccessible."

"What about the Green Shirts?"

Pepys shrugged. "They've chosen to blend in with the Walker factions—if we can placate the Walkers, the Shirts cannot afford to step out of line. Not now. We're too close to declaring martial law and that could hamper their opera-

tions here severely. No, they'll be somewhat circumspect."
He met Baadluster's gaze. "Don't you think?"

Vandover thought that the emperor had webs of his own
that he knew nothing of, and he did not like it. He considered the idea that Pepys had come to the end of his own
usefulness. The palms of his hands itched as he hid his
thoughts. "Put that way, I agree."

"Good. Make whatever arrangements with the WP and
the sweepers that you have to. I don't want the barracks
or training grounds breached."

"I'll make the arrangements," Vandover told him. Without seeming to be hasty, he brought the conversation to a
close and bowed his way out. Nothing in the emperor's
cold stare told him that the tone of his voice had been far
from subservient.

"I'd give my left nut to g' with you, boy, but that's not
my lot." The chunky sergeant strolled alongside Jack, his
beefy legs stretching to keep up with Storm's stride.

Jack smiled. "And take you away from the recruits?
Pepys would have *my* left nut if I suggested it." In rapid
time, they reached the cornerstone of the base, and stopped
where the massive walls closed off the parade and training
grounds, and where the shop buildings abutted the structure. He *knew* the grounds and yet did not . . . his memories
slip-sliding over one another as though he looked through
a camera obscura. One moment he knew exactly who he
was and where he'd been; the next moment his mind was
as blank as an unwritten page.

Lassaday cleared his throat. "I'm glad we got all that
traitor and deserter stuff put behind us."

Jack turned from the parade walls and looked down at
the NCO. "That's politics, Sarge. Pepys and Vandover and
who knows who else—and I don't guarantee that it's behind
us at all."

The white-hot Malthen sun glinted off Lassaday's well-
bronzed pate. He showed his teeth. "Them things can trip
up an honest soldier good, Commander." He jerked a
thumb to the walls. "Rawlins'll be dismissed in another
couple of minutes. I've got to get the racks out for the
suits."

"I'll be fine," Jack reassured him. The NCO hesitated,

then awkwardly rolled back into motion, leaving him alone and on his honor, as it were. Pepys did not exactly have Jack under house arrest, but neither had his status been cleared up. Storm would find himself exonerated if and when he found Colin.

It was as though he had blinked, looking after the NCO, and he found himself grasping after thoughts he no longer had under control. Jack shuddered and his palms grew sweaty as he fought the panic of being in an unknown area for unknown reasons. His body had brought him here and then abandoned him, and he knew . . . he knew that he was losing his mind. He steadied himself and, like a fading echo, remembered that he was here to meet someone.

He looked at the towering walls. He could hear a rumbling of distant warfare beyond them and then dulled silence. Maneuvers. He recognized the muffled sound of battle armor in use and smiled, remembering. Armor he *knew*. Armor was more than a second skin to him. He anticipated the tunnel opening and the men spilling out, the suits encasing them with a kind of power and grace foot soldiers had never thought to have. Mobile tanks, redesigned, sleeked down and yet massive. *No suit, no soldier,* he thought, as if his own days of training had been yesterday.

He shuddered a last time, just before the portals opened.

The soldier who approached him wore captain's insignia on his chest plate, and had his helmet off, hooked on his equipment belt. The battle armor smelled of fire and dirt and sweat. As Jack's eyes met those of the captain, he knew with a jolt that this man was an undiluted version of himself: piercing dark blue eyes, wheat-blond hair, steadily looking back at him. Sweat streaked his temples and dripped down the back of his neck. The young captain had been hard at work. He put a gauntlet out.

"Commander, it's good to see you again."

Jack took the gauntlet without hesitation, though he knew the power behind the suit could easily crush his hand. He also knew that a soldier wearing armor knew what he was doing. "Captain."

Behind them, recruits were thundering to the shop and the equipment racks Lassaday had set up. They were sweaty also, and tired to the bone, but the suits came first. The suits always came first. Once his armor was cleaned and serviced, a trooper could go home and soak his own weary muscles.

One yelled out as he went past, "Rawlins!" to which the young captain responded, "Later, Corporal," and turned his attention back to Jack.

Rawlins. Jack knew he should probably know this man intimately. He'd been an aide to Storm once. He grasped for recall and found nothing. Then it was there, briefly, like a wisp of cloud across the face of a too-hot sun: a faded scene of another world, Rawlins with blood on him, but whole, supporting a man he knew as St. Colin, as they walked through a carnage of Thrakian and otherworldly dead. What was the connection between the two of them? He found nothing else, but this memory at least stayed with him. He tucked it away. *I'll have you yet, all of you.*

Rawlins drew him aside. "Thanks for meeting with me, Commander. I wanted to talk to you first, before I did anything official."

"All right. I'm listening."

The young man unhooked his helmet from his belt and studied it, speaking quietly. "I want to go with you. I want to volunteer to find St. Colin."

Why the secrecy? Was Rawlins afraid Jack would refuse? Should Jack fear the tenuous connection between them? He studied the captain. He had nothing to go on but his gut feelings, and his instincts told him that this was an honorable man.

"If it can be arranged, Captain, I'd be pleased," he found himself saying.

Pleasure and determination flashed from those piercing eyes as Rawlins glanced up. "That's all I can ask, sir," the man answered.

"Is it?"

Rawlins' gaze dropped back to the helmet again and he seemed to be examining it minutely. "You could have your doubts about me, sir. I've been known to obey Colin instead of you, sir."

"Pepys could say the same about me. There are times when a good soldier has no choice but to disobey." He felt a tingling of knowledge within himself. There were times when a good soldier had no choice but mutiny. The truth of it rang throughout his very fiber like a clarion call. This was who he was—

Rawlins' voice interrupted his thought. "Commander K'rok," he finished.

Jack blinked. "Of course," he said. "I'll speak to him."

Rawlins relaxed and saluted. "Thank you, sir. I'll be waiting for you to make arrangements."

Storm saluted back and watched the young man leave, leonine grace in Flexalinks, his bared ,head a flaxen beacon. He thought of K'rok, the Milot commander of the Knights. He had no desire to meet with a smelly, hirsute, devious Milot. Another frame slid over his thoughts—hand to hand with the Milot, face to snarling face—and respect as well as defeat in the eyes of the other.

Jack clenched his hand, feeling a minor ache where his finger had been sheared off. Reaching for those elusive memories did no good; the harder he tried to grasp them, the more slippery they got. He thought of St. Colin and of resurrection. Beyond his orders from Pepys, there grew in him the burning need to find the man for himself. There would be truth and resurrection when he did. He stood staring after the battle suits as they carried their wearers thundering across the expanse and thought of his own suit, infected, dangerous to any who might covet it. There was a canker that needed to be cauterized as soon as possible. He was to claim his new armor later that day. He would have to remember to put out the word that the old suit was to be destroyed as soon as it was located.

Jack pivoted and returned to the dusky rose confines of the obsidite-walled palace.

When the summons came that was not a request but an order, Amber was ready. She chafed at the call, but did not flinch away because she had been prepared for it. Baadluster had her on a leash, it was axiomatic that he would yank it whenever he felt like reminding her. But the despair had given way to action, and she dressed for the meeting with a calm determination, secreting the circuitry and explosives about her body with special attention so that scanners and her dress would not give her away. There was a serenity to each of her movements, each placement of a tiny packet that would not raise alarm of itself, but combined with every other packet would be enough to vaporize Baadluster and anyone else within five feet of her when she triggered the detonator. Vandover might know that she was wired. Dealing with it would be another matter altogether. Nothing he could do could stop her.

It was strange that the decision had given her such calm. She smoothed the drape of her red dress over her hip. The fabric was lush and silken, its color the deep full ruby of blood. She looked at her face in the mirror—her hair thick and curling about her slender face with the chin she'd always thought too pointed—and retraced a pout about her lips. The open sensuality of the expression she made would hit Vandover like a fist below the belt. She intended it to. By the time the man recovered, it would be too late.

She patted the powder along her eyelids into a sultry shadow and straightened. The spidery webbing of the gossamer wires along her bare skin could not be detected under her dress's fine lines. She'd had some trouble smuggling in the goods. Malthen was a city under siege. The striking Walkers had closed down most businesses and even the Green Shirts had been damned hard to reach. But she still had her connections in under-Malthen and they'd served her well.

Amber blew a kiss at her reflection before turning away. The only ripple in her calm happened when she thought of Jack—Jack, whom she could no longer help and who could not help her. She swallowed down the lump in her throat. He would never forgive her for this. That would be her own private hell.

She felt a dampness at the corner of her eye and quickly put a fingertip to it, blotting it out. "I will *not* cry. Not any more." She keyed open her door and left before her determination failed her.

CHAPTER 14

Colin pushed away his gourd bowl in disgust. The steamed vegetable, which usually was his container and dinner in one, held what appeared to be a mass of squirming maggots. Hungry though he was, the wriggling knot of flesh turned his stomach. For reasons he could only attribute to the eating habits of his captors, these meals arrived sporadically. Usually he could not identify the living parasites that inhabited the gourd—the varieties changed from time to time—though crickets and maggots were close enough the last two times. Yet even though his stomach had shrunken terribly, he could not bring himself to eat what he had been given. Cooked perhaps—no, never. His resolve wavered as he shoved the gourd back through the door flap from which it had appeared.

He sat on his haunches and hugged his knees and tried not to think of the time span which might elapse before his next meal arrived. Once or twice, they had speedily given him new food, but most often they did not. He wondered if he insulted them by refusing his dinner even as his stomach growled in bitter protest. Food seemed to be the only common ground they had.

He felt a rumbling underneath him. For a moment, he thought that the clenching and growling of his hunger shook his entire body, then he knew that his cell responded to something else.

The walls shook. Colin got clumsily to his feet. He grabbed up his stool for whatever protection it might afford him as his cell peeled apart and he stood blinking in the harsh floodlights.

The Ash-farel had come seeking him.

He had seen the Ash-farel mummified on the dead moon of Lasertown. He'd walked among their remains on Co-

linada and detected their presence in Walker prehistory
sites. He had not known then who or what he dealt with,
but even a thousand thousand years dead, they had been
magnificent.

Now he quailed before the three who faced him, his
thoughts and rational reasoning blown from his mind by
winds of awe and terror. Angels, he thought for a moment,
inspired such feelings. And devils. Then even those reflec-
tions were driven from him.

They were massive, three times his size, and undoubtedly
saurian, but the scales of their skin were jewels that bedazzled his eyes, and their limbs were supple and quick, their
eyes coals of fire that lanced his soul. They emanated righteous anger and he dropped to his knees, the crude stool
he would have used for protection rolling out of numbed
fingers. As they reached for him, his heart fluttered wildly
in his chest.

"Oh, God," he cried out, knowing that he was dying, for
if they did not kill him, surely his heart was bursting in his
chest. He twisted his head to see where they carried him,
and when he saw, prayed that he might be lucky enough
to die first. The glittering sterility of table equipment, lights,
and tools met his eyes.

As alien as these beings were, the man knew a vivisection
lab when he saw one. He began to kick and scream
helplessly.

CHAPTER 15

Vandover had his back to the chamber doors when they opened. "Milady," he said, without turning. Amber cast a quick glance about the spacious private rooms: anteroom and library, and doors to the bedroom beyond, apartments nearly as gracious as those of the emperor himself. The chambers occupied the penthouse floor. Behind Baadluster was an unobstructed skyline view of the palace grounds and Malthen. The windows were glass, offering a crystalline sharp view to the horizon. Amber preferred plastic, the slight fuzziness of which lent a softer aspect to the cityscape.

On the other hand, glass could be kicked through a lot quicker. Smiling slightly to herself, she advanced far enough into the room to allow the doors to glide shut behind her.

Vandover turned. As quickly as his eyes widened to take her in, his gaze narrowed. "Milady," he repeated. Then, "Have you forgotten I have no heart?"

"Seduction," Amber said, moving closer, "doesn't rely on heart. And you do lust, Minister, I see it in your eyes. For power and . . . other things."

His mouth closed with a nearly audible snap. He had been working hard that day. Purple bruises of fatigue shadowed his dark eyes and his pasty complexion looked paler than usual. Whatever she expected him to say, it wasn't what he said next.

"I am the master here."

Amber felt her cheeks grow hot, knew that color tinged her face. She inclined her head in silence and waited, fearing that she had made him suspicious. Only let him come close enough for her to be sure that she would take him with her!

But he did not approach her. He kept his distance across the room and she felt his scrutiny, felt his rough probe that she fended off, being careful not to give away her power in relation to his—and wondered if he played the same game. Surely he could not be very powerful or else she would have sensed him years ago . . . and feared him.

It had been a long time since she had known fear. Oh, she had worried about Jack and herself many a time, but the strength-leeching fear that trying to survive on the streets brought, she hadn't felt that since leaving Rolf. She knew it now.

"I do not always have to be the master, but I will not play the game," he said, his voice as hollow as if it issued from a tomb. "I will not promise you that you can be my partner. We both know that is not your price."

Her mouth went dry as she whispered, "Jack is my price," and found to her shock that Vandover said it at the same time.

"Jack is your price." He paused. "I can't promise you his safety either. There are too many others involved in the struggle for this empire. But if he stays without his current memories, I can promise you that I won't be the one who calls for his death."

She looked up. There was both hope and damnation in his words. And the threat that she could be the one he called upon to end Jack's life if he came to that decision. "No," she said. "That's not good enough."

He shrugged. His robes rustled upon his lanky frame with the movement. "It's all I can offer. I can compel you whether you wish it or not."

"Not to kill Jack!"

He had a drink in one hand. He raised it now to sip at. "My dear girl," he said, bût his voice took an ugly tone and Amber knew he may have voiced girl, but he thought *whore*. "You'll do whatever I trigger you to."

"Over my dead body." She threw herself at him, one hand to claw at him and the other grasping at the detonator hidden in the necklace she wore.

He caught her. Glass crashed to the apartment floor and shattered, then ground to deadly shards beneath their shoes as he bent back her arms. He showed his teeth.

Amber brought her knee up. He gasped and let her go,

then quickly recaptured her left wrist as she twisted and tried to grasp the pendant again. Breathing quickly, harshly, he said, "What do you have planned, milady, eh?"

He forced her back, tripping over the edge of her dress which gave way with a loud rip. The wall caught her up sharply. Amber flinched as the wiring ground into her skin.

Vandover pressed into her, grinding her into the wall. She felt him quickening into hardness as their bodies clashed. His breath thickened. He pinioned her wrists above her head with one hand. She twisted and strove to free herself, but he was far stronger than she could ever have guessed. He stroked a wing of hair that had fallen loose upon her cheek.

"What trap have you set for me? Will you tell me?"

Despite the hardness that thrust at her, she leaned into him. Let their chests meet severely enough and the blow would set off the detonator.

He drew back a little warily, his face flushed. He caught her under the chin and held her face cupped in his hand, his hand which was as steely strong as the one bruising her wrists.

"Talk to me!"

Her teeth ground together. She parted her lips in contempt. "I will . . . never . . . murder for you!"

The heel of his hand stopped her words and she felt blood in her mouth, tasted its sudden leap. He thrust his pelvis into her and her stomach turned at the touch of his manhood, the silken fineness of her dress scant shield against him. The traitorous wall held her pressed to him.

"Remember," he said harshly. "You came to me."

Her mind erupted of its own accord, forgetting her suicide; the detonator, the explosives, the fine circuitry she wore like a web of undergarments. He would never have her. Psychic fire lashed out. She struck and struck deep, unheeding that he might yet have time to say the words she feared most. Her thoughts speared him. She poured herself into her attack until her very soul threatened to leave her body.

Lights exploded. Articles began to rise in the air and smash across the room. Pictures toppled from their moorings. Furniture danced in its place, stampeding upon the floor. Books took wing from the massive bookcases. The air filled with sound and fury and then the flying objects began to spiral inward until an immense maelstrom of destruction filled the center of the chamber.

When she realized what she had done, she held her breath, waiting.

Vandover staggered back a half step. The lust burning in his eyes went blank. His cruel mouth slackened. Their pelvises separated. His iron bar of a leg kept her own pinned or she would have kicked free.

Amber inhaled with a quavering sound. His hand should weaken on her wrists. She twisted, expecting the convulsion of death to break her free altogether.

His mouth fell open. He gasped for air. Then light flickered back into Vandover's eyes. The eddy whirling overhead began to settle, drifting gently to earth, tamed. The din quieted until all that could be heard was the sound of the books fluttering and then slapping to the ground.

He rocked back on his heels and roared with laughter. When he had done, he jerked her into his rough embrace. "Like fire you are," he told her. "But I am water. Deep and still. Muddied and polluted, perhaps. My power has always been feeble, but it feeds on yours. Feed me, Amber. Feel me grow stronger."

Fear lanced through her. Her breasts crushed against his chest. "Let me go!" Amber spat. She jerked and kicked, desperate to reach the pendant that would destroy him and set her free.

Their struggle rent open the neckline of her gown. His callused fingers grabbed for her breast and pinched her nipple. It tightened under his touch. Amber snapped at his face, but even as Vandover flinched away, he saw the spidery network of wires her gown had been concealing.

He tore the necklace from her throat. It took flesh with it. She let out a sound of pain as he threw her back against the wall and pinned her there, one massive hand clawlike upon her throat, so tight she could scarcely breathe. Black spots swam before her eyes.

Amber caught the sob before it could sound.

The pendant cupped in the palm of his hand, he clawed at her dress and ripped it away savagely, shred by shred. Ruby threads and patches drifted to the floor like pieces of flesh. Her skin grew cold and her pulse roared in her ears. Choked into submission, she leaned against the wall, helpless as he bared her body. His fingers probed and pinched at her until her nipples stood out in purple anger and her body throbbed in violation.

He tore the last fragment of her silkspun panties from her. With it, the last adhesive patch of explosive from her skin. He tossed it and the necklace pendant aside. He let her drop to her knees.

He knelt beside her on one knee. His left hand squeezed her throat tighter yet, and he stroked the inside of her thighs with the back of his right hand. "You would have killed us both," he said. His voice thickened. Amber thrashed feebly, her vision blinded, her limbs grown weak. "You won't defy me again."

He let go of her and she sagged into his arms. With a low, guttural sound, he let her drop to the floor. As she cried for breath, he stripped himself. She felt the heat from him scald her own chilled body. Then the power of his mind took her up and bound her as tightly as if he had used chains. Every attack she sent against him, he absorbed and turned back against her until she could do nothing but lie helplessly still, a prisoner of her own mind.

He raped her then. But not quickly, so that it might be over and done. He lingered over her, using and knowing every part of her, so that nothing of her might be untouched by him. So that nothing of herself might remain hers. So that nothing that might ever be touched by anyone else would ever forget the memory of his touch, his pain, his faint pleasure.

So that she might hate herself forever.

His kisses branded her. He whispered dull obscenities as he worked on her. He brought her flesh to life so that she moaned in spite of herself, knowing the edge of desire which he turned to pain, and then he started over again. He licked the salt sweat and sweet blood from her skin as if it was honey. When he was done with her mouth, her lips were swollen and throbbing, but she could not force a cry from them.

And when finally he was sated, he lay beside her and took her in his arms and felt her body shudder uncontrollably in shock and then he put his moist lips to her ear and whispered the name of the first person she must murder.

Then he loosened his bondage so that she might cry and struggle weakly against him.

When she had done with sobbing, he took her again. Then he told her that she would do whatever he wanted willingly, or the next name he spoke would be Jack's.

CHAPTER 16

Nighttime. Sensors adjusted to delicate shadows could not find the silent figure moving with a strange, broken grace just outside their range. Alarms that were keyed to weaponry passed over the figure without sounding any warning. With caution, the stalker ranged throughout the complex, lighted and dark, until it found its destination and paused, to watch unseen.

A woman sat and eyed her face in her mirror. It was an elegant, well-chiseled face showing little ravages of the passage of time and history with the exception of a singular frown line cutting deeply between her brows. It was an imperious mark. It reminded her that she wanted things and she was used to getting what she wanted. It did not tell her that she was one of a ruling triumvirate, a person whose will and orders affected whole planets.

With a sigh, the woman broke off her self-examination and quickly began to apply makeup. With fast strokes that betrayed how many times she had done this same routine without change, she finished her cosmetics. A few more strokes and pinnings and her dark, luxurious hair was upswept and captured. She pouted her lips and made a last, desultory examination before turning off the mirror lights and standing. She ran her hands down her flanks, settling her dress into position.

She was as ready to start a revolution as she would ever be.

"You're canny, Pepys," she said to the darkened mirror. "But you've made your moves too late. You should have unleashed Storm sooner."

The stalker in the hallway had been coming to its feet in a fluid move. It stuttered to a halt at the dialogue, then regathered itself and launched.

The in-house cameras recorded only a blur of light, energy too potent for the film to capture well, a levin-bolt of death. When the assassin finished, the body of the woman known familiarly as the Countess collapsed in a heap without ever having been touched. Blood ran from her delicate nostrils and diamond adorned ears and even in death, the imperious frown mark did not relax.

Vandover slid into the privacy booth, well aware of the unhappiness and hostility in the expression of the man waiting for him. He'd left his robes of office at the palace but still wore black as was his habit. The other shifted his bulky weight as Baadluster did so, as if to keep the table squarely between them. Vandover smiled to himself as he noted the unconscious movement.

The other was just past his prime, his black hair amply flecked with yellowish gray, his haircut out of style and becoming unruly. He looked altogether nondescript and Vandover knew the man's look was as affected as his own. "Naylor," he greeted.

Naylor gave a half-grunt in reply and ignored Baadluster's hand. He examined his own pinkish palm, which contrasted with the richness of his skin, instead. "You heard fast," he finally said, and there was a tone of defeat in his voice.

Baadluster spread his hands. "What point is there in having the WP and the sweepers, if not to know these things quickly? Still, the house had already been cleaned. Security tapes gone. Recordings gone."

"And you want to know what killed her?" Naylor met his glance with a hard, brown one of his own. "We don't know."

But Vandover was already shaking his head. "That's immaterial at this point. The Countess is gone. Without her, you're adrift."

"I came to meet you because you said you had something interesting to say. I won't sit and listen to you gloat."

"I'm not gloating, my friend. I am commiserating with you. Much good work has been done, but there's a great deal more to do."

Suddenly Vandover had Naylor's full attention. "What do you want with me?" the dusky man asked.

The Minister of War said nothing, but his long tapered fingers etched out the secret greeting of the Green Shirts on the tabletop.

Naylor sat very still on his side of the table, long after Baadluster's hand had ceased to move. Then he nervously wet his lips. "How can I trust you?"

"You can't know. Nor do I know if I can trust you. But I would think, in my position, that I have far more to lose, revealing myself to you." Vandover sat back in the booth. Crystal lights from the shabby bar played over them and the booth's noise curtain muffled what passed for music in the background. He watched and waited as the other came to a decision.

Finally, reluctantly, "What do you want from me?"

"What killed her?"

Naylor shrugged. "We think it was sonics, but we're not sure. The tapes don't reveal anything except some sort of energy surge across the film. It's not a beam of any type we're familiar with. Official cause of death is massive brain hemorrhaging. It could even be natural."

"But it wasn't."

"Not as far as we're concerned."

"How will you carry on without her?"

Naylor hesitated again. He took a drink, saying nothing.

Vandover leaned across the table. "What if I were to offer you cohesion instead of chaos?"

Queen Tricatada rattled her chitin with pleasure as General Guthul approached and did obeisance to her. Opening her back casings, she displayed her wings as only a queen might, their luminescent blue splendor casting a glamour over the Thraks bowed before her. Her body thrummed with the need to be mated, and she favored this warrior Thraks above any who might approach her, but this was not the time or place. She folded her ornamental wings back under her carapaces and settled, signaling Guthul that he might rise. She admired his mask as he levered himself upward.

In the clacks, hums, and trills of their voices, she said to him, "It is good to have you back under my wing, Guthul. Neither the leavings nor the matings have been so sweet."

He inclined his head. "Only duty could drive me from your side."

"How goes our interweaving?"

"The ancient enemy is strong and is as unreadable as ever." The warrior Thraks, in spite of his audience with his queen, could not hold his pose. He began to pace from side to side. "Only your vast superiority in egg-laying keeps them at bay."

The queen projected pride and sorrow in her mask, an artistic rendering of two opposite emotions done with such skill that Guthul stopped in his tracks to admire it. The queen's eyes shone. She had not missed that involuntary adulation. She lowered herself to all fours. "My time is short," she said.

As well the warrior Thraks knew. The burden of laying enough eggs to replenish their society was one no female could bear for long—and yet, the shame of their race was that no other fertile female had yet been hatched. When the queen could no longer bear, their race was doomed. And yet their hope lay in the knowledge that surely the more eggs she bore, the greater the chance of finding another fertile layer must be. Thus her sorrow . . . for the more she bore, the shorter her span as her body slowly, inexorably, gave out. Guthul knew that in his lifetime the ancient battle might well be lost, and his race gone.

Tricatada looked up. "How skillfully have you woven our plans?"

"So skillfully that, I believe, our past foe and current ally has no inkling of our true intent. We are a true mating, you and I," Guthul told her.

"The humans believe our forces intertwined, and yet we dominate with less than a third of our corps engaged."

"Only a third?"

Guthul thrilled to hear his queen suck her breath in with pleasure. It stirred him, made him think of things other than war to quicken his pulse. "As you ordered, it has been done."

"And the council backs me in full agreement." Tricatada rattled her carapaces. "They dare not cross me otherwise. I am the only hope."

Unspoken was the threat that she might withhold laying if the council crossed her. It was a ploy she had told Guthul she might use. The Thrakian League was united behind her because it had no choice. No other faction had a fertile queen it might bring forth to unseat her, and it would take nothing less to break her rule now.

The queen stood up again and looked down on him. "But you have not been entirely successful, General."

He brought his mask into humble statement. "No, my queen, I have not. The commander called Storm survived our clumsy attack. But I do not think it likely that he alone can sway the Triad Throne or the Dominion even if he should guess the truth. They are not like us. No one being can encompass the power and authority we do."

Tricatada paused in the process of stroking her flank. "Think you not? I think, my warrior, you had best turn your talents to finding that one known as Colin of the Blue Wheel. Our sources tell us that Pepys is mounting a search and rescue for that one. It will involve Storm. I do not like the implications. The Walkers have impeded our norcite mining long enough. He is bound to, if he has not already, discover that which we do not want known. If Colin is to be found, I want it to be by us."

Guthul bowed. "Yes, my queen." He knew an order when he heard one. Whatever misgivings he had about the assignment, he put them aside.

Tricatada paused. "Try to put K'rok into the detail. The Milot is a capable being and we have found him useful in the past."

"As you command." Guthul stopped. Without seeming to, he changed the projection of his mask slightly, dominating and courageous. He could no longer ignore the scent she had begun to secrete. He had been taken from her side for too long and though no Thraks claimed monogamy, he was her prime mate and thought to remind her of it. "The defense lines have been drawn, my queen. When the Ashfarel fall upon us this time, it will be the foreign bodies who protect us. The human realm from the Outward Bounds to the Dominion to the Triad Throne itself will be sacrificed to ensure your survival. And while they fight and die, the swarm will carry us far beyond their reach. I, Guthul, pledge this to you. We shall triumph."

Tricatada's throaty reply was nearly inaudible, sensually drowned by her call to mating. With a cry of his own, Gu-

thul mounted her, and she spread her wings over the two
of them as they answered a more primitive call to the survival of the species.

When Guthul left her, she lay upon her nesting, deep in
sleep, exhausted, the musky scent of their mating pervading
her chambers. She did not rouse when the chamberlain
slipped in to leave the evening meal. It would not have
mattered to her even had she been aware, for the chamberlain was a male drone, and drones by their very nature
were inferior and inconsequential. The drone did his duties
quietly, so as not to awaken the queen. As Thraks go, he
was far more graceful than the warriors, unhampered by
the almost metallic shielding of their carapaces and chiton.

When he should have left, he paused by the nest of the
queen. Her mating scent thrilled him as well. He was insig-
nificant, a nothing, his matings confined to the inconsequential drones of his caste, but he found himself irrevocably
aroused by his queen. In an act which would mean nothing
less than the annihilation of his familial nest if it were ever
discovered, the drone mounted the queen and sated himself
on her unconscious body. Tricatada moaned and thrashed
in dreamy awareness, for the drone's member was also unhampered by the body armor of a warrior Thraks and
pierced her with far more strength. As she responded to
his mating, the drone spent himself hastily and withdrew,
knowing that he had committed the most heinous sin one
of his caste could. In haste he fled the chambers, his mask
concealing his shame.

CHAPTER 17

His life was peeled away from him layer by layer, sometimes poignant and sometimes sweet, like the skin of an onion, but always painful. He hung onto his existence tenaciously, unwilling to let it go no matter how painful. No doubt the Ash-farel observed this about him as much as they did the veinings and ganglia they traced. He had no way of knowing their reaction to his humanness, but their surgical skill he could attest to in that he still lived at all.

Strange to be alive and yet disembodied, to search for comfort and find only more agony, to look for death and see instead the myriad points of his soul that were connected to others. He brushed the consciousness of Jack's armor and then Jack himself, emperors and knaves, and the shadowy glint of Amber's thoughts, nothing he could anchor himself to and yet interwoven strongly throughout himself. He found he could not pray to die, that to let go now would cause a vast unweaving of a pattern he couldn't yet admire. So he clung to the strands of his life and his soul with all the feeble weakness he could muster.

It must have been enough. He slowly became aware that the Ash-farel were putting him back together. The vastly separated stars of his life and thought rushed close and connected again. No longer was he strewn against the dark threshold of his own death.

He awoke to greater pain than he had ever known, to a body that was his and yet not his. The Ash-farel had taken him apart and put him back together. But for all their skill, they had not done it correctly.

CHAPTER 18

"I heard the emperor was taking appointments for audiences again." A frail, wispy white-haired man stood at the palace viewscreen. He shifted his weight nervously from one foot to the other. "I need to talk with him as soon as possible." His release from the Green Shirt lab kept him on edge, moving, fearful of being found. He'd been told to seek out the Minister of War, but to give his message in person.

An officious looking woman stared back at him. "State your name, Church ranking, and affiliation."

"Church? I—" the being stammered to a halt.

"You're not a Walker?"

"Why, no, I . . . I'm a xenobiologist," the man said, with the shreds of his dignity.

"I'm sorry," the hawk-nosed woman told him. "The audience chambers are being opened to Walkers only."

"But I—"

"I'm sorry," she repeated icily. "Strike negotiations must take precedence. Surely you understand that. Public audiences will be opening once the general strike has been settled."

"I *must* talk with Baadluster," Mierdan insisted. "I have something important to tell him that I cannot submit by com line. There must be something you can do—tell him—"

The woman had been seated on-screen. Now she got to her feet, and he knew instantly he'd been pleading with the wrong person as she came out from behind the shelter of her console. Not only was she massive, but the crude cross that vibrated with irritation on her heaving breast identified her as a Walker herself. "I've called for palace security," she told him. "I suggest you leave before they respond."

Mierdan turned and fled. He had no desire to be detained by the World Police. The street beyond the palace gates remained open and quiet. He paused. Having come this far. . . . He turned back, brushing at the front of his rather seedy clothing. His old security clearance had gotten him this far. Despite his reedy stature and frail nerve, he was not inclined to give up this easily. His lab work had been poorly funded and ill-received, but he had information which could change the entire structure of the Thrakian alliance. The rioting over St. Colin's disappearance aside, nothing could be more important than this, but he had to tell the minister face to face. The Thraks had infiltrated Malthen too thoroughly. With the loss of the countess, his benefactors had been thrown into chaotic inaction. Mierdan could wait no longer.

The sound of Thrakian chittering brought him to a halt and then a dash into the greenery bordering the grounds. His skin prickled with fear and he ground his teeth to keep them from chattering and to hold back the bile in his throat. He'd spent too many years as a Thrakian captive to lose his freedom now. He listened to them pass. He caught a little sense of their communication. The Walker situation was being closely watched. But these were warrior Thraks and most of their conversation was of eagerness to fight and wondering when they would be unleashed to do so. Mierdan found the warrior Thraks muscle-bound and dull, single-minded. The only warrior Thraks of any subtlety and guile the man had ever known had been Guthul. Guthul, he sensed, could easily have been a diplomatic Thraks as well.

When the aliens had passed, Mierdan crawled out on stomach and pointed elbows, to see where he had brought himself. He did not recognize the outbuildings or the massive, fire-walled stadium beyond but he knew he had to be near the barracks for the Dominion Knights. To be caught here might well cost him his life, if the Thraks did not get hold of him first. Mierdan scurried back into the foliage.

Voices carried, human voices. The tiny man ducked his face down and hoped that his thatch of now-white hair remained unseen among the greenery.

"That's done, then," growled a coarse voice. "Fitted for th' suit and backed as well as you can be, Commander."

The second voice was milder in tenor but it drew Mierdan's attention immediately. He strained against the impulse to look up, to match gazes with the owner of that voice. "K'rok surprised me."

"I'd give my left nut to know why queenie let him off the hook so's he could go with you, other than to spy."

"Me, too. K'rok has never been wholly loyal to his Thrakian host, but neither can I count on an alliance with him. I'll have Rawlins and Amber with me."

Mierdan edged his chin up over a leafy branch. He could clearly see the two men who spoke and he muffled his shock with a trembling hand. He knew he'd recognized that voice—he could not forget the man who'd saved his life and brought him home alive from Klaktut—but the man had been captured by Pepys as a traitor. What miracle was this?

The Knight's voice cut through his confusion. "I don't want Amber along."

Lassaday brayed in response, then said, "You won't be keepin' that one behind! Not anymore."

"She deserves better, Sarge. Pepys is letting me go after Colin—but I haven't been reinstated and I may not be, regardless of what he says. I'm a traitor and when the emperor has no further use for me, I won't have much of a future."

"You're no deserter, Commander," answered Lassaday with conviction.

Mierdan's mouth hurt from the pressure of his hand across it. He watched the two men continue walking, taking them out of ear and eyeshot. His information was privileged, yet no one would hear him . . . and he could think of no one else who would put it to better use than Commander Storm. Yet Mierdan was confused by the apparent resurrection and by the words "traitor" and "deserter." He brushed hesitation aside and stood up. Leaves tangled in his wispy hair.

A shadow darker than those of tree and limb fell across him. Mierdan looked up and shrank aside as the massive battle armor dwarfed him. He could not read what manner of face was behind the visor as the right gauntlet reached out and engulfed his shoulder.

"What you be doing here, little man?"

Mierdan's newfound resolve dried in his throat. "Storm," he got out. "I must see Commander Storm."

The gauntlet closed on his shoulder until bone and cartilage moved in protest and flesh pulped into bruises. "What say you?"

"I must find Commander Storm!" Mierdan's voice went falsetto as the gauntlet drew him up on his toes, dangling in pain. In sudden panic, he twisted loose, the fabric covering his shoulder tearing and he sprinted away, darting out of sight and through the palace gates. The hulking figure in battle armor looked after him, suit cameras taking a record of each and every step.

Mierdan reached dubious sanctuary in under-Malthen and closed his door behind him, panting with nervous energy. His shoulder twinged with every breath or movement, yet he could tell from gingerly testing it that nothing had been broken or permanently damaged. Those suits were powerful! With only a little more effort from the wearer, he would have been pulverized.

It was a long time after his heart and pulse calmed before he moved away from the door and crossed the shabby room where the Green Shirts had secreted him and his work. What use they'd have for him now, he did not know. His whole world had gone topsy-turvy once again. He did not know whom to trust. He put no stock in the expediency of politics.

He began to clean up the tiny lab, destroying tapes and disks as he went. His work was done, engraved indelibly in his memory. He would not leave evidence for others to misuse. He worked feverishly, heedless of the pain in his shoulder or of the growing hunger in his stomach. When done, he would destroy the lab and flee, to think about what he knew and decide what it was best to do with the information. He would be a hunted man, not only by the Green Shirts who would think he had betrayed them, but by the Thraks who wanted him back desperately. He would have to plan well.

Mierdan never heard his door being forced, but when the overhead lights blacked out, he turned to look—and saw the colossal being occupying the building, eclipsing the lights with its armored bulk.

The being reached up and took off its helmet. The biologist saw the furred and ursine face of a Milot. His heart sank. He knew of only one Milot who served both the Thrakian League and the Dominion Knights.

The being smiled widely, fangs glinting. "I be following you, little man. Now what is being so important you must talk to Commander Storm?"

His tongue clove to the roof of his mouth. Mierdan backed away, blinking frantically. The debris underfoot crunched. "I—I have information for him," he finally managed.

"Only for Jack?" the Milot swung about, looking the building over. He hunkered down in the battle armor, bringing his massive face level with Mierdan's. "Let's not be fooling one another, little man. I be K'rok and you be Mierdan. My queen wants you back very badly."

"I—I'm not property! I'm a f-free man!"

"And a frightened one." The Milot did not move. "I be telling you what few know. I also am free, though my queen would have my head and the grubs would feed off my body if she be knowing I say this. You came to find Storm. He is in great trouble now. But tell me your message and I will be giving it to him."

"And then you'll go?"

K'rok nodded his shaggy head affirmatively.

Mierdan stood in frightened shock a moment longer. Then, as K'rok's gauntleted hand came up, the pain of his shoulder decided him. The words bolted out of him. "It's about the norcite. Storm knows a little—he knows I've been working on the problem. You tell him. I lived among the Thraks. The grubs and drones are different from the others. The carapaces, the chiton, are much softer and flexible. I know why the Thraks covet the norcite. For a while we thought they might use a solution to coat themselves, like enamel, but that's not it. But Jack's old armor is coated with norcite and there were times when he was almost sure Thraks couldn't see him. Well, they could, but didn't."

"Slow down," K'rok growled.

Mierdan took a gulping breath. Then, "It's like this. They grind the ore to powder and ingest it. That greatly strengthens the armor. The lesser castes don't do it—it's not necessary. So when norcite is sensed in the composition of another—the Thraks don't see the way we do—they think they're sensing another Thraks. But now they know the enemy is using norcite, too, so they take that into account. But what they don't know is that norcite is affecting them adversely. Tell Jack norcite is the answer." Mierdan slowed to a halt. He clouded his last words deliberately, unwilling to give the Milot all his information. But Storm was savvy and would make the connection. The little man gave a quivery smile in relief.

"And that is being all?"

"Yes. Can you remember that?"

"Oh, yes." The Milot rose and shook himself. The Flexalinks gave a shimmering dance in the lights. "I be remembering all of this very well. And you?"

"I destroyed my records."

"Good." The Milot replaced his helmet. "I am sorry, little man." He reached out. Mierdan had a second to let out a terrified squeak, then his head cracked audibly and he went limp in K'rok's hands. He held the body until he was sure death had come, then he lowered it gently to the lab floor. The armor obscured the emotion in his voice. "No one is being entirely free," he said. "They would hound you to your death. Now you are being beyond them." With deliberate grace, he stepped over the body and left the shabby laboratory.

CHAPTER 19

Pepys shrugged on his red and gold threaded robes with great difficulty. The floor to ceiling com screen was filled with the visage of his caller and he had ordered his dressers to leave so that he might speak in private. The Thrakian queen looked at him with an amused glint in her faceted eyes. He wondered if she thought he put on body armor and found it amusing. His hair crackled in annoyance as he ran a hand through it.

"I do not threaten well, if at all," he told her. There was a long pause for transmittal during which he changed his slippers for dress boots.

Then, "It is not a threat. It is a promise. We have invested much in our alliance. You are on the brink of . . . internal warfare. We intend to step in before the Dominion decides that it has the option to do the same."

Fury ignited in him, burning deep in his stomach like a suddenly flaring ember. He fisted his hand. "I will declare the alliance at an end."

Could a Thraks laugh? Her gloriously colored blue and gold chitin appeared to shake. "How, Pepys? We are entangled among you. Your armor is our armor—to separate us will leave us both exposed to the Ash-farel. Put your nest in order before you tear us all down. We shall be close, waiting." Tricatada tilted her head. Her throat leather fluttered, and her mask closed into an expression of beauty and command. The screen went gray.

Pepys fastened his overrobes with shaking hands. The Dominion was to be his and his alone. Even if Storm somehow managed to find Colin and return with him, forcing Pepys to be true to his word and step down, the Dominion awaited him. Tricatada hinted at betrayal and conquest under the cloak of martial law. He would find a way to stave her off. Today's audience was only the first in a series of steps. Much depended on Storm and if the mind block Pepys had instituted was finally wearing off, he would be the weapon Pepys needed—when Storm was out of Vandover's range.

Pepys finished his outfitting. *I'll give you your saint, friend, and a kingdom beyond that. Pray God you'll never have to head it.* With a shrug, he signaled for his ministers and went out to meet the humble Walkers who threatened to topple his reign.

Jack woke with the bitter taste of *mordil* still on his tongue, the empty vial clenched in his hand. He released his grip gingerly and let the vial drop. He had beaten the night. His dreams and memories were still his own this morning. With a powerful stretch, he eased his muscles into waking and got up. His dress uniform hung on a stretcher, reminding him that Pepys was putting him on display.

His imprint slipped over him from time to time, leaving him with annoying gaps of time, and nighttime was the worst. There were other drugs he could use to sleep, but *mordil* was the least destructive. It was worth it if he could face himself in the mirror and remember his family. The blackouts worried him less and less—the memories always came back. There was only the worry that he might commit a fatal mistake with Pepys or Vandover—and he was more likely to do that as himself than as his imprint. He was not supposed to remember the years of intrigue and bad faith.

Nor was he expected to remember that Pepys had promised to step down if he found Colin With a wry smile, Jack made his way to the refresher. As he passed through the apartment, he caught a bare hint of perfume and stopped to inhale it.

Had Amber been here again while he slept? He cast about, trying to catch the perfume again, wondering if he'd only imagined it. Then, having grasped nothing, he continued to the refresher. He had not seen Amber for several days, though Lassaday told him she'd come in for a suit fitting. He would arouse suspicion if he sought her out.

He stepped into the shower and let it beat down on his neck and shoulders, hammering out tense muscles. He walked a razor's edge with Amber's life and knew it, and did not know how to tell her he knew it. There were too many others with too much at stake listening to every word he might say to her. He could only hope that Amber could take care of herself, as she always had. He stood in the shower until the fog in the stall enveloped him.

Vandover and Pepys wanted a tame act they could trot before the Walkers to placate them. Jack did not know the Walker organization well save for Colin, Jonathan, and Denaro, and Colin's harsh-faced secretary, Margaret—but he knew about the turmoil within the organization and that Colin's amenable philosophy had always been in danger. The Walkers would not settle for the crumbs Pepys was hoping to toss them. Jack wanted to be there, if for no other reason than that. The order had been, no suits. If Jack had been commanding, it would have been, no Thraks. Pepys would be doing well to keep the lid on.

This would be Jack's resurrection. The Triad Throne had declared him dead and buried, after all, months before tracking him down and bringing him back as a traitor and deserter. It wouldn't do to be late.

Anticipating action at last, after weeks of imprisonment, he put his dress uniform on.

Amber chose a dress that would not reveal her bruises, though her chapped and swollen lips she would have to disguise. She watched herself as she crossed the room to finish dressing. She moved like a cheap and crudely assembled doll. Amber paused, caught in the mesh of her own stare and the thoughts it precipitated.

She should tell Jack. She knew the gentlemanly creed that was at the core of the man she'd loved—it was still there. The imprint had probably made him stronger than ever. Jack would kill Vandover, remembering her or not. But there would be retribution and she would never ask Jack to give his life up for her justice. And there was always the chance that Jack would not be fast enough to kill Baadluster before he ordered her to kill Jack.

She smeared her thumb over her lips, harshly, savagely, as if assessing how much pain remained in them. It was just her flesh, after all. Just flesh. Amber turned away then, unable to meet the look in her own eyes. Vandover had spilled his foul, black seed in her mind as well and she could feel it growing there. He had chains for her very thoughts—and would not hesitate to use them.

She finished her hair and makeup quickly, unable to meet the accusation in her eyes. She'd let him do it. But no, she'd fought and been beaten. There was nothing she could have done. Was there? *Was there?*

A sound at her door kept the tears from welling in her eyes. She signaled it open and stood quickly, expecting to see Jack standing there, ready to escort her to the audience, and she secured the last of her knives in her gloves. "Jack, you're early—" Her words ground to a halt as Baadluster filled the portal.

He wore slate today, and a short overrobe that showed his whippet lean body. He looked, she thought, like one of the dark poisonous blades she had just hidden in her wrist sheath. He showed his teeth in a smile. "Milady," he said, in that tone that oozed other meanings into what he said. *Whore,* she thought. *He always means whore when he says that . . . and now he is right.* "You were expecting someone else?"

"Old habits die hard," Amber bit off. "What do you want?" She kept distance between them.

"Only the pleasure of your accompanying me to the hall. Pepys will be seated shortly."

"I can find my way there alone."

"Of a surety. But there is something I wish to say to you first." And he halved the distance.

Her pulse skidded. "I've already done a job for you."

"Amber, Amber. You don't think I wasted all that money and those years in training for one name and one name alone, do you? That was just a demonstration for you and some of my opponents. A little warning that disobedience is futile." His lips thinned. "Come here, Amber."

Nausea rocked her stomach. She stepped toward him. The room had gone suddenly cold. "Not Jack," she protested.

"No, no. Not Jack. Jack has to find St. Colin and, if we're very lucky, bring home the secrets of the Ash-farel." He crooked his finger. "Closer, milady. I know your aversion to security systems and that you have this room well sealed, but some things are meant to be whispered."

*　　*　　*

The hall looked resplendent. Laser holograms filled the domed roof with a silvery net of planets and stars depicting the worlds that mankind had touched. Banners rippled in the current of an unseen breeze. Voices filled the air, muted and multitudinous. Anyone and everyone who could possibly gain entrance had. They had not minded the wait since early dawn nor the shuffle through the weapons net for clearance nor even the near stifling crowding of the audience floor. All they had to do was stretch their necks and look upward, where the stars roamed freely above them.

A hush fell over the crowd as Pepys entered from the private chambers to the rear and took his place on the stage throne. A small, golden android came to the fore and cried out, "Oyez, oyez, his right honorable majesty, Emperor Pepys, sits in court to address the suits and grievances being brought before him. All hail Emperor Pepys."

As the crowd responded, the Minister of War emerged and took his shadowy place to the right of the throne. Pepys turned and their gazes met. Vandover had been late, too late to discuss last minute details in the private chambers, so late that Pepys had even wondered if his minister would be attending him. As the emperor studied him now, he saw a few blonde hairs trailing upon the minister's black vest. His attention immediately flicked back to the hall, but he could not see Amber among the throng. He did see Jack, to the left, his dress uniform bare of rank and honor, at attention.

Worriedly, Pepys turned his focus back to the ceremony at hand. He knew Baadluster intended to dispose of the girl soon. Looking at the crush of people before the dais, he wondered how and when Vandover would terminate her. An assassin could move through such a crowd easily. He got to his feet. The immense hall full of people fell to a hush.

"Good people. This is the first time the audience hall has been open since the known disappearance of Colin of the Blue Wheel, my friend and adviser, as well as the prelate of the Walker religion. Many of you have come to petition me to seek for him, unaware of the exhaustive search we have been conducting in conjunction with the Dominion and the Thrakian League. While his whereabouts are not certain, we do have some idea of where he intended to go when he disappeared.

It is my sad duty to inform you that he is not lost, he has been taken, in all probability, by the Ash-farel." Pepys paused dramatically, the vidscreens about the hall reflecting the vivid color of his green eyes in close-up. He listened to the gasps and cries of his distressed audience. His gaze lingered on the stern visage of Margaret, Colin's longtime secretary, who had helped him arrange this event. She stood in the cordoned off area before the platform along with others—Dominion senators, Walker ministers, ambassadors—who had specific permission to question him along with the different reporters and recorders. She showed no surprise on her hawklike face. He was only confirming what she was already privy to.

"I do not know why Colin placed himself in such jeopardy. It is our feeling that he hoped to treat with an enemy that has proven itself inscrutable as well as invincible. That would have been much like my old friend, to place the common good before his own welfare. But the fact remains that he is needed and wanted here, and if we can return him, we will!" Another pause, this one heralded by shouts and ovations. As he looked around, gauging the reaction, he saw Amber, in an emerald dress echoing the color of his eyes, edging closer. As if in response, Jack's head turned as well, to watch her.

There was a spate of questions being shouted at him from the cordoned off section. He put his hands out palms up to quiet them. "Military response," he said, "would prove futile. Our intelligence sources have not yet been able to pinpoint the sectors of space our enemy calls home. We cannot predict when or from where they will attack. We do feel that they have the capabilities to mount massive warships and leave them cruising at large, to take whatever opportunity they can to strike at us. This random pattern increases their invincibility as well as our vulnerability."

Pepys halted. He reached for the goblet on the side table and took a sip of water to clear his drying throat. Vandover looked up at him through flat black eyes and smiled bleakly. The emperor nodded at him.

"My capable Minister of War, Vandover Baadluster, however, has defended us most ably. Within our alliance, we have begun to mount a defensive line, a stellar demarcation and thus far, we have been able to turn the Ash-farel away along that front." *Hopeful lies,* Pepys thought, *but no one here with the information or the authority to contradict him.*

"As for Colin, myself and my advisers have concluded that a small, handpicked unit will be the most effective way to search for him. To that end, I have conducted a search of my own for the man to lead that unit. You have all heard the rumors and now it is time to set them to rest.

"About a year and a half ago, it was my sad duty to officiate at a funeral for an officer who had given much to our throne. Imagine my shock when information came to me indicating that this officer had not died, his body unrecoverable on a faraway world, but had instead deserted his command. We verified our intelligences and went in search of this officer. I brought him back with me for the sole purpose of locating Colin of the Blue Wheel and vindicating his desertion." Pepys looked to Jack and found Jack's attention already upon him. The rock steadiness of the man unnerved Pepys slightly. What confidence, to stand among a crowd which might well stone him to death for his betrayal. He motioned for Jack to join him on the dais.

There was a murmur of unrest, growing in volume, as Jack mounted the stage and came to parade rest to Pepys' left. "Ladies and gentleman, the last living Knight of the Sand Wars, Commander Jack Storm."

Pepys waited quietly through the commotion that followed, listening to the shouts and demands and half-scattered applause, timing his remarks to follow. After a few moments, he signaled his speaker and held up his hands for silence as the android called for it.

"Commander Storm is no stranger to controversy," Pepys said. "But I have found in him a man who has always done as he believes is his duty. He has undertaken trials for me that would have broken a lesser officer. His courage and ability to think independently under fire are qualities that cannot be forced upon a man. He is the only officer I can think of who has a chance of going after Colin and bringing him home, if he is still alive."

"He has asked me for this opportunity to vindicate himself against the charges of deserter and traitor." Pepys hesitated. "I have decided to give him this chance. Finding St. Colin is a challenge, and I have the man to meet it." He stepped back, leaving Jack alone to face the audience. "Ladies and gentleman, I give you Commander Storm." He returned to his throne.

There was a stunned silence, then a sudden clamor as reporters pressed close to hurl their questions at him. Jack did not turn to look after Pepys. He had been half-expecting such drama from the emperor. He pointed at an individual and prepared to field his question.

"Commander Storm, why did you leave your post? Was it cowardice?"

The vidscreens posted about the hall seemed to echo the question in the sudden silence. Jack wet his lips. He saw Amber edge into the cordoned area and stand at Margaret's elbow. The Walker secretary scarcely seemed to notice her.

He looked out. "Rather than answer individual questions, I would like to make a statement at this time. I left my command under Pepys because I felt the Thrakian alliance had compromised the security of the Dominion and the Triad Throne. I was wrong to do so. It was not my duty to question the decision." Jack paused again. He could feel Baadluster's stare on him, as well as that of Pepys. They had discussed this position with him and he did not know whether he betrayed his true self or not. "I took it upon myself to search out the nature of this new enemy, the Ash-farel. Emperor Pepys has taken this into account, along with my service record, and decided that I would be the best man to undertake this assignment. I'm not sure he's right—but I welcome the opportunity to prove myself a Knight worthy of the rank. Thank you."

Furor broke out as he stepped back to flank Pepys. The emperor gave him a bemused smile. Baadluster remained expressionless. Out of range of the speaker, Pepys said softly, "Now I know why I picked you for the job."

But the audience was not pleased. Accusations and questions were hurled at them until Jack was forced to step forward and say, "No comment." His silence drove them to further displays of their displeasure until Margaret approached the edge of the platform. Then the hall fell quiet.

"We will not," she said, and the speaker carried her firm

voice to the farthest corners of the chamber, "be placated by you. Your promises are as empty as most of the bellies on Malthen. You are an emperor who refuses to hear or represent our will and then tries to foist a traitor on us as a savior. It's not good enough and we won't stand for it. You no longer have a mandate to rule us, Pepys."

Jack searched the crowd and saw his fellow Knights moving quietly forward to form a bastion between the platform and the audience.

Pepys stood again. "We are at war with an enemy that threatens to destroy us utterly. We cannot win that war if we are divided against ourselves!"

"That is a choice you've made." Margaret pointed at him. She looked like a long-ago prophetess. "We are not divided against *you*."

The aureole of his frizzed red hair wavered as he moved to the very edge of the dais to meet the Walker's tall, commanding figure. "You threaten civil war. Officers, remove this woman."

Jack looked at Amber, standing in Margaret's wake. Vandover said something inaudible, and Amber's attention snapped toward him. Then, with a tiny frown, she turned her gaze on Pepys.

The emperor let out a sharp cry. He swayed as the crowd, sensing something was wrong, began to scream.

Only Jack was close enough to catch him as the man went down.

CHAPTER 20

Other forces were in motion even before Jack reached for his falling sovereign. He could see the ripple of movement throughout the immense hall. As he put out his arms to catch Pepys, he called out sharply. "Amber! Get clear!"

Vandover seemed like a puff of charcoal smoke as he turned and bolted for the exit behind the dais. Pepys hit Jack's embrace. Ribbons of crimson streamed from his ears and nose and one vermilion drop from his eye etched a tearlike path down his cheek. Amid the screams and jostling, Jack could hear the Knights and then the WP clearing the room, but his keen ears heard more—the sound of armed conflict in the hallways.

K'rok and his Thraks emerged at the portal, his armor streaked with smoke stains. The Thrakian Knights wore Enduros rather than the full battle armor, though they did have modified suits. The bracers and adapted headgear they wore now made them look like some kind of mutated cyborg. The immense Milot plowed to a halt.

"See this area is being secured," he ordered. The Thraks fanned out, pushing the last of the crowd out, oblivious to the hysteria around them.

Pepys moaned as Jack lowered him carefully to the dais. K'rok loomed over them.

"Medical is en route, but the palace is being overrun. The Walkers came with an army, eh. What happened?"

"I don't know." Jack checked the emperor's pulse. It was slow and erratic, but the man still breathed laboriously. He pulled aside the heavy imperial robes to give what ease he could. "He just collapsed." He heard something at his back and saw Amber standing there. "Are you all right?"

"Yes. Who would have thought Margaret could set off a revolution?"

"More likely she just gave a signal." He turned his attention back to the emperor. The man's hand was slack in his and the flesh was growing cooler by the moment. "K'rok, where's medical?"

The Milot swiveled. "The corridors up here have been sealed off. They're fighting their way through. Jack, I am getting reports that the airports and space berths have been taken."

"The streets of Malthen are running with blood," Amber said tonelessly. Jack turned quickly to her but could read nothing in her expression.

"Who's in control?"

"For the moment," Vandover said smoothly, as he returned from the secured privacy chambers to the stage's rear, "it appears no one is. I'm in charge as long as the emperor is incapacitated, but the Triad Throne is under siege." He looked at Amber and Jack. "I've just received word that the Thrakian League is closing in. They state that, as allies, they have no choice but to impose martial law in Pepys' name."

"Legal invasion," Jack muttered. He stared down at the man on the dais who fought for every breath. "You son of a bitch."

"Jack," said Amber softly, warningly.

He looked up and saw K'rok with his gauntlets leveled on him. Jack smiled. "Don't worry. He's either going to make it or not without my help."

The Milot in battle armor shifted away. By the time he reached the hall's doors, he was in full stride, the floor ringing under every strike of the Flexalink boots. As he reached the corridor, fire flash illuminated him for a moment as eerily as if he'd been struck by lightning. The boom and yells and noise of return fire echoed in the empty hall.

Then K'rok reappeared, medical teams streaming in in his wake. Jack let go of Pepys' cool hand and stood back to let them do their work.

Amber had changed from her gown to a jumpsuit of somber brown, a subtle resonance of the color of her eyes. She stood in the hospital wing, chewing a ragged edge of nail off one fingertip. She looked over at Jack. "If you were the man you're supposed to be," she said, "this wouldn't have happened."

"I'm not responsible for an aneurysm."

"No. Of course not." She looked smartly away.

Jack felt the edge of her scorn and anger. He also felt certain that he had given himself away before Vandover in the heat of the moment, but the minister had said little to him once Pepys had gotten out of surgery, the bleeding halted and his condition stabilized. The Triad Throne was under attack within and without and Baadluster had no time for him. Jack's gaze ran over the obsidite walls. He loathed infirmaries, spent as little time in them as possible and yet it seemed as if recently all his days had been spent here. He paced away from Amber. It suddenly seemed necessary to be somewhere, anywhere, else.

With no access to the port where the worst fighting was centered, it would be impossible to get off-planet. Intelligence reports seemed to indicate that even Walker factions were splintered—and getting off world to find Colin would depend on who had control of the port. The Thraks' heaviest concentration was being directed there and Vandover's latest reports seemed to indicate the aliens were gaining ground. But the port was built like a fort, made to withstand the backlash of spacing vehicles . . . squat and solid, damn near unconquerable. It would be a long battle.

Colin was running out of time. Jack could not wait for the tide to turn in a long, drawn out civil war. He had to get off-planet and get off now. He sensed it in every fiber of his being. In all probability, Pepys and Baadluster, too, were playing a game of power far beyond his expectations. The resulting struggles would leave the worlds of mankind open to the Ash-farel. Nothing would survive.

What had been a personal quest for truth and friendship now became something more, a responsibility he was not sure he could shoulder, but knew he had to try.

The care unit door opened and a nurse came through, looking for Jack. He saw Amber drop back fluidly, one hand going to her opposite wrist, as she took up a lethal stance just behind the nurse's shoulder. He had only a split second to wonder what she was doing when the frowning nurse spoke.

"Are you Commander Storm?"

"Yes."

"Good. He's conscious though not entirely lucid, but he refuses to rest until he's spoken with you." The technician hesitated. "Understand that the hemorrhaging has had strokelike aftereffects. He's difficult to understand and he's very weak."

Amber had relaxed her stance. "But he is alive," she asked softly.

"Oh, yes. Very much so." The nurse blocked Amber as she started to follow after Jack. "I'm sorry. Just the commander right now. He's too weak to have visitors."

Amber made a wry face at Jack and let him pass.

The emperor looked like a crumpled up version of himself, the crèche and tubing obscuring all of his body except for his face and hair. When Jack bent near to speak to the man, he noticed for the first time streaks of gray among the fiery red, and that the electricity had gone, leaving the fine strands limp upon the pillow bracing his head. His face had gone slack, and the left side was drawn and twisted, letting drool escape from the corner of his mouth. Jack leaned close, feeling mixed emotions, as he came to the fallen emperor's side.

Pepys' eyes flew open. He stared for a moment, unseeing, then focused on Jack. "Storm," he said, and his mouth and tongue seemed incapable of speaking. Then, with visible effort, he repeated Jack's name.

"Yes."

"What is happening. They won't tell me." Each word took a lifetime. Each breath was a pant.

Jack put his hand on Pepys' shoulder to calm him. "The Thraks have pulled in."

"Shit." The emperor closed his eyes briefly. He seemed to drift, then he opened them and looked back at Jack. "You must remember who you are. Take command from K'rok. Use the Knights. Fight your way out. Fight the Thraks and find Colin." Spent, the man lapsed into pants. Jack waited until his breathing eased.

He smiled briefly. "Is that an order?"

"It . . . is."

"I owe you no allegiance, highness. I swore my oath elsewhere. But I will find Colin and then we'll come to terms with who is to sit the Triad Throne.''

Pepys' eyes widened, then he nodded wearily, and gave a shuffling laugh. "I . . . should have known," he said.

"You should have." Jack straightened. "And you never had to order me to fight Thraks.''

Amber was not waiting for him when he left the care unit. The halls of the palace had been cleared of the insurgents, but the obsidite walls showed the scarring of the battle as he made his way past them. Rawlins was waiting for him at the barracks.

He saluted him. "Captain. Emperor Pepys has reinstated me and given me orders that nothing, repeat, *nothing* is to stand in the way of completing our mission.''

The fair-haired officer snapped off a return salute. "I'm waiting for orders, sir.''

Amber found Vandover in the war room, surrounded by a com net not unlike the sophisticated one Pepys used. Nervously, she combed her hair away from the side of her face as she waited for his attention.

Finally, Vandover swung about in his chair to glare at her. "You failed," he said flatly.

She had not known who her target had been until he'd said that final word from the dais, speaking an edict of death. But she could no more have halted her execution of the act than stopped breathing. Jack had thrown her off when he'd ordered her to get out of harm's way, but by then she was certain the damage had been done to Pepys as she'd seen him collapse in Jack's arms. She gave Baadluster a humorless laugh. "I did my best.''

"That I doubt. But the fact remains that it may be good enough. He is incapacitated. I sit where I wish to sit. And no one is the wiser that it was not a natural occurrence.''

Amber did not counter him. She'd overheard the technicians talking while Jack was in with Pepys. The aneurysm had not shown on the emperor's scans during his annual physical and there was some suspicion. But nothing could be proved. She kept her silence.

Vandover gestured. "Jack is giving orders. I'm anticipating that the search for St. Colin will still be launched. You, my dear, are among the volunteers. Hadn't you better ready yourself?"

Her nerve broke and she quailed inwardly. She could feel her skin go pale. "Don't make me go with him."

Vandover's lips tightened. "Milady, you promised him. And me."

The minister would trigger her against Jack. She knew it. She shut her eyes tightly. "I'll do anything," she said. The words stuck in her throat. Vandover made no response and she wondered if he had heard, so she repeated herself. "Anything. But don't make me go with Jack."

The lank and ugly man threw his head back to laugh. When he finished, he smiled coldly at her. "Amber, you keep underestimating yourself. You have a great deal of work yet to do for me. I need Jack alive and you're the best way I have of keeping him safe. Now go get ready."

Almost out of reach of the man, she turned to flee. He caught her wrist at the last second and pulled her roughly to him. The wires and cables of the com net twisted about her, biting at her bare arms.

"And you should remember that I enjoy what I take much more than what I am given," he told her as he felt himself growing hard.

She tried not to struggle, but could not help it as he began to punish her flesh for her disobedience.

CHAPTER 21

"And those are the options as I see it," Jack said quietly to the people assembled before him. The barracks fell silent. He put a hand to his forehead and wiped the sweat off. The Malthen season was blazingly hot. The air conditioners were failing, as warfare affected all of the utility services where guerrilla action took its toll. The central wings of the palace had backup solars and generators, of course, but the barracks lay on the outer grounds. He had recircuited some of his available power to create white noise barriers and sound buffers to override the emperor's security equipment. Even as he wiped his hand on his trousers to dry it, the machinery sputtered and the lukewarm air circulating shut off.

"Jeez-a-mighty," Lassaday said, getting to his feet. "I'm going to have t'kick a door open, Commander."

"Not just yet, Sergeant," Jack told him. His mind wavered. Was he going to lose it again, just when he needed to be most steady? He could still achieve what he had to, but this one step forward, two steps backward progress would hinder dangerously what he had to attend to now. "Are we agreed on this? There'll be no coming back if we don't succeed in what we set out to do." He did not need to add that there might be nothing to come back to. If the Thraks broke the backs of the remaining Knights and Pepys' troops, Malthen might well become *sand*. If not, the resultant destruction would bring the world shields down, leaving them vulnerable to the Ash-farel.

"What about Pepys?" Rawlins said, a glint deep in his blue eyes.

"Stabilized. Baadluster has taken over for him. There's no knowing which way the wind lies with that one yet."

Jack felt sweat trickling through his scalp and down the back of his neck. The room was becoming stifling.

Lassaday leaned against the wall. "We're agreed, sir."

"Whatever it takes," Rawlins seconded.

Jack took a deep breath. He did not like pitting Walker against Walker, but it was the only way he could gain access to the port berths. The militant faction remained firmly entrenched. Only their brethren could safely approach though it was unlikely they could talk their brothers in arms into relinquishing the port. But he didn't need that. All he needed was a shield to get them that far.

From there, he had his own methods of persuasion. There was only one Walker he knew who could face a battle suit, and he was daring Jack to come get him . . . off-planet.

"All right, then. Sarge, get some air in here."

Lassaday, his bronzed pate gleaming with sweat, keyed the door open. It began to slide, then ground to a halt with a dull whine. A huge, shaggy booted leg kicked it off its tracks.

K'rok leaned in. He grinned hugely. "I be left out of the meeting, eh, Jack?" A detail of Thraks filled the background behind him.

K'rok had gotten cool air piped in. He sat, massively conquering one of Jack's chairs, clad in Enduro bracers and a modified jumpsuit for modesty's sake, his hair and bulk armoring him effectively. The musky and rancid oil smell of him filled Jack's quarters.

"Finding Colin be one of the critical factors of our fate, Jack," the Milot said solemnly. "We cannot turn away from it. I am being here because of my masters—and also because I want to be." He leaned across the table separating the two of them. "Milos is losing *sand*."

"What?"

K'rok leaned back cagily. "I will not say it a second time. You be hearing me, my friend."

"It's failing?"

"Yes. My homeland is too tough to be defeated. I am too tough to be defeated."

Jack sat back in his chair eyeing his fellow commander. He knew that K'rok was only the most visible of a small community of Milots who had survived the desecration of their homeworld. He also knew that K'rok had grown sons and daughters—and dreams of someday going back. Now that someday was a concrete possibility. If *sand* failed, the Thraks would leave. Milos could be terraformed. K'rok might never live to see the day, but his children could. An officer of the Thrakian League would never hope to see such a day, but he knew K'rok survived for it. The Milot was the same as telling him of his divided loyalties. But that meant Jack couldn't trust him completely either and K'rok seemed unaware of the paradox he presented Storm.

K'rok's headset was down around his neck, but he wore an abstracted look as if listening to it now and again. He clenched his bulky hand now. "We are out of time, friend Jack." He got to his feet and signaled the Thrakian officers waiting just outside the sound curtain shielding Jack's doorway. "A massive attack is being launched. It appears that the insurgents are calling for Pepys' head."

Jack got up hastily. He reached for the pack he intended to take off world with him. "We'd better suit up," he said. "And it's time to decide who the real enemy is."

K'rok responded with a growling laugh. As he passed through the brace of guards, he moved with a speed that belied his bulk and laid the two Thraks out. Jack dealt a mercy blow to one while K'rok handled the second. Then he stood.

"Casualties of the rebellion, eh?"

"Looks like. How many Thraks are in the barracks?"

"Close to a hundred."

"May I suggest, Commander, that you put them to the fore of our defense against the assault coming in?"

"Good idea."

Jack reshouldered his pack. "We will take the shop and secure it, and work our way back to the palace. Then we work our way out until we meet the front."

With stiff, jerky movements, Amber gathered up her belongings and packed them. Her arms felt as though they had been pulled from their sockets and her ribs protested the new bruises laid over the old. But he had not taken her again—she'd struggled vigorously enough that he'd been forced to let her go, or risk damaging his communication equipment. Vandover had not seemed to mind it as she fled from him. He took more joy from the pain than from the sex.

But she could no longer flee his thoughts. They followed her, smoldering, like the guttering flame of a trash dump fire, rancid and smutty, choking her own thoughts down. As if he'd realized that she was aware of his invasion, there was an echoing, guttural laugh and he was gone.

Amber staggered to a chair. She sat, holding her face in her hands, trying to breathe. Clean air, clean lungs, clean thought. With a shudder, she looked up. He *would* make her kill Jack, she had no doubt of that. But when? When would he be done with the two of them? Could she break Vandover's hold over her? She wouldn't even hear the words when he whispered them in her ear—how could she turn them away?

She dashed away the tears that threatened to spill. Tears would not help. She had asked for this, in a way. She had wanted to be deadly, to be lethal again. Now she was. How could she face Jack this way? How could she reach out to him? He would never be able to love her again.

She clenched her fist. The sinews on her thin but powerful wrist stood out. She stared at it. The delicate skin on the inside of her wrist was bare where most denizens of Malthen wore a microchip just under the surface. She did not carry a computer ident and never would. She had fought to stay free of that chain. She raised her fist higher.

The first thing she had to do was keep Jack alive. Then she would worry about the rest.

A klaxon broke the stream of her thoughts. In the corner of her tiny room, the com came on. "General alert. Repeat, this is a general alert. We are under attack."

Muttering a street slang curse from the roughest part of under-Malthen, Amber grabbed her kit and ran.

The rebels broke through before they could establish a line. Jack felt good in his suit; despite its bulk and the room he had inside of it, a good soldier wore his armor like a second skin. Point a gauntlet and fire. Or shoulder the field pack and laser cannon. He was a human tank, damn near invincible—but not quite invincible enough.

For the first time in his fighting life, he looked out across a field of enemy who were not the enemy, though they had brought the battle to him. They were flesh he did not want to see burned or blasted. They were fighting for something he might well be fighting for himself, except that he had been trapped on this side.

K'rok bellowed over the com, "Keep it defensive!" He strode over the outer perimeter like some massive mountain come to the aid of the emperor. "Link together and hold the front!"

There would be no holding of this front without killing. Jack swung about. "Rawlins!"

"Yessir."

"Is the shop clear?"

"Shut down and shielded, sir."

The equipment not in use would remain safe—and out of insurgent hands. Jack shrugged into his shoulder pads, feeling the leads and wires clipped to his bare torso pinch more tightly in reaction. If necessary, they could all fall back to the main wing of the palace and shield there as well—but it would only be a matter of time before they would have to come out for supplies. It was not a strategic position one wanted to be in.

He had no time for further thought as his front cameras and grid showed him incoming rebels. With screams that broke into static over his sensors, the enemy charged. He fired over their heads. He brought down trees in their path, exploded ditches before their feet . . . and, in the end, he shot a few.

The numbers were overwhelming. He caught sight of K'rok's suit. "We're going to be up to our helmets in bodies," he said.

A heavy grunt answered. Then K'rok said, "There is always being plan two, Jack."

Plan two might well prove to be the lesser of two evils. "All right," Jack told him.

"Good. Listen up, this is being Commander K'rok. Fall back!"

Pepys slowly became aware that someone sat on the edge of his medical crèche. His head ached, and one eye seemed out of focus—the barely seen visitor took a damp cloth and wiped it for him.

"Thank you," he said, and found his voice in a hot, hoarse whisper, barely audible.

"Don't mention it."

The emperor smiled. "I cannot see you well, Amber, but my hearing is fine."

"Yeah, well, it's about all you've got going for you. Take your ice chips."

Pepys took a cup being folded into his hand—weak, he was so incredibly weak—and the crèche shifted so that he could sit up. He tapped a few chips into his mouth, felt a couple skid off his chin, and tried to suck on the remaining cold miracles. Their refreshing strength trickled down his throat. His eye cleared a little, as well.

Amber was watching the corridor outside the care unit.

"What's happening?"

"Someone started a civil war. I think it was a religious fanatic and a half-assed emperor."

Pepys started to laugh, found himself choking and at her mercy as she helped him to spit up the dust clogging his throat. He sat back, hands shaking as he feebly tried to straighten his covers. "I know that," he said, a little peevishly. "What's happening now?"

"The hospital wing is the most secure part of the palace. We're about to be up to our neck in WP and battle armor."

He tried to think. It eluded him for a moment, then he grasped that they were mounting a last ditch stand and hold effort. "My God." He gasped. "Has it come to that?"

"For the moment." Amber faced him. He thought she looked both tough and beautiful. "Got any ideas?"

"None." He lay back and took a deep breath. He hurt all over, and was strangely numb in places he shouldn't be. "Where are the nurses?"

"Most of your palace staff fled along with your psychics, valets, cooks and maids, and medical staff. But you still have your Knights." She gave him a crooked grin.

"Yes. I would, wouldn't I." No matter what he had done to Storm, the man had stayed with him, kept there by his own brand of ethics. "Where's Vandover?"

"He's deploying the WP officers. He's been running your show, you know."

"I know, my dear. I know." Pepys coughed again. She

got up and held his head until he'd finished, then wiped his mouth with a cold cloth, and gave him a tiny sip of water.

She frowned at him. "Unfortunately, I think you'll live."

"Do you?" He blinked. The bad eye was beginning to blur again. "I wish I had your faith."

"Faith about what," Vandover said, as he entered the care unit. "Pepys, you're looking better."

"What's happening?"

The minister looked at Amber. There was an expression deep in those dark eyes that Pepys had never seen before and wasn't sure he liked. "Can't keep him down. K'rok has ordered a fallback to avoid a bloodbath. A good decision, I think—we don't need to give them any more martyrs at this point than they already have."

"What are you doing in the way of containment?"

Amber looked away. Pepys caught the expression of distance that had fallen across her features. If only he had not given over her destiny into Baadluster's hands. If only he had thought more about the decision. Concern made him cough again, and this time, no one moved to his aid. By the time he had caught his breath, the corridor had filled with noise as battle armored soldiers filed in.

CHAPTER 22

"They'll fight for me," Pepys said later, with confidence, his voice no longer a whisper, but thin and reedy for all that. The day had been long and the din from the armor in the hallways tumultuous. He felt weary unto death, but he clung to his wakeful state as if it were the only indicator that he still lived. All was quiet now.

Amber's suit hung in the corner of the care unit, near the life monitors. She eyed it as she stabbed a piece of protein from her packaged dinner. "They'll fight to survive. What's important, your highness, is that the two objectives coincide." She delicately picked the morsel from her fork and ate it.

Pepys stared at her. He debated about chiding her for the lack of respect in her tone of voice, but he knew Amber well . . . and knew that manners were like a suit of clothes to her, that she used them depending on whether or not she needed the disguise. He ended up sighing. She was right, of course. Wired to this crèche he was as helpless as a scraggly, thrown-away babe. He began to understand what Jack had seen in her, beyond her grace and beauty. She had an innate ability to filter the truth out, however fine, and retain its clarity. "I made a mistake with you," he said, to his utter surprise.

She shot him a look then, with such hatred in her eyes that he shrank back. It faded as quickly as he recognized it and Pepys wondered if he had really seen it at all. "Tell me you tampered with Jack and I'll unhook your crèche right now."

His shallow breathing rose and fell only with the help of that unit. He would get better, but for now . . . she threatened his very life. Pepys waved a hand, a reflection of his old imperious self, unaware that he did so. "On the contrary, I did all I could to help him."

"Then it was Vandover."

He nodded, a feeble movement that merely dropped his chin to his chest and left it there.

Amber's face twisted. "We're all spiders in that web." She polished off the last of her dinner, crumpled the packet as if it were an enemy, and tossed it away.

"But I left you to him," Pepys said softly, so softly that he was not even sure she'd heard him as she stood and crossed the room to her armor. It was coated with norcite, which gave it a gleam over its blue-black enameling. He thought it was a dark and deadly color for a beautiful woman. Did she murmur something back, or was it an unconscious echo of his own mind? *I made a mistake with you as well.*

His eyes felt terribly heavy. She had already fed him and now his thoughts spun away as quickly as a cloud across the merciless Malthen sky. "I think . . . I'll sleep now," he said.

"Good." Amber did not turn. The last thing he saw was a bleary image of her stretching out her hand and stroking the empty sleeve of the war suit.

He awoke to thunder. The corridors were filled with suits, running, and Amber came to his side, angling the crèche bed up so he could see better. Strain showed on her face.

"What is it?"

"They've fallen back. I'm not sure—"

One of the colossal armored bodies entered the care unit. Jack took off his helmet and hung it from his belt clip.

"Jack—" Amber blurted, then bit her lip as he gave her no notice.

He approached the emperor, had eyes for him alone. "We've been holding a defensive position." Sweat slicked back his sandy hair. Pain faded the blue of his eyes. "We can't hold it any longer, and I'll tell you, sir, that none of us wants to stage a full-scale war against what we're facing out there. And there's a Thrakian mother ship overhead, threatening to come in as well. *They* won't think twice about fighting."

Pepys wet his lips. "Vandover," he croaked, then took a sip of water from a glass Amber held for him. "Where is Vandover?"

"Monitoring Ash-farel activity. Something is happening out there. I've got to get to Colin. We can't wait any longer."

Pepys licked his lips again. "Speaker," he got out. "Hook me up to a speaker."

Jack watched the curtain of night. Flames of light spouted upward, orange-red against the blackness, then sputtered out. He could hear the percussion of explosions and the high-pitched singing of laser fire. His helmet bumped the hip of the suit. Against the relative silence of muted battle came the weakened voice of the emperor.

"This is Emperor Pepys. People of the Triad Throne, you work to your own undoing. Lay down your arms. Give our mission safe passage to search for St. Colin. I call on you to come to the bargaining table, not the battlefield."

The message repeated endlessly for nearly half an hour. Jack replaced his helmet and focused his cameras and sensors, searching for a response to the message being broadcast. None came. He had not expected any. He opened his com line.

"K'rok. They're calling our bluff. Give the signal. Rawlins, prepare to move out. Lassaday—watch your nuts." He fell back, anticipating renewed attack. Inside the suit, sweat dripped off his brow. He felt suffocated. His thoughts and memories tangled again. Where was he? *When* was he? He was a *Knight,* for god's sake, fighting the "Pure" war. He held onto that tenet as if it were a lifeline and strode into the night.

K'rok swelled out of his suit neckline as he removed his helmet. "I am being sorry, Minister," he said to Vandover. "We have done all we could, without a massacre."

Vandover paced the length of Pepys' care unit, his long black robes alive with the movement like a pair of immense wings at his back. He gave the Milot an ugly stare. "You don't win battles by retreating."

"No, sir." The Milot met his look, baring yellow-ivory

canines of immense length. "But there will be another fight."

"Where's Jack?" Amber asked quietly in the tense silence that followed K'rok's statement.

"He be coming in last. There was a suit down, and the Dead Man circuit was triggered. The armor is lost, but our man might be injured. Jack be looking for our lost man."

"What about the Thrakian contingent of the guard?"

K'rok gave an eloquent shrug which the Flexalinks copied, a wave of movement down the length of the battle armor. Whatever he might have said was lost in the commotion at the corridor's end as the doors were opened up to the outside and Jack came in, bearing an injured man in his arms.

"Let's get this man in a crèche."

Fire and smoke framed him in the doorway. There was a moment of hesitation, then Rawlins leapt to his aid, his own suit gored and charred. Jack himself turned to secure the doors he'd come through. As they clanged shut, he removed his helmet and took deep gulps of air. Lassaday handed him a cold glass of beer. Jack took it and then grinned.

"Short rations, eh?"

The sergeant gave a bellowing laugh in response before trailing his men to the care unit where they swiftly installed the wounded Knight. Jack watched them go before sucking down a deep draught. Vandover met him in the corridor outside Pepys' room.

"What now?"

"We don't shield, at least, not yet. Can't afford the power drain. This building can take an assault or two without damage." Jack paused for another drink. He rested the cooling glass against his forehead. "We need time." He saluted K'rok with his drink. "Commander."

"Commander," returned the Milot. He shouldered past Jack and for a moment the corridor was filled floor to ceiling with battle armor. The Milot growled, "I could use one of those."

Jack let him by. He smiled at Amber and Pepys and said, "It's going to be a long night."

Vandover scowled heavily. "What do you think you're doing?"

"Well, Baadluster, we're fighting the battle and right now, we're taking a break while the other side regroups and does some thinking. You see, up until now, we've only been deflecting them. We've done some heavy damage without being on the offensive. Even though we're dealing with fanatics here, some cooler heads are going to realize the kind of damage we can do if we take the offensive. Someone's going to hesitate." Jack paused for another drink. He lifted the empty glass in salute to Vandover. "You've got to remember that none of these people here have ever really seen us in combat. A demonstration or two in the stadium, but that's it. Now they have. Now they know just what to be scared of." He stifled a mild burp. "And now, if you'll excuse me, I'm going to get some sleep." He crossed the care unit and sat down, the Flexa-link suit folding gracefully to lower him to the hard floor. He leaned his head back against the wall and closed his eyes.

Amber knew Vandover shot an angry glare at her, but she refused to meet his expression. She took up her post, curling up on a countertop, bracing her shoulders where the cabinet met the wall.

Pepys was either chuckling to himself or snoring lightly as Vandover made a disgusted noise and left the care unit.

The clangor came just before dawn. Jack got to his feet quickly, heading toward the secured doors. Rawlins, Lassaday, and K'rok joined him immediately. Pepys made a mewling noise as Amber sat him up a little. He seemed disoriented, then grasped her sleeve as she said, "Watch Jack."

"Open the doors," he ordered.

"Commander, scanners show they're—"

"I know what they are," Jack snapped, interrupting. "Get those doors open."

Lassaday pointed and two privates hurried to unshield and unbar the portal. It came open, the stink of smoke and ash flooding in.

Jack stepped forward. "General Guthul. How fortunate you've dropped in. We place ourselves at your mercy."

Amber gasped in disbelief as Storm knelt at the feet of the Thrakian warrior.

*   *   *

"I wish," Pepys said peevishly, "that someone had told me about all this."

Wearing her own armor and shouldering her pack, Amber said, "You're out of the loop, emperor. And so, apparently, am I." She pointed at the Thraks rolling the crèche out into the loading dock. "Watch it, bugface." She looked around the grounds, where landing ships had fused the landscape into a burnt, glassy surface. "Your gardeners are going to be real pissed."

Pepys laughed in spite of himself. The rose obsidite walls of the palace stood with scarcely a scar, but the grounds surrounding it looked as if they'd been through a firestorm. The carnage had marked them deeply. He could only thank K'rok's and Jack's intuition that the Walkers would hesitate before a full-scale Thrakian attack. Letting the allies come in had begun a cease-fire. The bad news was that Guthul was taking them in hand. Queen Tricatada wanted to talk to Pepys very badly. He dared show no weakness before the Thrakian queen.

Amber patted Pepys on the shoulder as if knowing his hesitant thoughts. Vandover led the caravan, his hands filled with the valises he carried, his shoulders bowed under the weight. Jack and the small handful of Knights going with them took up the rear. "It's going to be a rough trip," she commented, looking at the shuttle docked in a make-shift berth as they approached it.

"I'll make it," Pepys said grimly.

"You don't have much choice," Amber returned. She looked at the Thraks flanking them. They were as much prisoners as allies. She twisted about to glance at Jack. He'd been strangely quiet since his capitulation to Guthul, his longtime nemesis. She could not fathom what was going on behind his pale, careful expression.

Jack watched the loading caravan approach the shuttle. His thoughts slipped and tumbled over one another. He was walking into the enemy's jaws and none of them would make it out again if he couldn't keep himself together. He fought to hold on, to stay in control just one moment longer. Fatigue and stress leeched his strength when he needed it most. He would have stumbled, but the suit held him up, kept him moving. He looked at K'rok and for a frightening instant, Milos and Malthen overlapped one another, time over time.

The Milot brushed against him lightly, the jarring clearing his mind again, and he ducked his head as they reached the loading bay. The Thraks ensconced them all in hammocklike seats, the bay closed, and the ship began to thrum as it powered up.

Jack closed his eyes against the hammering thrust of the takeoff. He could hear Pepys' moaning over the roar of the engines. The little man might not survive the gs of the takeoff although the aneurysm was supposed to have been lasered off and cauterized, its damage already having been done. Would he care if Pepys died? He had time for no further wondering as the shuttle left its berth and the body-crushing punishment of leaving Malthen's gravity began. His memories could take no more.

He awoke to find Thraks unwrapping his armor from takeoff netting. They chittered in derision at his weakness. Jack put his boots on the floor and straightened, standing head and shoulders taller than their own giant forms. He looked about and saw the other humans and knew his own actions were hostage to theirs. He had been defeated and why he was not dead, he did not know. Flanked by Thraks, he was marched out of the shuttle and into the belly of a much larger vessel, probably a mother ship.

As they crossed the hangar, he saw the dais and the honor guard flanking the brilliant iridescent blue body of a queen Thraks. She levered herself upward, her face plates settling into a mask of exotic beauty as she looked at him.

"Welcome, my valorous warrior," she said to Guthul, speaking in the humans' language for the prisoners' sakes, then repeating it in her chirps and trills. The warrior Thraks made a deep obeisance to her.

The gorge rose in Jack's throat. He could bring the queen down from where he stood, but that meant that all of the prisoners' lives would be forfeit. He weighed the option as the queen turned to him.

"I bring you Commander Jack Storm," Guthul said formally. "Of whom you have heard so much sung about."

Sung? Caught off guard, he watched as a hangar door opened to her right. She indicated it.

"I have a surprise for you, Jack Storm, befitting your status as a warrior."

As the portal opened, his breath caught in his chest. Pearly armor faced him, helmet set beside its boots, scarred from battle and gallant—his armor, lost to the ages. Now he knew what his captors intended for him—he would be fed to his own armor, and left to be consumed by the parasite infesting it. *They* knew, the Thraks did, of the horrors of the Sand Wars on Milos.

Jack lunged at the armor, intent upon destroying it, upon ripping out the bestial life-form inhabiting it.

Amber screamed. "Jack! Don't! It's Bogie!"

CHAPTER 23

Under the weight of Jack's attack, the battle armor dropped to its knees, swaying. Amber lunged at him and hung on to his sleeve, crying, "Jack, don't do this."

He shook her off unthinkingly. Guthul moved to place himself between his queen and Jack, but Tricatada stopped him.

"It is his to deal with," she said, intrigued.

Jack reached into the neck of the armor where a chamoislike thing pulsed, woven within and without the gadgetry of the war suit. It was alive and yet not—unformed, embryonic—and it controlled the armor. Its empty sleeves clawed beseechingly upon his own armor.

Amber got to her feet. "No," she said. "I won't let you. *Don't make me do this.*"

His mind felt as though a whirlwind was blasting through it, tossing leaves of thought and memory to and fro, forward and backward, spinning around. Milos and Malthen, Dorman's Stand and *sand* . . . he awoke to find himself with his gauntlet down Bogie's gullet, with Amber's voice ringing in his ears.

He turned to look at her. She stood defiantly, chin out, engulfed by her own war suit, only her face and tangled mane of hair visible. Bright color illuminated her fine cheekbones and he knew he had not imagined what he remembered her saying. *Don't make me hurt you.* He could feel the edge of her mind now, like a blade against his neck. With great restraint, he kept himself from turning and looking at Pepys.

He knew now what she had done to protect herself and him when she thought she'd lost him. He knew now what had struck the emperor down. She had somehow gone and retrieved that dark part of herself they had worked so hard to purge—reimprinted herself, perhaps, just as he had done—and now she stood ready to protect Bogie as well.

He withdrew his hand, swallowing down a tightness in his aching throat. The near empty armor stopped clawing at him and slumped to its side. Jack kept himself from responding to Bogie's weakness. He must have gone berserk when he'd seen it. Rawlins stood guard over Pepys, his visor shielding his youthful expression. Jack wondered what he must think of his erratic commander.

"I am curious," Tricatada trilled, "as to what animates the armor."

I'll bet you are, Jack thought. "Robotics," he said.

"Curious," Guthul said, edging his body between them. "I thought robot arms were banned by your races."

"They are," Vandover Baadluster interjected smoothly. "This was an experimental model to retest them. As you can see, it is a failure."

Jack hooked his old helmet onto his belt and hefted the white armor in his arms. "It will be destroyed as soon as we can retrieve the data."

The Thraks turned her attention to him again. "Data?"

"This armor was with St. Colin when he disappeared. It's a good assumption that our in-suit cameras will have some recording of the incident."

"Ahhh." She waved a signal to Guthul. "I am pleased that we have salvaged it for you, then. Your quarters have been made ready. Then we shall talk."

Amber entered his quarters on his heels and knocked his gauntlets away as he set the collapsed armor down in a corner. She'd shed her suit and was still breathless with the effort as she knelt down by Bogie.

"What are you doing?"

She didn't look up at him but her voice was filled with scorn. "I'm powering your armor." With deft hands and a few small probes and tools she had secreted about a jump-suit he could have sworn was skintight, she rigged a plug-in for the armor. When she was done, she swiveled on her heels. "You wouldn't want to lose all your precious *data.*"

Boss. Bogie's voice, its basso profundo tone a mere shadow of itself. *You have found me. And Amber is angry.*

Amber is indeed angry, but don't let her know we've talked.

The war suit shifted. Amber made a pleased sound and stroked it as if the Flexalinks could feel her touch. With Bogie hooked up inside it, it could.

I am a signpost, the being told him. *Colin said for me to point the way.*

Jack felt a thrill go through him. "We'll check it out later," he said aloud. "The systems look pretty drained."

Amber got to her feet then. "Don't let anybody else at this suit. It knows too much."

He met her level gaze. "Why did you threaten me?"

"I had no other way to stop you from harming . . . Bogie."

"It's a parasitic infestation."

Amber tossed her head. "It's *alive,* Jack and at least it knows who it is!"

He blocked her from leaving the tiny cabin cubicle. "Maybe you should tell me who I am."

Her hands worked. "You're a back-assed farm boy who just fell off the shuttle and wouldn't amount to slag if it hadn't been—hadn't been for me."

He couldn't take the pain in her voice and eyes any longer. He made a decision he hoped he wouldn't regret and answered, "I thought I was your White Knight."

Her mouth made a tiny "o." Then she kicked the door shut behind her and ran at Jack. He opened his arms to take her in, saying, "Quietly, quietly, we're not out of harm's way yet."

But instead of hugging him, she pummeled the chest of the armor until her hands were red with pain and he finally got hold of her.

"Son of a bitch," she cried and put her face to the Flexalinks. He could feel her shoulders heave with emotion. "What you've put me through."

"I know," he said softly, leaning down and putting his mouth to her ear. Mixed with the soft perfume that was uniquely hers, he could smell the plastic and metallic flavor of the armor she'd been wearing. "They tampered with my imprinting. For days I had no current memory. Now it slips and slides. Pepys has all but told me it was Vandover and to watch my back."

She snuffled. "Pepys is no angel either."

"I know. Amber . . . I know what you've done."

She pulled back. She looked up at him. She shook her head slowly. "No, I don't think so."

"I know about Pepys."

Something shadowed her golden-brown eyes. Then she shook her head again. "I couldn't help it. Are you going to turn me in?"

"No. Whether they've declared it or not, this is war, and," he smiled, "I need you on my side."

"Always."

"It's going to be painful. Until we're in the clear, until I've got a vessel and what I need to go after Colin, I have to keep you at arm's length."

She took a deep breath and answered, "I think I can make it that far."

He released her then. She gained the door and stopped. "What about Bogie? What happened to you just now?"

"I thought I was back on Milos . . . the evacuation . . . I'm not always here."

"And when you're not here . . . you're there?"

"Yes." He did not need to explain further. His torment reflected in her eyes.

"Still fighting the Sand Wars."

"Always."

She left him then, the tiny cabin growing darker as if she alone had kept it illuminated. Jack shook himself as he realized it was only Bogie, draining power. He went to the suit. "Now show me," he said, "what you know of Colin." Whatever he thought had happened, he was not prepared for what did happen—for the scream of fear and anguish Bogie had recorded.

CHAPTER 24

"There is a fine line between guests and prisoners, your majesty," Vandover said smoothly. "The slightest interruption in the power supply of my emperor's medical care unit can place him at risk. Intelligence tells me that our troops have resecured the palace grounds and the city-state known familiarly as Upper Malthen. I urge you to return us there, before we stage any further talks." Baadluster held the center of attention in the hangar as they gathered for a conference. The queen's dais had been moved into the loading dock as had Pepys' crèche. Amber hung behind Jack and watched them all intently, particularly K'rok, who now flanked his queen and general.

The queen hummed as the Minister of War spoke, her faceted eyes watching them all in turn with a placid, even benevolent expression on her mask. "Who is in charge if Pepys is weak?"

"I am his co-counsel, majesty, and let me assure you that Pepys is not weak, merely incapacitated for the moment. He speaks for himself and I do his will. As for the Triad Throne—"

"Shut up, Vandover," Pepys said, face white.

"The Triad Throne is secure in all respects—"

"*Shut up,* Vandover," the emperor repeated, his crèche fairly shaking with agitation. Rawlins moved toward it protectively, but Pepys waved him off.

Tricatada let out a trill which Jack interpreted as laughter. The Thrakian ruler bent down. "Let us discuss this incapacitation."

"A stroke, your highness, an attack upon the brain." Vandover smiled thinly.

Pepys glared at Vandover, but said nothing.

"Pepys, do you expect to return to your throne?"

"Yes," he answered loudly, a spark of his old self apparent in his words. "I warn you, Tricatada, that any effort by you to go beyond those measures allowed by our convention of alliance will be construed by myself as an act of war." His eyes flashed.

Amber murmured to Jack, "He doesn't sound afraid that she might pull his plug."

"He can't," Jack answered back carefully. "The Thraks don't believe in wounded or infirm. They take no prisoners."

"Unless they're stocking the larder." She shifted her weight. "What's K'rok up to?"

"I'm not sure." Jack watched the Milot. He got the impression the commander was aiding with the finer nuances of translation, but he had no real confirmation of that. Did Guthul or Tricatada know how close K'rok had come to throwing away his allegiance altogether? Had the Walker forces been smaller or less adamant, K'rok would not be standing with them now. He listened to Tricatada giving Pepys assurances of their actions. It was impossible to tell if the Thraks had a patronizing tone.

When Tricatada finished her speech, she turned to Jack. "What news do you have of your missing man?"

Her directness took him aback. "I report to my superiors, majesty, and the information you ask me to divulge is privileged. The power drain on my armor was severe and the recordings damaged, but I do know Colin was in search of the Ash-farel, hoping to make peaceful contact. How he predicted that they would come to Claron, I don't know. But he was right and he left enough data for me to follow."

"Follow the Ash-farel," the queen repeated. "With what purpose? He had been named envoy by you, Pepys? What could he have had in mind?"

Jack's gaze flicked to the emperor.

"Come now, Storm," Guthul said. "Your emperor and minister ask us for a vessel and outfitting for your mission. There must be a price paid for everything." He rattled his chitin in emphasis, like an irritated beetle. "And the armor is a gift from my queen."

Jack frowned at him. "I'd like to ask just how you acquired it, if we're trading information."

"Jack," Vandover soothed, as Guthul drew himself upward.

The Thrakian general sputtered as his queen rearranged her mask. "This is a fitting question," she answered. "We were investigating Ash-farel intrusion in the quadrant which contains the rehabilitating planet Claron. This intrusion was most unique. It appeared to be a reconnoitering flight . . . something our ancient enemy rarely does. We found a rescue pod, a tiny vessel, from a larger Walker cruiser. It was empty except for the armor. It tried to defend the vessel, but its resources were too drained. Why, Minister Baadluster, would a Walker be this far out? We have had several encounters with those of the Walker persuasion. We seem to have similar interests in norcite deposits."

"I'm afraid the norcite veins are coincidental to the archaeological sites which are also near. The Walkers, while in need of funding, are not interested in mining norcite. It has a very limited market. They will mine gold and platinum deposits if located, but they are most interested in the archaeological finds." Baadluster put his hands behind his back and took a stance. Oddly, it mirrored Guthul's position near his queen.

Tricatada leaned close to K'rok and a slender but muscular, lean-bodied drone all but hidden by the Milot's bulk. She trilled and chirped with the two of them for a few moments. Hearing K'rok imitate Thrakian speech was a different experience, Jack decided. After a moment, the queen looked up. Her blue carapaces shimmered as she gestured.

"If the Walkers have no use for norcite as we do, yet we find them disputing our mining claims so often, who is to say they do not seek to negotiate those claims with our enemy? And if this is so, why should we aid those who might be the friends of our enemy?"

"One might ask us the same of you," Jack said tightly.

Guthul swung on him. "You are a warrior," he spat out in Thrakian agitation. "You presume to answer for your emperor? You presume to have your speech inflicted upon my queen? I will not tolerate your insults. I have heard far too much from you already."

Vandover apologized, but General Guthul was alive with

quivering movement. Jack's lips drew into a fine line as he recognized the Thrakian battle rage. He gave a hand signal to Rawlins. The shock-haired officer took it in and answered with a grave nod. He was prepared to die protecting Pepys' crèche.

Jack looked to Pepys. "A Thraks' concept of a ruler is different from ours, your highness. As the only fertile egg-layer, a Thrakian queen is solely responsible for the continuation of their race. She approaches godhood in status. Your responsibility, Pepys, is far exceeded by hers. However, failure in any ruler is not tolerated by those ruled," he ended deliberately, shifting the Thraks' attention from his emperor to himself.

There was a snap in the air as the queen's wings thrashed out, a canopy spanning those two or three near her as well as herself. Amber made a sound of awe at Jack's back.

"I didn't know she had those."

The awesome spectacle of the queen's wingspan took him by surprise as well. "I didn't either," he answered, as he took a step backward, taking Amber with him. It was his fault the queen had taken umbrage over a remark he had meant for Pepys. He had forgotten for a moment her inability to lay another queen. At the opening snap, Guthul had gone prone where he knelt still, head down, at his monarch's feet.

Vandover looked toward Jack, his blotchy face ashen. "Someone," he said in an undertone, "must pay for this."

Jack nodded. "It was my insult. Let Guthul take it out of my hide."

K'rok moved forward as Guthul raised upward, his mask frozen in hideous Thrakian fury. Amber held onto Jack's arm. "Don't."

"I have to. They'll only outfit us if they think we're strong enough to take what we want anyway. How do you think K'rok's stayed in her graces this long? She knows he's never really capitulated to her. The Thraks don't respect the weak."

"You can't fight him unarmored," Pepys husked from his crèche. His spark had gone and he seemed shrunken, weary.

Rawlins seconded him. "It's suicide, Commander."

K'rok interrupted. "My queen has taken offense from

your remark, friend Jack. My commander is bringing challenge to you."

"And I accept, K'rok."

The hairy Milot bent closer. "You have hit home. She fears that you know her innermost shame. Guthul will not rest until you're dead, but I don't think she will be allowing that."

"Tell her I fight for Pepys' honor as well as my own. She thinks him too weak to rule . . . she's toying with all of us now."

The Milot inclined his shaggy head. "You be knowing her well, Jack." He stepped back and spoke rapidly to the Thraks.

Guthul snarled back. K'rok gestured and humped his shoulders. Amber's hands tightened on Jack's arm. "What's happening? Are we going to get out of here?"

"We're as good as prisoners if the queen doesn't respect our ability to assert ourselves. Vandover can spread as many honeyed words as he wants—it won't get us a ship to go after Colin, or get Pepys back to Malthen."

Vandover had moved to the other side of Pepys' medical crèche, standing over him like a storm cloud. "They wouldn't dare harm us."

Jack let out a humorless laugh. It drew Guthul's attention and the two stared at each other across the hangar floor. "You see," Jack said quietly. "He wonders what we're laughing about. He wonders how we can be so brazen as to laugh now, in the midst of crisis. The only way to get respect out of a Thraks is to beat it out of him."

Guthul dropped his hard stare and chattered rapidly at K'rok. The Milot officer made a motion with his pawlike hands. The Thraks gestured abruptly.

K'rok turned around. "The challenge is agreed to. Guthul has asked for personal combat."

Amber thrust herself forward, her hair flying with her movement. "Not under those terms. Jack is bare-handed." Jack pulled her back, but the Milot stared at her for a few instants.

K'rok showed his teeth. "A moment, little missy." He turned back and argued briefly with the Thraks. Then he came around again. "Jack, as befits a Knight, in armor. Guthul will be wearing Thrakian bracers."

Jack thought rapidly. His new armor was still being powered. The only armor he had that was fit to wear was his old armor. He shuddered as his memories warred with one another, and the Sand Wars won. He had no desire to wear an infested battle suit. K'rok drew close. His rumbling voice lowered. "You must be wearing your old suit, Jack. It is the only way. I know the secret of norcite. The Thraks eat it powdered to strengthen their body armor. Your old suit has been enameled with it. Guthul will not be seeing you so easily . . . he will be thinking it another Thraks."

The Milot looked at him intently. Jack nodded, momentarily confused. Who was he? He got a grip on himself as he considered the importance of what the Milot had told him, and whether K'rok could be trusted. Norcite . . . eaten by the Thraks? He watched K'rok rejoin the queen, Guthul, and her drone. The difference between the drone and the warrior Thraks was astounding—but the Thraks bred for that difference. And had begun to ingest norcite to augment it. Eaten a tremendous amount of it, if their avid search for new norcite deposits was any indication.

How had the Milot known? Jack only knew of one man beyond the Thrakian League who might have known that secret—and Mierdan was safely hidden among the Green Shirts' ranks. The little xenobiologist had spent more than twenty years among the Thraks and since Jack had brought him home, Tricatada had searched tirelessly for him. It was Mierdan who had told Jack why the Thraks swarmed so militantly, because of their sterility, in a desperate attempt to prolong their existence.

He gently shook Amber off and stepped forward. Tricatada still extended her wingspan, colors shimmering in the hangar's lighting. "I welcome the opportunity to prove my bravery," he said, watching her. He was careful not to let his interior battle show . . . old Jack and young Jack, as he'd grown to think of himselves. Young Jack was thrilled to fight Guthul but feared his own armor. Old Jack was dismayed to fight yet again but trusted Bogie. As both identities tried to possess him, he eyed the Thrakian queen. Her body was full and pulsing—did she swell with eggs yet again?

Was Malthen destined to become the next *sand* world if they failed here and now to convince the Thraks of their ability to hold the Triad Throne? Pepys had taken a grave chance in allying with this enemy. The queen's throat leather swelled. "And if you win, Pepys' champion, we will abide by our alliance and will return Malthen to its rightful ruler, and you will be given our fastest ship to go after St. Colin. If you lose . . . we must talk long and hard about our futures."

"How are you doing?"

Sweat sprang up on his brow as he closed the inner seams and the chamois that was Bogie settled about his shoulders and down his bare back. "I'm fine."

Amber looked at him. "You don't look fine."

He fought the impulse to tear the armor from him as his mind warred against itself. "I'm losing it," he said.

She mopped the perspiration from his brow with the palm of her hand, and combed his hair away from his face with gentle fingers. "Try to hang on."

He nodded and busied himself clipping leads on his torso before putting his arms into his sleeves.

Boss, rumbled Bogie comfortingly. For a moment, their emotions intertwined, and he felt the jubilant warrior spirit that was the other. What was Bogie, anyway, if not a Milot berserker? *I am a signpost* the other answered him.

The road to Colin and truth.

"I have to make this a good fight," Jack said. "We can't afford to have Bogie damaged."

Amber paused in her work on his left gauntlet. She smiled gently. "Jack, he'll fry you."

"Only if he gets the chance. Why do you think K'rok maneuvered me into armor? He wants to bring the general down as Tricatada's right hand . . . why, I don't know, but he's always followed his own game plan. Give me the helmet." He shoved his arms into his sleeves, felt the electric tingle at his wrists telling him he was powered up and armed, as Amber gave him his helmet. He screwed it in place.

The outside world was not muffled away, but keener and sharper than ever before. Bogie's hardwired senses joined into those of the armor made it like a second skin. He was aware of every curve and nuance of Amber's body as she leaned forward into the Flexalinks, checking the helmet's fit. He felt himself sifting emotions and thoughts.

"Let me go," he said. "I'm as ready as I'll ever be."

"All right." She pushed a tangle of tawny hair back. "Whatever happens, I'll be backing you up."

Her expression was serious and Jack knew she meant what she said. He started to nod, stopped because that was one of the few movements the suit could not imitate, and saluted her instead.

"I shall kill him," Guthul promised his queen.

"I would be pleased," Tricatada murmured. "I want Malthen for our own, and this alliance has grown as cumbersome as an old egg casing." She stroked her warrior's brow. "Do as little damage to the armor as you can, now that we know its worth. Handled properly, it will lead us to the nest of our ancient enemy and we can at last strike at their vulnerable undersides."

Guthul froze under her touch, his desires raging. Her body glistened with the egg sacs swelling inside of her—*his* get, *his* seed—and without a doubt, one of them might well prove to be the savior of their race. He would not fail her. She dropped her arm/leg as if guessing the fever of his thoughts.

"I will be watching," she sang to him.

The loading hangar had been cleared. The audience watched from above, from mechanics' booths. Pepys labored in his crèche and Amber put a hand on his shoulder. He was cool to her touch. She immediately ordered a covering, and prepared to watch over the emperor. She had done this, and if she could give her own life to undo it, she would. He had never shown any fear or suspicion of her and guilt bit into her deeply. He patted her hand back.

"You need to be home," she said. For this man, this enemy who had so confounded her and Jack's lives, she found pity and understanding when she would rather have hated him. If this had been Vandover instead of Pepys— she would have struck him dead, but instead she found herself grasping the creed that motivated the emperor.

"Jack knows more about the Thraks than just about any man alive," Pepys said. He did not notice the sharp look

Vandover gave him suddenly. The emperor let go of Amber's hand. "Here they come."

The metal hangar clanged and thrummed as the stock portals opened and let the two combatants into it.

Even to onlookers from above, they had not lost their grace or immense stature as they approached one another in a *pas de deux de guerre.* Amber tightened her grip on Pepys' shoulder. She did not know if she could strike quickly enough to save Jack's life, if it came to that, or even if she could strike at all, the Thraks were so alien. Her glance slid away from Jack and Guthul as they sized one another up, thinking that if she could strike, it would be at Vandover.

As if sensing her thoughts, the Minister of War looked up. His brown hair had an unhealthy luster in the booth's dim light. His thick lips curled. "Good luck to your commander, milady," he said.

Amber shivered. She looked back to the battle. Rawlins shifted beside her, equally intent on what was happening below.

Jack let Guthul strike first, determining the method of combat they would be using. The Thraks wore wrist lasers, signaling his intent to do some serious damage if Jack's shields ever weakened. Jack couldn't remember ever having engaged in hand to hand combat with a Thraks, but he knew of those who had—literally torn from their armor. That was why suits came with a Dead Man circuit, to destroy the armor rather than let it fall into enemy hands. A Thraks could be incredibly strong, though Jack believed that battle rage enhanced the power.

Bogie still lacked full power. The suit could not keep his body heat down properly. Sweat poured off his face, blurred his eyesight and one of the leads clipped to his torso slipped off with a snap. Bogie pulsed across his shoulder blades. *Go for the throat leather, boss.*

"I just want to bring him down." Jack felt the armor rock back on its heels as the Thraks reared and kicked out. The shock drilled him to the roots of his teeth.

I think he wants us in pieces, boss Bogie rumbled back.

Jack got in motion, using all. the strength and agility of his war suit, hitting the power vault.

Guthul matched him, malice glittering redly in his dark, faceted eyes. Then Jack spun away and for a split second, hesitation was masked on the Thraks' face. He's lost me, Jack thought, and then the Thraks responded as Jack landed and pivoted, but not fast enough to evade the Knight as Jack threw him across the hangar floor. Sparks flew as the wrist lasers dragged across the metal plating under Guthul.

K'rok had been right. There was something about the battle armor that Guthul could not quite see—but even as Jack realized it, Guthul fired and the wash of the energy threw Jack off his knee and rolling across the hangar floor. He could feel the heat through his second skin.

The armor could take so much fire—was made for it— but with his evaporation and temperature regulation systems down—enough fire would be the death of Jack. He'd cook inside the suit. He did a backward flip out of harm's way of a second blast, and leapt to close instead, where armed fire would hurt Guthul as much as himself.

As they closed, the hangar floor vibrated under them. Guthul slammed Jack in the chestplate. The blow reverberated into Jack's own chest. As he gasped for air, he kicked back and around, seeking to dislodge the Thraks. Guthul went down. He rolled quickly and came up. From the angle of the general's head, Jack knew the Thraks was looking for him.

But he could not move for a second, doing everything he could to just *breathe*, the wind knocked out of him. His lungs felt as though a giant fist squeezed them shut.

The Thraks came up. His sight scrolled past Jack. Jack blinked the sweat out of his eyes and gulped a swallow of air as his diaphragm loosened. *Son of a bitch,* K'rok had been more than right. Guthul could only spot him as long as he stayed in motion.

The Lasertown miners' gift of having had Bogie coated in norcite years ago had probably saved Jack's life several times over, since. With irony, Jack told Bogie that. The problem now was to defeat Guthul without destroying him and incurring the further wrath of the queen. And to defeat

him, Jack would have to move, drawing the Thraks'
attention.

"What's he doing?" Baadluster's face twisted.

"I don't know. Circuitry damage maybe—he took quite
a hit."

Pepys sucked in a rasping breath. "He'll be all right."

"I know," Amber whispered. "I know."

"We're running out of time," Vandover protested. "He's
got to move and move now."

As if in answer to his objection, the battle armor twisted
and kicked high, just under Guthul's Kabuki mask of rage.
The Thraks fell back, arms flailing in pain. Jack laid down
a line of fire that scored the hangar plates, sending the
Thraks leaping into his embrace. The two soldiers closed a
last time and when Amber opened her eyes, the Thraks lay
still on the floor, Jack's booted foot firmly on his throat
leather, the only vulnerable spot on a Thrakian soldier's
body.

They had won.

CHAPTER 25

The shuttle to Malthen lay in the bay of the mother ship, its ramps down and berth ready for disembarkation. Pepys rested in his crèche, waiting to be loaded, his breathing a little easier than it had been in days, but his color still pallid. K'rok shadowed him as the emperor reached out and took Jack's hand.

"Against all charges of desertion and treason, I hereby find you guiltless and absolved. Baadluster and Commander K'rok, witness me."

There was a hearty glint in the Milot's eyes as he growled, "I witness," his hale voice drowning out Vandover's quiet response.

Jack found a tremble in his hand as he removed it from the emperor's. "Why now?" he asked. "My job isn't done yet."

"You've earned it. If anything should happen to me or to you, this shadow will be lifted. You've protected me from everything but myself. I could not ask you to do more. This needed to be done now."

He eyed his emperor. "I'll be back," he said. "You promised me a throne." He stepped back as the Thraks approached.

Vandover turned his back on the aliens, his face as dark and clouded as the robes he wore. "Pepys, I ask you to reconsider my returning with you. I prepared to go with Commander Storm and this change of plans is most distressing."

"I need you with me," Pepys answered simply.

"My value with St. Colin—"

"Your value is with me."

Baadluster shut his mouth. Then, shuttering away the abrupt look of hatred in his dark, flat eyes, he bowed his head and stepped out of the way so that the Thrakian guard could wheel the medical crèche up the ramp. As soon as Pepys was out of his sight, he wheeled on Amber and took her by the elbow. He bent his lips to her ear before she could pull away in startlement.

"Do not think yourself free of me. My thoughts will find yours wherever you hide."

He let go so suddenly she rocked back on her heels, even as she swung her head about to protest his catching her up.

"What was that about?" Jack said.

She shook her head. "A threat to remember him by," she answered quietly, troubled. She watched Vandover mount the ramp in Pepys' wake, never looking back. As the shuttle ramp pulled close, she felt him tug at her thoughts, unclean and revolting mental touch followed by his mocking laughter. Unconsciously, she stepped closer to Jack for protection.

K'rok dropped his heavy hand on Jack's shoulder. "Now it is my time to say good-bye." With his other hand, he signaled the Thraks to hold up securing the shuttle ramp. It paused, half-shut. "I am being given orders by my queen to go with Pepys."

"I thought you were going with us." An unexpected sadness washed through Jack.

"So I was also thinking. But Tricatada has asked me to go to make sure our alliance is strong." He scratched his thick jowl. "We each be facing our destinies now, Jack. Good luck to you."

Jack clasped the Milot's wrist. "And you, K'rok."

The brace of Thrakian guards began to chitter in agitation. K'rok answered them rapidly and strode across the dock's floor. He jumped to catch the ramp and as soon as his booted feet rang upon its surface, it began to close again.

Left with only Rawlins and Amber at his side, Jack watched the shuttle engines begin to burn. Amber pulled him through the air lock so the bay could be evacuated and then opened to space. Jack did not linger at the viewing portal. "Suit up," he told them. "I want them to see us leave in armor."

"Yessir," Rawlins said, and grinned.

* * *

Pepys mopped at the corner of his droopy eye. The crèche hindered him more than it aided him as the Thraks escorted him across the sere grounds of the palace. He snapped at Vandover, "I want the place staffed again, immediately. And get a medical team in—I want to be out of this thing as soon as possible. Get me a scooter instead. See to it."

Without replying, Vandover dropped back in the caravan so that Pepys could no longer see him as the crèche rolled past.

"I want the WP out here and this area kept secured. See if we can get them in armor if need be."

K'rok rumbled, "The suits are being dangerous to amateurs, emperor."

"Whatever it takes, then, Commander. I'm still emperor here and I think our citizens should know it.

The Milot gave a half-bow. "Your wish is my command."

"And Vandover—" Pepys attempted to twist around in his bed. "I want a listening post set up to keep track of what Storm is doing."

"Of course," Baadluster said neutrally. He gathered himself as if walking into a strong wind, chin down in thought. The battle-scarred ground crunched beneath his steps. Beyond the side yards, if he looked up, he could see the sentries set up and the sonic watch posts. In the far distance, if he listened, he could hear the faint "pop-pop" of artillery. But the war in Upper and Under-Malthen was nothing compared to the battle raging in his thoughts at the moment.

"We'll pick up a pilot on Claron. There'll be somebody there who's free-lancing; until then, we've got the auto. Rawlins here tells me he's been studying and can make manual adjustments if he has to."

The younger man looked at Jack, color high on his fair face. Amber laughed at Rawlins' reaction to the mild teasing. "Better you than a Thraks," she added.

Rawlins finally shrugged and strapped in. "They could have this baby rigged to blow, for all I know."

Jack sobered. "They don't. They're letting us go too easily. I think they have almost as much at stake in this venture as we do. They've been fighting the Ash farel far longer—and all it's done is drive them farther afield." He motioned Amber to a net. "Better settle in."

Rawlins maneuvered himself into a seat meant for a Thrakian pilot, his armor folding to meet the demands of his body. He looked the control board over. "They've ripped stuff out of here, sir. I think they're not too anxious for us to have one of their ships at our disposal." He pointed at the dash curving in front of him with open slots and blank areas where clips and leads dangled.

Jack scanned the board. "As long as we have what we need to make the trip."

"As near as I can tell."

"Then signal them to get the bay open. We've wasted enough time." Jack loomed over Rawlins a second or two longer, then backed toward his own webbing. Bogie brushed over his thoughts. Jack flinched away from the contact without thinking of his reaction. He could not bear to hear once again his friend's voice echoing in the scream of fear and anguish that Bogie had recorded. How long could a saint live in the hands of the enemy?

Long enough, he hoped, to be rescued.

CHAPTER 26

The physician shook her head as she watched the readout. "You will never be the man you were," she said to Pepys. The emperor squirmed in anger in the crèche.

"Never mind that," he said. "How soon can you get me out of this thing?"

The woman turned, and a slight smile warmed her cool features, drawing her almond eyes into a graceful curve. "That thing is what is keeping you breathing. Look here and here—these shaded areas are those affected by your stroke. That's permanent damage and, unfortunately, in an area where even repatterning will not be of very great benefit. This area here—" she traced it with a light pen—"we have bypassed the involuntary muscle stimulus center successfully. Yes, you'll be off the respirator soon—but your arm and leg will be permanently weakened. And you're extremely susceptible to another attack."

"Will I be competent or not?" Pepys' green eyes darkened as he glared at her.

"You'll be somewhat handicapped, but I suppose you'll be as competent as you wish to be . . ." Her soft voice trailed off.

"That is all I wanted to know. Vandover!" Pepys snapped.

The minister had been watching and listening to the examination with an abstracted expression of his own. He came to the bedside when the emperor summoned him. "Vandover, you're relived of the burden my illness placed on you."

"So soon? Perhaps you should wait until you are out of the crèche, at least. There are other susceptibilities. . . ." Baadluster's voice trailed off as the emperor struggled to sit up despite the shell of the respirator over his chest.

Pepys waved the physician out of the care unit. She left, whisper-quiet. As soon as the door shut behind her, he said, "Take care, Vandover. Take great care. Don't let your ambitions trip you up now. There is more than enough in all of this for both of us."

Baadluster held his breath until he had forced his emotions to calm. Then he answered, "You are a ruthless man."

Pepys smiled. "And it takes one to recognize that, does it not?"

Baadluster did not answer. The emperor plucked at the corner of his sheeting. "Do you still have your contacts among the Green Shirts?"

"Some."

"Good. I want you to spread the word that, when St. Colin is found, he will be held hostage against Walker good behavior."

The minister paused, then said, "That may not be necessary. I've gotten reports of renewed fighting between Thrakian forces and our outer continents. Even with the Green Shirts among them, how long can the Walkers hold out?"

Pepys lay back. Tricatada dared to invade anyway, under the guise of bringing the entire planet to order. Then he shrugged. "Well, then. As long as they are fighting each other, they cannot fight us."

"I shall keep that in mind." Vandover bowed gravely and left the emperor alone in his sick room, staring in thought. Then he called for Commander K'rok.

When the Milot commander turned up, he was slightly winded, his pelt ruffled as though he'd been in a rush. He smelled of laser fire and sweat. He came to a halt at Pepys' side, with a nod that was far less than subservient.

"Have you men I can trust?"

The Milot's eyes narrowed as if he'd been insulted. Pepys met his glare with an innocent expression. "I want a man to follow one of the WP."

"Ahh," the commander said. He frowned. "But the World Police are your own."

"No. Never mine. First Winton's and now, I fear, Vandover's."

"I be seeing," answered K'rok. "I have one or two we can trust."

"Good. Baadluster will be leaving the palace shortly, if he has not already. I want him followed. Recorded, if possible, but probably not—if he wanted to leave himself open to recording, he would communicate from here. No, he'll probably be shielded, but try anyway."

"I will have it done," K'rok rumbled.

Pepys nodded, closing his eyes, his flare of strength ebbing rapidly. His last waking thoughts carried the echo of the Milot's heavy footsteps leaving the care unit.

K'rok trusted the assignment to no one but himself. As torn and littered by warfare as the streets were, he wore armor and easily kept abreast of the vehicle Baadluster ordered up. The hover car wove painstakingly in and out of the warrens of the city while the Milot found the broken concrete canyons to his advantage, keeping to their shadows and barricades. When at last the automated vehicle came to a stop, Baadluster sat in it until another shadow joined him. K'rok keyed open his suit sensors to full capacity and watched his targeting grid in case other shadows thought of besieging him.

"Well done, Naylor," came Baadluster's reedy voice. "I thought to wait half the night for you."

"My bunker's not far from here. This area isn't secured, minister. This meeting isn't safe for either of us."

"Some risks are worth taking. Pepys is gathering in the reins of power again."

"Pepys?" Surprise in the other's voice. "I thought he'd had a severe stroke."

"It is not well for him, but he doesn't care if he walks or stands alone, as long as he can continue to govern alone. He will recover."

K'rok listened to an intake of breath, and then silence. There was then a sound as if something were being exchanged between hands.

"I've coded your instructions on this, but all depends on how well you've infiltrated the Walkers."

"You cannot separate one weave from the other."

Vandover's voice. "Good! You'll find this more detailed. Bring them down, lay them open. I want them gutted."

Disbelief registered in the other's, this Naylor's, voice. "The Thraks will sweep through us."

"Preciscly. Keep your men clear when it happens."

"And what'll happen then?"

"Then," answered Baadluster, "then they'll give me the Triad Throne."

K'rok's target grid showed him moving figures to his flank, and there was static over the receivers as the shadowy occupant left the taxi hastily. The Milot withdrew then, knowing he had heard all he could. He pondered his information as he returned to Upper Malthen, sifting through his memory, wondering what he would choose to tell Pepys and what he would not. It was clear to him that the emperor expected treachery. But did he expect collusion with the Thrakian League? In all probability not—or he would not have passed this task to K'rok.

Or perhaps he knew what K'rok had hidden in his own black heart.

Lengthening his stride, the Milot crossed the war zones of the city.

Pepys woke to thunder in the halls again—battle suits running the corridors. His heart took a skip and jump, and he peered through his one clear eye as the saggy one blurred. Dark armor loomed up beside him, and a heavy gauntlet fell upon his shoulder.

"Do not be worrying," K'rok said in his gravelly voice. Before he could say more, the emergency lights flickered on, and Baadluster swept in, illuminated by the orange glow.

"Arrest him," Baadluster ordered. His hand shook with fury as he targeted K'rok.

Armor flanked the corridor, but no one moved to do as Vandover ordered. The man looked from side to side as he realized his bidding was being ignored.

"I be thinking not," said K'rok. "These are Knights. I am a Knight." Pride echoed in his heavy voice.

"Explain this," Pepys got out. His voice croaked each word. He did not know if he felt reassured or threatened by K'rok's presence.

"I have purged your command of the Thraks," the Milot told him.

"You what?"

The bulky Flexalinked personage of Sergeant Lassaday

bulled forward into the doorway. The sergeant cleared his throat. "There ain't a Thraks left among us. Sir." If he could have spat, he would have.

Pepys rubbed at his bleary eye carefully as if it might clear his perspective. "What did you do?"

"I be putting them on the shuttle and shipping them back. And I be allowing no further incoming landings."

Baadluster's mouth twisted. "Guthul will split a gut. Tricatada will lay waste to the entire planet if she thinks you've gone back on your alliance."

"Or you yours," Pepys said, watching K'rok intently as the Milot took his helmet off. The shaggy being grinned at him. He felt pleasure surge through him. He had guessed Vandover's game and here stood K'rok verifying it to him.

The Milot saluted. "I be commander of your Knights, emperor. We will die defending you."

Vandover gathered himself under his robes. Pepys now turned his gaze on his minister.

"Have you anything to say?"

"I," Baadluster ground out, "have nothing to say."

"That is very circumspect of you. I might almost suspect that you are waiting for the Thraks to break through. Would you wish that, minister?"

"They are our allies."

"Mmmm." Pepys then ran his hand through his red hair. The fine strands which had lain lankly upon his pillow since he'd been struck down, began to crackle and rise with electricity as though newly invigorated. "Well done, Commander," he said to K'rok. "Now pray you can hold this island free until Commander Storm returns."

"Aye," answered K'rok. "I be praying."

He remained at Pepys' side as Vandover left in a swirl of robes and anger, escorted down the corridor by Lassaday and the troops, as if knowing the emperor wished to talk to him privately. When they had been left alone, Pepys merely turned an inquiring stare on the Milot.

K'rok showed his teeth happily. "I be following him myself," he said. "He met with a Green Shirt by the name of Naylor."

Pepys sucked in a breath. "Verified?"

"Voice print ident."

"All right. Go on. I ordered him to do that."

"They met in under-Malthen, near the firing zones. He be ordering Naylor to abandon the Walker lines, leaving them open to Thrakian attack. He be thinking grateful Thraks would make him emperor."

"He's probably right, too. The Thraks abhor weakness. My . . . infirmity . . . would lead them to this, and Vandover would take advantage of it. Why didn't you come to me first?"

K'rok's shoulders rolled in an eloquent shrug. "You probably not be allowing me to do what I did."

Pepys gave a dry laugh. "Probably not," he agreed. "I owe you one."

"More than one, emperor. Shall I tell you the price now?"

They were alone in the shadowed hospital wing. Pepys suddenly felt cold, and shook it off. It would be better to know, he told himself. "All right."

"Who ruled Milos?"

"Your people did, under the aegis of the Triad Throne, of course—that's what we were doing there fighting, protecting you and the considerable Dominion investments." Pepys reflected that the loss of those investments were what had given him financial sway over the Dominion, which was in part why he and Winton and Baadluster had arranged the military defeat there, but he had no intention of telling K'rok that.

"And if the Thraks left Milos now?"

"Milos is *sand,* dammit, you thick-headed woolly. What use is it to anyone, even if the Thraks did pull out?"

"It's my home," K'rok rumbled.

The emperor heard the edge in his words. "Yes, I understand that. What are you asking of me?"

"I want to go back. I want to go back as governor and ruler of Milos."

Pepys shook his head. "Oh, please. I have no control over this—"

"The *sand* is failing. Did Storm not tell you?"

"No. No, he didn't. And how do you know?"

K'rok's eyes shone. "I never forget my home. Queen Tricatada is most distressed over Milos' failure. *Sand* comes from the first nest. It has never failed before. But now it has. She has thinned it too much, perhaps, overswarming.

She does not know. I do not know, though I guess much. Milos will be abandoned. As long as you hold the Triad Throne, it is yours. Give it to me, Pepys. That is my price."

"As long as I hold the throne," Pepys repeated. "Done, Commander. Milos is yours if the Thraks should abandon it. More than that I cannot promise you."

The gauntlet squeezed tight on his shoulder. "That be fine. I will take care of the rest. Now we wait for Jack to come back."

CHAPTER 27

She awoke in fear and hunger, pain cramping in her stomach, her hands digging into her flesh as if she could knead it out. Agony lanced through her temples as her dreams leeched away into wakefulness amid the awful echo of Baadluster's laughter. She panted once or twice to clear her thoughts, but he'd been in them again and the smutty residue she could not cleanse.

A crowded room, an argument, a stern looking woman pointing at the man dressed richly in robes of crimson and gold, and the weapon of her mind lashing out. . . . She wouldn't do it again. Couldn't. She'd do whatever she had to, to keep Jack safe. *Milady.* A last, sickening jab from Baadluster and then he was gone for the moment. Her torment slowly ebbed away. The Thrakian hammock twisted about her as she got out, finally dumping her on the floor with a thud. Amber sat in the dim light. It was almost her turn on watch, anyway, and she knew that sleep was impossible now. She was getting to be like Jack, she thought ironically.

The hunger she could handle. They'd all eaten lightly for dinner, bypassing what the Thraks had stocked for meat. But there were legumes and dried fruits and even breads aplenty, so she picked out an assortment of baggies to take with her to the deck. There was no sense in shorting herself, the stores had been packed for a full crew and Jack figured they'd be pulling out of FTL and turning the corner for Claron within the next twenty-four hours. The three of them practically rattled around in the Thrakian cruiser.

Jack turned his head as she padded softly on deck and came to rest at his shoulder. He was getting used to her sleeplessness. The week or so they'd been aboard, she'd been early for every watch.

"What's up?"

"Nothing," he answered, turning his attention back to the screens. "We'll be going into decel and turning the corner in about nine hours. You'd better buckle up after you get off watch."

Amber made an "ummm" sound in her throat as she nodded. The lighting from the panels was subdued and had an odd coloration that she had no description for because it was in the visual spectrum of the Thraks. It cast an eerie glow over Jack's features, highlighting the strain in them.

"Bad night?" she said, leaning close.

"Ummm."

"Which one are you?"

"I'm always me. What happens now is like a drift, a daydream. It's a mask that someone drops over me. If I'm lucky," and Jack leaned back in the chair to look her in the face, "I remember Mom making cookies while I chop vegetables for a salad. Or I'm fighting with my brother or we're getting homework off the tutor. But if I'm not . . . then I'm fighting *sand*."

"Anything I can do to help?"

He inhaled deeply and she knew he was breathing in the fragrance of her hair and skin. The corner of her mouth quirked as he answered, "Nothing that wouldn't make Rawlins awfully uncomfortable."

She pouted at him. "The problem with being one of the boys is that I have to act like one of the boys." She smoothed his hair from his forehead. "It's my watch."

He got to his feet. "Let me know if anything happens."

Amber made no answer but watched him leave the deck. She wondered if he would be any more successful than she at getting some sleep. She sat down in the warm chair he'd just vacated. Constructed for a warrior Thraks, it dwarfed her lithe form. She pressed the back of her hand to her forehead, mopping up a dewy film of sweat. Damn Vandover. She could not sleep, she could not wake from the nightmare, and it took all her discipline to keep from flinching when someone like Jack was near. How could she ever tell him what had happened . . . how could she ever take comforting from him if she could not bear for anyone to touch her. *Dark child,* she thought. *How do you grow in my mind?*

There must be that within her which was very fertile.

She shivered away from those thoughts and forced her attention to the screens and displays as the cruiser arced through nothingness toward somethingness.

Rawlins was on watch when the ship came out of hyperdrive and began braking into the decel-maneuver known as turning the corner and he was on watch again when Claron came into view. He let out a yell that echoed through the near-empty cruiser, waking Amber and alerting Jack.

Jack put aside the tool he was using on Bogie. The opalescent armor shifted, levering itself to its feet. "What is it, boss?"

"I'd say we've reached Claron. Rawlins'll be putting us into orbit there until we can pick up traces of Colin."

Flexalink shimmered. Did the armor tremble in eagerness? Jack put a hand on the gauntlet.

"I know the way," Bogie said, his deep voice hollow within the battle armor.

Rawlins yelled again, "On deck, sir!"

"I know you do," Jack said soothingly. He disconnected the power lines to his tools. "I'll be back, or you can come up. Just don't break anything."

Under the suit's power, Bogie was like an overgrown, very uncoordinated child. Jack left in answer to the captain's summons without looking back to see if the armor followed him.

He was not prepared for the sight that met him in the control room. Rawlins had boosted the display and put it on the big screen—there it was, the wreckage that had once been a verdant, promising planet. To know that he had been the cause of its destruction had put a lump in his throat before he'd even stepped on deck.

And now this. Cloud cover and oceans—and a tinge of green snaking among the char. Amber was there ahead of him. Her hair streamed loose about her shoulders and there was a glow in her eyes as she reached for him.

"You did this! You did."

"Out of the ashes," Rawlins murmured. "You made them bring it back out of the ashes."

Jack gripped the railing in front of the observation screen. Claron filled his vision—newborn, hopeful, promising yet again. "I didn't do it. The terraformers did. Look at it. Think your parents will apply again?"

Rawlins shook his head. His deep blue eyes looked from Jack back to the screen. "No," he said. "They've resettled. But I just might." He tapped the control back. "I've sent out a new ident . . . they might not be too happy to sight Thraks."

On the heels of his statement, the com board lit up. Rawlins gave Jack a grin and bent his head over the missive, tapping back a quick reply, the keyboard being more reliable than the verbal sending because of Thrakian mechanics.

"Oh, my," Amber said as Rawlins replaced Claron with a deciphered version of the communication. "Such language."

The harshness of the displayed jargon drove the wonderment out of Jack. He *had* done it, in his way. He had been responsible for the firestorming and now he'd made them turn the clock back. An ending, and a beginning.

Rawlins snorted at Amber, saying, "Only a guttersnipe from under-Malthen would even know what most of that meant."

Instead of flaying him alive with his own words, she went as white as if she'd been whipped, shrinking back. Rawlins didn't see her reaction, but Jack did. She recovered quickly, snapping out a retort at the captain who laughed, leaving Storm wondering if he'd seen what he'd seen. Rawlins knew Amber's background, anyone who had been with Jack over the last seven years knew Amber as well, so why should she be bothered?

Vandover, he thought. His fist closed along his thigh. Baadluster was the only one who called her a lady but treated her like dirt. He thought of Baadluster's whispered farewell. Amber had all her deadly skills back. What had she to fear from the Minister of War? There was no one alive who could make Amber fear with the exception of the unseen master for whom she'd originally been trained.

Vandover, he thought again. Why hadn't he seen it? Vandover, who'd replaced Winton as smoothly and neatly as any succession into power he'd ever seen. Winton, who'd ordered retreat on Milos when there had been no need for one, who'd betrayed the Knights into a foul and disgraceful history. Jack had known there'd been other hands besides

Winton's in that plot. Baadluster, the link between Winton and Pepys, unseen, uninvolved until Winton's untimely death made it necessary for him to step forward. How could he have been so blind?

"Amber," he said quietly, thinking to draw her aside and share the truth with her, but static began to spew forth and Rawlins clucked his tongue against his teeth, saying, "There's someone who wants to talk to you, Commander."

Finally, he got the com line open. Battle armor filled the big screen, the helmet tucked under the man's elbow, and Jack smiled thinly as he recognized the darkly handsome head of the man who wore it.

"Denaro. Am I late?"

The Walker militant bared his teeth before replying, "I left little clues for you on the way out, but you didn't stop for them. You came straight here. How did you know?"

"I know Colin," Jack said quietly. Flanking him, both Amber and Rawlins watched the screen intently.

"Ah." Denaro twisted to look off-camera, then back. "Come on down, Jack. We've got a lot to talk about."

"All right. I've got armor this time." Jack said to Rawlins, "Get the coords."

"Yessir."

Amber slipped back to Jack's side as the display went dark. "Let me go down there with you."

How could he trust her, knowing what he did? What if he were right and Vandover was her master now? Guilt and distrust filtered through him. If Amber had fallen into Vandover's hands, it was because he had driven her there. And yet. . . . The thought must have flickered through his eyes, for she shrank away then, with that same whipped look on her face.

Rawlins said, "We all go or we all stay." He stood up from the control board, quiet determination written on his young face.

Surprised, Jack looked at him. Then he nodded. "All right."

Amber said nothing.

Rawlins added, "And we all wear armor."

Jack, whose ribs still felt the knots of recent injuries, nodded a second time.

CHAPTER 28

Claron still had that edge to its scent, like an exotic spice, and now it was tinged with smoke and another smell, one that Jack breathed in deeply and which brought a smile to his face. It was that of newly turned loam, rich soil, and he knew that Claron was truly reborn. The banks of greenhouses replaced what he had known as a mining and colonial town, but the enterprise was no less raucous. Skimmer traffic patterned the approaching lanes and he wove in and out of it to reach the lot where they'd been directed after berthing the Thrakian cruiser. Amber was sandwiched between the two of them on the skimmer and she was so subdued it was as if she wasn't even there. Clouds of lace-winged, tiny insects billowed up as he brought the skimmer down on a pad.

The windscreen shielded them until they emerged. Then, for a moment, the insects obscured even the target grids of the suits, there were so many of them.

Amber asked in amazement, "What are they?"

"Don't know," Jack answered. "Possibly they give the terraforming microbes a hand."

"Likely they keep them from getting out of hand," Rawlins commented as he got out. The blue sky reflected off his armor like a mirage off flatlands. His visor was on sunscreen and its darkness did not show his face. "It looks good."

Jack agreed. As the cloud of insects spiraled upward and away from the skimmer lot, Jack caught the approach of another war suit. He pivoted to face it dead on.

He saw Denaro, but not Jonathan's hulking form. "Where's Jonathan?"

Denaro pushed his sunscreen up so his face was clearly

visible through the visor. "He's in the quonset. He's not well, Storm."

Amber came to life. "Let me see him." She made as if to brush past Denaro, but he caught her. There was a sound of clashing as the two sets of Flexalinks met and ground on each other.

"Not so fast. This is Walker ground. This whole complex," and Denaro waved, "is Walker reserve. If you've come under Pepys' tyranny, you've got no authority here."

"And if I didn't?"

Denaro dropped his glove from Amber's sleeve. "Then we can talk. Follow me in where we can shed suits."

"I'll keep mine on," said Amber stonily.

"They're weapons as well as defensive skins. This is a sanctuary."

Jack shrugged. He motioned Rawlins back to the skimmer. "We're ready to talk when you're ready to be realistic. We're not the ones who kidnapped a patient and blasted our way out of the imperial hospital wing."

"No," Denaro agreed. "But I wasn't the one who put you in a crèche for two weeks. The Thraks did that."

Jack made a half-bow. "I'm holding no grudges . . . yet."

"All right, then. Follow me." Denaro snapped his sun-screen back down, turned in front of Amber and led the way, angling across the complex where patches of lawn were as green and new as spring shoots.

They had to duck to enter the prefab where Denaro led them. Jack eyed the building with interest. It was well thought out and well stocked—and planning boards were covered with sounding diagrams as well as fly-over maps. "Looking for something?"

"No. Initial surveys we always do, given permission. We found norcite on the far side, where there was also some evidence of a Thrakian infestation—burned out nest and *sand* remnants. If Claron hadn't been firestormed, there's a good chance we'd be up to our necks in Thraks now." Denaro indicated a right-hand corridor. "Third room on the left. We'll be a bit crowded in the armor, but—"

"I can stand crowded," Amber said tartly. She swung past him. Inside the building, Denaro put his sunscreen up again and now Jack caught a bemused expression on his face. The Walker had, after all, been the man who'd taught Amber how to use armor, albeit the lessons had been strictly clandestine.

Rawlins and Denaro fetched up against one another ahead of Jack. He watched as they sorted themselves out awkwardly. Both men had been profoundly affected by Colin in their lifetimes, but what a difference there was between them. Denaro, quick-tempered, ambitious, embittered that the passive way of Walker life was endangering their religious survival. Rawlins, quiet, confident, not Walker born or taught, but linked to Colin by the act of healing performed on him.

Denaro finally deferred to the taciturn blond and let him follow after Amber who managed to put a sway and grace even into the walk of a battle suit.

Jack drew Denaro back for a moment. "Is there anything I should know going in?"

"You should know that Jonathan is dying. I don't know what happened to Colin and Jonathan out there, or who took Colin after they separated—"

"I do," Jack interrupted gently. "He came to meet the Ash-farel."

"Shit." Denaro stopped in his tracks. "I knew it—he told me—but I kept thinking that something else must have happened. The Thraks or one of Pepys' freebooters."

"No."

"You can't go after him alone." Denaro locked gazes with him.

Jack smiled and said, "Let me talk with Jonathan first."

The burly aide had shrunken, was now a clammy white shadow of his former self. Amber had shed her helmet and knelt by the simple cot in a room ill-equipped for hospitalization, her gauntlet dwarfing his hand. There were shiny tracks on her face.

Jonathan turned his skull-like face to Jack. "Commander Storm," he said, and his voice husked. "St. Colin had hoped you'd catch up in time to join us."

"I'm sorry I disappointed him."

"You've never disappointed him. He always said you were a man who always tried to do the right thing." Jonathan wheezed. They all shared his struggle to catch his breath. "Denaro said you would come after me . . . I told him there was never any doubt that you would come after me and Colin. But he is a young and impetuous man . . ."

"We all start out that way," Jack said. The praise from Colin had embarrassed him. He questioned Denaro. "How often do ships go back to Malthen or the Dominion—any place with decent facilities?"

"Bi weekly. Next week."

"Make arrangements to leave him behind and see Jonathan is on it."

"Now wait a minute. We got this far, but now the trail is cold—"

Jack felt Bogie's warmth along his shoulders and back. "We don't need Jonathan. We'll find the Ash-farel without him. I'll hold you," and he pointed at Denaro, "personally responsible for any more suffering this man goes through. Do you have room for us at the compound or do I need to check in elsewhere?"

"Here," Denaro got out. "You can stow your gear here. But as far as Jonathan is concerned, he has to stay with us—he's my witness—"

"He's seen enough," Amber said. She got to her feet, eyes alive with her anger. "We got this far without you. We can find St. Colin without you."

Jack saw the expression come and go. That was a prospect that disturbed Denaro. He made a tough decision, then nodded to Jack. "All right. I don't want to see him go any more than you do."

Rawlins left the tiny room, saying, "I'll get the gear from the skimmer." He blocked Denaro's suit for a moment, and when he'd passed, the expression was gone from Denaro's face. But Jack hadn't missed it. Denaro had let the Walker go only because the man's death would avail him nothing.

Jack left Amber with Jonathan and followed Rawlins to the skimmer. The captain worked with short, energetic bursts of movement that Storm knew concealed anger. Jack caught a crate and held it between them.

"What is it?"

The clarity of Rawlins' blue eyes met his own, somewhat faded gaze. "I don't trust Denaro."

"Neither do I—but I want to have him where I can watch him rather than trailing us. All right with you?"

The subtlety of the battle armor was such that Jack could see it echo the relaxation of Rawlins' own body. The captain nodded. "All right." He took the crate from Jack's hands.

Jack would not let Jonathan hear or see the playback of Bogie's records. After dinner, he took them to a sound-proofed room that he had Denaro set up and there played back what the suit had documented, limited though it was. Amber let out a long, shivery breath.

"Good God," she said. It fell into silence in the dimmed room.

They had all shed their armor, although Bogie rested on a rack in the corner, his presence a reminder that what they had just heard and seen had happened.

Denaro had a tumbler of the local rotgut in his hand. He sucked it halfway down before saying, "Colin's been around a long time. He's seen and done a lot. What in God's name could have frightened him like that?"

"Whatever it was, that's what we're going after."

"We've no lead. The trail is stone cold—what do you think I've been doing for weeks here? The Ash-farel come and they go. No warning, no tracks. Even the Thraks, who've been fighting them for a century or two, *don't know where they come from.* There's a lot of space we haven't traversed yet. They could even be coming from behind us." Denaro set his glass down in front of him.

Jack leaned forward in his chair. "Changed your mind about coming with us?"

"No. Someone's got to bring back the body." The Walker militant got to his feet. "You said you could point the way. I suggest you be prepared to do it quickly . . . before the rebellion on Malthen spreads."

"Thinking of giving the word?" Rawlins asked, head up, body stilled, poised with the quiet strength of a powerful animal waiting to strike. Denaro didn't seem to notice it.

"Colin has a devoted following. If disinterest from the Triad Throne and, yes, even the Dominion, has cost us his life, and from all indications it may well have, we aren't going to take it."

"Don't threaten us," Amber said. Shadows of fatigue lined her eyes. She scarcely looked at Denaro as he paused in the doorway.

"I don't need to threaten you. I'm just reminding you. We'll want answers in the morning." He turned on his heel and he was gone.

Amber waited until his presence faded from her awareness, then said tiredly, "I wonder what his stake is."

"What it's always been. He wants to take over Colin's job," Jack told her. "Only Jonathan could have prevented it and he's made sure Jonathan's in no shape to do it."

Rawlins got up. "What do you think the chances are he's still alive after that?"

"I don't know. I just think he is. How about you?"

The captain gave a sudden, boyish grin. "Damned if I know. But I think he is, too. We're kind of connected, you know."

"I know." Jack watched Rawlins leave for the room he'd been given.

Amber folded herself up tighter, defensively, in her chair. She retreated to her old habit of hiding part of her face under a wave of her long, golden-brown hair. The unhidden eye stared at him. "Do you really think he's still alive?" she asked finally.

"I do. But I don't know how much longer he's going to stay that way when we find him if I take you with me. What I don't know is how Vandover hopes to trigger you from Malthen."

She flinched. She opened her mouth to say something, then looked away, shut her mouth, and remained silent.

Something was wrenching inside of him. He thought for a moment it was the battle between his two selves, but his thoughts were crystal clear. He fought for a calm breath. His chest felt tight.

"How much," she said softly, looking at her tucked under feet as if contemplation would reveal to her the mystery of life, "do you know?"

"Only that you were desperate enough to reimprint, and that Vandover has his hooks into you. He couldn't do that unless you were afraid of him. You wouldn't be afraid of him unless he's the one who could trigger you."

"And I thought you were an ass-backward country boy." She sighed. "I can't fight him. He feeds on me. Everything I do just adds fuel to him."

"Who's he stalking?"

She shook her head, the movement freeing her pale face from the curtain of hair. "I don't know. Even when he's triggered me, I don't know until it's too late."

"Pepys."

She hid her face in her hands, muffling a sob. "Yes. Jack, I—"

"Who else?"

"The Countess. That's why the Green Shirts didn't rally behind us when the Walkers broke loose."

"What about Colin?"

"I—I don't know." She brought her hands down, wiped her nose on her sleeve, oddly like the girl-child he'd met years ago. "You and I both know it's probable. Colin's death would throw suspicion on Pepys, break him completely—and break the Walkers, too."

"Denaro doesn't have what it takes to take over without bloodshed." Jack reached for his own glass of homebrew, untouched until now. He didn't ask if she had orders to do him in. He didn't want to hear the answer. The liquor went down, burning his throat, anything but smooth. He coughed.

Amber made a rueful face. "I could use a drink. What do you recommend?"

"Anything but this, but this is all we've got." He refilled his glass and passed it to her. "At least it'll help you sleep." The knot in his chest mellowed out. "I can't help you. I can love you, but I can't help you."

Her hand touched his briefly as they exchanged the glass. She looked up. "I think . . . if you love me . . . I can do almost anything. But he's always with me . . . in my thoughts, my dreams, like a blackness grafted onto me. Sometimes I think I'm looking into what Colin calls hell."

"Dig deep and fight it. You were always at my back. Now I'm at yours. I can't help you, but you're not alone. And whatever happens, I won't let you kill Colin."

Her lower lip trembling, she raised her glass to Jack in

a salute. Eyes brimming, she downed the liquor. She stifled her cough with the back of her hand. "Now, just how are we going to find him?"

Jack turned and looked at Bogie. "He tells me he's the signpost. Now, Bogie, tell me what you didn't record."

CHAPTER 29

He was the rose, the attar, with thorns on the inside. They pinioned his soul to flesh that could no longer stand to bear it . . . and they wouldn't let him go.

It made little difference that now the Ash-farel could talk to him, and he could understand. He was pain incarnate in a body that only remotely resembled humankind, that creaked and wobbled when it would stand, that bent when it should be rigid, that wept when it should be dry. He only had peace when he left it and discord when they pulled him back.

His best memories were those of when he'd gone to seminary school, a rough man, too old to be called a boy, a man who had already worked a miracle, and now had to learn the rules and laws governing what he had done. Those were the days, the days when he thought he could accomplish anything by the laying on of hands. Among his schoolmates was a quiet, sardonic red-haired lad who would have been the butt of jokes except that he was from a family of considerable power and had a way of remembering grievances and paying them back later in a sly, undetectable way. The redhead had an earthy intelligence and though he left later for the military school he'd prayed for, Colin and Pepys had gotten along well with one another. The key had been mutual respect.

His fondest memory of the seminary had been his basement room. He was lucky enough to have one with windows, a wall of them, and though they were near the ceiling, they looked out across the lawn. If he stood on a chair, his eyes were level with the grass. If he watched from his normal height, he saw the dirt pressed up against the glass pane, and the roots in that earth as they stretched their tiny tendrils out and thrust forth life from dirt and moisture. Sometimes the dean's little black and white dog would look in at Colin while he studied and bark insulting noises at him as if he were a rat gone underground.

He hadn't thought of those windows in a long time. Yet he knew that they had inspired him a lot during his first, fiery years. People were like seeds and if they could be struck with the right inspirations, they, too, would grow and flourish. He'd spent a lifetime trying to emit enough god-spark for nations to thrive on.

In the end, he hadn't done all that much, really. He'd been much more successful in his smaller ambitions. He dreamed now and pondered those windows, with the seeds bursting forth and growing flowers or grass stalks. The Ashfarel were calling him back, he could feel their blasted tugging just when he was about to know why he'd failed. Where he had gone wrong in trying to find the proof he needed that God Incarnate had walked other worlds as well. Why he had failed to provide the right stimulus for the seed of mankind to thrive.

As they pulled him back, memories of other worlds whirled past him . . . weeds poking up through broken concrete streets, flowers growing through cracks in rock . . . *how odd,* he thought. *How odd I should be seeing these things.*

And then it struck him that each seed carried the god-spark inside itself—and would be what it would be. It was not a spark imparted from outside, it came from within. All it needed was encouragement to free itself. *Why, I've been going at it backward,* Colin thought, as they made him become conscious.

Now that he knew, he needed to live. He had to live. He reached out for that strange bond he'd made before he'd been taken, his signpost, to guide him.

Bogie heard the call. It stirred him as he'd known it would, striking like wild lightning into his very being. His new flesh quivered, cells swirled in a dervish of activity, cilia stretched forth. And even as the call came to him, he knew he would not answer it.

He could not. The good man had walked into a maw of strangeness and fear . . . a maw Bogie would not look into, for fear he'd find himself.

He'd thought about it for a long time. He was not berserker, though similar, and he was not Thraks or Milot. He
was not human nor one of the genetically altered humanoid
races colonizing planets on the far borders of space. He
was either nothing . . . or one of the enemy, the Ash-farel.
And if he was Ash-farel, his symbiosis with Jack had so
changed him that he was still nothing, for there would be
nothing else like him in all the universes.

Would Jack destroy him if he knew Bogie was the
enemy? He and Jack were warriors. It would be fitting.

But he did not want to be defeated. He wanted to live.
He wanted to flesh out his entire body, his soul had been
homeless long enough. He wanted to look upon himself as
he could look upon Jack and Amber through the suit. As
the clarion call came to him, he turned it away.

"It's been days," Amber said. "If Denaro knew the answer was in Bogie, he'd have him scrapped."

"I'm not far from it myself." Jack dropped the printouts
he'd been scanning. "He's right . . . the trail is completely
cold. The Ash-farel literally drop out of a pocket in the
sky and drop back in."

"Meaning what?"

"Meaning their FTL is probably instantaneous. They
don't have to accelerate into it or turn the corner coming
out of it, signaling their presence. One minute they're here
and the next, they're gone."

Amber sat down opposite him. She looked as though
she'd gotten some sleep at last, her eyes clearer than he'd
seen them in a long time. She had brewed up a batch of
an herbal concoction the locals swore was a substitute for
tea. It wasn't, but it was hot and wet, with a smoky sweetness. "No wonder we can't fight them."

"No, all we can do is lay down a line of defense and
hope they trip over us from time to time. But I'm not
convinced we have to fight them. Amber, all the colonies
they've hit . . . the land remains intact. Civilization is gone,
yes, but the land regenerates."

"Ready to be recolonized?"

"Not that, but what," he frowned and rubbed his lower
rib cage, "I'm not sure. But there's more destructive ways

to carry on a war. It's the flesh that destroys the land and it's the flesh that they war against."

She looked at him across the rim of her teacup. "You're giving them human motives. From what little we know of them, they're totally alien to us. Jack, if we have to go against them to bring back Colin, you'd better be able to fight."

"I'll do what I have to," he bit off, then buried his anger. Amber wisely said nothing and turned her attention to blowing her tea cool. He shoved himself to his feet and went to the makeshift shop where the suits hung on racks to be geared up. Opalescent Flexalinks shimmered briefly as Bogie stirred.

Old memories resurfaced and for a moment Jack fought his revulsion against the life-form harbored there, and then the moment was past. Now he felt only the cold disappointment that, if Bogie did indeed know the way to Colin, he was hiding it. Before he could approach the armor, steps told him someone was behind him.

"Excuse me, sir," said Rawlins as Jack turned to him. The young captain held a plastisheet in his hand. "We've word that a fairly large contingent of Thrakian ships has come out of hyperspace and is turning the corner to Claron."

"We've been followed."

Rawlins nodded, the shock of his white-blond hair falling over his forehead. "Looks like it."

Jack thought rapidly. There was nothing on Claron for them. The Thraks must be hoping that Jack would lead them to the Ash-farel. "Thank you, Captain."

"Is there . . . anything else?"

"Not for now. I think they'll take up position and wait for us to make a move." If they could make a move. Jack eyed the armor on the racks. "You might alert the locals and let them know that this is nothing hostile . . . yet."

"Yes, sir." Rawlins hesitated.

Jack hid a smile. "Questions?"

"What are we waiting for?"

"We're waiting for the enemy to make a move."

"Which enemy is that, sir? The Thraks, the Ash-farel, or Baadluster?"

Jack let his smile show. "If I knew that, Rawlins, I wouldn't be waiting."

With a shake of his head, Rawlins left the shop room. Jack waited a moment, then approached his armor and sat at its boots, crossing his legs. The Dominion Knights had been an order of mental strength as well as physical. Most of the old disciplines had died out when they'd been disbanded and although Jack had tried to reinstitute them when Pepys had revived the guard, he hadn't been entirely successful. But the old rites were ingrained in him and he sought refuge in them now, breathing deeply.

There was strength in pure thought, just as there was in pure action. There was hope in every breath the body took, just as there was potential victory in every movement. He followed the lines and swoops of his exercises to their conclusion. He opened his eyes.

Bogie had moved a gauntlet over where it curved in the air just above his head. Jack reached up and took the hand in his. "No suit, no soldier," he said. "We've been there and back again. Our last battle is close, Bogie, very close. I'm ready."

He felt the flicker of touch that was Bogie rising to meet him. He was not psychic, like Amber . . . if the alien had not inhabited his armor, he would never have known its thoughts, but he did not regret it.

I have been shamed, Bogie said. *I have run from battle.*

"You've always done all I've asked of you. You've carried me when I was dying, filled me when I was empty. You've been as good a friend as anyone I know."

You gave me life. Now I run from doing the hard thing. A profound sadness tinged the deep, rumbling mental voice.

Jack wondered what bothered the sentience and thought again of the haunting scream Bogie had recorded. Was facing the Ash-farel so terrifying that Bogie could not do the duty Colin had given him—could not be the signpost Colin had intended? "What frightens you?"

Not living. Not fighting. Bogie paused. *Not knowing what it is I am meant to be.*

"Ah, Bogie. At last you know what it is to be human." Jack sighed.

I am not human.

"You might as well be. You're going to have to dig deep for those answers."

Did you . . . dig deep?

"I think so. I'm trying, anyway." Jack got to his feet. "Tell me where Colin is."

I . . . don't know.

"I think you do. I think you're afraid of knowing. Turning away will kill you just as surely as anything else."

Stony silence. Then, *You do not have to search for the enemy. Take off the helmet and look inside. I am the enemy, boss. I am Ash-farel. Your search is over. I have called them to us.*

The corridor filled with the sound of running. Rawlins and Amber hit the shop room at the same time.

"Incoming, Jack. And I don't think we're talking Thraks."

Jack turned. Rawlins had gone pale. "What are we talking about?"

"Out of nowhere, sir. Three of the biggest damn warships I've ever scoped. We're in trouble."

Jack kicked Amber's suit rack across the room. "Get in armor, and then broadcast an alert."

Amber collapsed her suit and opened up its seams. "Claron's got no shields. We're dead in the air unless you've got a plan."

"Let's just get aboard ship and see if we can get off-planet. Then we'll start thinking." Jack grabbed for Bogie. The seams did not open to pressure.

No, boss, Bogie said. *Not this time. I want to become alive. There is no more room for both of us, not enough energy.*

Jack paused, then reached for the hooks holding the suit on the rack and released them. It dropped to its boots with a dull thud. Amber and Rawlins both hesitated, their helmets in their gauntleted hands.

"What are you doing?"

"Nothing. Where's Denaro?"

"Getting defenses up around the compound." Rawlins screwed his helmet into place. "I've got him, sir. He says he'll meet us at the cruiser."

"What about Jonathan?"

Jack slapped Bogie out of the equipment room, saying, "He's better off down here if we're going to decoy them away. Rawlins, get our gear."

The officer left as bid. Amber turned to him. "What's wrong?"

"Bogie won't let me in. He says it'll kill him."

She bit on her lower lip. "Take my suit."

Jack laughed. "I haven't the right curves. Come on, let's go."

"You can't do this. There isn't even a deepsuit aboard that cruiser. Jack, you're in your bare skin. You can't survive any kind of a firelight if we get hit."

"We're not going up there to fight, we're going to find Colin. We don't know why they're here—now get a move on."

She moved, with a string of Malthenian curses that blistered the air.

CHAPTER 30

"I've got something to tell the emperor," Vandover said, as he stood there at the door, stubbornly blocked by K'rok's massive form.

The Milot's heavy jowls worked as though thinking of forming a word, and his shaggy brows beetled. "No," said the commander.

"It will be of interest to Pepys, I think." Baadluster refused to be intimidated any longer. He could not see his influence waning any further than it already had. He was little more than a prisoner in the obsidite palace.

"No," repeated K'rok.

"You big hairy lump of shit. Go tell his majesty that the Ash-farel are closing in on Claron and see if that interests him enough to talk with me." Vandover's lips tightened into a thin, pale line.

K'rok moved deliberately, shutting a door shield between them as he left his post. Vandover made an inaudible sound and whirled about, pacing the corridor. His hands worked in and out of fists as he strode, his long vested overrobe unfurling in his wake. He heard the *whirr* of servos behind him before Pepys' thin voice.

"Vandover. What is it?"

Baadluster pulled up. Pepys signaled K'rok to disarm the door shields and drove into the hallway. Much color had returned to his face, and his aura of hair crackled with energy. But nothing could be done to restore movement to that portion of his face frozen by the stroke. Baadluster could see the butterfly stitches surgically put in to keep the eyelid from drooping too unpleasantly over his eye. He cleared his throat to make it appear as if he had not been staring. Pepys smiled. Vandover wondered for a moment how many muscles of the face and even the light of the eye made up that expression. He also wondered if his own eyes glimmered pleasantly when he smiled. Somehow, he doubted it.

"Your sources are better than mine," Pepys persisted. "What have you come to tell me?"

"Only that the Ash-farel have returned to Claron. It appears we no longer have to go in search of them, they have come to us."

"Bearing Colin, perhaps." Pepys wheeled his conveyance about. "I wish I could be there." His voice trailed off. He looked back over his shoulder. "Thank you, Vandover." He disappeared beyond the bulk of the Milot commander's form, lost once again to Baadluster.

K'rok showed his teeth. He stepped back and brought the door shield down. Vandover stood there in frustration. It was clear to him that Amber must be brought back, for she had more work to do. And the Green Shirts would regret most bitterly that they had hesitated to rally to him at this crucial time. Plotting drove his chin down to his chest in thought as he left the emperor's quarters.

The Thrakian cruiser shuddered under them. Bogie's presence loomed on deck while the four of them rocked in their chair-webs as the Ash-farel warship thundered over them, flanked on either side by the other two.

"Come about!" Jack yelled.

Sweat dappled Rawlins' face. "I can't do it, sir. It's not that maneuverable."

"Damn it's not," Storm retorted. He'd seen Thrakian ships in motion, knew that they could fly rings around the warships—but Rawlins was not a Thrakian pilot. Neither, for that matter, was he. "Bring it about any way you can," he amended.

Denaro said, "No fire yet, but they have us targeted."

"No," Amber contradicted. "They have Claron targeted."

Something clenched in Jack's gut. Claron's fragile life would not survive a scourging by the Ashfarel. Not Claron. *"Rawlins, I don't care how you do it, but get us between them and dirtside."* He hadn't come this far to lose.

Bogie, linked to him by the warrior spirit they had in common, felt the fire of his determination. His grids gave him confused readings over the suit cameras. The flooring suddenly gave way under him as the cruiser went into a rollover. The armor went to its knees.

"Hang on," Denaro called, too late for most of them. Amber gave a brief cry as her chair swung about and she was thrown from one side of its webbing to the other, her tawny hair awash about her face as if she were seaborne.

The cruiser slammed forward. Rawlins let out a yell of triumph. "That does it!"

The ship surged past the warships as it flew over them. Denaro muttered to himself, "Watch it, watch it, we're still being targeted by *something* down there."

Their monitors filled with the topside deck views of the ships they were passing. Jack felt awed at the armament he spotted, at the sheer massive power of the vehicles. "I don't think," he said slowly, "that they *have* a home planet. We're looking at a goddamn city, a fortress."

"The Thraks will be happy to hear that." Denaro swiveled in his chair. "Rawlins, can you put a shield up over our ass?"

"I'm steering. You cover our rear if it's so damned important to you."

Jack leaned over the board in front of him. He had done a lot of looking at this board during sleepless nights while coming to Claron. He found a shield button, studied the pattern. He punched one with the heel of his hand. "That should do it."

"Got it," said Denaro. "That should help some." The cruiser rocked suddenly, viciously. "Just testing." Harmless orange fire washed over the screen and reflected upon his face.

"Now they know we've got our defenses up." Jack looked at Amber. "Keep your helmet where you can get to it easily. If anything happens, remember armor can act as a deepsuit."

She turned her golden eyes to him. "We're not going anywhere," she said.

"You wish," Denaro's voice carried a sardonic edge.

Jack looked at his monitor. The warships were gaining on them and fanning out. He knew a flanking maneuver when he saw one. "Rawlins."

"I see it, sir. I don't know how to push this baby any more."

Amber saw it, too. "They're driving us back toward Claron."

"All right, then. Just keep us in between."

"What are we going to do?" Worry, not fear, colored her voice. "They're driving us down."

"We start firing back before that happens. They're not picking up our signal. If they won't listen to our hailing, we'll see if our firepower can get their attention." Jack rubbed his hand over the back of his neck. "Give me a range, Denaro."

"We'll be within Pequena's orbit in five minutes and hit the ionosphere about twenty beyond that."

Pequena was a very small and very close moon. It was about three times larger than the Thrakian cruiser and its proximity made her appear much more prominent on the Claronian horizon than it would have in a more normal orbit. It was too much to hope she'd be on the darkside, away from them. "Where does she lie?"

"We're going to trip over her going in."

"Can you do a slingshot around her?"

Rawlins looked up. His dark blue eyes blinked slowly. "You've been listening to some real hotshot pilots. I don't think Pequena has enough gravity to get ahold of us."

The theory was good, the hope that Pequena's hold on them could slingshot them out of their present course, angling them unpredictably away from the Ash-farel. Not too many pilots he had known would have tried it. Jack smiled. "Just a thought. Okay, we'll use her as a shield, then, if we decide to return fire." He felt Amber's presence behind him, her gauntlet on his shoulder.

"I'm going to find Colin."

"Amber . . ."

"I can do it. Let me try."

Jack closed his eyes briefly, not wanting to make this decision. If she could find him, could she also strike at him? Before he could answer, a strangled noise came from Bogie in his armor.

"Jay-sus," Rawlins said, startled. "What was that?" On top of his exclamation, Denaro cried, "Here's Pequena."

They shot past it so closely they must have kicked up

dust on the moon's surface, Jack thought. Its pocked and rilled terrain filled the portside monitors. The vision exploded and the Thrakian cruiser jumped violently as the shock waves hit it. Rawlins cursed as he wrestled with the steering. A thin ping followed by a violent *whoosh* filled the air, and silence followed it as suddenly.

"Leak stopped," Denaro said grimly.

The back cameras displayed the shower of destruction of what had been Pequena. Gravel and dust sprayed out, glowing red with fire. One of those bulletlike rocks had pierced the Thrakian ship. The miracle was that more hadn't.

"Amber, I've got to know which ship Colin is on, *if* he's on a ship. We've got to be able to fight back." Jack turned to Denaro. "Got any gunnery turrets ready?"

"Powering up now," the Walker said.

Amber bent her head. This was a hell of a time to take calming breaths and begin soul-searching. The chair rocked violently about her as more shock waves reached them. She closed her eyes.

Dark child in her mind. Groping, probing, pain that should be pleasure . . . oh, gods, Vandover. . . .

She bit her lip hard, hoping that small agony would chase away her haunt. Hard, dark eyes staring back at her . . . *you can't escape me, milady. . . .* She couldn't break free of this waking nightmare, she had no choice but to take him with her looking for Colin. *Oh, gods, don't make me kill him. . . .* Amber looked up, wildly, heart pounding. "Help me," she cried, but her voice stuck in her throat and the others were too busy to notice. Her mouth worked without sound.

Then a gauntlet gripped her forearm. The armor pressed close. *I know the way,* Bogie said. He took her with him.

The contact came with a blazing shock. White light branded her mind, shearing Vandover away with its force. For a split second, she thought it had purged her mind of everything, but then she saw that, no, it was a beacon and everything stood out crystal clear. Vandover stood, hunched into his dark cape at one end of her mind, the light so blinding that he could be seen only as a shadow, and at the beacon's beginning was another figure, squarish, thinning hair ruffled about a mature face, the clothes that of a mining workman—"Colin!" she cried out, the name bursting from her throat.

Her mind went dark. The light gone. Vandover stilled. Bogie held her arm tightly and she wondered if he had felt what she had. She swallowed down the lump in her throat.

"I've got him," she said. "Lead ship. In the . . . the middle. Jack, he's alive."

"Damn." Jack came about. "Denaro, shut down the guns. We can't risk taking the offensive."

"They're bringing us down," Rawlins warned. Screens lit up as they hit the ionosphere and heat shields went up. Claron filled the displays.

"Try to stay away from the installations," Jack said. "We've got some control."

Amber sat back in her chair and took a deep breath. Bogie stayed at her side, silent. The ship spiraled down as its shepherds stubbornly forced it planetward.

"It's going to be a rough landing," Rawlins said. "Belly down."

They braced themselves for the hit. The Thrakian cruiser burst through the clouds, through mist and downward, dragging atmosphere and gravity with it. There would be no mat to brake it, no berthing to cradle it at journey's end, no hope that they could ever land intact enough to take off again. The only hope they had was to survive the landing at all.

"They're coming with us," Denaro warned.

Amber felt the gauntlet on her arm close. Was Bogie frightened? Did he share her sense of mortality? She made a soothing noise that did not finish. It got caught in her tightening throat.

Denaro said, very calmly, "They're coming in firing, Jack. We'll never make it down."

Bogie let out a howl.

CHAPTER 31

I know the way. Colin froze on the bridge as the words burned into his mind. The Ash-farel had herded him on deck, urged him quietly as he tottered his painful body where they wished him to be.

"We are hunting," they said, and he knew despair. The Ash-farel did not make war, as he knew it. They hunted and eradicated. He knew they might well be hunting his people.

"We have heard a call," they told him. "We are unsure. Listen with us."

And then his thoughts had lit up as if novaed. He reached for Bogie with all his hope and joy, embraced Amber for an incredible moment, lost her but stayed with Bogie, warmth blazing through him as they melded and when a howl of terror eclipsed that joy, the Ash-farel reacted.

The ship's bridge pitched under him. He clung to the shoulder of Na-dara for strength in his physical self as his thoughts interwove with Bogie's fear and desperation.

"I hear," Colin said. And he showed Na-dara what it was he heard, all the while trembling, knowing his friends' lives were being measured in seconds, if he could stop the Ash-farel from hunting, if he could get the Ash-farel to listen to his friends. The screen in front of him filled with the vision of the slender, dwarfed Thrakian vessel as it plummeted groundward toward Claron's new soil.

"If you hear, we also must hear," Na-dara said reluctantly. He reached out to the control board. The tractor beams came on, seizing the Thrakian ship, controlling its rapid descent into a safe landing, and they followed it down, the keels of the warships plowing into the loam.

The Ash-farel turned to Colin. Its saurian face was avid.

"You must help us to listen," Na-dara said. "We hear the echo of one of our lost children in your thoughts."

Colin wondered about that. The warship shuddered as its great bay opened. He painstakingly left the bridge and tottered to the tongue of ramp that lowered him to Claron.

Fresh air touched him. There was mist in it, comforting to the burn of his skin. He saw the Thrakian ship pop its air lock, and figures tumble out . . . armored, all of them, except for Jack—Colin's heart swelled at the sight of Storm—and he spread his arms in welcome.

They stared unknowingly at the white-robed figure and then the dark blue armored soldier reached up and took his helmet off. Rawlins said slowly, "My god. It's Colin."

The Walker could have wept, did weep, knowing that someone recognized him, beyond all hope that they could have done so.

Amber could not tell if it was the Claron mist on her face, or the tears she shed, as she stood back after gingerly embracing Colin. The man in her thoughts and memories did not stand in front of her. She searched for remnants of him in this tortured, elongated caricature of humanity. Only the voice remained the same, and the hair, and the eyes— she did not know how Rawlins had recognized him.

Denaro paced the virgin soil, not caring that his armored boots churned up new seeds and shoots, trampling them. Colin looked at him. "Have a care, my son," he said. "You are being listened to."

Jack had kept his arm about Colin's waist as if knowing instinctively that the older man found it difficult to stand. He looked up the ramp into the darkened interior of the warship. It was cavernous and held secrets. "By them?"

"Yes. You must understand that any attempt at communication at all is miraculous. To them, we are parasites. Vermin. The worlds are better off without us. Would we talk to such creatures, in their position?"

Understanding illuminated Jack's face as Colin spoke. "That explains their warfare."

"Yes. Only they call it hunting."

Denaro stopped short. "Tell them we've come for you."

Colin made an abrupt movement, lost his balance and would have fallen but for Jack's bracing. His face twisted.

"Knees don't always lock," he said by way of explanation, then turned to Denaro. "You don't know what you ask. Could I live like this among you? I think not. I see myself mirrored in your eyes. I am a grasshopper of a man . . . a walking skeleton. My pain numbers my days. But," and he looked at Amber kindly. "The price paid is not without reward. I talk, and they listen."

"They threw a tractor beam on us," Rawlins said. "I think it kept us from splattering the landscape. You did that?"

"I asked. They listened. We were both fortunate." Deliberately, Denaro spat over one armored shoulder. He held his helmet in one glove as if it were a weapon he might throw. "You have obligations."

"You do not need to remind me of my former life."

"I need to bring you back."

The two Walkers stared into one another's eyes. A faint tinge of pink dusted Colin's painfully boned face. "If for no other reason than to pick a successor?" he asked carefully.

Denaro flushed then. "The streets of Malthen run with blood. My brethren chose to fight, but now is not the time. We are wasting good men, good weapons."

Amber felt chilled by his words. Colin made a desultory wave. "I have other matters to settle first. The Ash-farel are listening, and they're growing impatient. Bogie." He turned to the opalescent armor.

I hear you.

"Bogie, there is a good chance that these are your people. They cannot quite hear you, as they put it, but they can listen to you through me. Do you wish it?"

The sentience did not answer immediately. Jack reached out with his free hard and clasped the shoulder of the battle suit. Colin said gently, "I know the way."

There was another muffled howl as Colin swept him up, and Bogie could not fight the torrent of thought as it took him. Without moving a physical step, Bogie and the Walker saint joined the Ash-farel who had been observing them from the shadowy interior of the warship.

He felt their exultation and more, the fierce burning warrior spirits that he knew were kindred to his own, but when he spoke, they did not quite hear. It was only when Colin bridged him that he could touch them, could know that his flesh had once been their flesh.

And the difference that must be spanned was that which he had taken from Jack. He could hear them, but they would not, could not hear him without Colin. He railed at the difference. He was theirs, but not theirs. And finally, in sadness, Bogie pulled away from them and from Colin, knowing that he could not return to them.

He was alone.

No. In his flesh was Jack and Amber, in his spirit, in his thoughts. They made the difference, but they also transformed him.

He would not be alone again.

Colin released him. They stood once again in the misty morning breeze off Claron. Jack's hand touched the Flexalinks which Bogie used as skin and shell both.

"I am," Bogie said, "Ash-farel. And I am not."

Colin's face had grayed with strain. He nodded wearily. He had no chance to turn away as Denaro strode over and snatched him up, tearing him away from Jack. He brought his armored knee up viciously into Jack, knocking him aside.

Colin cried out, "Don't. The Ash-farel—"

Denaro leapt past Amber as she grabbed for him, their armor clashing, and her gauntlet slipping away.

Colin bumped on the shoulder epaulets, his breath torn from him, gasping, "Denaro, you don't know what you're doing—"

The ground fell away from under them. Denaro snarled, "I know the Ash-farel won't touch me as long as I've got you. I need you, old man, just long enough to make a statement in front of witnesses—"

White armor landed in front of them, and Bogie threw up his arms, saying only, "No."

They clashed, Walker and alien, the man hampered by the burden of frail flesh over his shoulder. Denaro kicked out. Bogie turned, catching the boot on his flank. He hit his power vault and returned the blow, staggering Denaro backward. He came back with his fist and their armor pealed out as they made contact. Denaro shook himself loose of his burden, throwing Colin away, heedless of the white-robed figure tumbling away from him.

He brought his gauntlet up and fired, laser wash scouring Bogie's chest and helmet. Amber ran to Colin's side and knelt over him, protecting his body with her own armor. Bogie reeled, straightened, and jumped at Denaro. They bowled over and then Denaro shook free.

Rawlins helped Jack stand. Jack fought to breathe, winded. He felt broken in two or three different spots. He managed to gasp down some air and his diaphragm loosened slightly. He looked up. He launched himself across the broken field at Amber.

Rawlins saw what Jack saw even as the man dove at Amber and Colin to protect them. Denaro, at close range, cocked his wrist to fire, heedless of the damage the backwash from a wrist rocket would do. The white armor was his sole target, his obsession.

He fired. The rocket exploded, taking the white armor dead on. It staggered back, flowering open, Flexalinks splitting. Rawlins unhooked his helmet and screwed it on, as Denaro began to pivot toward the three huddled on the ground just as the explosion washed over them. The ragged hem of Colin's robe caught fire spontaneously. As the orange flames gouted upward, Jack smothered them with his body.

Rawlins hit his vault. He smacked into Denaro just below the shoulder. Before the armored Walker could right himself, Rawlins locked his arm about the man's upper torso, and tore the helmet off. Denaro yelled in fury.

His shout was cut short as Rawlins reached in and broke his neck.

The battle suit slumped over in response to its wearer's death. Rawlins dropped back to the ground. He tore his own helmet off.

"My God," he said, as if unsure himself just what he'd done. He stumbled to Jack's side as he levered himself off Colin's body.

The Walker saint lay crumpled, his robes sooty and stained. His broken form looked as if it had finally taken all the punishment it could. Amber let out a sob. Rawlins fell into a kneeling position beside his friend's body. The pallor of his face matched the winter-wheat color of his hair, Jack thought. Aloud, he said, "You did what you could. It's too late, that's all." And he wondered who the

Ash-farel would listen to now, if indeed they would listen at all.

Thunder rolled sullenly in the sky. Rawlins caught his breath and reached for Colin's hand.

What happened next, neither Jack nor Amber could be sure, nor could they ever describe it except to say that the gauntlet took on a glow, an infusion of light and dark as it met Colin's flesh. Rawlins never saw it, for the tears obscured his dark blue eyes. He held the dead saint's hand for a long moment and when he let go, the radiance faded. The spicy air of Claron filled with an aroma that made Amber think of roses.

With a deep, shuddering sigh, Colin rolled over and sat up. They could see life shimmering into him, through him. He reached for Rawlins' hands. "My boy," he said. "You have returned the gift I gave to you."

Rawlins' mouth dropped open. Then, he shook his head. "I'm no Walker."

"No? Well, then, I'm sure we can find someone who will teach you. But a good man is a good man, a saint is a saint, regardless of his religion. If my Walkers won't accept you, there will always be those who will. You'll do." Colin released his gauntlets and looked at his own hands briefly. "You took away my pain. That'll make listening with the Ash-farel a little easier."

Jack looked up. He frowned. "If there are any left. Rawlins—that's reentry rumble! The Thraks are coming in! And the Ash-farel are on the ground—Amber, get Colin up and in the ship. We've led them into a trap."

CHAPTER 32

Vandover sat in his com net, face furrowed with anger. Amber had been able to brush him away, but he'd sifted through her mind well enough to know that the team had found Colin, been in touch with him. He would not be turned away from his goal now. She would do his will.

He took a cleansing breath. He knew her well, he did, the silken feel of her skin, the curves and valleys of her body as well as the twists of her mind. With every heartbeat, he drew closer to her again and she would be his. . . .

"What are you doing, Vandover?"

The minister jerked upward in his chair. He looked at Pepys, weakened, hapless Pepys, and smiled even as he sent his questing thoughts out farther, closer to his quarry. He made a steeple out of his hands. "I do my work, emperor."

"You've been relieved of your duties." It was night on Malthen, and the emperor had been asleep. Lines from his pillow still creased his face and his frizzy red hair was matted down. He ran his good hand through it as if aware of Vandover's observation.

"Not all of them, I'm afraid. Not my duty as I see it."

The cables and wires of the com net prevented Pepys' scooter from bringing him closer. The emperor remained in the doorway, frustrated. His anger showed on his face. "What are you doing?"

Vandover smiled that humorless smile of his. "A little long-distance assassination, my dear Pepys. The cease fire you've instituted won't last long when the Walkers discover what you've done to their much beloved saint."

"They've found Colin?"

"Oh, yes. And the Ash-farel. And," he smiled with real satisfaction now as he found Amber's mind and sunk his hooks mercilessly into her, "I have found them." He laughed dryly. "Remember the east wing? Remember the quorum of psychics you used to keep ensconced there, just in case one of them could sense or predict something for you?" He leaned forward, the comnet trailing about his head like an obscene tiara. "Well, my dear emperor, you've had the genuine article under your nose for years without a clue. She's beautiful and deadly—but she's mine."

Pepys' mouth worked silently. He saw his soul suddenly stretched out before him and knew that the stain of Colin's death was a stain he could not bear upon it. He had to stop Vandover even if he had to kill him to do it. He tried to thrust himself from his conveyance.

They left their wounded and dead upon the field. Rawlins shut the Thrakian cruiser after them, Amber strangely pale as she helped Colin into a webbed chair. Jack climbed above, into the overhead turret. The cruiser vibrated into life.

Colin said, "Since this is a Thrakian vessel, I presume you can open channels for me?"

"Yes, sir, but—"

The Walker leaned his head back against the molded chair. He looked above. "Jack, hold your fire."

Jack looked at the Thrakian warships coming in lean and mean on his grid. "Guthul won't let us go. I don't know what you have in mind—"

"Norcite. The Ash-farel know far more about norcite than you and I ever will. I think the Thraks will trade our lives for the location of additional deposits."

Jack came about in the turret, staring down. Amber sat in her chair next to Colin. The shock of all they'd gone through was written in tiny lines about her eyes and mouth. She gave him a stricken look.

Giving norcite to the Thraks was like giving weapons to a baby. Even if it meant bargaining for his life now, it also meant he would spend the rest of his life fighting Thraks and *sand,* until Tricatada gave out and her generation died fighting his—

"Shit." The realization hit him.

Colin jerked in his chair. "What is it?"

Jack began to slide out of the turret. "Open up that channel, Rawlins. I've got something better to trade."

An explosion rocked the cruiser. "Close," said Rawlins. "They're getting our range." He opened up the monitors. They showed one of the Ash-farel vessels beginning to lift off.

Jack faced the screen. "Guthul, I know you're on-line."

The screen came to life with the Thraks' Kabuki mask looming fiercely at him. "I am, Commander, and this time I will find victory and honor!"

"There's honor for all of us, but only if you call a cease-fire." He looked to Colin. "Can you keep the Ash-farel from fighting back?"

The man looked bemused. "I can," he answered slowly, "try."

Amber shuddered.

Jack faced Guthul's visage again. "I know," he said, "the answer to Tricatada's infertility. I think our lives are worth that, don't you?"

The mask reformed slowly. Then, "You trick us."

"No. But I won't tell you if we're under attack."

"You have allied with our ancient enemy . . ."

Jack shook his head. "The Ash-farel don't need us and they don't need you. Fire on us and you've signed your own death warrant. Do you want fertile eggs or not?"

Behind him Rawlins cautioned, "One of the Ash-farel ships is up. We're on borrowed time."

As if he'd heard him, the Thrakian general bowed abruptly. "We will talk."

Colin let out his breath abruptly. He said, "The Ash-farel are listening. They will allow Guthul's ship to land. The others must, however, pull back."

Vandover laughed as Pepys fell from the scooter. His weakened wrist doubled under him. It broke with a dull pop. The emperor let out a squeak of pain and writhed on the floor. Baadluster spoke and his words dripped venom. "Do you think to stop me now? You should have thought to do it years ago when you still held power." He threw his head back and closed his eyes, discounting the broken emperor across the room.

Pepys closed his lips tightly upon his whimpering. Quietly, so as not to warn Vandover, he began to crawl across the floor.

*   *   *

They met on the valley floor. Jack recognized the land with a shock—it had once been the lush Ataract forest, where he'd done much of his rangering when Claron was still verdant, and now the blast of the landing vehicles had welded the new soil into glassy fields. As he strode over the obsidian surface to the ramp of the Ash-farel vessel, Guthul's contingent waited for him. Amber leaned on him, her breath rasping as she fought to keep pace with him. They had shed their armor. Colin thought it best. He tottered alongside Jack. Only Rawlins wore his suit, and he carried Bogie's remains in his arms. He laid the shattered armor down on the ramp as they came to a halt.

Guthul twisted about. Jack knew Thrakian masks well enough to recognize an expression of pure hatred. Before the Thraks could speak, the Ash-farel finally emerged from the cavernous belly of their ship.

Jack had seen them before, their mummified remains on a dead moon mining colony, in a Walker dig on Colinada, and now in the flesh. They were saurian, immense, and yet curiously avian; they were three times his size and their eyes were large, and knowingly arrogant. But they were listening.

He could not speak directly to them. Only Colin could translate what he would say now, so he turned to his old friend as Guthul made impatient chittering noises. Seeing the face of his ancient enemy did not seem to impress the Thraks.

"I can give you only the reason, not a solution. But if we can create a true alliance between us, I can promise you we'll help with the solution."

Guthul and his aides rattled their armor. "Empty words are like empty egg sacs. Flaunt them and we will return to our vessels." He pointed his mask up the ramp to where the Ashfarel milled about. "We will leave the field to fight another day."

"If I give you the reason, you'll come to treaty?"

Guthul bowed. "So my queen has ordered me."

Jack smiled wryly. That was as good as he was going to get from the Thraks. "All right. Norcite has been among the Thraks for a long time. It's a strengthening agent, highly prized for its effects upon armor."

Guthul nodded and said warningly, "You waste my time."

"No. Not by half. When you first began to contend with the Ash-farel, you needed norcite to protect yourselves. At the beginning, you painted it on. It did well. Then, some time ago, you discovered the virtues of ingesting it. Drinking or eating it . . . it not only increased the strength of your armor, but its size. You began to develop your warrior classes and your warfare against your enemies. The end result of all the fighting was a drop in population. Your queens, of necessity, began to work harder laying eggs. You swarmed, taking over whole planets for *sand* nests to hatch and feed those younglings."

The general's mandibles worked. He rumbled, "The enemy knows enough of our secrets."

"But it's no secret now. Tricatada cannot lay a fertile egg. You've come as far as you can. In the last thirty years, you've gone through a frenzy of swarming, driven out of your own lands by the Ash-farel and conquering ours. The Ash-farel have long known of your uses of norcite—every deposit we've found, the two of you have fought over. This has been revealed in archaeological records as well as in present history. But what you didn't know, Guthul, was that it was not the warfare dooming you. It was the norcite. *Norcite makes you sterile.* The warrior class cannot fertilize the queen. Oh, she can lay eggs from now until the stars grow cold, but there isn't a mate alive who can finish the job."

"I am not impotent!"

Jack stared at the enraged Thraks who towered above him. He blinked. "I don't doubt it—but you can't give the queen fertility, either. Maybe only the lowliest Thraks, those never allowed to consume norcite still carry the ability. Maybe not. That answer I can't give you. I can only tell you what happened."

Guthul rattled his chitin in deafening agitation. "Our enemies will destroy us!"

Colin moved forward. "No," he said. "They are listening, and they have compassion. I think I can say. . . ." He trailed off, a quizzical expression on his face. He pivoted very slowly toward Amber. "Amber, what are you—"

Jack saw it in her face, in the intense struggle suddenly

imprinted on her features. He jumped and brought her down, their bodies hitting the metal ramp, she fighting him like a wild thing.

"Don't," he begged. "Don't do this. Listen to me, not Vandover. Love, listen to me!" He bore her body down with his and took her face between his hands. Her eyes went wild and she screamed in fury at him.

Colin put his hand to his temple. He closed his eyes in sudden pain.

His arm hurt as if he'd been knifed. He held his breath for fear of whimpering too loudly. He crawled another foot upon the floor. He was close enough now to touch the edge of Vandover's over-robe. To smell the sweat of the man's booted feet. Pepys wrinkled his nose. All those years, and he'd never noticed how Baadluster's feet stank. He pulled himself forward again. With a sudden upheaval, he wrapped his good hand in Vandover's robe and pulled himself to his knees. Vandover exploded in snarling hatred and the smaller man saw his death in those flat, dark eyes.

Jack stroked her heated face, feeling her body heave under him, not caring if all the Thraks and Ash-farel in the universes saw him struggle with her. "Dig deep," he told her. "I'm here. Fight him. Don't give in. I'm with you."

Rawlins let out a shout and caught Colin's toppling body. The saint said weakly, "I'm all right. Help Amber." The Ash-farel let out the first sounds he'd heard them make—it was like whale-song. He understood nothing they said and he thought that perhaps he couldn't even hear all that they sang and boomed. Amber thrashed under him again, and a tear leaked out from her eyes.

"Jack," she rasped. "Don't lose me."

"Never."

She shuddered, her eyes rolling back until he could only see their whites. She cried out, "Dark child!"

Pepys screamed as Vandover shook him like a broken doll. He heard K'rok's thundering voice, "What be happening here!" as the Milot leaped over the scooter and into the room. The impact of their bodies sounded like the clash of giants as Baadluster dropped him, forgotten. The hairy

Milot and the black-clad man joined in battle, the com net tiara trailing a tail of sparks as it tore loose. A powerknife buzzed to life in Vandover's hand.

Blood splattered Pepys. He wiped it from his cheek and looked up, to see the Milot dripping upon him as the knife cut him yet again. K'rok snarled in outrage, reached out, and punched Vandover in the chest. There was a sickening crunch of bone. Baadluster staggered back, gasping. He clawed at his chest and the powerknife dropped to the floor where its blades whirred angrily. He looked at Pepys as he sank to his knees. His pasty complexion turned purple. Then Vandover collapsed face first, burying the knife to its hilt in his shattered chest.

K'rok lifted Pepys to his feet. The emperor clung to him as if to life itself.

Bodiless, Vandover's thoughts clung to their foul anchorage in Amber's mind. She gasped and bucked as Jack's words made their way to her. She thought of the light Colin had made in her once, the light that had driven Baadluster out. She had to make such a light now.

"Together," Jack said.

She looked into his eyes. He loved her. She had lost him and gotten him back. "I won't let him have you," he told her.

If he only knew. If she did not burn Vandover from her mind now, she would be forever possessed.

"I love you!" she cried. He kept her face between his hands and his eyes became her world. Eyes of rainwater blue. Eyes she had once told someone could never lie. He loved her back.

Happiness roared up like a fire fed by the look in those eyes. It spewed its light throughout her and Amber let it burn.

With a howling, that dark child which was Vandover burned out and was gone.

CHAPTER 33

"If they can take a man apart and put him back together, it stands to reason they can do the same to armor," Colin said. He smiled at the gleaming opalescent suit standing before them with the radiance of a newly born sun. "And as for Bogie, the suit did its job. It protected the life within it."

Jack smiled. Amber stood within the cradle of his arm. The Ash-farel had dressed her, decorating her like some wild exotic creature, silks and feathers and beads about her. "I wish you'd reconsider coming back with us."

Colin tilted his head. He had the look of the Ash-farel about him when he did it. "No," he answered. "I've passed that robe to Rawlins. He'll do much better than I. I've told him a few of the hard things I've learned along the way. He's got a head start on the job."

Rawlins ducked his head, suddenly and embarrassingly humble.

"Forget Rawlins. I can use your help dealing with Pepys and K'rok."

"My friend. There is no one who can do what I can do here. Even Bogie cannot. But with your help, he will. You've brought the Thraks to bay and you'll have the time you need to rebuild. The Ash-farel are listening, and that is no small feat. I'd say you've more than met the challenges Pepys handed you."

Jack shook his head. "I was given a job. I did my best. Denaro—"

"You couldn't help him any more than you could save Vandover from himself. Pepys has dismantled his throne, K'rok has his regency over Milos, my Walkers await Rawlins. You've done well. The only thing I regret," and Colin put a finger to his lips as he smiled, "the only thing I regret is not being able to give the vows to bond you two officially."

Amber laughed. "What's stopping you?"

"What? Here and now?" Colin looked about him. The Claron sky was midday bright and clear. The warships perched like gigantic nesting birds and Amber stood among the warriors, a brilliant rainbow-hued nestling.

"We're among friends," she said. "There's no time better. Is there?"

Jack cleared his throat. "Now I know what Pepys felt like with K'rok staring him down the throat demanding a regency." He smiled. "Go ahead, Colin. Do your worst."

It was fitting, Jack thought, to begin again on Claron.